12 Heartwarming Historical Romances for the Season of Love

THE

12 Brides of

Christmas

COLLECTION

Margaret Brownley, Mary Connealy,
Diana Lesire Brandmeyer, Amanda Cabot, Susan Page Davis,
Miralee Ferrell, Pam Hillman, Maureen Lang, Amy Lillard,
Vickie McDonough, Davalynn Spencer, Michelle Ule

BARBOUR BOOKS
An Imprint of Barbour Publishing, Inc.

Print ISBN 978-1-63058-489-4

eBook Editions:
Adobe Digital Edition (.epub) 978-1-63409-194-7
Kindle and MobiPocket Edition (.prc) 978-1-63409-195-4

Published by Barbour Books, an imprint of Barbour Publishing, Inc., P.O. Box 719, Uhrichsville, OH 44683, www.barbourbooks.com

Our mission is to publish and distribute inspirational products offering exceptional value and biblical encouragement to the masses.

 Member of the
Evangelical Christian
Publishers Association

Printed in the United States of America.

Contents

The Festive Bride

by Diana Lesire Brandmeyer

Chapter 1

Southern Illinois, 1886

Roy Gibbons stirred the pot of oatmeal while doing his best to ignore the state of his kitchen.

"Papa, it shouldn't look like that." Eight-year-old Elisbet glared at him. "I can't wait until our Christmas mama gets here."

If Janie were here, everything would be in the cupboards where it belonged, not shoved into nooks and crannies. He never thought he'd be making breakfast for his daughters, much less trying to keep their frocks clean and pressed. He missed his wife more and more every day. Roy didn't know how she'd made his home run so smoothly. Not once had he needed to worry about how to get tomato stains off his shirt or when to cut his hair. She'd say in her musical voice, "It's time, sit down and let me trim that head, Roy."

When Elisbet asked him for a mother for Christmas, he'd said yes, thinking it couldn't be that hard to find one.

"Papa, do you think Becky will have sugar cookies at her party?" Frances, his youngest and his shadow, tugged his pant leg.

"Franny, she's going to have cake. That's what you have at a birthday party, right, Papa?" Elisbet never had trouble correcting her younger sister.

"But I like sugar cookies." Frances tugged again. "Can we make cookies when we come home? Mama makes the best kind."

"Mama *made* not makes. She's in heaven. Remember?" Elisbet patted her sister's shoulder. "When our Christmas mama comes, she'll make cookies with us."

"Stop telling her that, Elisbet. It's not that easy to get a mother. I can't order one from the catalog." He slid the pot from the burner, his little shadow still clinging to his leg as he moved. "Sit down, girls, and I'll fill your bowls." Roy was still stinging from Widow Percy's rejection. She'd have been a perfect fill-in for his deceased wife. Seemed logical—she didn't have a father for her boys, and his girls didn't have a mother. When he suggested they marry for the common good of their families, she'd done all but slap his face.

Trouble was, he hadn't lived here long enough to know people. Maybe he'd made a mistake moving here after Janie died. If he'd stayed in Collinsville, he'd have a mother for the girls by now. The whole reason he'd left was because too many young hopefuls were knocking on the door with some treat and mooning over him and the girls. At the time he didn't want another wife. No one could fill Janie's shoes, and these women would be expecting to have children of their own. He couldn't face that, not after losing Janie and the baby. No, he didn't need a companion. Just someone to take care of his house and his family.

He scooped up the oatmeal and plopped a lump in each girl's bowl.

He sat at the head of the table, a daughter on either side of him, and pushed back the hurt that came from seeing Janie's chair at the other end. The house was different, but the spot across the table was as empty as if he hadn't left Collinsville. "Grace, then food." He watched until little hands were folded and heads bowed, then said the prayer followed by an "Amen."

Frances stuck her fingers on the inside of her bowl to pull it closer. "Hot!" The bowl went spinning from the table to her lap and then crashed to the floor. She wailed.

"Are you all right? Are your fingers burned?" Roy sprung from his chair and pulled his daughter from hers. He grabbed her hands and flipped them palm up. They weren't red. Relieved to avoid a crisis, he planted a kiss on her fingertips the way he'd seen Janie do so many times.

"My dress," Frances whimpered. "It's dirty. I don't have another one for the party."

"Shh, Frances, stop crying. Your fingers look fine, and no one will notice your dress." Kneeling, he reached under the table for the offending bowl and spoon that had spoiled Frances's morning.

"If we had a mama, this wouldn't have happened, Papa." Elisbet already held a wet rag in her hand. She dabbed at her sister's dress. "It's only a little bit of oatmeal. Look, Franny. See? I got it off."

It bothered him that Elisbet tried to be like Janie, and he had no idea how to prevent it.

"But it's my favorite and it's. . ." Frances hiccupped. "Wet!"

Roy wondered how he would ever raise these girls without help.

∞

Alma Pickens tugged her cape closer to guard against the sharp fangs of the November wind and leaned across the buggy seat. Her father had returned to the very subject she'd asked him not to speak about at breakfast. "Papa,

8

you're a dreamer. Maybe I'm not the only one God will send a spouse for. I do believe I'll pray as hard as you do for me, that you'll marry again. A doctor should have a wife."

And she would take it to God in her prayers. She'd grown weary of her father's constant efforts to see her married. It wasn't that she was against the idea, but she'd made a promise to her mother to take care of him. And it would be a rare man who would marry her and take in her father as well.

Besides, she had her painting and taking care of her father's home. That gave her plenty to do. Why, just this morning she'd risen earlier than normal and put in a full day's work so she could come to town with him despite the cold to make a deposit at the bank and to visit her friend Jewel.

"Little Bit, it's not right for you to devote your life to me."

"Papa, I told you not to worry about me. I have you, and I don't need anyone else. Besides, there isn't anyone left in Trenton that I'd care to marry."

"Alma my girl, you'll make a good wife and mother. I can't sit back and watch you miss out. God will bring someone." He stopped the horse in front of Bossman's Bank and stepped out of the wagon. He tied the horse to the hitching post and helped Alma dismount. "I'm too old to get married again. It's you I worry about. I'll pick you up at Jewel's when I'm through at the Detterman's. And don't start making lists of promising wives for me. Go on, get in the bank and put your pennies away."

"I'm going." Who would be a good match for him? And who could she find that wouldn't mind her presence in the house as well?

Maybe she should hold off ordering from the Montgomery Ward catalog. She had her heart set on the Oil Painting Outfit Complete. It was outrageously expensive, but it came with twenty-five colors of paint. If she weren't able to sell her paintings right away, and her father married a woman who valued their privacy, she would need that money to rent a room somewhere. And without the paints and lessons that came with the painting outfit, how would she have anything to sell? Well, she wouldn't worry about that today, seeing as how there weren't any women who interested Papa. The irony that this town held no one for either of them struck her. Maybe Papa would consider moving to St. Louis, where her paintings would be discovered, and she'd be famous and wealthy. He could be a doctor there, and the number of people in that city would increase his chance of finding another wife.

She needed to talk this new idea of St. Louis over with Jewel. Together they'd find a solution.

Inside the bank, Alma waited her turn. Two little blond girls in front of her clung to their father. She knew who they were—the Gibbons family minus the mother who had died last spring giving birth. Mrs. Remik at the store said everyone was speculating on when Mr. Gibbons would take another wife to help with Elisbet and Frances.

The oldest, Elisbet, played peekaboo with her sister. Their giggles captured one hiding in Alma. She clenched her lips to contain it, but it escaped.

Mr. Gibbons turned and smiled. Alma had an unusual urge to slide her finger into the indentation on his cheek. Dimples. Then she noticed what looked like oatmeal in his hair. She shuddered. The man needed help.

"I apologize if my girls disturbed you, miss."

"They didn't. Their giggles captivated me along with those dark blue eyes." If she were painting them, she'd use cobalt blue to capture their intensity.

"We're going to a birthday party," Elisbet said.

Alma leaned down. "I love birthday parties, lots of games and cake to eat."

"I have oatmeal on my dress." Frances looked so sorrowful that Alma wanted to take her down to the store and buy her a new frock.

"Franny, it's okay. Remember I got it off and your dress dried on the way here. Papa, we have to get Becky a gift, don't forget. I want to get her red hair ribbons."

Had that man brought his daughter out in this cold weather with a wet dress? Was he touched in the head? No doubt her own father would end up at their place tending to the little girl for pneumonia.

"I don't. I think we should get her a knife." Frances held up her hands and pretended to open one. "It would be grand to have one. Papa, can I have one for my birthday?"

"We'll see. We best get moving if there's shopping and lunch to do yet." He turned to Alma. "Nice to meet you."

"Papa, can she be the mama you're getting us for Christmas? She doesn't have a wedding ring. I looked like you showed me." Elisbet smiled a got-you-now smile at her father.

Mr. Gibbons's green eyes flashed to Alma's, and his face flushed. "Let's go, girls." He ushered them out without another word to Alma.

Alma watched them leave, noticing the hem on Elisbet's coat was torn. She understood the child's desire for a mother but sincerely hoped her father didn't run into Mr. Gibbons before Christmas.

Chapter 2

Roy covered Frances's shivering body with the blanket from his bedroom and tucked it around her. Her teeth chattered, and he brushed his hand against her forehead. Hot. Nothing good ever came from fevers. He couldn't let his daughters see his worry, especially Elisbet. "You'll be right as rain soon. I sent Pete to fetch the doctor. He'll be here before long."

"Not the doctor!" Frances sobbed. "I want Mama."

Her words cut him, opening a scar he'd thought healed. "We all do. The doctor will help you feel better, sweetheart." He'd taken to calling his daughters by the terms of endearment he'd heard Janie use. It seemed to settle them down when they were in a state he didn't understand. He should never have left Collinsville. Right now his mother could be helping him with this sick child.

Frances coughed again and again. Her body shook, and her chest had a rattle Roy didn't like. "Elisbet, sit and read to your sister until the doctor and Pete get here or I get done milking the cows."

Elisbet, eyes wide and face pale, didn't object but grabbed the picture book Frances loved. "Can I get under the covers with Franny?"

"I want Elisbet!" Frances threw off the covers.

Frances didn't know what she wanted, but he would give her what he could. "Didn't I just tuck you in, little girl?"

"Please, Papa?" Frances coughed again.

Roy slid back the covers. "Climb in." He waited for Elisbet to snuggle in next to her sister. *Please God, don't let her get sick, too.* "I'll be back as soon as I can."

Roy knew Elisbet was terrified. He wished he didn't understand her fear, but he did—all too well. The last time they'd seen a doctor, Janie died. He left his heart with his daughters as he headed outside. You couldn't let a cow go unmilked, even if you had somewhere better to be.

He shivered. He should have grabbed his coat. No matter, the barn would hold back the chill. He'd have to keep Elisbet home from school tomorrow to help him with Frances. He couldn't take care of a sick child, do barn chores, and work at the mill. This illness pushed him to fulfill his daughters' Christmas wish. He'd write to his mother, asking her who back home was still looking to get married. He wanted a widow, someone who'd already known love and didn't expect it to happen again. Someone who'd understand she couldn't replace his wife any more than he could replace her husband.

∾

Alma convinced her father to take her for an afternoon drive before the winter snows came and forced them to stay close to town. Outside of town, the roads suffered from last week's gully washer, making the smooth rides of summer a memory to be cherished. The buggy springs bounced, squeaking as the wheels dipped in and out of holes in the dirt road. Alma held on to the edge of her seat. "Thanksgiving makes me sad. It makes me think of Mama."

"I think about her every day. Holidays are the hardest for me. But you've your mother's happy attitude about life, and that helps me." Her father winked at her. "Yes, you do many things that remind me of her."

"Tell me how, Papa." Alma drew the buggy blanket up higher on her lap. The warmth of fall had been shoved aside as winter gained a foothold. The trees held tight to a few weather-beaten leaves. Another strong wind and they'd be bare.

"The way you want to make small things into a celebration. Like Thursday, you invited friends to eat with us, but it wasn't enough to have all those platters of food. You decorated the table with red and gold leaves. That's not something I would do."

"Too many germs, Dr. Pickens? Those tiny little things no one can see?" Alma tried to raise an eyebrow the way her father did when making a point. It wouldn't go.

Dr. Pickens raised his brow. "Still can't do it? Neither could your mother. And yes, there is a new study out about germs being in unexpected places. It's possible leaves would carry bacteria spores, but your happiness matters more to me, so I kept quiet."

"Thank you. The decorations made the entire dinner party more festive. If the leaves make people sick, wouldn't everyone be ill when they fall from the trees?"

"It does seem I have more patients in the winter, doesn't it?"

"That's because it's cold and we don't get enough fresh air. You taught me that. So I'm like you, too, Papa."

"I'd like you to be more like your mother and me—married."

This conversation was going down a corduroy road she didn't wish to travel. Distraction always worked with her father. "Who was the letter from that you were reading last night?"

"Someone you don't know. How about Mr. Bruin? He'd make a good husband."

"I can't marry him. I won't. I know you're concerned for me, but I'd never be happy married to a miner. I'm surprised you would even consider him. He must bring home lots of germs every night. Why, I could catch something and die before spring if I were to marry him." She tried one more time to arch her eyebrow. It wouldn't go, so she pushed it up with her finger.

In the distance, Alma saw a horse and a rider coming up on them fast. "Look, someone else is out for a ride today."

"Doesn't appear he's riding for fun. Must be an emergency. He's got that horse running at a gallop." Dr. Pickens pulled back on the reins. "Wise to slow down and let him pass. No need to give our boy Charlie here a reason to bolt."

The horseback rider whipped off his hat and waved. "Dr. Pickens! We need you at the Gibbonses'." He stopped his horse next to the buggy.

"Pete, you came up so fast I didn't recognize you. What's the problem?"

"Roy Gibbons's little one is sick. She can't stop coughing, and he said she's burning hot as a barn afire. He sent me to get you. Can you come straight away?"

Her father wore his serious face; she knew he wouldn't hesitate. "We'll follow you." Doctor Pickens urged Charlie into a trot.

"What does Mr. Gibbons do for a living, Papa?"

"I heard he bought Becker's farm." His forehead furrowed like a freshly plowed field.

"He's not married. Jewel says he never comes to town without the girls. Why do you suppose that is?"

"I take you places."

"Yes, but not all the time. Do you think he's taking care of the girls by himself? That would explain the oatmeal in his hair and the torn hem."

"Oatmeal? What are you talking about?"

"I saw them at the bank. The girls were going to a birthday party and were excited, but they weren't dressed for the occasion. I wanted to take them home, curl their hair, and buy them pretty dresses. I hope the other children weren't mean to them."

"Were they mean to you?" Her father's mouth turned down.

She hadn't meant to hurt him. "No. Well, sometimes. It didn't happen

13

after you asked for help from Mrs. Wilson."

"She was a saint to step in. I'm not sure you would have learned how to be a lady if not for her."

"You tried, Papa." Alma pushed back memories of the times she missed her mother. She'd kept many of them from her father.

The two-story farmhouse appeared when they came around the bend in the road. A house built for a large family, not a father and two little girls.

"Will you let me help?"

"Don't believe you've become a doctor since lunch, have you?"

"No."

"You can carry my bag."

"I'm no longer a child."

"Believe me, I'm aware."

The door opened, and Mr. Gibbons stepped onto the porch. "In here, Doctor. Franny is sick. I don't know what to do."

Alma followed her father into the house. She'd learned early to step back when her father was needed. Too many times she'd landed on the floor as he rushed by her.

Mr. Gibbons hadn't waited for either of them, but it wasn't difficult to locate him or the patient. The coughing led them to the sick child.

Dr. Pickens felt Frances's forehead. "Definitely a fever. You need to take those blankets off of her right now. You're making the fever climb higher. I need a basin of cold water and a cloth, please."

When Mr. Gibbons removed the covers, Frances cried out. "I'm cold!"

Alma rushed to the child's side and stroked her arm. "Do you like to build snowmen? I bet you're as cold as one, aren't you?"

Frances quieted. "Yes."

"Mr. Gibbons, the water please?" Papa dug in his black bag. It was a good thing he'd acquired the habit of tossing it into the buggy whenever he left home.

Alma spoke to Mr. Gibbons. "I'll watch over her while you're gone. It won't take but a minute to get what Papa needs."

He nodded and hastened from the room. Alma felt compassion for the man. Not having a wife to help him through this trying time had to be difficult.

"I'm cold."

"Keeping the covers on will make you sicker longer. Then you'll be sad if it snows and you can't go outside to build a snowman." Alma sat on the bed next to Frances and picked up a book. "Were you reading this?"

"Sissy read it to me."

"Where is Sissy?"

Frances pointed to the corner where Elisbet stood, her eyes focused on Alma's father. She seemed frozen in fear.

Alma smoothed Frances's hair. "My papa will take good care of you. Right now, I'm going to talk to Sissy." She went to Elisbet and knelt in front of her.

She grasped the child's hand. "You don't need to be afraid. My papa is a good doctor. He can make your sister well. Do you want to watch?"

Elisbet yanked her hand away, eyes wide. "No! She's going to die like Mama."

∽∾

"No, she's not going to die." Roy strode into the room in time to hear Elisbet. "Right, Doc? Tell them everything is going to be fine." *Tell me, too.* He couldn't bear losing Frances. *God, please don't take her, too.* He'd been praying for her to get better. But then, he'd prayed for Janie, and it didn't make a difference.

Dr. Pickens removed the stethoscope from around his neck and returned it to his bag. "She'll be fine. She's got the croup. Feed her soup and give her tea with honey to soothe her throat and cough. I have a tincture you'll need to give her three times a day."

"Will Elisbet catch this, too?" If both girls were sick, he wouldn't be able to work at the mill. As it was, the idea of leaving Elisbet alone with Franny caused him some concern.

"She might. If she does, follow the same procedure. Keep a cool cloth on Frances's forehead for the night. Dip it in cold water when it warms. That will help bring down her fever. Keep her in bed for a few days."

"I don't have to go to school?" Frances propped herself up on her elbows.

"Then I'm not going either." Elisbet strutted from the corner. "I'll take care of Franny."

"We'll discuss it when the doctor has gone."

"Mr. Gibbons, do you have someone to watch the girls?" Dr. Pickens asked. "They are too small to stay home alone."

"I don't have a choice. You don't understand. It's the three of us that looks out after each other."

"I'll watch them."

He turned and noticed the doctor's daughter was the woman from

15

the bank. She held Elisbet's small hand in hers. It took him back in time. Janie with her daughters. Would it hurt them to have another woman look after them? Would they become attached, or worse, badger her about marrying him?

"Please, Papa?"

"Pretty please, Papa?"

Roy rubbed his forehead. He needed help. He'd deal with the consequences later.

Chapter 3

Alma's father waited in the buggy at the Gibbons farm. The sun cracked open the morning sky. Alma had brought fresh eggs, since she wasn't sure what their pantry held.

Mr. Gibbons met her with a finger over his lips. "They're still sleeping." He yawned. "Sorry, I was up most of the night."

"Is Frances better? Papa wants to know before he drives back to town."

"I think so. She doesn't feel as hot this morning, and she's not restless."

She turned and waved to her father. He tipped his hat in her direction and jiggled the reins. Charlie shook his head, pawed the ground, and the buggy wheels turned.

She didn't smell coffee brewing. "You haven't eaten?"

"No, you woke me up. It's a good thing, too. I need to do the barn chores first. I would have been late to work if you hadn't come when you did."

Alma held out the basket she'd brought along. "I brought eggs. If you don't mind, I can make breakfast." She didn't think twice about offering, but the grin on Mr. Gibbons's face said she'd given him a large gift.

"You wouldn't mind?" He was already sticking his arms into his coat sleeves.

"Not at all." Especially if he kept flashing those dimples at her.

"None of us are too picky about food. If you can make the oatmeal, I'd appreciate it." He took off out the door.

The minute she walked into the kitchen, Alma knew Mr. Gibbons didn't have a woman helping him. The stove was filthy, and there were dishes caked with dried oatmeal stacked on the table. She shrugged off her cloak and searched for an apron. Mr. Gibbons had left a shirt draped over a chair. With a sigh, she tied the sleeves around her waist. Not the best use of a shirt, but maybe it would save her favorite day dress.

She stoked the stove and put on the coffee. Next, she gathered the dirty dishes and put them in the sink to soak. She hadn't had breakfast either, and she hated oatmeal. There had to be something else for her to make that would be easy for Frances to eat. A quick search of the food supply and she had the makings for griddle cakes. The syrup would go down Frances's throat easier than lumpy oatmeal.

She found a clean bowl and mixed the ingredients.

"What are you doing?" Elisbet, hair tousled and in her nightclothes, peeked around the corner.

"Griddle cakes. Do you and your sister like them?"

"Better than oatmeal." Elisbet skipped across the floor. "Can I help?"

"Can you get out the griddle for me?"

Elisbet disappeared into the pantry and brought out the heavy cast-iron piece. "I can grease it. Mama showed me how."

"That would be helpful, thank you. Before you do that, could you get dressed and check to see if your sister is awake?"

"She's sleeping, but I bet she wakes up when she smells these cooking. Don't grease it, promise?"

"I promise. Off you go, and put on some warm clothes. It's cold today."

While the batter was resting, Alma started cleaning. She was wiping down the table when Mr. Gibbons came in the back door.

"Thanks for starting breakfast. I can finish up."

"I'm making griddle cakes, not oatmeal."

His dimples came out to torment her again. She needed a diversion. "Why don't you check on Frances? See if you can get her to come to breakfast?"

"You have flour on your face." Mr. Gibbons reached over and brushed her cheek then withdrew his fingers fast, as if he'd been burnt. He whirled around and headed for the bedroom, muttering something about checking on Frances.

Alma touched her cheek where his fingers had been. If she were made of butter, she'd be a puddle on the floor.

⌒◌◌⌒

Next to the window in her bedroom sat Alma's art studio. She'd tried to capture the playfulness of the barn kittens from last spring. The laundry basket looked right, but the kittens in it were giving her a great amount of difficulty. Jewel had been instrumental in helping her find an outlet for her creativity after her attempt at weaving palm leaves together to make hats failed.

Would it be easier painting children? Frances and Elisbet would make good subjects, with their big blue eyes and blond curls. Curls that were a mess. After she'd cleaned the kitchen to a tolerable standard, she'd spent the rest of the day with the girls. She'd combed and braided their hair, even found ribbons to tie at the ends.

Their imaginations sparked hers, and they made up stories of castles and trolls. She could feel how they wanted her attention, and she was happy to give it. She prayed Elisbet's Christmas wish would come true, and they would get a mother.

Splat. Black paint hit the canvas in the wrong spot and trailed like a tear. She ought not be thinking of those little ones. God would see to them. After all, He'd helped her father take care of her.

As the sun set, the light faded from golden to silver, making it difficult to see. Alma set her paintbrush and palette on the table next to her easel. Time to stop for today, which, by the look of the work she had accomplished this afternoon, was a good thing. Kittens shouldn't have cone-shaped heads, but she couldn't quite get them more rounded. Frustrated, she removed her painting apron and draped it over the chair. She had to get that painting kit and discover how to do it correctly.

Heavyhearted, she headed to the kitchen. On Wednesdays she always made stew. Papa made calls that day and was often late to dinner, which gave her time to work on her art.

She couldn't let the problem of the kittens' misshapen heads alone. How did other painters get those round shapes? How did they paint children's heads? Did they trace something until they learned to do it freehand? Maybe she could use one of her mother's china cups. But would a real artist resort to something so amateur? She would ponder that. Maybe for this painting it would be okay. The next time she saw Jewel, she'd inquire about the rules. She was determined to be a real artist, not just occupy her time, even though that's what Papa said she was doing.

Her shoulders drooped. If this painting didn't sell, he would surely start talking about husbands again. He'd given her three choices and asked her to pick one. She shuddered. She'd known all of them since grade school and had never been fond of any of them.

She gave the stew a quick stir. The kitchen felt closed in and dark this evening. There were so many things she wanted to do in here. Despite being dirty, the Gibbons' kitchen was cheerful and full of light. Jewel had painted candlesticks with sunflowers in her kitchen and planned to paint her hutch with flowers. It was time to broach the topic with Papa again about brightening up this room. Could she convince him to let her paint the corner cabinet?

He hated change. If you asked her, he lived too much in the past. Mama wasn't going to come back to life and complain about the look of the kitchen. Not when she was living in heaven, where everyone knew Christ had built her a mansion. Mama must love it there, all those bright colors and the sparkles on the streets. It was a shame they couldn't experience a bit of that here at home.

"It's time for a change. I'll tell him right after supper. I live here, too, and since neither of us is getting married and I do the cooking, the kitchen is as good as mine." Her hand flew to her mouth. Had she said that out loud? It was a good thing Papa wasn't lurking around the corner. He'd think she was daft. No, best find a way to ease into this change. He was a stubborn man, set in his ways, and his rules applied in this house. Maybe she should go to St. Louis on her own and take painting classes. That's what Jewel suggested, but Alma couldn't leave. Not when she'd promised to watch over him. Which brought her back to her plan of finding Papa a wife.

Alma stirred the stew again. Papa was late, and she didn't know if she should continue to keep the food warm. Sometimes when he stayed out this long, the family that needed him fed him.

The back door creaked open, and she spun around. The air rushed in, making the kerosene flames dance in their glass, casting graceful shadows across the room. "Papa, you're so late. What happened? Did you deliver a baby?"

"Not tonight. Is supper still warm?"

"Yes, but I do believe I'll warm it a bit more for you."

"Not too long, I'm hungry. Been looking forward to a hearty meal tonight." Papa took off his coat, slung it over his bent arm, and grabbed his hat. "I'll put these away later." He dropped them on a kitchen chair and sat at the table. "How was your afternoon?"

Papa asking about her day before eating sent a shiver up Alma's back. He was up to something. Food always came before conversation. She turned to face him. "You know that it's painting day. Are you getting too old to remember? It's a good thing you have me around to help you through your days."

He had the grace to flush and bend his head. Yes, there was something he was about to say, and Alma knew she wouldn't like it.

"Don't sass me, Alma. I was being polite."

"I'm sorry, Papa. I was teasing. Your last call must have been difficult. You haven't complained about my joshing with you in a long time. Did you lose a patient? Would you like me to make you some cocoa?"

"Forgive me for snapping at you. It's been a long day." He scrubbed his hands across his face. "There's something I need to tell you, and I know you won't like it, but what's done is done. We'll discuss it later, after I've eaten."

Alma slid a plate of stew across the table in front of her father and took a seat. "What do you mean, it's done? And what does it have to do with me?"

Chapter 4

What's done is done? Inside Alma, tension built like steam collecting in a covered pot of boiling water. If Papa didn't finish his stew soon, she was going to snatch it off the table. How dare he drop a loaded statement that begged for questions and then say he'd discuss it with her as soon as he'd finished his supper? For once she was glad she hadn't remembered to make the biscuits.

Chew and swallow, her father ate slower than a snake swallowing a mouse. "Papa, can't you tell me anything?"

Dr. Pickens held up a finger and shook his head no.

Alma jumped from her chair. "I don't understand why you would keep something from me. It must be unpleasant, or you would have told me straight away. This isn't like you." She tugged her ear.

"Don't pull on your ear."

Her hand dropped to her side. It had taken her years to break that tugging habit, and with one sentence Papa brought back her insecurities.

"You'll know soon enough. I want to eat and think about how I want to say what I have to say."

"Eat faster, please, because I'm imagining all kinds of things." Alma paced the kitchen, which gave her no satisfaction, since it only took four steps to cross the room. She slid back into her chair, propped her elbows on the table, and then rested her chin on her palms. Fine. She'd wait him out by staring at him.

He didn't look her in the eye or tell her to remove her elbows from the table. Alma refused to change her position. Even if it wasn't working, it made her feel like she was doing something.

When the last bit of stew disappeared, Alma grabbed the bowl. "Let me put this in the sink."

Her father squinted at her then frowned. "Why do you have feathers in your hair?"

"I was creating a new hair ornament."

"Did you glue them in?"

"No, I glued them to a leather strip, but the glue wasn't quite dry and

21

some of the feathers stuck. I'll get them out. Like most of the things I attempt to create, this was a failure, but I'm not giving up my creative works. Are you ready to tell me what you mean by 'what's done is done'?"

Dr. Pickens wiped his chin with a napkin and scooted his chair away from the table. "I've made a decision. I've signed up for a surgical course in St. Louis."

"St. Louis!" Alma clapped her hands. "That's wonderful! It will be a perfect place for us to live. Why, Jewel and I were discussing this on Saturday. When do we have to leave?"

"I'm leaving at the end of the year. You aren't."

"I don't understand."

"You can't go with me. I'm renting a room by the school."

"How long will you be gone? You don't need to worry. I can watch over the house."

"No, you can't. I've rented it out. I'll be gone a year, and you, my dear, will be getting married before I leave."

Anger chased fear down her back like a cat running over piano keys. "Married? Who to? Papa! This is so wrong. I don't want to get married, you know that."

"So you've said. It's my job as a father to make sure you are taken care of, and that's what I've done."

"Who did you pick? The man who works at Bassler Brewery and stumbles home at night? The coal miner who coughs so much he's probably going to die soon? Or the man who beats his dog?"

"Daughter, I listened to you."

His forehead wrinkled the way it did when he was concerned for her. Could it be he would change his mind? Alma stacked reasons why she needed to go with him to St. Louis, ready to use them all. "Good, then let's put this leaving me behind business away. There will—"

"Stop. I'm not finished. Yes, your reasons were sound for not picking one of those men. I've found a better one. Roy Gibbons. He's a good family man and goes to church. With Pastor Elrich's help, I obtained his mother's address. She wrote back. He's a good man and moved here to remove himself from memories of his deceased wife. The two of you are well suited. We've shaken hands. There will be a marriage."

⸱⸱⸱⸱⸱

Roy had hoped the dishes he'd tossed in to soak after dinner would clean up quick. He was wrong. Dried food seemed to have planted roots in the stoneware. He noticed the kitchen had lost the appetizing appeal it had held after Alma had cleaned it.

He used a knife to scratch the surface of the plate. Marrying Alma would solve quite a few problems. She wasn't a widow, but she seemed to like Elisbet and Frances. They'd taken to her, too. He could keep his Christmas promise to them. That made him smile. He'd wanted to tell them tonight but decided to wait until after Dr. Pickens talked to Alma.

As far as he was concerned, a quick trip to see the minister after work one day next week would work out well. They'd be married, and Alma could start helping out right away. He'd already been through the courting of a woman and a wedding. He paused his chipping at the dried food. It had been nice the first time, but now it would be a waste of time. He and Alma would get to know each other after they were married.

Unless she expected to be courted. Her father had avoided that question when Roy brought it up. He'd said, "Alma will be happy to get married. She knows the little ones need a mother's care as soon as possible."

Seems her mother had died when she was a young'un. He went back to prying off the dried eggs. Roy figured God had sent him to Trenton because He knew Alma was here. That had to be it. A woman as pretty as she should be married by now, with children of her own.

Why wasn't she? Was there something wrong with her? Maybe she was too picky in whom she wanted to marry? Add that to her father being willing to let her get married without a courting period.

It had been his experience with Janie that women didn't always say what they wanted. Perhaps this Alma was different? She must be, or her father wouldn't be so confident in arranging this marriage without talking to her first.

‿✀‿

"All you have is the word of his mother? What mother would say anything bad about her son?" Alma sucked in her anger.

"You might have a point about that, but like I said, I've seen how he treats his daughters. I figure how he takes care of them is a good indication of what he'll be like as a husband."

"So I can go around with dried oatmeal in my hair and the hem of my dress torn and dragging in the streets?"

"Alma, calm down. You'll fix those things as their mother. What I see is the way he gets them candy at the store, the way the littlest one hangs onto his pants leg and he doesn't mind. The oldest holds his hand while they walk into church."

"So as long as I have candy, hang on his pants leg, and hold his hand, I'll be treated special as his wife?"

"Alma Gail Pickens. Enough. The matter is settled. He'll be over here tomorrow to discuss the details with you. I've given my word that you'll marry him, and there won't be a fuss about not having a season of courting."

"And I have no say in this? I'm to marry him without knowing him? Without being in love?"

"There isn't time for courting. I'm leaving the day after Christmas, and I want this settled before then." Dr. Pickens reached across the table for his daughter's hand. "I promise, you'll grow to love each other."

Tears stung her eyes. "But I promised Mama that I'd take care of you."

"I know, and you have done that longer than you should. Mr. Gibbons is a good man and needs help. You saw that; you even told me about the sad state of his home and how his daughters are taken with you."

"That doesn't mean he's the marrying kind!" She yanked her hand away from him and pushed back her chair. Married by Christmas might be what her father and Mr. Gibbons wanted, but not her.

"You know that's false, Alma. Think about what you're saying. He's been married before, and from what I can tell, still loves his wife. That means a lot to me. I'm glad. I feel good about handing you over to him."

"Glad? You're glad about giving me to a man who still loves another?"

"Yes, to me it means he's wanting to have the same kind of comfort and companionship he had before."

"Does that mean you didn't love Mama enough to want to marry again?"

"No, it means I never found someone I could love as much. Roy Gibbons has."

"I don't believe that. I won't do it." She snatched up the stew pan and scraped the metal spoon against the sides, not caring how much noise it made. She pushed the scraps into the garbage pail. She wasn't saving any leftovers. As far as she was concerned, Papa could make his own dinner from now on. See how glad he'd be about that.

Chapter 5

Roy thought it best to meet with Miss Pickens without his daughters. He'd left them with Pete, his farmhand. To their delight, Pete promised to take them out to play with the barn cats. They were so excited they forgot to ask where he was going and why they couldn't come with him. Even Frances had let go of his leg and attached herself to Pete.

Dr. Pickens's two-story brick home was much nicer than his. Guess it made sense to be located close to town where most of the people lived, quicker to get to emergencies. He raised his hand to knock on the door and then lowered it. Maybe this wasn't a good idea. It seemed reasonably sound yesterday, but now that he'd slept on it, the idea of marrying so quick felt wrong. His shoulders tightened. He and Miss Pickens would benefit from this arrangement. But would she like living on a farm so far from town? In a house that seemed too small when Frances and Elisbet got to squealing and shrieking? He'd given the doc his word, though, so he best follow through. He and Miss Pickens wouldn't be the first couple necessity had brought to the altar.

He tapped on the door, deciding a polite knock would be best. He stepped back and waited.

Miss Pickens opened the door. "Mr. Gibbons."

"Miss Pickens, your father suggested we meet this evening."

"Yes, he did."

Wasn't she going to ask him inside? "May I come in?"

She swung the door wide. "Please do. Papa is in the kitchen."

He'd remembered her blond hair and that's about all. When she'd rescued him during Frances's illness, he hadn't noticed her dark blue eyes or how the top of her head didn't come up to his shoulder. "I came to see you, not him."

"Perhaps you did, but since the two of you have arranged my life for me, you might as well work out the details and fill me in later." She turned, back straight, and walked away from him like royalty. "Shut the door behind you."

So this wouldn't be as easy as the doc suggested. Miss Pickens would be a challenge. He closed the door, and for the first time in quite a while found himself excited about the prospect of winning a woman's attention.

⤫

Alma, still spitting mad, led Mr. Gibbons into the kitchen where her father waited. "Mr. Gibbons is here. I think you two should chat and then let me know when I'm to leave the house."

"Alma, that's not how this is going to work. I know you're angry, but sit and get to know him before you stomp upstairs." Dr. Pickens pulled out a chair for her. "Evening, Roy."

"Doc." Roy stooped his shoulders to get though the doorway.

Alma hadn't noticed before how tall he stood or the width of his chest. The man and his dimples took her breath away. Maybe it wouldn't be so bad being married to him. At least she'd have something worth looking at every day. She found her way to the chair her father stood behind, and sat. "Thank you. How are the girls?"

Roy sat across the table from her. "They're fine. Pete's letting them play with the barn cats while I'm here."

"What do they think of you getting married?" She heard the terse tone in her voice and didn't like it. She'd been taught better than this. "Love your neighbor as yourself" came to mind.

Dr. Pickens slid a cup of coffee onto the table in front of Mr. Gibbons and gave Alma a look she knew too well as he handed her one. She had taken this as far as she could.

"I know they are anticipating a mother for Christmas, so I wondered about their excitement at the news." There, that was better.

"I haven't told them. Thought I ought to talk to the woman I was marrying first and make sure there would be a wedding." He gave her a slow grin then took a sip of his drink.

He'd considered her feelings? Her heart fluttered. She hadn't expected that. "I don't understand. I thought. . ."

"Well, I agreed to marry you, but not until after I decided you would be interested. I can't be bringing home just anyone to be a mother to my daughters. There's enough fairy tales out there to scare them without getting them their own wicked stepmother."

"But. . ."

"Sorry, Miss Pickens, I didn't mean to imply that you would be like that. I think it best for both parties to be agreeable to marriage." He set his cup down. "What about you?"

Alma's tongue-twisted words couldn't make it past her lips. He had to be the most beautiful man she'd ever been this close to. She wrenched herself out of an imaginary embrace and felt the loss. "I—I think. . .yes."

Mr. Gibbons slapped his hands together, making her jump. "Then we have a deal. You're right, Doc, she did say yes."

Alma gasped.

"I talked to the reverend, and we can get married Sunday, Miss Pickens."

"No!" Alma's stomach contents slid and jerked, bumping into her throat. "Not Sunday. I have a few things to say about this wedding, and the first thing is—it won't be this weekend."

Roy couldn't be more confused. The woman had said she'd marry him. Why would she want to delay? Her father had said courting her wasn't necessary.

"Mr. Gibbons, I will marry you on Christmas Eve."

"Why wait? Four weeks isn't going to change anything, and I need a wife now."

"I refuse to be a replacement for your wife. I know you still love her, and I think that's admirable."

He felt his head nodding and wondered where this would go.

"Here are my demands. If I'm to be thrown into a marriage by my father's wishes, you will have to court me until we get married. It's the only wedding I intend to have, and I'm not going to walk into this one on Sunday, get up on Monday and make your breakfast and clean your house without some kind of happy memory to cling to."

"Demands?" He shoved his chair away from the table. "I don't—"

"Alma, I told you to give it time, and you'll fall in love with each other."

"You told her that, Doc? How can you promise her that?"

"Papa, it may or may not happen, and that's the way life is. Mr. Gibbons needs a mother for his girls more than he needs a wife, so I'm willing to do that. Before that happens, though, I want to be treated special. Right now, I feel like Mr. Gibbons ordered me from a catalog. He knows nothing about me or I him. It's only fair that I get to know him before we get married. I'm not asking for a year, only four weeks."

Miss Pickens had a good point. Roy settled his back against the chair. "What do you have in mind?"

"I'll make a list and give it to you when you pick me up for our first outing. You can choose where to take me." She rose from her chair and nodded. "This time tomorrow would be fine, unless you care to provide dinner?"

Roy's lips moved, though his mind couldn't grasp what he was saying. "Dinner. Yes, we have to eat."

"Tomorrow, then. Let me walk you to the door. I know you're needed at home, and I must work on my list."

Before he knew what had happened, Roy found himself escorted out by the pretty and spirited woman and left standing on the porch. How had she done that? Small as she was, he'd been moved to the door and hadn't felt a thing.

Chapter 6

Alma checked the mirror again for stray hairs that may be out of place. She wouldn't admit it to anyone, but she was excited to be seeing Mr. Gibbons. Her cheeks couldn't hide that, flushed as they were against her pale skin.

Should she be waiting for him when he arrived or make him wait a little bit? She missed her mother. Her papa did his best, but when it came to being a female, he was lost.

Making him wait didn't feel comfortable. She should have asked Jewel what to do. She picked up the list, folded it, and stuck it in her dress pocket.

Her dress. Was it all right? She didn't put on her fanciest one but picked the blue wool one. It kept her warm, and Papa said it made her eyes bright as a July sky.

In the parlor, she settled on a chair. Papa had started a fire. He'd come home early to see her off. Most likely to make sure she would go with Mr. Gibbons.

"You look nice, my dear." Papa walked across the room and stoked the fire. "Mr. Gibbons should be here soon."

"Are you sure about this marriage, Papa? It's not too late. We haven't told anyone."

"I am."

"I understand you don't want me to come with you to St. Louis and you rented out my home, but I could stay with Jewel and her husband. Or perhaps one of the widows from church? It's only for a year."

"No. I considered those things, but it's not fair to you. Suppose I find a wife in St. Louis. Then what will you do? You need your own home and family. A place where you can paint the furniture if you want to."

"I don't have to change things," Alma whispered.

"I want the best for you." He dabbed his eye and turned back to the fire.

Footsteps landed heavy on the wooden porch. There was a pause, then a knock. He was here. Why did her heart flip like a griddle cake? Goodness, she would need to get this emotion controlled before she faced him.

"That's your intended. I'll get the door, you wait here. A little bit of mystery is a good thing. Your mother told me that. Guess I should have mentioned a few of those bits of wisdom to you sooner."

"There's still time, Papa."

"I love you, Little Bit. Don't forget that ever." He gave her a quick hug and released her.

"I won't. You're making me cry. My face will be all red."

"You're beautiful, like your mother." He stepped out of the room.

Alma blinked and looked at the ceiling to keep the tears from falling. She turned to see Mr. Gibbons standing in front of her father. He smiled. She caught the schoolgirl sigh before it escaped.

⌒⌒

Roy had cleaned the carriage the best he could in the cold weather. He didn't think Miss Pickens would notice, but she sure would if it were a mess. "I hope you don't mind. We'll be dining at my house tonight. The girls are excited that you'll be eating with us." More than that, they'd been collecting pinecones after school and arranging them multiple ways across the tabletop.

"We're eating at your house?" Alma pivoted to look at him.

"That's what I said. The girls helped me set the table, even made some decorations, though I told them it's not a holiday."

"Nothing wrong with expressing creativity. It will be fun to see what they've come up with. Did they collect things from inside or outside?"

"You'll have to wait and see. They like you—the girls."

"I like them, too." She rubbed her hands together.

"Are you cold? I have a blanket if you need it." He reached behind her, brought it over the carriage seat, and handed it to her.

Alma covered her lap and stuck her hands underneath. "Thank you. I should have brought my muff, but I didn't want to give in to it being winter yet. I dread its full-blown arrival."

"There, I've learned something about you. Winter is not your favorite season."

"I didn't say that. I love snow and ice skating, but the season lasts too long."

"I can never decide. In the heat of summer, I long for the cold. When it comes, I get tired of splitting wood and I want it to be July." He pulled up in front of the house, stopped the horse, and helped her out of the carriage.

Pete stepped out the door. "I'll take care of Dolly and get her in the barn. Those girls are wound tighter than a top. It'll be a rest to brush down the horse."

Inside, the girls wrapped their arms around Alma's waist.

"You came!" Frances said.

"Of course she did. Papa said she would," Elisbet said. "May I take your cloak, Miss Pickens?"

"Yes, you may. Thank you." Alma slid it from her shoulders and folded it in half before handing it to Elisbet. "There, maybe it won't be quite so hard to carry now."

His girls made him proud. "Thank you, Elisbet."

Elisbet buried her nose in the fabric and came up smiling. "You smell good, like cookies."

"And she has the most beautiful dress." Frances stroked the fabric. "Blue is my favorite color."

"Thank you." Alma's face flushed cranberry red.

Frances snuggled her hand into Alma's and tugged her toward the kitchen. "Come see the table."

Alma looked back at Roy. Was she trying to arch her eyebrow? He couldn't help but grin at her. He figured she didn't know how much his daughters craved a woman's attention. "I'll be right behind you." A place he didn't mind being, because his daughter was right. Alma smelled good.

⤞⤝

Dinner went well. Alma exclaimed over the girls' efforts to make the kitchen "festive," as she called it. He hadn't seen Elisbet's face hold so much joy in months.

"Thank you for tucking them in while I checked on the calf."

"It was fun. I haven't read that princess book in years."

"I can't say the same. It's the same book, or a variation, every night. Think you'll be able to stand that after we're married?" He stood in the parlor. Should he sit next to her on the sofa or in the chair across from her? They'd sat together in the carriage, but that didn't count. Still, it was intimate sitting with a woman without a chaperone. Maybe he'd poke the fire again. "You mentioned a list?"

"I brought it with me." She slid her hand into her dress pocket and pulled out a folded paper. She did that little thing with her eyebrow that was a slight imitation of her father's. On Alma it was downright cute. "You won't toss it in the fire?"

"Maybe after I read it."

"Then sit next to me and I'll read it to you. That will eliminate the chance of its being destroyed." She patted the sofa. "The fire is fine. It's rather warm in here."

Was she bossy? Or practical? Janie never told him what to do. They'd married young, and she thought he could do anything. It had scared him to have someone think he was that capable. He'd let her down in the end. Maybe it would be better to have a wife with her own opinions, used to doing for herself. It would be harder to disappoint her.

He sat by her but not close enough to touch. "Let's hear the demands."

Alma unfolded the paper and held it up. "Isn't it pretty?"

The paper was bordered with tiny birds and flowers. Were those real pieces of ribbons glued to it? Roy nodded.

"I like to paint. I'm learning more about it, and I've been saving for the Oil Painting Outfit Complete with twenty-five colors of paint so I can increase my skills."

Her eyes were wide open and not at all showing any fear that he might disapprove. Not that he would. She'd find out soon enough how little time there would be to paint. "It's good to have something you love to do."

"I do love it. That's why it's on my list."

"Painting?"

"Yes, I want to paint the furniture."

Janie had picked out the furniture he hadn't made for them. "What's wrong with—" Alma dropped her gaze to the floor. He hadn't meant to hurt her, but those were changes he couldn't allow. He'd discuss it with her later. Surely she would understand when he explained what the pieces meant to him. "What else is on that list?"

"First, I want a real wedding at the church, and after it, I want to have cake and punch for our friends. I can make my own wedding dress. Elisbet and Frances should have new ones, too, and shoes, maybe hair ribbons to match."

Roy grasped the paper and slipped it from her hand. "Let me read this." She wanted him to bring her flowers. Where did the woman think he was going to find flowers in November in Illinois? Did she think he had special growing powers that could make them bloom in the middle of winter? It became clear to him there might be a reason she hadn't married. He continued reading. Spend time together every day and. . . "Exchange special gifts at Christmas?" What did that mean?

Chapter 7

Settled on Jewel's sofa, Alma and her friend hunched over a fashion plate in *Godey's Lady's Book*, admiring a dress.

Alma caressed the page. "It's perfect."

"You'll be beautiful. The bottle-green satin will make your eyes look bluer, and with the touches of red on the cuffs and inside the stand-up collar, it's perfect for Christmas."

"I think the cuffs should be red velvet."

"What about the hat?" Jewel wore a cat-grin.

"I'm not wearing a bird, especially a brown one!" Alma put her hands together on top of her head and flapped her fingers as if they were wings. "That would make quite a stir."

"I'm sure the bird is stuffed."

"Doesn't matter. Feathers are fine, but a dead bird is not." Alma frowned. "I have to find a gift for Mr. Gibbons, too." Why had she thought it would be a wonderful idea to make him a special present?

"Shouldn't you call him Roy?"

"I suppose. It feels too soon." And it was. Since she'd agreed to this marriage, her old life had disappeared. Precious objects were packed and stored; furniture had been moved as well. Papa had wasted no time readying to leave. Her body ached with sadness. "Jewel, this is the first time I won't be spending Christmas with Papa."

Jewel slid her arm around Alma's shoulder. "It's going to be fine. You'll be Mrs. Roy Gibbons on Christmas, and you'll have two excited daughters to wake you."

"I don't know what to make him."

"What does he like? What's his favorite color? You could knit a cap."

"I don't know. I wanted to do this because Mama and Papa did, but they were married almost a year before Christmas came." She, of course, had to do this the hard way. Meet a man, agree to marry him, and make him a meaningful gift in four weeks.

Jewel's son, Caleb, woke with a scream. "Time for me to go back to being

33

a mother and not a schoolgirl. Why don't you ask around at the store and see if you can discover anything. Mrs. Remik up at the Star Store knows about everyone."

Alma felt light as relief pushed out the sadness. "She does!" She grabbed the Godey's *Lady's Book* and held it to her chest. "I'd love to stay and play with Caleb, but I have to go on a spying adventure."

⁓

Roy rode up to the front porch and slid down from the saddle. He was worked up about what he'd heard in town. He and Miss Pickens were in need of a serious talk. He rubbed the back of his neck. He'd fallen asleep reading to the girls last night and slept there for a few hours before realizing he wasn't in his own bed.

Alma opened the door with red-rimmed eyes. She'd been crying. His shoulders tensed as he waited for a problem to show up he'd be expected to solve.

"Evening, Mr. Gibbons. Papa isn't home, so I can't let you in." She sniffed.

"He's a few minutes behind me. Told me to tell you not to keep me standing outside."

Alma backed away and held the door open. "I always honor my father's requests."

So that's what the crying was about. She still didn't want to marry him. He wasn't sure he wanted to marry her, either, but he'd shaken hands with her father. "It's time you started calling me Roy, don't you think?"

"I suppose so. . .Roy." She closed the door. "I've got dinner about ready to serve for Papa. Would you like some?"

"I came to talk to you, then I need to get home. Pete's with the girls, but I'm feeling bad about having him watch them so I can see you every night." She looked as if she might burst into tears. "Alma, that didn't come out right. Would you be agreeable to a few nights a week instead of—"

"No, I wouldn't. We need to know each other better."

"Is that why you've been asking around town what color shirts I like best and what I buy at the store?"

"Mrs. Remik told you?" Her eyes were wide as a doe's.

"Yes, and when she couldn't understand why you were so interested, I told her we were getting married."

"So now everyone in town knows." Her shoulders sagged as she turned away.

"They'll know soon anyway. I don't see a problem."

"Of course not. Why would you? This is an arrangement between Papa and you. I don't have a choice."

"Is that why you've been crying, Alma?" His heart softened, and he put his hand on her shoulder. He prayed his daughters would never be in this situation. He would do his best from now on to make her feel treasured. Starting with taking her flowers, as soon as he could figure out some way to get some.

"No. It's because. . .I can't get my kitten heads to be round." She rested her hand on his for a moment then brushed it away. "I need to stir. . .something."

Roy scratched his forehead and followed her into the kitchen. He would never understand women, but he knew enough not to ask about the kittens. When it came to females, he'd learned a small problem generally covered a bigger one.

⟡

Alma shivered on the porch step. Elisbet and Frances had rushed past her. "It's early. Why are you here, Roy?"

"I saw your father in town. He said you wouldn't be opposed to watching the girls. I've taken on extra work at the mill and won't be able to meet them after school."

"Papa said to bring them?" How was she to continue packing the house, making her dress, and figuring out what to give Roy for a gift with two little girls running around?

"He thought it'd be a good idea for you all to get to know each other better. He'll watch them while we sit in the parlor after dinner. Doc wants to get to know them, too. Since he'll be their grandfather."

"If he wants to be one, he should stay here in Trenton." She wrapped her arms tightly around her waist. Had he said supper? She needed to cook for all of them every night?

"Then, sweetheart"—he reached out and stroked her cheek—"we might not be getting married." Roy flashed his dimples and then winked.

Sweetheart? Her knees went weak. Her body felt the way it did when she'd been double dosed with Mrs. Winslow's Soothing Syrup—all warm and happy. Did that mean. . . ? Could it be that he did care for her?

Chapter 8

Ten inches of snow covered the ground. On his one day off in over a week, Roy ought to be inside doing chores. Instead, once again, he stood on Alma's porch at an odd time of day. Under a heavy blanket, his girls waited in the sleigh. Music-box giggles floated through the air.

Alma squealed with delight at the sight behind him. "Sleigh ride!"

"Would you like to go with us?" Was she bouncing on her toes? "Can you get ready fast? I don't want to undress those two while we wait. It takes too long to put them back together."

"I'll hurry!"

She meant it, because when she appeared less than five minutes later, the twist of hair on the nape of her neck was off-center and the yellow ribbon didn't match the skirt he saw hanging from underneath her cloak. The fashionable Miss Pickens had turned into a little girl. She bounded past him, twisting a scarf around her neck. "How long can we ride?"

"Until the first one whines." He helped Alma into the sleigh and slid in next to her. When his arm brushed against hers, sparks he hadn't felt in a long time ignited. He urged the horse forward.

Alma rubbed her muffed hand under her chin. "It's the most beautiful thing, isn't it? Snow? Wouldn't it be perfect if there were bells on the sleigh, Elisbet?"

"Papa! Can we get bells?"

"Bells!" Frances chimed in.

"Please, don't encourage them." Roy glanced at Alma. "What's wrong with your eyebrow?"

"When Papa wants to make a point, he arches his. I can't, not yet. I'm training it." She used her finger to arch it. "Bells are not extravagant, if they make you happy."

Roy pursed his lips then rolled them under. This was not a moment to laugh. "Look, there's a hill and sledders. The snow must be well packed. Anyone want to give it a try?"

A chorus of "I dos" rang from behind him.

He helped everyone from the sleigh and untied the wooden sled he'd brought. "Who's first?"

"Me!" Elisbet said.

"Me!" Frances jumped in front of Elisbet, lost her balance, and toppled in the snow.

"Me!" Alma helped Frances get up. "Let's make snow angels before we go home. That way we won't be as cold and can sled longer."

Alma took him by surprise. He hadn't imagined she'd want to fly down a snowy hill. "I think this sled can hold two, so Franny and I'll go first. Unless, Elisbet, you want to ride with her. She is covered in snow."

Roy lost track of how many runs Alma and the girls, even he, made down the hill. Finally he had to say, "I think it's time to go."

"No, you have to ride with Miss Pickens!" Elisbet insisted.

He started to refuse, but Alma had already climbed on the sled. He settled behind her, the closeness of her, the sweet scent of her hair clutching his heart. Before he let his mind run off the rails, he sent the sled down the hill and into a snow bank. Snow covered her face. Before he could help her up, she giggled then went into a full-throttle laugh, fell backward, and made a snow angel.

"I want to do that again!"

"Maybe next time. I think it's best to get all the red-cheeked women in my life home and warmed up so there aren't any more colds." He couldn't handle another close ride with her. Not until they were married, anyway.

He loaded everyone on the sleigh then went to attach the sled to the back. On his way, he noticed a yellow ribbon. He picked it up and slid it into his pocket with a smile. He had his first piece of the gift he'd make Alma.

⟡

In the Gibbonses' warm kitchen, Alma yanked on Frances's boot until it gave up and released her foot. "Your stockings are wet. Are yours, Elisbet?"

Elisbet nodded.

"Let's find dry clothes for you two before you catch a chill. While we're gone, Roy, could you make some hot chocolate for us?"

"You have to say please." Frances's teeth chattered.

"Please." Alma bent down in front of Frances. "You're right. I should have said that." She stood and took the child's hand. "Shall we?"

Once Alma had the girls in warm clothes, they returned to the kitchen. She'd brought along their brush. "Frances, you're first. Let's get the knots out of your hair." The little girl stood still while her hair was put back in order.

Elisbet took her place. "You hurt less than Papa."

"I've had years of practice unsnarling hair."

"That's true. My hair has never been that long and won't be. Enjoy it, girls, because it's still a few weeks until Christmas."

"And we get Miss Pickens for our mama!" Frances shouted.

"Settle down. The cocoa is ready." He ladled it into cups.

The girls slid into their chairs. Chilled, Alma hesitated. She wanted to sit next to the stove, but that was Roy's seat.

"Sit here," Elisbet demanded, then added, "please."

Roy set cups in front of Frances and Elisbet. "Yes, that's a good spot for you. I'm sure you're cold and wet, too. We should have taken you home first."

"I don't mind. I only did one snow angel, so I wasn't as wet as these two."

Roy placed a cup in front of her. "This will help warm you. Good suggestion, Janie."

If a heart could make a sound when it broke, Alma's would have. Janie. His dead wife's name. She wanted to disappear, be anywhere but Roy Gibbons's kitchen. Her throat closed.

Roy's pale face swam through her watery eyes. "Alma, I'm so sorry. For a moment it felt like we were a family, and I guess that's why I called you Janie. You've filled a vacancy today, and my heart felt whole. Thank you. Can you forgive me, Alma?"

"Is Papa in trouble?" Frances hopped from her chair and was by his side, hot chocolate forgotten.

"No. Everything is fine." Alma offered a forced smile but looked away from Roy. It wasn't good that he took her as a replacement for Janie. He had to understand that before they married. She wasn't sure he would. She loved his children, but Roy never spent time alone with her. He didn't want a wife, he wanted a caretaker. "I am feeling chilled. Would you take me home now?"

Roy could have kicked himself. He had called her Janie. Alma had done her best not to let him touch her while he helped her into her cloak. He had to make this better. He could have offered her dry clothes, but that wouldn't do. She wouldn't want to wear the dress of Janie's that he'd kept.

Once in the sleigh, he thought he'd go for distraction. It worked for his daughters. Maybe it would for Alma. "Have you considered what you'd like to bring to the house?"

"My painting equipment, and Papa offered Mama's china. I'd like to bring it." She spoke to the side of the sleigh instead of turning his way.

"We'll probably find a place to store things in the barn. Janie's china is still serviceable, and I'm not sure where we'd put your paints."

"As you wish."

This wasn't going well. He'd planned to kiss her when he took her home, but now? He'd best wait.

Chapter 9

Something roused Roy. Had Frances cried out? He pushed against the chair arms and rose. He didn't hear her now.

He was heartsick about calling Alma the wrong name. Even thought of getting Pete to watch the girls so he could go talk to her. Get her to understand he liked having her in his kitchen. Instead, after getting the girls down for the night, he had sat down to rest and had drifted off.

A knock sounded. "Gibbons!"

Roy jerked open the door. "Dr. Pickens. Is Alma all right?"

"No, she is not." Dr. Pickens marched past him. "I thought you were a decent man." He paced the room. "I'm giving you my most valuable possession because I thought you were worthy. It seems I'm wrong."

"Doc, can I—"

"No sir, you cannot. I have a lot to say. My little girl has been in her room since you brought her home. She's crying, and I can't make her stop." He faced Roy. "Do you know how that feels?"

Not sure if he was allowed to speak, Roy just nodded.

"I know you do, because you've been raising those girls alone. That's why this match is a good one. You need each other, but you can't be calling my Alma by your wife's name." He lowered himself into a chair. "Now, what is your explanation?"

Roy sat across from the doctor, dipped his head, and held his forehead with his hands. "It slipped out. Everything felt normal, like we were a family again. I tried to tell her that."

"She doesn't expect you to quit loving Janie. She knows what it's like to lose someone you love, but son, you have to do what your vows said."

What vows? He and Alma hadn't said any yet. Confused, Roy straightened his back and gaped at him.

"Remember the part that says, 'until death do us part'? You have to release Janie and let Alma move into your heart. She needs the bigger space now. Show her you care enough to remember her name. All this coming over to our house in the evening is nice, but it's not enough. Alma was right. You need to court her so you mean it when you say those vows to her. You better repair this mess right away. Otherwise, you might as well hire a woman to come help in this house."

"I took her sledding."

"With your children."

"She didn't mind." He stopped from squirming like a ten-year-old caught with his hand in the cookie jar. Why had he thought this would be easy? Alma didn't know him, and he shouldn't expect her to.

"Take her out alone. There's always a bonfire on the weekend down by the pond at Sauer's place. Bring her candy. Take her ice skating. Hold her hand. Stare into her eyes. Make her feel like she's the only one in the world. Janie agreed to marry you, so you must know how to court a woman. Do you remember?"

Yes, he did, and the memory hurt. Could he do those things with Alma?

Alma's heart wasn't in making Roy's gift. She'd failed to find out more about him. She knew he cared about his family, but beyond that, she hadn't even discovered his favorite color. She strolled the store aisle searching for something to use to craft an ornament.

She fingered silk ribbons. Elisbet and Frances would like these. They were easy to buy for, not like their father. If God would send her an idea of what to make, something Roy would save and treasure, she'd be grateful.

The door opened and the sunlight struck something, sending a rainbow through the room. She picked up her pace, and there it was. A beautiful, clear, glass teardrop ornament. The perfect size for painting. She purchased it along with the ribbons and hurried home as the sun set.

She slowed her step. Roy sat on the porch rail waiting for her.

"I heard there was a bonfire tonight. I'd like to take you, just you, if you'll go with me," he asked.

Thrilled, Alma ran upstairs and put away her purchases, found warm clothes, and met him at the door. Minutes later they were at Sauer's pond sitting by a bonfire and lacing on their skates. He'd said little to her on the ride and even now remained quiet. Maybe it was time for her to let go of her anger and give him an opportunity to start over.

She could either continue to be furious or take it as a compliment that Roy was comfortable with her. The fire crackled and popped behind her. "Are we going to be like the wild young ones and take a chance on the ice, or stay by the fire like our elders?"

Roy's eyes flashed in the firelight. Then he took her hand. "I'm not feeling like an elder, so let's be young, but not wild. Unless you want to be?"

Was that uncertainty or fear in his voice? "Not up to falling and spinning on the ice tonight?"

"Not when I have to be a father in the morning. If I could lie around in bed like you all day, counting the flowers on the wallpaper, then I might."

She playfully slapped his arm. "I have never lain in bed all day."

"What do you do with your days?"

"Lots of things. Paint, feed the chickens, gather feathers for projects." Alma waved at her friend Katie and her brother as they swished by. "Make dinner for Papa."

"Feathers? What do you do with them?"

"I'm working on a dye to color them, or sometimes I try to paint them." Her foot slipped. "Oh!"

Roy caught her, brought her upright, and steadied her. "You paint them and then what?"

"I haven't found the best application for them, yet. They may have something to do with your special Christmas gift." She gave her best mystery-smile and skated away. Feathers. Perhaps she could find some way to adhere them to his gift.

Roy circled her then slipped in next to her, taking her hand. "Want to play a game?"

She attempted the eyebrow arch and felt it go a tiny bit higher. "What kind?"

"A getting-to-know-you game. I'll give you two choices and you guess which one I like. Then you get a turn."

"I'm first." She dropped his hand, skated ahead and did a spin, and returned with a question. "Christmas or Fourth of July?"

"You like Christmas because we'll be married by then."

"I do like it best, but not because we'll be married. I love the Nativity story and that's when Jesus was born."

"I like that you'll be my wife and you get to be there when the girls jump out of bed and their eyes are wide with excitement. I can't wait for you to see that."

The thin layer of ice around her heart began to drip. He did want to marry her. He'd said that first before anything else. She should apologize for leaving in a huff the other day. Roy pulled her tightly to him as they rounded the end of the frozen pond. "Working in the field or with wood?"

"I think"—she tilted her head and studied his face—"the field, because it provides for your family."

"Both do, and while I'm grateful, the fields don't provide much enjoyment. I like making things out of wood."

"So my gift is made of wood?" She giggled.

"Still a secret. You might be getting nothing more than a splinter."

"Orange or black?"

"Odd choices for favorite colors. Orange?"

"Black. I like black cats." A small group of boys began to race on the ice, whizzing past at dizzying speeds. The bonfire looked appealing.

"Cats make me sneeze. Do you think I'd rather eat pork chops or roast and potatoes?"

"Pork chops."

"Roast, because the next day I can have a delicious sandwich. I haven't had a good roast since Janie—"

A few boys raced past. One tripped, and his arms went in wild circles as he attempted to stay on his feet. He fell, sliding in their direction. Alma squealed.

Roy whipped Alma away from the sharp blades before they reached her. She ought to be grateful, but all she remembered was hearing the name Janie—again.

∽∾

In the barn, Roy caressed a piece of wood. He had to prove to Alma he cared. He'd seen the look on her face when he'd mentioned Janie again. If he wanted, and he did, to build a life with her, he needed to start with a good foundation.

He hadn't lied to her when he'd said she'd get a splinter for Christmas, because she surely would. But it wasn't her only gift. He had the special one finished, ready for Christmas.

Chapter 10

"Remember you can't tell your father about this." Alma tied Frances's apron and then checked to make sure Elisbet was well covered.

Before the girls arrived, Alma had covered the kitchen table with last week's *Trenton Gazette* to protect it from the red and green paint she'd mixed for them to use.

"We won't." Elisbet shoved her fists under her chin and squealed. "We keep secrets, don't we, Franny?"

"Yeth." Franny gave a missing-tooth grin. Her front tooth had fallen out last week, making her even more adorable.

Alma was unsure about these two. They tended to tell their father about their day the moment they saw him. "Let's sit at the kitchen table. Be careful—" They were in their chairs, feet kicking against the bottom rungs before she finished her sentence. "Not to knock over the paint."

"What are we painting?" Elisbet turned in her chair. "I don't see anything worth keeping a secret."

"I get the green!" Frances shouted.

"Frances, no yelling. There is enough of both colors. Turn back around, Elisbet. What we are painting is in my apron pocket."

The room grew quiet as Alma reached into her pocket and withdrew the ornament wrapped in brown paper. "This is it." She sat between them, set the package on the table, and lifted an edge of the paper, gently unwinding it. "It's made of glass. We have to be careful."

Alma held the ornament up for them to see. "We are going to paint our names on it. What do you think?"

No response. No excitement. No anything. She looked at each girl. No smiles. "What's wrong?"

"Franny can't write her name."

"I'll help her. Would that be okay, Frances?"

"Yeth. Can we paint the paper, too?"

"That's a good idea. While Elisbet paints her name on the ornament, you can work on half of the wrapping paper. Then we can switch."

The girls worked with occasional giggles, and Alma had to wipe paint from the ends of their hair a few times.

"Finished!" Frances glowed. "All my letterth are on there."

Including an adorable fingerprint. Alma didn't know if Roy would cherish it, but she would.

"Can we put your name and Papa's on it?" Elisbet asked. "Because Papa said we're going to be a family. So, can we?"

Alma's heart swelled with love. "Yes, and we'll hang it on our tree every year."

She finished the last stroke on Roy's *y*. The back door swung open. Her father rushed in, breathless. "The church is on fire. The wedding's canceled. Roy's on his way. Meet him at the front door, and I'll hide this."

∽

"We are getting married." Roy shivered in the cold air. The water on his pants had turned to ice. "Can I come in?"

"Yes, of course. You're wet. Go in the parlor where it's warm. I'll get hot chocolate for you, to chase the chill."

"I want—need you to come with me." He grasped her hand and pulled her along with him. Standing with his back to the fire, willing his teeth not to chatter, he drew her close and kissed her. "Alma Gail Pickens, will you marry me?"

"I don't under—"

"Just answer the question."

"Yes."

Her face crinkled, and her eyebrow arched. Did she realize it? He wanted to laugh and then shout, "I love Alma Pickens!"

"Roy?" Her questioning eyes begged for more.

He kissed her again, feeling the heat thaw his lips. "I saw the church in flames, and I knew the wedding would be called off. Then I realized, if this had happened tomorrow while we were there, I might have lost you, and I haven't told you how I feel. That I love the way you make every activity fun, the way you practice your eyebrow arch, and the way you make me feel like more than a father. You've given me my life back, and I never even proposed to you. You deserve that. So I'll ask you again, Alma, would you marry me? Could you love me the rest of our lives?"

"Yes! I love you, too. But how will we get married? The girls are counting on having a mother on Christmas morning."

"Don't worry. I have a plan. If you keep Elisbet and Frances tonight, I promise to make tomorrow a special memory, even without the church." He tipped her head and kissed her again.

"Are you going to kiss me a lot when we're married?"

"Yes, I am."

"I'm glad. I didn't know I'd like it so much." Her face flushed a bright red. "I should get you something to drink, to warm you."

"I don't need anything. You've thawed my frozen bones, sweetheart."

∾

Alma waited in Roy's bedroom, trying hard not to think that it would be her bedroom, too, tonight. Her father had covered her eyes when they entered the house, and the girls led her in so she couldn't see the decorations. Her hands shook. How she wished Mama was here. Jewel had explained a few things to her, with a scarlet face. Her father had come to her room last night to discuss with her the duties of a wife. Horrified, she'd sent him away.

She'd helped Elisbet and Frances into their red velvet dresses and tied bows in their hair. Their faces were blinding with joy as they scooted from the room. Jewel had helped her put on her dress. The satin, soft as a kitten, slid over her head. She rubbed the red velvet cuff between her fingers. It was perfect. Even more so, she knew she would honor her mother and father by marrying Roy.

It was almost time. Soon she'd be Mrs. Roy Gibbons. Her stomach twirled. She promised God she would be the best wife and mother possible. The door opened, and her father stepped inside, beaming.

He held out his arm. "You're beautiful, Little Bit. So much like your mother. Are you ready?"

Alma took his elbow and they strolled past the dining room. Roy had placed Mama's embroidered tablecloth under heaping platters of bread and meat. China dishes and. . .were those Mama's cups? They were. Her eyes watered. It felt right, almost as if Mama were here, smiling. It was beautiful, festive.

But the parlor took her breath away. Candles in crystal holders ambled across the mantel, sending warm, dancing lights across the room. A music box played in the background, and Roy waited for her by the fire with the preacher. He'd kept his promise. He'd given her a wedding to remember.

∾

The bedroom door creaked. Alma started. She heard giggles and opened her eyes.

"Good morning, Mrs. Gibbons." Roy stood inside the door, holding

46

tight to his daughters' shoulders. "They have something to say." He let go, and blond hair flew as Elisbet and Frances ran and jumped on the bed.

Elisbet tapped Frances's shoulder. "One, two, three."

"Merry Christmas, Mama!" Alma treasured the unison of the sweet voices.

"Come on, girls, let's let your mama get dressed and meet us in the parlor." Alma smiled at her new husband with gratitude.

The girls waited by the tree, pointing out decorations they liked. They asked questions about how the tree got into the house without them knowing, and when could they open presents. They were elated at the ribbons from Alma and the gifts from Roy.

"Mrs. Gibbons? I believe you are to give me a special gift?"

Alma giggled. "It's here." She hopped to her feet and brought out a package.

"We painted the paper!" Frances shouted. "And we—"

"Hush, Franny." Elisbet covered Frances's mouth. "You're giving it away. Open it, Papa!"

"Remove your hand from your sister's mouth, please." Roy unwrapped the ornament and, if possible, the dimples in his cheeks grew deeper as he smiled.

"Do you like it?" Alma thought so but wanted to hear him say it.

"I do. I see our names and one fingerprint. The feather is a nice touch. That's from you, Alma?"

"Yes, and the fingerprint is from Frances. I thought it was special."

"It is, and we will cherish this. One day, this will hang on your tree, Frances."

Elisbet frowned. "Why does she get to have it?"

"Just wait." Roy drew a package from his pocket. "Here is my gift, Alma."

She opened the paper. Inside was an ornament made of blond braided hair shaped into a heart and glued to a small piece of wood. A yellow ribbon twisted with a piece of a black string tie wove through a hole and tied to use as a hanger. "Is this my ribbon?"

"And my tie. I wanted this gift to represent our family."

"I love it." Alma pressed it to her heart. "Elisbet, someday this will be yours."

⁓∞⁓

Later, Roy slipped a kiss on Alma's neck. "Remember when I said you were going to get a splinter for Christmas?"

"But I didn't. You sanded the wood smoothly."

"I made you something else." Roy's heart beat fast, ready to explode.

Alma's face filled with excitement.

"Come to the barn with me." Once they were inside, he led her to a stall and yanked off the tattered quilt covering the blanket chest he'd built. "I wanted to start this marriage off with a piece of furniture we both made. I've done my part. Now it's up to you to paint it any way you like."

Alma dropped to her knees. She ran her hand across the daises he'd carved on the front panel. "Daisies."

"To get you through the winter until I can bring you real ones."

"It's so beautiful." She opened the lid and gasped. "The Oil Painting Outfit Complete!" She jumped up and wrapped her arms around him. "I love you, Roy Gibbons."

"I love you, too." She fit him more perfectly than he ever could have imagined. God had replaced his pain and loss with Alma, who taught him true love could come more than once in a lifetime.

About the Author

Diana Lesire Brandmeyer writes historical and contemporary romances. She is the author of *Mind of Her Own*, *A Bride's Dilemma in Friendship, Tennessee*, and *We're Not Blended, We're Pureed: A Survivor's Guide to Blended Families*. Once widowed and now remarried, she writes with humor and experience on the difficulty of joining two families, be it fictional or real life.

Please visit her webpage, www.dianabrandmeyer.com

Bigger. Better. Together.
Stories of love, blending and bonding.

The Nutcracker Bride

by Margaret Brownley

Be not forgetful to entertain strangers:
for thereby some have entertained angels unawares.

HEBREWS 13:2

Chapter 1

Kansas, 1880

Thunderous hoofbeats broke the silence on that gray December day. Even the air crackled with urgency.

Lucy Langdon dumped a handful of hulled nuts into her bucket and looked up from beneath the walnut tree. Someone was in a big hurry. Such haste generally meant an emergency: a tornado, prairie fire, or locust invasion—a doctor needed. Or maybe Mr. Jones had been attacked by one of his chickens again.

She craned her neck, but the road curved around the Holbrook orchard, preventing her from seeing much beyond the bend.

Even her sorrel, hitched to the wagon, sensed something amiss. Ears pricked forward, she pawed the ground and whinnied.

"It's all right, Penny," Lucy called as she hastened to calm her skittish mare. As the pounding hooves moved closer, Penny tried pulling free from the traces. In the struggle to contain her horse, Lucy's straw bonnet flew off.

A shiny black steed sprang into view and galloped at full speed toward her. The horseman reined in next to her wagon, his powerful mount rearing back on its hind legs and pawing the air. A flash of blue eyes and a handsome square face greeted her from beneath his wide-brimmed hat.

"Save that for me!" the stranger yelled, spinning his mount around in a tight circle beside the wagon.

Startled, she called back, "Save what?" But her question went unanswered, for already the man had raced away.

No sooner had he vanished than three more horsemen rode into view, their faces half hidden by scarlet kerchiefs. A shiver of panic raced through her. Outlaws!

Lucy released Penny and grabbed her shotgun from the back of the wagon. Her rapid heartbeats all but drowned out the pounding of hooves as the desperados raced past.

Paying her no heed, the masked men headed in the direction of her house. Her first thought was for her grandfather. *God, please don't let them stop there!*

She swooped up her bonnet, reached for the bucket, and tossed them into the wagon along with her shotgun. She would have to pay Old Man Holbrook later for the nuts.

Scrambling onto the driver's seat, she grabbed the reins and released the brake. "Gid-up!" she shouted. Cracking her whip, she drove home helter-skelter, the wheels of her wagon kicking up dust in her wake.

Less than twenty minutes later, Lucy ran into her house, calling out to her neighbor. "Mrs. Abernathy! Mrs. Abernathy!"

The older woman looked up from her needlepoint, her spectacles slipping down her nose. "Good heavens, child. Why are you yelling? You'll wake your grandfather, if you haven't already."

Lucy locked the door and ran around checking all the windows. It wasn't like her to lose her ladylike composure, but this was an emergency.

"You won't believe what happened—" She talked so fast her tongue tripped over her words. On and on she went. "—and then he said, 'Save that for me' and—"

Mrs. Abernathy stared at her with rounded eyes. "Are you saying that a handsome black horse stole your nuts?"

Lucy drew her gaze from the window. "What?"

"I was asking about the handsome horse that stole your nuts."

"The man was handsome, not the horse. And the robbers—"

"My word. Did you say robbers? Are you all right, child?"

"I'm fine." Lucy collapsed in a chair and pulled off her bonnet. She wished she could say the same for the stranger on the black steed. Three against one; that wasn't very good odds by anyone's count.

Mrs. Abernathy looked visibly shaken, and Lucy felt bad for worrying her. "The highwaymen are probably gone by now," she said, sounding more confident than she felt.

"I certainly hope you're right."

In an effort to ease her neighbor's mind, Lucy changed the subject. "Did Grandfather give you any trouble?" What would she do without this kind-hearted neighbor's help? Mrs. Abernathy sat with Opa every Wednesday while Lucy drove into town for supplies and to deliver baked goods to her customers.

Lucy's tactic worked, and Mrs. Abernathy's worried frown faded away.

"Your grandfather is a love. He and I had a nice chat about old times."

"A nice chat" meant Mrs. Abernathy had done all the talking. The only word Grandfather had uttered in more than two years was his late wife's name. Mrs. Abernathy probably preferred his silence. She never could understand his German accent, which had remained as thick as the day he landed in America thirty-five years earlier.

Mrs. Abernathy gathered up her sewing. "I better take these old bones home, dear."

"Maybe you should wait." The bandits were probably gone, but it never paid to take chances.

"I only have a mile to go. Besides, what would a robber do with an old lady like me? The only things I own of any value are my wedding ring and the family Bible."

After donning her woolen shawl, gloves, and hat, Mrs. Abernathy reached for her sewing basket. She was round as a barrel and waddled as she walked to the door.

"I wish you would reconsider," Lucy said.

Mrs. Abernathy patted her on the arm. "It's better that I go now while it's still light and before it begins to snow."

Lucy kissed her on a parched cheek. The old woman smelled like violets and cloves. "Be careful, and don't forget your pastries." She handed Mrs. Abernathy a tin of her special fruit-and-nut Christmas cakes.

The woman chuckled. "Harold would never forgive me if I did."

Lucy followed her outside to the horse and wagon parked in front. The road was deserted, and a cold wind cut through her woolen skirt. A strand of coppery hair pulled free from her bun, and she brushed it away from her face.

"Take care."

"Don't you go worryin' none, you hear? You have enough troubles as it is." Mrs. Abernathy climbed onto the seat of her wagon. "I wish you would let me watch him on Sunday so you could go to meeting." Nobody in town went to "church." It was always "go to meeting," a phrase left over from the days the town had no church and worship was held in private homes.

"It's kind of you to offer, but I wouldn't feel right keeping you from worshipping with your husband."

Mrs. Abernathy discounted her concern with a flutter of her hand. "Harold wouldn't mind, long as you don't wake him when he falls asleep. The reverend believes that 'life everlasting' refers to the length of the sermon." She chuckled as she gathered the reins in her hands. "I just hope that handsome horse returns with your walnuts."

The memory of blue eyes flashed through Lucy's mind. "I do, too," she said, and laughed. Hugging herself for warmth, she watched until the back of her neighbor's wagon vanished behind a wall of gray haze.

A few snowflakes began to fall. Winter was here at last. Turning toward the house with a shiver, Lucy caught a glimpse of her grandfather wandering about the yard dressed only in his red long johns. Oh no, not again!

Lately, all he wanted was to escape outside. . .searching, always searching for Eva, her dear, deceased grandmother and his beloved wife.

Chiding herself for not closing the door all the way, she hastened across the yard. Just before leading him back inside, she glanced at the dark, angry sky, and a feeling of foreboding washed over her.

Chapter 2

Good intentions to the contrary, Lucy sat on tenterhooks the rest of the day. The brave front she'd managed for Mrs. Abernathy's benefit had long since deserted her.

The narrow dirt road was deserted, but that didn't keep her from flying to the parlor window every few minutes in search of lurkers. She'd posted signs on the wooden fence in front of her property, warning any passersby to watch for outlaws.

Sensing her anxiety, her grandfather seemed especially restless. Every time she turned her back, he made a beeline for the front door.

She pulled him away for perhaps the tenth or eleventh time. "You don't want to go outside, Opa," she explained patiently. "It's cold." He'd always insisted she call him Opa, the German word for grandfather.

"Don't worry," she added for her own benefit. "The thieves are probably miles away by now." She didn't want to think about what might have happened to the man on the black steed. She only hoped his commanding presence was enough to save him.

She seated her grandfather on a chair in front of the blazing fire. The doctor had a term for Opa's condition, which she refused to embrace. She didn't know why a kind and loving man had, through the years, become an empty shell, but she refused to believe him insane.

How much he heard or understood, she couldn't guess, but talking to him helped her feel better. At least it made the silence bearable, though it did little to abate the loneliness.

"Stay here and I'll get our supper, Opa." She had made his favorite lamb stew, and the delicious smell wafting into the parlor made her mouth water.

She walked into the kitchen and grabbed an apron. Orders for her baked goods were stacked on the counter next to her recipe file and notebook. The numbers assured her that it would be a merry Christmas indeed. With the money left over after living expenses, she would finally be able to hire someone to make much-needed repairs on the sod house and barn.

The house had been built by her grandfather's own hands thirty years earlier. He'd cut the sod into blocks, sawed cottonwood for rafters, and made the wooden roof shingles by hand.

Through the years, additional rooms had been added as needed, like tiles in a game of dominoes. Now they had the luxury of three bedrooms. But the kitchen remained her favorite place. Not only did it remind her of the many happy hours spent learning the baking trade at her grandmother's side, but the process of sifting flour and cracking nuts also offered a welcome respite from her troubles.

She set to work at once, pulling ingredients from her pantry. Dumplings would go nicely with the stew. She reached for the bag of flour and found the shelf empty. It was then that she remembered leaving her groceries and walnuts in the back of the wagon. She'd been so upset by her earlier encounter, she'd unharnessed the horse but had forgotten to unload.

Donning her shawl, she left the house quietly, hoping her grandfather wouldn't try to follow. It was still light enough to see her way to the barn without benefit of a lantern.

The wind was icy and the air hung thick with the promise of more snow. Penny greeted her in the barn with a soft neigh, and a hen clucked from its roost.

Her nuts were scattered on the bottom of the wagon, and she decided to leave them till the following day, when the light would be better. Tomorrow she would remove the hulls and start the curing process by spreading the black walnuts out to dry for next year's baking.

She reached for the crate of groceries purchased from Walden's Mercantile. As she lifted the wooden box out of the wagon, an unfamiliar gunnysack caught her attention.

"Now where did that come from?" It hadn't been there when she'd loaded her groceries. Of that she was certain.

Curious, she set the crate down and pulled the coarse cloth sack out of the wagon. Setting it on the barn floor, she released the drawstring tie, and her eyes widened in astonishment.

Heart pounding, she jerked her hand back. Had she seen what she thought she saw?

With a nervous glance around, she grabbed hold of the gunnysack and dragged it over to the open barn door where the light was brighter. This time the shock of discovery hit her full force.

The sack was full of money!

⊸∞⊷

Lucy stared at the stacks of banknotes spread across her kitchen table. Each bundle of hundred-dollar bills was bound with a paper band. The grand total was seventy thousand dollars. Never could she have imagined so much money in one place.

Save this for me.

The memory of the man's puzzling request triggered a disturbing thought. Perhaps she'd gotten it all wrong. Maybe the blue-eyed stranger on the black horse was also a thief. That meant. . .

Panic bubbled up inside. What if he came looking for her? There were very few houses in the area. She wouldn't be that difficult to find.

Forcing herself to breathe, Lucy tried to think. This was no time to go off the deep end. She needed a clear head to consider her options.

Riding into town to the marshal's office was out of the question. That would require taking her grandfather out in the cold. Besides, it was almost dark. And what if it started to snow or she ran into bandits on the road?

A sound from the other room made her jump. Quickly rising from her chair, she hurried to the parlor. It was just her grandfather trying to open the front door again. Thank God he hadn't yet learned how to turn the newly installed lock.

Taking him gently by the arm, she spoke in a soothing voice. "You don't want to go outside, Opa. Your supper is almost ready."

She steered him away from the door and, with an anxious glance out the front window, walked him back to his chair in front of the blazing fire. She had a feeling it was going to be a very long night.

⊸∞⊷

Texas Ranger Chad Prescott tugged on the reins of his black horse. "Whoa, boy."

He turned up his coat collar and stared in the direction of the house. A light shone from the window, and the smell of smoke told him a fire blazed within. He could use a bit of warmth right now. He'd been riding for hours and was colder than a Montana well digger.

After leading the notorious Dobson gang on a merry chase, he was finally able to double back. He'd planned to sneak up from behind, but somehow he lost them.

No matter. He'd find them—all three of them. He always got his man, or in this case, men. First he had to locate a certain pretty, copper-haired woman with eyes the color of a Texas bluebonnet. If he didn't retrieve the money in her possession, he'd have a lot of explaining to do.

As the night wore on, his worries increased. For a state as flat as Kansas, it didn't seem possible that people could so quickly disappear. The sooner he finished his business here and hailed back to Texas, the better.

The temperature had dropped the moment night fell. He was cold and hungry and could sure use some shut-eye. Riding back to town sounded like a good idea. He would begin his search again first thing in the morning.

No sooner had he made the decision than he heard something flapping against the fence that ran parallel to the road. A closer look revealed some sort of sign. He dismounted and pulled a box of safety matches out of his saddlebag. His back against the wind, he lit a match, cupping his hand around the flame.

He was able to pick out the word *bandits* before the match went out. His mouth curved upward as he pulled the sign down and stuffed it in his pocket. Well now. Looka there. A certain young woman had sounded the alarm. Unless he was mistaken, he was standing in front of her house.

As tempting as it was to march up to her door and ask for the money tossed in her wagon for safekeeping, he decided to check in back first. If Frank Dobson and his brothers were hiding inside, he wanted to know about it before walking into a trap.

Chapter 3

It was late, nearly nine o'clock, before Lucy took the last batch of cookies out of the oven and set them on a rack to cool. The only time she could fill her orders uninterrupted was when her grandfather was asleep.

She'd hidden the money beneath a loose floorboard in the parlor and covered it with a rag rug. Tomorrow she would decide what to do next. Maybe she could flag down one of her neighbors and ask him to take it to the marshal. That would save her the hassle of dragging her grandfather along.

Or maybe—

Startled by a loud thud, she dropped her wooden spoon and flew to the window over the kitchen sink. It was too dark to see out, but it sure did sound like the barn door.

In all the confusion of finding the money, she must have forgotten to latch it. Penny and the other animals could freeze to death if she didn't do something.

Reaching for her shawl, she hesitated a moment before grabbing the shotgun. After lighting a lantern, she cautiously opened the door. A blast of frigid air blew out the flame. Knowing the futility of lighting it again, she hung the lantern back on the hook.

Anxious to get the job done and return to the house before freezing her fanny off, she stepped out on the porch. The robbers still very much on her mind, she kept her finger on the trigger.

The wind whistled through the eaves, and her skirt whipped against her legs. The barn door kept up a steady rhythm, like a drummer during a death march. Stomach clenched tight and senses alert, she moved forward.

She reached the end of the porch and was just about to descend the steps when a dark form loomed in front of her.

Jumping back, Lucy's breath caught audibly in her throat and her hand jerked. A flash of light and deafening blast from her shotgun sent her reeling.

Thinking with her feet, she managed to get back inside and slam the door shut. She stared down at her weapon, and reality hit her. Dear God,

61

what had she done? The shotgun slid from her hands and fell to the floor with a clatter.

Breathing hard, she listened. Only the moaning wind and banging barn door could be heard over her pounding heart.

Cold fear gripped her as she walked on silent feet to the sink. Moving the curtain, she peered out the window. Seeing only the reflection of her own pale face, she dropped the curtain. Frightful images raced through her head.

A sudden pounding startled her, followed by a man's rough voice. "Open up!"

She retrieved her shotgun from the floor. "What. . .what do you want?" she called in a wavering voice.

"I need help, lady." Silence followed and then, "I've been shot."

She lowered her weapon until the muzzle pointed downward. Had she really shot him, or was it a trick? "H–how do I know you're telling the truth?"

"You'll know when you open the door." His voice sounded weaker. Maybe he really was hurt. Then again, maybe it was a trick. *God, please tell me what to do.*

"I c–can't. You might have evil intentions."

"Lady. . ." Pause. "Right now. . ." More silence. "I couldn't hurt a fly."

It sounded like he was telling the truth, but how could she be sure? Then she remembered something Opa had told her long ago. The fastest way to know a man's true character is through his relationship to God.

"Can. . .can you recite a Bible verse?"

It took so long for an answer to come, she feared the man was dead. Finally, she heard his muffled voice. "What?"

"A Bible verse." A man who knew his Bible couldn't be all bad. "What is your favorite verse? It'll help me know if I can trust you."

"Thou shalt not. . .*kill.*"

She pursed her lips. "Actually, the Bible doesn't say that. It says thou shalt not *murder.*" An important distinction, in her estimation. "Of course, a lot of people say 'kill' when they mean—" She was yammering on about nothing but couldn't seem to help herself. It was how she dealt with nerves. "But I'm sure God forgives—"

"Open the blasted door!"

⁂

The moment he stumbled into her kitchen Lucy recognized him as the man on the black horse.

Blood dripped onto the floor, and he leaned heavily on her as she half dragged him to the spare bedroom. No sooner had they reached the bed than he collapsed on the straw mattress in a state of unconsciousness.

He was a large man—even larger than her grandfather—with wide shoulders and a broad chest. He was also tall, and his feet hung over the bottom of the mattress. It took every bit of strength she possessed to roll him over so she could tend to his wound. The amount of blood alarmed her, and she feared she'd done him serious harm.

She worked frantically to pull off his coat, vest, and shirt. *Please don't let him die, God.*

Fortunately, she was no stranger to bullet wounds, thanks to her work as Doc Hathaway's assistant.

Her steady hand and sharp mind made her a quick study, but none of those other bullets had been her fault. That alone unnerved her. What if she did something wrong? What if the man died? Would that make her a murderer? *Dear God, no!*

Pushing such terrifying thoughts aside, she focused on the task at hand. She bound her patient's wound with strips of cotton fabric to stop the bleeding and hastened to the kitchen. After lighting the fire under the kettle, she searched through the kitchen drawers. The kitchen tongs were too large for pulling out a bullet, so she settled on two teaspoons.

Fortunately, the gunshot blast hadn't awakened her grandfather. The man could sleep through anything, and for that, she was grateful.

The barn door was still banging, but that would have to wait until after she'd taken care of her patient. The thought of going back outside filled her with dread, but concern for the animals took precedence over fear.

Calming her still-pounding heart, she reached into the sewing basket.

Doc Hathaway believed that unless a wound was deep, it was best to let it heal naturally. Just in case, she pulled out needle and thread. Recalling that more men had died during the War between the States from infection than bullet wounds, she grabbed a bottle of tincture of iodine.

After gathering her supplies and arranging them on a tray, along with a bottle of medicinal whiskey, she hurried to her patient's side.

She adjusted the lamp and set to work. He was still bleeding quite a bit, but as far as she could tell, the bullet hadn't penetrated any vital organs. That alone was a blessing. As long as the slug hadn't lodged in a bone, it shouldn't be that hard to remove.

With some careful probing, Lucy managed to locate the bullet in the fleshy area of the chest next to the man's armpit. It took several tries before she managed to grab hold of the pellet between the spoons and ease it out. The slug made a pinging sound as it hit the bottom of the porcelain bowl.

After packing the wound to stop the bleeding, she covered it with iodine-painted gauze and strips of clean muslin. After mopping up the blood and washing her hands, she laid a damp cloth on his forehead.

Doc Hathaway had impressed on her the importance of keeping a professional attitude at all times when treating a patient. But, God forgive her, it was hard not to notice what a handsome man this was. He had a firm, square jaw, a straight patrician nose, and a nicely shaped mouth. His manly chest wasn't bad to look at either.

Surprised and even dismayed by such unladylike thoughts, she checked his forehead for fever before slipping out of the room to take care of that barn door.

Tomorrow, if the weather permitted, she would fetch the doctor. Meanwhile, there was nothing to do but wait and pray. Oh yes, and try to maintain a professional attitude.

Chapter 4

Chad had a hard time letting go of the darkness. When at last his eyes fluttered open, it took a moment to gather his bearings. His lips were parched and his mouth as dry as the desert sands. Worse, it felt like someone was inside his head pounding with a hammer. Where was he? He blinked, and gradually his vision cleared.

It took longer for his memory to kick in. Bits and pieces dwindled back, but none made sense. He remembered pain—and then softness. He recalled thinking he was burning up. . .until a featherlight coolness touched his brow.

Blue eyes—he remembered those, too. And hair the color of a coppery Texas sun.

He tried to move, and groaned. The memories might not be real, but the pain sure was, though he had a hard time locating it.

Only a sliver of gray light filtered through the curtains. It sure didn't look like his room at Mrs. Compton's boardinghouse. It didn't look like heaven either. For one thing, there was a row of wooden puppets staring down from a shelf, their garish painted faces mocking him.

He moved his legs and froze. His gun and boots were missing. So, for that matter, were his trousers, but that was of less concern.

He tried sitting up, but the room turned topsy-turvy. One moment the puppets were on the floor; next they were on the raftered ceiling. He fell back against the pillow. Something was wrong with his arm. His shoulder was wrapped in a bandage, and when he tried moving it, pain shot down his arm.

He grimaced, and all at once it came back to him. He'd been shot.

A sound alerted him. Footsteps. The door opened with a creak of its leather hinges. The dim light revealed a curvy feminine form.

Not till she stepped into the room could he see the woman's delicate features. Her eyes—those he remembered. How could he not? They reminded him of the bluebonnets that grew in wild abundance back home in Texas. So the angel of his dreams was real.

He moved and heard her intake of breath.

"You're awake," she said.

"Barely." He waited for her to come near the bed. She leaned over to check his bandage and a delicate lavender scent wafted toward him. Her eyes were sharp and assessing as she probed, and only when he flinched did she pull away.

"Sorry," she said. "How do you feel?"

"Like I've been shot." He studied her, and the fog in his head cleared. "Why'd you do that? Why'd you shoot me?"

She stared at him accusingly. "You scared me."

"Not as much as you scared me."

Her eyes widened. "You shouldn't have jumped out at me like that."

He frowned. Is that what he'd done? He remembered checking her barn for her horse and wagon and, recognizing both, walking to the house. He didn't even know she was on the porch until she fired at him.

When he failed to respond, she added, "I never meant to cause you harm. My gun went off accidentally."

Since it was partly his fault, he might have let her off the hook had she looked halfway apologetic or even vulnerable. Instead, she looked like a force to be reckoned with. She held herself erect, her features composed. Her copper hair was pulled into a tight bun and her pleated shirtwaist buttoned up to her chin. A model of prudence, modesty, and efficiency. He doubted she did anything by chance, and that might include firing a gun.

"Hard to tell the difference between an accident or good aim," he said. "I reckon they both hurt the same."

Not that he was an expert. As a Texas Ranger, he'd chased more trigger-itching outlaws than he cared to count, and not once had he taken a bullet. Being shot at was bad enough. But having his perfect record broken by a pint-size woman who probably weighed no more than a goose-down pillow was doggone galling.

She reached for the pitcher on the table by his bedside and picked up a clean glass. Every movement was precise and unhurried. He seemed to remember her forcing liquids down his throat, for which he was grateful.

"If I scared you so much, how come you let me in the house?"

Affording him a wary glance, she filled the glass and set the pitcher down. "I asked you for a Bible verse. I figured a man able to recite scripture couldn't be all bad."

He shook his head in wonder. The woman was either terribly naive or terribly trusting. Either way, he lucked out, or he might have bled to death on her doorstep.

"You better drink this."

His dry mouth told him it was probably good advice. He managed to pull himself upright while she fluffed his pillow with her free hand. Taking the glass from her, he gulped the water down his prickly throat and then checked his bandaged shoulder.

"The swelling has gone down," she said. "And it doesn't look quite as red."

That was good to hear. If only his head would stop pounding. "Who else lives here?"

Suspicion crossed her face and her eyes narrowed. "Why do you ask?"

He frowned. Obviously she didn't trust him. "Just want to know who took care of me."

"I did," she said.

Considering her size, that was hard to believe. "Does that mean you undressed me, too?"

She refused to meet his gaze but couldn't hide her reddening cheeks. "Your trousers and shirt were covered in blood."

"How did you get fluids down me?"

This time she looked straight at him. "With a funnel."

He thought about that for a moment. "What did the doctor say?"

She took the empty glass from him and set it on the bedside table. "Doctor?"

"A doctor removed the bullet, right?"

"No, I did," she said.

"You?" The woman was full of surprises.

"The doctor lives an hour away, and it was snowing hard."

He clenched his teeth. Going out in the snow seemed like a small price to pay for shooting him, even if it was partly his fault. Still, judging by the feel of things, she'd done a pretty good job without a physician's help.

"How many bullets have you taken out, anyway?"

"Yours was the fourth, or maybe the fifth," she said in the same straight-forward tone he'd already come to expect.

He stared at her. "That many?"

"Yes, and they weren't all accidents."

"Something to keep in mind," he muttered. It was just his luck to have a run-in with a trigger-happy damsel. "Did you shoot them yourself, or did you have help?"

His question brought a shadow of a smile to her lips. "Neither. I worked as a doctor's assistant."

"Ah, that explains it," he said. "By the way, my name's Chad Prescott."

"Miss Langdon. Miss Lucy Langdon."

"How long have I been here?"

"Four days," she said.

Four! He couldn't believe his ears. Now, wasn't that just fine and dandy? That gang of outlaws he'd trailed all the way from Texas was probably long gone by now.

"What about my horse?"

"He has been well cared for and is in the barn." After a moment, she asked, "What's his name?"

"I call him Spirit."

She repeated the name, and coming from her, it sounded almost musical. "That suits him."

Anxious to get down to business, Chad tried moving his legs, but they felt like lead. "I tossed something in your wagon."

"Oh?" She busied herself smoothing the bedcovers. "I hope it was a change of clothes."

The woman was joking, right? "Not clothes. A gunnysack."

Her gaze locked with his. "Why would you do such a thing? Toss something in my wagon, I mean?"

"If you recall, I was being chased by three hombres. I didn't want them getting their hands on it."

She studied him as if to determine whether he spoke the truth. "When it stops snowing, I'll check the wagon to see if. . .your bag is still there," she said.

"Never mind. I'll check myself, if you will kindly tell me where I can find my shirt and trousers."

"Your clothes are drying in front of the fire. Like I said, they were soaked with blood, so I washed them."

"What about my gun and boots?" he asked. "Did you wash those, too?"

She lifted her gaze to his. "You won't be needing those, Mr. Prescott. At least not for a while."

He tossed the blanket away and was surprised by the effort it took to swing his legs over the side of the bed.

Looking as prim as a preacher's wife at a prayer meeting, Miss Langdon folded her arms across her chest. "You're not in any condition to walk, Mr. Prescott."

"Wanna bet?" He planted his feet firmly on the floor—or at least that's what he meant to do. Instead, he somehow landed on his knees.

She stared down at him. "Would you like me to help you back in bed?"

"Never mind. I'll do it myself." He pulled himself upright and flopped facedown across the mattress. At least the woman had the decency to let him keep the bottom of his long johns on.

"I'll fix you something to eat, then." She pulled the sheet and blanket over him. "You need to get your strength back."

He heard her leave the room and gritted his teeth. Like it or not, he wasn't going anywhere. Not for a while, anyway.

Chapter 5

The following morning, Lucy pulled the baking sheet of *pfeffernüsse* out of the oven, and the sweet smell of cinnamon and cloves filled the air. Nudging the bowl of freshly cracked nuts and the tall wooden nutcracker aside, she set the metal sheet on the counter. She then sprinkled the cookies with spiced sugar.

The cookie recipe had been handed down by her German grandmother, who got it from her grandmother. After the cookies cooled, Lucy would pack them into tins to distribute to her customers.

A blizzard had raged for three days, piling drifts against the house and barn. The only person to come to her door in all that time was dear old Mr. Abernathy to check up on her. She made no mention of her guest. It would only worry him and his wife.

She hoped it would stop snowing long enough to allow her to make deliveries. If she could reach the Brookstone farm down the road a ways, perhaps they would let her use their sleigh.

She reached for another baking sheet and turned toward the oven. Just then the back door sprang open. Startled, she dropped the tray, and cookie dough spattered across the floor.

"Mr. Prescott!" Her mouth fell open. Never had she seen such a frightful sight. His bare feet were red, and his uncombed hair and unshaven chin were peppered with fresh-fallen snow. Over his long johns he wore one of Opa's shirts.

"You nearly scared the life out of me," she scolded. The shirt barely stretched across his massive shoulders and allowed for an intriguing glimpse of his broad, muscular chest. Much to her annoyance, she felt her cheeks blaze.

He slammed the door shut behind him, his face livid. "Where is it?"

"Please keep your voice down. My grandfather—"

"Where is it?" he asked again, advancing toward her with a menacing look.

Refusing to be intimidated, she lifted her chin. "Where is what?"

He stopped a few feet in front of her. "The bag I tossed in your wagon." The more she felt herself wilt beneath his angry gaze, the more determined she was not to back down. "I don't know what you're talking about."

"I don't believe you."

He took another step forward, and she leaned back. "I—It's the truth," she stammered. She hated lying, but she had no intention of turning the money over to anyone but the sheriff.

Trapped by the counter behind her, Lucy felt for the wooden nutcracker. But before she could reach it, Mr. Prescott grabbed her arm. Yanking her toward him, his bare chest pressed against her.

"I'll ask you one more time. What did you do with the bag?"

She glared up at him. "I don't know what you're talking about."

Suddenly, he released her, and a pensive look crossed his face. "What's your favorite Bible verse?" he asked.

So now he was playing her game. "Thou shalt not steal!"

He laughed. "So you think I'm a thief, do you?"

"Are you?"

Just as he started to reply, her grandfather shuffled into the room. Mr. Prescott hesitated a moment before turning and leaving the kitchen.

∞

Lucy was so shaken by the encounter with Mr. Prescott, she almost didn't hear her grandfather at the front door later that morning. Rushing into the parlor, she grabbed him firmly but gently by the arm.

"Eva," he murmured. "Eva."

"Eva's not out there, Opa," she said. How could she make her grandfather understand that his wife was not coming back? She opened the door, and wind-driven snow blew inside. "Brrr." She closed the door. "You don't want to go out there."

Never had she known her grandfather to be so restless. His determination to escape these last couple of days had exhausted her. Was Mr. Prescott's presence causing Opa's distress? Or was his condition growing worse?

"Come along." She drew him away from the door and helped him into his chair. Tossing another log onto the fire, she then wrapped a knitted shawl around his thin shoulders.

Intent on making him as comfortable as possible, she failed to notice Mr. Prescott's presence until he spoke.

"What's wrong with him?" he asked.

She looked up to where he stood in the kitchen doorway, his long, lean form propped against the wooden frame. He had shaved with the razor she set out for him, and his smooth jaw emphasized his good looks, as did his neatly combed hair. Despite his uncommon dress, he exuded a powerful presence, but it was the sudden change in demeanor that disarmed her. He looked genuinely concerned, with none of his earlier rancor.

"The doctor says he's lost his mind."

He studied her. "What do you think?"

"I think his mind is still there. It's just locked inside."

He broke away from the doorway. "And you take care of him all by yourself?"

She nodded. "I'm the only family he has left." Her father had died in 1858 during the Kansas Border War when Lucy was only three. The news of his death sent her expectant mother into labor, which neither she nor her unborn baby survived. Had her grandparents not taken Lucy into their hearts and home, she would have ended up in an orphanage. Now she returned the favor by caring for her dear, sweet grandfather.

Mr. Prescott sat on an upholstered chair. "It must be hard on you."

Heaving a sigh, Lucy dropped to her knees to check the clothes drying next to the fire. "It's getting harder. My grandmother died this past summer. I don't know why, but lately Grandfather keeps trying to leave the house to search for her. He thinks she's outside."

"Why would he think that?"

"The last time he saw her alive was when she walked out that door." Her grandmother had driven into town on that fatal day and never returned. "The doctor said it was her heart."

"I'm sorry," he said.

Observing him through lowered lashes, she moistened her lips. "Your shirt is dry, but I'm afraid your trousers and coat are still damp." The heavy wool fabric took forever to dry.

Her fingers touched his as she handed him the shirt, and she quickly pulled her hand away. He yanked off her grandfather's shirt and tossed it aside. Next to the white bandage at his shoulder, his bare chest looked as golden brown as tanned leather.

Confused by the way he affected her, Lucy quickly turned to the hearth and reached for the poker. As if to free herself of his mesmerizing hold, she stabbed at the burning log until sparks flew up the chimney.

"You can look now," he said, and she detected a note of amusement in his voice.

Replacing the poker, she transferred her gaze to him. His shirt was securely buttoned, and relief flooded through her.

He sat forward on the chair, hands clasped between his knees. "I'm afraid we got off to a bad start."

She tried to maintain the impersonal and professional demeanor she'd learned from the doctor. "You have been rather difficult," she said, her voice cool and precise.

"Actually, I was referring to the bullet you pumped into me."

She faltered in her efforts to remain aloof. "I hope you find it in your heart to forgive me." As it was, she was having a hard time forgiving herself. She was lucky her carelessness hadn't done more damage.

"Yes, well. . ." He rubbed his hands together. "I'm willing to let bygones be bygones. That is, providing you come clean and tell me what happened to the gunnysack I tossed in your wagon."

She sat back on her heels. "I have no idea what you're talking about."

"I think you do, but we'll get to that in a minute. First, I think you should know that I'm a Texas Ranger and I've been trailing a gang of outlaws for weeks. Followed them clear up here from the Panhandle."

Lucy frowned. Could he be telling the truth? "That's a long way to travel."

"I reckon I'll wear out another saddle or two before I'm done." His face hardened, but his eyes filled with pain. Not physical pain, but something deeper and more private. "There are three of them, and they killed my best friend. Shot him in the back."

"How awful for you," she whispered, speaking from the heart. "I'm so sorry."

"Thanks." He blew out his breath. "I'm out for justice, and until I get it. . ." He shrugged. "I guess you could say I have a one-track mind."

He looked and sounded sincere, but she was still hesitant to believe him. "Don't you rangers have to wear a badge or something?"

"What?"

"A badge. Nothing on your person led me to believe you were a lawman."

"The Texas Rangers don't wear badges. Not unless we make them ourselves. A few made badges out of Mexican coins, but I never did. Never saw a need. I figured my warrant of authority was enough."

"And where is your warrant of authority now, Mr. Prescott?"

"At the boardinghouse where I've been staying," he said.

A likely story. . . Or was it? "And the bag you claim you tossed in my wagon?"

"I surprised the gang while they were robbing a stage. They dropped it and I grabbed it."

His story sounded plausible, but what if he was a crook? What if he was only trying to trick her into revealing the whereabouts of the stolen money?

"There's really no way for me to know that you're telling the truth," she said.

He rubbed the back of his neck. "Guess not, ma'am. That kind of puts us in the same boat, doesn't it?"

"How do you mean?"

He locked her gaze in his. "You told me you know nothing about the bag I left in your wagon. Now, either you're lying or you're not. No way for me to know, is there?"

She hesitated, torn by conflicting emotions. She wanted to believe him, she did. But something held her back. "Has it ever occurred to you that perhaps those three bandits might have found it?"

He stared her square in the eye. "No, ma'am. That never occurred to me."

She smiled. "Well then." She rose to signal that their discussion was over. "Mystery solved."

Chapter 6

Chad spent the rest of the morning conducting a thorough search of the premises.

For the most part, Miss Langdon ignored him. Though he noticed her mouth grew tighter as he pawed his way through the kitchen cupboards. Wire whisk in hand, she never said a word when he started on the pantry, but whatever was in that bowl of hers took a terrible beating.

"Aha!" he crowed upon finding his holstered gun on a shelf next to a sack of flour.

He found his boots stashed behind the butter churn.

He worked his way meticulously through the house, room by room and inch by inch. Not till he reached the lady's chamber did she react.

"Mr. Prescott!" She came charging into the room after him, looking as indignant as a newly shorn sheep. "You've gone too far this time."

"Now don't go off half-cocked," he said.

For some reason, this only seemed to incense her more. Eyes flashing, she tossed her head, and her chest rose and fell like angry waves.

"I have never gone off half-cocked in my life. But you have no right going through my personal belongings."

He bent over her until his nose practically touched hers. "And you have no right keeping that money from me."

Glowering, she tightened her hands into fists. "You won't find any money here."

"I guess you won't mind my looking, then." He straightened. "Unless you have something to hide."

She clenched her teeth and seethed with rage. "I have to say, Mr. Prescott, you are the most annoying man I've ever met."

"And you, Miss Langdon, are the most annoying woman." Though he had to admit, she sure did make outrage look enticing. "Now that we've found something we can agree on, you'll have to excuse me while I continue my search."

"Don't let me stop you!" She left the room, slamming the door so hard a picture fell off the wall.

Grinning, he picked up the picture. The lady was a force to be reckoned with, that's for sure. Better watch his step. The last thing he needed was another bullet wound.

He glanced around the tidy room and decided to start the search with the large wooden chest at the foot of the bed.

He lifted the lid and got the shock of his life. A stack of satin and lace under-riggins—the likes of which he had never seen—greeted his startled eyes. Hers? Were they really hers? And if so, what was an unmarried woman doing with a chest full of apparel more likely to be found in a bordello than a farmhouse?

He hesitated before plunging his hands into the provocative depths. It felt wrong pawing through such personal attire, but a lot of money was at stake—money for which he was responsible.

The sheer femininity of the corsets, petticoats, and camisoles was enough to make even the most jaded man blush. As it was, he had trouble breathing as he rummaged through the feminine finery.

Finding no gunnysack, he pulled back and lowered the lid, but that did nothing to quell his wayward thoughts.

Well now. What do you know? The lady wasn't quite as straitlaced as she'd led him to believe. What else didn't he know about her?

∽∾

It was 11:00 p.m., and Lucy was exhausted. Not only had her grandfather worn her to a frazzle by constantly trying to escape, but Mr. Prescott's disturbing presence also made her feel—what? Anxious? Nervous? Confused?

Whatever it was, he had somehow aroused a womanly response that was all at once frightening and exciting. Never had a man affected her more.

Banishing such thoughts, she stifled a yawn and glanced around the kitchen. Dirty dishes were still stacked on the counter, but that was the least of it. She still had nuts to crack and flour to sift and butter to melt and. . .

Feeling overwhelmed, she sank onto a chair. She folded her arms on the kitchen table and laid her head down. If only Grandmother hadn't died. If only Opa could somehow miraculously return to his former fun-loving self. If only. . .

She groaned. How she hated feeling sorry for herself, but she couldn't seem to help it. Her grandmother had taken care of Opa when she was alive, and not once had she complained.

Lucy could still hear her grandmother's voice admonishing her not to act sad around her grandfather. "*The Bible says a cheerful heart is good medicine.*"

It wasn't until after Grandmother's death that Lucy found out the amount of work involved in Opa's care. Poor Oma. Is that why her heart had given out? From the strain of taking care of her husband? It was possible. And now the job had fallen squarely on Lucy's shoulders.

No matter how hard she tried to shoulder the responsibility of her grandfather's care with a loving spirit, she couldn't help but feel resentful. While her friends enjoyed barn dances, sewing bees, and socials, she was stuck at home with her silent and helpless grandfather.

To make matters worse, she was always behind schedule and barely had a moment to herself. Except for her daily Bible reading, she couldn't remember the last time she'd read a book or chatted with friends her own age.

To save time, she'd stopped shaving her grandfather, and he now sported a white beard. He would probably benefit from a bath, but he was unsteady on his feet, and she didn't want to take a chance on him falling. Sponging him off daily with hot water and soap was the most she could manage.

She wiped a damp strand of hair away from her face with the back of her hand.

Had God deserted her? It certainly felt like it, but He wasn't the only one. That awful Jason Mills sure did desert her last spring when she told him she wouldn't marry him unless he promised to care for her aging grandparents. Well, good riddance! All she had to show for a year-long courtship was the carefully sewn trousseau in her hope chest.

She sighed. What a mess. Not only had she nearly killed Mr. Prescott, but she now also had seventy thousand dollars of stolen money hidden away. With a blizzard raging outside, there was little chance of riding into town anytime soon. If the weather didn't clear, she wasn't even certain she could deliver her orders in time for Christmas.

Where are You, God? And how much longer do You think I can hold on?

∽

It was late, and still Chad couldn't sleep. Outside a blizzard raged as he applied a new bandage to his wound. The windows rattled and the shutters banged. By the sound of it, he wasn't going anywhere soon.

Had the Dobson gang found the money in the wagon as Miss Langdon suggested? It was possible but highly unlikely. Still, he'd searched the house high and low and had come up empty-handed.

He'd also searched the barn. Maybe she'd buried it. If so, there wasn't much he could do about it. Not with the storm raging outside and the snow piled high.

Maybe he'd handled the lady all wrong. Perhaps he should try appealing to her softer side. Now that he knew she had a softer side. . .

No sooner had the thought occurred to him than a vision of silk corsets and lace petticoats came to mind. God forgive him, but he hadn't been able to stop thinking about Miss Langdon and all that silken frippery since finding it stashed in that wooden chest. It was almost as if he'd been given a peek into the deepest regions of the lady's heart.

Surprised by his fanciful thoughts, he shook his head. He'd been cooped up too long. It was the only explanation he could think of to explain this sudden obsession with his hostess. What had it been? Five or six days? Yep, that explained it. He had cabin fever.

He was just about ready to undress for bed when something caught his ear. Crossing the room, he cracked open the door.

Was that Miss Langdon crying?

Chapter 7

At the sound of Mr. Prescott's footsteps, Lucy quickly wiped away her tears. What was he doing up at this hour of night? Couldn't a woman succumb to a moment of self-pity in privacy?

He stepped into the kitchen, fully dressed. "You all right, ma'am?" he asked, his voice edged in concern.

Lifting her chin, Lucy cleared her throat. She was certain her eyes were red and her face splotchy, but there was nothing she could do about it.

"I'm perfectly fine. Thank you."

"I thought I heard—" A look of bewilderment replaced his usual swagger. Outlaws didn't seem to faze him, but a woman in distress apparently put him in a state of confusion.

"Uh. . ." He raked his hair with his fingers. "Something smells good," he said at last.

"I'm making *zimt makronen*," she said, grateful for the change of subject. "Hazelnut cookies."

An awkward silence followed. She tried to act like she hadn't been crying, and he pretended not to notice her tearstained cheeks.

Finally, he cleared his throat. "Like I said. The tears. . .uh. . .cookies sure do smell good."

"Would you care to sample one?"

"If it's not too much bother."

Grateful for an excuse to escape his scrutiny, she left her seat. "Not at all."

He pulled out a chair and sat while she fixed two cups of tea and arranged the freshly baked cookies on a plate.

He picked up a carved wooden king and moved the handle on its back up and down. "What's with all the puppets?" he asked.

"They're not puppets. They're nutcrackers." She set the plate of cookies on the table and sat down. "My grandfather made them and my grandmother painted them."

He set the colorful monarch upright and helped himself to a cookie. "Never saw nutcrackers like that," he said.

"My grandfather learned the trade as a young man in Germany. Poor villagers enjoyed giving kings and other figures of authority the menial task of cracking nuts."

He chuckled. "I can see where they might."

"Unfortunately, Americans didn't have the same regard for his craft. After coming to this country, his business failed, leaving dozens of nutcrackers unsold." With a family to support, Opa had turned to farming.

"Only dozens?" he asked.

She smiled. "It does seem like more, doesn't it?" She pointed to the windowsill where several nutcrackers faced outward, including her grandmother's treasured nutcracker bride.

"It's a German tradition to keep a nutcracker in the window to protect the house from danger."

He rubbed his injured shoulder. "But not visitors?"

Her cheeks grew warm under the heat of his gaze. "Only certain ones," she said.

He bit into the cookie. "Hmm. Can't remember tasting anything this good."

She sighed and tossed a nod at the stack of tins waiting to be delivered. "I just hope I'll be able to deliver all these before Christmas. But if this storm continues—"

He dumped a spoonful of sugar in his tea and stirred. "It must be hard taking care of your grandfather and running a business."

Maybe it was his kind words or sympathetic look. Or perhaps she was just tired, but much to Lucy's dismay she burst into tears.

A look of sheer horror crossed his face. "I'm sorry, ma'am. Never meant to upset you." He dug into his pocket and handed her a clean handkerchief.

"You didn't upset me. It's just. . ." She dabbed at her wet cheeks. "I'm not complaining, mind you. The orders are a blessing. But running a bakery and taking care of the farm and animals, I'm afraid poor Grandfather"— she was practically sobbing—"hasn't had a bath in weeks."

A combination of relief and puzzlement crossed his face. "Is that all that's got you riled?"

She blinked. "All?"

"Don't mean to make light of your troubles, ma'am, but it's been my experience that women put more stock in baths than do men. As for the other problem. . .I'll be happy to help you with deliveries. My shoulder isn't fully healed, but I'm getting stronger every day."

"That's very kind of you to offer, Mr. Prescott, but I couldn't let you go out in this weather."

"Chad," he said. "Call me Chad."

She stared at him. He really did have nice eyes, and now that she thought about it, a nice honest face as well. "I'm afraid that under the circumstances that wouldn't be proper."

He looked at her askance. "What circumstances are those?"

"Grandfather is rather old-fashioned, and since you're staying under our roof—"

He rubbed the back of his neck. "I hope you don't take this the wrong way, ma'am, but I don't think your grandfather cares one way or the other what you call me."

"Perhaps not. But on the outside chance that he does, I would prefer it if we kept things proper between us."

He thought about that for a long moment. He took a sip of his tea and thought about it some more. "By proper, does that mean I can't kiss you?"

"*Mr. Prescott!*"

He rose from the chair. "Just thought I'd ask. Don't want to do anything to offend your grandfather." Grabbing a handful of cookies, he left the room, whistling.

She stared after him. Her heart hammered against her ribs, and fire seemed to race though her veins. Of all the nerve—

The very thought of kissing Mr. Prescott was. . .what? Alarming? Shocking? *Intriguing?* Surprised by the last thought, her fingers flew to her mouth just in time to cover a most unladylike titter.

Chapter 8

The next morning, Lucy woke to the sound of a dying bull. It was only after she slipped out of bed and put her ear to the door that she was able to identify the ungodly howl as Mr. Prescott singing. Glancing at the mechanical clock, she was surprised—shocked, really—to discover she had overslept.

It was still snowing hard, and no visitors were expected in such weather. Still, she took special pains with her morning ablutions. After brushing her hair until it shone, she pinned it into a neat bun and finger-fluffed her bangs.

It took forever to decide between the blue woolen dress that matched her eyes or the pretty pink one that showed off her tiny waist. Finally, she settled on the blue.

Pinching her cheeks and moistening her lips, she left her room and entered the parlor voice first. "Must you make such a dreadful—?"

She stopped midstep. A chair had been removed from in front of the blazing fire and the metal bathtub put in its place. Her grandfather sat in the tub, with water up to his armpits and looking perfectly content.

Speechless, Lucy lifted her gaze to Mr. Prescott, who was singing a most improper ditty about drunken sailors. Stripped from the waist up except for the bandage, he poured water into the tub from a kettle. He was soaked, and damp hair fell over his brow. His gaze suddenly fell on her, and he stopped singing.

"You're giving him a bath?" She felt something tug at her heart. "I—I don't know what to say. Except. . .it's hard to know which of you is wetter."

He set the empty kettle on the hearth. "Bathing your grandfather is harder than bathing a cow."

"You bathe cows, Mr. Prescott?"

He grinned, and her heart did a flip-flop. "Only when necessary."

Recalling his last words to her the night before, she felt her face redden. She backed out of the room. "I—I guess he's in good hands."

"At least one good hand," Mr. Prescott said, gesturing to his shoulder.

Lucy escaped to the kitchen and got another shock. Mr. Prescott had done the dishes she'd been too tired to tackle the night before. For the second time in two days, she broke down and cried.

❧

By the time Mr. Prescott joined her in the kitchen fully dressed, Lucy was busy decorating a batch of gingerbread men.

She felt oddly shy in his presence and not at all like herself. No matter how much she tried to maintain her composure, he managed to weaken her defenses.

"It was a kind thing you did," she said.

"Gotta do something to earn my keep," he replied, helping himself to one of the newly baked cookies.

His gaze clung to hers for a moment before they both looked away. She bent over to pipe eyes and mouth onto a gingerbread face, and he examined the nutcrackers guarding the window.

"This one is different." He lifted the white one off the sill and turned it over in his hands. "It looks like a bride."

She straightened, pastry bag in hand. "It *is* a bride," she said. "My grandfather gave it to my grandmother on the day he proposed marriage."

"And she still married him?" he asked with a smile.

"Why wouldn't she?"

"Most women would expect a ring," he said.

"It's a family tradition. A man places a nutcracker bride in front of his lady love. If she picks it up, it means yes, she will marry him. If she doesn't, the answer is no."

He set the bride back on the windowsill and reached for another nutcracker. "What does it mean when I pick up a king?" he asked.

"It means you're about to crack nuts." She slanted her head toward a bowl full of walnuts harvested the year before. "All you have to do is put the nut in the mouth and pull down on the lever."

"Sounds easier than giving your grandfather a bath," he said amicably.

❧

After the midday meal, Lucy put her grandfather down for his afternoon nap and walked into the kitchen. She immediately noticed the tins of baked goods missing.

Puzzled, she went in search of Mr. Prescott, but he wasn't in the house. Grabbing a wrap, she let herself out the back door. It was still snowing but not as hard as it had been. Traipsing through the knee-deep snow, she followed his footprints to the barn. She found him attaching a canvas bag to his saddled horse.

Her heart turned over in dismay. "What are you doing?"

"Don't look so worried." He rested a hand on the saddle. "I'm not leaving. I'm just getting ready to deliver your baked goods."

"I wasn't wor—" She cleared her throat. "You shouldn't be out in this cold. Your shoulder—"

"It's not my shoulder I'm worried about. It's my fingers and toes."

She bit her lip. "This is ridiculous. You don't even know where to make the deliveries."

He reached into his coat pocket with his left hand and pulled out the notebook containing her customer orders.

"I think I passed most of these houses looking for you."

She studied him. "Why are you being so nice to me?"

He mounted his horse and gazed down at her. "I have my reasons."

A sudden and disturbing thought occurred to her. "And would those reasons happen to have anything to do with seventy thousand dollars?"

"Seventy thousand, Miss Langdon?" His eyes gleamed. "Is that how much is in the bag you know nothing about?"

Chiding herself for her carelessness, Lucy flushed furiously. "How am I supposed to know what was in that bag?"

"Well now, I'd say that was a mighty good question." He gave her a knowing look before touching a finger to the brim of his hat. With a click of his tongue, he rode out of the barn.

Chapter 9

Lucy couldn't stay away from the parlor window for long. As much as she hated to admit it, she missed the man. She even missed his sardonic smile. But that was the least of it—she was also worried. It was snowing even harder now, and a gale force wind had started to blow.

What if he didn't come back? She discounted the possibility at once. Thanks to the slip of her tongue, he now knew for certain she had the gunnysack in her possession. Oh yes, he'd be back—of that she had no doubt.

His only concern was the money and catching those outlaws. Even he had admitted to having a one-track mind. Still, she couldn't help but wish he'd return for another reason. A more personal reason.

The thought made her grimace. Of all the dumb things that had ever crossed her mind, that had to be the dumbest. Why would a man like Mr. Prescott be interested in her? Next to his exciting life as a Texas Ranger, he must think her dull and uninteresting.

Nor was she much to look at. She didn't have time to do herself up like some of the other single women in town. She always had flour in her hair, and oftentimes her hands were chapped, and. . .

She sighed. There she went again. Feeling sorry for herself. *God forgive me.* Her duty was to take care of her grandfather and not have silly schoolgirl fantasies about a man she could never have.

⁓◎⁓

The next day was Christmas Eve.

Rising early, Lucy sat at the kitchen table counting the money Mr. Prescott had collected from her customers. It was enough to get the roof repaired and maybe a new pair of shoes for Opa. Her prayers had been answered.

After hiding the money in a cookie jar, she straightened the nutcracker bride on the windowsill so that it faced outward. She also said a prayer. As long as those outlaws were still on the loose, the house needed as much protection as possible.

It had stopped snowing, and a patch of blue sky stretched between the divided clouds. Pristine snow spread as far as the eye could see. The white landscape looked as stark and barren as her future.

Shaking away the depressing thought, she was just about to move from the window when a movement caught her eye. She leaned over the sink for a closer look. That's when she noticed the barn door open. Funny. She could have sworn. . .

Had Opa escaped the house?

Barely had she thought it than she spotted a man she didn't recognize walking out of the barn. Gasping, she ducked out of sight. Was that a gun in his hand?

Heart pounding, she ran to Mr. Prescott's room and, without knocking, rushed inside. "Mr. Prescott." She shook him. "Wake up!"

He turned over and stared up at her. "What the—"

"Shh. There's someone outside. A stranger. He was in the barn. I think he has a gun."

Throwing the covers aside, Mr. Prescott jumped out of bed and reached for his trousers, pulling them on over his long johns. "What did he look like?"

"I don't know. I only caught a glimpse."

He quickly finished dressing, grabbed his holster on the bedpost, and raced out of the room.

Moments later the two of them were crouched in front of the parlor window. Three horses were tethered to the front fence.

"It's them," he said grimly. "The Dobson gang. Guess we were wrong."

"Wrong about what, Mr. Prescott?"

He gave her a meaningful look. "About them taking the money out of your wagon. If the money was in their hands, they'd have no reason to come back."

He had her there. "How. . .how did they know where to find you?"

"Good question. Maybe they spotted me yesterday delivering baked goods. I should have taken your horse instead of mine. Spirit tends to stand out."

Grabbing him by the arm, Lucy dug her fingers into his flesh. "What are we going to do?" she whispered.

"Letting go of my arm would be a good start," he whispered back.

"Oh, sorry."

Something banged against the kitchen door, and Lucy jumped. A rough voice called out. "We know you're in there, Ranger."

Mr. Prescott transferred his weapon to his right hand, but he had trouble lifting his arm above his waist, so he switched back to his left.

"What kind of shot are you?" he asked.

"Accidentally or on purpose?"

"Right now I'll take it any way you can dish it out."

"In that case, I'm an excellent shot."

He nodded. "You hold down the fort while I sneak up behind them."

Cold fear knotted inside her. "That sounds like a bad idea."

"The way I see it, a bad idea is better than none." He opened a side window and checked outside. Seeing no one, he climbed over the sill. "Close it behind me," he whispered.

She slid the window shut and rushed to the kitchen for her shotgun. A sound made her whirl around. "Opa!"

Lowering her weapon, she grabbed him by the arm and led him back to the parlor.

"Eva," he muttered.

"Sit, Opa! Sit," she said in a stern voice. After settling him in his chair, she waited. The silence that followed was almost worse than the banging. She glanced out the front window. The three horses were still tethered to her fence. One by one, she checked all the windows in the house.

Just as she reached the kitchen, a gunshot rent the air. Fearful visions filled her head, and she imaged Mr. Prescott lying in the snow bleeding. *Oh God, no! Don't let anything happen to him. Please, don't!*

Holding her shotgun rigid, she moved through the kitchen, muzzle first.

Another shot, this time from a distance away. A barrage of gunfire followed. Glass shattered and sprayed over her sink.

Rising on tiptoe, Lucy chanced a quick glance outside then ducked. The three men were on her porch, backs toward her. One man was loading his gun, and the others had their weapons aimed in the direction of the barn.

The men were talking among themselves, their low voices drifting through the broken windowpane. They were planning something. No time to lose. . .

Careful not to step on the broken glass, she aimed the tip of her muzzle through the shattered window. She didn't want to hurt anyone. She just wanted to chase them away.

Counting to three, she pulled back on the trigger and fired just as one of the men stood. He fell back, grabbing his arm.

"Ow, I've been hit!"

"We're surrounded," cried another.

"Let's get outta here," yelled the third, and all three fled her porch.

∽∾

Moments later Lucy peered through the draperies of her parlor window and watched two of the outlaws struggle to help the injured man on his horse. She waited until they had ridden out of sight before racing through the house and out the back door.

Stumbling through the snow, she called his name. "Mr. Prescott!" She was breathing hard, and her breath came out in misty white plumes. *Please God, don't let him be hurt.*

Stomach clenched, she trudged forward, her feet sinking deep into the snow.

"Mr. Prescott!" And then, "Chad!"

He stepped out from behind the barn, grinning, and her heart leaped with joy. Another prayer answered.

"Oops! You called me by my Christian name," he said. "What will your grandfather say?"

At that moment she didn't care. All that mattered was that he was alive. Closing the distance between them, she flung her arms around his neck.

"I thought you were dead," she cried.

His one good arm circled her waist, and he held her close. "Thought or hoped?"

"Don't tease," she whispered.

He gazed deep into her eyes. "If I'm dead, then this has got to be heaven," he said, his voice husky. And with that, he lowered his head and captured her lips with his own.

∽∾

Chad watched Lucy traipse back to the house to check on her grandfather. He had stayed behind to calm the animals and secure the barn. He also needed to look for a board to cover the broken window.

Lucy. Just her name made the blood pound through his veins. She was a complication he hadn't counted on. Somehow she had worked her way into his heart, and that was a problem. His job was to track down the Dobson gang, and now that he knew they were still in the area, his job got a whole lot easier.

Had his firing arm not been injured, he would have caught the scoundrels while he had the chance. No matter. He'd trailed them this far; he'd trail them to the end of the earth if necessary.

He quickly finished his tasks and headed for the house. Brrr, it was cold, and it had started snowing again. That was a blessing. He doubted the Dobson gang would make another move in this weather. Not with one being injured. That gave him a distinct advantage, but only if he acted quickly. That meant leaving the comfort of Lucy's house and getting back to work.

He paused on the porch and blew out his breath. His mouth still throbbed with the memory of her sweet lips. No matter. He had to leave, and the sooner the better, for both their sakes.

Weighed down by his thoughts, he stomped the snow off his boots and walked inside.

"Lu—"

He paused upon seeing her on the kitchen floor. She held broken pieces of wood in her hands. The bullet that shot out the windowpane had shattered the nutcracker bride.

Knowing how much that particular nutcracker meant to her, he grimaced. All of this was his fault. Tossing that money into her wagon had involved her in a way he never would have imagined.

He stood the board next to the counter and dropped to the floor by her side.

For the second time that day, he pulled her close and buried his face in her sweet-scented hair.

"What. . .what if they come back?" she whispered.

"That's why I must leave," he said. "I need to find them before they cause any more trouble."

She pulled away and looked at him. "But there're three of them, and your arm. . ."

"I won't do anything without the sheriff's help. He knows the area."

Her eyes welled with tears. "I don't want you to go."

He didn't want to go either, and that made no sense. He wasn't one to hang around in one place for long. A week or two at the most. . .

"Staying here was a mistake. It put you and your grandfather in danger."

"You had no choice," she said. "I'm the one to blame, and—"

He pressed a finger to her pretty pink lips. "It's time, Lucy."

She took his hand in hers and held it to her chest. "Today's Christmas Eve." She gave him a beseeching look. "Can't you at least stay till tomorrow?"

Common sense told him to say no, but his heart spoke louder and with more persistence.

"All right," he said. "Till tomorrow."

Chapter 10

It was snowing outside when Lucy lit the candles in the parlor that night. Her grandfather sat motionless and stared at the fire.

Chad sat whittling on a piece of wood, his trousers covered with white chips.

He'd assured her that the outlaws weren't likely to return that night, but she noticed he never strayed far from the window and was alert to every sound.

She blew out the match and tossed it into the fire. She then reached for the wooden box she'd dug out of a cupboard earlier.

"My grandfather made this crèche, and each year my grandmother set it out on the mantel," she said.

She pulled a wooden figure from its wrappings and held it up for Chad to see. It was a gray-haired shepherd in a blue robe.

Chad paused from his whittling. "Your grandfather sure did know how to dig out the best from a piece of wood."

"That he did," she said. "Each year Opa carved a new figure for the crèche and kept it secret until Christmas Eve." She smiled at the memory. "Oma and I always tried to guess in advance what he'd made, but we always got it wrong."

Altogether there were forty-six pieces. The last piece—a camel—had been made three years earlier. Never would she have guessed that it would be the last piece Opa would carve. But shortly after that Christmas, her grandfather started showing signs of forgetfulness. Soon he couldn't even remember the names of simple household items and once was unable to find his way back from the barn.

She spread a white cloth on the mantel and ran a finger across the gold stars embroidered by her grandmother. Opa'd had a fit once upon finding his initials embroidered on his long johns. "Confound it," he'd railed, "if your grandmother can't bake it, she'll embroidery it." The memory made her smile.

One by one she set each artfully crafted figure on the cloth. There were shepherds, angels, animals, and, of course, the Christ child.

She normally loved celebrating the birth of Jesus, but this year—God forgive her—sadness filled her heart. Not only would it be the first Christmas without her beloved grandmother, but tonight would also be the last night spent with Chad.

She drew her strength from the Lord, but she now knew the joy of having a strong shoulder to cry on. It had only been a short while, but already she had grown accustomed to Chad's presence. She would dearly miss him.

No sooner had she put the last piece in place and stepped back to admire the holy scene than her grandfather made a funny grunting sound. He rose from his seat and headed for the door.

"Eva."

"Opa, no."

Hurrying to his side, she took hold of his arm. "It's dark and cold outside," she said gently.

"Eva!" he said again. He pulled his arm away so hard, Lucy fell back. The look on his face frightened her. Something wasn't right.

"I think the crèche upset him," Chad said.

"The crè—" Suddenly, understanding dawned. Of course. All the signs of Christmas—the crèche, the baking, the snow—reminded Opa of his wife, who loved this time of year. That's why he had been so restless of late.

Lucy reached for her grandfather's arm. This time his expression softened, and he turned away from the door of his own accord.

Only then was she aware of a soft warbling sound. Her gaze settled on Chad, who was playing what looked like a musical instrument.

Much to her surprise, her grandfather walked back to his chair unassisted.

"What is that?" she asked.

Chad pulled the wooden tube away from his mouth. "An Indian flute." He blew into the instrument again, working his fingers across the holes. "I hope you don't mind. This is the wood from the nutcracker bride."

"So that's what you've been working on." Delighted that he was able to put the broken pieces to good use, she smiled. "My grandmother loved music. It would have made her very happy to see her treasured bride turned into a musical instrument."

"Legend has it that Indians came up with the idea of making a flute after hearing the wind blow through woodpecker holes," he explained.

It was the first Lucy had ever heard of woodpeckers causing anything but problems, and she was intrigued. Mr. Holbrook often complained about the damage the birds did to his walnut trees. Just wait till she told him about the Indian flute.

She glanced at her grandfather, who looked perfectly at peace. "The music seems to calm him."

"I noticed how much he likes music," Chad said. "Thought he might enjoy some Christmas carols."

"He was fond of music, but that was a long time ago." She sighed away the memories of the past.

"He still likes music," Chad said.

Her gaze sharpened. "What makes you say that?"

"I sang while giving him a bath, and that's how I was able to get him into the water."

"You mean that awful sound—" She stopped, and he laughed.

"Yep, that awful sound." The warm humor in his eyes told her he hadn't taken offense.

Chad lifted the flute to his mouth, and she recognized the tune at once as "Silent Night"—her grandmother's favorite carol—and one she called "*Stille Nacht.*"

Lucy's gaze settled on her grandfather. Something like recognition flickered in his eyes, and her heart practically burst with joy. She had almost given up hope of ever reaching him. But Chad had found a way.

She lifted her voice in song, singing first in German as Oma had often done, and then in English. She'd almost forgotten how much she enjoyed singing. Her grandmother never failed to sing while doing her chores, but Lucy had felt so overwhelmed these last few months, singing had been the last thing on her mind.

Her grandfather stayed perfectly still while she sang and Chad played. But at the song's end, a silver tear rolled down his cheek.

A cry of joy fell from Lucy's lips as she rushed to his side. It was the first real emotion he had shown in a very long time. "Don't cry, Opa." She wrapped her arms around him and held him tight, and for one glorious moment, he hugged her back.

cↄSo

After putting Opa to bed, Lucy returned to the parlor to find Chad sitting on the floor in front of the fire, stirring the flames with the poker. She dropped to her knees by his side.

"Thank you," she whispered.

He turned his head to look at her, the flames from the fire reflected in his eyes. "For what?"

"For bringing Opa back to me." His hug had lasted only a fleeting moment, but it was something she would never forget. "You're right. Music does have a calming effect on him." For the first time in more than a month, he'd stopped trying to escape.

"Maybe music helps him feel close to his wife, and he has no need to go searching for her," Chad said.

She smiled at the thought. "Maybe you're right." She watched the dimple on his cheek fade away. "I have a present for you," she said.

"For me?"

Instead of answering him, she stood and ordered him to do the same. He replaced the poker before rising.

She turned the corner of the rug over and lifted a floorboard.

He peered down the hole. "That's not—"

"Don't look so surprised. You knew the money was here all along."

"I had my doubts," he said. "At least at first." He slanted his head and studied her. "Why now?" he asked. "Why didn't you tell me before?"

She gazed up at him and thought her heart would break. "Because I knew that the day I gave you the money was the day you would—"

Something flickered in the depths of his eyes. "Leave?"

"I didn't want you to go." She wasn't proud of what she had done, but neither could she keep lying to him.

"And now? Do you want me to go now?"

"No, but I know you must." He would not rest until he tracked down the men who killed his friend. Nor would he forgive himself for failing to do so.

"Lucy—" His hands at her waist, he gazed down at her.

She wrapped her arms around his neck. "You don't have to explain," she whispered. "But after you wear out your saddles, I hope—I pray—you'll come back."

He didn't answer her, didn't make any promises, and her heart broke into a million pieces. But even as she gazed up at him, she heard her grandmother's voice. *"They call the here and now the present, Lucy, for it is a gift."*

And since the present was all that was left to them, she pushed all other thoughts aside and concentrated on memorizing every inch of his face as they talked.

And talk they did.

He told her about his sheriff father and Irish mother. About working on a Texas cattle ranch. About his friend Paul, killed in the line of duty while chasing the Dobson gang.

"He's the one who talked me into become a ranger," he said. "Between the two of us, we captured some of the worst outlaws that ever set foot in the Panhandle."

With his prompting, Lucy told him about her parents. How her grandmother instilled in her a love of literature and taught her everything she knew about cooking.

"My grandfather taught me to ride and plant crops," she said, smiling at the memory. "He also taught me how to care for animals and even showed me how to deliver a calf." It was during that time that she first became interested in anatomy. "When I told him I wanted to be a doctor, he didn't laugh. Instead, he encouraged me to work for Doc Hathaway."

Chad stared at her. "You wanted to be a doctor?"

"In the worst possible way." She smiled. "Can you imagine? A woman physician? Even the doctor was dubious, and I had to prove I was sincere. Before he would hire me, he made me stare at pictures of nudes."

Chad studied her. "Why?"

"He said I had to learn to look past the obvious so that I could concentrate on the wondrous body that God had created and learn how it worked."

"What happened? Why did you give up medicine?"

She took a deep breath. "Grandmother needed me. Taking care of Opa and running the farm and bakery was too much for her." It was too much for anyone.

"Any regrets?"

She thought about her grandfather and the tear that rolled down his cheek as he hugged her. Smiling, she shook her head. "None."

The tall case clock began to chime. "It's midnight, Lucy," Chad whispered between kisses. "Merry Christmas."

Startled by how quickly the time had passed, Lucy reached up to smooth a wayward lock from his forehead. "Merry Christmas, Chad."

Epilogue

Spring came late that year. It was almost April, and the wildflowers were just beginning to bloom.

Lucy had worked all morning on the three-layered cake for Mary Hampton's wedding. Her grandmother had taught her how to pipe icing borders and mold flowers out of marzipan.

She forced herself to sing as she worked, though she had little heart to do so. It was only for her grandfather that she sang, as it kept him happy and content.

It was the third wedding cake she'd done that month, and each served to remind her of all she'd lost. Chad had been gone for three months, and she'd not heard a word. No letter, no telegram—nothing.

Even the sheriff had no knowledge of his whereabouts. Chad had returned the money to the bank and vanished, presumably on the trail of the Dobson gang. Was he even alive?

The possibility that he might be dead nearly crushed her, and she refused to dwell on it. She much preferred to think of him riding his black horse and wearing out his saddles.

If only she could forget his kisses. If only he didn't haunt her dreams. If only she didn't imagine seeing him, hearing him, feeling him.

She stepped back and gave the cake a critical once-over. Satisfied, she tossed the empty icing bowl into the sink and put on the kettle for tea.

A knock on the back door surprised her. Her customers usually came to the front door to pick up baked goods.

She opened the door, but no one was there. Now she was hearing things.

Moments later she heard another knock. Again, no one was there. Puzzled, her gaze traveled to the steps and her eyes widened. Something—she wasn't sure what—stood at the bottom of the porch. Something with a garish face. She walked out for a closer look and blinked.

Thinking her eyes were playing tricks on her, she ran down the steps and picked it up. This time there was no question. It was a nutcracker bride—or at least she thought it was.

The bride's gown was white and her eyes blue. Thick lashes made her look like she'd been in a fight. She had a crooked red mouth and a strange pointed chin. It was nothing like the wooden bride her grandfather gave her grandmother the day he proposed nearly half a century ago, but. . .

Puzzled, she lifted her gaze and her heart lurched. Chad stood a short distance away with a silly grin on his face. He looked even handsomer than she remembered, and much, much taller.

"Did. . .did you make this?" she asked, her voice thick with emotion.

He gave her a sheepish look and shrugged. "Not only am I a terrible singer; I'm lousy at making nutcracker brides."

She held the wooden figure to her chest. "I think it's. . .beautiful," she said, and laughed. It was the ugliest, most beautiful thing she had ever seen. She swallowed the lump that rose to her throat. "What about the Dobson gang?"

"I'm better at catching criminals. You'll be glad to know their outlaw days are over." After a beat, he added, "And so are my ranger days. I've been hired by your local county as a cattle detective. It looks like I'm gonna have to wear out my saddles chasing rustlers."

Lucy's heart leaped with joy, but she was still having a hard time believing this was real and not just another dream. "So. . .so does that mean you're staying?"

"It depends," he said.

"On w–what?" she stammered.

"On whether or not my nutcracker bride does its job."

As the meaning of his words became clear, ripples of pure happiness rushed through her. With a yelp of delight, she flew into his waiting arms.

German Zimt Makronen Cookies

(A recipe handed down from Lucy's grandmother)

1 cup ground hazelnuts

1 teaspoon cinnamon

1 teaspoon nutmeg

1 teaspoon vanilla

4 large eggs, separated
(need only the whites)

1 teaspoon lemon juice

Pinch salt

1 cup sugar

Whole hazelnuts to top cookies

Mix together ground nuts, cinnamon, and vanilla. Beat egg whites. When eggs are stiff, add lemon juice and salt. Continue to beat until stiff. Gradually fold sugar into beaten egg whites and fold in nut mixture.

Using two small spoons, place small mounds of cookie dough onto greased baking sheet. Top each cookie with a whole hazelnut and bake in a preheated oven at 350 degrees for about 20 to 25 minutes. Leave to cool. Enjoy with friends and family.

About the Author

Margaret Brownley is a bestselling author of more than thirty books. Her story was inspired by Tchaikovsky's *Nutcracker Suite* and her own collection of nutcrackers. Look for her exciting new Undercover Ladies series beginning with the release of *Petticoat Detective*, December 2014.
www.margaret-brownley.com

The Christmas Star Bride

by Amanda Cabot

The Lord redeemeth the soul of his servants:
and none of them that trust in him shall be desolate.

PSALM 34:22

Chapter 1

There had to be a way. Esther Hathaway punched the dough with more force than normal. A good kneading was just what her trademark pumpernickel needed. She could—and would—provide that. If only she could find what *she* needed as easily.

Four weeks from today was Christmas, the day to celebrate the most wonderful gift ever given. It was also the day her niece would become Mrs. Lieutenant Michael Porter. Esther sighed as she gave the dough another punch. Susan's dress was almost finished. They had chosen the cake Esther would bake. Michael's parents had their train tickets and hotel reservations. Everything was on schedule with one exception: Esther's gift.

With the kneading complete, she slid the ball of dough into the lightly greased bowl and covered it with a towel to let it rise. The sweet white dough that would become cinnamon rolls for her early morning customers had already completed its first rising and was ready to be rolled out and filled with the rich butter and cinnamon filling.

Esther's hands moved mechanically, performing the tasks they did each morning, while her mind focused on the problem that had wakened her in the middle of the night. Susan claimed it didn't matter, but it did. Four generations of Hathaway women had had their Christmas stars, and Susan would, too.

A smile crossed Esther's face as she thought of the stars, now carefully wrapped in soft flannel, waiting for their annual unveiling and placement on the tree. Each was as different as the happy brides and grooms whose portraits were highlighted by the star-shaped frames: Esther's great-grandparents, her grandparents, her own parents, and her sister and brother-in-law. Having each couple immortalized in a Christmas ornament had become a Hathaway family tradition.

Esther, of course, had no star-shaped portrait to display on the mantel or

THE *12 Brides of* Christmas COLLECTION

hang on the tree. Her hopes for that had died on the blood-soaked fields of Gettysburg more than twenty years before, but Susan—the niece she loved as dearly as if she were her daughter—would carry on the tradition. If only Esther could find a suitable artist.

Once the filling had been spread over the dough, she lifted one of the long edges and began to form it into a log that would then be cut into individual pieces and baked in one of the large, round cake tins that did double duty for cinnamon rolls.

Esther's smile turned into a frown as she thought of her search for someone capable of painting Susan and Michael's portrait. Quality. That's what she sought. When she'd taken over running the bakery, she had insisted on using nothing but the highest quality ingredients and the best pans she could find. Susan's portrait deserved the same high quality.

Esther had interviewed every portrait painter in Cheyenne, but none of them had been right. Some were too busy to take on her commission. Others lacked the talent she sought. Still others admitted they'd never painted a miniature. Though they were willing to try, Esther wasn't willing to take a chance on failure. She had found the perfect frame, a simple gold star, the only embellishment being Susan and Michael's initials engraved in each point. Now she needed an artist.

Bowing her head, Esther sent a prayer heavenward. Though she knew the good Lord had many more important things to do, she prayed that He'd send her the painter she sought. There was no answer. Of course not. It was silly to have expected an artist to knock on her door this early in the morning. She would wait.

Once the rolls were in the oven, Esther poured herself a cup of coffee and retrieved the morning paper from the front step. Settling into a chair at the kitchen table, she began to peruse the news, turning the pages slowly as she learned what had happened in Cheyenne yesterday and what events were planned for today.

Her gaze stopped and her eyes widened. The ad was so small that Esther almost missed it, but there it was, buried deep inside the paper. *Jeremy Snyder, artist. Portraits, landscapes, oils, watercolors.*

Her heart singing with happiness, she reached for a piece of stationery and an envelope. This was no coincidence. God had answered her prayers.

⁓

Cheyenne was a fine city, Jeremy Snyder reflected as he headed past the train depot on Fifteenth Street. Some might complain about the noise when an iron horse chugged and whistled its way to the depot, but Jeremy wasn't one of them. He recognized the trains for what they were: the lifeblood of the city. Thanks to President Lincoln's vision of a transcontinental railroad and the Union Pacific's part in turning that vision into reality, Cheyenne existed.

Jeremy crossed Hill Street. Just one more block and he'd be able to rest his legs. Though the doctors had told him that walking was good for him, even after more than two decades it remained a painful experience if he went too far or too quickly. He'd done both today, searching for work.

Other end-of-the-rails towns had disappeared, but Cheyenne had flourished. In less than twenty years, it had grown from a rough-and-tumble tent town to one of the wealthiest cities in the country. That was why Jeremy had come. He'd reasoned that all those cattle baron millionaires would want family portraits or pretty landscapes to hang on their walls. He'd been right. They did want artwork, but not from an itinerant painter like him. They could afford artists who'd gathered a following in the East. Some had even commissioned work from famous European painters.

Jeremy winced as pain radiated up his left leg, but the pain was not only physical. As much as he enjoyed living in Cheyenne, if he didn't get work soon, he'd have to move on. Though he'd hoped to stay until spring, that was beginning to seem unrealistic. The boardinghouse where he stayed was one of the cheapest in town, and he'd arranged to eat dinner only three nights a week to save money. But even with those economies, his small reserve would soon be depleted and he'd have no choice but to leave.

He climbed the five steps leading to his boardinghouse, deliberately ignoring the peeling paint and the squeaking boards beneath his feet. At least the roof did not leak, and his room had enough light that he could work there. . .if he had a commission. Lately all he'd been able to afford to paint had been watercolor landscapes. Though they filled his heart with joy, they did nothing to fill an empty stomach.

"Mr. Snyder." As Jeremy entered the boardinghouse, his landlady emerged from the kitchen, an envelope in her hand. "This just came for you."

It was probably rude, but Jeremy ripped the envelope open and withdrew the single sheet of paper, his eyes scanning the few words. His heart began to thud, and he grinned at the kindly woman. "Thank you, Mrs. Tyson."

"Is it work for you?"

"I hope so."

Back in his room, Jeremy buffed his shoes, then studied his reflection in the small mirror over the bureau. No one would call him handsome, but at forty, that was no longer important. What mattered was what he was able to create with brushes and paint. He pulled his leather case from under the bed, trying to decide which items to take. Since Miss Hathaway hadn't specified whether she wanted oil or watercolor for her niece's portrait, Jeremy included a watercolor landscape along with the oil portrait of his father that he'd done from memory and the miniature of his mother.

Sitting on the one chair the room boasted, he tightened the straps that held his left foot in place. Wood didn't flex like flesh and sinews, but at least it allowed him to walk without crutches or a cane. There was nothing he could do about the limp. That was a permanent reminder of what had happened at Antietam, but it was also a reminder that he'd been fortunate. He had lived, and now, if Miss Esther Hathaway liked his work, he would be able to spend Christmas in Cheyenne.

Mindful of the leg that protested each step, he walked slowly east. Instead of retracing his steps, this time he took Sixteenth Street, heading for the Mitchell-Hathaway Bakery on the corner of Sixteenth and Central. Jeremy had passed it numerous times on his walks through the city and had been enticed by the delicious aromas that wafted through the air each time the door opened, but he'd never been inside. The few commissions he'd obtained had barely covered room and board and the cost of supplies. There'd been nothing left for treats.

There it was, a small brick building on the southeast corner, facing Central. One plate-glass window held a display of tempting baked goods, while the other revealed four round tables that encouraged customers to enjoy a cup of coffee or tea with a pastry. Jeremy saw a second door on the Sixteenth Street side and suspected it led to the proprietor's living quarters. He'd been told that many shopkeepers lived either behind or on top of their establishments.

As Jeremy opened the front door, he was assailed by the smell of freshly baked bread and pastries, and his mouth began to water. He took another step inside, carefully closing the door behind him, thankful there were no customers to hear the rumbling of his stomach. Fixing a smile on his face, he turned. An instant later the smile froze and Jeremy felt the blood drain from his face. Instinctively, he gripped the doorframe to keep his legs from collapsing.

It couldn't be. He blinked once, twice, then a third time to clear his vision, but nothing changed. There was no mistaking that light brown hair, those clear blue eyes, and the patrician features that had haunted his memory for so many years.

"Diana, what on earth are you doing here?"

Chapter 2

Esther stared at the man who was looking at her with such horror in his eyes. Close to six-feet tall, he had medium brown hair with only a few strands of gray, and brown eyes that under other circumstances might have been warm. His features were regular, almost handsome; his clothing well made; his shoes freshly polished. He might have been a customer, but the leather portfolio he held in his left hand told Esther otherwise. Unless she was sorely mistaken, this was Jeremy Snyder, her last hope for Susan's portrait.

She took a step forward, seeking to defuse his tension by introducing herself. She wouldn't ask about Diana. Indeed, she would not. That would be unspeakably rude. "I'm Esther Hathaway," she said with the warmest smile she could muster, "and I suspect you're Mr. Snyder." Before she realized what was happening, the question slipped out. "Who is Diana?"

So much for good intentions.

The muscles in Mr. Snyder's cheek twitched as if he were trying to keep from shouting, but his voice was level as he said, "No one important."

It was a lie. Esther recognized the expression in his eyes. The shock had disappeared, only to be replaced by sorrow and longing. It was the same expression she'd seen in the mirror too many mornings, but there was more. Mr. Snyder's face had the pinched, gray look of a man who hasn't eaten well. Esther had seen that look on countless faces as men made their way home after the war. The Union might have won, but the soldiers who'd filed through town had shown no sign of celebration.

"Please have a seat, Mr. Snyder." Esther gestured toward one of the four tables that filled the right side of the store. "I'll be with you in a moment."

Fortunately, this was a quiet time at the bakery, and with no customers to wait on, she could devote her attention to the man who might be the painter she sought. A slight shuffling sound made Esther glance behind her as she walked toward the kitchen, and she realized that Mr. Snyder was limping. Hungry and lame. The poor, poor man.

As she sliced and buttered bread, Esther wished she had something more substantial to offer him, but there was nothing left from her midday meal.

Fortunately, two cinnamon rolls remained. She placed them on a separate plate, filled a mug with coffee, then positioned everything on a tray.

"I thought that while I was studying samples of your work, you could sample mine," she said as she arranged the plates and mug in front of him.

Though his eyes brightened momentarily, Mr. Snyder shook his head. "This isn't necessary, ma'am."

"Oh, but it is," she countered. "I can tell a lot about a man from his reaction to food. I insist."

He nodded slowly before opening his portfolio and extracting three framed pictures. "I wasn't certain whether you wanted oil or watercolors," he explained as he laid them in front of her.

Esther's eyes widened at the sight of a landscape, a man's formal portrait, and a more casual painting of a woman. "I had thought oil," she said as she picked up the watercolor landscape, "but this is magnificent. The flowers look so real I want to pick them. It's excellent work, Mr. Snyder."

"And this is the best pumpernickel I've ever eaten. There's something unique about it—a hint of coffee, perhaps?"

Esther didn't bother to mask her surprise. "You're the first person to identify it."

He shrugged as if it were of no account. "I've drunk a lot of coffee over the years, and I've learned to recognize good brews." Raising his mug in a toast, he added, "This is one of the best."

It was a simple compliment, no reason for color to rise to her cheeks, yet Esther's face warmed at the praise. To hide her confusion, she lowered her head and studied the three paintings. Each was wonderful in its own way. There was no question about it: Jeremy Snyder was the man she wanted to paint Susan and Michael's portrait.

Fearing that he might stop eating if she spoke again, Esther kept her eyes focused on the miniature of a woman she suspected was the artist's mother, waiting until he'd finished the last bite of cinnamon roll before she spoke.

"These are exactly what I was looking for. Mr. Snyder, you're the answer to my prayers."

∽∾

"That's the first time anyone's called me that." Jeremy took another sip of coffee, as much to avoid having to look at the woman who sat on the opposite side of the table as to wash down the last bite of that incredibly delicious cinnamon roll. She didn't sound like Diana. Her voice was firmer, a bit lower pitched than Diana's, but there was no denying the resemblance. This woman could be Diana's twin, and that hurt. Every time he looked at Miss Esther Hathaway, memories threatened to choke him.

"Tell me more about this portrait you want me to paint." Though he had every intention of refusing the commission, Jeremy had eaten the woman's food. He owed her at least a few minutes' consideration. And the truth was, other than Miss Hathaway's unfortunate resemblance to Diana, he was enjoying being here.

The bakery was warm, clean, and filled with tantalizing aromas. A pressed-tin ceiling complemented the pale blue walls and the dark wooden floors. The tables were made of a lighter shade of wood than the floor, the chair cushions a deeper blue than the walls. Though the room was not overtly feminine, Jeremy suspected it appealed to a mostly female clientele.

"I'll do more than tell you," Miss Hathaway said in response to his request. "I'll show you."

She returned from the back of the bakery a minute later, a large flannel package in her hands. Unwrapping it carefully, she withdrew four star-shaped frames and laid them on the table. To Jeremy's surprise, though he'd expected each to hold a woman's portrait, two people had their likenesses painted in each one.

"It's a family tradition," Miss Hathaway continued, "to have the bride and groom's portrait painted for their first Christmas together. My niece will be married on Christmas Day, and this will be my gift to her." The woman who looked so much like Diana gazed directly at Jeremy, not bothering to hide the eagerness in her expression. "Will you do it, Mr. Snyder?"

I can't. The words almost escaped his lips, but then he reconsidered. As painful as it would be to spend days in the company of a woman who looked so much like Diana, there was no denying that he needed the money. He needed to be practical.

Jeremy nodded slowly. "My fee for a miniature portrait is. . ." As he quoted a figure, he studied Miss Hathaway, his eyes cataloging the simple gray dress that skimmed her curves, the white collar and cuffs giving it a festive look without seeming too fancy for a shopkeeper. Though she was as beautiful as Diana, Jeremy suspected that Miss Hathaway deliberately underplayed her looks, perhaps not wanting to compete with her customers.

"You're selling yourself short, Mr. Snyder," she said with a small smile. "The other artists I've considered would have charged considerably more than that and for only one portrait. Since you'll be painting two people, it seems only fair to pay you twice that amount."

Diana would never have said anything like that, but then again, Diana would not have thought to offer a hungry man food.

"I'm not looking for charity."

Miss Hathaway gave him a piercing look. "I didn't think you were. I'm looking for excellence, and I'm willing to pay well to ensure I receive it. Now, do we have a deal, Mr. Snyder?"

There was a challenge in her voice. It was almost as if she'd read his doubts and was daring him to conquer them. They'd only just met. The woman had no way of knowing that Jeremy Snyder was not one to back down from a challenge, and yet. . .

More intrigued than he'd thought possible, Jeremy nodded. "We do."

"I tell you, Susan, the man is the answer to my prayers." It was several hours later, and Esther and her niece were seated at the kitchen table, their supper laid out before them. Though many shopkeepers had totally separate living quarters, when Esther's sister, Lydia, and Daniel had built the bakery, they'd seen no need for two kitchens. The apartment had two bedrooms and a sitting room but shared the bakery's kitchen. That arrangement had worked for Esther's sister and brother-in-law, and she'd seen no need to change it.

"Mr. Snyder's work is outstanding." Esther gazed at the girl who'd inherited her father's dark brown hair and eyes but her mother's delicate features, wishing Lydia and Daniel were here to share the joy of Susan's wedding plans. "You and Michael will be proud of your portrait."

Susan smiled as she buttered a piece of rye bread. "I'm glad you found him. I know I told you it didn't matter if Michael and I didn't have our star, but. . ."

"You really wanted it." Esther finished the sentence.

Blinking in surprise, Susan stared at her. "How did you know?"

"I've lived with you for the past ten years. I'd like to think I've learned a bit about you in that time." It had been a joy and at times a trial, watching Susan change from the bewildered eight-year-old whose parents had died of a cholera epidemic into a poised young woman of eighteen, but Esther did not regret a single moment.

Susan's smile softened. "Then you also know that as much as I'm looking forward to being Michael's wife, I hate the idea of leaving you." She reached across the table and touched Esther's hand. "Won't you reconsider? Michael and I want you to live with us."

Trying not to sigh at the fact that this was far from the first time Susan had raised the subject, Esther shook her head. "I appreciate the offer. You know I do. But I don't want to give up the bakery. People depend on it." Perhaps it was wrong, but Esther couldn't help being proud of the way she turned her sister and brother-in-law's struggling enterprise into one of the most successful bakeries in Wyoming's capital.

"There are other bakeries in Cheyenne."

"But none that feed the hungry." Knowing that it was sometimes the only food they'd have, at the close of each day, Esther took bread to the boardinghouses and cheap hotels where the poorest stayed.

"I know others might not consider it a mission, but I believe I'm doing God's will. I can feel His approval in the way He's blessed me with a home of my own and you to love."

Susan had no way of knowing how important that home was to Esther. Esther had lived with her parents, caring for them until their deaths ten years ago, and then she'd moved to Cheyenne to live with Lydia and her husband.

Though she would have given anything to have had Lydia and Daniel survive the cholera and be able to raise Susan to adulthood, Esther could not deny that she had flourished in the ten years since their deaths. Forced to make her living, she'd discovered that she had a flair for both baking and attracting customers. And for the first time in her life, she had a home that was hers and hers alone. A home and independence. She couldn't—she wouldn't—give that up.

"This is my place," she said softly. "I can't leave."

Chapter 3

They were an attractive couple. Jeremy took a step to the right, studying the subjects of his next painting. Michael's golden-blond hair and blue eyes provided a pleasing contrast to Susan's darker coloring, while her yellow dress shone against the dark blue of his uniform. But what impressed Jeremy the most and what he planned to capture in their portrait was the love they shared. He took another step, wanting to see them from every angle. That love was evident in the way their smiles softened when they looked at each other and the way Michael kept Susan's hand clasped in his.

Jeremy paused, wondering whether he and Diana had been so deeply in love before the war. Though he wanted to believe they had, the way their love had ended said otherwise. But there was no point in dwelling on that, even less in envying this young couple their happiness and their bright future. While it seemed unlikely, it was still possible that God's plans for Jeremy included a wife and the kind of happiness Michael and Susan shared. In the meantime, he had work to do. Jeremy settled onto a stool and began to sketch.

He'd been sketching for the better part of an hour when the clock chimed and Michael rose. "I'm sorry, Mr. Snyder," the young man said, his voice ringing with regret, "but I need to return to the fort."

Trying not to smile at the realization that Michael's regret was over leaving his fiancée rather than the portrait session, Jeremy nodded. "That's not a problem. Miss Hathaway explained your schedule. I've spent most of today making sketches of you. Those will be the foundation. I can fill in the details after I've finished Susan's portrait."

The truth was, Jeremy did not need to have his subject in front of him when he painted a portrait. Once he'd made the preliminary sketches, he could work from them, but since most people were accustomed to posing while the artist painted, he continued with what was almost a charade.

As Susan rose to accompany Michael to the door, Esther approached the corner of the store where Jeremy had set up his easel. Esther. Jeremy smiled. He wasn't sure when it had happened, but he'd ceased to think of her as Miss

Hathaway. Of course, he wouldn't presume to address her that way, but in his mind she was Esther.

"Are you certain it's all right to work here in the main room?" She'd removed one of the tables to give Jeremy space for his equipment and the high stools that Michael and Susan had used. "Our sitting room is more private, but it just wouldn't be proper. This way Susan is chaperoned."

Esther smiled, a sweet smile that made Jeremy pause. While it was true that she resembled Diana, their smiles were not at all alike.

"I have to confess that I had a mercenary motive, too," Esther said with another smile. "I thought having you here would be good for business."

"Yours or mine?" Though he'd been in the bakery for less than two hours, Jeremy had noticed that several people had lingered to watch him. They'd bought a cup of coffee or tea and a cookie or pastry to give them a reason for sitting at one of the tables.

Esther's smile broadened. "To be honest, both. I can't compete with the variety of goods Mr. Ellis's Bakery and Confectionary offers, but at this point, I run the only bakery in Cheyenne with its own artist-in-residence."

Though she looked at the easel, she made no comment. Jeremy appreciated that. Preliminary sketches were exactly that: preliminary.

"I haven't had additional customers today, but some of those who've come have stayed longer and spent more money than usual. Monday will be different, because word will have spread. That'll be good for me."

Jeremy grinned. "And it's free advertising for me."

"Exactly. I wouldn't be surprised if you got several commissions in the next few days."

"I won't complain if that happens." This could be the boost his career needed, a way to stay in Cheyenne until spring, maybe even longer. "I appreciate your help, Miss Hathaway."

Those lovely blue eyes twinkled with what appeared to be amusement. "We're going to be seeing a lot of each other over the next month. Please call me Esther."

Jeremy blinked in surprise. The woman was amazing. Had she read his mind and known that he no longer appreciated the formality society demanded?

"I'd like that. . .Esther."

⁂

Esther bit the inside of her cheek as she tried to control her reaction. It was silly how the sound of her name on Jeremy's lips made her feel all tingly inside. The last time she'd felt that way had been before the war, and that had been a long time ago. She was no longer a girl of less than twenty pledging her love to her dearest friend; now she was a confirmed spinster with a business to run.

As Susan returned to her stool, her smile a little less bright now that Michael was no longer with her, Esther returned to the kitchen to prepare a tray with coffee and cookies. She didn't want to embarrass the man, and so she'd decided to wait until tomorrow to add a sandwich or two to the plate. She had it all planned, how she'd claim that she'd cooked too much beef and that she was afraid it might spoil. Always a gentleman, Jeremy wouldn't refuse to eat it.

"I thought you might like a break," Esther said a few minutes later as she placed the tray on the empty table next to Jeremy's easel and darted a glance at his foot.

Though Esther had always thought artists stood while they painted, Jeremy perched on a stool, undoubtedly to rest his leg. She wouldn't ask about the limp, but she'd studied the way he walked and sat and had decided that he had lost his left foot. The wooden replacement allowed him to walk, but since it did not flex like flesh and bones, it couldn't be comfortable to stand for long periods.

Susan rose, her expression once more eager. "Are we done for today? I promised Pamela I'd help her choose a dress pattern."

Jeremy nodded. "I've got enough to work with tonight."

Esther raised an eyebrow. She hadn't expected him to work nights. Didn't artists need good light? Before she could ask, Susan clapped her hands like a small child.

"Good. Aunt Esther can keep you company." Susan kissed Esther's cheek and hurried to their apartment for her hat and cloak.

"I hope you like oatmeal cookies." The words sounded stilted, but somehow with the buffer of Susan removed and the store momentarily empty of customers, Esther felt awkward sitting across from Jeremy. She hadn't been alone with a man since the day Chester had donned his uniform and left for what they'd believed would be only a few months of fighting.

Jeremy took a bite of the cookie, chewed thoughtfully, then washed it down with a slug of coffee. "It's delicious," he said, his brown eyes serious as they met her gaze. "You added nutmeg as well as cinnamon, didn't you?"

Esther nodded. Perhaps it was foolish to be so pleased that this man appreciated the special touches she put into her baked goods, but Esther couldn't help it.

He finished the first cookie and reached for a second. "I noticed the bakery's name is Mitchell-Hathaway. Is Susan a part owner?"

This time Esther shook her head. "When I moved to Cheyenne, my sister and her husband were running it—Lydia and Daniel Mitchell. After they died, I took over. People kept calling me Miss Mitchell, so rather than explain every time, I decided to add my name to the sign."

"But you kept theirs, too."

Esther wondered why Jeremy was so interested in the bakery and its name. "They were the ones who started the business."

"From what I've heard, it was struggling, and you're the one who made it the success it is today."

"Who said that?" As color rose to her cheeks, Esther tried to tamp down her embarrassment. She shouldn't be blushing simply because this man had called her a success.

He shrugged. "Does it matter if it's true?"

"I suppose not. I am proud of the way the business has grown. I hadn't expected it, but it's very rewarding—and I don't mean only monetarily—to create a new recipe and watch people enjoy it. I feel as if I was called to do this."

The instant the words were out of her mouth, Esther regretted them. Why was she confiding her inner thoughts to a man who was practically a stranger? The answer came quickly: for some reason, Jeremy didn't feel like a stranger.

"Have you always been a painter?" she asked, determined to turn the focus away from herself.

A brief shake of the head was Jeremy's response. He was silent for a moment before saying, "Only since the war. Before that I was a farmer." He took another sip of coffee, and Esther suspected he was corralling his emotions. Mention of the war had that effect on many.

"The war changed my life," he said, confirming her supposition. "At night, after we'd been marching all day, men would play the harmonica or sing. I couldn't do either, so I started making sketches for them to send to their mothers or sweethearts. They liked the results, and I realized that I enjoyed sketching. It was one good thing that came out of the war."

The way he said *one* told Esther there was at least one other. "What were the others?"

"There's only one. I discovered the joy of traveling and exploring new places. Before the war, I had never been more than ten miles from my home.

Now I've seen almost every part of this great country."

It was a life Esther could not imagine. She hadn't particularly enjoyed the trip from Central New York to Cheyenne, and now that she was here, she had no desire to travel farther.

"So you don't have a permanent home?" That was even more difficult to understand.

"No. I haven't yet found a place where I wanted to stay."

And she was firmly rooted in Wyoming Territory.

It didn't matter that Jeremy was the most intriguing man Esther had ever met. He was like the jackrabbit that had fascinated Susan one winter when it had apparently taken residence under one of their lilac bushes. Susan would check each morning and every afternoon when she returned from school, giggling with delight when the rabbit was still there. And then one day it had disappeared, leaving Susan feeling bereft. Like the rabbit, Jeremy was merely passing through Cheyenne and Esther's life.

Chapter 4

Five days. It had been five days since he'd met Esther, five days since his life had changed. Jeremy couldn't claim he understood the reason, but he found himself dreaming of her every night. And now he was here, in the warm, aromatic building that had become his studio as well as her bakery.

"I'm so excited about having my own home." Susan's smile turned into a grin. Though she was good about remaining motionless while Jeremy captured her likeness on canvas, the instant he lifted his brush, she began to speak, her words as effervescent as the fizzy drinks he'd enjoyed as a boy.

"Michael showed me what officers' housing is like," she continued. "Did you know that families have to move if a higher ranking person comes to the fort? Sometimes they only get a day's notice." Susan shuddered in apparent dismay. "I don't imagine that'll happen to us, though. We're going to be in one of the smallest houses at the fort. That doesn't matter, though, because it'll be ours."

To Jeremy's surprise, the corners of Susan's mouth turned downward. "I only wish Aunt Esther was going with us."

Jeremy doubted any newlyweds really wanted company, but Susan seemed sincere. "You'll still be able to see her."

"It won't be the same. I don't know what I'd have done without her. She's been like a mother to me ever since my parents died." Susan continued talking, repeating the story Jeremy had heard about how Esther had revived the bakery at the same time that she'd adopted her orphaned niece.

"She's a remarkable woman." That must be the reason Esther dominated his thoughts. The only reason.

"Mrs. Bradford is here for your fitting, Susan." Esther smiled at Jeremy as her niece rose from the stool, shaking her arms and legs as if to relieve a cramp. "It shouldn't take too long." Pointing to the wall that divided the bakery from her sitting room, she smiled again. "Just knock on the wall if a customer arrives."

Jeremy shrugged as he swirled the tip of his brush on the palette. "I have plenty to do. You needn't worry about me."

But she did worry about him, Esther admitted as she followed Susan to their apartment where Mrs. Bradford waited with the wedding gown. Though she couldn't explain it, Esther dreamed about Jeremy every night. When she awakened, all she could remember were fragments, but they were enough to convince her that Jeremy Snyder's life had not been an easy one. It wasn't only his limp or the painful thinness that worried her. More important was the sadness she saw in his eyes when he didn't realize she was watching.

"You're a good Christian woman, Miss Hathaway," Mrs. Bradford said as they waited for Susan to slip out of her daytime dress. She smoothed the hair that had once been a bright auburn but was now fading and threaded with silver, and gave Esther a look that could only be called patronizing. "I admire you for taking pity on that poor man. It's such a shame that he's been afflicted with that limp, but it explains why he's not married. No woman would want to be shackled to a man like that."

How dare she say that! Esther felt her hackles rise. "You're wrong, Mrs. Bradford." What she wanted to do was slap the woman who'd insulted Jeremy, but good manners kept her hands at her side. "There is nothing pitiful about Jeremy. He's a strong man and a very talented artist. Any woman would be proud to be seen in his company."

The seamstress raised an eyebrow, her expression calculating. "Jeremy, is it? Just what is going on here?" Her tone left no doubt she thought the worst.

Esther took a deep breath, exhaling slowly as she corralled her anger. "What is going on? Simple. I've employed Jeremy"—she stressed his name—"to paint my niece's portrait, just as I've employed you to sew her gown." She stared at the woman who was one of Cheyenne's premier seamstresses. "I can see that you don't believe me. That's your prerogative, but if I hear any scurrilous gossip, you may be certain I will tell my customers that, although you are skilled with a needle, you are less skilled at minding your own business."

The woman's eyes widened, and a flush stained her cheeks. "I didn't mean I thought anything wrong was going on."

Esther let the lie slide. There was nothing to be gained by continuing the confrontation. As Susan emerged from her bedroom, Esther forced a bright smile to her face. "What do you think about adding another row of ruffles to the skirt?"

Though anger still simmered, by the time she and Susan had made a decision about the ruffles, Esther felt calm enough to face Jeremy. She hadn't wanted to do that when she feared her face would reveal her fury with the outspoken seamstress, but a quick glance in the mirror told her that her color had returned to normal.

"I wondered if you could start coming earlier, perhaps around eleven," she said as she approached Jeremy. He was cleaning his brushes, the pungent smell of turpentine mingling with the more pleasing aromas of yeast and chocolate. When he raised a questioning eyebrow, she continued. "Susan and I would like you to join us for our midday meal. That will give us an opportunity to discuss the portrait."

It was an excuse, nothing more, to ensure that he had at least one good meal a day. If it also gave her the opportunity to spend more time with him, well. . .that was an added benefit.

Curiosity turned to surprise, and Jeremy raised one eyebrow. "I can certainly arrange that, if you think it's wise." The way he phrased the acceptance made Esther suspect he'd overheard Mrs. Bradford's comments and her response through the thin walls.

"I do." Oh, that hadn't come out the way she had planned. "I do think it's wise," she amended, lest his thoughts had turned the direction hers had, to wedding vows. "Michael will come whenever he can, but you realize the army has first call on him."

Jeremy's eyes crinkled as he smiled. "That I do. And that leads me to something I wanted to discuss with you." He gestured toward his easel. "I studied the other portraits, because I know you want this one to be similar. I'd like to suggest one change, though. Their backgrounds are all plain. I wondered if you might want something different for Susan and Michael."

Esther hadn't thought about backgrounds. Her focus had been entirely on finding an artist talented enough to convey the young couple's likeness onto canvas. "What would you suggest?"

"Perhaps some aspect of Fort Russell. After all, that's where their married life will begin."

As happiness bubbled up from deep inside her, Esther gave Jeremy a warm smile. In all likelihood, the men who'd painted the other family portraits hadn't been skilled at landscapes. Jeremy was. "What a wonderful idea! That would make Susan's star even more special."

He nodded, obviously pleased by her enthusiasm. "There's only one problem. I haven't seen the fort, and I don't know which location they'd prefer."

Esther doubted either Susan or Michael did, either. "If you can wait a few days, we can all go together. I can't leave the store, so that means Sunday." She took a shallow breath before she continued. "Would next Sunday after church and dinner be a good time for you?"

"Perfect. I'm looking forward to it."

So was she.

Chapter 5

It was the perfect day for a ride. The deep blue Wyoming sky accented by a few puffy cumulus clouds always brought a smile to Esther's face. Though at this altitude the sun made the air feel warmer than the thermometer claimed, the presence of the man at her side warmed her far more than the sun. It had been so long—half a lifetime—since she'd gone for a Sunday ride with a man.

Susan had taken the backseat, insisting that Esther sit in front with Jeremy, and though they had tried to involve her in the conversation, she had closed her eyes as if she were dozing. Esther knew it was feigned sleep. Susan was playing matchmaker, wanting her aunt to have time alone with Jeremy.

More pleased by her niece's ploy than she wanted to admit, Esther shifted slightly on the seat and gazed at the man who'd captured her imagination. They talked about everything and nothing. Jeremy told her how grateful he was to be painting in the bakery, because he already had three new commissions. Esther confided that her business had improved since he'd been there. They spoke of the weather, of the harsh beauty of the Wyoming prairie. They discussed the relative merits of pumpernickel and rye bread and the different uses for watercolors and oil paints. The one thing they did not discuss was Diana.

Esther took a deep breath, exhaling slowly as she unclenched her fists. Ever since the day she'd met Jeremy, she had known that Diana—whoever she was—was an important part of his life. While Mrs. Bradford might claim otherwise, Esther believed that Jeremy had chosen to remain unmarried, that Diana, and not his wooden foot, was the reason he was a bachelor. Though she longed to know the story, Esther wouldn't ask. That wouldn't be polite, and if there was one thing Esther had been raised to be, it was polite. But she couldn't help wanting to learn more about Diana and her role in Jeremy's life.

⁘

Jeremy smiled and loosened his grip on the reins. The horses seemed content to amble along. Perhaps they recognized that he was more than content to continue riding, so long as Esther was at his side. He took a deep breath as he gazed at the woman who'd captured his thoughts. She was remarkable, the kindest person Jeremy had ever met. Look at the way she'd invited him to have dinner with her every day.

The need to discuss Susan's portrait had been only an excuse. Jeremy knew that. What Esther really wanted was to ensure that he was well fed. Perhaps he should have refused, but he hadn't, for there was nothing he'd wanted more than to spend time in Miss Esther Hathaway's company.

The food wasn't the attraction, although she was a superb cook. No, the simple fact was that he enjoyed being with Esther. He admired her quick wit, her friendly smile, the obvious love she lavished on her niece. Even more, he enjoyed the way she made him feel almost as if he were part of the family.

Perhaps he was mistaken. Perhaps this was the way she treated everyone, but Jeremy did not want to believe that. What he wanted to believe was that she had begun to harbor some of the tender feelings that welled up inside him every time he was with her, every time he thought of her.

It was too soon to ask her that, and so Jeremy posed the first question that popped into his brain. "Do many of the officers' wives visit your bakery?" Though the answer affected his plans, what he really wanted to ask was why a woman as wonderful as Esther had never married. Susan chattered about almost everything else, but that was one subject she had never mentioned, and Jeremy hadn't wanted to pry.

"A few. Why?"

For a second he wondered what Esther was saying. Then he remembered the question he'd posed. Clearing his throat, he said, "I was hoping some of them might be interested in my paintings. I thought perhaps they'd want a landscape to remind them of their time in Wyoming Territory." And if they did, he would have a little more spare cash to do some of the things he'd begun to dream of.

Esther tipped her head to the side, as if considering. "I don't know any of the wives well, so I can't predict their reaction. Why don't you bring the landscape you showed me to the store? That way we can see if they're interested."

We? Jeremy felt a bubble of hope well up deep inside him at Esther's casual use of the plural pronoun. It might mean nothing, and yet it could mean that she'd begun to feel the way he did. "I have other landscapes finished," he admitted, pleased that his voice did not betray his excitement. "Portraits are easier to sell, but landscapes are what I enjoy most."

"Then you should focus on them. Life is too short to do things you don't enjoy."

Jeremy couldn't agree more. Though part of him wanted the ride to last forever, Fort Russell was only a few miles northwest of Cheyenne, and they soon reached it. The collection of mostly frame buildings around the diamond-shaped parade ground caught Jeremy's eye, and he could envision that as the background for the portrait, but after touring the whole fort, looking for possible sites for their portrait's background, Michael and Susan chose the house they'd share.

Though it wouldn't have been Jeremy's choice, he understood their reasons. Pulling out the folding chair Esther had insisted they bring, he began to work. While Jeremy sketched the simple building with the modest front porch and the young couple strolled along the walkways, he couldn't help noticing that Esther was deep in conversation with two women who'd come out of neighboring houses.

"You're right," the taller of the women said, her voice loud enough that Jeremy had no trouble distinguishing her words. "A painting would make a wonderful Christmas gift. I'll come into town tomorrow to see which one I like best."

"And I'll be with her." The second woman's giggle made Jeremy think she was no older than Susan. "My husband deserves one, too."

Jeremy grinned. Unless he was mistaken, Esther had just sold two of his landscapes. She was a truly remarkable woman.

❧

"I'm so glad we went to the fort." Susan smiled as she drew the brush through her hair one last time. "My star will be the most beautiful of them all."

If there was one thing Esther could count on, it was her niece's enthusiasm. "Jeremy's very talented," she said.

"He's handsome, too. . .for an older man," Susan added, the corners of her lips turning into a grin. "Don't shake your head, Aunt Esther. I know you've noticed, and *I've* noticed the way your eyes sparkle when he's around." She started to braid her hair, then turned back to look at Esther. "I think you're harboring special feelings for him."

"Nonsense!" Esther glared at her niece. It was true Jeremy was never far from her thoughts. It was true she treasured the time they spent together. It was true she had begun to dream of a future that somehow included him. But Esther wasn't ready to admit that to Susan.

That night she dreamed of Jeremy again. The dream began the way it always did, with him walking down a deserted lane. Then it changed, and it became clear that this was no aimless strolling. His stride was purposeful, the purpose soon apparent. A beautiful woman was waiting at the end of the lane. Diana.

❦

"Who's Diana?" Taking advantage of the momentary lull between customers, Esther was sharing coffee and dried apple pie with Jeremy when the words popped out of her mouth. She hadn't intended to ask, but now that the question was in the air, she did not regret it.

Jeremy did. That was apparent from the way he shook his head, his lips tightening and his expression darkening. He stared at the pie on his plate as if the answers were there, and Esther suspected he would not speak. Then, after a few seconds, he raised his eyes to meet her gaze. "I don't like to talk about her," he said softly, "but you deserve to know." He took a sip of coffee before continuing. "Diana is the woman I wanted to marry."

Is, present tense. That meant she was still alive. "What happened?"

Gesturing toward his left foot, Jeremy scowled. "Antietam is what happened. I lost my foot and my fiancée the same day. I just didn't know it at the time."

He ran his finger over the rim of the cup in a nervous gesture Esther had not seen before today. "I wasn't much good to the army with only one foot, so they sent me home. Despite the pain, I was glad. You see, all the time I was traveling, I pictured a joyful reunion with Diana. Instead, she stared at me, horrified. Three days after I returned, she gave me back my ring, telling me she wanted to marry a farmer and that I couldn't be a good farmer with only one foot."

Esther gasped, horrified by the evidence that Diana's love had been so shallow and by the realization that although more than two decades had passed, Jeremy was still suffering from Diana's rejection.

"I can't believe anyone would be so cruel." Though she'd known Jeremy less than two weeks, Esther knew he was a good, honorable man, the kind of man who made dreams come true. But Diana had thrown his love away.

"The war destroyed so many dreams," she said softly.

❦

Jeremy stared at Esther, more touched than he had thought possible by the sheen of tears in her eyes. She'd cared—really cared—about what had happened between him and Diana all those years ago. And now, if he read her correctly, she was opening the door to her past.

"Is that what happened to you? Your dreams were destroyed?"

She nodded. "We weren't officially betrothed, but Chester and I had an unspoken agreement that we'd marry when the war was over." A bittersweet smile crossed her face as she said, "I'd known him my whole life."

As her eyes darkened at the memory, Jeremy felt a twinge of jealousy at the evidence of a love far stronger than what he and Diana had shared. Esther and Chester had been fortunate.

"Everyone joked that we were meant to be together because our names were so similar," Esther continued. "We thought we were invincible, but we weren't. Chester was killed in the first day of fighting at Gettysburg."

"And you've never married."

"No."

"Why not?" Jeremy couldn't imagine that she'd lacked for suitors, especially here where men far outnumbered women.

Esther's eyes were somber. "No one else could compare."

It was what he'd feared.

Chapter 6

"You look happy, Mr. Snyder." Jeremy's landlady wiped her hands on a towel as he entered the kitchen looking for a cup of coffee to keep him awake while he painted.

"I am happy," he admitted, though he was surprised it was obvious. "I'm beginning to think I might settle down in Cheyenne."

Though he had felt a moment of despair when he'd heard the story of Chester, the last few days had given him hope that there might be a future for him here and that Esther might be part of that future.

Mrs. Tyson nodded, her eyes narrowing as she studied him. "It's a good place to live. When Abel went to heaven, my sister wanted me to move back to Illinois. I was tempted for a day or two, but then I realized that Cheyenne's my home."

Like Esther. The difference was, Esther had never had a husband. Jeremy felt his heart clench at all that she had missed. Anyone could see that she would have been a wonderful wife and mother. All you had to do was look at how she'd raised Susan and the way she treated her customers to know that she had an abundance of love to share. And then there was the way she'd dealt with him, paying him more than he'd asked, serving him dinner each day, helping him find new clients. That was wonderful, but there was more. Jeremy sighed softly, remembering the glances Esther had given him, the sparkle in her eyes, the sweet smile that accompanied those looks. It was enough to make a man dream. And so he had.

"I guess you'll be looking for a permanent place to live once you marry." Mrs. Tyson's words brought him back to the present. "I'll miss you," she said, "but it's plain as the nose on my face that you've changed in the last few weeks. You're wearing the look of a man in love."

Jeremy hadn't realized it was so obvious. It was true that he'd never felt like this, not even with Diana. Everything seemed different. Colors were brighter, sounds sweeter, even his painting was better. When he sat by the easel, he felt as if his ideas were being translated into images almost without conscious effort. He'd completed two new landscapes in less time than ever before, but the quality had not suffered. To the contrary, this was the best work he'd ever done.

He smiled as he pushed open the door to his room and set the carafe of coffee on the bureau. If this was what love brought, he never wanted it to end. And maybe, just maybe, it wouldn't have to.

Opening one of the drawers, he pulled out his money sack and counted the contents. It would be a stretch, but this was something he wanted to do.

∞

"He's courting you."

"Nonsense!" The idea was appealing—very appealing—but Esther knew better than to assign too much importance to the invitation. "He simply wants to thank me for all the meals I've cooked."

Susan shook her head and returned to brushing Esther's hair. Though Esther had protested the extra effort, saying she could wear her normal hairstyle, Susan had been adamant that a special evening demanded a special coiffure and a special dress.

"That might be what he said, but I have eyes." Susan shook her head again. "I've seen the way he looks at you, and it's not like you're a cook. Besides, if all he wanted to do was thank you, he wouldn't have invited you to the InterOcean. There are plenty of other restaurants in Cheyenne, but he chose the most exclusive one."

"I know." And that had bothered Esther. Though she'd never eaten there, she knew that the hotel's dining room was renowned for both its fine cuisine and its high prices. "I told Jeremy it was too expensive, but he insisted."

Susan wrapped a lock of Esther's hair around the curling iron. "It's what I told you. He's courting you, and only the best will do." She released the curl and studied the way it framed Esther's face. "Perfect. Jeremy will like this."

When he arrived an hour later, it appeared that Susan had been correct, for Jeremy was speechless for a second. Clearing his throat, he said, "You look beautiful, Esther."

As color flooded her cheeks, Esther tried to control her reaction. It had been many years since she'd dressed to please a man, and she hadn't been certain she would succeed. The fact that Jeremy's eyes gleamed with admiration set her heart to pounding.

"It's the dress," she said, running her hands over the purple silk. "I had it made for the wedding, but Susan insisted I wear it tonight." The gown had been beautiful when Mrs. Bradford had finished it, but unbeknownst to Esther, Susan had spent countless hours embroidering a row of lilacs around the hem. The delicate flowers captured in floss had turned a beautiful gown into one that was truly spectacular.

Jeremy shook his head. "Your beauty is more than the dress. I'll be the envy of every man at the hotel." He reached for Esther's heavy woolen cloak and settled it over her shoulders. "And now, if you're ready. . ." He bent his arm and placed Esther's hand on it. "I hope you don't mind walking."

Esther did not. Though Jeremy had proposed hiring a carriage, she had insisted that she was capable of walking the one block to the InterOcean. Her initial thought had been to save him the expense, but now that they were on their way, she realized how much she enjoyed walking at Jeremy's side, having her hand nestled on his arm, feeling as if she was part of a couple. This was the stuff of dreams. And when they entered the hotel and were ushered to the dining room, the pleasure only increased.

"This is even more beautiful than I'd expected," Esther said when they were seated. With its polished dark wainscoting and coffered ceiling, the dining room exuded elegance, while the white table linens and shiny wallpaper brightened what could have been a dark room.

"You mean you've never been here?"

She shook her head. There were so many things she'd never done, and dining with a handsome man was one of them. "A woman alone doesn't eat in places like this. It would have been awkward." There were no tables for one.

"Then I'm doubly glad we came." Jeremy smiled, and the warmth in his expression made Esther's pulse begin to race. Was Susan right? Could Jeremy be courting her? Was it possible that her dreams of marriage and happily-ever-after might come true?

"I feel honored to be the one who introduced you to this restaurant." Though his words were matter-of-fact, Jeremy's tone caused her heart to skip a beat. Truly, this was the most wonderful evening imaginable.

When the food arrived, Jeremy bowed his head and offered thanks for the meal, then waited until Esther had tasted her trout before he picked up his fork.

"The food is delicious," she said, savoring the delicate sauce. Perfectly prepared food shared with the perfect companion. She could ask for nothing more.

Jeremy cut a piece of his meat and chewed slowly before he said, "It's not as good as yours."

Esther did not believe that. "There's no need for flattery."

"It's not flattery. It's the truth. The stew you served on Wednesday was more flavorful than this bison."

It couldn't be true, but Esther appreciated the thought, just as she appreciated everything Jeremy was doing to make the night so special. "I enjoy cooking," she told him, "and I'm more than happy to share it with you." It felt so good—so right—having Jeremy at her kitchen table. His presence there made her heart pound and fueled her dreams.

He nodded, as if he'd heard her unspoken words, and Esther blushed. "Your cooking is superb," Jeremy said, "but the company is even better. I've enjoyed these past few weeks more than any I can recall."

And then the bubble of happiness burst. Though his words touched her heart, Esther heard the finality in them. Tonight wasn't simply a thank-you. It was an early good-bye. Jeremy was reminding her that he would soon be leaving Cheyenne.

Mustering every bit of strength she possessed, Esther smiled. "I'm the one who's grateful. If it weren't for you, my dream of giving Susan her Christmas star would have remained just that—a dream. Thanks to you, she will have something she can treasure for the rest of her life."

And Esther would have memories of these few sweet weeks when Jeremy was part of her life. He filled the empty spaces deep inside her. He made ordinary days special. He brought color to what had been a gray life. Esther lowered her eyes and pretended that the trout demanded her attention. She didn't want Jeremy to read the emotion in her eyes.

Just being in the same room with him lifted her spirits, and when he smiled at her, Esther's heart overflowed with happiness. She placed a piece of trout on her fork and raised it to her lips. She could deny it no longer. She loved Jeremy. He was the man who'd put a spring in her step. He was kind, talented, and generous. Oh, why mince words? Jeremy was everything she'd dreamed of in a man. If only they had a future.

But they did not. He was leaving, and she was staying. That was the way it had to be. Even if Jeremy had asked her to go with him, Esther would have refused. If there was one thing she knew, it was that she would be miserable sharing the itinerant life that was so important to him. And misery was the quickest way to destroy love. Esther wouldn't take that risk, for it wasn't only her heart that was at stake. Jeremy had been hurt once. She would not be the one to hurt him a second time.

Chapter 7

"I don't understand it." Jeremy muttered the words under his breath as he sat on the edge of the chair and unstrapped his left foot. He'd believed Esther would be pleased by dinner at the InterOcean, and for a while it had seemed that she was enjoying not just the food and atmosphere but also his company. Her eyes had shone with what he thought was genuine happiness, and her cheeks had borne a most becoming flush. Then suddenly the lovely glow had faded, and only a blind man would have missed the sadness in her eyes. Esther had said all the right words, but Jeremy could tell that she wasn't happy, and that had spoiled the evening for him.

He wanted Esther to be happy. Oh, how he wanted her to be happy. But she wasn't, and he wasn't certain why. Though he'd replayed the evening a dozen times, trying to understand what had caused the change, the only clue he had was that she'd looked sorrowful when she spoke of the Christmas star. Perhaps Esther's thoughts had returned to the past and she'd wished she'd had her own star, that Chester had survived the war and given her the life she'd dreamed of.

Jeremy rubbed petroleum jelly into his stump as he did each night. Though that eased the pain in his leg, it did nothing to assuage the pain in his heart. He hadn't been lying when he told Esther that he enjoyed seeing new parts of the country. What he hadn't told her was that the itinerant life was lonely. For years, Jeremy had prayed for a home of his own and a woman to share it. And now when it seemed that his prayers were close to being answered, he feared that once again they'd be dashed, unless he could find a way to make Esther happy. Jeremy couldn't bring Chester back to life, but surely there was something he could do to make her eyes sparkle again.

All he had to do was find it.

❧

What a fool she was! Esther winced as the brush tangled in her hair, but that pain was nothing compared to the pain in her heart. She had spoiled a perfectly wonderful evening by worrying about her future. Hadn't she learned anything in her thirty-eight years? She knew she couldn't control the future.

Only God could. She knew she needed to trust Him. He'd healed her heart after Chester's death; He'd brought her here and shown her the way to succeed. He would guide her to her future, if only she would let Him.

Her hair needed to be braided, but that could wait. There was a greater need right now. Esther reached for the Bible on her bedside table and opened it to the book of Jeremiah. Chapter 29, verse 11 had always brought her comfort, and it did not fail her now: "For I know the thoughts that I think toward you, saith the Lord, thoughts of peace, and not of evil, to give you an expected end."

Esther closed her eyes, letting the words sink into her heart. When she felt the familiar comfort settle over her, she read the next verse. "Then shall ye call upon me, and ye shall go and pray unto me, and I will hearken unto you." The promise of peace was there, but if she wanted it, she needed to ask for it.

Kneeling beside her bed, Esther bowed her head. "Dear Lord, help me find joy in each day. Show me the path You have prepared for me."

Though the future was still clouded, that night she slept better than she had in months.

From her vantage point behind the counter, Esther watched as Jeremy put the final brushstroke on the painting.

"We're finished, Susan."

"Can I see it?" Susan asked as she slid from the stool. "You've been so secretive."

Jeremy shook his head. "Your aunt told me that's part of the tradition. Although others can see the portrait, you need to wait until your wedding day."

Susan's pout drew Esther to her niece's side, and if that meant that she was near to Jeremy, that was all right, too. Though she'd tried her best to regain the special feeling of closeness they'd shared at the InterOcean, Esther had failed. It seemed as though a barrier had been erected between them, and nothing she said or did demolished it. Jeremy seemed preoccupied. He'd even stopped eating with her and Susan, claiming he had work to do and couldn't afford the time. The worst part was that although Esther suspected she had created the barrier, she had no idea how to make it disappear.

"Jeremy's right. It's only eight more days." A quick glance at the canvas confirmed what Esther had thought: the painting was magnificent. Turning to Jeremy, she raised an eyebrow. "When will you have it framed?"

"Two days. It needs to be completely dry first. If it's convenient for you,

I'll bring it Saturday afternoon on my way back from Mrs. Edgar's house."

This was what Esther had feared. Today would be the end of her time with Jeremy. Oh, she'd see him occasionally while he was still in Cheyenne, but those wonderful days of sharing meals and conversations with him, of having only to look across the room to see him, were over.

"The offer of using the bakery as your studio is still open," she said, hoping she didn't sound as if she were pleading.

He nodded as he dipped his brush into turpentine. "I appreciate that, but Mrs. Edgar doesn't want anyone to know she's having her portrait painted. Apparently her husband has been asking for a miniature to put in his watch for years. When Mrs. Edgar heard about Susan and Michael's portrait, she decided this would be the year Mr. Edgar got his wish."

"Will you have enough time to finish it?" Susan's portrait had taken almost three weeks to complete.

Jeremy nodded again. "I just won't be sleeping very much." Or sharing meals with her.

"I'm sure it'll be as wonderful as Susan's portrait." Esther darted another glance at the finished work. Jeremy had captured more than Susan and Michael's features; he'd captured their love. Though the other Christmas stars were beautiful, this one was spectacular. "I can never thank you enough."

"It was truly my pleasure." For the first time since the night at the Inter-Ocean, Jeremy's smile seemed unfettered. As the clock chimed, the smile turned into a frown. "I'm sorry to rush away, but I have another appointment this afternoon."

A minute later he was gone, leaving Esther with an enormous void deep inside her.

⸱⸱⸱

Jeremy pulled his watch from his pocket, trying not to scowl when he realized that the store would close in five minutes. If he were able, he'd run, but running had not been a possibility since Antietam. When he opened the door to Mullen's Fine Jewelry, the clock was striking five, and the proprietor seemed on the verge of locking the door.

"Thank you for waiting for me. I'm sorry I'm so late." Jeremy brushed snow from his coat. "Were you able to find one?"

As the jeweler shook his head, his elaborately waxed and curled mustache wiggled. "I sent telegrams to my best suppliers, but no one had what you want."

Though he'd feared this would be the case, Jeremy could not disguise his disappointment. "I know I didn't give you much notice."

Mr. Mullen stepped behind the main display case. The assortment of gold and silver pieces, many decorated with gemstones or pearls, was the best in Cheyenne, yet it held no appeal for Jeremy. There was only one thing he wanted.

"That's true," Mr. Mullen agreed. "You didn't give me much notice. On top of that, it's a busy time of the year for every jeweler. I was afraid I would not be able to find it. That's why—"

Jeremy had heard enough. This was one dream that would not come true. "There's no need to apologize, Mr. Mullen. I know you did your best. The fault is mine."

The jeweler fingered his mustache, almost as if he were trying to hide a smile. That was absurd. There was no reason to smile.

"If you'd let me finish, you'd know that I wasn't going to apologize." Mr. Mullen's words came out as little more than a reprimand. "When you first approached me, I knew it was unlikely anyone would have what you need. That's why I took the liberty of making one." He reached under the counter and brought out a cloth bag. "Is this what you had in mind?"

Jeremy stared in amazement at the object in Mr. Mullen's hand. It was everything he'd dreamed of and more. "It's perfect."

∞

"Is something wrong, Aunt Esther?"

Startled by her niece's approach, Esther dropped the rolling pin. As she bent down to retrieve it, she frowned when she saw the amount of flour she'd spilled onto the floor. This wasn't like her. But then the way she'd been feeling for the past few days wasn't like her, either. Despite her prayers, the future was still unclear.

"Nothing's wrong." Though Esther had hoped that her indecision hadn't been obvious, Susan had seen behind the mask she'd been wearing. "I'm simply extra busy this year." That wasn't a lie, but it also wasn't the whole truth. Esther had spent far too much time dreaming about a future that would never happen.

Susan perched on the edge of a chair. "It's my wedding, isn't it? I should never have planned a Christmas wedding. I know how busy the bakery is during December."

After rinsing the rolling pin, Esther resumed her work on the piecrusts, grateful that the task kept her back to Susan. She didn't want her niece to see the confusion she knew was reflected in her eyes. "It's not your fault,

Susan. This is the perfect time for you and Michael to marry. I wouldn't have it any other way." Being busy should have kept her mind focused on happier thoughts than Jeremy's absence.

"But something is wrong," Susan persisted. "I can tell."

Esther hadn't planned to say anything to Susan until she'd made her decision, but the girl's obvious concern made her admit, "I've been thinking about my future. I'm trying to decide whether I should sell the bakery."

"What?" Susan jumped up from the chair and put her arm around Esther's waist, turning her until they were facing. "You said this was your home. Your life."

Esther nodded slowly. "That's true. You and the bakery have been my life for the last ten years." She laid a finger under Susan's chin, tipping it upward. "They've been wonderful years, but it feels as if they've been a season in my life and now that season is ending."

Susan was silent for a moment, her eyes searching Esther's face as if she sought a meaning behind the words. "If you do sell the bakery, you can live with Michael and me."

Her niece's generous offer did not surprise Esther, but there was only one possible answer. "Thank you, Susan, but I cannot do that. You and Michael are starting your life together. As much as I love you, I know it would be wrong for me to be part of that life."

Susan looked bewildered. "But what would you do?"

"I'm not sure." That was the reason Esther hadn't slept last night. "I know what I want to do, but I'm not sure that's possible." If wishes came true and prayers were answered, she would spend the rest of her life with Jeremy, but he'd never spoken of love or of wanting her to be a permanent part of his life.

Bewilderment turned to a calculating look as Susan stared at her, and for the briefest of moments Esther feared her niece had read her thoughts. Impossible.

"Aren't you the one who told me Grandma Hathaway said Christmas was the season of miracles?"

Esther nodded, remembering the number of times her mother had said exactly that. "Yes, but. . ."

"Then start praying for one."

Esther did.

Chapter 8

Three days until Christmas. Jeremy peered into the mirror as he wielded his razor. No point in nicking sensitive skin. They'd be a busy three days, but he wasn't complaining. No, sirree. If everything went the way he prayed it would, if he had enough courage to do all that he planned, this would be his best Christmas ever.

The first part was easy. He would finish Mrs. Edgar's portrait this afternoon, frame it tomorrow night, and then deliver it early on Christmas Eve morning. The second part was more difficult. Laying down the razor, he studied his face. No whiskers visible. He rinsed the bits of shaving cream from his face, then toweled it dry. Those were all mechanical tasks, things he did every day. What he was contemplating was far more difficult.

He'd completed the other painting last night so that it, too, would be ready for delivery on Christmas Eve or perhaps Christmas morning. The question was whether he could muster the courage to do that. While it had seemed like a good idea when he'd first considered it, now he wasn't so certain. But there was no need to make a decision this morning. He had three more days.

Dressing quickly, he descended the stairs for breakfast. First things first. He'd put the final touches on Mrs. Edgar's portrait, then think about the other one.

"You have a letter, Mr. Snyder." Mrs. Tyson grinned as she handed him a cream-colored envelope. "A young woman just delivered it."

Jeremy hadn't been expecting mail, and he didn't recognize the handwriting. Carefully running his finger beneath the flap, he opened the envelope and withdrew the heavy card, his eyes widening in surprise when he realized it was an invitation to Susan's wedding. Why had she invited him? Susan had said it was going to be a fairly small wedding, with only her and Michael's family and a few close friends. Jeremy didn't fit into either category.

Uncertain how to reply, he slid the card back into the envelope, then realized there was a second piece of paper inside it. That was ordinary stationery, not the heavier vellum of the invitation. Curious, he unfolded the sheet and read:

> *Dear Mr. Snyder,*
> *I hope you will join us on Christmas Eve. We attend services at 11:00 p.m. Afterward, Michael's parents have invited us all for supper at their hotel. I know this is short notice, but it would bring me much pleasure to have you as part of our group. You need not reply, but if you can come, please arrive at our home at 10:30 p.m.*
>
> Sincerely yours,
Susan Mitchell

Jeremy sank onto the hallway bench, trying to regain his equilibrium in the face of this extraordinary missive. By rights, the invitation should have come from Esther, not Susan. By rights, Jeremy should refuse it. Yet what if this was the answer he sought, the impetus he needed to gather his courage?

Jeremy nodded. When he'd read Susan's note, he'd envisioned himself walking to church with Esther at his side, sitting next to her, sharing a hymnal with her, and afterward. . .

This was one invitation he would not refuse.

∽

"Now, aren't you glad I convinced you to wear this gown?" As Susan slid the last button into its loop, she turned Esther toward the cheval glass. "Look."

Esther stared at her reflection in the mirror, not quite believing what she saw. The burgundy silk with the elaborate bustle and the double box pleats circling the hem was the most elegant garment she had ever owned, and the intricate hairstyle Susan had insisted complemented the gown left Esther feeling as if she were looking at a stranger. An elegant stranger.

"Are you sure this is me?"

Susan nodded. "The new you. You want to make a good impression on Michael's parents, don't you?" Though Esther had had more than a few minutes' worry over her first meeting with the elder Porters, Susan's almost secretive smile made her think her niece had something else in mind. That was silly, of course, for what else could Susan be thinking of?

"It's very kind of Michael's parents to host supper tonight." The couple had arrived in town only this morning but had made all the arrangements in advance, telling Esther they wanted to thank her for the many meals she had given Michael over the course of his courtship.

It was the same argument Jeremy had made when he'd invited her to dine at the InterOcean, but tonight would be far different from that evening. Though Esther had no doubt that the meal would be enjoyable, she was not filled with the same anticipation she'd felt before. The reason was simple: instead of being half of a couple, tonight Esther would be part of a group, a group that did not include Jeremy.

A firm knock on the door broke her reverie. "The Porters are early," she said, glancing at the clock on the bureau.

"Do you mind going?" Susan gestured toward the lock of hair that had somehow come loose from her coiffure.

Knowing her niece wanted everything to be perfect, Esther headed toward the door. When she opened it, she stared in amazement as the blood drained from her face.

"Jeremy! Is something wrong?"

His heart sank. This was not the reception he'd expected. Though he'd suspected that Susan had sent the invitation without consulting Esther, he had assumed she would have told her before now. The shock on Esther's face made it clear that she had not expected him.

"As far as I know, nothing's wrong," Jeremy said, trying not to stare at the woman who held his heart in her hands. "Susan invited me to join you tonight. I thought you knew."

Though she was clearly flustered, Esther looked more than usually pretty tonight. It might be the fancy dress or those loose curls that danced against her cheeks. It could simply be the flush that colored her face. Jeremy didn't care about the reason. All he cared about was whether or not this beautiful woman would allow him to share Christmas Eve with her.

"Come in," she said, ushering him into the sitting room. "We'll be ready to leave in a few minutes."

Though the words were ordinary, Esther's voice sounded strained. It could be nothing more than the shock of an unexpected guest, but Jeremy feared the reason was more serious. Perhaps he'd misread her earlier friendliness. Perhaps it had been nothing more than charity that had made her be so kind. Perhaps she saw him only as the man who'd painted Susan's portrait. All of that was possible, but Jeremy refused to believe it. He wouldn't give up so easily.

"I can see that my coming is a surprise. I should have considered that, but to be honest, since the day I received Susan's invitation, all I've thought about was being with you again."

Esther's eyes darkened, and her lips turned up in a sweet smile. Before she could speak, Jeremy continued. "If you'd rather I leave. . ." He had to make the offer, though he hoped against hope that she would refuse.

"No, of course not." The color in her cheeks deepened. "I'm so happy to see you again." Though Esther started to say something more, Susan rushed into the room, her brown eyes twinkling with what appeared to be mischief. "Aunt Esther and I are glad you're here."

"Yes, we are." The warmth in Esther's expression sent a rush of pleasure through Jeremy's veins. It appeared that coming here tonight had not been a mistake.

Perhaps it was a mistake, but if it was, Esther would have all her tomorrows to regret it. No matter what the morning brought, she intended to enjoy the simple pleasure of being with Jeremy tonight. Perhaps she should have chided Susan for issuing such an inappropriate invitation and neglecting to tell her about it, but Esther could not, not when that invitation had brought her what she longed for: time with Jeremy.

There was no time for private conversation, for the once-quiet sitting room felt as crowded and noisy as the train depot when Michael and his parents arrived. Though the Porters appeared to be as charming as their son, Esther barely heard a word they said. Instead, her gaze kept meeting Jeremy's, and she found herself wishing they were alone. The opportunity came sooner than she had thought possible.

"Esther and I can walk," Jeremy said when Mr. Porter explained that he had hired a carriage but that it might be a bit crowded with six passengers. "If she agrees."

Esther did. Minutes later they were walking down Sixteenth Street. It felt like the night they'd dined at the InterOcean as they strolled along the street with Esther's hand nestled in the crook of Jeremy's arm. But tonight would be different. Esther was determined to do nothing to spoil the evening. Tonight was a night to celebrate the wonder of God's love and the greatest gift the world had ever received. Sharing that joyous message and the hope that accompanied it with Jeremy only made the night more special.

As happened each year, the church was crowded, the scents of perfume and Macassar oil mingled with the pungent odors of candle wax and wet wool. Yet no one seemed to mind the crowding or the smells, least of all Esther. Even if it was only for a few hours, she was with Jeremy.

When the first hymn began, she discovered that his voice was as off-key as her own, but that didn't matter. What mattered was that they were worshipping together. Judging from the expression on his face, Jeremy was as moved as she by the minister's reading from the Gospel of Luke.

"'Fear not: for, behold, I bring you good tidings of great joy, which shall be to all people.'"

Esther felt the prickle of tears in her eyes as joy filled her heart. Even if her prayer for a miracle was not answered, this was a Christmas she would never forget.

"Are you certain you want to walk again?" Mr. Porter asked when the service had ended and they'd filed outside. "We could let the young people do that."

Jeremy turned toward Esther. "If Esther's willing, I'd prefer to walk. It's a beautiful night."

It was indeed. The wind had subsided, leaving a star-studded sky with a few lazy snowflakes drifting to the ground.

"I'd like to walk." And to share more of this night with the man who had captured her heart.

They strolled in silence for a few minutes. When they were two blocks from the church and the crowd had dispersed, Jeremy stopped.

"The beautiful night wasn't the only reason I wanted to walk." He reached into his greatcoat pocket and withdrew a cloth bag. "I have a gift for you." His voice sounded almost hesitant, as if he were afraid of her reaction.

Esther stared at the dark green velvet sack, her heart leaping at the thought that this wonderful man had brought her a gift. "I didn't expect anything." Just being here with Jeremy was more than she had expected.

"I know you didn't, but I want you to have this." He placed the bag in her hand.

As her fingers reached inside and touched the familiar shape, Esther gasped. It couldn't be, yet it was. Gently she pulled out the star-shaped frame. Similar in size to the one she'd bought for Susan's portrait, this frame was more ornate, with open filigree decorating each of the points. And in the center. . . Esther took a deep breath, hardly able to believe her eyes. All her life she had longed for her own Christmas star, and now Jeremy had given it to her. Looking back at her from one side of the painting was her portrait. The other side was nothing more than blank canvas.

"It's beautiful, Jeremy, but I don't understand. I didn't pose for this." What Esther really didn't understand was what he meant by the gift. He knew the tradition.

He gave her a smile so sweet it brought tears to her eyes. "You didn't need to pose. Your image is engraved on my heart. All I had to do was close my eyes, and I pictured you."

Esther nodded. Though she was not an artist, she had no trouble picturing Jeremy when they were apart.

His expression sobered. "I wanted to give you a finished star, but I couldn't, because I wasn't certain what you wanted on the other side." He paused for a second. "I can paint a landscape there. That may not be like the others, but it's important to me that you have your own star. I know you've dreamed of one, and I want to make your dreams come true."

Esther looked at the star, marveling at the way Jeremy had portrayed her. It was her face, yet it wasn't. She had never seen herself looking so beautiful, so in love. Was this how Jeremy saw her?

He took a shallow breath before he continued. "I know how I want to finish the portrait. In my dreams, it's my face next to yours." Jeremy's voice rang with emotion. "More than anything, I want to be part of your Christmas star and part of your life."

Esther stared at the man she loved so dearly, the man whose words were making her heart pound with excitement. He said he wanted to make her dreams come true, and he was doing exactly that. When she opened her mouth to speak, he raised a cautioning hand.

"I know I can't take Chester's place, but I want whatever place in your life you can give me." Jeremy paused for a second and took her left hand in his. "I love you with all my heart. Will you marry me?"

Her heart overflowing with love, Esther nodded. Susan had been right. All she needed to do was ask God for a miracle, and He'd granted it. "Oh, Jeremy, there is nothing I want more than to marry you. It's true that I loved Chester and that he'll always have a place in my heart, but my love for you is stronger than anything I've ever known." The words came tumbling out like water over a falls as Esther tried to express the depth of her love.

She squeezed Jeremy's hand, wishing the cold night hadn't dictated gloves. "I think I fell in love with you that first day when you walked into the bakery. I had never felt that kind of instant connection before, but it was there, and it's only grown stronger since then. Marrying you will make my life complete."

"And mine." Jeremy's eyes shone with happiness that rivaled the stars' brilliance. "Oh, my love, you've made me happier than I dreamed possible."

When Esther smiled, he drew her into his arms and pressed his lips to hers, giving her the sweetest of kisses. His lips were warm and tender, his caress more wonderful than even her wildest dreams, and in that moment Esther knew this was where she belonged: in Jeremy's arms.

When at length they broke apart, she smiled at the man she loved, the man who was going to be her husband. "It may take awhile, but I'll sell the bakery so we can travel wherever you want."

His eyes widened, and she saw him swallow, as if trying to control his emotions. "You'd do that for me?" Jeremy's voice cracked as he pronounced the words.

Nodding, Esther explained. "A month ago, I felt as if the bakery and Cheyenne were my home. Then I met you, and I learned that home is more than a building or even a city. Home is the place you share with the person you love."

Jeremy matched her nod. "Will you share your home with me?" Esther's confusion must have shown, for he continued. "I've learned a few things, too. One is that I want to stay here. Cheyenne will be my home as long as I'm with the woman I love."

"Oh, Jeremy!" Esther raised her lips for another kiss as snowflakes drifted past them. "You've made all my dreams come true."

"And so have you, my Christmas star bride."

About the Author

Amanda Cabot is the author of more than thirty novels, including the CBA bestseller *Christmas Roses* and *Waiting for Spring*, which is also set in Cheyenne. A Christmastime bride herself, Amanda now lives in Cheyenne with her high-school sweetheart husband. You can find her at www.amandacabot.com.

The Advent Bride

by Mary Connealy

This book is dedicated to Steven Curtis Chapman, who sang a really encouraging song, "Love Take Me Over," at a time I really needed encouragement. Thank you to all the wonderful, blessed artists in contemporary Christian music.

Chapter 1

Being a teacher was turning out to be a little like having the flu.

Simon O'Keeffe. Her heart broke for him at the same time her stomach twisted with dread for herself. The churning innards this boy caused in her made a case of influenza fun and games.

The small form on the front steps of the Lone Tree schoolhouse huddled against the cold. Shivering herself, she wondered how long seven-year-old Simon had been sitting with his back pressed against the building to get out of the wind.

On these smooth, treeless highlands the wind blew nearly all the time. No matter where a person sought shelter outside, there was no escape from the Nebraska cold.

Just as there was no escape from Simon.

Picking up her pace and shoving her dread down deep, she hurried to the door, produced the key her position as schoolmarm had granted her, and said, "Let's get inside, Simon. You must be freezing."

And what was his worthless father thinking to let him get to school so early?

Simon's eyes, sullen and far too smart, lifted to hers.

"Did you walk to school?" Melanie tried to sound pleasant. But it didn't matter. Simon would take it wrong. The cantankerous little guy had a gift for it. She swung the door open and waved her hand to shoo him in.

The spark of rebellion in his eyes clashed with his trembling. He wanted to defy her—Simon always wanted to defy her—but he was just too cold.

"My pa ain't gonna leave me to walk to school in this cold, Miss Douglas." Simon was offended on his father's behalf.

"So he drove you in?" Melanie should just quit talking. Nothing she said would make Simon respond well, the poor little holy terror.

"We live in town now. . .leastways we're living here for the winter."

And that explained Simon's presence. He'd started the school year, then he'd stayed home to help with harvest—or maybe his pa had just been too busy to get the boy out the door. And before harvest was over, the weather turned bitter cold. The five-mile walk was too hard, and apparently his pa wouldn't drive him.

The day Simon had stopped coming to school, her life as the teacher had improved dramatically. That didn't mean the rest of her life wasn't miserable, but at least school had been good. And now here came her little arch enemy back to school. It was all she could do to suppress a groan.

Closing the door, Melanie rushed to set her books on her desk in the frigid room. She headed straight for the potbellied stove to get a fire going.

Gathering an armful of logs, she pulled open the creaking door and knelt to stuff kindling into the stove. She added shredded bits of bark and touched a match to it. A crash startled her. She knocked her head into the cast iron.

Whirling around, expecting the worst. . .she got it.

Simon.

Glaring at her.

Around his scruffy boots lay a pile of books that had previously sat in a tidy pile on her desk.

Dear God, I'm already weary, and it's just gone seven in the morning, with nearly two hours until the other children show up. She was on her knees. What better to do than pray?

The prayer helped her fight back her temper. After seeing no harm was done—not counting the new bump on her forehead—she turned and went back to stoking the fire.

Melanie swung the little iron door shut and twisted the flat knob that kept the fire inside. "Come on over and get warm, Simon." Kneeling by the slowly warming stove put heart into her. Her room at Mrs. Rathbone's was miserable. She spent every night in a mostly unheated attic.

Simon came close, he must have been freezing to move next to her.

The little boy's dark curls were too long. He was dressed in near rags. Was his father poor? Maybe a widower didn't notice worn-out knees and threadbare cuffs. And it didn't cost a thing to get a haircut, not if Henry O'Keeffe did the cutting himself. Water was certainly free, but the boy had black curves under his ragged fingernails and dirt on his neck.

Pieces of cooked egg stuck on the front of Simon's shirt, too. Sloppy as that was, it gave Melanie some encouragement to know the boy had been served a hot breakfast.

The crackling fire was heartening, and the boy was close enough to get warm. She reached out her hands to garner those first precious waves of heat.

"Soon, I'll have to get to work, Simon. But you can stay here, just sit by the stove and keep warm."

A scowl twisted his face. What had she said now?

"It ain't my pa's doing that I was out there. He told me to go to school at schooltime. I'm the one that got the time wrong."

Leave a seven-year-old to get himself to school. Henry O'Keeffe had a lot to answer for.

"Well, I hope you weren't waiting long. I'm usually here by seven, so you can come on over early if you want." The twisting stomach came back. She didn't want this little imp here from early morning on.

But she'd just invited the most unruly little boy in town to share her peaceful time at the school. Just the thought of dealing with him for more hours than absolutely necessary reminded Melanie of influenza again. Her stomach twisted with dismay.

But what could be done? The boy couldn't sit out in the cold.

God had no words of wisdom for her except the plain truth. She was stuck with Simon O'Keeffe. She'd have to make the best of it and help the boy any way she could.

Chapter 2

"Class dismissed." Melanie clasped the *McGuffey Reader* in both hands and did her best to keep her face serene while she strangled the book. It had to be better than strangling a seven-year-old.

Every child in the place erupted from their seats and ran for the nails where their coats hung.

"Simon." Melanie's voice cut through the clatter. Simon stood, belligerent. He held his desktop in his hands.

The three boys older than Simon laughed and shoved each other. There had been none of this roughhousing last week. They'd been acting up all day, reacting to Simon's bold defiance. She'd lost all control of the older boys. Four older girls giggled. Two little boys just a year older than Simon slid looks of pity his way. They all scrambled for their coats and lunch pails.

It hadn't helped that she'd started practice today for a Christmas program, scheduled for Christmas Eve, here at the school. Melanie had been warned that the entire town, not just parents, would be attending.

"Yes, Miss Douglas?"

Do not render evil for evil.

Why, that was right there in the Bible. Was disassembling a desk evil? Normally Melanie would have said no, but this was Simon.

"You will stay after school until you've put that desk back together." Melanie hadn't even known the desks could be taken apart. They'd always seemed very sturdy to her. But she'd underestimated her little foe.

"I can finish it tomorrow. Pa will worry about me." Simon stood, holding that desktop, the little rat trying to wriggle his way out of this trap. The boy was apparently bored to death with school. Studying would've made the day go faster, but that was too much to ask.

"When you don't arrive home on time, he'll come hunting for you, and this is the first place he'll check."

"But he said he might be late."

"How late?" Melanie clamped her mouth shut.

Simon's eyes blazed. The boy was always ready to take offense on his father's behalf.

Melanie had to stop saying a single word Simon could take as a criticism of his pa and address her concerns directly to Henry. But she wasn't letting Simon leave for a possibly cold house with no father at home. Simon's after-school time was, as of this moment, lasting until his pa turned up to fetch him.

"Get on with repairing the desk. Then you can bring your books close to the stove, and we'll study until you've made up for the schooltime you wasted taking your desk apart."

Simon glared at her, but he turned back to the desk. Melanie opened her book to study for tomorrow's lesson. The two of them got along very well, as long as the whole room was between them and neither spoke.

"It's done. Can I go now?"

Melanie lifted her head. She'd gotten lost in her reading. One of the older children, Lisa Manchon, was in an advanced arithmetic book. The girl was restless, ready to be done with school and, at fifteen years old, find a husband and get on with a life of her own.

Her folks, though, wouldn't hear of such a thing, or perhaps there were no offers. For whatever reason, Lisa was kept in school. Melanie worked hard to keep her interested in her work.

"No, you *may* not go." Melanie stressed the correct grammar. "Bring your reader to the stove, and we'll go over tomorrow's lesson together."

November days were short in Nebraska, and the sun was low in the sky. Obviously Henry was not yet home, or he'd have come to find his son. Melanie carried her heavy desk chair to the stove and stood, brows arched, waiting for Simon to come join her.

It helped that it was cold.

As they worked, Simon proved, as he always did when he bothered to try, that he was one of the brightest children in the school.

The school door slammed open.

"Simon is missing!" In charged a tall man wrapped up in a thick coat with a scarf and Stetson, gloves and heavy boots.

Henry O'Keeffe—here at last.

He skidded to a halt. His light blue eyes flashed like cold fire—at her. Then he looked more warmly at his son. "Simon, I told you to go home after school."

"Pa, she wouldn't—" The little tattletale.

"Your son," Melanie cut through their talk, "had to stay after school for misbehaving, Mr. O'Keeffe." Unlike her unruly young student, she had no trouble taking full responsibility for her actions.

She rose from her chair by the fire. "Is it a long way home?" It was approaching dusk. She didn't want Simon out alone in the cold, dark town.

"No, just a couple of blocks. What did he—"

"Simon, get your coat on, then, and head for home. I need to have a talk with your father." She noticed that Henry carried a rifle. Did he always have it with him, or was he armed to hunt his missing son?

"Miss Douglas," Simon began, clearly upset with her.

"Is that all right with you, Mr. O'Keeffe? Will your son be safe walking home alone?" Melanie wouldn't press the point if Henry wasn't comfortable with it.

"Of course. There's nothing in this town more dangerous than a tumbleweed, and even they are frozen to the ground these days. I need to get supper. It's getting late."

"Let Simon head for home, then. I promise to be brief. You're right, it is getting late." She arched a brow at him and saw the man get the message.

"Run on home, Simon. I'll be two minutes behind you."

Simon took a long, hard look at Melanie, almost as if he wanted to stay and protect his pa.

"We won't be long, Simon." Melanie tilted her head toward the door. With a huff, Simon dragged on his coat and left the building.

Melanie knew then he was really worried because the door didn't even slam.

Chapter 3

Why did all the pretty women want to yell at him?

Hank turned from watching Simon leave, then dropped his voice, not putting it past Simon to listen in.

"What's the problem, Miss Douglas?" Those snapping green eyes jolted him. He'd felt the jolt before, every time he'd gotten close to her in fact. And that surprised him because since Greta had died, no woman, no matter how pretty, had drawn so much as a whisper of reaction, let alone a jolt.

He'd gotten used to the idea that his heart had died with his wife. Melanie made him question that, but of course, all she wanted to do was yell at him. He braced himself to take the criticism. He deserved it.

"Mr. O'Keeffe, your son is a very bright boy. It's possible he's the smartest youngster in this school."

That wasn't what he expected to hear. Had she kept him here to compliment Simon? Maybe she wanted to pass Simon into a higher class? He *was* a bright boy. Hank felt his chest swell with pride, and he started to relax.

"But he is disrupting the whole school. We have to do something, between the two of us, to get him to behave."

Hank's gut twisted. It was fear. He tried to make himself admit it. But that effort was overridden by a need to fight anyone who spoke ill of his boy.

"You're saying you can't keep order in school?" Simon was all he had. Hank knew he didn't give the young'un enough attention, but a man had to feed his child, and that meant work, long hours of work.

"I was doing fine until today." Miss Douglas's voice rose, and she plunked her fists on her trim waist.

Hank looked at those pretty pink lips, pursed in annoyance. He'd never had much luck with women. He still had trouble believing Greta had married him. She'd seemed to like him, too, and it hadn't even been hard.

Now, when he needed to handle a woman right, calm her down, soothe her ruffled feathers, all he could think of was snapping at her.

He clamped his mouth shut until he could speak calmly. "What do you want from me, Miss Douglas? You want me to threaten him? Tell him if he gets a thrashing at school he'll get one at home?"

Hank didn't thrash Simon. Maybe he should. Maybe sparing the rod was wrong, but the hurt in the boy since his ma died had made it impossible for Hank to deal him out more pain.

"I don't thrash my students, Mr. O'Keeffe. I have never found it necessary, and I don't intend to start now. What I want is—"

The schoolhouse door slammed open. "Hank, come quick; a fight broke out in the saloon."

Mr. Garland at the general store stuck his face in the room then vanished. Hank took one step.

A slap on his arm stopped him. Miss Douglas had a grip that'd shame a burr.

"I'm not done talking to you yet." She'd stumbled along for a couple of feet but she held on doggedly.

"We're done talking. I have to go. My Simon is a good boy. You just need to learn to manage him better." He pried her little claws from his sleeve and managed to pull his coat open. "Let loose. You heard Ian. There's a fight."

"Why do you have to go just because there's a fight at the saloon?"

"I have to stop it."

"But why?"

His coat finally flapped all the way open, and he impatiently shoved it back even farther so she could see his chest.

And see the star pinned right above his heart. "Because just today I started a job as the town sheriff. That was the only way I could find a house in town. Now, if you can't handle one little boy, just say so and I'll get him a job running errands at the general store. Schoolin's a waste of time anyway for a bright boy like my Simon. Most likely the reason you can't handle him is he's smarter than you." A tiny smile curved his lips. "I got a suspicion he's smarter than me."

Then he turned and ran after Ian.

Chapter 4

About once a minute, while she closed up the school, put on her wrap, gathered up her books, locked the building, walked to Mrs. Rathbone's, and let herself in the back door, Melanie caught herself shaking her head.

"He's smarter than you."

There was no doubt in her mind that Simon was very bright. Was Mr. O'Keeffe right? Was it her fault?

"My Simon is a good boy. You just need to learn to manage him better."

Was it all about managing rather than discipline? She shook her head again. Not in denial, though there might be a bit of that, but to clear her head so she could think.

How long would Henry be dealing with that saloon fight? Simon was home, and he'd be expecting his father. Had Henry thought of that?

"You're finally here, Melanie?"

That cold, disapproving voice drove all thoughts of the O'Keeffe family from her head.

"Yes, Mrs. Rathbone." As if the old battle-ax ever had a thing to do with her. Melanie hadn't even gotten the back door closed before the woman started her complaining. Mrs. Rathbone had made it clear as glass that Melanie was to always use the back door, never the front—that was for invited guests, not schoolmarms living on charity.

"I've eaten without you."

Melanie walked through the back entry and through the kitchen, where she saw a plate, uncovered, sitting on the table, without a doubt cold and caked in congealed grease.

She walked down a short hall that opened onto an elegant dining room and on into a front sitting room. Mrs. Rathbone called it the parlor. She sat alone before a crackling fire, needlework in hand. She glanced up from the bit of lace she was tatting, peering over the top of her glasses, scowling.

"Good evening, Mrs. Rathbone."

The older woman sniffed. "A fine thing, a woman cavorting until all hours. The school board would not approve."

Always Magda Rathbone seemed on the verge of throwing Melanie to the wolves, ruining her career, and blackening her name with the whole town if she was forced to tell the truth of how poorly Melanie behaved.

Melanie happened to think she behaved with the restraint of a nun—a muzzled nun—a muzzled nun wearing a straitjacket. But no matter how carefully she spoke and how utterly alone she remained in the upper room, Mrs. Rathbone found fault.

"One of my students was left at school. His father is the new sheriff in town, and he was delayed. I minded the boy until his father could come."

"Hank O'Keeffe." Another sniff. "Everyone knows that boy of his is a terror, and as for Mr. O'Keeffe, he's got a lot of nerve being a lawman when he himself should be taken up on charges for the way he neglected his wife."

Melanie froze. What was this about Henry's wife?

"She'd still be alive if that man hadn't been so hard on her."

What sort of demands? Was she expected to work on the homestead? Or was there a darker meaning. Had Henry abused his wife? And was he now abusing his son?

"Go to your room now. I prefer quiet in the evening. Disturbances give me a headache."

Sent to her room like a naughty child. *I'll show you a disturbance, you old battle-ax.* Melanie had a wild urge to start dancing around the room, singing at the top of her lungs. Disturbance? She'd show Simon a thing or two about disturbances.

Melanie, of course, did nothing of the sort. "Good night, Mrs. Rathbone."

"One more thing."

Melanie froze. She knew what was coming, the same thing that came every Monday, after Melanie had worked hard cleaning Mrs. Rathbone's house all weekend to earn her keep.

"Yes, ma'am?" What had the woman found to criticize now?

"I distinctly told you I wanted the library dusted this weekend. It's as filthy as ever."

The library. Two or three thousand books at least. And from what Melanie could see, judging by the undisturbed dust, Mrs. Rathbone had never read a one of them.

"I'll get to it, ma'am, but Sunday you specifically stopped me from dusting to clean out the cellar. There weren't enough hours this weekend to do both."

"You'd have gotten far more done if you hadn't spent a half a day idling."

"I spend half a day in church." Melanie squared her shoulders. She would never give in on this, even if it meant being cast into the streets in the bitter cold. "I will always spend Sunday morning attending services. I've made that clear, ma'am. In fact, the Lord's Day should be for rest. But I worked all afternoon and evening on the cellar."

Melanie clamped her mouth shut. Defending herself just stirred up the old harpy. And Melanie knew how miserably unhappy Mrs. Rathbone was. Her constant unkindness was rooted in her lonely life—a friendless existence shaped by her cruel tongue, a heart hardened to God, and her condemnation of anyone and everyone.

The people in Lone Tree endured Mrs. Rathbone, in part because of her wealth that she sprinkled onto the needs of the town, not generously, but she gave enough so that no one wanted to out-and-out offend her. Instead they avoided her and spoke ill of her behind her back.

It was a poor situation.

Melanie did her best to do as she was asked, even though the school board had said nothing about Melanie having to work as a housekeeper to earn her room. She suspected the board had no idea what was going on.

But it was a small town, most houses one or two rooms. There was nowhere else for Melanie to stay. She remembered what Mr. O'Keeffe had said about needing to take the job of sheriff to get a house. She had little doubt there were no empty houses in the raw little Nebraska town.

"I don't appreciate your tone. Get on to your room."

Because no *tone* could possibly come out of Melanie's mouth at this moment that would be appreciated, she went back to the kitchen, picked up the plate of food, and walked up the back staircase.

Melanie worked like a slave for Mrs. Rathbone at the same time being told she lived on charity. Each step she took upstairs wore on her as if the weight of the world rested on her shoulders.

The narrow stairs had a door at the bottom and top. Both were to be kept firmly closed, which also kept out any heat.

In Melanie's room, a chimney went up through the roof. It was the only source of heat—a chimney bearing warmth from two floors down.

It wasn't a small room; the attic stretched nearly the whole length of the house before the roof sloped. But Mrs. Rathbone had stored years of junk up here. There was barely room for Melanie's bed and a small basket with her clothing. She had to walk downstairs for a basin of water and bring it back up to bathe or wash out her clothing.

She spoke the most heartfelt prayer of her life, asking God to control her temper with Mrs. Rathbone and with Simon and, while she was at it, with Henry. She prayed for strength sufficient for the day.

The prayers struck deep. Her impatience with Simon was sinful. It was easier to admit this now, with the boy away from her. While she was dealing with him, she felt justified in her anger.

Continuing to pray, she ate the unappetizing chicken—though it looked like it might have been good an hour ago. She swallowed cold mashed potatoes coated in congealed gravy. She was hungry enough she forced herself to eat every crumb of a piece of dried-out bread. She reached in her heart for true thankfulness for this food.

Only four days after Thanksgiving—a meal she'd cooked and served to Mrs. Rathbone, who had then told her to eat upstairs in her room. But Melanie knew she had plenty to be thankful for: first and foremost, a heavenly Father who loved her even if she was otherwise alone in the world.

She set her empty plate aside with a quick prayer of thanks that she wasn't hungry. She'd known hunger, and this was most definitely better. Turning her prayers to Simon, she remembered Henry's words: *"My Simon is a good boy. You just need to learn to manage him better."*

She begged God for wisdom to figure that out. If it was about managing Simon, then how would she do it?

Changing quickly into her nightgown in the chilly room, Melanie took her hair down and brushed it out, speaking silently to God all the while.

In the midst of her prayer, she remembered that moment earlier when she'd wondered about Simon going home alone tonight. She should have gone with him and stayed with him until his father arrived.

She worried enough about the trouble that little boy could get into alone that she was tempted to go make sure he was all right, though his father had to be home by now.

Her worry deepened along with her prayers as she set the hair combs and pins aside. Then her eyes fell on a large wooden box sitting on one of the many chests jumbled into the room. Strange that she'd never noticed it before, because right now it drew her eye so powerfully the dull wood seemed to nearly glow.

It was an odd little thing. Crudely made thing, the wood in a strange pattern, like a patchwork of little squares as if it had been put together with scraps of wood. About ten inches tall and as much deep and wide, a little cube. Four pairs of drawers were in the front, each with a little wooden knob. It wasn't particularly pretty, but there was something about it.

Her eyes went from the box to the combs and pins. They would fit in there perfectly. She should ask Mrs. Rathbone before she used the grouchy woman's things, but those little drawers seemed to almost beckon her.

With a shrug, Melanie decided she'd ask Mrs. Rathbone about the box in the morning, but for now, on impulse, she pulled open a drawer, which was much narrower and not as deep as she expected. Staring at the strangely undersized drawer, Melanie wondered at it for a moment then slipped her hair things in.

A whisper of pleasure that made no sense eased the worst of her exhaustion and helped her realize the waste of energy worrying about Simon was at this late hour. Her chance to help was when Henry got called away. Now she was just letting sin gnaw at her mind and rob her of her peace.

The prayers and somehow the little box replaced her worry with a calm that could only come from God.

Prayer she understood, but why would a box do such a thing?

Chapter 5

Melanie asked about the box the next morning. Mrs. Rathbone snorted with contempt.

"I remember that shabby thing. It belonged to my husband's grandmother. His mother's mother. He adored that strange old lady and wouldn't part with any of her old keepsakes. That's what most everything is up in the attic. She was covered in wrinkles and dressed in the same old faded clothes, even though there was money for better. Those rags are probably still up in that attic, too. *Mamó* Cullen—that's what he called her—*Mamó*, what kind of name is that?"

An Irish word, most likely for mother or grandmother?

"She was ancient and blind by the time I came into the family and a completely selfish old woman. She seemed to be well into her dotage to me. The old crone seemed to never speak except to tell stories of the 'old country.' She always called Ireland 'the old country.' She was an embarrassment with her lower-class accent. I could hardly understand her. I hadn't met her before my marriage, or I might have had second thoughts."

Mrs. Rathbone waved a dismissive hand. "You can have that old box. I remember it well. My husband refused to part with it after his mother died. I'm not up to climbing all those stairs anymore. I'd forgotten it was up there, or I'd have thrown it away by now. Now as to dusting the library. . ."

Melanie listened politely while Magda found fault. Being given the box lifted her spirits, and her prayers last night combined with her renewed determination to be thankful got her through breakfast and the packing of her meager lunch. The packing was done under Magda's watchful eye, lest Melanie become greedy and take two slices of bread.

Setting out for the short, cold walk to school before seven, Melanie feared Simon would be sitting there in the cold. He wasn't, but he appeared minutes later and came straight for the stove Melanie had burning.

∞

The plucky thankfulness was sorely tested for the next eight hours. Simon started a fist fight, then two other boys ended up in a fight all their own. He tripped one of the older girls walking past his desk. The whole classroom erupted in laughter. During arithmetic he used his slate to draw a picture of a dog biting a man in the backside and passed it around the room to the wriggling delight of the other boys.

And through it all, the heightened noise and constant distraction, Simon hadn't learned a thing. And that was the worst of it. Neither Simon nor the other children were doing much work.

"My Simon is a good boy. You just need to learn to manage him better."

Manage him.

But how?

When the children were let out at twelve for lunch, they all ran home, except for Simon.

Her heart sank at the sight of him fetching a lunch pail and bringing it back to his desk. She'd planned for the noon hour to be spent in prayer that God would help her through the afternoon.

After eating his lunch far too quickly, Simon ran around the room—it was too cold to go outside. He complained and asked questions and just generally was as much trouble on his own as he was in the group. Instead of being able to sit in silence and listen for the still, small voice of God, she'd sent up short, desperate prayers for patience and wisdom—with no time to listen for God's answer.

He tore a page out of another child's reading book, broke a slate, spilled ink—and then he lifted the flat wooden top of his desk into the air and dropped it with a clap so loud Melanie squeaked and jumped out of her chair.

Her temper snapped. "Simon, why are you so careless?"

A sullen glare was his only answer.

Maybe if she threw him outside and told him to run in circles around the schoolhouse to burn off some energy...

"Hyah!" Simon dropped to his knees and shoved the desktop forward. He swung one arm wide like he was lashing an imaginary horse's rump and made a sound that was probably supposed to be a cracking whip.

Fighting to sound like it was a simple question, rather than the dearest dream of her heart, she asked, "Wouldn't you rather go home to eat?"

"Pa rides out to the homestead every day to do chores. We've got cattle out there. He can't get there, do his work, and get back in time to make a meal, so he packs a sandwich and milk for me."

The little boy had a better lunch than she did.

"Get off the floor and get to work putting your desk back together."

Simon stopped. "It was wobbly. I didn't take it apart on purpose."

He most certainly had.

"You have to stop taking things apart. Even if they're wobbly." It sounded like begging—and maybe that about described it. She was at her wit's end.

"It came apart on its own. I'll put it back together." His begrudging tone made it sound like she'd just told him his "horse" desktop had a broken leg and had to be shot.

"You took another desk apart, and you didn't get it put back together well. Which is why I moved you. Now this one will be wobbly, too, if you reassemble it poorly. I'll be out of desks by Friday."

"I'm going to get to work putting this back together right away."

"Is there a chance you can improve on yesterday's task?" Melanie heard the scold in her voice and fought to keep it under control.

Simon sat up straight. His eyes lit up.

Melanie nearly quaked with fear.

"I'll bet doing it a second time will help me improve. Once I'm done with this one, I'll work on the one from last night. This is good practice for me."

What did he mean "practice"? "Are you thinking of doing this sort of thing for a career, Simon?"

That was a form of teaching, she supposed.

"Yep. Pa's already given me a knife to whittle with, and I've carved a toy soldier."

The thought of Simon with a sharp knife nearly wrung a gasp out of her.

"I'm going to keep at it until I've got an army." He was so enthused. "Then Pa's gonna show me how to build a toy-sized barn and a corral. He said pretty soon I'll be helping him build big buildings. We need a chicken coop come spring."

This excited him. "That is fine to learn a skill, but you're supposed to be studying reading, writing, and arithmetic while you're here at school. You shouldn't have time to practice your building skills."

Simon's face went sullen again. All the brightness and enthusiasm went out like a fire doused in cold water.

"Just get on with the desk, Simon. Maybe we can figure out a way you can work on your building skills after you're done with your studies." She tried to sound perky, but all she could imagine in her future was one disaster after another.

Then a thought struck her. "Say, Simon, is your pa a good carpenter?"

"Yep, he built our sod house, and it's the best one all around."

The best house made of dirt. What a thrill.

"And he built a sod barn."

"Will the chicken coop be made of sod, too?"

Simon shrugged. "I reckon. Where would he get wood? There ain't no trees around. They didn't name this town Lone Tree for nothing."

Melanie thought of the majestic cottonwood that stood just outside of town. Alone. But the folks in town were planting trees. They'd tilled up the ground around the tree so seedlings had a fighting chance to sprout. Now little trees poked up every spring and were quickly transplanted. There were hundreds of slender saplings scattered around, but they were a long way from trees.

"Let's see if you can do a better job repairing this desk than you did last night. It will be a test of your skills. And please don't take anything else apart."

"But it was *wobbly*. It needed me to fix it."

Melanie decided then and there to impose on Mr. O'Keeffe and his admirable carpentry skills to keep the building standing—if working with sod translated to working with desks. What his son took apart, Mr. O'Keeffe could just reassemble.

And she'd start tonight because she wasn't going to let Simon go home to an empty house, no matter how late she had to stay at school. She'd felt the Lord telling her not to do that again.

Judging by last night, she could be here very late.

And wasn't Mrs. Rathbone going to have something to say about that?

Chapter 6

"Miss Douglas, Simon would be fine at home alone."

Melanie arched a brow at Henry O'Keeffe as she rose from beside the stove, where she'd been working on a desk, with Simon beside her. "He will stay here at school every day until you come for him. The only way to stop him from staying late is for you to get here at a reasonable hour."

She brushed at her skirt, and Hank suspected she had no idea what a mess she was. Her blond curls were about half escaped from the tidy bun she usually wore. Her hands were filthy. Her nose was smudged with grease or maybe ash. Something black was smeared here and there. She didn't seem aware of it, or she'd have given up on smoothing her dress: that wasn't the worst of her problems.

Hank's temper flared, but he knew himself well. The temper was just a mask for guilt. Simon had spent too much time alone in his young life. The schoolmarm was right.

"I can try and find someone around town who will let him come to their house after school. I know it's not fair to ask you to stay here with him. I apologize that you got stuck—"

"Mr. O'Keeffe," she cut him off.

Then she gave him a green-eyed glare he couldn't understand—except it was pretty clear she wanted him to stop talking.

There was a crash that drew both of their attention. Simon had just tipped over a bucket of coal, and black dust puffed up in the air around him.

"It is fine for him to be here. I enjoy his company." Her face twisted when she spoke as if she'd swallowed something sour. So she must not want him to say she was stuck with Simon. Which she most certainly was. Where did the woman get a notion that speaking the truth was a bad idea?

"Simon, clean up that coal and stay by the stove where it's warm. Miss Douglas and I need to speak privately for a moment." He clamped one hand on her wrist and towed her to the far corner of the room, which wasn't all that far in the one-room building.

She came right along, so maybe she had a few things to say, too. All complaints, he was sure.

"Mr. O'Keeffe—"

"Call me Hank, for heaven's sake." Hank enjoyed cutting her off this time. "It takes too long to say Mr. O'Keeffe every time."

"That would be improper."

She might be right, because Hank didn't know one thing about being proper. Dropping his voice to a whisper, he leaned close and said, "I'm sorry about this, but I work long hours and I see no way to run my farm and keep this job without working so long. And this job supplies us with a house in town—which we need because our sod house is too cold to live in through the winter."

She tugged against his hold and startled him. He hadn't realized he'd hung on. "You need to figure something out. Simon is running wild. He's undisciplined, and I think a lot of what he gets up to is a poorly chosen method of getting someone, anyone, to pay attention to him."

"He's just a curious boy."

A clatter turned them both to look at Simon, who had stepped well away from the coal bucket and was tossing in the little black rocks one at a time. A cloud of black dust rose higher with every moment, coating Simon and the room in soot.

To get her to look at him so he could finish and get out of there, Hank gently caught her upper arm and turned her back to face him. "Things are hard when a man loses his wife and a boy loses his ma. I know we aren't getting by as well as we could, but that's just going to be part of Simon's growing-up years. Short of—" Hank dropped his voice low. "Short of letting someone else raise him, I don't know what else to do. And I won't give him up. I love my son, and his place is with me."

"Clearly, what you need to do, Mr. O'Keeffe—"

"Hank."

"No, Mr. O'Keeffe."

"No, Hank. Everyone here calls me that. Men and women both. Nebraska is a mighty friendly place, and you sound unfriendly when you call me Mr. O'Keeffe."

"Not unfriendly, proper."

"Call me Hank, or I'm going to start letting Simon sleep at school." Hank had to keep from laughing at her look of horror.

"Fine, Hank then. But—"

"He can stay then? Until I get done with work each night?" She'd offered.

Her offer was laced with sarcasm and completely insincere, but it was too late to take it back now. Hank knew he was supposed to promise to get here on time, but he couldn't do any better than he had been doing, and besides, making those green eyes flash was the most fun he'd had in a long time.

She didn't disappoint him. Burning green arrows shot him right in the chest. He got that same jolt he always got from her, and it occurred to him that he'd never had any idea what his wife had been thinking. Greta had always been a complete mystery.

Just thinking about it drew all the misery of living without her around him and all the fun went out of teasing Miss Douglas, who had never invited him to call her Melanie. Hank decided not to let that stop him. And if it annoyed her, all the better, because he needed her to stay away from him. He'd never again put himself in a position to face pain like he had when Greta died birthing their second child.

With that memory of pain, suddenly he couldn't wait to get away from the green-eyed schoolmarm and her fault-finding ways.

"Let's go, Simon. We've kept Melanie here late enough."

Her gasp followed him as he rushed to get Simon, who was now in desperate need of a bath. They were gone before the bickering with Melanie could start up again.

⌒≫

"Late again?"

You are a master of the obvious. "Good evening, Mrs. Rathbone. It's been a long day."

She waited. Maybe tonight would be the night Mrs. Rathbone would be agreeable. Or at least send her to bed with her supper and not a single word of criticism.

"If I told anyone on the school board that you're out at such a late hour, you'd be dismissed immediately. You are supposed to be a young lady of exemplary morals."

Melanie wasn't sure what the point was of that comment. She almost expected Magda to start blackmailing her.

"Split your thirty-dollar-a-month salary with me, or I will tell the school board about your sinfully late hours."

They wouldn't fire her. But Magda might kick her out of the house. Melanie wondered if the school board would object to her sleeping at the school. She was tempted to hunt them up and ask, but she knew it was improper for her to live alone, and sleeping at the school would certainly be alone. Unless, of course, Hank got any later and Melanie started sleeping there with Simon. A woman and her—sort of—child could stay alone together.

If she walked away, Magda would call her back, upset at her impertinence. If she defended herself, Magda would only speak louder and become more critical. If she sat down to have a long, reasonable chat with the old bat, Magda would take offense at the familiarity of a woman living on charity thinking to sit with her as an equal.

Melanie suddenly couldn't stand it anymore, and she opened her mouth to tell the awful old woman to go ahead and report her. Melanie would sleep outside through a Nebraska winter before she'd take any more of this.

Then out of nowhere came her memory of that box. And with it came peace. Calm. How odd. She was able, without any trouble, to stand and take the harsh words Mrs. Rathbone handed out, and when the inevitable "go to your room" moment came, it was as easy as if the poor old lady had just politely said good night.

"I'll see you in the morning, ma'am." Melanie turned away to the sound of an inelegant snort of disgust.

She picked up her supper, even colder than last night, and walked up to her room. The moment she entered, her eyes went to that box. What was it about that box that seemed an answer to prayer?

Even though that made no sense, Melanie knew it was true. She'd prayed for patience and that box had. . .had. . .glowed at her.

She ate quickly and removed the pins and combs from her hair, eager to put them away. Lifting the box from the trunk where it sat, Melanie sat on her bed, the closest the room had to a chair, and held the box in her lap.

Mamó Cullen. Melanie pictured an old Irish lady, wrinkled and full of charming stories of the old country. Was it possible Mamó Cullen hadn't been that thrilled with her new granddaughter-in-law and had, in fact, been unkind?

With a wry smile, Melanie knew that was entirely possible. She studied the odd box. The outside of it was full of seams, little squares of wood, some longer slats, and a few decorative brass knobs that didn't move when she tugged on them. There was nothing beautiful about it, but it was very old, and that alone made it charming.

Melanie slipped her pins and combs into the top drawer on the left. Then, on impulse and because she really didn't want to put it down, Melanie pulled the little drawer all the way out and set it aside. Why was the drawer so small? She looked into the space where the drawer had been and saw solid wood. Then she pulled out the seven other drawers that went down the front of the box, each with a little brass knob just like those that didn't do anything. Each drawer was undersized. But this box wasn't heavy enough to be solid wood through and through.

Reaching in she touched the back of one drawer—playing with it, tipping the box sideways, holding it up to the lantern light so she could see the back, she touched and then pressed and thought the back gave just a bit. Not solid wood.

There had to be something in that unaccounted for space. She worked over the box for nearly an hour when she heard a little click and the back of one drawer slid sideways just a fraction of an inch. For a moment she thought she'd broken something, but looking in, she decided it wasn't broken, that piece was meant to move.

Finally she got it to slide farther, and that was accidental, too. She must have gripped something in just the right way, because the back of that drawer tipped forward, and Melanie could see it was on little hinges that showed when the cunning slat of wood fell flat. Something was in there.

Reaching, Melanie realized her fingertips trembled. She pulled a small scrap out, old, yellowed with age. A bit of cloth, no, a delicate handkerchief, very fine and nearly a foot square when she brushed it flat.

It was embroidered in each corner with a piece of a Nativity scene. Mary, Joseph, and the baby Jesus in one corner. Two shepherds—one with a shepherd's crook and the other with a lamb around his neck—filled the next corner. Three wise men and a camel were in the third corner. In the fourth, in beautiful flowing script, stood the words *Peace on Earth*.

The delicate stitches made each small picture a work of art. It was the most beautiful thing she'd ever seen.

Now that she knew how to open the one back, Melanie set to work on another and found it didn't work. The back had to come out, but not in the same way as the first. An idea sparked to life as surely as a match touched to a kerosene wick. An idea she knew was straight from God.

There would be something in each of these drawers. Almost certainly there would.

And finding them would be an activity to keep her. . .or better yet, an overactive little boy. . .occupied for hours.

A little boy who loved carpentry.

With a sudden smile, she set the box aside and went to her reticule and found a copper penny and put it in the hidden space. She closed it up, packed the box in her satchel and made plans to lure her unmanageable little student into a quest.

As she lay down, she realized the next day was December 1. The beginning of the Christmas month. One of the first days in the season of Advent.

How many more drawers were there?

She'd have to find them before he did, and—judging by the size of the one drawer she'd found—she'd have to seek out tiny gifts to put in each.

Maybe Melanie could do more than bribe her little rapscallion into good behavior. Maybe with this Advent box, she could begin a journey to Bethlehem, to the Christ child, to a new, happier time for a sad and neglected little boy.

That was a lot to ask of an old, homely wooden box, but she couldn't help but believe that God was guiding her, and He would use her to guide Simon.

They'd do it together. One secret drawer at a time.

Chapter 7

Hank felt a chill slide up his spine that had nothing to do with the cold December evening. His son, sitting right next to Melanie Douglas, their heads bent over. . .something. Hank wasn't sure what.

Just as he stepped in, they looked at each other and shared the friendliest smile. It terrified him.

Melanie looked up, but he could tell she was reluctant. Whatever they were looking for had them both lassoed tight.

Her eyes focused on him, and that jolt hit. "Come on in, Hank."

Then she gave him that same friendly smile she'd shared with Simon. Up to now, she'd never been real friendly to him. This was the first time she'd called him Hank without an argument. The pleasure of it curved up his lips. They smiled at each other for too long, and Hank forgot all about his chilly backbone.

"You got here just in time, Pa." Simon sounded happier than he had since before Greta died.

"Just in time for what?" Hank decided then and there that whatever Melanie had done to make his boy this happy, he was going to encourage it.

"Look at this, Pa." Simon held up some dark thing about the size of a man's head. "I found a secret drawer."

Hank came toward the teacher's desk, trying to see what his son had.

Finally, when he got up close, he saw a stack of small wooden objects beside Simon. The knobs on them helped Hank figure out what he was looking at.

"Those are drawers you took out of this thing?"

"Yep, it's an Advent box, Pa."

"An Advent box? I've never heard of that."

"I just named it that because there are more drawers, maybe enough to last until Christmas. Simon will search for one each day after school."

Melanie turned to Simon, and with mock severity waggled her finger under his nose. "If his school work is done."

Hank knew how curious Simon was and how much he liked working with his hands. He'd taken to whittling like he was born to it.

"And there was a present in the drawer I found, Pa." Simon held up a penny. "Miss Douglas said it's a Christmas present for me. This box is full of secret drawers. And I have to stop disrupting class, too. Then I can spend the after-school time searching for another secret drawer."

Hank met those green eyes again. He was the one who'd challenged her to manage his son better. And she had come up with the perfect way.

"Can I see the box?" Hank grinned, unable to stop it. He wanted to search for hidden drawers, too. Melanie could probably make him behave and study with this box.

Simon and Melanie shared a conspiratorial smile.

Simon snapped something inside what looked like the opening for one of the drawers. "You try and find it, Pa."

Hank took the box before he noticed it was full dark. "I want to, but we've got to go home. We'll be late for supper as it is."

"Maybe you could try and get here a bit earlier tomorrow night, Hank." The asperity caught his attention; then he saw the sparkle of amusement in her eyes.

It widened his grin. "Maybe I can think of a way to get here. I wouldn't mind helping with the hunt." His hands tightened on the box, and he was surprised at how badly he wanted to sit down and search or maybe run off with the box and spend the evening with it.

Melanie snatched it from his hand. "I see that look. Simon had it, too. No, you may not take the box. The only way for Simon to spend time with it is to study and behave. And the only way for you to spend time with it, Hank, is to get here earlier. The rest of the time, this box is mine alone."

She tucked the box into a satchel that stood open on the desktop. "Well, it is time to close up for the day, gentlemen. I will see you early tomorrow morning, Simon. And you, Hank, I'll see perhaps late tomorrow afternoon."

Hank tugged on the brim of his Stetson. She had him caught just like a spider with a web. He'd work faster tomorrow, and he'd be here closer to school closing than he had been. And spend a bit of time with his son.

Chapter 8

Melanie woke up exhausted the next morning. She'd stayed up terribly late last night. It took forever to find the rest of the drawers, and she had to do it before Simon did.

She'd managed to finagle each of the backs of the eight drawers open—none of them worked the same way—and she hoped the bright little boy didn't find a drawer she hadn't, because there'd be no gift.

With a smile she knew if he found an empty drawer, he'd just have to keep searching for the day anyway, and the gift wasn't the thing. It was the search. If he found a drawer she hadn't, he'd probably crow with delight at having bested her.

Then she had to produce a small gift to put in each one. She had no opportunity to buy anything. She had to be at school by 7:00 a.m. to beat her little friend's arrival and stay until nearly six at night waiting for Hank to come for him.

She had to come up with a few tiny gifts before Saturday, when finally she'd have a chance to go to the general store.

She looked among her own meager things—she hadn't left the orphanage for this job with many possessions.

Two things for Thursday and Friday. A little red pin, circular with a white cross painted on it. She'd earned this for perfect Sunday school attendance. She could find only one more thing small enough. A tiny, silver angel that she'd had all her life. At the orphanage, she'd been told it was sewn into the hem of the little dress she'd been wearing when she was found left in a basket on a church doorstep.

The kind ladies who'd raised her kept it until she was old enough to care for it. It was her most treasured possession. Praying for a generous spirit, she thought of that unruly and loveable little Simon and smiled. It was easy to tuck the angel into the drawer.

If she thought of anything else to put in, and he didn't find this first, she might retrieve it. But where better to place an angel than in an Advent box? As she left, with Mrs. Rathbone's nagging still ringing in her ears, she wondered if she should tell the old woman about the secret drawers. There was no question that Mrs. Rathbone had given her the box, but maybe if she knew about the hidden drawers, she'd want it back. After the first piece of embroidery, Melanie had found nothing in those drawers, and if she did, she would most certainly give anything she found to her landlady.

She'd spread the handkerchief on a flat surface to be a doily, and it felt as if she'd decorated for Christmas.

Melanie didn't ask. Simon was too excited about the box. What if Magda decided she did want it? Then what would happen to Simon and his behavior?

Melanie decided she'd wait until after Christmas to show Magda the hidden drawers. Though Melanie found herself loving the little chest, she'd return it to Magda if the woman wanted it.

⌒∾⌒

Monday, December 13
The Sixteenth Day of Advent

"Have you found a new one yet?" Hank found himself nearly running during the day to get all his chores done. And he could have stayed longer at the farm and walked a patrol around the town to make sure everyone knew the sheriff was on duty. But he loved helping Simon and Melanie play with that box.

And each hidden space was harder to find. He had a feeling the hard part was just beginning.

"Hi, Pa." Simon lit up. "I've been hunting awhile, but we've found all the easy ones."

"The easy ones?" Hank laughed as he hung up his coat and hat.

At the sight of his son's cheerful welcome, Hank kept a smile on his face, but honestly he wanted to kick his own backside. How many times had he been too busy to make sure his son was happy?

"Those hidden spaces in the backs of the drawers weren't easy."

Simon laughed, and Melanie's sweet, musical laughter joined in. She was so pretty. Hank pulled a chair up to the desk on Simon's right while Melanie sat on the boy's left. He'd brought the chairs over the third day they'd worked together; before that there'd only been Melanie's teacher's chair in the schoolhouse.

Simon turned the box so the side with the drawers lay facedown on the table. "The whole back half is still not open, Pa. The drawers and spaces behind 'em don't come close to taking up all the space." Simon held the box up so it was between them, his eyes intent as he examined the back.

"These thin slats of wood must open." Hank wanted to grab the box and push and slide those slats. Instead, he let his son work on it. Hank quietly pointed here and there, making suggestions.

"Try sliding two at a time. Remember that one hidden compartment that only opened when all the other compartments were closed and the drawers were back in place, except for the one we were working on?" Melanie reached for the box, checked herself, and pulled her hand back. Hank laughed quietly and looked up at her.

"Hard to be patient, huh?"

She laughed.

"Thanks for letting me find them." Simon looked up. Hanks's son's blue eyes gleamed as bright as a guiding star.

"Get back to work." Hank jabbed a finger at the box, but he smiled all the way from his heart. A heart that'd felt more dead than alive for the last two years. "It ain't easy to be so generous."

Melanie laughed. Simon joined in then bent his head back to the box, still chuckling. The boy focused intently on the job—but with a smile on his face.

Melanie brushed a yellow curl off her cheek and tucked it behind her ear in a move so graceful Hank could've sworn he heard music. She rested a hand on Simon's head with an amazingly motherly gesture. Hank looked up and met Melanie's green gaze. She quietly snickered and smoothed Simon's unruly black curls.

Her laughter, the affectionate touch, the change in his boy, the few inches that separated them—all hit Hank in a different way than the usual jolt.

Something so deep, so strong.

He cared about her, and not in a way that had anything to do with a good teacher who'd found a way to manage an unruly student. The feeling had nothing to do with Simon at all.

He cared about her. He knew he could love her.

Their eyes held. The moment stretched. Hank felt himself lean closer. With Simon here, he couldn't think of kissing her, but—he was thinking of kissing her.

He was drawn to her warmth and heat. She leaned his direction, just an inch, two inches, three. He lifted his hand to rest it on top of hers, still caressing Simon's hair.

When he touched that soft, smooth skin, he remembered Greta. They'd been this close, with Simon between them, as she died, their unborn child forever trapped inside her.

He'd touched her just this way. Simon, her hand, his. And felt the life go out of her. Seen the moment her eyes had lost vitality. Her hand had slid from Simon to the bed, and all Hank's love couldn't hold her. As she lay dying in childbirth, he felt as if his love had killed her.

Pain like he'd never known swept over him. He'd barely survived losing her. In a lot of ways he hadn't survived—neither had Simon. They'd stayed alive, but there was no life in either of them, no joy, no family, no love.

And now here he was touching another woman. He would *never* put himself through that much pain again.

Only a fool risked that. He didn't know what went across his face, but right there, with Simon so intent on the Advent box that they might as well have been alone, her spark of laughter died. Her hand slid from between Hank's hand and Simon's head, just as Greta's had.

She looked down and brushed some bit of nothing off her dress and cleared her throat. "I need to spend a little time getting tomorrow's lesson together."

"No, Miss Douglas." Simon looked up from the box, wheedling. "Stay and help."

"Let me get a few things done for the Christmas program practice for tomorrow. I ask you to do your work before you can work on the Advent box, so it's only fair I behave by the same rules." Melanie reached, froze, then almost as if she couldn't stop herself she brushed Simon's dark, over-long hair off his forehead. His curls flopped back right where they had been.

"I'll come back as soon as I'm finished." She smiled at Simon, too decent to let the boy see she needed to get away. "In the meantime, you and your pa work together."

He'd hurt her to protect himself. A shameful thing for a man to do.

Simon let her go without an argument. And Simon hadn't done anything without an argument in two years. His tears had dried after Greta's funeral and he'd started causing trouble. And Hank had found enough work so that he could avoid dealing with his troublesome son.

Only since Melanie had Hank been able to see a ray of hope that his son might stop being such an angry youngster. So, he'd thank her for it and thank God for bringing such a good teacher into town, but he would not let any feelings for her take root.

She moved away, and he focused on this strange box-full-of-secrets. As he studied it, he wondered if he was like this box. Full of hidden places. Guarded, impossible to open unless someone worked really hard.

Hank decided he liked it that way. He would open enough to let his son in, but no more. And just as well, because what woman would work so hard for the doubtful pleasure of finding all the private places in Hank's heart, especially if he hurt them when they got close?

With regret, but feeling far less afraid, he went back to working with Simon. They were at it for a long time, completely lost in testing each and every piece of wood in every way they could think of. Then while he held a small slat of wood that sprung back into place whenever they let it go, Simon tipped the box on its side and they heard a faint click. Hank's eyes rose and met his son's.

"Did you hear that, Pa?" Simon almost vibrated with excitement.

It hit Hank hard that Simon had been sitting still, working hard, showing great patience for a long time. Hank had, too. He remembered how hard it'd been for him to stay in his desk when he was a sprout. One of these days he ought to tell Simon he was a pretty normal child. In looks Hank and Simon were a match, but it appeared that they were a match inside as well.

For now, Hank smiled at his boy; then the two of them turned back to the box. Simon went right back to his diligent work, but it only took a couple of seconds for him to slide one of the thin boards on the back. It slid all the way out and revealed a skinny compartment, as tall as the box but less than an inch deep. And inside the little space was—

"Miss Douglas, it's a tin soldier." Simon's voice shook with excitement. He'd been whittling, and he'd made a little soldier. Hank knew the boy had plans to build his own army. Now he could add this little tin man to it. The soldier shone in the lantern light, and that's when Hank realized it had gotten dark. Every day was shorter as they closed in on the first day of winter.

"Miss Douglas, come and see." Simon lifted up the toy. Hank realized, not for the first time, that Simon didn't understand where these toys came from. The boy thought they were just there, maybe miraculously, put there by God as Christmas gifts.

Melanie hadn't taken credit for the gifts herself.

She came close, her attention all on Simon, and smiled at the intricately shaped toy. "That's beautiful. Didn't you say you were whittling a toy soldier?"

"Yep and now I've got two. By the time I'm done, I'm going to have a big enough army to protect everyone."

Hank wanted that, too, a way to protect everyone.

But first Hank had failed his wife. Then by neglect, he'd failed his son. Now he was busy protecting himself from another broken heart.

Did that mean for once he was doing right by protecting himself? He looked at Melanie, who'd never spared him a glance, and wondered if instead it meant he was failing again.

Chapter 9

"And don't think I won't talk to the school board!"

Melanie could usually remain calm, but the way Hank had looked at her tonight—as if he wanted her as far away from himself as possible—had shredded her normal calm. She'd prayed almost desperately while she tried to find something to do to keep busy until Hank and Simon left.

In the end, she'd rewritten some of the lines of the play, sewn hems in two costumes, worked on some decorations she wanted the children to finish, and read through the highest level arithmetic book she had, a book she was familiar with and understood completely.

Through it all, she prayed.

Memories of the years at the orphanage haunted her and seemed tied to that look in Hank's blue eyes. She'd always borne this heavy feeling there was something wrong with a little girl who had no parents, an older child who was never adopted, a young woman who'd never found a man to love her.

She didn't have those thoughts so much anymore. Living alone in an attic and working all day with children, she was too busy or too alone to be rejected.

Until now. By Hank.

"I know you're spending time in that schoolhouse—alone with a man. There's talk all over town."

Melanie had to dig deep to find the calm needed to keep from snapping back at Magda's verbal assault. Every day it was harder to turn the other cheek, to return good for Mrs. Rathbone's evil. And today—thanks to Hank—holding her tongue was harder than ever.

"Simon is there, Mrs. Rathbone. We're certainly not spending time alone, and Hank, uh, that is Mr. O'Keeffe is often occupied with his work as sheriff. I won't send a little boy home to an empty house. I'm trying to get Simon more interested in schoolwork and less interested in causing trouble. And he's doing very well. Often when Hank gets there, Simon is in the middle of something. . . ." *Trying to open hidden compartments in the box you gave me, which I should tell you about. But I don't dare, for fear you'll take it from*

174

me. "I hope a few more nights"—twelve: there were twelve more days until Christmas—"and Simon won't need extra help anymore."

The Advent box in her satchel seemed to weigh more with each passing moment. Melanie felt heat climbing up her neck, and she knew she had to get upstairs before she said something that got her thrown out of this house—the only available home for her in town.

"One word from me to the parson and the doctor and Mr. Weber at the general store," Magda rattled off the names of the men on the school board, "and I can blacken your name to the point you'll be fired." Mrs. Rathbone waggled a finger from her chair by the warm fire.

"And it's a wonder I can breathe with the dust you kicked up cleaning the library last weekend."

"I'll dust the rest of the house this weekend, ma'am." Prayer. Melanie clung to prayer.

God, don't let me shame myself with my foolish temper. I need this home. Surround me with protection from this enemy.

"I won't have a woman of questionable character in my home. No Christian woman should have to put up with it."

Melanie knew it was either run or say something absolutely dreadful. Terrible, sinful words burned in her throat, and it wasn't even Mrs. Rathbone's fault. All of her need to rage could be laid right at the feet of Hank O'Keeffe because of his withdrawal from her.

She chose to run. "Good night, Mrs. Rathbone."

Grabbing her plate, ignoring Mrs. Rathbone's insistent demand to come back, she rushed up those cold stairs. Every day the weather was worse. Melanie had been able to see her breath in the room when she got dressed that morning.

Today was Monday, and the weekend had allowed Melanie to find a few more drawers in the box, but she knew the strange object still held some unaccounted-for space. She'd become nearly obsessed with finding them all. She'd bought enough tiny toys and candy to last until Christmas; whether the hidden compartments would last that long, she didn't know.

Of course, she only had to find enough drawers to keep Simon busy on school days. A smile crossed her lips as she remembered Simon sidling up to her at church to plead for a look at the box right then.

The little pill was as eager as she was.

Melanie gained her room, set her plate on the bed, drew the Advent box out of her satchel, and set it on the trunk. She studied it and felt led to pray as she ate her cold meal.

The entire center of the box was still unexplored. The little drawers on the front and back were accounted for. . .by her. Simon still had a while to go finding them.

The meal was decent enough, if a girl had spent her entire life in an orphanage with a meager budget. She finished it quickly and picked up the box. She'd been listening for that click as Simon and Hank worked.

She'd been all weekend finding it herself.

Now which of the many little seams between wooden slats and tiles was the one that needed to be tipped just so, pressed just so. . . Often two things moved at the same time. . .

At last, because she'd learned tipping the box made a difference, Melanie finally pushed the right boards with the box tilted at the perfect angle, and the whole box popped. A seam appeared right down the middle, separating the front with the visible drawers from the back with the other compartments they'd found. Hinged on one side, she found more little tiles and slats of wood. But a grin broke across her face. She was learning how this strange box worked. There were little nooks and crannies to be found all over in this new section.

Not easy, because nothing about the Advent box was easy. But findable. She could do it. Simon could do it. And very possibly, just based on the small sizes of the drawers they'd found up until now, there might be enough spaces to last until Christmas.

After that, she'd tell Mrs. Rathbone about the little drawers, and if the contentious old lady agreed to let Melanie keep it, she'd give it to Simon as a Christmas gift.

The discovery of the new stash of drawers helped set aside the hurt from Hank. Well, not set it aside really, just accept it. More pain in a life that had dosed her with a lot of it. Nothing new, not even a surprise.

She got ready for bed with a prayer of thanks in her heart.

Chapter 10

Tuesday, December 14
The Seventeenth Day of Advent

They found several slender lengths of wood painted bright red.

"What's this, Miss Douglas?"

Hank looked at Melanie, who was busy writing, always working on her Christmas play. Or so she said.

With a sweet, sad smile that made Hank's heart ache—because he'd put that sadness there—she shook her head. "I don't know. What do you think it could be?"

She did a very good job of acting mystified.

It had been left to Hank to notice the little slots that fit together to form an outlined A-frame building.

～∞～

*Wednesday, December 15
The Eighteenth Day of Advent*

"It looks like a little ball of yarn, Pa." Simon's brow furrowed as if he had no idea what to make of a knotted up ball of yarn.

Hank noticed Melanie lean a bit toward them from where she sat by the potbellied stove, with a pair of knitting needles and a ball of white yarn.

"Look closer, son. It's got a little red nose and two blue knots for eyes. And these little sticks are legs. It's a lamb."

Simon had brought the strange little A-frame sticks with him, and suddenly Hank knew what it was.

"The sheep goes in the barn, only it's a stable, like the stable in Bethlehem."

Melanie eased back in her chair without comment and went back to her knitting.

c⊗ɔ

Thursday, December 16
The Nineteenth Day of Advent

"It's a star." Simon's voice rang with excitement. He knew now what was coming. The stable, the sheep, the star.

Hank watched as Simon examined it. The star was sewn with felt and just the tiniest bit padded like a tiny star-shaped pillow. It was stitched onto a button, the whole thing painted bright yellow. Melanie had made this with her own hands, just like the sheep.

A loop of thread on the button was perfect to hang the star on a little notch on the stable. Hank hadn't noticed that notch until just now.

What else had she made? There had to be an entire Nativity scene coming. Each of the few pieces were clever. But how did she make the people? She should have come to him. But of course he'd made it impossible.

He looked over, and her gaze met his. He got his jolt for the day. Then she looked back at the piece of white fabric she was cross-stitching. She wasn't even pretending to be busy with schoolwork anymore.

c⊗ɔ

Friday, December 17
The Twentieth Day of Advent

Simon squealed over the tiny piece of carved wood. It was Mary, the mother of Jesus. Hank knew then what she'd done. He'd seen these figures in the general store and had never given them a second thought. For one thing their price was a bit dear. But Melanie had bought the set, and now they'd be introduced to the Holy Family one at a time.

Family. Hank rested his eyes on Melanie. Her head bent over her work. How he'd loved having a real family.

c⊗ɔ

Monday, December 20
The Twenty-third Day of Advent

A little donkey.

"Donkey's are stubborn things, ain't they, Pa?"

"It's *aren't*, Simon, not *ain't*. You must use proper grammar." Melanie's voice drew Hank's attention, as if he wasn't already paying too much attention to her.

"They are stubborn, Simon," she said. "Almost as stubborn as men."

Melanie's lips quirked in a smile. A real smile. He detected no sadness. But the smile was gone, and she didn't look up.

He needed to find a way to make her look up. He needed his daily dose of her pretty eyes.

∽

Tuesday, December 21
The Twenty-fourth Day of Advent

"Was Joseph Jesus' father, or was God?" Simon studied the little bit of wood, perfectly painted, about as tall as his little finger.

"Well, God was Jesus' real Father, but Joseph was like the father God gave Him here on earth."

"Like Mike Andrews has a new pa? I hear Mike call him a stepfather, but he acts just like a regular pa."

"I don't know if Joseph is exactly Jesus' stepfather, because that's what you get when your own pa is dead, and Jesus' heavenly Father was with Him in spirit."

"Is Ma with us in spirit, Pa?"

Hank looked down at Simon and saw only curiosity. No hurt. He probably could barely remember Greta. Hank's thoughts faltered because, for a few seconds, he couldn't picture her. Couldn't bring her face to mind. Then it came back to him, Greta's face. But he pictured her as his young bride. Happy, working hard, a good cook, a pretty woman with a nice singing voice and a tendency to nag. She was usually right, so Hank didn't hold that against her.

He realized that he'd always before pictured her as she was when she was dying. In pain, ashen white, bleeding. But now the good memories came flooding in and replaced the bad. He felt a part of his heart heal.

And he looked at Melanie, who for once didn't have her eyes fixed on her work. She watched Simon with concern and kindness. Maybe afraid Hank would say some boneheaded thing that made Simon feel bad.

"She is indeed, Simon. But that isn't exactly how it was with Jesus being God's Son." Hank told Simon the Christmas story in a way that was more real than the usual reading from the Bible. Precious as those words were, talking with his son, discussing a heavenly Father, a stepfather, a mother who'd died, the story of Jesus was more real to Hank than it had ever been. And he owed that to Melanie.

He looked up at her as he talked, and for once she smiled at him as she had before he'd driven her away from the desk and the Advent box.

She'd never by so much as a tone in her voice punished Hank for his harsh rejection.

◦∞◦

Wednesday, December 22
The Twenty-fifth Day of Advent

"Melanie, come over and see what we found." Hank didn't betray himself, but Melanie looked up, and her eyes flashed.

"What is it?" She knew good and well what it was. She'd put it there.

"Come and see, Miss Douglas." Simon sounded excited, and Hank knew that however unhappy Melanie might be with him, she'd not deny Simon her attention.

Rising with great reluctance, she set aside her needlework and came to the desk to see Simon hold up the tiny angel. Hank had no idea where she'd gotten this.

But he couldn't ask without letting Simon know she'd put it in there. He was willing to believe this box was just for him, maybe the gifts put there by God. Hank wasn't sure just what his son thought about this box, only that he loved it, was fascinated by it, and that as he'd opened the secret drawers, he'd also opened his heart. Hank had regained his son's love. And he'd have never done it without the generous schoolmarm.

"It's an angel, Melanie." Hank didn't take it from Simon; he'd have had a tug-of-war. But he lifted Simon's hand and turned it a bit so the angel shone in the lantern light. This drawer had taken hours to find. Hank couldn't believe how well Simon had learned to concentrate and stick with a task.

Rising from his chair, he stepped around his son so he was just that little bit closer to Melanie. "An angel put in this box by an angel."

Melanie looked past Hank to Simon. But his son was busy finding the perfect place for the angel in his nearly complete Nativity set.

Hank touched her arm and gained her full attention. "Thank you, Melanie. And I'm sorry I've made it so you"—he dropped his voice to a whisper—"couldn't help. So sorry. God bless you for letting Simon and me take this journey to Christmas together. But I'd like it if you joined us. I let fear and my grief push you away, but I've found my way past it now. I have you to thank for it, and if you'll forgive me, please help us, these last two days before Christmas, search for the last drawers."

180

Melanie looked scared, like a woman might who'd been hurt too many times. But she nodded. "I'd like that. Thank you."

∽

Thursday, December 23
The Twenty-sixth Day of Advent

When they opened the next little cranny, Simon said, "It's a baby Jesus."

He reached his chubby little fingers into the ridiculously well-hidden spot and pulled out a tiny baby in a manger. Hank wasn't too surprised. His eyes went to the little Nativity scene set up on Melanie's desk. Simon brought them every day and set them up before he started hunting.

"Pa, it's just like when Jesus was born." Simon looked up and smiled. All of the pain his boy had carried for two years seemed to be gone. Hank was at fault that the boy had been so unhappy. He'd blamed it on Greta's death, but spending this time with Simon had shown Hank the truth.

And it was because of Melanie's wisdom that they'd come so far, taken a journey just as the Holy Family had.

Smiling, uncritical, Simon asked. "But what's left now? Finding the baby Jesus should have happened Christmas Day."

Hank didn't know. Had Melanie hoped they wouldn't find Jesus until tomorrow? Christmas day was Saturday. But the Nativity was completed. What else could there be?

And though she'd joined them in their search today, after he'd asked her to forgive him, she hadn't steered them. They found whatever they found. So, it's possible this wasn't the order she'd hoped the compartments would be opened.

He looked at her, and she was watching Simon, smiling. Not a flicker of alarm that they'd found the wrong drawer.

"Let's go ahead and put Jesus in by Mary and Joseph." Melanie and Simon turned to arrange all the little figures.

While they did it, Hank, his hands moving idly on the box did something and a new drawer popped open. A drawer Hank could see had nothing in it. The oddest little slit in the wood. She hadn't found it yet. He knew if she had there'd be some bit of a thing in there.

But this drawer, well, Hank knew exactly what belonged in this one. He took a second to study the cunning little space before he snapped it shut.

And then he made his plan while Melanie and Simon talked about the first Christmas.

181

∽

Thursday, December 24
The Twenty-seventh Day of Advent

Melanie lined the children up to sing their final song. They were so bursting with Christmas cheer it had been hard to get them to do their parts, but in the end, with a few funny mix-ups, they'd done a wonderful job.

When the school finally was almost emptied out, she smiled at the two who remained. She'd asked Magda's permission to keep the box, even opened a few of the little drawers. Magda had waved it off as if it smelled bad.

"Simon, can you come here, please?" As always, Simon came rushing up, eager to search. But tonight there was to be no search.

She reached under her desk to get her satchel. "It's gone." She straightened to see Hank holding the box.

"I wanted to look at it closer." He handed it to Melanie.

"We've found all the drawers, but I do have one final gift for you."

She extended the Advent box to him. "This is for you and your pa." Her eyes raised to Hank.

"It's mine?" Simon gasped then grabbed the box and hugged it, his face beaming with joy.

"Yes, merry Christmas."

Hank stood beside her, both of them facing Simon.

The sweet little boy set the box down. "I'm going to open every little compartment just for the fun of it."

"Simon, it's too late. We can't—"

"Let him work on it for a while, Melanie."

Melanie saw a look pass between the two and wondered at it.

The warmth of Hank's voice drew her eyes from the boy to the man. Hank rested one strong hand on Melanie's arm. Smiling, knowing he wanted space between them and Simon so they could talk, she let him pull her over to the stove. All of ten feet away from the distracted child.

"Melanie—" Hank rested both hands on her upper arms. His blue gaze locked on hers, and it drew her in just as his hands drew her closer.

"Y–yes?" She hoped that yesterday had changed things between them. But she was a woman who had learned so long ago not to hope.

"Melanie, it's taken me too long. I've been stubborn, and mostly I've been afraid. But I'm not afraid anymore."

His voice charmed her. His hands, so strong, could protect her from the whole world. Oh yes, she wanted to hope.

His head lowered. His lips touched hers.

The first kiss of her life. The sweetest kiss she could imagine.

"Melanie, that box has one more secret to tell."

"What?"

Then he kissed her again, and she didn't care much about that box, no matter how it had taken them on a journey to find each other.

"There!" A harsh voice shocked Melanie out of the romantic daze, and she jerked her head toward the schoolhouse door.

"I demand she be fired." Mrs. Rathbone stormed into the schoolhouse with the parson, the doctor, and Mr. Weber right behind her.

Parson Howard arched a brow. "Hank, what's going on?"

"That's a stupid question, Parson." Doc Cross smiled at Melanie.

Mr. Weber alone looked shocked. "I can see how upsetting this is to you, Magda. Of course, we can't keep a young lady who'd behave so scandalously working here."

"What?" Melanie needed a job.

"And she won't sleep another night under my roof."

Gasping, Melanie said, "It's snowing out and bitter cold. And you'd throw me out of your home?"

"And what's more, she's a thief."

"Thief?" Melanie cried. "I am not a thief."

"What about that box?" Mrs. Rathbone jabbed a finger at the box just as Simon came up beside her, holding it, its many hidden drawers now wide open.

"But you told me I could have it. I asked again this morning."

"You did no such thing. You're a thief and a liar. Mr. Weber, Hank can't be trusted to do the sheriff's job. Please take over."

The fear that swept through Melanie nearly choked her. Mrs. Rathbone was just spiteful enough to demand Melanie be arrested.

Simon stormed right up to Mrs. Rathbone.

"No, Simon, come back." Melanie remembered in a flash all the changes that had come over Simon in the last month. But now he nearly quaked with anger. If he believed Melanie had lied and stolen—for heaven's sake, stolen a gift for him—would it undo all the good Melanie had done?

He shoved the box right at Mrs. Rathbone's ample belly. "Here, take the box. Miss Douglas isn't a thief. But if you want it back, you can have it."

Magna caught the box by reflex then gave it a distasteful look. Melanie knew the old bat didn't want that box. She just wanted to cause trouble. Walking in on a kiss was one good way to accomplish her goal. Had the woman agreed Melanie could have that box with the plan of accusing her of theft? Or had the woman just seen it in the schoolhouse and seized on another accusation.

With one quick move, Hank snatched the box out of Magda's hands.

Mrs. Rathbone squawked like an angry rooster.

"You can have it back in just a minute." Hank looked at the three men standing a step behind her. "And you can all just stay right here for a while longer. I think I can clear all this up."

"I'd appreciate it if you would," Doc Cross said with weary amusement that didn't match the emotional temperature of this upsetting meeting. "And be quick about it. My wife is holding supper."

Hank turned with the box and brought it to Melanie. He let go of it with one hand and touched Simon's shoulder. "Stay right here with me, Son. This is from both of us."

"You can't give her that box as a gift; it's mine." Magda was still storming around.

"I won't give her the box." Hank manipulated two boards while holding the box nearly on its side and the slot tipped open.

"Reach in. Today it was my turn to bring a gift for you."

Melanie saw the sincerity in his eyes and slowly reached in the tiny dark gap he'd opened. She grasped something and pulled it out. "A ring."

Nodding, Hank said, "A wedding ring. Marry me, Melanie. You have no home to go to, so we can marry and you'll come home with me."

Her stomach sank as she heard the practical reasons she should marry. And a lonely child who'd never been loved couldn't help noticing he hadn't said the one thing she wanted above all to hear. "Th–that isn't a good reason to get married."

"Then just marry me because I love you."

She gasped in delight. Hank leaned down and caught that gasp with his kiss. He pulled back. "Say yes, Melanie, marry me. Then let's finish this Advent journey we've been on. Let's end it at our home."

Hank's hand left her arm to rest on Simon's head. The little boy grinned up at her in what looked like glee. "Marry us, Miss Douglas. We love you."

Melanie couldn't stop the grin that spread across her face, though so many looked on and she'd been accused of terrible things.

"Yes, I'll marry you." She looked at sweet Simon. Then her eyes lifted to meet Hank's gaze. She couldn't look away. "I'll marry you for one reason only, Hank. Because I love you, too."

Hank turned to face the four people who'd witnessed his proposal. He handed the now-empty box back to Mrs. Rathbone. "You can have that, ma'am."

Magda looked at it with a scowl. "Oh, just keep the ugly old thing." She slammed it onto a desktop and walked out in a huff.

"Parson, as long as you're here, will you say some vows and give us your blessing?" Hank asked. "And, Doc, Mr. Weber, will you be witnesses?"

Both men grinned. Doc Cross said, "Make it quick, Parson, my wife is a fine cook."

They said their vows, and Melanie received the finest gift of all. The gift of being an Advent bride.

Hank slid the ring on Melanie's finger at just the right time. Simon hugged the Advent box tight. Then the three of them walked home.

Just as Mary and Joseph, on that long-ago Christmas, had completed their Advent journey, now Melanie, Hank, and Simon completed theirs: a journey that brought them to Christmas, to family, to love.

About the Author

Mary Connealy writes romantic comedy about cowboys. She is a Carol Award winner and a Rita, Christy, and Inspirational Reader's Choice finalist. She is the bestselling author of the Wild at Heart series, which recently began with book number one, *Tried & True*. She is also the author of the Trouble in Texas series, Kincaid Bride series, Lassoed in Texas Trilogy, Montana Marriages Trilogy, Sophie's Daughters Trilogy, and many other books. Mary is married to a Nebraska rancher and has four grown daughters and three spectacular grandchildren. Find Mary online at www.maryconnealy.com.

The Christmas Tree Bride

by Susan Page Davis

Chapter 1

Polly Winfield dashed about the dining room, setting up. On days the stage came through, she and her mother always prepared to serve a full table. The passengers would eat quickly, reboard the stagecoach, and hurry away toward the next station.

Polly didn't mind the hectic mornings on Wednesdays. The stage was heading west, and that meant Jacob Tierney would be driving it. He would blow the brass horn to announce their arrival and canter the horses the last few hundred yards, to put on a good show. After the passengers gulped down Ma's stew and biscuits and pie, they would go on, but Jacob would stay.

The young man had recently landed the job as replacement driver for old Norm Hatfield, who had been injured in a driving mishap when his team was spooked by lightning and ran away with the stage. If Norm recovered, or if the division agent hired another permanent driver, Jacob wouldn't come by the Winfield Station anymore. But that wouldn't happen for a while. At least, Polly hoped not. She liked Jacob enormously, and he had told her he expected to drive the route another three or four weeks, until the line stopped operation for the winter.

The best part of the arrangement was that Jacob stayed at the Winfields' home station from Wednesday until Saturday, when the stage returned, heading east. The driver on that run, Harry Smith, would stay there from Saturday until Jacob returned the following Wednesday. They each had a run of 120 miles or so, covering six stations. On their days between runs, the drivers could do whatever they pleased. If Polly had anything to say about it, Jacob would be pleased to further their acquaintance.

Ma bustled through the kitchen doorway carrying two covered baskets. "They'll be here any minute. Set these out and fill the water pitchers."

Polly took the baskets and set them on the table, enjoying the fresh scent of baking. The passengers always raved about Ma's flaky biscuits. Polly had heard more than once that the Winfield Station had the best food of any along the line from Fort Laramie to Salt Lake City.

She filled the pitchers with water straight from the well and made sure each place setting was perfect. Ma would serve the stew in shallow ironstone soup plates, and the diners could set their biscuits on the broad edge.

The faint call of Jacob's horn reached her. The stage was coming down the slope from the bluffs. She longed to run outside and watch him guide the team in, but Ma would have a fit if she disappeared now. Their job was to get the meal on the table and make sure every passenger was satisfied, while Pa collected the price of dinner and the tenders swapped the tired horses for a fresh team.

Jacob's duties ended when the last passenger stepped down from the coach. He'd give Pa and Harry any news he'd picked up along the way and then mosey out back to use the necessary and wash up. When the passengers were done eating and were scrambling back into the coach, he would stroll into the dining room and grin at Polly and say, "What's to eat?"

Polly smiled as the first passenger came through the door. The next quarter hour would be hectic but so worth the fuss. Her mother earned nearly as much with her cooking as Pa earned for running the station.

Eight men paid up and came to the table today. Ma was smiling, and Polly knew she was adding up the money in her head. The coaches had been full every week in the summer and autumn, but now cold weather was setting in and sometimes Jacob had only one or two riders. People hated riding the stage in freezing weather.

Polly filled coffee cups, brought more biscuits, and distributed slices of apple pie. She glanced out the window once. The tenders were guiding the fresh team into place.

"Got more coffee, miss?" one of the diners asked, and Polly hurried to get it.

A moment later, Harry poked his head in the doorway and yelled, "All aboard!"

Men grabbed one last bite of their dessert or a final swallow of coffee and headed out to the yard.

And there he was, leaning against the doorjamb, grinning, his whip coiled in his hand.

"What's to eat, Polly?" he asked.

She laughed. "You know we always have beef stew on Wednesday."

He stepped forward and took a seat at the end of the long table. "Did you save me any biscuits?"

"I always do." Polly whisked away the dirty dishes from the table in front of him and hurried to the kitchen. "Jacob's ready to eat."

"What about the shotgun messenger?" Ma asked. "Is Billy Clyde with him?"

"Haven't seen him yet," Polly said.

Ma ladled a generous serving of stew into a soup plate. "I'm saving enough for him. Didn't expect so many passengers today, though. They nearly cleaned me out."

Polly carried the stew and a basket of warm biscuits into the dining room.

"Where's Billy Clyde?" she asked Jacob.

"Out yonder, jawing with your pappy." Jacob's eyes lit up when she put the plate of stew before him. "I've been dreaming of this stew all week."

"Naw, he ain't," Billy Clyde said from the doorway. "Miss Polly, he's been dreamin''bout you."

Polly laughed and felt her cheeks warm. "Hush you, Billy Clyde." The shotgun rider had been with the line since it opened and stayed with it when Wells Fargo bought out the previous owners. He was nearly Pa's age, lean and lithe. His beard showed some gray, and he limped from a wound he'd received courtesy of a road agent three years back.

Billy Clyde always teased Polly—and any other female in sight—but they said he'd never seriously courted a woman. He complained a lot, especially in bad weather when his leg ached, but he'd become a fixture at Winfield Station, and he was Pa's closest friend.

Ma came in from the kitchen carrying a soup plate, for Billy Clyde, and two mugs.

"There you are." She smiled at Billy Clyde.

"Couldn't stay away," he replied.

Polly began to stack the passengers' dishes while Ma poured coffee and lingered to banter with Billy Clyde. Jacob tucked into his meal and seemed disinclined to talk until his belly was filled.

Pa had warned Polly when they first moved here last year to keep away from the men, but she was sure he mostly meant the tenders. They were rough-hewn and loud, and they cursed and played poker in the bunkroom that was part of the barn. Billy Clyde might be unpolished, and he might even join the poker game now and then, but he was always polite, and Pa seemed confident that his women were safe around him.

Jacob was altogether different, quieter and more courteous than the others. When a chore needed doing, he offered to help, whether it was sweeping the dining room or toting firewood. He never gambled with the other men. Last week, Polly heard Billy Clyde confide to Pa, "Young Tierney won't even go near the saloon at the fort. And I offered to buy." Maybe Billy Clyde considered that unmanly, but it was music to Polly's ears.

She hummed a hymn as she washed the dishes. From the dining room, the men's cheerful voices reached her. Wednesday was Polly's favorite day of the week, hands down.

Pa came in, carrying two coffee mugs. "New pot ready?"

"Should be." Polly resumed her humming as she scrubbed the empty stew pot.

"Oh, there's something for you in the mail, Polly."

"For me?"

"Yes—from your friend Ava."

Polly dried her hands on her apron and dashed into the dining room. The small pile of mail lay on the table by Pa's empty chair. Beneath two envelopes he had opened, she found a colorful square postal card. She gasped and picked it up.

"Pretty, isn't it?" Jacob said.

Polly nodded. "It's a Christmas tree."

"I've never seen one," Billy Clyde said.

The pictured evergreen was decked in glass ornaments and small candles, the way the Germans trimmed their trees. Polly turned the card over and smiled at the sight of Ava's handwriting.

Miss you. Hope you have a good Christmas. We are going to my grandmother Neal's. Love, Ava

Her father came in from the kitchen carrying the mugs, now filled with steaming coffee.

"Pa, can we have a Christmas tree this year?" Polly asked.

"What do you want with that foolishness?" Pa asked, but his tone wasn't sharp.

"Oh, come on, Pa. We always had one back home."

Pa set one mug in front of Billy Clyde and the other before Jacob and sat down. "Polly, this is home now. And trees are hard to come by in Wyoming. I'm a busy man, and I don't have time to traipse around looking for a Christmas tree."

Polly sighed and turned the card over to gaze at the beautiful tree. The artist had drawn it in a background of fluffy snow, but she doubted anyone would really decorate a tree outdoors like that. Still, it was pretty, and a saucy red bird perched on the highest branch, more beautiful than the hand-blown ornaments.

"Polly," her mother called from the kitchen.

She tucked the card into the pocket of her dress and hurried back to her chores.

A few minutes later, her father poked his head in the doorway. "The men are done eating. You can clear the table."

Polly turned partway around and caught his eye. "Are you sure we can't find a tree somewhere, Pa?"

He sighed. "I told you, I don't have time. But the men don't have much to do for the next couple of days. Why don't you ask them to get you one?"

Pa left the kitchen, but Polly didn't go back to humming. Was a Christmas tree such a hard thing to find out here? Of course, they had fewer trees than back in New England. But still. . .

She missed a lot of things about Massachusetts, and no matter what Pa said, she still thought of it as home.

On her arrival at the stage stop with her mother a year and a half ago, Polly was excited by the newness of everything. She had immediately been pressed into service, but she didn't mind. She was contributing to the family's income.

She kept very active in the summer and autumn. When she wasn't needed to prepare meals, serve, do dishes, or perform other chores, she explored the rolling grasslands around their new home. She loved the wildflowers and her frequent sightings of birds, prairie dogs, coyotes, and now and then a herd of antelope. But the birds and flowers here looked different, and there were no neat little villages or close neighbors. She missed her friends, especially Ava. She missed the trees, too. No spreading maples out here, no hardy oaks or waving birches.

And she had not been prepared for the bleak winter of the prairie.

Last winter she had keenly felt the isolation of the station. She and Ma had stitched a quilt, curtains, and several items of clothing for the family. The stagecoaches couldn't get through for nearly three months, and in all that time they'd had only one another to talk to, besides an occasional hardy trapper who ventured out on snowshoes, one cavalry detail, and a couple of small bands of Shoshone who stopped in, hoping to trade.

The Indians had frightened Polly a little, but they seemed friendly enough. Pa had allowed Polly to trade a pair of outgrown shoes for a small beaded pouch that now housed her embroidery needle and silk thread. The items for her fancywork had been a gift from her grandmother one Christmas, and the thought lowered Polly's spirits even further. No more Christmas gifts under the tree. No more Christmas Day visits to Grandpa and Grandma Winfield's house for a huge turkey dinner with her aunts and uncles and cousins.

As she tossed the dishwater out the back door, Polly noticed how dark the sky was. Maybe they would have snow before nightfall. The air was certainly cold enough.

She determined to ask Jacob if he would find a tree for her. They may not have relatives to share the holiday with, and there may be no ornaments for the tree, but a Christmas tree would fill a small piece of the gap in her heart.

Chapter 2

Jacob was reading in the room he shared with Billy Clyde when someone knocked firmly on the door. He laid aside his book and went to answer it. Polly stood under the overhanging eaves at the back of the house, smiling at him with her dimples showing in her cheeks.

"Hello," Jacob said.

"Hello, yourself. Ma thinks we should do laundry since it's warm today. Got anything you want washed?"

"That's very kind of you. Hold on." Hastily, Jacob gathered up a few things. He hadn't put on his long johns this morning, so he rolled them up in his dirtiest shirt, along with a pair of socks. He was glad he had spread up his bunk earlier, as Polly stood in the doorway, gazing unabashedly around the room. Billy Clyde's bunk was a heap of quilts and linen, and Jacob hoped Polly wouldn't take offense.

"Here you go." He passed her the bundle, a wave of heat passing over him as he realized she'd be seeing his longies. "Uh, what about Billy Clyde?"

"I asked him before he and Pa went hunting, and he said he didn't need anything washed." Polly wrinkled her nose as if she disagreed strongly with Billy Clyde on what constituted "clean enough."

"Well, thanks."

Polly looked up at him suddenly and grinned. "Say, would you get me a Christmas tree?"

Jacob couldn't have been more surprised if the tenders had brought a team of bison out of the barn for his next run.

"A Christmas tree?"

"Yes. Pa says he's too busy to look for one, but he said I could ask you fellows if you'd have time."

"Well, now, I'd have to think on where I could find one." Jacob scratched his chin.

"I know it'd be a ways. Pa has to go miles and miles to find any firewood." Polly's blue eyes held a wistful, faraway look.

"Means a lot to you, does it?" Jacob asked.

She smiled as though a little embarrassed. "More than I realized. It's pretty out here, but it's so different."

"I guess you had a lot of forests where you came from."

She nodded. "My friend Ava and I used to hang our skates around our necks and walk to the pond."

"Ice skates? I never had any," Jacob said. "It hardly froze for a minute down in Arkansas."

"You poor thing. I loved skating on the pond. It was grand fun. Sometimes Pa would build a bonfire on the bank at dusk, and everyone would come from miles around to join in the party. It was almost like going to a dance."

"Sounds like a good time. But what's all that got to do with trees?"

Polly chuckled ruefully. "I thought of it when you asked me about the forest. To get to the pond, we'd pass through a big pine grove, where it was all shadowy and spooky some days. But in summer, it was cool and shady in there."

"Which did you like best?"

"Summer, I guess, but winter wasn't so bad. Here, it's lonesome. Everything's dead as far as you can see. The line shuts down. Nobody comes to visit. And last Christmas, we didn't even have a tree. It just seemed wrong and sort of. . .depressing."

She looked lost then, and more than anything, Jacob wanted to bring the merry smile back to her face. He squared his shoulders. "There's some scrub pines in the hills between here and Fort Laramie. I'll see what I can do on my next run."

Her whole face lit up, and she clutched the bundle of laundry tighter. "Thank you ever so much!"

"It'd be an honor. That is, if I can find one."

"We always had a balsam fir in Massachusetts." Her eyes took on that yearning look again. "We had a few ornaments—not many. I'm not even sure Ma brought them along. But we'd string popcorn and cranberries and cut stars and snowflakes out of paper. And when it was all trimmed, it looked grand."

"Well, I don't know as I can find a fir tree. Would a pine or a cedar do, if I can't?"

Polly laid a hand on his sleeve, and Jacob felt her warmth through the flannel. "At this point, I'll take any kind of an evergreen. Just a small one—I don't want it scraping the ceiling in the parlor—but maybe six feet or so. Of course, I don't want you to spend days and days looking for one, but it would mean so much to me."

Jacob smiled and nodded, feeling kind of like his insides had turned to pudding. Like his smile was crooked, and maybe his thinking was, too. Polly didn't have the dignified beauty of a fairy princess, but she was pretty, and she sure did make him see that pond in the woods where she skated and the tree festooned with popcorn garlands. If he could keep that look on her face for a few days by bringing her a scraggly little pine tree, it would certainly be worthwhile. Somehow, the thought of making her happy made him happy.

That evening, Jacob enjoyed dinner with the family, Billy Clyde, and the tenders. Mrs. Winfield outdid herself with fried chicken, potatoes, and gravy. She'd cooked up a squash and some beets, too. Jacob didn't see too many fresh vegetables this time of year. The Winfields must have a well-stocked root cellar. And the cake that came after—now, that was something. Mrs. Winfield let on that Polly had made it. Polly blushed and giggled and thanked the men prettily for their compliments. Jacob thought that was fine—that a girl who worked hard and showed winsome ways could cook to boot.

The tenders headed out for the barn when the cake and coffee were gone, and Billy Clyde followed shortly after. Mr. Winfield pushed back his chair and said he thought he'd go and check the stock.

"Those Mormon fellows that came through from Fort Bridger said there's a band of Arapahoe on the move. Seems late for them to migrate to their winter camp. I want to make sure they don't take a fancy to any of our horses or mules."

"Can I help you, sir?" Jacob asked.

"Maybe so. I think I'll run them inside for the night. The boys won't like it. They'll have to clean out the barn in the morning."

"That's better than losing your teams," Jacob said.

When Jacob came back to the house twenty minutes later, Polly was elbow-deep in dishwater, and her mother was putting away the supper things.

"Anything I can help with, ma'am?" he asked from the kitchen doorway.

"Oh, thank you, Jacob," Mrs. Winfield replied with a smile. "I think we have it in hand. Everything all right in the barn?"

"Yes, ma'am. All the horses and mules are inside now. Well, good night."

Polly looked at him over her shoulder with that saucy little dimpled smile. "Good night!"

Oh, she was pretty all right.

Two wagons full of supplies for the winter arrived Friday, and Jacob and Billy Clyde helped Pa and the tenders unload it. They lugged sacks of feed to the barn and boxes to the lean-to behind the kitchen.

Polly helped her mother bake bread and pies for the stagecoach trade that would come on Saturday, and she and Jacob smiled at each other every time he passed through the kitchen with a load.

"Guess the rest will have to go in the barn," Pa said after they'd made about a dozen trips each.

"I just toted two buckets of axle grease in," Jacob said, "but I guess it should go to the barn."

"Land, yes. Anything that's for the stagecoach or the livestock, put out there," Pa said. "Just foodstuffs and coal in the lean-to."

"Yes, sir." Jacob looked a little embarrassed that he had made such a mistake. He went into the lean-to and returned with two five-gallon buckets.

"Oh, Jacob, when you're finished, I've got your clean clothes for you," Polly called after him.

"Thank you kindly." His face was a dull red as he went out.

"Now, Polly," Ma said gently, "men don't like to think of ladies handling their unmentionables. Best let me give him his things when he comes back."

"All right." Polly went back to rolling out piecrust. How was she supposed to know these things if no one told her?

Jacob and Billy Clyde were invited to spend a leisurely evening with the family. Pa played checkers with the other two men in turns, but neither of them could beat him. Polly sat demurely on the settee beside her mother in the cozy parlor, embroidering a special center square for her next quilt, while Ma knitted. With a coal fire in the potbellied stove, the room stayed warm, though outside the wind buffeted the station.

"I won't wonder if we get snow soon," Ma said.

"Maybe you boys will get snowed in here," Pa added.

"It'd have to be a lot of snow to do that." Billy Clyde moved his checkers with a click-click-click. "There! King me!"

Pa chuckled. "Pratt sent word with the supply wagons that they'll keep the stages running as long as they possibly can."

"I don't fancy getting stuck in a snowdrift with a stage full of drummers," Billy Clyde said.

"What about you, Jacob?" Pa asked. "Do you like driving in snow?"

"I don't mind, so long as I've got warm gloves and a good wool hat." Jacob stacked up the checkers Pa had already taken from Billy Clyde. "I hope we can keep on for a couple more weeks at least."

"Wanting to draw your full pay for the month, eh?" Billy Clyde said.

Jacob nodded. "This position's just temporary for me. If I'm going to be out of a job soon, I'd like to have enough to buy a good saddle horse, so's I can set out and find another place to work."

Polly's spirits plummeted. She had hoped Jacob would stay in the area. If he was leaving soon for parts unknown, the hopes she had nourished were nothing but childish dreams.

She tried not to look at Jacob too often, but the next time she glanced his way, their gazes caught and he smiled at her. The shock of warmth that washed over her almost knocked her off the settee.

After an hour or so of checkers, fancywork, and placid conversation, Ma put aside her knitting and stood. "Would you fellows like some gingerbread before you go to bed?"

Polly stuck her needle through the material of her quilt square and tucked it into her workbag while her mother took beverage orders. She hurried to the kitchen to help.

"I left a jug of milk in the lean-to," Ma said. "Will you get that?"

Polly retrieved it and poured a cup for Jacob and one for herself. Ma had poured out mugs of coffee and opened the pie safe. She set the pan of gingerbread on the table.

"You cut that, and I'll whip some cream."

Polly cut generous squares of the fragrant gingerbread for each of the men and more modest ones for herself and Ma. She took the men's beverages into the parlor on a tray. Pa was engrossed in his checker strategy, but Jacob smiled up at her as he took his milk.

"Thanks, Polly."

"Makes me hate to leave this station." Billy Clyde raised his cup and blew on the surface of his steaming coffee. "Why, if I had my druthers, I'd stay here all week."

"You could sign on as a tender," Pa said grimly. "We'll likely lose Roberts soon." He'd been having some trouble with the men lately, getting them to stick to their tasks of keeping the harness in good shape and the horses immaculately groomed. Polly knew that the stocky man called Roberts wasn't happy at the prospect of getting stranded here for the winter and was talking about quitting.

Billy Clyde snorted a laugh. "As if I'd take less pay to sleep in the barn and never get to town. Although Miz Winfield's vittles would be a benefit to consider."

"You'd get so fat and lazy, come spring you wouldn't be able to roll out of your bunk to harness a team," Pa said.

Polly smiled at that. Billy Clyde was so thin, she doubted he would ever be fat, even if he spent a whole winter eating Ma's cooking and getting no exercise.

"It might be nice to have friends here at Christmas," Ma said.

"Was you all alone last year?" Billy Clyde asked.

"You should know," Pa said, looking over the checkerboard. "You left with the tenders, a week before Christmas, and then the snow came. I didn't mind. It was restful. But I began to think Bertha and Polly would go a mite crazy."

Ma smiled. "We three had to celebrate Christmas and New Year's alone and didn't see a soul for most of January either. Finally a bunch of troopers came through, breaking trail."

"I wish we could go back East for Christmas," Polly said. Pa frowned at her, and she added, "Oh, I don't mean to stay. The holidays just don't seem the same without the decorations and the carols and our loved ones all around us."

"I'll try to bring you that tree you hanker for," Jacob said.

"Oh, so this is the one you've drawn into your scheme." Pa shook his head.

"I don't mind." Jacob looked at Polly, as if for support.

"He said he might have time, Pa, and you did say I could ask."

"Yes, I did."

"Better you than me," Billy Clyde said, reaching to move one of his checkers.

They said no more about the tree or Christmas, and Polly hoped she hadn't embarrassed Jacob too badly by enlisting his help.

While Ma resumed her knitting, Jacob said quietly, "That was mighty fine gingerbread, Mrs. Winfield."

"Thank you, Jacob. Now, tell us where you're from and how long you expect to be driving this run."

"I'm from Arkansas originally, ma'am, but I came out here from Independence. The division agent hired me just temporary."

"He ought to keep you on," Billy Clyde said. "You're doing all right driving."

"Thanks. I've always wanted to drive stage. I was driving a freight wagon in Independence, but that's not the same."

Billy Clyde snorted. "Not hardly."

"I do need the job badly. I don't know where I'll go when they turn me loose."

"Well, don't waste time on your run looking for a tree for my daughter," Pa said.

"He can't do that," Billy Clyde assured him. "Can't stop the stage unless it's an emergency."

"Yeah, I'd lose my place for sure if I did that." Jacob looked over at Polly and smiled. "Don't you worry, though. I'll keep my eyes open, and if I see a likely tree, I'll ride out on Monday and get it."

Polly couldn't help smiling back at him. Pa's thoughtful frown may have dulled the radiance of that smile a little but not much. Jacob Tierney was the sweetest man she'd ever met.

Chapter 3

The next morning at precisely ten fifteen, Polly stood with her mother on the front stoop and waved to Jacob and Billy Clyde as the stage pulled out, heading east.

"Thank you again for looking for a tree," she called, and Jacob touched his whip to his hat brim in reply.

Polly let out a big sigh and leaned back against the doorjamb.

"He's a nice young man," Ma said.

Polly tried to guard her expression, but Ma could always read her. "Sure, he is. He's polite, hardworking, and considerate."

"Not to mention long on looks."

"Ma!" Polly knew her cheeks were red. She ducked inside and began to clear the dishes left by the latest batch of passengers. No matter what time the stage arrived, they always got "dinner." Ma made sure the travelers got their money's worth, too. Today's chicken pie and spice cake had disappeared like magic—the same as every Saturday.

"Well, we'd best change the sheets out back," Ma said as she came in and shut the door. Every time the driver and shotgun rider left and the incoming pair took their place, Ma changed their beds. When bad weather prevented her from doing laundry, she stripped the beds anyway and kept each bundle of sheets separate, so that when the men returned, they could at least sleep in their own linen, not someone else's. If Billy Clyde were to be believed, this was not the case at every home station. In the summer, when things were busy, he'd sworn one station agent hadn't changed the beds for all of June and July, regardless of who slept in them.

The chores tired Polly out, and she was glad the next day would be their day of rest. The tenders, Harry, and the shotgun messenger who accompanied him—Lyman Towne—did not share the Winfields' faith or Pa's belief that Sunday should be a day of rest and contemplation. They came for their meals on that day and, for the most part, avoided the house the rest of it. Ma said they probably carried on with the poker games in the barn, even on the Lord's Day, but Polly had never ventured to find out.

After breakfast and the kitchen work were done on Sundays, Polly sat with her parents in the parlor. Pa would read scripture for an hour. Then they would pray aloud for all their kinfolk back East, for daily sustenance, for the safety of the drivers and shotgun riders, and for the souls of the tenders. Today Pa's petition for Roberts was especially fervent, and Polly wondered what the man had done now.

After the amen, she opened her eyes.

"Pa, why don't you just fire him?"

"Who?" her father asked, as though he hadn't a clue.

"Roberts. If he's so bad. . ."

"Never you mind, missy."

"Really, Russell," Ma said. "Polly may be right. If he vexes you so. . ."

Pa sighed. "I suppose he's no worse than most—at least most that are available out here. I found an empty whiskey bottle in the hay, and he admitted it was his. Seems he's been having Towne bring him bottles on the Saturday run."

"You'd be justified in letting him go," Ma said.

"But no one will come to replace him this time of year."

Ma shook her head. "No matter. The stages will stop soon. You can get by for a couple of weeks."

"I'll think about it."

After dinner, Polly was allowed to go to her room and read, and she took a nap before joining her mother to prepare supper. On Sunday evening they put out bread, meat, cheese, fruit preserves, and pickles, and the men were invited to help themselves while the family ate in the kitchen.

Harry, Lyman, and Ernest, the other tender, came in to fill their plates, and Polly took them a pitcher of water and the coffeepot.

"Where's Roberts tonight?" she asked.

"Oh, he ain't feeling up to snuff," Ernest said.

When Polly went back to the kitchen, she told her father.

"I'll see about that." He shoved back his chair.

"Oh, Russell, finish your food," Ma said. "If the man is drunk, he'll still be that way when you're done."

"Yes, but the others will go back out there once they've had their cake and coffee. I'd rather speak to him alone."

Pa went out, and Polly looked at her mother. "Do you think it's safe for him to confront Roberts alone?"

"I expect so." Ma frowned but continued eating as though nothing was wrong, so Polly did the same.

About ten minutes later, to her relief, the front door opened, and Pa's voice carried in from the dining room.

"Boys, just so's you know, I'm discharging Roberts. He'll be going out with you Wednesday, Harry."

"Yes, sir," Harry said, as though he had expected this and it bothered him not at all.

"And Towne?"

"Yes, Mr. Winfield?" came the apprehensive response.

"I shall report your actions to the division agent. It will be up to him whether to discipline you or not, but if you ever bring in liquor for any of the stage line's employees again, you'll be out."

"Yes, sir."

Pa came into the kitchen. "You heard?" he asked.

Ma nodded. "You can help Ernest with the teams until we get someone else."

"Yes, and Jacob will pitch in when he's here. Probably Harry will, too."

Pa finished his supper, and the family spent a quieter evening than usual, even for Sunday. Polly finished knitting one of the wool socks she was making for her father. The difficulty in making the heel gave her second thoughts about knitting a pair for Jacob. She wanted to do something for him, since he was being so nice about the tree. Would socks be too personal a gift for a young man? She'd better ask Ma before she went ahead with that plan. Anyway, as soon as Pa's socks were finished, she wanted to start making ornaments for her tree.

~∞~

The stagecoach arrived on time Sunday at the station near the fort, after a long, cold run from Winfields'. Jacob attended chapel at the fort and spent the rest of the day resting, reading, and talking to the other people at the Newton Station, which was his home on that end of the run. The drop in temperature overnight ruined his plans to search for Polly's Christmas tree on Monday.

"A man shouldn't set out in this cold if he doesn't have to," Mr. Newton, the station agent, said. "In fact, I pity the drivers if they have to bring the stage along today."

"They won't stop it, will they?" The thought that the line would be suspended early for the winter and he might never get back to the Winfields' made Jacob unaccountably sad.

"Not yet," Mr. Newton said. "They'll stop it when the snow gets deep but not before."

"Too bad we don't have some of Mrs. Winfield's soapstones here," Billy Clyde said.

"How's that?" Jacob asked.

"The passengers complained so much of the cold last year in the fall that she ordered half a dozen soapstones. She'll heat 'em and wrap 'em in burlap and rent 'em to passengers for two bits. It'll be up to you to collect 'em at the end of the stage and get 'em back to her. Norm had that job last year. I think they only lost one, and Mrs. Winfield made a tidy sum. A little extry, she'd say."

Jacob smiled. "Sounds like a good investment. Does she give one to drivers?"

"If the passengers don't take 'em all," Billy Clyde said. "Of course, if you was on her good side—or Miss Polly's—you might get special treatment."

Jacob laughed. He wouldn't butter up Mrs. Winfield or flirt with her daughter to gain special favors, but maybe he could work something out to keep his feet warm. He had a little chat with Mr. Newton later that day.

The mercury stayed close to zero during his whole layover at Newton's home station, but only about three inches of snow fell. By the time the westbound stage pulled in on Tuesday, the road had been packed down enough so that they could travel at their usual pace most of the way, and the horses were eager to go. Jacob was glad to be heading for the Winfields' again. He only wished he wasn't going empty-handed.

Mr. Newton came out as Billy Clyde loaded the last of the three passengers' luggage. He handed Jacob two bundles.

"What's this?" Billy Clyde asked when he climbed up to the driver's box beside Jacob.

"Hot bricks wrapped in burlap sacks. They won't stay hot as long as Mrs. Winfield's soapstones, but it will help."

The warmth from the bricks did keep the soles of their boots warm for the first five miles or so. When they got to the next swing station, Jacob asked the agent to let him put them on top of his stove during the brief stop. They didn't have time to heat thoroughly, but every bit of warmth helped on the two to three hours between stations.

By the time they approached the third stop, Jacob's fingers were nearly frozen inside his gloves. He could barely hold the reins. He could still feel his toes, though, thanks to the bricks. Even so, the extra warmth in them was long since sapped by the bitter cold.

Jacob awkwardly took the reins in his right hand and put his left hand to his face so he could blow on his fingers through the gloves. He couldn't wear mittens on this job, or he wouldn't be able to handle the reins of the six-horse hitch properly.

Billy Clyde, from beneath layers of the muffler wound around his neck and face, said, "I sure wish I'd ordered me a soapstone."

"I put in an order for two," Jacob said. "Mr. Newton will send it with his supply order to St. Louis on the next eastbound."

"One for me?" Billy Clyde asked.

"If you want to pay for it. Three dollars, with the shipping."

Billy Clyde blinked at him. "That's a lot."

"If you don't want to buy it, I'll use one for my hands, too."

"I'll think about it," Billy Clyde said.

Jacob would have smiled, but his lips felt frozen. He'd have to grease them with lard at the next station. Billy Clyde wasn't known for saving his pay for anything. He spent it on whatever took his eye at the moment.

"Polly's gonna be disappointed," Billy Clyde said a little later. He had his hands tucked under his arms and had stood his shotgun between his knees, pointing up. If they were held up, Billy Clyde would be sadly unprepared. Of course, most road agents wouldn't be out in this cold to rob stagecoaches anyway.

"I wish I could have gotten her that tree," Jacob said.

"Only one more run to their place before Christmas."

"I know." Jacob concentrated on shifting the reins to his left hand so he could blow on the right. Two more miles to the next way station. The passengers weren't complaining, but he was certain they would be glad when they got to Winfields' and ate a fine hot meal and had the opportunity to rent a soapstone. A person had to be crazy to travel in this cold.

⌒

Polly waited eagerly for the stage on Wednesday. Half a dozen times she went to the window between her tasks of setting up the dining room. Ma caught her at it when she brought in the butter and jelly for the biscuits.

"They'll be here," Ma said, "but they won't come any faster with you gawking out the window."

"It's so cold."

"Not so cold as yesterday, and your father says the road is passable. They'll be here."

The stage pulled in a half hour later than usual, a rare event on the line.

The passengers hurried in and huddled around the stove. Billy Clyde and Jacob didn't linger outside but gladly turned the team over to the tenders while the passengers moved to the table to get their meal down before Harry called them to board. Jacob and Billy Clyde stepped closer to the stove and warmed themselves thoroughly.

"The going was a little heavy in spots," Jacob said, flexing his hands above the stove top, "and the creeks were frozen, but the horses broke through on some of the ice. It wasn't deep, but the wheels tore it all up. That's hard on the team."

"Looked like the off wheeler had a cut on his fetlock," Billy Clyde said mournfully.

Jacob nodded. "Soon's they get the new team hitched and I can feel my fingers, I'm going out and check on them. Some of the horses might need some doctoring."

"The tenders will do it," Billy Clyde said.

Jacob shook his head. "I want to see to them myself."

One of the passengers called for more coffee, and Polly moved to get the coffeepot. "Pa's been keeping the horses inside this week."

"That's good," Jacob said, "but I don't envy Harry and Lyman going out on this next run."

Polly went about her duties. Ma came in while the three passengers ate dessert and offered to rent them a hot soapstone. The men willingly accepted her offer and thanked her fervently.

"Just be sure you give them to the driver when you get out at his last stop," Ma said. "He brings them back to me. I'm sorry you can't get one at every station."

Ten minutes later, the coach pulled out with all three men aboard, and Harry Smith and Lyman Towne on the box with two of the extra soapstones. Pa came inside with his eyes glinting. Even though fewer passengers rode today, between the dinners and the stones, Ma was turning a profit.

Not until the dishes were done and the dining room swept did Polly broach the subject of the Christmas tree. Pa had invited Jacob and Billy Clyde into the parlor, which was much warmer than their bunk room at the back of the house, and the checker game was in play once more, between Jacob and Billy Clyde. Pa sat on the settee, leafing through a newspaper that Billy Clyde had brought from the other end of the run.

"What's going on in the world, Pa?" Polly asked, taking a seat beside him.

"Well, this is a month old, so it's mostly election news."

"We already knew General Grant was elected," Polly said.

"Yes, but they have a lot of rhetoric about the new governors and con-gressmen, too," Pa said, turning the page. "Looks like Spain has tossed out its queen, and she'll be spending Christmas in France—in exile."

"That wasn't very nice of them." Polly looked at Jacob, who was studying the checkerboard. "Speaking of Christmas, I don't suppose you were able to get me a tree, Jacob?"

He looked so remorseful that she wished she hadn't asked.

"No, and I'm sorry."

"Please don't let it distress you," she said quickly. "I understand."

"Thank you."

Her father lowered the newspaper and gazed at Jacob. "Don't look on it as a critical task, Tierney. No one expects you to freeze to death getting a Christmas tree."

"That's right," Polly said. "If it were a simple thing, Pa would have done it."

Her father harrumphed and went back to his reading.

Polly reached for her workbag and took out her knitting. Likely she would have to do without her tree. If they got another snow, Jacob would probably not return.

∽∾

Jacob enjoyed the next two days, spent quietly with the family. The tree was not mentioned again, and he tried not to think about it. Mr. Winfield was right—it wouldn't do any good to feel guilty about it. Meanwhile, he spent several pleasant interludes conversing with Polly, usually under the sharp eye of her mother.

He and Billy Clyde ate their dinner early on Saturday and got their gear ready to leave. Jacob went to the barn and inspected the team himself. They all seemed in fine shape and ready for the road. The weather had turned, and the breeze was once more warm and inviting. The snow had melted on the road and shrunk down in other places. As long as the wind stayed light, the next run should not be too unpleasant.

He wandered into the dining room. He had nothing to do until the stage arrived. Then he could grease the wheels. Some drivers let the tenders do that, but Jacob had learned from old Norm that it paid for the driver to do it himself and know it was done right.

Polly was setting up the long table for the passengers. She always set it for eight after the family and crew had eaten, though often these days fewer travelers came on the coach.

The stage pulled in on time, with Harry sounding a blast of his horn.

Jacob sidled into a corner and watched six passengers come in. So, quite a few men were taking advantage of the break in the cold and hoping to get across the plains without too much discomfort.

"What kind of place is this, that you don't serve beer?" one man snarled at Polly as he unbuttoned his overcoat.

"It's a decent home where you'll find a welcome and a good hot meal, sir," she replied. "Let me bring you a glass of sweet cider with your dinner."

The man frowned but accepted the offer. Polly looked Jacob's way as she turned away from the disgruntled man, and she smiled at him. Jacob smiled back and clapped his hat on his head. High time he tended to the grease pot.

The Winfield Station was beginning to seem like home—the closest he'd had to a home for the last three years, anyway. Mrs. Winfield mothered him, while her husband treated him like a responsible man who was welcome in the family circle. And Polly made it extra special.

Despite occasional moments when she seemed younger than her eighteen years, Jacob couldn't think of her as a child. She helped her mother willingly, not in sulky obedience but as a work partner for the business, and she handled unhappy passengers with grace. Her request for a Christmas tree had amused him at first, but it meant a lot to her, and he knew it wasn't just a childish whim. Having the tree would make her feel more settled in this wilderness.

He still had one more run before Christmas—provided the weather didn't turn nasty again. Mr. Winfield might think it frivolous, but Jacob determined as he mounted the driver's box to get that tree and deliver it on time.

Chapter 4

The following Wednesday, Polly fidgeted more than usual. She and her mother prepared dinner for twelve, though they had no assurance the stage would come. Her father went out to the barn several times during the morning to help Ernest get everything ready. Each time he returned to the kitchen, his predictions were more dire.

"The sky is low and black to the south and west, and the wind is picking up. I'm afraid we'll see snow anytime now."

"But if it's to the west, the stage will be ahead of it," Ma said. "They're coming from the east, so they should get this far all right."

Pa frowned and looked out the window. "They might not have sent the stage out. They don't want the passengers to be stuck here for weeks. If they don't think they can get all the way through, they might not set out."

So this is it, Polly thought. Jacob would not return. She wouldn't get her Christmas tree, and the family would celebrate the holiday without him or Billy Clyde. Funny how her heart ached more to see Jacob than for her precious tree. Two weeks ago, she could think of hardly anything but that tree.

The festive table would feel empty. Roberts was gone. They would invite Ernest, the lone tender remaining, to eat Christmas dinner with them. He wanted to leave for the winter, and he'd planned to go out on this week's eastbound stage. Then it would be just the family here. Pa would have to tend the stock alone. If by some miracle the stagecoaches kept running, he would have to change the teams by himself. Polly supposed she could dress in her cold weather clothing and help him, and the drivers and shotgun riders would pitch in if needed, in an attempt to keep the schedule.

"This is why Butterfield used the southern route," Pa said glumly. "When people send mail out, they expect it to get through."

The stage company had a hard time making a profit on this line. The Winfields did everything they could to ensure good service and keep the line running. After all, this was their livelihood.

About eleven o'clock, the snow began. Small flakes plummeted down, so thick Polly couldn't see to the barn.

"This means business," Pa said.

They went on with the dinner preparations, but as noon approached they feared they would have no guests that day.

Ernest came into the house and stamped his feet on the rag rug by the door. "The team's all set—harnessed and ready to go—but I doubt they'll be coming, Mr. Winfield."

Pa sighed. "I fear you're right, Ernest. Let's sit down and have our dinner."

Ma ladled out generous portions of the stew. Probably they would eat it for the next three days, since she had made much more than the four of them needed.

"I held back on the biscuits," she said. "If the stage comes in, I'll throw more in the oven."

"I sure hope they're not out there in this storm," Ernest said a few minutes later.

They'd all been thinking it, but nobody liked hearing the words.

Polly stood. "I'll start the dishes. Call me if they make it."

"They might surprise us," Ma said. She got up and helped Polly clear and reset the table.

In the kitchen, Polly filled the dishpan and put more water on the stove to heat. Ma went about putting away the food, but Polly noticed that she made a full pot of fresh coffee and set it on the stove top.

They worked in silence. When Polly had washed all the tableware and begun to scrub the pans, she said, "You don't think they're out there in the snow somewhere, do you?"

"Of course not," Ma said. "If they left the fort last night, they're probably holed up at one of the swing stations. I don't know if Jacob has the experience for it, but Billy Clyde's old enough to know when a storm is coming."

"He said once he can taste snow in the air before it falls," Polly said. She would miss Billy Clyde this winter, too. "I made presents for them."

Ma smiled. "So did I. A vest for each of them. Did you make socks?"

"No. I barely got Pa's done. I made a tobacco pouch for Billy Clyde and a muffler for Jacob. You saw the gray and white yarn."

"Oh yes, and a muffler's much quicker than a pair of stockings."

"Much simpler, too," Polly said. She'd had trouble turning the heels on Pa's socks, and her mother had helped her redo them.

"Ma, this was going to be the last run."

"I know, dear. Likely the division agent canceled it."

Polly sighed and walked to the stove for a dipperful of hot water. She poured it over the clean biscuit pan to rinse off the soap. "I'll try not to fret about it, but I keep thinking of them all huddled in a stagecoach in some snowdrift, slowly freezing to death."

She tackled the stewpot then dried all the clean dishes. Ma helped her put them away.

"Want me to take the things off the dining table?" Polly asked.

"Let's leave the place settings, just in case. If no one shows up by suppertime, we'll put it all away."

Pa opened the door from the family parlor. "Bertha, I thought I'd saddle my horse and ride down the road a ways."

"In this storm?" Ma's eyebrows shot up almost to her hairline.

"The snow's let up some," Pa said.

"How much is on the ground?" Polly asked.

"Three or four inches so far. They could make it through that, with a stout team. But I doubt they ever left the fort. I just want to make sure."

"Let me come with you, Pa." Polly tossed her apron onto its peg.

He frowned. "I don't know, Polly. It's cold, and you're not dressed for it."

"I'll bundle up. Wait for me, please? I won't be long."

She dashed to her room and opened her top dresser drawer. She had a long, thick pair of woolen stockings that she wore in coldest weather. She pulled them on over her regular stockings and added a pair of sturdy cotton pantalets. They were old-fashioned things, but in extreme times, warmth was more important than fashion.

Knowing her father was waiting, she jerked on a second petticoat—this one flannel—beneath her skirt. A hood, a muffler, boots, her thick woolen coat, and mittens lined in lamb's fleece completed her ensemble.

She ran back to the kitchen. Her mother was putting food into a basket.

"Where's Pa?" Polly asked.

"He went out to saddle the horses. Take these things."

She placed a small box in the basket, tucked a clean towel over the top, and handed it to Polly. "There's a few bandages and things in that little box. And here's your pa's canteen, full of water. Now, Polly, you be careful. And do whatever your father says."

"I will." Polly scurried through the dining room and outside. The chilly air snatched her breath, and she slowed down. The snow still fell, and the ground, the roofs, even the fence posts, were frosted in several inches of white fluff. The only tracks were those Pa had made. Polly tried to walk in them, but her stride was shorter than his, and the heavy basket threw her off balance. At least the snow was not deeper than her boot tops. Lifting and setting each foot carefully, she made her way to the barn.

Inside, the air was warmer. The fresh team of horses for the coach stamped in their stalls. Pa's horse, Ranger, was already saddled and tied to an iron ring in the wall. In the dimness, Polly made out Pa, saddling the buckskin mare she sometimes rode, and Ernest throwing a blanket across the back of a mule from the extra team they kept on hand, in case anything happened to the horses regularly used on this run.

"Are you going with us?" Polly asked Ernest.

"Thought I would. Getting a little batty just sitting inside all day."

"We're only going a mile or two down the track," Pa said. "I don't want your mother to be left home worrying about us very long."

Polly nodded and carried the basket over to him.

"What's this?"

"Things Ma packed. Food, mostly, and medical supplies."

Pa sighed and pulled the dish towel off the top of the basket. "Have you got saddlebags on your rig?" Pa called to Ernest.

He shook his head.

"Well, take the canteen." Pa nodded at Polly, and she took the water over to Ernest.

When she got back to her father's side, he was tying the basket as securely as he could to the back of Lucy's saddle. He already had a blanket rolled up and tied to the cantle of Ranger's. "Try not to jostle this too much."

He handed her Lucy's reins and led his gelding to the large rolling door. When he pushed it back, a gust of wind blew in, bringing a cloud of swirling snow. Polly adjusted her muffler so that it covered most of her face and led Lucy outside. Ernest brought his mule out and rolled the door shut behind them. Already, the snow seemed deeper than when Polly had come to the barn. A skim of fresh flakes had softened her footprints into dimples in the surface.

"Need a boost?" Pa asked.

Usually Polly didn't, but with all her extra clothing weighing her down, she decided it might help.

"If you don't mind."

She got her foot to the stirrup, and Pa helped her bounce up into the sidesaddle.

"All set?"

She nodded. The harsh wind blew snowflakes into her eyes, and she blinked at them.

"Having second thoughts?"

"No," she said. "I want to go."

Pa hesitated. "All right, but we won't stay out long, like I said. That wind won't be kind to us."

He and Ernest mounted, and the three of them set out, with Ranger and Pa breaking trail. The snow drifted before the angry wind, sometimes making a sheet in front of Polly that nearly prevented her from seeing Ranger's black tail. At other moments, she could see for yards all around. Small eddies of wind picked up snow and whirled it around before dropping it again. She couldn't tell how much new snow was still descending until she looked up and saw myriad flakes falling, always falling.

A huge boulder loomed beside the trail. That landmark told Polly they had come a mile from the house. The small part of her face exposed to the wind began to feel stiff, and the cold seeped through her sturdy boots and layered socks. She clamped her teeth together so they wouldn't chatter, but she wasn't sure how long she could keep this up.

By the time they rounded the bend that was another half mile along, she wondered if they had made a mistake. The snow was coming down harder, and she could barely make out Pa's white-covered form ahead. Lucy plodded along with her head down. Polly didn't want to stop Pa, but she didn't want them to get off the trail and lose the way or to be overcome by the cold and unable to return home.

Her unease grew, and just as she was about to shout to her father over the wind, Ranger stopped, and Lucy nearly ran into his hindquarters. She stopped, too. Polly clucked to her and pressed her leg against Lucy's side to ease her up next to Ranger.

Pa said nothing but raised his arm and pointed ahead, down the trail. Polly squinted. A shadowy figure materialized out of nothing then disappeared again behind a whoosh of snowflakes propelled by the wind.

"Hey!" Pa's shout was blown back at them by a gust, but the cloud of snow passed, and now the form was closer—so close that Polly jumped.

A muffled cry reached them, and they waited. She could see now that a large horse was coming toward them, and hunched over, clinging to its back, was a person. Only when the horse's nose nearly touched Ranger's could she tell that it was one of the regular coach horses, still wearing his harness. The man perched on his back, clutching one of the straps and a handful of mane, was Jacob.

Chapter 5

"What happened?" Pa yelled.

Jacob leaned toward them. "Wreck!"

"How far?"

"Maybe a mile."

Polly shivered. A mile might as well be a thousand in this storm. At least the stage was closer to the Winfields' than to the next station.

"Anyone hurt?" Pa bellowed, and she realized the wind had momentarily dropped.

Ernest edged his mule up next to Lucy so he could hear what was said.

"Two of them are bad," Jacob said. "I would have set out sooner, but I stayed to build a fire for them."

"Billy Clyde?"

"He fell on his arm, but he's trying to help the others."

Pa nodded. "How many horses do you have?"

"Two more that can travel," Jacob said. "I only set out with four, though I asked for six."

Polly grimaced. That meant one horse was badly injured or dead.

"I'd have brought people along on them, but I wasn't sure I could make it through," Jacob said. "Figured they'd do better to stick together."

The wind picked up again, howling around them and driving a maelstrom of snow into their faces. Polly ducked her chin and closed her eyes until the worst of it had passed, but its icy fingers pierced even her woolen coat now.

"How many people in all?" Pa shouted.

"Seven passengers and Billy."

"Ernest and I will go back for the oxen and the sled."

That made sense to Polly. More than six inches of snow now covered the ground, and it was drifting much deeper in some spots. But the oxen Pa was fattening to sell in the spring could break through it. They would go slowly, and it might take them a couple of hours to reach the stranded travelers, but Pa would see to it. The injured passengers could ride on the sled that he used in winter to haul supplies and firewood.

Jacob nodded. "I'll stay with the stage."

"Can I go with Jacob?" Polly yelled.

Pa frowned at her then said to Jacob, "Can she get warm if she stays with you?"

"Fuel is hard to come by," Jacob said, "but there are a few scrub trees. I think we can keep the fire going until you come back if we burn the broken tongue off the coach."

Pa's eyes flickered, and he hesitated. Burning the equipment was a drastic step, but people were badly injured, and the tongue would have to be replaced anyway, by the sound of things.

"All right. Polly, take the food and this blanket." They transferred the items from Ranger's saddle and the canteen from Ernest's.

"We'll try to be there in two hours," Pa said. "It may take longer. Don't give up on us."

"I could send some of the passengers out on the coach horses," Jacob said.

Pa swiveled in the saddle and gazed at their back trail. "They might not be able to see our prints all the way. It's blowing and drifting something fierce."

"I could send Billy Clyde with them. He knows this trail better'n just about anyone."

Pa nodded. "Do it. We won't stick around waiting for them, but we'll look for them on our way back with the ox team."

Polly watched Pa and Ernest ride off, back toward the station. She was shocked by how suddenly they disappeared into blowing snow. The wind howled around her and Jacob.

"We'd better get moving," he said.

"I'll follow you." She had to shout again to make him hear. He pivoted the coach horse. The big animal seemed clumsy compared to Lucy. Riding close behind, Polly had the benefit of shelter. The coach horse's body broke the force of the wind. She huddled low. Lucy didn't need much guidance now. She followed the bigger horse, walking in the trail he had carved in the new snow. They plodded on for what seemed a long time.

Polly grew so cold she thought about unrolling the blanket Pa had given her and wrapping it around her, over her coat. She looked ahead at Jacob's back, wondering if she could make him hear her. Then, to one side and still a ways ahead, she saw a warm orange glow and took heart.

The horses slogged along slowly until they came to the fire. It had burned low, and Polly could see that for lack of fuel it would soon go out. A few yards away, the stagecoach lay on its side. One wheel looked hopelessly smashed, with several of the spokes broken.

"We got off the trail in the storm," Jacob said. "Ran over some rocks. The front axle's bent. It's my fault."

Before Polly could reply, he turned toward Billy Clyde and the seven passengers huddled around the fire and shouted, "This is Polly Winfield, from the next station. I met her and her father and another fellow. Mr. Winfield and Ernest are headed back to the station for an ox team and sled so we can carry the injured people in."

Several of the passengers got to their feet, staring at Polly, as if she were a ghost appearing out of the snowstorm.

Billy Clyde came over, holding on to his left arm just below the shoulder. "Miss Polly, you oughtn't to be out here! We're like to freeze to death."

"We brought you some sandwiches and water." Polly ignored his dire prediction and swung the canteen toward him. "I have a blanket, too. You can put it over the two hurt folks."

"That sounds mighty good," Billy Clyde said. "I'd help you down, but I think my arm's busted."

"I'm sorry." Polly didn't need any help swinging down off Lucy's back, and in a moment she stood beside him in the snow.

"We need more fuel for the fire," Jacob said. "Mr. Thomas and Mr. Percival, could you help me, please? Mr. Winfield said we can burn the broken wagon tongue. I don't have an ax, but we can burn the two pieces that broke off from the end." He looked at Billy Clyde. "Let Miss Polly warm herself."

Polly hated displacing anyone at the meager fireside, but she couldn't deny that she needed the heat. Her fingers began to warm soon, but what little warmth radiated from the remains of the fire didn't penetrate her woolen skirts or her boots. The poor fire flickered, and the flames threatened to die.

"It needs more kindling," she said.

"We busted up all the branches we could find," one of the passengers said, and Polly realized the speaker was a woman.

"Ma'am, are you hurt?"

"No, but my husband is. He was thrown from the stage. Thank you for bringing the blanket. I'll put it over him and Mr. O'Neal."

"I've got bandages, too," Polly said. "Perhaps that would help."

"It would indeed."

Polly hurried to her horse and took the basket down. "They're in here, with some food my mother sent." She handed the basket to the woman. "Could you please ask someone to distribute the food? There are a few sandwiches and some apples and oatmeal cookies."

"That sounds wonderful," the woman said. "I'm Mrs. Ricker."

"I'm sorry you're not enjoying my mother's hospitality this minute, ma'am. But if you'll see to passing out the food, I'll scrounge around and see if I can find anything else burnable. Jacob will need something smaller to feed the fire, if he wants it to catch onto that broken wagon tongue."

The men had struggled with the equipment while she spoke, and now Jacob came to the fire carrying a five-foot piece of the broken timber.

"We need something else," he said, eyeing the smoldering embers.

"I was just going to look for more fuel," Polly said.

"All right. Stay within sight of us. And do you have anything we can use for a sling for Billy Clyde's arm?"

Polly thought for a moment. "There's a towel covering the food in my basket. Ask Mrs. Ricker for it."

Jacob nodded and pointed beyond the overturned stagecoach. "There were a few scrub trees over that way. But I meant what I said about staying close. We don't want to lose you."

She went in the direction he indicated, wading in snow that was nearly as deep as her boots now. She rounded the coach and stared at the luggage spilling from the back. Tied to the roof of the coach, which was now vertical, was a bushy form that could only be one thing. Jacob had brought her Christmas tree.

⌒∾

Jacob helped Mrs. Ricker tend her husband and the other injured man, Mr. O'Neal. Meanwhile, Polly went off into the darkness. Two of the able-bodied passengers helped her look for wood, and they came back with enough small branches among them to perk up the fire until it took hold of the wagon tongue. Everyone couldn't get around the small blaze at once, so they took turns, with the two seriously injured men on one side of the fire, huddled under the blanket, and the others standing around the circle, extending their hands toward the flames.

"It was kind of your mother to send food," said Mr. Percival, a drummer from Kansas City.

"She was happy to do it," Polly said.

Billy Clyde, who was now wearing the towel tied around his neck for a sling, came over to stand beside Jacob. "I could make it to the station on one of those horses."

"Yes, I think you could," Jacob said. "Take Percival and Thomas and head out, while Mr. Winfield's tracks are still visible. I'll wait here with the others." He ticked them off mentally—Mrs. Ricker, the two badly injured men, along with two other fellows who had received no more than a good shaking up and a bruising. They would probably want to know why they couldn't be the ones to ride the horses to the way station, but they hadn't been as ready to help out as Percival and Thomas, so Jacob thought those two had earned the privilege.

"What about Polly?" Billy Clyde asked.

"I'll ask her if she wants to go." Jacob walked over to where Polly stood.

Her smile gleamed in the firelight. "I was thinking that we might do well to build a snow wall around the patients, to shelter them from the wind. It's not too bad right now, but it could pick up again."

"I'm sending Billy Clyde and two others off on the three good coach horses," Jacob said. "Do you want to take your mount and go with them?"

Polly hesitated. "I'd rather stay here, if you think I could be of some help."

"I do. You've already been very helpful, and I'm sure Mrs. Ricker is glad to have some female company. But it may be some time before your father gets back here with those oxen. You could go along with Billy now and be safe at home."

Polly's smile looked a bit sad. "I should feel very guilty if I did that, and I would go wild, wondering if you were all right."

Her words warmed Jacob's heart, though he told himself she meant all of them, not just him.

"All right."

Polly glanced toward where the team stood and then away. Jacob feared the sight of the one dead horse had upset her.

"We had to put him down. That is, Billy Clyde did. He'd broken a leg, and he was screaming awfully."

She nodded, and he wondered if he had said too much.

"Anyway, I'll be back in a few minutes."

She reached out her mittened hand and touched his sleeve. "Tell Billy and the others to warm themselves thoroughly before they set out. It's a good two miles, and it was quite a journey out here."

Jacob helped the three men get the horses ready. Mr. Percival and Mr. Thomas assured him they could ride the two miles without saddles.

"Can't get much colder than we are out here," Thomas said. "I'm game."

Jacob gave Billy Clyde a boost up onto the large wheeler's back. Billy Clyde moaned before he straightened and took the single rein in his good hand.

"You sure you'll be all right?" Jacob asked.

"I'll make it." Billy Clyde clucked to the horse and moved out ahead of the other two.

When Jacob got back to the fire, Mrs. Ricker and the two uninjured men were huddled around it. The others had brought over two large satchels from the luggage boot and were now seated on them.

"Shove that timber in a little farther," Jacob said to one of the men.

Polly was at the fringe of the circle of light, patting snow into a low barrier behind where the sick men lay.

"Is it sticky enough?" Jacob asked.

"I think so. We used to make snow forts when I was a child."

"I'll help you." The wind gusted, throwing a bushel of loose flakes into the air.

Polly shook them off her head.

"It seems awfully flaky and dry for this." Jacob scooped up handfuls and tried to pack a snowball, but it wouldn't hold together. "If we had a shovel..."

"We just have to keep at it," Polly insisted.

"Maybe what you're using is closer to the fire." Jacob settled in to work beside her, determined not to quit, no matter what. He hoped the next gale wouldn't blow away their wall. At least this exercise kept Polly moving. The others seemed content to stay seated on their luggage near the fire.

"It could be hours before your father comes back," Jacob said. "I'm thinking of busting up the coach wheels to burn."

"I think we've exhausted the supply of bushes nearby," Polly said.

"Yes. I'm not sure I can break up anything else without tools, though. And I hate to start busting up the coach." Jacob looked toward the damaged stagecoach. The division agent would be upset enough when he heard about the accident, let alone if they burned the whole coach, but the broken wheel at least could be sacrificed.

"There's my Christmas tree," Polly said.

So, she had seen it. He was surprised the passengers hadn't already tried to burn it. "I really don't want to use that," he said. "It's small, and it would burn up fast. I don't think it would do much good, really."

Polly smiled at him. "All right, but if we get desperate, it goes on the fire. Agreed?"

"Agreed."

Mrs. Ricker walked over to where they worked.

"I hate to trouble you, Mr. Tierney, but if you could find my husband's valise, he had another jacket in it, and I thought perhaps I could get it on him. He's shivering violently."

"Of course."

Jacob left Polly to work on the snow wall and went to help Mrs. Ricker. One of the other men came to the overturned coach and helped him retrieve Mr. Ricker's valise. Jacob wrenched three loose spokes from the broken wheel and added them to the fire.

Polly's barrier was now nearly two feet high and about eight feet long. Mr. Ricker and the other injured man were sheltered behind it, and Jacob could feel the difference it made.

Polly smiled up at him. "This work is keeping me warm."

"Good, because I don't think we'll find anything else to burn."

Jacob set to work with her, and they completed a semicircular snow wall that he estimated to be thirty feet long. Toward the last of it, one of the disgruntled men came to help them.

"Might as well move about," he muttered, and began to pack more snow along the top of the barrier.

The fire burned down, but the snow had stopped falling, and the wall helped cut the wind. "Come on over here," Jacob called to the other man, who sat stubbornly near the cooling ashes. Jacob, Polly, the two male passengers, and Mrs. Ricker sat shoulder to shoulder, near the makeshift pallet for the two wounded.

"I suppose we could play Twenty Questions," Polly said.

One of the men laughed at her suggestion, but soon they all joined in, and the grumblers quit complaining.

Jacob judged that two hours had passed since Mr. Winfield left them. Finally, he spotted a speck of light in the distance. He rose stiffly and plodded onto the trail. The tracks of those who had gone on were no longer visible, concealed by drifting snow, but he could still see the contour of the road. Far in the distance was the light he had glimpsed. He was now sure it was a lantern, shining for the oxen that trudged along pulling the sled.

He turned back toward the group. "It's Mr. Winfield. He's coming!"

Polly rose and staggered toward him. Jacob seized her hand and pulled her along through the snow.

"Is it over your boot tops?" he asked.

"I don't know. I can't feel my feet." But she managed to advance toward the ox team.

Mr. Winfield shouted, and when they at last met, Jacob saw that Ernest had returned with him.

"We've got four hot soapstones," Polly's father said. "Is everyone all right?"

"Nearly frozen," Jacob told him. "We ran out of wood. Bring the sled closer, and I'll help you load the two injured men. Can Mrs. Ricker ride as well?"

"Yes, and there's room for Polly," Mr. Winfield said.

"Pa, if you just let me warm my feet on one of those stones first, I'll ride Lucy back," Polly said.

"If you're sure." Her father eyed her doubtfully. "We met Billy Clyde and the others a mile out from the house. I'm sure they made it in, but those horses were about done."

"You brought the mules," Jacob said, peering through the dimness toward the shadowy forms behind the ox sled. Ernest rode one of the mule team and appeared to have the rest strung together on a lead line.

"They don't like it, but they've come along in the track of the sled. We've got only four, so you decide who rides what."

Jacob helped situate the injured men on the sled while Polly warmed her feet and her father got the other passengers onto mules. Mr. Winfield gave soapstones to Mrs. Ricker to use for the patients, and she settled down to ride beside her husband. Jacob and Ernest took the other two mules, and Polly's father boosted her into Lucy's saddle. The poor little buckskin would be glad to get back to the shelter of the barn, Jacob was sure.

He took a last look back at the stagecoach and remembered one more thing. "I'll be right back," he told Polly.

He urged his mule over to the side of the coach. It was mostly covered in snow now. By leaning over and scooping off six or eight inches of fluff with his arm, he was able to uncover his prize—the scraggly little tree he'd tied to the top of the vehicle.

His fingers were too stiff to untie the knots, but he took out his knife and sliced through the rope. A moment later, he had the tree dragging behind him. The mule didn't like it but was too tired to put up much of a fuss.

Polly's eyes were huge above the fold of scarf covering her mouth. "You're going to bring it!"

"Why not?" Jacob said. "After all the trouble I went to to get it, I don't want to leave it behind."

She laughed. "Thank you! Come on, even the oxen are ahead of us."

They started out for the trek through the snow.

Chapter 6

Ma had lanterns burning on the front porch, and lamps cast their cheery light out the dining room windows. Polly's heart cheered when she saw the welcoming glow. Billy Clyde, Mr. Thomas, and Mr. Percival waded out into the yard to meet them.

"Go right in and get warm, folks," Billy Clyde shouted. "Mrs. Winfield's got a roaring fire going and hot vittles for ya."

Mr. Percival stepped forward to take Lucy's bridle. "Are you all right, Miss Winfield?"

"Yes, thank you."

"Your mother was quite worried about you," he told her.

"I was in good hands, but I'll go right in and show her that I'm safe."

Mr. Thomas and Pa carried Mr. Ricker inside on a woolen blanket. Polly hurried past Jacob, who was untying the rope on his saddle horn so Billy Clyde could take the mule to the barn and unsaddle it.

"Ma," Polly shouted as she entered the house.

Her mother came out of the kitchen, her cheeks rosy and her hands covered with flour.

"Polly! You must be near frozen, child."

"Not so bad." As she unwound her scarf, Polly hurried through to the kitchen stove. The guests could have the fireplace in the dining room, and no doubt her parents would let them into the parlor, too, by the small coal stove. "What can I do to help? We've all these extra people for at least the night, probably longer."

"Yes, I've thought of that. Billy Clyde helped me work out the arrangements." Her mother wiped her hands. "First we'll feed them and get them warm. I shall help with the injured gentlemen if needed. You'll have to sleep in my room with me tonight, dear. We'll give the Rickers your room, and your father can bunk with Jacob and Billy Clyde."

"That makes sense." Polly doffed her mittens and stretched out her aching fingers toward the kitchen range. "What of the others?"

"The men who aren't hurt can sleep in the tenders' room with Ernest. It will be snug, but at least it's warm out there, and we'll have more privacy. The

223

injured ones will have to be in here, where we can care for them."

Polly unbuttoned her coat. "Well, I'm ready to work. Just tell me what to do."

"Take the biscuits out of the oven and put the sheet cake in. The stew has been simmering all evening. If you can serve it up and give them all hot coffee, I'll distribute bedding. I expect your father will be tied up in the barn for a while, caring for the livestock, but we can make Mrs. Ricker comfortable and provide whatever she thinks will help her husband."

Polly put on her apron and went to work, humming a hymn as she flitted about the kitchen. When she entered the dining room with four steaming soup plates on a tray, the four male passengers who were able were seated at the table, along with Billy Clyde.

"Hungry, gents?" Polly asked with a smile.

"Famished," said Mr. Percival. "Young lady, that smells delicious."

"My mother made it, so of course it is." She set a dish before him and made her rounds of the table, setting a serving before each passenger. "Billy Clyde, I'll bring yours in a trice, along with coffee and biscuits."

"Take your time, missy. It's not like I'll eat more than the tablecloth if you don't hurry."

Polly laughed and scuttled into the kitchen to reload her tray.

By the time the men had eaten their stew and were starting on the cake, Polly's mother came in from the family quarters carrying an armful of quilts and linen.

"Gentlemen, I apologize for the lack of order here. We don't often have overnight guests."

"You owe us no penance, madam," Mr. Percival said. "We've eaten like kings, and I'm told we'll have a warm place to cast our bedrolls on the floor."

"Yes, there's a stove in the tenders' room," Ma said. "I've brought out every extra blanket and sheet we own, and I'll let you divvy them up as you see fit. We've settled Mr. O'Neal on the parlor sofa so we can keep an eye on him."

"How are he and Mr. Ricker doing?" Billy Clyde asked.

"I think they'll be much better for some warm broth and a good night's sleep," Ma said. "Mr. O'Neal seems to have a broken arm and quite a bump on his head. It's Mr. Ricker I'm more worried about. He appears to have taken a blow to the head when the coach overset, and he's terribly bruised. Broken ribs, I shouldn't wonder."

"Too bad we didn't have a doctor among us," said Mr. Thomas, holding his cup out to Polly for more coffee.

Pa, Jacob, and Ernest came through the front door after stamping the snow off their feet on the porch.

"Time for the second sitting, gentlemen," Polly told those at the table. "Perhaps Billy Clyde will show you your accommodations."

The four passengers went out carrying the bedding, and some of them their coffee mugs. It seemed very quiet when only Pa, Jacob, and Ernest remained.

"I'll take these dirty dishes off and bring you some stew," Polly said.

"I ate my supper," Pa said, "but I could do with some of that cake, and I expect Jacob wants his stew."

"Whenever it's convenient," Jacob said.

Ernest laughed. "Listen to him. You're too polite, boy!"

Jacob looked a little flustered, but he reached for one of the dirty plates. "Let me help you, Miss Polly."

"Sure," Ernest said. "That way, we'll get our eats quicker."

Polly piled her tray with crockery and flatware, and Jacob came around the table.

"I'll take that out for you. It looks heavy."

Ernest laughed again, and Polly felt her cheeks go scarlet.

"Don't mind him," Jacob said when they reached the sanctuary of the kitchen.

"He's got no manners," Polly said. "I've never once heard him offer to help Ma or me."

"Perhaps he didn't grow up in a home with a nice mother who taught him to be polite and lend a hand," Jacob said.

Polly smiled as she lifted dishes into the dishpan. "I never thought of it that way."

Jacob's return smile made her stomach queasy.

"By the way, I left your tree out on the porch. Didn't want to bring it in with snow all over it. I'll see about it tomorrow, though. Where do you want it?"

"In the parlor, if Mr. O'Neal's not too sick to have us working around him." Polly set the last of the dishes off the tray and took it from him. "Thank you, Jacob. I really appreciate that you took extra trouble to get that tree for me and that you thought to bring it here from the stage."

"I was glad to do it."

Their gazes held for a moment, and Polly thought she could stare into his twinkling brown eyes forever. Jacob looked away first, a half smile on his lips. "Shall I get my own stew?"

"Oh, I'm sorry. I need to wash a bowl for you. We ran out of dishes tonight."

She washed and dried one of the soup plates and ladled it full of stew.

"I'll bring in the biscuits, but the fresh coffee won't be ready for a few minutes. Would you like water now?"

"That'd be fine." Jacob carried his dish into the dining room. While Polly put the last half-dozen biscuits on the serving plate, her mother came in with another tray of dishes.

"I'm pleased. Mrs. Ricker got her husband to take some broth, and she ate a good supper herself. She's a very sweet woman."

"I hope Mr. Ricker is going to be all right." Polly hesitated then said, "Ma, how does a girl find a husband out here?"

Her mother set her tray on the worktable. "You like Jacob, don't you?"

"Well, yes. Don't you?"

"He's a very nice young man. Oh, Polly, back in Massachusetts, you'd meet suitable young men at church, or in town, or at neighbors' houses. Here we have only those who pass by on the road. So far, I think Jacob is the best of the lot."

"So do I," Polly said, smiling.

"But you must be careful. And your father and I must get to know him better and make sure of his intentions. Just because he is the first decent, eligible man to come along, does not mean he's the one for you."

Polly nodded slowly, but she could barely hold back her smile. "I understand, Ma."

Christmas day dawned cold but sunny, with the Winfields and Jacob eating a hearty breakfast of eggs, sausage, and pancakes. The division agent had sent a crew two days previous with two sleighs, each pulled by six draft horses. They had taken away the stranded passengers. Ernest had gone with them, to spend the winter with his parents near St. Joseph, and Billy Clyde had joined the others in hopes of seeing the fort's doctor about his arm.

Jacob felt a bit awkward as the only guest for the holiday, but the Winfields assured him that he was welcome to stay.

"We've got the stagecoach fixed right as rain," Mr. Winfield said as he helped himself to seconds on sausage and pancakes. "As soon as the roads are good for wheeling again, Jacob will be able to resume his work."

"That's if the line decides to keep me on," Jacob said.

Mr. Winfield reached for the molasses pitcher. "They should. You've proved you can repair your chariot as well as drive it."

Jacob laughed. "I suppose a driver who is handy with tools is an asset to the company."

"Indeed. And I'll put in a good word for you."

When the meal was finished and the dishes done, they gathered in the parlor. Jacob didn't dare sit down beside Polly on the sofa but took a chair opposite, where he had a good view of her yule tree. She had cajoled him, Billy Clyde, and Ernest into helping her decorate it. Though it came a foot short of the ceiling and its limbs drooped a little, it now stood resplendent in the corner, reaching its branches into the room, as though offering the popcorn strings and paper stars and angels that festooned it. Mrs. Winfield had brought out six glass ornaments from some recess in the house, and they seemed all the finer because they were few.

Mr. Winfield opened the large family Bible on his lap as his wife settled down beside Polly, her knitting bag in her hands.

"I like to read the second chapter of Luke on Christmas morning," he said.

Jacob nodded. He looked forward to hearing the familiar words once more.

Mr. Winfield held the book up closer to his face and opened his mouth to read.

A loud knock sounded at the front door, followed by Billy Clyde's muffled shout of, "Hello! Anyone home this morning?"

Polly jumped up and hurried out of the room, returning seconds later with Billy Clyde.

"Merry Christmas, folks," the shotgun rider said. "Sorry to interrupt."

"Nonsense," Mrs. Winfield said. "Grab a seat. You're just in time for the scripture reading."

Billy Clyde crossed to sit beside her, on the other end of the couch from Polly, his hat crumpled in his hands.

"Any news, before we begin?" Mr. Winfield asked.

"A few bits. I'm to wear this sling for a month, and Mr. Ricker is on the mend."

"Oh, I'm so glad," Mrs. Winfield said. "What about Mr. O'Neal?"

"He'll recover. He's gone on already, back to Independence. And, Jacob—" Billy Clyde fixed his gaze on his friend. "The division agent said to tell you that Mr. O'Neal was a heavy investor in the line."

"You don't say," Mr. Winfield put in.

"I certainly didn't know it," Jacob said.

"He commended you for getting everyone to safety last week," Billy Clyde said, triumph in his eyes. "You can keep your job, sonny. Don't expect to drive the stagecoach out of here soon, but he wants to send sleigh runs through and see how that works. You're to be ready on Saturday, weather permitting."

"Do you think you'll have many passengers?" Mrs. Winfield asked.

"Probably not, but we've contracted a mail run through to Boise for the next six months."

Polly had kept silent during this exchange, but now she beamed at Jacob. "There! Your job is secure, at least for a while, Jacob."

Mr. Winfield read the chapter, and then he brought out the parcels from beneath Polly's bedraggled little tree. He put the small box Jacob had brought for Polly in her hands, and Jacob held his breath while she opened it.

"Oh! It's lovely." She passed the box to her mother.

"Yes, indeed. Very nice." Mrs. Winfield touched a finger to the silver necklace.

The filigree cross had seemed right to Jacob when he saw it at the trader's on his last run to the fort. Polly looked at him and smiled.

"Thank you. It's beautiful."

Jacob exhaled carefully. Her mother hadn't protested or said the gift was too personal for her daughter to accept. Did that mean Polly's parents would receive him as a suitor for her? He hoped so, because the more time he spent with them, the more he wanted to become part of the family.

Mr. Winfield placed a parcel in his hands, and Jacob turned his attention to it. A striped muffler, knit by Polly herself. The others opened their packages, exclaiming over the thoughtful items each had made or purchased. Jacob had a new vest from the Winfields and a bag of penny sweets from Billy Clyde. But perhaps the nicest gift he received was seeing the pure joy on Polly's face as she sat in the shadow of the Christmas tree.

꙳

After supper, Polly couldn't sit still. Jacob and her father had gone to the barn to tend the livestock, and Jacob had told Billy Clyde to stay in the house and rest his poor arm. His look had been so meaningful and Billy Clyde's answering smile so mischievous, that Polly knew something was up. She wasn't sure she could last until Pa and Jacob returned, and Billy Clyde's teasing didn't help.

"So, you've got some fine jewelry now, missy," he said when her mother had gone to the kitchen for a moment.

"What do you know about it?" Polly said, feigning disinterest.

"Oh, I know heaps," Billy Clyde said.

Stomping footsteps came from outside, and soon Jacob appeared in the doorway. "Any coffee, Polly?"

"Certainly. I'll get it." She jumped up, but Jacob held up a hand to stop her.

"No, I thought maybe Billy Clyde could get it. Your pa said there was more of that pie, too." He looked keenly at Billy Clyde.

"Oh, I'm wanted in the kitchen, am I?" Billy Clyde lumbered up awkwardly from his chair, trying to keep from bumping his injured arm. "Half an hour ago, I was no help, and now you want me to do everything."

"Hush," Jacob said. "Just go make yourself useful."

"I can take a hint." Billy Clyde shuffled toward the kitchen.

Polly hardly dared look at Jacob. Her cheeks were flaming hot, and if asked, she would have to agree that it was very odd for Jacob to clear the room.

"Is everything all right in the stable?" she asked.

"Oh yes." Jacob stepped toward her. "Polly, I spoke to your father."

"Did you?" She could barely breathe. She gazed up from beneath her eyelashes. "And?"

"He—he said I could court you. If you wished it. Polly, please say you wish it. I think you're the nicest girl I've ever met, and the way you helped Mrs. Ricker and nearly froze your toes off to build that snow wall. . .well, I think you're wonderful."

Polly laughed, a little giddy from the suddenness of it. "You're no slouch, Jacob Tierney. And I've thought a lot about our talk a couple of weeks ago."

"Have you?"

"Yes."

He stepped closer. "Do you mean when you were telling me all the things you missed about the East?"

She nodded. "I'm ready for Wyoming now. To make this my home. Well, it is my home," she hurried on, "but I don't think I'd fully accepted that until after we talked, and until you brought me that silly, beautiful little tree." She looked over her shoulder, smiling, at the Christmas tree. When she turned back toward him, Jacob stepped closer and put his arms around her.

"I'm glad I got snowed in here and not at the fort."

In the shadow of the Christmas tree, he leaned toward her and kissed her. In the most glorious moment of her life, Polly kissed him back.

"Do you think you might share that Wyoming future with me?" he asked softly.

"Oh yes," Polly said. "I believe we can make something of it together."

About the Author

Susan Page Davis is the author of more than forty novels, in the romance, mystery, suspense, and historical romance genres. A Maine native, she now lives in western Kentucky with her husband, Jim, a retired news editor. They are the parents of six and the grandparents of nine fantastic kids. She is a past winner of the Carol Award, the Will Rogers Medallion for Western Fiction, and the Inspirational Readers' Choice Award. Susan was named Favorite Author of the Year in the 18th Annual Heartsong Awards. Visit her website at: www.susanpagedavis.com.

The Nativity Bride

by Miralee Ferrell

Chapter 1

Goldendale, Washington
September 1875

A pillow connected with Curt Warren's backside, and he staggered but caught himself. "Where did you come from, Deb? I didn't even see you there." He raised his down-filled pillow above his head and ran across the Summers' kitchen after sixteen-year-old Deborah Summers as her laughter filled the air.

"You may have longer legs than me, Curt, but I'm quicker." She darted to the side of the woodstove, her breath coming in gasps, then raced out again to cover the expanse of the room and slipped into their dining area, where she skidded to a halt, her pillow raised in defense. "I got the last lick in, so I win."

"Who says we're done?" He frowned in mock anger and inched forward, hoping she wouldn't notice.

She giggled and sidled the opposite direction. "Your father, that's who. He's expecting you home to do chores, and you know how grumpy he gets if you're late. Admit it, you don't want to get beaten by a girl, even if it's a girl you're sweet on." She arched a sassy brow and winked.

Curt tossed the pillow onto a chair, and as her gaze followed it, he lunged forward and grasped her upper arms before she could scamper away. "A girl I'm sweet on, huh? Let's just see about that." As quick as a hummingbird swooping for nectar, he dipped his head and attempted to steal a kiss, but the little minx turned her head, and his lips landed on her cheek. "Ah, Deborah, come on. Just one little kiss before I go?"

She squealed but didn't try too hard to get away. She put her hand on his chest and pushed, smirking as she did so. "I didn't hear you say you're sweet on me, and we're not betrothed yet, so no kisses for you."

She danced across the floor and waved her hand toward the door. "It's a good thing Ma's upstairs on the far end of the house, or you'd have waked her by now. You'd best get before your pa comes looking for you." Her pretty face sobered. "Will I see you tomorrow when you're done with chores?"

"Yep, I reckon you will, as long as Pa doesn't keep me till after dark." His heart thudded at the quirk of Deborah's lips. If only he could kiss her! He rolled his eyes as she pointed at the door again. "All right, I'm going. You don't have to shove me out, you know."

"From the expression I glimpsed a second ago, I think I do." Her smile faded, and she ducked her head. "I'll see you tomorrow."

He eased toward the door then pivoted after he grasped the knob. "I love you, Deborah." He jerked on the knob and bolted down the steps, not waiting for her reply. He believed she felt the same, but he wasn't taking any chances. As soon as she turned seventeen, he'd ask her to marry him.

Curt raced across the fields that connected his father's farm with the Summers' then slowed his pace as he neared the barn. Hopefully Pa would still be in the east pasture. He slipped inside, waiting a minute for his eyes to adjust to the dim light, then groaned. The cows were already in their stations, ready to milk.

Pa stepped around a corner and glared. "You're late. Bringing in the cows is your job."

"I know, Pa. I'm sorry." He grabbed a milk pail and pulled up the milking stool.

"You need to stop seeing Deborah." Pa crossed his arms over his chest and kept his eyes riveted on Curt. "The way you're going, you'll ruin her life. You aren't interested in this farm, and all you want to do is play. Maybe it's time you figured out what you *do* want to do."

Curt stared at his father, certain he hadn't heard correctly. "What?" He shook his head. "I love Deborah, and there's no way I'm going to stop seeing her. I can't believe Ma feels the same way."

Pa leaned his forearms on the rough surface of the half wall next to the milking stall. "Your mother is too soft and has spoiled you all your life. You're eighteen—a man now—and you need to start making good decisions. Think about someone besides yourself for a change. This will be your farm one day."

Curt couldn't stand this any longer. He pushed to his feet, wanting the advantage, even if it was only to be had by towering over his father. Why did the man have the power to unsettle him so or stir such a deep anger? "*I am* thinking about someone else. Deborah. She loves me and wants to marry me."

"She's sixteen and has an ailing mother who needs her. If I didn't oversee her farm help, they'd have lost that place when her father died ten years ago."

Curt sucked in a breath, wanting to retaliate, but the response died on his lips. Pa had sacrificed much to keep his own farm going as well as that of the Summers' and never said a word of complaint.

Pa thumped the flat of his hand against the wall. "Are you going to put aside your foolish notions and settle down to farming so Deborah is guaranteed a good life?"

Curt's spine stiffened. "You know the answer to that. I kill everything I try to grow. I wasn't cut out to herd cattle or plant crops. All I've ever wanted to do is work with wood—to make furniture and create things for people's homes—why can't you respect my choice? Deborah does, and she supports me in it."

"That's all well and good, but is it going to put food on the table? You have no training or experience. It takes years to build a name for yourself before you start making a living."

"I know all that, Pa. You've said it often enough over the years." Curt tried to keep the growl out of his voice. Pa meant well, and Ma would be disappointed in him if he showed disrespect to his father, even if the older man refused to understand. "But I found a man in The Dalles—a master craftsman who's offered to take me on as an apprentice. In four years or so, I could open my own shop, or if I'm good enough, he might take me on as a partner. I could do well for myself and Deborah."

Pa shook his head. "Four or five years from now you'll *try* to start your own business. Until then, you'll not make any money. The man will feed you and teach you a craft, but that's all. How can you support a wife and the babies that will follow? Your grandfather tried his hand at furniture making and couldn't make a living." He frowned. "And there's one more thing you've given no thought to."

Curt wondered what could possibly come next. "Yes, sir? And what is that?"

"You don't share the same faith as Deborah. She's lived her whole life with an aim to please God, and you've spent your whole life pleasing yourself."

This time Curt couldn't keep the irritation from his voice. Pa was wading in where he didn't belong. "I attend church with you and Ma."

"That's not what I'm talking about, and you know it. Deborah lives out her faith every day. She cares for her ma, she works at the church, and she loves God with a devotion I've never seen in someone so young.

"You barely tolerate church and have no relationship with God at all. Oil and water don't mix, Curt. Deborah loves you now, but if you continue down the path you've been walking, rebelling against all she holds dear, you'll break her heart and destroy that love. Better you let her go while she's young and still able to find a man who will care for her—one who believes as she does—rather than drag her off to a life of poverty without the strength of a living faith to carry you through the trials that lay ahead."

"I don't agree." Curt kept his tone even while pushing down the anger that simmered inside. "The love we share will overcome anything. She'll move to The Dalles with me, and we'll be happy together."

"So you'll force her to choose between you and her ailing mother instead of settling down and working her farm?"

"Why does it have to come to that? Maybe her mother would come with us. Have you thought about that? Why should Deborah be the one to sacrifice everything?"

Pa stared down for several moments then finally looked up. "Because even at sixteen years of age, Deborah is the type of woman who will do the right thing. Her father is buried on that land, and it would be hard on her ma to leave. You'll destroy Deborah's respect and love for you if you try to force her to do otherwise. Listen to me, boy. Don't put her in that position."

Curt clenched his hands then stuffed them into his trouser pockets. "I've had enough of this talk. I'm going to see Deborah."

Pa thumped the palm of his hand against the stall wall. "Don't be foolish, Son. If you go off half-cocked and leave the farm, don't come back begging for handouts. You can stay here and work like you ought to, or don't bother returning."

❦

Five years later—December 1880

Deborah Summers folded a shawl and tried to smooth out the creases, admiring the intricate flowers Sarah Warren had stitched in each corner. She wanted to do the best she could by Jarrod Warren after all he'd done to help them over the years. The poor man had lost his wife yesterday, and he was in no shape to get his house ready for the service tomorrow.

She placed the shawl in Sarah's bureau drawer then lifted her head and met her mother's gaze. "I don't plan to marry, Ma. I don't mean to be disrespectful, but even if a dozen farmers or store owners offer for my hand, I'll stay single."

Her mother sank onto the hand-knitted coverlet draped across the neatly made bed and sighed. "You should have married Timothy Bates, instead of breaking it off a few weeks before you were to wed. It wasn't fair, Deborah."

Deborah bit her lip to keep from saying something she shouldn't and gave her mother a weak smile.

Ma gripped her shaking hands in her lap and leaned against the ornate headboard. "I'm not long for this world, and I don't want you left alone when

I pass. You're twenty-one, my dear, and you need a good man to provide for you. We're not wealthy folks, and I won't leave you much besides a small farm that barely pays its way."

Deborah's brow puckered. She loved her mother but despaired of convincing her she wasn't on her deathbed. "You aren't dying, Ma. I know you've been weak lately and you lost some weight, but I believe you're getting better."

She plucked a stack of lace-edged kerchiefs from their place on a chair arm and moved them to another bureau drawer, wishing Mr. Warren had given better instructions on where he wanted them to store Sarah's belongings. A trunk lid yawned open against the far wall, and two or three wooden boxes sat empty near the open bedroom door.

Her mother reached out and touched Deborah's arm, bringing her activity to a halt. "I'll never get completely well, Deborah—not after having scarlet fever years ago. You avoided my comment about Timothy Bates, Daughter."

Ma swept a hand around the room. "Even Mr. Warren acknowledges his son isn't coming back. If the death of his own mother didn't draw Curt back to Goldendale, then you need to face the fact he'll never return. It's been five years since he left. You must move on with your life."

Deborah winced, not wanting her mother to see how much her well-meaning words had pierced her heart. She fought against the truth in Ma's comment. Before he'd left, Curt had come to her house and told her he was leaving, that he wasn't good enough for her, but she couldn't accept that then and wouldn't accept it—not ever.

She knew he loved her and had left because he believed it was right, but it stung, nevertheless. She should have had some say in the matter. How could he walk away and not even stay close enough to visit? Worse yet, he'd only written twice after leaving, and not at all in the past four years.

"You had an excellent chance with Timothy Bates."

Deborah sighed. "I didn't love Timothy, Ma. I never should have agreed to marry him. I was still hurting over Curt, and Timothy's kind words eased some of the pain. But that's not a good reason to marry. I knew he'd be happier with Nadine Garvey. I did him a favor by ending our agreement."

Her mother clucked her tongue. "Be that as it may, it didn't help your future by letting him go. You're a lovely woman now, with plenty of skills that any man would be happy to acquire. But if you wait much longer, you'll be alone the rest of your life."

Deborah shut the drawer a little harder than she'd planned then swung around. "Better to be alone than to marry someone I don't love, while my heart is still tied to another."

"Then untie it, girl. You're being more than a little foolish." Ma flicked a hand at the wardrobe standing open against the far wall. "We'd best get to work and finish this off. I promised Mr. Warren we'd be done before the service tomorrow."

"Not with all the cleaning, too? We can have the front room and kitchen tidied and shining before folks show up but not the rest of the house. Sarah was ailing for such a long time. I'm afraid Mr. Warren kept up on the farm but not the house. It's going to take at least a week to set this place back to rights."

"If only I had more energy and strength, we'd get done faster." Ma's voice ended on a weak note, but she pushed to her feet and wobbled across the floor to the walnut wardrobe.

Deborah's heart lurched. Maybe her mother hadn't been exaggerating. "Come sit, and let me do that. There's no need to push yourself."

She wrapped her arm around her mother's shoulders, shocked anew by the sharp bones where there used to be soft flesh. She settled her mother onto the bed again then straightened. "I'll step into Sarah's sitting room and bring a few things in here. We'll need that area somewhat clear before guests arrive, and the easiest course of action is to store things in this room for now."

"Fine, dear. I'll rest, and when I get my breath, I'll help."

"No ma'am. You stay put." Deborah shook her finger and smiled. "That's an order." She headed for the door to the adjoining room, thankful it was close. She'd leave it ajar and listen in case Ma called.

She stepped into the sitting room and stopped, her breath caught in her throat. A man stood with his back toward her. It wasn't Mr. Warren, but something was disturbingly familiar about the set of his shoulders and the fringe of dark brown hair she could see beneath his hat. "Hello? May I help you?"

He pivoted, his hand on the mantel above the fireplace, and his warm brown eyes captured hers. "Deborah Summers. Well, I'll be. You're the last person I expected to see here."

She dropped the crocheted doilies, her fingers numb and her brain refusing to function. She must be seeing things. It wasn't possible that Curt Warren was standing there, his face wreathed in a nonchalant smile. The shock passed in moments, however, and anger took its place. How dare he return after all these years and act as though nothing had changed! She sank to the floor, blindly groping for the bits of lace, while a storm gathered in the pit of her stomach, ready to erupt.

Chapter 2

Curt held himself steady against the mantel, working hard to stay composed. He wanted to rush across the room and pluck the bits of lace from the floor and present them to the stunning young woman on bended knee. But it had been far too long since he'd seen her, and his tongue was as frozen as his limbs. Couldn't he have come up with something more fascinating than she was the last person he expected to see? She must think him a complete dunderhead—if not worse.

Finally, he pushed himself erect and straightened his jacket, wishing he'd worn his usual everyday clothing and not crammed himself into this suit. But Pa needed to see that he'd attained some measure of success in his chosen career. He held out his hand and smiled. "Let me help you."

She hesitated, and he saw a flicker of what appeared to be anger flash in her eyes, but she finally extended her hand.

"Thank you." Standing, she withdrew and stepped away, putting a wider distance between them.

Curt grimaced at the frown marring Deborah's face. "I came home for Ma's service, but I didn't realize you'd be here. Have I done something wrong?"

"Wrong?" Deborah's frown deepened. "Whatever would give you that idea? It's only been five years since I saw you, and yet you act as though it was last week." She crossed her arms and tossed her head. "Not a single letter in the last four years, even after I told you I'd wait."

Curt's blood thrummed in his ears. "But I told you. . ." He licked his lips. "Did you wait? Are you married? I mean. . ." Warmth rushed into his face at the fury clouding Deborah's expression. "Pardon me. That was rude and disrespectful. As I remember, I told you not to wait—that I wouldn't be back, and you should move on with your life. Dragging you away from your mother wouldn't be fair. I'm sorry if I caused you distress by not continuing to write. I truly thought you understood."

❧

Deborah hunched a shoulder. "It doesn't matter now; and no, I'm not married or betrothed." She lifted her head. "Not that I haven't had offers."

She had no idea why she'd tacked on that last. Maybe due to the flicker of joy she saw in his eyes when she'd said no—a perverse desire to show him she wasn't an old maid with no one who cared to marry her. But she couldn't deny the attraction she still felt for this man or the longing that had rushed over her when he'd clasped her fingers for those few seconds it had taken her to stand.

She tipped her head toward the next room. "I'm surprised Ma hasn't appeared. I left her resting on the bed, but I'd better check on her."

"Your mother is here, too? I haven't seen Pa yet, so I'm not sure what's going on."

Deborah gave him a slight smile. "I must say I'm quite surprised to see you. You haven't visited since you left." She rested her hand on the doorframe leading into the adjoining room and turned. "Your father asked Ma and me to ready the house for the service and clean out some of your mother's things, but he didn't mention you were coming."

A belated thought struck her, and she sucked in a quick breath. "Curt, I'm so sorry about your ma. She was a good woman, and my mother treasured her friendship."

He nodded, his face grave. "Thank you. Someone from the church sent word, or I wouldn't have known. I wish I could have arrived before she passed." He bowed his head for a moment. "I didn't tell Pa I was coming, so I'm not sure what he'll say when he finds out I'm here."

From listening to Mr. Warren over the past five years, Deborah had a good idea what he might say to his son, but she couldn't destroy Curt's look of tentative hope. "I hope he'll be surprised and happy to see you." She smiled and pushed open the door to the bedroom. "Ma? Are you awake?"

Peeking into the room, she hesitated then walked softly to the bed, hating to disturb her mother. The older woman lay on the coverlet, eyes closed and hands clasped over her waist. The same pose Deborah had seen her father in, lying in his casket.

Panic gripped her, and she rushed to the bed, certain her mother's words about dying had been prophetic. "Mama?" She touched her mother's cheek, and relief swamped her at the warmth that met her fingertips. "Are you all right?"

She sensed Curt behind her but ignored him, intent on making sure her mother was well. "Wake up, Ma. Someone is here."

"Hmm? Who? What?" Her mother's eyelids fluttered, and she struggled to sit up. She pushed against the headboard and attempted to straighten her skirt. "Oh my!" Her gaze lifted to just over Deborah's shoulder. "My stars! Is that young Curt Warren, or am I dreaming?"

The bedroom door swung open and thumped against the wall. Deborah and Curt swiveled and stared. Mr. Warren stood in the opening, a scowl marring his otherwise pleasant visage to the extent Deborah barely recognized him.

He pointed at Curt as his bellow filled the room. "What in thunder are you doing here?"

Curt stiffened, ready to do battle as he'd always done as a young man, then forced his tight muscles to relax. He was no longer the rebellious youth who'd lived in this home. He was a man who'd matured into the kind of person his parents had always hoped for—but somehow he doubted his father would believe that. He could only pray Deborah would, once he had a chance to talk to her alone.

But right now he must deal with the man who stood before him, trembling with anger. Curt held out his hand and stepped forward, forcing a smile he didn't feel. "Pa. It's good to see you, sir."

His father's gaze didn't waver, and his arms stayed at his sides. "I asked you a question. Why are you here?"

Curt flinched at the harsh words. He'd prayed so many times about this reunion. In fact, he'd longed to come home, but his mother's letters had begged him to wait. She'd worked hard to soften his father's attitude, but for some reason Curt couldn't understand, Pa seemed determined to keep him a prodigal for as long as he continued in his chosen career.

"I heard about Ma. She wrote and told me she was sick, but she was certain she was doing better. Then a friend wrote and told me she'd passed." He hung his head and his body shuddered. "I'm sorry, Pa." He raised damp eyes. "I would have been here if I'd known how bad it was."

Pa flicked a hand toward the door. "If you cared, you never would have left in the first place. Maybe you'd best go back to your home. You don't belong in these parts any longer."

Deborah had stood silent beside the bed where her mother sat, but now she moved to stand beside Curt. "Mr. Warren, maybe it would be good to set this aside for the moment. At least until Mrs. Warren is put to rest. Curt didn't have a chance to tell his mother good-bye. Perhaps you could give him a few days before you ask him to leave?"

241

Pa swung his gaze to Deborah, and Curt saw his hard expression soften, then he heaved a sigh. "All right. I'll do that for you, girl. I appreciate your help here, and yours, Winifred, and I don't want to appear callous or unfeeling at a time when charity should abide in our hearts."

His glare returned to Curt. "You can use your old room and stay—for one week. One week from today, if you decide you want to give up your foolish notions and return to working the farm, we'll talk. Otherwise, you'd best get along home."

Curt winced but gave a slight nod. "Thank you, sir." He had to bite his tongue to keep from saying he'd never push a plow again. There was no sense in riling his father more when he'd opened the door to possible reconciliation—but at what cost? Certainly one Curt would never be able to pay. All he could do now was pray that somehow God would soften his father's heart.

He glanced at Deborah in time to see a flicker of despair cross her face, and he held in a groan. Maybe coming home had been a mistake. All his old feelings for her were returning in a rush, and it appeared he'd opened several old wounds that should have been left closed.

Chapter 3

Deborah clenched her hands in the folds of her skirt and shut her eyes as anxiety turned into relief. Mr. Warren had given in, something she'd prayed the man would do but had not expected. But why hadn't Curt told him he'd stay for good? Surely now that he was back, he'd see how much he was needed. Was there a reason he couldn't do his woodworking here, now that he'd learned a trade?

She longed to throw her arms around him and beg him to heed his father's words—to give them another chance at love and a life together—but fear kept her arms pinned to her sides. His vocation apparently meant more to him than she did, and he'd never seemed to regret what he'd given up for his new life. No matter how much she'd longed for his return, she didn't know if she'd ever be able to trust her life to him again. But was it possible God might be giving them a second chance?

She turned to her mother. "Ma? We should get you home to bed."

Curt touched Deborah's arm. "May I drive you? Is your buggy in the barn? I can tie my horse to it and ride back."

Deborah's breath caught in her throat as memories returned of past buggy rides. "I don't know, Curt. You should stay here and visit with your father."

Mr. Warren grunted. "I've been without him for five years; I can muddle along for another hour. Besides, Winifred doesn't look well." He shot a hard glance at Curt. "Hitch the buggy and take them home."

Curt nodded, but a mask slipped over his features. "Yes, sir." He pivoted and walked out the door without looking back.

Deborah's heart plummeted. Would he be able to tolerate his father for a full week, or would he leave town again right after the service? She'd better guard her emotions and not allow herself to hope.

She placed her arm around her mother's waist, and Mr. Warren moved aside as they crossed the threshold into the other room. "I'll return after I get Mother settled, if that's all right? If Curt drives the buggy, I'll ride back with him and work a little longer."

Mr. Warren rushed past them and opened the door. "Please don't worry about it, Deborah." He glanced over his shoulder at the still untidy living area. "I'm sure the neighbors will understand if everything's not perfect."

She shook her head. "Ma just needs to sleep for a bit. If she's worse by the time we get home, I'll stay with her. Otherwise, I'll return."

Her mother waved her hand. "I'm fine. Quit worrying. I'll take a nap and be right as rain in a couple of hours."

Mr. Warren followed them out and helped them into the buggy as Curt held the reins of the restless horse. "Now, Winifred, don't you even think about doing any more work. I won't stand for you making yourself sick on my account. Sarah would have had my hide." Sadness crept across his face, and he choked on the last words.

The drive to their home passed in silence as Curt kept his eyes on the road and Deborah and her mother sat quietly in the seat behind him. Disappointment grew in Deborah as they neared the house and Curt still hadn't spoken. Was he already regretting his decision to spend a few days on his father's farm?

She softly cleared her throat and leaned forward. "If you'll wait, I'd like to get Ma settled then return with you and continue cleaning."

His shoulders tightened, but he gave a brief nod. "Of course."

He pulled the horse to a stop then climbed down and helped them from the buggy. Deborah got her mother in bed, kissed her forehead, and tiptoed out of the room to a still silent Curt. A brief smile flickered then vanished before he handed her up to the front seat, where he sank down beside her. He picked up the reins, released the brake, and urged the horse forward.

Deborah waited, wondering how to broach the subject she longed to know about and hoping he'd be the one to speak first. Finally, she could stand it no longer. "Curt?"

He turned a warm gaze toward her and smiled.

A soft sigh escaped her lips, and she relaxed. "What was it like there?"

His brows knit together. "You mean in The Dalles? Or at my job?"

"Both. And the man you work for, is he. . .kind?" She struggled to not pour all her questions out at once, not wanting to overwhelm him but hoping he'd be willing to talk.

A full grin split his handsome face, and the dimple she'd always loved appeared. "Mr. Colson is one of the finest men I've ever met. He's honest, hardworking, and a true man of God. He doesn't preach at you but shows you the right way by how he lives. I've never met a man I respect more."

"More than your father?" As soon as the words left her lips, Deborah wished she could snatch them back again. She knew what a turbulent relationship Curt and his father had maintained throughout Curt's later teen years and how far apart they'd drifted.

Curt's grin faded, and he faced forward again. "Yes. Although I hate to admit that to anyone, I know you understand. You saw how things were between my father and me when I lived at home. It was. . .hard. He was always preaching, always trying to force me to be the person he wanted me to be and never listening to my hopes or dreams."

He pulled back on the reins and drew the horse to a halt, then swiveled to face her. "But now I know it wasn't all his fault. Much of it was mine. I've come to understand how rebellious I was and how I must have hurt both my parents." He winced. "And you."

She gripped her hands in her lap, barely daring to breathe, hoping he'd continue and she'd hear the words she longed to hear. "So, are you staying this time? Here on the farm with your father?"

His face paled, then flushed. "You know I can't do that. You heard him. The only way he'd accept me is if I give up my trade. I'm no longer an apprentice. Mr. Colson told me I'm ready to go out on my own now. I can't credit his words, but he says I've exceeded even what he knows, and I could teach others or have my own shop. He's willing to take me on as a partner if I don't care to start my own business, but I haven't decided what's best." He bowed his head for a brief moment then met her gaze. "I want to spend time praying about it first."

⁓

Curt heard Deborah's soft gasp and knew he'd surprised her—possibly even shocked her—with his declaration about prayer. He'd wanted to tell her this entire last year, ever since he'd made the decision to follow in Mr. Colson's footsteps and put God first in his life. He waited, but she still didn't speak. "I thought you might be glad."

The dazed look turned to one of joy. "Oh, but I am! So very glad. I've prayed for this for years. If going away is what it took for you to open your heart to God's love, then I'm glad you did." Her face softened. "But I still don't see why you can't stay here. Your father will come around if you give him time."

"You saw him today. The anger and resentment, demanding I return to farming." He shook his head. "I'll admit, I don't understand. I've *never* understood why he's so against me working with wood. It's a good trade. His own father made furniture for a living."

She shifted beside him, and her arm pressed against his. A jolt shot through him, and he sucked in his breath, surprised that having Deborah near could still affect him. Or had she never stopped affecting him, and he'd simply buried his feelings as deeply as possible to deal with the hurt of having to leave her? He longed to take her in his arms and pour it all out—the full truth of what happened. How his father had insisted he break it off with her, due to her mother's lingering illness and Curt's inability to provide. How he'd come to her home to persuade her to run off with him, only to find her nursing her sick mother and frightened she might die. But he could provide now and would happily do so, for Deborah, and her mother as well. He'd allowed her to believe he wanted a career and didn't care to remain in Goldendale—and while that was partly true, there had been so much more.

Then his mind returned to the scene in his mother's bedroom with Mrs. Summers today, and the fear he'd seen on Deborah's face as she'd rushed to her. Would it be any more fair now to make Deborah choose between them than it had been when she was sixteen?

She touched his sleeve. "What are you thinking, Curt? What's wrong?" Her imploring eyes probed deep.

He shook his head, not wanting to reveal how much he cared. He picked up the reins. Maybe he should slip away after the service tomorrow and never return. Deborah said she'd had offers, and like five years ago, he couldn't stand the thought of remaining and see her married to some other man. That would destroy him.

◦◦◦

The service for Sarah Warren was heavily attended, and with Deborah and Curt's efforts, the parts of the house open to guests shone. Deborah awoke two days later, ready to finish the rest of the Warrens' home but dreading what she might find when she arrived. Pushing open the door, she slipped inside, praying Curt wouldn't be gone.

A cheery whistle emanated from the kitchen, and relief weakened her muscles. She'd know Curt's whistle anywhere. She tapped on the doorframe, waited a second, then stepped into the kitchen as he swung around. A smile brightened his countenance. "You're up early. There's no need for you to keep cleaning the house. I'm sure you have plenty of work to do at home, with your mother not well."

Deborah's smile faded as the realization struck her that Curt apparently wasn't as pleased to see her as she'd hoped. She moved into the room, her chin high, and reached for a towel lying beside the stack of wet dishes. "I see you've learned how to tackle a few household chores, but this is my job, not yours. Your father has been a blessing to me and Ma since Pa died, and I see this as a way to pay back a small part of our debt. Ma is stronger today, and she's doing a few of the inside chores and leaving the supper preparations to me."

"Ah, I see. All right, then. Let's have at it together." Curt plucked the towel out of her hand and tossed it on the countertop with an impish glance. "Those will dry fine on their own. What else is on your list of things that must be done? Sorting clothing again, or something else?"

"Boxes, I think. There are several crates in the attic your father wants me to go through, to see if there's anything worth saving. He believes most of them are full of old clothing or yardage your mother saved that might be ruined by now, but he asked that I check."

Curt nodded. "I'll get a pry bar to remove the nails. Once all the lids are off, I might run out to the barn to clean my horse's stall then tote anything downstairs you've decided needs to be moved. Will that work?"

Joy bubbled inside that he wanted to help—better yet, that he planned to spend time alone with her. Other than the ride back to his farm, she'd had only snatches of time without his father or her mother or a helpful neighbor stopping by. "Yes, thank you. I'd like that." She tried to keep the eagerness out of her voice, but something in his answering glance told her she might not have succeeded.

They climbed the stairs to the attic, and Curt pushed open the narrow door at the top of the steps. "Whew." He waved his hand in front of his nose. "It's not too pleasant up here. Want me to bring a few boxes downstairs to work where the air is fresher?" He looked around the cramped space. "You'll have better light, as well."

She shrugged, not anxious to return to the living area where some well-meaning person might drop by and interrupt whatever conversation could develop. "Let's stay here for a bit. Maybe open a few boxes and see if they look like something I need to sort through. If most of them are musty old clothing, you can take those down."

"Fair enough." He dragged a wooden crate from a dark corner and rolled up his sleeves. "I'm glad you wore a full apron. It's pretty dusty up here." Sticking the edge of a bar under the lip of the crate, he pressed down, the muscles in his forearms bulging.

Deborah tried not to stare but couldn't quite help herself. He'd changed so much since she saw him five years ago. He'd gone away a boy of eighteen and returned as a mature man. One who had made his way in the world and knew what he wanted from life—and one who had learned to turn to the Lord during times of indecision and trial. The kind of man she'd always hoped he would become.

He glanced up, the final nail screeching as it reluctantly released its hold. "That's the last one. Looks like you were right; this one is full of clothes." He moved to the next and repeated the process. "Yard goods? Ma loved to sew. I'm guessing we'll find several of these boxes. If any of the cloth is still good, the church ladies might want it for sewing projects."

Deborah nodded and set about digging to the bottom of the crate he'd pried open, sneezing from the dust as she did so. "They'll have to be laundered and checked for holes, but some of this is still good."

He sat back on his haunches. "Want me to tote them downstairs? Or open a few others first?"

She gazed around and spotted a stack in another corner then noticed a lone box pushed under the eaves. "If you don't mind opening that one first, then a couple of those others, I'll have plenty to do until you return."

He nodded and set to work, pausing occasionally to wipe perspiration from his forehead. "All right, looks like that's it. I'll take a couple of these with me. I won't be gone long."

She watched him cross the room, carrying the heavy load as though it were feather pillows. "I'll be here."

A warm chuckle drifted from the top of the staircase, and she thought she heard him say, "I'm glad," as his steps echoed on the hard wood, but she couldn't be sure.

She moved to the crate that had been off to one side, her mind wandering to what might have been if Curt hadn't left town. Would they be married and living in their own home, with possibly a baby or two? If only he could reconcile with his father and find a way to stay.

Removing the loosened lid from the crate, she glanced inside, certain she'd see more clothing or sewing goods. A variety of odd-shaped objects wrapped in cloth surprised her instead. She touched the linen, only to note its fragility. How long had this been stored, and did Curt have any idea what it might be? She hesitated, wondering if she should unwrap the objects. But Mr. Warren had been firm. Go through the boxes and determine what should stay and what should be donated or thrown.

She plucked out a long object and carefully unwrapped it. Her breath caught, and she stared at an exquisite hand-carved statue of a woman, clothed in a robe and sandals, her face alight with joy. Hurriedly, Deborah removed the remaining objects and placed them reverently on the floor around her. A beautiful Nativity scene stood revealed, complete with a manger, cows and sheep, wise men and shepherds, and the most lifelike depiction she'd ever seen of the baby Jesus and His family. Amazing. From the condition of the cloth, the pieces had to have been wrapped decades ago, and it was obvious they'd not been touched in years.

Boots clomped up the final few steps, and she raised her head. "Curt?" As soon as he appeared through the door, she waved him over. "Do you know where these came from?"

Chapter 4

Curt stared at Deborah sitting on the dusty floor, her skirt flared around her and the beautifully carved pieces of wood standing just beyond. He knelt beside her, barely daring to breathe. "What in the world?" He gently cradled the figure of baby Jesus lying in a manger and stroked the wood with his fingertip. "These are exquisite. I've never seen such fine detail. These were in that box?"

She nodded, a frown puckering her lovely face. "Yes. I assume you didn't carve them, as the cloth protecting them is so old. Your grandfather was a woodworker, correct? Do you suppose they were his?"

Curt examined each piece before he replied then set the last wise man reverently on the floor. "Very possible, although I don't see why Ma wouldn't have brought these out each Christmas. What do you want to do with them?"

Deborah brightened, her blue eyes sparkling. "I'd love to take them downstairs and put them on the mantel for Christmas. It's only two weeks away. Do you think your father would mind?"

"I can't imagine why he would. I'll move them for you. Do you want to do more today?" He glanced around, taking in the small pile of boxes not yet sorted and the streaks of dirt smudging Deborah's face. "Or have you had quite enough of the dirt and stale air by now?"

She giggled. "I must look a sight. But you aren't a lot better yourself." She pointed to his head, where a hat usually resided. "It looks like you're trying a new hairstyle, with little points all over the place."

He slapped his hand to his hair and groaned. "I guess if we still care after seeing each other at our worst then. . ." He snapped his lips closed, horrified at what he'd almost said and shocked that he'd truly meant it. Where was he headed with that kind of statement? Was he ready to declare himself and choose to stay in Goldendale?

No. As much as he cared for Deborah, he needed to think this through. He must pray before he dove into anything. There was no room for regrets in his life, and he certainly didn't want Deborah to have to deal with the sorrow of a hastily made decision. He'd experienced enough of that as a youth.

"I'm sorry. Please forgive me for speaking out of turn."

She hunched one shoulder and turned her head. "I knew you were teasing. It's all right."

But it wasn't all right. He'd seen the disappointment reflected on her face and watched the joy drain from her eyes before she'd turned away. If only he could find a way to reconcile with his father, or move back to The Dalles and marry Deborah without taking her mother from her home.

"Here. I'll help you pack these and take them to the parlor. In fact, if you want to go clear the mantel, I'll be a few minutes behind you, then you can set these out. We can even find fir boughs to tuck around them if you'd like." He kept his voice light, hoping her smile would return—praying he hadn't hurt her too deeply—again.

A few minutes later he arrived in the cozy parlor that his mother had loved so much. Deborah had removed the old clock from the wide oak mantel and readied it for the holy family that would reside there.

He breathed easier, loving Deborah's excitement as she clasped her hands in front of her waist and rocked back and forth from her tiptoes to her heels. "I'll set the crate on the chair where you can easily reach it. I need to make one more trip to the barn. Do you want me to wait and help you set up the figures?"

She shook her head. "No, thank you. I'd love to do it, if you don't mind. Then you can tell me what you think when you return and help me move them if they need it."

He nodded then stepped forward, unable to resist any longer. As he drew close, she froze, staring up at him with an expectant expression. He lifted a finger and tucked a loose curl behind her ear then stroked her cheek. "I do care, Deborah. I wasn't teasing upstairs. I simply don't know how to make it all work, but I care. Can you accept that much for now?"

She looked at him, her eyes brimming with tears. "Yes. I think so. But I'm afraid."

"I'll talk to you first if I decide to leave. I promise."

She wiped her damp cheek and stepped away. "But you won't promise not to leave?"

He hesitated, not sure how to reply. His heart longed to promise he'd stay forever—that he'd never leave her again—but could he keep that promise and not take her away from the mother she needed to care for? It all came back to the problem of five years ago. His father wouldn't tolerate him living in this house or being part of his life if he didn't take up farming, and Curt couldn't imagine abandoning his woodworking.

"I'll promise to do my best to find a way to make this work. I promise to pray, and I ask that you do the same. Can that be enough for today?"

She gave a silent nod then smiled. "It can. Now, let me get busy." She waved him toward the door. "You do what you need to do, and let me rejoice in the beauty of this Nativity."

⸺

Curt rushed through the chores he'd put off too long, knowing it would be one more strike against him if his father noticed they weren't done on time. He longed to return to the woman who'd captured his heart at a deeper level than he'd thought possible. He realized now he hadn't really loved her as a wayward, eighteen-year-old boy—not in the way she deserved to be loved. He had been too selfish, too thoughtless at the time. But what was he now, if he couldn't set aside his own desires and show her true love?

He hurried to the house, wanting to see her again, praying they could find a way to sort through this dilemma. Pushing open the front door, he stepped inside then closed it and drew a deep breath. He strode through the entry and stopped just inside the parlor door in time to see his father raise a fist in the air and shake it.

The older man's bellow filled the room. "What is going on here? Where did you get those?"

Deborah stood pressed against the wall next to the fireplace, bewilderment covering her face. Curt strode across the room and stopped by her side. He took her hand in his and turned to confront his red-faced father. "Quit shouting, Pa. You're scaring her. You can do that with me but not Deborah."

The red didn't fade from his father's face, and his entire body shook, but the force of his words diminished a little. "I asked you a question, and I demand an answer. Where did those come from, and why have you put them on my mantel?"

Deborah squeezed Curt's hand then released it. "I found them in the attic while sorting through boxes, sir. I assumed they were a family heirloom that you'd forgotten about and that you might enjoy displaying them. I apologize for not asking you first."

The tension seemed to ease from his father's stiff frame as a shudder ran through him. "I don't want them there. Pack them back in the box and put them in the attic. Or take them out to the refuse pile for all I care. I never want to see them again."

Curt placed his hand on Deborah's shoulder as she moved toward the mantel. "Wait, please." He leveled a hard gaze on his father. "What's going on here? I'm not tossing this work of art. Where did it come from? Was it grandfather's?"

Color started to build in the older man's face again, and he swiveled and headed for the door. "Don't ask questions about what doesn't concern you." He stormed out of the room, and the front door slammed so hard the pieces on the mantel shivered.

Deborah sank into the nearest chair and put her hands over her face. "What have I done? Your father must hate me for touching something I shouldn't have."

Curt knelt beside her and cradled one of her hands in his own. "Look at me, dearest." He waited until she complied. "This is not your fault. You followed his instructions by going through the boxes, so you did nothing wrong. I'll help box them up and take you home. There's no need for you to do any more today. Or ever, for that matter. If you choose not to return, no one will blame you."

She burrowed her hand deeper inside his. "I'm truly not afraid of your father; he just startled me. I thought he'd be pleased, especially if I'd found something his father made. I wish I knew what was wrong and how to help."

Curt shook his head. "I've wondered most of my life about why he despises my grandfather's woodworking. I've never understood, and he won't talk about it. Don't worry yourself. It's his problem, not yours."

"But he's your father, Curt. We need to care about what's worrying him."

"I know, dear, but I've tried, and it's never done any good." He released her hand and smiled. "Now, will you let me take you home?"

"I don't think so. We'll take these up to the attic then I want to finish the boxes you uncovered." She gave him a warm smile. "Truly, I'm fine, and when I go home, I can drive myself. Your father has been so kind to Ma and me over the years. He's allowed one outburst when something is bothering him."

Curt stood and moved to the mantel. "How about we pack these, and then I'll take them up while you work on something else downstairs?"

"All right, thank you."

They finished in a companionable silence, and then Curt toted the crate to the attic. He tacked the lid on then perched on the hard surface, his chin propped on his hands. That scene with his father had shaken him more than he'd realized. He'd been especially disturbed by the shock on Deborah's face. There was no way he could return to The Dalles and leave her behind.

He knew that now. He loved her more than his passion for woodworking. Maybe it was time to declare himself and do his best to mend fences with Papa, even if that meant returning to farmwork and building furniture on the side. Surely he could work something out to satisfy them both.

He lunged to his feet as relief flooded through him, then took the stairs as fast as he could, eager to share his decision with Deborah and see if she'd be willing to be his wife. He didn't want to startle her, so he slowed his pace and walked quietly toward the living room, pausing when he heard his father's voice. It was quieter than last time, but Curt wasn't about to allow the man to bully Deborah or chastise her again. He reached the open doorway and paused, wanting to understand what he might be dealing with before bursting in.

He leaned closer to better hear his father.

"I'm sorry for my behavior, Deborah. It was unkind of me to take my anger out on you. I hope you'll forgive me."

Curt heaved a sigh and relaxed. He didn't want to walk in and embarrass his father when he'd humbled himself to this degree. Better to wait till Deborah accepted the apology and the conversation moved to something new.

Deborah's soft voice barely reached his ears. "It's all right, Mr. Warren, truly. I'm so sorry my actions caused you pain, but neither Curt nor I knew the Nativity would do so. It's a lovely piece, one I'd be proud to call my own. I would never have brought it out if I'd known you didn't care to see it displayed."

The older man harrumphed then cleared his throat. "Speaking of Curt, there's something I feel I must say, if you're willing to listen."

There was no response, and Curt assumed she must have given silent assent, as he heard his father rush on.

"I'm afraid you're going to get your heart broken again. The boy isn't stable. He has no intention of staying here. He values the new life he's built and plans to leave again. I hope you'll guard yourself against getting involved, and focus on your mother."

Curt waited several long moments for Deborah to reply, praying she'd spurn his father's declaration and declare her own feelings for him. Finally, he heard a rustle of her skirts, and he leaned closer to hear her reply.

"I see. Thank you for sharing your concerns."

Another moment passed with nothing further, and Curt's stomach twisted into a knot. She must no longer trust him. She believed his father's assessment of his character and chose to listen to him rather than take a chance on loving Curt. Not that he blamed her. He'd brought this on himself by leaving the first time and not keeping in touch. He backed away from the doorway as carefully as he could and left the house, his heart too sore to listen further.

Chapter 5

Deborah thought long and hard about what her answer should be to Curt's father—a man she'd come to respect and care for over the years since her own father had died. She didn't want to reject his declaration outright, but she didn't believe he understood his son or had noted how much he'd changed. She gripped her hands in her lap and worked to compose herself then lifted her eyes to his.

"I'm sorry you feel that way, Mr. Warren. I know Curt disappointed and hurt you when he left the first time, but I believe he's a changed man. I can't say for sure he won't leave again, but if he does, I believe it will be because he's prayed and thinks it's the right thing to do. He promised he'll talk with me before he makes a final decision, and I trust him. I wish you could open your heart and see the man he's become."

"Humph." Mr. Warren jerked upright from his stance against the wall. "Then he has you fooled, the same way he fooled his mother. She always believed he'd come home one day a changed man, serving the Lord and willing to settle down, but he never did. The boy never had any real faith of his own. He wanted his own way and wasn't willing to pray about anything. What makes you think he will now?"

"Because he told me." Deborah bit her lip, not willing to share that Mr. Colson had been more of a fatherly influence on Curt's life than the man standing before her. But she must tell him something. "He said that circumstances and people where he lives now had opened his eyes to the truth of the Gospel—that he sees what his immaturity cost others and how he'd lived a selfish life. He's changed, Mr. Warren. Curt's made a true commitment, and I believe he'll walk it out."

"I hope you're right, but I hoped that before and nothing came of it." His voice was gruff, and he shook his head. "I'll try to keep an open mind, though, and not be so quick to judge. I thank you for telling me. I just wish he'd done so himself."

Deborah rose to her feet and stepped close, placing her hand on his arm. "I think he's afraid to, sir—afraid that you might reject him again."

The man reared back as though he'd been burned. "I love my boy. That's a foolish thing for him to think or say. Besides, he left, not me. He's the one who needs to apologize and make things right. I'll forgive him if he does that, but it's on his shoulders, not mine."

He pivoted and walked away, his body stiff and unyielding.

Deborah sighed and shook her head. Mr. Warren hadn't changed as much as she'd hoped. Now she'd better pray his obstinate attitude didn't discourage Curt to the point he'd fulfill his father's dire prediction.

⁓

The next day, Curt finished the morning chores in the barn. He'd done the milking before breakfast and returned now to clean out the stalls. The one thing he enjoyed about farmwork was milking—there was something soothing about the repetitive action and the mesmerizing splash of the milk in the pail.

He was at a total loss as to what to do next. His father had made it clear he didn't want or need his help in the fields or with the few cows he owned, and there was little else to do in this farming community.

If only he had his woodworking tools. Even more than that, he wished Deborah would welcome his presence as she finished sorting his mother's personal items. But he'd determined to give her time—to not press her for a day or two. After the conversation he overheard, he feared she'd lost hope that he'd ever really change.

He pitched a forkful of dirty straw into a pile and wiped his sleeve across his forehead. He couldn't blame her, since he'd not contacted her in the last four years. It had been too hard, knowing things could never work out between them and that she'd probably be married to someone else soon. A friend in Goldendale had written him, letting him know that more than one young man was interested in Deborah, and then wrote again, telling him when she'd gotten engaged. That almost killed him—he was sick for a week and had produced the worst work of his life.

He rested his chin on the handle of the pitchfork. This uncertainty was even worse. When he'd seen her that first day after he'd returned and realized she wasn't married, hope had returned. Now it came close to withering again, and despair gripped him in talons so tight he could barely breathe. Maybe he'd stay in the barn all day until she was gone.

The crunch of buggy wheels on the pebbles outside drew him to a large chink in the wood. Deborah climbed down from the seat and walked to the horse's head. She'd want to unhitch and turn the horse into a stall. Time to quit being a coward. He swung open the door as she reached it, and mustered what he hoped would pass as a pleasant look, but he couldn't manage a smile. "Good morning. I'll unhitch for you if you want to get started inside."

Her brows drew together, and she stared up at him. "Is your father upset again?"

He groaned inwardly. She'd always been too good at reading him, but he didn't see the slightest flicker of personal interest beyond worry about his father. "No, he's fine."

She drew the horse forward into the alley between the stalls but didn't reply.

He extended a hand. "There's no need for you to get your skirts dirty."

She hesitated then sniffed. "Fine. If you don't care to talk about it, I'll get to work." The barn door creaked again as she let herself out, but Curt didn't stir. It hurt too much to see the woman he loved walking away from him. Now he understood a tiny bit what she must have felt all those years ago, when he left Goldendale and didn't return.

☙

Deborah flounced out of the barn but slowed her pace halfway to the house, her steps beginning to drag. It was obvious something was bothering Curt, but he didn't appear interested in telling her what it might be. That irritated her even more than his cool reply. When they were young and in love, he'd told her everything—except for how much he must have hated farming. She'd known he chafed at the chores and longed to work with wood for a living, but she'd never truly believed he'd strike off on his own and leave the farm and his father—and her—behind.

She hadn't believed it even when he'd come to the house that horrible day and said he was leaving to apprentice in The Dalles, Oregon. Deep inside, she'd known he'd last a few weeks or months at most and come home to her. But his letters had stopped completely that first year, and her hope had begun to fade.

Her chin lifted then she marched the rest of the way to the house. Maybe she should have married when she'd had the chance.

Her pace slowed—was that fair? Curt could have had a bad morning with his father again and didn't want her to worry. Surely that was the case. Once he finished stabling the mare, he'd come in and help her, as he had the past few days.

She wished she could decorate the house for Christmas. It seemed such a shame that Mr. Warren wouldn't allow her to display the lovely Nativity set. Fir and pine abounded in the region. Her lips curved at a new thought. Maybe Curt would take her in the sleigh to gather some if the snow arrived soon. They'd had several flurries, but it hadn't stayed long, which was certainly not typical for this time of year.

She slipped into the house, wondering if Mr. Warren was around or out in the fields. Drawing off her heavy coat, she headed for Sarah Warren's private room, wanting to finish the last few drawers and a trunk that she had yet to open. Sometimes she felt funny about going through another woman's personal things, but it seemed neither Mr. Warren nor Curt cared to tackle the tasks.

The flat-topped trunk sat under the window. A cream-colored cloth with delicate, hand-stitched embroidery in each corner covered most of the top, with a piece of cut glass perched in the center. Sarah fingered the lovely bowl then set it aside and removed the cloth cover.

She lifted her head and listened, wondering when Curt would come in, then she shoved the thought aside. If he didn't care to spend time with her, she certainly didn't plan to pursue him.

The lid opened with a slight squeak, as though the hinges hadn't been worked in years. She lifted out a tray with shallow, open compartments after giving it a quick glance. It appeared to be mostly sewing supplies that she could sort later. More sewing goods lay beneath, along with a stack of books.

Deborah plucked out the top three and set them aside. The next book caught her attention, as did three more identical ones beneath—all cloth-bound volumes that showed little sign of wear, the corners still crisp, and the dark brown color not dimmed by exposure to light.

She looked at the spine of the one on top and drew in a breath. It appeared to be a journal or diary of some sort, as did the rest. Was she trespassing on Mr. Warren's property again? Her hands trembled as she considered whether to ask him first or place it back inside and shut the lid. But he'd told her only to avoid his room and the desk in the living area—he'd been very explicit that all the items in his wife's rooms were to be thoroughly examined, as he didn't feel up to doing so.

The first page was dated December 26, but there was no indication of ownership. Perhaps if she read a page or two, she might get a sense of whom it belonged to. She supposed it must be Sarah Warren's, although without an identifying year, it could belong to a parent or grandparent. She read the first page with interest, intrigued by the sweeping script and conversational style.

I'm so worried about Jarrod—I wish he would talk to me. Something is wrong, but he won't say what it is. He gave me a lovely gift yesterday, a cut-glass bowl that I plan to keep in my room where I can see it as soon as I awaken. But he's been glum and unresponsive. Not that he didn't show enthusiasm over the shirt I made for him, but he turned aside with very little comment over the whittling knife that I was certain he'd love. I must try to find out what the matter is when he visits again tomorrow.

Deborah turned the page, wondering if it was right to read more but unable to resist the story for long. The second page was dated December 28. Had Sarah had a busy day and been unable to write the day before?

Jarrod came to visit last night so we could talk about wedding plans, but I had a hard time breaking through his silence. Finally, before he left, he went out to his buggy and returned with a crate, which he shoved into my arms. I asked if it was another Christmas gift and assured him he'd already given me enough. He gave a harsh laugh and shook his head. "Not a gift that was meant for you in the beginning, but if you don't take it, I'll destroy it."

I peeked inside the cloth wrappings and was amazed at what met my gaze. A beautiful carved Nativity, each piece intricate. I had withdrawn three when he grabbed one, the figure of a shepherd, and drew back his arm as though he planned to throw it. I stopped him in time and demanded he explain.

"I made it for my father for Christmas," he said. "When he saw it, all he could do was criticize. It was no good. I would never be able to make a living from this type of work. He said he had struggled to provide for our family all these years and I'd do the same, only worse, since I had no talent to speak of. I never want to see them again. Take them and put them away where I can't find them, or I'll burn them."

I saw that he meant it, and I wrapped up the wonderful creations and took the crate to my room. There was no use trying to dissuade him. I will try to broach the subject again in a few days.

Deborah's hand shook as she turned the page, knowing that she was unlocking the key to Mr. Warren's anger at her discovery of the Nativity set in the attic. Would Sarah say any more about it, or was this where the matter was left? The following page shed very little light on the subject.

December 31. I tried talking to Jarrod again tonight about his gift to his father, hoping he might attempt once more to give it to Mr. Warren, but he turned away in obvious pain. I assured him the pieces were magnificent, but he only scoffed. His father is considered one of the best woodworkers in the valley, and he should know whether Jarrod has talent or not. His father had only been able to eke out a living with his woodworking and must farm on the side to get by, so Jarrod believes that farming is the more sensible career.

I told him not to give up on his carving, but he said he'd stored his tools and will never touch them again. His father's words cut deep. The man might have meant well, trying to save his son the pain of being a poor provider, but I fear he's wounded my love's spirit to the point where he might never recover.

More than anything, I want Jarrod to reconcile with his father. I fear that if he doesn't, he'll carry his hurt and bitterness into our marriage and pass it along to any children we might have. I pray that somehow God heals his heart and brings him to a place of peace, before it's too late.

Deborah picked up another journal from the bottom of the pile and glanced at the first page, noting it was penned only a few months before Sarah's death. She turned to the last page and sucked in a quick breath as her eyes caught Curt's name. She read the final paragraph then closed the book, suddenly ashamed of reading such a personal entry. Should she give the diaries to Curt, so he could see his father through his mother's eyes? Or would he be angry at her because she'd read his mother's private thoughts and turn away from her in disgust? She'd put this back where she found it for now and spend a day or two praying before she decided. Maybe God would help her find a way to reconcile the two men before Curt's week was up.

Chapter 6

Curt wished he'd driven over to get Deborah in his buggy so he could offer to drive her home later. The snow was falling and the wind had picked up, but that wasn't what had stopped him. He'd do it if he thought she'd care to have his company, but after what his father had said to her, he doubted that was the case.

He finished harnessing Deborah's horse, knowing she'd be leaving soon. It had taken all his willpower to stay away from the part of the house where she was working today.

He sucked in a breath and patted the mare's neck then strode to the house. He'd see what her attitude toward him might be then take it from there. Swinging open the door, he almost collided with Deborah. Her words were stiff as he glimpsed her solemn expression. "I apologize. I'll slow down and watch where I'm going next time." No smile warmed her features; no light shone in her eyes.

"I'll drive you home, if you'd like. I can keep the buggy and drive over to get you in the morning."

She shook her head, her dark curls dancing under her bonnet. She buttoned the neck of her heavy coat as she moved past him, not meeting his eyes. "I've driven that short section of road hundreds of times without you, Curt. There's no reason for you to come out in the cold."

"I don't mind." He bit his tongue before he blurted out how much he longed to spend time with her—how much he'd missed her company today and regretted not offering to help. If only she'd say something to let him know how she felt.

"Thank you, but no. I don't care to be without a conveyance, in case Ma needs a doctor. Besides, if the snow moves in and gets deep, I'll probably stay home tomorrow." Sadness flickered over her face as she glanced at him.

He scrambled to think of something to say but couldn't come up with a thing. Had she believed Pa that he planned to leave? Didn't she trust him after he'd told her he'd discuss his plans with her, if he made the decision to return to The Dalles?

Curt stepped aside. "As you wish. But if you'd like to come tomorrow, I'll hitch the sleigh and pick you up—if there's enough snow."

Her eyes lit with something akin to expectation, then after several seconds she looked away. "I do have a few things to finish, so that would be nice. I'd better hurry on home now and fix supper before Ma starts to worry."

"How is she?" Curt walked beside her to the barn and tugged open the door, anxious to get them both out of the wind.

"A little better. I'm not so worried about leaving her now. I'm being cautious about wanting a buggy close-by, but I don't think she'll take a turn for the worse."

They continued in silence, and Curt shoved down the hope trying to bubble to the surface. Just because Mrs. Summers was better now didn't mean it would last. The poor woman had struggled with health issues for years, and Curt well remembered Deborah's fear when they were young that she'd lose her mother soon.

He helped her into the buggy and held her hand a few moments longer than necessary. "Deborah?"

She settled onto the seat and released his hand to pick up the reins. "Yes?" The word had a breathless aspect.

"Is everything. . .all right? Is there anything you'd like to tell me?"

"That *I'd* like to tell *you?*" She shook her head. "No. Should there be?"

"I suppose not." He hesitated a moment then rushed on, still praying she'd show some indication of her feelings. "Well, I won't keep you. The wind will cut through your warm clothing, so you'd better hurry." He kept his voice neutral, not wanting to press her but wishing she'd feel safe to confide her fears.

She averted her head and stared between the horse's ears. "Yes, you're right." She shook the reins and clucked to the mare. "Get along there. It's time we got home."

Curt stared after the departing buggy, praying he could find a way to make things right.

∽

Deborah looked out the window at dawn, hoping for enough snow that Curt would come for her in the sleigh. Unfortunately, the wind had blown the storm somewhere else before it had a chance to drop more than an inch or two. Her horse would have no problem drawing the buggy, and the runners on the sleigh would scrape and bump over the ruts and rocks in the road.

Two hours later, with her mother fed, the kitchen clean, and a pot of stew simmering on the stove for dinner, Deborah pulled her horse to a stop in front of the Warren home. She waited for Curt's cheerful whistle but didn't hear it, so she climbed down and tied the mare to the hitching rail. The wind had calmed, and the horse would be fine while she saw if anyone was home.

She knocked on the door, not expecting anyone to answer, and was startled when it swung open and Mr. Warren stood inside.

His face crinkled in a welcoming smile. "Deborah. Come in out of the cold. I didn't expect you today. You've done so much already. I assumed you'd take a day or two to get caught up at home."

"Is Curt here?" She wished she could retract her words as the smile on the older man's face dimmed.

"I sent him to town to get a few supplies. He should be back in an hour or two, although I don't expect he'll be around much longer. He's getting itchy feet, I can tell. Just you wait and see, he'll disappear soon." He wagged his head then took her coat as she slipped out of it.

Deborah drew in a quick breath. "Mr. Warren? Would you have a minute to talk?"

He wrinkled his forehead but nodded. "It's always a pleasure to visit with you, Deborah. I have a pot of coffee on. Come into the kitchen and sit."

They settled down at the table with their mugs. Fragrant steam rose, making Deborah's mouth water. She almost decided not to broach the subject of his wife's journal, in the hope of continuing this genial atmosphere, but forced herself to press on. "I found some things while sorting items in Mrs. Warren's trunk that I wanted to ask you about."

Pain washed Mr. Warren's features, and then he nodded. "Go ahead."

She bit her lip then plunged forward. "It's a set of journals."

He brightened, and a smile curved his mouth. "Ah, yes. Sarah was always one to write down her thoughts. Someday I'll read her journals. But I thought she'd given me all of them for safekeeping. You say you found more?"

"Yes. In the trunk in her room. They didn't have her name on them, and I wasn't sure who they belonged to or what I should do with them." Sudden panic assailed her as she realized she'd have to admit she'd read a few pages. "I'm so sorry. I fear I've overstepped again. I read parts of them, as I thought it might be from an older relative. I got so caught up in her wonderful narrative that I'd read more than I planned before I realized. I do hope you'll forgive me."

He grinned. "My girl could tell a story, that's for sure. I don't mind you reading it, as long as it wasn't too personal."

"Well. . ." She winced and averted her gaze. "It was personal. She shared how proud she was of your talent. Then, on the last page, years later, she talked about Curt and his love for the same craft—carving and working with wood. She was so sad—she longed for the two of you to reconcile. . ." She sucked in a deep breath then rushed on. "She talked about the Nativity you made for your father."

Mr. Warren's expression turned to granite, his hands so tight around his mug it looked like he might crush it. "I don't want to talk about that."

Deborah couldn't help herself. "But I care for you and Curt, Mr. Warren. I understand your wife's pain and longing for the two of you to reconcile. He's following in his grandfather's footsteps, but they're your footsteps as well. Curt longs for your approval and acceptance. Please think about it, for his mother's sake, if not for mine." She pushed up from her chair. "I think I'll go home now. I've imposed enough. If you still want me to come tomorrow, I'll finish up then."

He gave a bare nod, his lips pressed in a tight line. "Tomorrow is fine."

"I'll see myself out." She moved with heavy tread to the door, wondering yet again if she'd done the right thing. Mr. Warren had only recently lost his wife, but if something didn't change soon, he'd lose his son, as well.

⁕

Curt dragged himself out of bed the next morning. Deborah had seemed so preoccupied and distant of late. Pa hadn't come in the house the entire evening last night but stayed in the barn until long after bedtime. Could his father be so disgruntled with him that he didn't care to even be in the same house?

It was time to return to The Dalles, even though his heart longed to remain here. Swiftly, he packed his saddlebags with his few clothes and personal items and headed to the kitchen. He found a paper and pencil and scribbled a note for his father, on the chance he might not see him before he left. This time he wouldn't disappear and not return—but he had to talk to Mr. Colson and explain that he needed more time to decide a course of action. He wanted to marry Deborah, but it might take weeks, if not months, to regain her trust.

He'd ride to her farm and say good-bye—he'd given his word not to leave again without telling her. Slinging the saddlebags over his shoulder, he headed outside. There was no point in delaying this. Hopefully Pa would come in from feeding the cows in the pasture, but if he didn't, he'd find the note and know his son would return. It should only take him a few days to ride to The Dalles and back, as long as a snowstorm didn't dump too much snow to make the return trip.

His stomach churned, and he swallowed hard, not wanting to give way to grief. What if Deborah would never accept his suit or learn to trust him? It didn't matter. He'd wait the rest of his life, if that's what it took, and put up with whatever his father saw fit to dish out, for as long as the man continued to live. If only he and Pa could repair their relationship. He grunted. Not that there was much to repair. They'd been close years ago, before he'd decided he didn't want to farm and turned to woodworking instead.

He saddled his horse and slung the bags over its rump then secured them with leather straps. The air had a harsh bite to it, and he buttoned up his coat and tucked the woolen scarf that Deborah had given him so many years ago around his neck.

The front door of the house banged, and Curt's head whipped up. Pa must be back. But why hadn't he come to the barn first? He waited, wondering if he should go inside or wait for Pa to read the note and come see if he'd gone. He swung into the saddle, his decision made. If Pa wanted to talk, he'd come out. If he didn't show up in the next minute or two, he'd ride for Deborah's farm.

The barn door crashed open and Pa stood silhouetted in the dim light of the winter morning. He strode forward and grabbed the horse's reins. "What do you think you're doing? What's wrong with you, boy? Get off that horse. I've got something to say."

Chapter 7

Deborah drew her buggy to a stop in front of Mr. Warren's house and swiveled toward her mother, happy Ma felt strong enough to come. She turned toward the barn. Was that Mr. Warren she heard bellowing at the top of his voice? What in the world could be the matter? She prayed he wasn't injured or sick and calling for help. She plucked up her skirts to keep them from dragging in the mud and rushed toward the open door.

"Deborah! That you?" Mr. Warren's voice boomed from the interior. "Come in here."

Hands shaking, Deborah turned to her mother. "Will you be all right if I run in for a minute, or would you like to come?"

Ma smiled. "From the sound of things, you might need some support. I'll stay inside the door in case I'm not wanted, but I'd like to come."

Deborah tied the horse to the rail and helped her mother down, then hurried inside. She waited for her eyes to adjust then spotted Curt standing beside his saddled horse, and Mr. Warren all aquiver beside him. She left her mother by the door and walked forward. "I'm here. Is something wrong?"

Mr. Warren beckoned to her, and as she drew near, he took her hand, giving it a light squeeze. "Do you love this son of mine?"

She gasped and felt the blood drain from her face. "Mr. Warren! What kind of question is that?"

He swiveled to Curt. "You've been mooning over Deborah every day since you got home, but now you're going to ride off and leave again. What's wrong with you, boy?"

Curt stared at his father, seemingly unable to find a reply. His gaze shifted to Deborah and stark longing blazed from his eyes.

Mr. Warren drew Deborah close by his side and wrapped an arm around her. "Deborah Summers is the best thing God's brought to our lives since your mother, but you don't seem to have the good sense to figure that out. Why aren't you staying here and trying to win her, instead of acting like a man who doesn't have a lick of sense?"

Curt shook himself and straightened. "Didn't you read my note? I told you I was going to stop to see Deborah on my way out of town and that I'd be back soon. I do love her, but from what I can tell the past few days, she doesn't feel the same." He grasped his horse's reins and patted his neck. "I heard what you told her a few days ago, that I'd leave her and not return this time. Apparently, she believed you."

Relief hit Deborah so hard she thought she might swoon. "So that's why you've been acting as though I don't exist?" She moved away from Mr. Warren and touched Curt's sleeve. "If you'd listened a minute or two longer, you'd have heard me tell your father I don't believe that, and that I care for you."

Curt's lips parted, but nothing came out. "I'm so sorry. I'm ashamed I didn't give you a chance to explain." The words were mere whispers.

Mr. Warren shook his head. "Then you'd better ask her to marry you, boy. Women like Deborah and your ma only come along once in a lifetime. You let her go, you'll live to regret it." He scrubbed at his chin with his fingers. "I don't regret a day I spent with Sarah, but I do regret plenty of other days. I've not been the father I should have been to you."

He glanced at Deborah. "I stayed up half the night reading Sarah's journals. I'm ashamed of the pain I caused her all these years."

He turned his attention back to Curt. "And I'm ashamed of the way I've treated you, and all because of the anger I harbored against my own father. I made the Nativity set for him for Christmas a year before I married your mother. He cut me deeply when he rejected my gift, and all these years I've taken it out on you, because you wanted to follow his chosen path rather than mine."

His gaze dropped for a moment, and then he raised his eyes and met Curt's. "I hope you'll be able to forgive this old man his foolish ways and accept something I'd like to give you both." He tapped Curt on the chest with his finger. "But first, do you plan on marrying this gal?"

Curt smiled. "If she'll have me." He took a step toward Deborah then hesitated and glanced toward the door. "Mrs. Summers? I need to ask your permission first. Would you do me the honor of allowing me to ask for your daughter's hand?"

Deborah pivoted, her heart swelling with delight as she spotted her mother's beaming face.

Ma walked toward them and stopped beside Mr. Warren. "I agree with your father, Curt. It's better late than never, and I hope she has the good sense to say yes."

Curt bowed his head then turned his attention back to Deborah. "I'm sorry I misjudged you. I've loved you for as long as I can remember. Like Pa said, I've made some foolish choices, but all that's behind me now. Would you make me the happiest man on earth and marry me?"

Joy spiraled through Deborah like a spring wind kicking up its heels in a grove of trees, setting the leaves to dancing. "I will, Curt. I love you, too. I always have."

He took her hands in his. "We'll make it work. I'll help take care of your mother and work your farm, if that's what you want. I'll even give up my woodworking. I plan to be a good provider, and I don't want to ever let you down."

Mr. Warren strode across the barn to a workbench covered by tack and other supplies. "You keep doing what God designed you to do, Son, and you'll never let her down. Now, I hope both of you will accept this as a wedding gift—if you see fit to have it in your home, that is." He removed a large cloth to reveal the beautiful Nativity set then stepped aside as she and Curt drew close.

A small gasp left her mother's lips, and Deborah glanced at her, noting a tear trickling down her cheek. Had Sarah shared her husband's pain with her mother and Ma had kept it a secret all these years?

Awe filled Deborah as she saw the pieces in the light filtering through the window above the workbench. Each one had been cleaned and polished until they shone with a burnished light. They were even more beautiful than she remembered.

Curt breathed out an exclamation of wonder. "You made these, Pa? They're exquisite. I've never seen such fine craftsmanship." He gazed at his father as he cradled a figure in his hands. "This is the finest wedding gift I could imagine."

Tears welled in Mr. Warren's eyes. "You truly think so? My pa told me they were no good, and I believed him. I was younger than you were when you went away, and I decided never to touch wood again, other than hammering a board across a stall or building a crate for storage."

As the four stood in reverent silence gazing at the Nativity, Deborah looped her arm through her mother's, and Curt put his arm around her shoulder and his other hand on his father's shoulder. "I agree with Curt. This is a precious gift, and one we'll treasure forever. And it will look perfect at our wedding, if Curt wants to marry me on Christmas Day."

Curt turned adoring eyes on her and whooped. "You'd marry me next week? That soon? Don't you need to make a dress?"

She shook her head. "I've always wanted to wear Ma's dress. It fits me perfectly, and I love it. This Nativity will be the centerpiece on a table at the front of the church, and that's all the beauty we need, besides our love and that of our families." She stood on tiptoe and kissed Curt square on the lips then blushed and peeked at Mr. Warren. "That is, if you don't object to us marrying so soon."

Curt stiffened beside her, but Mr. Warren chuckled and threw his arms around them both, drawing them into a hug. "I feel as though my soul has gained peace at last, and a Christmas wedding sounds perfect to me. Don't just stand there, boy. I'll unsaddle your horse while you kiss your bride-to-be."

About the Author

Miralee Ferrell and her husband, Allen, live on eleven acres in Washington State. Miralee loves interacting with people, ministering at her church (she is a certified lay counselor with the AACC), riding her horse, and playing with her dogs. An award-winning and bestselling author, she speaks at various women's functions and has taught at writers' conferences. Since 2007, she's had ten books released, both in women's contemporary fiction and historical romance. Miralee recently started a newsletter, and you can sign up for it on her website/blog. www.miraleeferrell.com

The Evergreen Bride

by Pam Hillman

Chapter 1

Samuel Frazier's heart skittered into double time when Annabelle Denson rushed into the sawmill. She grabbed his arm, her touch sending a jolt of awareness coursing through him.

"Papa said I could go!" Annabelle's evergreen eyes danced beneath the woolen scarf draped over her hair.

Had Pastor Denson given in, then? Samuel looked away, dread filling his chest. "Where?"

Annabelle swatted his arm and moved away to sit on the low stool he'd made just for her. Every day, after she rang the school bell and the Sipsey Creek schoolchildren swarmed out of the schoolhouse and raced toward home, Samuel dusted the sawdust from the stool, hoping she'd stop by on her way home. Most days she did.

"To Illinois, of course. As if you didn't know."

Of course.

It was all she'd talked about for weeks, for months, actually. A trip to Chicago, Illinois, to visit her cousin Lucy. So she could have a white Christmas. He turned away from the excitement on her face, back to the board he'd been working to smooth. He made another swipe at the piece, the scrape of the plane filling the void left by his silence. It wasn't his place to derail Annabelle's dream of a little snow-filled adventure. But maybe when she returned, when he and Jack got the old sawmill fully operational again, he'd get up the nerve...

Annabelle tossed the woolen scarf back, and the feeble sunlight streaming through the open shop door landed on hair the same dark mahogany as the hope chest he'd made for her last Christmas. She pulled an envelope from her pocket and waved it in his face. "Aunt Eugenia is going to visit, and Papa said I could go, too. He says the train isn't a safe place for a lady traveling alone."

"You don't agree?"

"In this day and age?" Her nose scrunched up, reminding him of Lilly, her two-year-old sister, refusing to eat boiled okra. But, although Annabelle might be cute as a button, she definitely wasn't a child. Not by a long shot. She'd turn twenty next summer. "Goodness, Samuel, it's almost the turn of the century, and women travel alone all the time these days."

"Some women, maybe, but not the sister and daughter of a respected minister from the Mississippi pine belt." He couldn't resist teasing her. "Maybe Reverend Denson should reconsider."

"Oh no, he's already agreed, so it's settled. He can't change his mind now." Annabelle clasped the letter to her chest with both hands. "My very own white Christmas. It'll be glorious."

The snow couldn't be half as glorious as the glow on her face as she talked about it. Reluctantly, Samuel lowered his gaze and brushed the film of sawdust off the board. Smooth as silk and perfect for a slat in the rocking chair Reverend Denson had ordered for his wife. "But you'll miss Christmas here with—"

With us. With me.

He bit back the words he wanted to say and finished instead, "—with your family."

"They'll hardly know I'm gone come Christmas morning. And besides, Jack will probably spend the entire day with Maggie's family anyway." She swiveled on the stool. "By the way, where is my brother? I can't wait to tell him my news."

"Gone to take a load of logs to Abe's." He and Jack snaked logs out of the woods around Sipsey Creek and hauled them to Abe Jensen's sawmill twice a week. Two days lost in travel that could be spent harvesting trees if they had their own circular saw.

"Why does Jack always go?"

"You know Jack." He shrugged. "He likes to be out and about, meeting people. And besides, I've got to finish this rocking chair."

Annabelle stood and ran her hand along one of the rungs of the half-finished chair. "Mama's going to love this."

The scent of rose petals, or lavender, or whatever women tucked between the folds of their clothes in a chest of drawers still clung to her dress even after a day of teaching. Flustered by her nearness, he concentrated on the chair and muttered, "Hope so."

"Of course she will." She dusted off her hands. "Speaking of Mama, I need to get on home and help her with supper. Don't forget to tell Jack my news."

"I'll tell him."

She headed toward the door but whirled around, cocked her head to one side, and studied him, tiny frown lines on her forehead. "You're excited for me, aren't you, Samuel?"

"Of course I am, Annie-girl. It's what you've always dreamed of." He tossed a handful of sawdust toward her. She dodged away, laughing as she brushed the flecks from the hem of her brown skirt. "Just don't run off up north and forget all about us poor ol' folks here at home."

"I'd never forget y'all." She flashed him a bright smile as she headed out the wide barnlike door he'd propped open to let in a bit of sunlight. "See you Sunday."

Samuel watched her go, her dark skirts swaying with each step. The loblolly pines, with their bright wintergreen needles that towered along each side of the road, marked her path, and he couldn't help but remember how her green eyes lit up with excitement when she told him about her trip.

As she rounded the bend out of sight, the smile slipped from his face and he turned back, his gaze surveying the dilapidated building he and Jack owned. Summer before last, they'd bought it on credit when Old Man Porter had called it quits. They'd poured every dollar they could into the business, working their fingers to the bone to get it up and running again.

They could fill small orders for lumber by cutting boards with a crosscut saw in a saw pit, but Samuel dreamed of a steam engine and circular saw like Abe's. They'd never make a decent living with just a crosscut and the sweat of their brow. Porter hadn't been able to make a go of it either. He'd said he couldn't compete with the newfangled saws. But Jack and Samuel were young and eager.

And broke.

But they had dreams of expanding, one step at a time. In the meantime, he'd keep making furniture and hope chests, snaking logs out of the swamp, and hauling them to Abe. But someday, he and Jack would have their own steam-powered saw.

And then he'd court Annabelle.

Chapter 2

As soon as supper was over, dishes washed, and the kitchen spotless, Annabelle excused herself to write a letter to Lucy. An excited buzz built inside as she penned questions, asking her cousin what to pack, how many changes of clothes she would need, how many outings Lucy had planned.

She frowned, thinking about how fashion might be different in Illinois than it was in Mississippi. Was there time for Lucy to send her a couple of catalogs of the latest styles? She tapped her pencil against the letter, thinking. Between teaching and helping her mother around the house, she didn't have time to make a new dress. She'd just have to make do. Scrapping the idea of a new outfit, she continued her letter, urging Lucy to ask her father about accompanying Annabelle back home to Mississippi.

Lucy, you really should come for a visit. It's been seven years since you moved away. You tell me that none of the young men there catch your fancy. Well, there are plenty here that I think you'd do well to set your cap for.

Do you remember Amos Rosenthal? He's taking over his father's dry goods store and would be a good catch. And Willie Godfries started working for the railroad just last week. No, never mind about Willie. From what I've heard, he's a bit wild, although I shouldn't say things like that without proof. But as they say, where's there's smoke, there's fire.

Annabelle studied her letter, trying to think of someone else that would entice Lucy to come back to Mississippi. She grinned. If her cousin came for a visit and just happened to fall in love with someone local, then they'd get to see each other all the time.

Her gaze landed on the hope chest in the corner of her room.

Samuel.

Oh my goodness! Why hadn't she thought of it before? Samuel would be perfect for Lucy. She chewed her pencil, trying to think of a way to describe her brother's partner and best friend. Her words filled the page.

I have the most perfect beau in mind for you. Do you remember Jack's partner, Samuel Frazier? He and Jack have started their own business, and he makes the most exquisite furniture. He made my hope chest last Christmas. I'm sure I told you about it. It's so beautiful, and sturdy, too.

But I'm sure you're not interested in the quality of his furniture, are you?

Samuel is tall, but not too tall, mind you. And he's very handsome, at least all the girls say so. Mama would skin me alive if she saw this letter, but he really is just perfect. He does like to tease me, though, and that's a bit bothersome, but it's all in good fun. I don't think he realizes it, but sometimes I can tell when he's teasing because he'll act like he's ignoring me by keeping his hands busy, but then he'll give me this funny little crooked smile.

Annabelle stopped writing and let her thoughts wander back to the afternoon at the sawmill, trying to visualize how Samuel had looked when she'd barged inside. He'd been engrossed in his work, his large hands smoothing a slat for her mother's rocking chair, his hair mussed from a hard day's work, a late afternoon shadow covering his lean cheeks.

She bit her lip.

How could she explain to Lucy how Samuel's dark hair curled over his ears just so, even though he'd been promising to get a haircut for weeks? Or how his brown eyes twinkled when he teased her about her trip to Illinois? Or even how respectful he was when her mother invited him over for Sunday dinner? He always thanked Mama for the meal and never asked for seconds of dessert.

She smiled. But that didn't stop Jack from reaching across the table and cutting two extra large pieces of pie and plopping one on Samuel's plate. Samuel never said a word, just threw her a wink and gave her his crooked little grin.

Her heart tripped a little at the thought of that grin. Without even trying, he'd probably gotten his way with that dimpled smile from the time he was knee-high to a cricket.

But how to explain all that in a letter to Lucy, in such a way that would make her cousin want to come to Mississippi to visit? She shook her head. She'd just have to tell Lucy more about Samuel when she got there. It shouldn't be too hard to convince her. Pleased with her plan, Annabelle finished her letter and addressed it.

She stored her writing supplies in her hope chest, smiling as she ran her hand over the smooth lid, stained dark and polished to a high sheen. Samuel did make beautiful furniture, and he really did have a nice smile.

He'd be the perfect beau.

Chapter 3

"Timber!"

Samuel scrambled out of the way, Jack right on his heels. They didn't stop until they'd put a safe distance between themselves and the severed pine. Samuel held his breath. Would it fall true?

For a split second, time stood still; then a faint groan wafted across the clearing. The sound sent a shaft of excitement through Samuel's veins, along with a healthy dose of fear in case the tree went wild.

The faint cracking and groaning grew louder until a great rent split the air and the trunk tilted, slowly at first, then gaining speed as it fell toward the forest floor littered with pine needles.

Limbs the size of a man's thigh split and rent the air with cracking, popping noises. Mere seconds later, the long, tall, loblolly pine slapped against the forest floor with a heavy thud that shook the ground where they stood.

Samuel let out his breath and slapped Jack on the back. His partner grinned, wiped the sweat glistening on his brow, and settled his hat more firmly on his head. "Mighty glad that's done."

"Laying 'er down is just the beginning."

"The rest can wait. I'm starving." Jack walked away, and Samuel followed, stomach growling. Come to think of it, lunch did sound like a good idea.

They found the rucksacks they'd hung on a low-lying limb to keep safe from prowling critters and settled in for a well-deserved break. They tucked into thick slabs of ham and leftover biscuits Jack's mother had sent with him that morning.

Samuel swallowed the last of a biscuit and rested his head against the rough pine at his back. If they didn't have to delimb the tree and snake it out to the road, he'd take a short nap right then and there.

"You should see Abe's new circular saw." Jack spread his arms wide. "Forty-eight-inch blade. I've never seen the like."

Samuel snapped to attention. "Did you ask him about his old saw?"

"Yep." Jack picked up a pine needle and threaded it through his fingers.

"He'll let us have it for half the profits on the lumber we cut. But we have to dismantel it and haul it ourselves."

"What about the saw blade?"

"Still has all its teeth. All it needs is a good sharpening. You think it's worth it?"

"Maybe." Samuel pondered Jack's question. "Having a circular saw, even one that small, would be better than using the crosscut in the saw pit."

"But on halves? That don't seem rightly fair for Abe to get half of what we make sawing logs."

"It's his saw, and we can't afford to buy it outright." Samuel shrugged. "And besides, he'd keep a tally and eventually we'd own it, fair and square."

"We'd still need bigger machinery eventually, if we're gonna make a go of it."

"Gotta start somewhere."

"I know, but time's a wastin'."

Samuel squinted at his friend. "Maggie?"

"Yeah." Jack tossed the pine needle away, and it bounced off the nearest tree.

"Have you popped the question?"

"Not yet." Jack grimaced as he swiped crumbs from his trousers.

"You know she'll say yes." Why wouldn't she? Jack and Maggie had been courting nigh on to two years now. Everybody expected them to get married. It wasn't a matter of if, but when.

Jack cleared his throat. "I've been meaning to talk to you about that."

Samuel arched a brow. Jack's gaze met his then skittered away to focus on the evergreens swaying in the breeze high above their heads. He acted plumb nervous, and nothing fazed happy-go-lucky Jack.

"I can't ask Maggie to marry me without a place to live. And we barely squeaked by last year, what with buying that freight wagon and another pair of mules."

"Is that all that's stopping you?"

"I'd ask her tomorrow if I knew I could provide for her." Jack's eyes took on a look of desperation. "Her pa's been making noises about moving on, out west somewhere."

No surprise there. It was a known fact that Maggie's pa had wandering feet and uprooted his family every couple of years. Jack's reasons for not asking Maggie to marry him were the same ones that kept Samuel from courting Jack's sister, except Samuel had plenty of time to get up the nerve to court Annabelle.

Jack didn't have the luxury of waiting.

"Then let's accept Abe's offer. As soon as we get the saw up and running, we can start cutting lumber to sell, and also stockpile some to build a house for Maggie." Jack stood, slapped his hat against his pants, and grumbled, "And when are we going to have time to do all this cuttin' and sawin'? We're already working from sunup to sundown."

"You're just gonna have to do less courtin' and more working. Come on, let's get started. If we get this pine snaked out, we'll earmark some more trees before nightfall."

Chapter 4

"Do you think it might snow?" Annabelle asked Maggie as the congregation filed out of church after Sunday morning worship.

"I doubt it." Maggie pulled on a frayed woolen coat and buttoned it up. "It'll just be cold and wet and muddy, but it probably won't snow."

"Jack thinks it will. Here I am headed to Illinois in a couple of weeks and everyone's talking about it snowing here in Sipsey." Annabelle laughed as she settled her scarf over her head. "God sure does have a sense of humor."

"We lived up in the mountains of Tennessee once, and it snowed so much Pa couldn't even get to the barn. I thought I would freeze to death." Maggie's features softened as her attention veered toward Jack standing with the men at the potbellied stove. "You can keep your snow and your white Christmas. I'm happy right where I am."

"You'd be happy anywhere as long as Jack was there, and you know it."

A shy smile twisted the corners of Maggie's mouth, and color bloomed in her cheeks. "Well, maybe."

"Maybe, my foot." Annabelle grinned and bumped her shoulder against Maggie's.

Soon the church emptied, and Annabelle helped her mother gather up the little ones as her father brought the wagon around.

"Maggie, I hope you'll join us for dinner." Annabelle's mother tossed the invitation over her shoulder as she herded her brood out the door. "Samuel, that goes for you, too."

"What about me?" Jack called out as he closed the damper on the woodstove.

"I couldn't beat you off with a stick, Jack, so I guess that means you're invited."

"Maggie, see how my own mother treats me." Jack threw a hand to his chest and staggered back as if mortally wounded. The children giggled at their older brother's antics.

Annabelle caught Maggie's attention, raised her eyebrows, and nodded toward her brother. "That is what you have to look forward to."

Her friend just smiled, and they all trooped outside. Jack sidled up to Maggie and whispered, "Walk with me?"

She blushed and nodded. Jack snagged Annabelle's arm. "You, too, Sis."

"Walk? Have you lost your mind?" Annabelle sputtered, and made a half-hearted attempt to pull free, knowing full well that Jack only wanted her along as chaperone. "It's too cold to walk. And besides, I need to help Mama put dinner on the table."

"Sally can help until you get there." Her mother's lips twitched as her gaze landed pointedly on Jack. "Don't dally, now. You hear?"

"Yes, ma'am."

The wagon rattled off toward home, and Annabelle and Samuel fell into step together, Jack and Maggie bringing up the rear. As the distance between the two couples widened, Annabelle pursed her lips. "I think we've been hornswoggled."

A tiny smile kicked up one side of Samuel's mouth, and he stuffed his hands in his coat pockets and sauntered along like he didn't have a care in the world. "How's that?"

Annabelle huffed. "We're walking along this muddy, wagon-wheel-gutted road—in the wind, mind you—so that those two lovebirds can get all flutterpated."

Samuel laughed. "It's hard for them to get any time alone, and they needed a chaperone."

"Well, they could wait till spring."

"They might not have until spring."

"What's that supposed to mean?"

"Maggie's pa is talking about heading west."

"Oh." Annabelle pulled her coat closer to ward off the chill. No wonder Jack wanted to spend as much time with Maggie as he could. The scripture about contentment flitted across her mind. Why couldn't Maggie's pa be content wherever he was? It wasn't like he didn't have good Christian neighbors, plenty of food, and a homestead any man would be proud of. His oldest daughter certainly didn't want to leave Sipsey, and her mother and younger siblings seemed happy as well. Maybe he didn't think that being content in whatsoever state he was in meant in the state of Mississippi.

They walked a bit farther, the wind cutting through Annabelle's woolen scarf. She shuddered.

"Cold?" Samuel asked.

"Yes. That wind cuts right through me."

"It's going to be a lot colder in Illinois."

"Maybe, but it's a different kind of cold. Or at least that's what Lucy says."

"Cold is cold to my way of thinking."

"But the snow will make it worth it."

Maggie's soft giggle floated to them on the brisk wind. Annabelle glanced back and saw her brother pulling Maggie close to his side. She tapped Samuel's arm. "Look. Some chaperones we're turning out to be." She turned around, walking backward, and called out, "Hey, you two, stop that."

Jack shot her a look that would melt snow faster than a bonfire at a sing-along.

Samuel reached out, snaked an arm around her waist, and lifted her off the ground. "Leave 'em alone. They deserve a bit of privacy."

"Put me down, you big oaf." Laughing, Annabelle squirmed, plucking at his coat sleeve, knowing the effort was futile. Samuel's arms were like bands of steel around her waist, and he'd put her down when he was good and ready.

He let her go, his brown eyes laughing. Her feet on firm ground once again, she attempted to peek at Jack and Maggie. Samuel took a step toward her. "Don't even think about it."

She laughed and let him have his way. They passed the sawmill, the weathered building still and silent on a Sunday. No welcoming smoke rose from the chimney like it did on weekdays when Samuel and Jack were there, the warmth a welcome break halfway between the school and home. Annabelle frowned, her thoughtful gaze on the small barnlike structure tucked in a clearing away from prying eyes. "Sometimes I wonder about propriety."

Samuel lifted a brow and grunted. Clearly, he had no idea what she was talking about.

"Take those two back there. They've been courting for two years now. Why is it that society still expects them to have a chaperone?"

"Because they're courting."

"But that's just it. People should expect them to want to spend some time together."

"But not alone." Samuel shook his head. "They should never, ever be alone."

"Aha." Annabelle turned around and walked backward, enjoying the banter and knowing she had him trapped. "They're alone now. Maybe we should wait."

"They'll be along shortly." Samuel gave her a lopsided smile. "Turn around."

She grinned at him, still trying to walk backward and carry on a conversation at the same time. "Nobody thinks anything about it when I stop at the sawmill. Why is that?"

A funny expression crossed Samuel's face, and she laughed. "What? What did I say?"

"Nothing." He shook his head, a half smile turning up the corners of his mouth, as if the topic amused him. She made a note to tell Lucy what a nice smile he had.

The heel of her boot caught on a wagon wheel rut, and she stumbled. Samuel grabbed her just before she fell flat on her back in the muddy road. As he held her close, the lingering scent of bay rum tickled her nose. She lifted her gaze to meet his, a teasing remark about her clumsiness on the tip of her tongue.

But when their eyes met, she froze, suspended for a moment in time. She'd never seen Samuel's eyes quite this close. They were brown, with flecks of gold. Mesmerized, she wondered why she'd never noticed that before. His gaze flickered then lowered, sweeping across her face before settling on her lips.

"Hey, you two, stop that."

At the sound of Jack's teasing laughter, Samuel set her on her feet and let her go. Annabelle concentrated on her footing, all thoughts of teasing and laughter completely forgotten as she willed her heart rate to slow to normal.

One near fall today was enough, thank you very much.

Chapter 5

Samuel stuffed his hands in his pockets, heart pounding like a runaway mule. What just happened? One minute they'd been walking along, Annabelle teasing him with silly questions about propriety and courting and such, then the next minute she'd been in his arms.

If Jack and Maggie hadn't rounded the bend, he would have kissed her for sure.

What had come over him?

Annabelle had.

Her laughing green eyes and soft, silky hair that smelled like roses in springtime; her willowy frame that no amount of layered winter coats could disguise.

He chanced a glance at her, walking two steps ahead and to his right, her scarf blocking her face from his view. Had she realized what had almost transpired? Surely she had. He wanted to kick himself. He hadn't meant to let his feelings be known so soon. Not with her about to leave for Illinois.

The Denson homestead came into view, and Annabelle's little brother Ike raced out the door and launched himself at Samuel. Samuel hoisted the boy high, grateful for the distraction. He held the door open as he'd done more times than he could count, but this time Annabelle's gaze ricocheted off his and she murmured a thank-you before hurrying inside.

Little Ike wrapped his arms around Samuel's neck and squeezed tight, but not as tight as the vice wrapped around his chest. Had Annabelle been distracted by the need to help her mother with dinner, or had his actions caused her to avoid him?

Mrs. Denson's Sunday dinner was as good as ever, but Samuel's stomach was too tied up in knots to enjoy it. Seated between Ike and Ander, he teased the boys and concentrated on eating, simply because it kept his mind off Annabelle. He couldn't bear to see the confusion in her eyes, on her face. The conversation centered around the sawmill equipment he and Samuel planned to get from Abe Jensen.

"What do you think, Pa?" Jack asked before shoveling a helping of field peas in his mouth, followed by a generous bite of corn bread.

"Abe Jenson is a good businessman, and he's looking to make some money. He wouldn't bother if he didn't think the old engine still had some life in her." Reverend Denson nodded, considering the offer. "If you boys can get her to run, I think it's a fair offer."

A weight lifted off Samuel's shoulders. He valued Reverend Denson's opinion. "We'll need to make several trips."

"I'll hook up the wagon tomorrow and go along with you."

Jack grinned. "Thanks, Pa. We could sure use the help."

The conversation turned to Annabelle's trip, with Maggie peppering Annabelle with questions and Sally begging her mother to let her go to Illinois with her sister. Samuel didn't join in the conversation, unwilling to risk letting anyone know how he really felt about Annabelle leaving.

"Are you going to the Art Institute?" Maggie asked.

"Yes, if the weather permits. And to the library. Lucy says there are two, the Newberry Library and the Chicago Public Library. Can you imagine all those books in one place?"

"Are you going to any Christmas balls?" Sally piped up.

"I don't think your aunt and uncle know anybody that would hold a ball, Sally." Mrs. Denson nodded at Sally's plate. "Eat your peas if you want some dessert."

"You gonna eat that pie?" Jack stabbed a fork at Samuel's plate.

"Get away." Samuel braced his forearms on each side of his dessert plate and pushed Jack's fork away. "Eat your own pie."

"Well, I was just wondering. You've been staring at it for half an hour. Pa's sermon get to you this morning?"

"Something like that." Samuel shoved a forkful of pie into his mouth and chewed, hoping Jack would take his answer for fact and leave him be.

For the first time ever, Mrs. Denson's hot apple pie with its flaky crust stuck in his throat like he'd inhaled a mouthful of sawdust.

Chapter 6

Sunday evening worship and chores done, Annabelle took her writing supplies from her hope chest. She had just enough time to pen a letter to Lucy before bedtime. She peeked into the sitting room on her way to the kitchen, the warmest—and the *quietest*—room in her parents' drafty old house.

Her mother darned socks while her pa dozed and rocked Lilly, humming under his breath. Her little brothers played with the wooden logs and toy soldiers Samuel had carved for them.

Samuel.

Annabelle's heart lurched. She'd managed to push thoughts of today to the back of her mind, what with helping her mother clean up after Sunday dinner, evening chores, and family worship right after supper.

But now, in the quiet before bed, it all came rushing back.

She sank into a chair at the kitchen table and untied the ribbon that held her writing supplies, the events of today's almost-kiss flooding her thoughts.

What would it be like to be kissed? By *Samuel* even? She'd imagined her first kiss, and a few times she'd tried to picture her first beau, but never in a million years had she imagined being held securely in Samuel's strong arms, his gaze capturing her lips.

Samuel kissing her.

Samuel even *wanting* to kiss her.

Maybe she'd read too much into the thud of his heart as he held her, his face so close to hers, his gaze drifting down and settling on her lips. Cheeks flaming, she flipped open her leather writing satchel. She'd do well not to dwell on what had happened today. Samuel had eaten his dinner as usual, accepted Jack's teasing with a crooked smile, defended his dessert, but for the most part, remained quiet.

Just like always.

He hadn't acted as if anything out of the ordinary had transpired. But she'd been so flustered by her own reaction to being held in his arms that she'd avoided looking at him. She pulled out a piece of paper and found her pencil, teeth worrying her bottom lip.

What if he had tried to catch her eye during Sunday dinner? Their gazes had met and held for a moment when the men were discussing business. And his expression hadn't held even a hint that the incident on the road had meant anything to him. Clearly, she'd blown the whole thing out of proportion, when he'd already forgotten it. Just because she'd glimpsed one of those crooked little smiles of his as he held her close didn't mean a thing. For heaven's sake, she might have had mud on her face or a smudge of soot and he'd been laughing at her as usual. If Jack hadn't yelled out about that time, Samuel would have made some teasing remark about her clumsiness.

She sighed. All would be back to normal when she returned from her trip to Illinois.

Is that what you want?

Annabelle blinked, staring at the blank paper. Except the stationery was no longer blank. Sweeping swirls of romantic doodles covered the page. Hearts and flowers and curling garnishes surrounded the name *Samuel*, penned dreamily in her very own flowing, fanciful hand.

Chapter 7

"Matt, put that peashooter away this instant."

Several boys giggled, and Matt grinned. "Sorry, Annabelle, I was just showing it to Ander."

"*Miss* Annabelle." Annabelle glared at him, knowing full well he'd been doing more than just showing his new peashooter to her brother. Why on earth had she ever thought she could teach children who'd known her all their lives? Papa had put the fear into her three siblings, and they behaved well enough, but sometimes she had trouble keeping the rest of them in line.

Of course, the youngest ones adored her and applied themselves to their lessons with gusto. It was the children who'd been in school when she graduated that caused the most problems. They had a hard time separating the Annabelle they'd gone to school with from Miss Annabelle, the teacher. When she'd agreed to take on this task, she hadn't realized how difficult it would be to teach in her own community. She'd stick it out until school dismissed for the summer then see about transferring somewhere else.

Matt stuffed the peashooter into his pocket and grinned at Sally. Sally concentrated on her ciphering, as if she didn't have a care in the world. But Annabelle had seen the spitball land in Sally's hair. She shook her head. Why Matt thought shooting spitballs at Sally would get her sister's attention was beyond her. But she remembered being that age and Amos Rosenthal doing the same thing. Well, it had certainly earned him her attention, but not necessarily in a good way.

The clock said they had thirty more minutes, and then she could let the children go for the day. They'd become more and more restless as Christmas drew near, and she had a feeling this last week was going to be trying for all of them.

"Let's continue. Matt, start up where Beth left off."

Matt groaned but did as he was told. "Johnny Reed was a li–lit. . ."

"Little."

"Little boy who ne–ne–ver had seen a sn–snow. . ."

"Snowstorm."

"Snowstorm, um. . .until he was six years old. Be–before this he had l–lived in. . ."

The back door opened, and Matt trailed off. Maggie stuck her head in, eyebrows lifted as if asking permission to enter. A ripple of excitement wafted over the students at the intrusion. Visitors at school were few and far between, and Annabelle knew she'd lost their attention for the day. She closed her book, and Matt sat up straight, a grin splitting his face. She gave him what she hoped was a stern look.

"All right, children. Gather your things. I think we can leave a few minutes early today. Sally, you may ring the bell."

Pandemonium erupted and within minutes, the children had donned coats, gloves, and hats, and scattered for the door, whooping and hollering.

Maggie flattened herself against the wall, out of the way. "My goodness, what a stampede."

"You don't want to be caught in their path at the end of the day, that's for sure."

"I'll say." Her friend watched as Annabelle closed the damper on the woodstove and straightened the papers on her desk. "Sometimes I envy you."

"Me?" Annabelle lifted an eyebrow, surprised. "What in the world for?"

"You get to experience something new and exciting every day, while my life is the same thing day after day out on the farm." Maggie toyed with a paperweight on Annabelle's desk. "Well, except today. Today was different. I helped Pa shell corn and haul it to the gristmill."

"Oh, so that's why you stopped by today. You've been to the gristmill."

"Pa went on without me. I asked him to drop me off and pick me up at your house on his way home." Maggie followed Annabelle to the door. "I hope you don't mind."

"Of course not." Annabelle reached for her coat. "I don't get to see you often enough."

Maggie looked away, but not before Annabelle saw the tears in her eyes. "Maggie? What's wrong? Is your pa talking about heading west again?"

"It's all he talks about." She blinked back the tears and sniffed. "Annabelle, I don't know if I can bear to leave Jack."

"If I know my brother, he'll find a way to keep you here."

Color bloomed on Maggie's face, and she whispered, "But he hasn't asked me yet."

"Asked you what?"

"To marry him. Do you. . .do you think he loves me? Enough to want to marry me?"

"I do." Annabelle hugged her then held her at arm's length. "Who knows why he hasn't asked you yet? He could be waiting until Christmas, or he could just think you already know what he wants."

"How would I know that?"

Annabelle gathered up a stack of books and handed them to Maggie. "Because, my friend, he expects you to read his mind."

"I'll never understand men."

"Me neither." Annabelle locked the door, joined Maggie at the bottom of the porch stairs, and linked arms with her friend. "And I certainly don't understand my brother."

Their laughter lightened the mood as they headed toward home, and Annabelle was grateful for Maggie's assistance with the books and papers she had to carry and more than a little grateful for the company. With Maggie along, the decision on whether to stop at the sawmill was out of her hands. Of course Maggie would want to stop and see Jack.

More than once today, she'd wrestled with whether she should drop in as usual or just walk on by. Knowing that she hadn't quite put yesterday's incident behind her, she didn't know if she could pretend nothing had happened if she found Samuel alone.

Her face flamed. With her newfound awareness of him, she knew now why a chaperone was necessary for her brother and Maggie. Goodness, she'd been tempted to ask Sally to stay after school and walk with her just so she'd have an excuse not to stop.

But she hadn't said anything. Because truth be told, she wanted to see Samuel.

Chapter 8

"Just my luck."

Jack's outburst barely registered as Samuel adjusted the tension on the belt that powered the saw blade. He knew a bit about steam engines from working with Abe. He just hoped he knew enough to get this one up and running without blowing them to smithereens.

"Are you listening?" Jack waved a piece of paper in front of Samuel's face. "Maggie and Annabelle stopped by yesterday while we were gone to Abe's."

Mention of Annabelle pulled Samuel's thoughts from the work set before him. He'd wondered if she'd come after what happened Sunday, but it couldn't be helped that he'd missed her. It had taken most of the afternoon to dismantel the machinery at Abe's and load everything in the wagons. They hadn't made it back until nearly dark.

He frowned. Maggie? "What was Maggie doing with her? Is something wrong?"

"No. She stopped off to visit Annabelle at the school while her pa went to the gristmill." Jack stuffed the note in his pocket. "She said she had something important to tell me but didn't want to put it in writing."

"Do you think it might be about her pa's itch to move on?"

"What else could it be?" Jack scowled.

Samuel didn't answer. Since the threat of separation hung over Jack and Maggie, Jack was probably right. What encouragement could he offer? None, but he could keep his friend busy. He gave the steam engine a pat. "Let's give this saw a run."

The chug-chug of the engine and the whir of the blade filled the air, and Samuel's heart sang along as he and Jack tested out the blade. They debarked a log then eased it through the blade. Sawdust flew in every direction, but they concentrated on the task at hand as the blade sliced into their very first board.

Jack grinned at their handiwork. "I know exactly where I'm going to use this."

Samuel quirked a brow. "Where?"

"Over the front door."

"One board does not a house make." Samuel nodded toward the block of wood as they readied it for another pass. "Steady now."

As the afternoon wore on, Jack and Samuel realized just how temperamental the old steam engine was and how exhausting hefting logs onto the ramp and rolling them into position could be. Midafternoon, the blade jerked, lodging itself against the log, and the belt started spinning.

Heart pounding, Samuel scrambled to kill the power to the engine before something blew. As he and Jack tinkered with the cantankerous old equipment, their early excitement waned.

"I'm not sure if this is worth it." Jack wiped his brow and took a long swig of water from a canning jar. He wiped his mouth on his sleeve. "At this rate, we'd be better off hauling logs to Abe just like we've been doing."

Samuel searched for the problem, determined not to give up so easily. His heart sank when he saw that one of the braces that held the blade straight and true had cracked. He pointed. "Look."

"Piece of junk. No wonder Abe wanted to get rid of it."

"It's not so bad. If we can get this piece off, Zeke might be able to forge it back together."

An hour later, Jack headed to the blacksmith's with the iron bar in hand, and Samuel eyed the saw blade wedged against the log, trying to decide the best course of action. The one thing he didn't want to do was ruin that blade, or Jack's dream of building a house and a life with Maggie would be even further out of reach.

He loosened the belt that provided traction for the blade, but the blade held fast, wedged tight against the unforgiving pine log. Nothing for it. He grabbed a saw. Better to waste part of the log than ruin their only blade.

He'd worked up a sweat by the time he sawed away the board and the blade jerked back into alignment. *Lord, please don't let any of these teeth be chipped.*

A rain of sawdust fell on his head, and he looked up to see Annabelle smiling at him, her cheeks glowing from the cold. His heart rate spiked at the sight of her. She slapped her gloved hands together, and sawdust fluttered on the slight breeze and peppered her coat and scarf, reminding him of the snow she longed to see in Illinois. A smile wreathed her face. "You got the saw to work!"

"Well, yes and no."

Her smile slipped. "No?"

"It worked fine until a piece broke." He showed her where the broken brace had been.

She moved closer and peered at the spot. "Oh no. Can it be fixed?"

"Maybe." Samuel shoved his hat back. "Jack took it to Zeke."

"That's good. Zeke should be able to make it good as new."

The breeze blew her soft floral scent toward him, and he swallowed, trying not to think about how she'd felt in his arms on Sunday. How her lips had softened and parted just before Jack had called out. He pulled his gaze from her face and settled on the multicolored scarf covering her hair. "You're covered in sawdust."

"Uh-oh." She brushed at the flecks clinging to her scarf. "That won't be easy to get out."

"Reminds me of snow."

"It does, doesn't it?"

He couldn't resist her laugh and found himself looking into her eyes again. Did she feel the electric charge in the air? A charge he'd managed to keep buried deep down inside.

At least until last Sunday.

She cleared her throat and moved away. "I got another letter from Lucy. She said that it started snowing and they've already put sled runners on the wagons. Did you know that? I never really thought about it, since we've never had any need for sled runners here in Mississippi. And there's going to be a Christmas play at her church, and her pastor's wife invited us to dinner one night. She said we could go sledding, and ice skating—that is, if the ice on the pond is thick enough. She said everybody comes out on Saturday afternoon to skate since it's not every year that they get the chance."

Samuel watched the emotions playing across Annabelle's face as she prattled on and on about all the things she'd do and see in Illinois. Her eyes danced with excitement, and her cheeks bloomed with color that didn't have anything to do with the slight chill in the air.

"What?" Annabelle gave him a tentative smile, and he realized she'd stopped talking about Illinois and was staring at him.

He said the first thing that popped into his head. "With so much to do, you're liable to end up staying in Illinois."

"Oh, no, I can't imagine that happening." She laughed, a bit shakily, before looking away and picking up the canning jar Jack had left sitting on the windowsill, sawdust settling in the water. "I mean, what would I do there?"

Samuel's heart slammed against his ribcage as the truth hit him. She had considered moving to Illinois. Why hadn't he seen it?

She shook the jar, and the tiny flecks of wood swirled in the water. She lifted her gaze, all trace of teasing and laughter gone. Her eyes, the exact color of the pines towering behind her, met his briefly before she looked away and gathered up her school satchel. "I'd better go. I hope you and Jack get the saw going again."

Long after she'd gone, Samuel turned the conversation over in his mind. What if she met someone in Illinois? She was smart and beautiful and would make some man a good wife. There'd be any number of men who'd want to court her, and he'd given her no reason to come back to Mississippi.

What a fool he'd been.

Pride in having enough to provide for a wife and family had kept him from making the slightest move to let Annabelle know how he felt. He needed to do something, say something before she left to let her know that he cared. That he wanted her to come back.

His gaze landed on the canning jar half full of water, the sawdust swirling slower and slower until it gradually began to sink to the bottom like softly falling flakes of snow. He reached out, lifted the jar, and gave it a gentle shake as an idea began to form.

Chapter 9

Samuel pictured the carving in his mind as he turned the block of wood in his hand. The entire carving wouldn't be much bigger than the palm of his hand, and the details would be small and delicate. He itched to be out in the woods felling timber, but falling temperatures and a steady rain earlier in the day had kept them from the woods. Even so, the time hadn't been wasted. It had taken two days for Zeke to fix the brace on the engine, and Samuel and Jack had cut up the rest of the logs small enough to run through the saw blade.

He chuckled. Actually, they'd cut up anything and everything that even looked like it could be used in Jack's house. They were a long way from having enough lumber, but that hadn't stopped Jack from sketching his dream house out on paper.

"What do you think about this?"

Samuel paused in his carving and eyed the crude drawing Jack had made. He pointed with his knife. "I'd put a door right there, off the main room. That'll make it easy to add on an extra room when you need it."

"Good idea." Jack nodded toward the block of wood as he scratched in a door with his snubby-nosed pencil. "What are you making?"

Samuel hefted the three-sided carving, the image of their small country church beginning to take shape on one side. "Christmas present for Annabelle."

"She's not going to be here for Christmas."

"I know."

Jack laughed, still fiddling with his plans. Suddenly, his pencil poised in midair, he squinted at Samuel, an odd look on his face. "You sweet on my sister?"

Samuel didn't see any sense in denying it. He nodded toward the open sawmill doors. "It's stopped raining. Maybe you should hook up the mules and head on in to town with that load of logs."

Jack ignored him. "I should have noticed before now, I guess. She doesn't stop by here every day to see me."

"Sure she does."

"What about last Sunday?"

"She tripped and I caught her. That's all."

Jack crossed his arms over his chest, the worn fabric of his work shirt stretched tight. "Looked like more than that to me."

Samuel gritted his teeth. It was more. A lot more. But Jack didn't need to know that. "It wasn't."

Jack snorted. "When are you going to tell her how you feel?"

Samuel sighed. There was no use trying to deny that he had feelings for Annabelle. "I'm not."

"Why not? She's going to Illinois next week."

"And that's why I'm not going to say anything. She's got her heart set on a white Christmas, and I won't do anything to ruin it for her."

Jack stretched and reached for his hat. "You just keep thinking like that, buddy, and she's liable to meet some yahoo up in Illinois, and then where will you be?"

After Jack left, Samuel stared at the block of wood where he carved his hopes and dreams for the future. Would it be enough? Enough to bring Annabelle back to him?

Chapter 10

Weary from a long day of teaching, Annabelle locked the schoolhouse, thankful for the Christmas break that gave her three glorious weeks of freedom. It had been all she could do to keep the children under control all week but practically impossible today, they'd been so excited.

From the schoolhouse steps, she stood on tiptoe and squinted through the cloudy midwinter haze. She could barely see Miller's Mercantile at the crossroads on the other side of the church. Sipsey couldn't even be called a town unless you counted the church and the school, along with Mr. Miller's store, and you couldn't always count the store.

The tiny mercantile consisted of two wagons butted end to end. The space was so tight, you just entered from one end and exited the other, and every nook and cranny was stuffed full of nonperishables, spices, sundry items, and a bit of cloth and thread. Mr. Miller moved his store to a new location whenever the mood struck him. She hurried toward the wagons, thankful he hadn't packed up and moved today. Regardless of the lateness of the hour, her mother had asked her to pick up some salt, and with school out, she didn't know when she'd have another chance to stop in.

In no time at all, she made her purchases and headed toward home, carefully avoiding the puddles left by the recent rain. Free of trying to corral a dozen children, the fluttery feeling of anticipation she'd become familiar with this week niggled at her the closer she got to the sawmill.

When she'd stopped by the last two days, Zeke, Jack, and Samuel had been up to their eyeballs trying to get the old steam engine running. With her brother and the crotchety old blacksmith there, it had been easy to make small talk for a few minutes before heading on home.

On one hand, she'd been relieved not to find Samuel alone, since the opportunity to see him without having to talk put her at ease over Sunday's episode; but on the other, she'd been disappointed. Which would have seemed downright silly a week ago. But today, the feeling was anything but silly or trivial.

In the distance, she spotted a wisp of smoke curling above the tops of the pine trees. She rounded the last bend, and her gaze swept the familiar weathered boards of the barnlike structure, the lean-to on the left that housed the steam engine, the barn and pasture out back. Zeke's wagon, with all his scraps of iron, was nowhere to be seen, but the fresh pile of cut lumber stacked under the lean-to was testament that they'd gotten the saw going again. And the big freight wagon Samuel and Jack used to transport logs to town was gone.

Her steps faltered, and her heart skittered. Was Samuel here? Or Jack? Had they both gone to deliver logs? Should she stop in or not? The lure of the woodstove's warmth drew her, and she hurried toward the doors pulled shut against the cold.

She pushed one of the huge doors open just enough to slip inside. Disappointment filled her as she realized the room was empty. She'd convinced herself that she hadn't longed to see Samuel, that her concern was just for their business and her brother and Maggie's plans for the future.

Well, nothing for it. Jack was gone, and so was Samuel. A pot of coffee sat on the stove. Ah, coffee. She sniffed and closed her eyes in appreciation. Just what she needed to warm her for the walk home. She removed her gloves, snagged a cup from one of the pegs, and poured, then sat on the stool next to the stove. As she sipped the brew—a bit bitter but not too bad—her gaze landed on Samuel's tools and the partially carved train set spread across the table. Probably a Christmas present for one of her brothers. She leaned closer to inspect one of the boxcars, complete with working wheels and tiny axles fashioned from nails.

The door creaked open and she jumped, almost spilling her coffee. Samuel entered, a load of firewood in his arms. He turned, eyes widening at the sight of her before a slight smile turned up the corners of his mouth. "I'd given up on you today."

He'd been watching for her?

Warmth filled her, and it had nothing to do with the coffee. "I had to run to Miller's Mercantile for a few things."

"Still at the crossroads, then?" He took off his coat and hung it on a peg by the door.

"Still there. But not for long. He said to tell everybody that he's thinking of moving to Kitchener next week, so if you need anything, you'd better get it now."

"He says that every Christmas."

"True."

He opened the firebox and poked at the burning embers. Sparks flew, illuminating a days-old shadow on his cheeks, a shadow that he'd shave off come Sunday morning. She studied his profile underneath the brim of his hat. He tossed a couple of sticks of wood into the firebox and threw her a glance, his dark eyes reflecting the flames. "That should warm you up for the trip home."

Annabelle laughed. "Are you trying to get rid of me already?"

"Nope. You're welcome to stay as long as you want." A tiny smile kicked up one side of his mouth again. His shirt stretched taut across his shoulders as he reached for the coffeepot. "More coffee?"

"No, thank you." Annabelle quelled the flutter in her stomach. Heart pounding, she lowered her gaze and stared into her coffee cup. What was wrong with her? When had she become so aware of every move Samuel made? Since Sunday, when she'd tripped and somehow got it into her head that he'd wanted to kiss her, that's when. She'd wrestled with questioning him about it all week. But what could she say?

Were you going to kiss me?

No, she couldn't. She wouldn't ask him such a question. Her cheeks flamed as she tried to think of a way to broach the subject without embarrassing either of them.

A jingle of harness alerted her that Jack had returned. She placed the cup on the table and stood, panic at what she'd almost said mingled with a wild desire to know the answer to the question that had kept her awake five nights in a row. "I'd better get home."

"I'll take you in the wagon."

"No, that's not necessary."

"It'll be dark soon, and the temperature is dropping." He moved to the door and called out, "Hey, Jack, just leave 'em hitched. I'm going to take Annabelle home."

Thankful that she didn't have to walk the rest of the way home after today's rain, Annabelle headed outside. Her brother grumbled good-naturedly as he set the brake and jumped down, grinning at her. "What's the matter, Sis? Afraid you'll get a little mud on ya?"

"You know good and well I'm not afraid of a little mud, Jack Denson."

Samuel climbed into the tall freight wagon then reached for Annabelle's hand as Jack hoisted her up. Her brother winked up at her. "Y'all have fun. Straight there and back, now, you hear?"

The ride home took less than ten minutes, but Annabelle was too mortified to even look at Samuel. Jack acted like she and Samuel were courting, for heaven's sake, and Samuel hadn't even said one word to her that would make her think he was interested.

Samuel reined in the mules, set the brake, and jumped down, only to be swarmed by Ike and Ander running out to meet them. Annabelle eyed the distance to the ground from the lowest rung on the wagon. She clambered over the side before Samuel could untangle himself, only to find herself a good foot or more off the ground, with no foothold.

Samuel glanced at her, her little brothers dangling from his arms. "Need help?"

"Well, it seems I do. There's no way to get down."

"Sorry. This wagon wasn't built for ladies." He shooed her brothers away and moved closer. His hands encircled her waist, and even though she could barely feel his touch through the bulk of her coat, her heart fluttered. Her hands landed on his shoulders, and he lowered her to the ground, so close she could see the golden flecks in his brown eyes. Not a trace of laughter lingered in their depths. "It wouldn't do for you to fall right before your trip to Illinois."

"Like last time?" she blurted out, regretting the question immediately. If he didn't remember or made some teasing remark about her clumsiness, then she'd know the event meant nothing to him.

His gaze softened, dipped, and settled on her mouth before flicking to meet hers again. "Like last time."

Chapter 11

The sun barely peeked over the horizon, and Annabelle looked around her room, trying to determine what she'd missed. Two bags sat beside the door, and she mentally ticked off the contents carefully folded and stuffed inside. She couldn't think of a thing she'd forgotten.

Then why did she feel so unsettled? *Discontented*, even.

Guilt stabbed her. She'd brushed off Maggie's father's desire to uproot his family as discontentment. Did she harbor a bit of unhappiness in her own heart? A longing for change for the sake of change, regardless of whether it was for the better or even good for her?

She plopped down on the bed and stared out the window. Where had the excitement over her trip gone? For as long as she could remember, she'd dreamed of a white Christmas. Every year, without fail, it was the one thing she'd wished for. Oh, there'd been a little snow here and there, but nothing to compare with what her cousin described. Surely the desire for one short trip wasn't the sign of a discontented heart.

She lifted the lid of her hope chest, just to be sure she hadn't forgotten anything. As she riffled through pillowcases, dishes, and hand towels embroidered with snowflakes against a background of evergreens, and all the other things a young woman stored away in anticipation of the day she'd set up housekeeping in her own home, she finally admitted to herself what was bothering her.

What she'd left undone.

Unbeknownst to anyone, other than maybe to Lucy, Annabelle's dream of a white Christmas was just a small part of her trip. She dreamed of finally meeting the one man who could make her heart sing, the one man who would look at her with stars in his eyes and who'd say sweet things to her, bring her wildflowers in the springtime. The one man who would tell her he couldn't live without her. She'd thought she'd find that man in Illinois. But what if he was right here, here in Mississippi, underneath the pines?

What if Samuel is that man?

But she didn't know how he felt. Did he even think about her like she'd begun to think about him? He'd wished her well on her trip and teased her about coming back. But he hadn't given any indication that he might care for her in any way other than as his partner's sister and as a friend.

A light knock sounded on the door, and Annabelle's mother poked her head in, a smile on her face. "You ready for your big adventure?"

"I can't believe it's finally here." Annabelle smiled, struggling to push thoughts of Samuel to the back of her mind.

"Enjoy it. Two weeks will go faster than you ever dreamed." Her mother hugged her and held her at arm's length. "Now, you be good, mind your manners, and don't go off alone with any young man, no matter how respectable your aunt claims he is."

"Mama, you know I'd never. . ."

"I know, but it's a mama's duty to issue these warnings. And I just don't trust those big-city boys, not by a long shot." She reached for a soft-sided carpetbag. "Now, gather your things. Jack's downstairs and rarin' to go."

"Jack?" Annabelle grabbed the other bag and followed her mother down the hall. "I thought Papa was taking us to the train station."

"He got called away. Old Mr. Hedricks is in a bad way and asked for him. Your pa asked Jack to take you and your aunt to the train station."

"Oh no. Is Mr. Hedricks going to be all right?"

"Don't worry, now. Just his stomach ulcers giving him fits. I'm sure he'll be fine." They hurried outside, and Jack put her bags in the wagon bed. Her mother shaded her eyes and glanced at the sky. "Thank goodness it's not raining today, or you'd have to take Eugenia's buggy."

"Knowing Aunt Eugenia, we might have to anyway." Jack helped Annabelle into the wagon and climbed up beside her.

"Well, get on, then. You don't want to be late. Mind what I told you, Annabelle."

"Yes, ma'am."

Jack slapped the reins against the horses' flanks and they headed out. A package slid along the seat, and Annabelle grabbed it to keep it from falling. "What's this?"

"Oh, Samuel sent that. Said to give it to you and that you weren't to open it until Christmas morning."

"Really? How sweet." Annabelle ran the tips of her fingers over the odd-shaped package wrapped in plain brown wrapping paper and tied with a string. Her heart fluttered. How could she wait another week to see what Samuel had gotten her?

Her brother scowled. "Samuel? Sweet?"

"Of course he's sweet."

Jack rested his elbows on his knees, the reins clasped between his fingers. "Then why are you gallivanting off to Illinois chasing after some beau if you think my partner is sweet?"

"I'm not chasing off after a beau." Annabelle glared at her brother then shrugged. "You know I just want a white Christmas."

He arched a brow at her. "So you're saying that you won't even look at a man while you're there? That you and Lucy haven't talked about men in all those letters y'all have sent back and forth, back and forth, day after day? Nobody can write that much about snow and dresses and such nonsense."

Annabelle squirmed. "Well, Lucy might have mentioned a few fellows that she wants me to meet."

Jack grinned. "See, I told you."

"But it doesn't mean a thing."

"Just like you calling Samuel sweet doesn't mean a thing either?" He nodded at the package. "Or him taking the time to make you a present, knowing you weren't even going to be here for Christmas."

"He made it?"

Her brother grimaced. "I wasn't supposed to tell you that part."

Annabelle fingered the string. What could it be? Something made from wood, no doubt. A small box for trinkets and ribbons? A carving of some kind? Smoke from the mill curled above the treetops around the next bend. She needed to thank Samuel. His was the only present she was taking from home.

As they rounded the bend and the mill came into view, Annabelle put a hand on her brother's arm. "Stop."

"No time." Jack didn't slack up. "Aunt Eugenia's waiting."

"Jack. Please." Annabelle held up the package. "I can't leave without thanking him."

Chapter 12

Samuel had kept himself busy from the moment Reverend Denson had stopped by to ask Jack to drive Annabelle and Miss Eugenia into town. Jack would be gone most of the day, so they wouldn't be able to cut any logs, but he could finish up the last of his projects for Christmas, starting with the rocking chair for Mrs. Denson.

The reverend wanted him to deliver it bright and early Christmas morning, and had even invited him to stay for dinner, but Samuel wouldn't be eatingChristmas dinner with the Densons this year. He couldn't stomach the thought of sitting there listening to the family's laughter with Annabelle's empty chair across from him.

He sanded the chair runners, the scraping filling the quietness of the shop.

"Samuel?"

His stomach did a slow roll at the unexpected sound of Annabelle's soft voice. Turning, he saw her silhouetted in the open doorway, in a dark green dress that brought out the color of her eyes, and her best Sunday coat and scarf.

"What are you doing here?" He smiled to take the sting out of his blunt question. "Don't you have a train to catch?"

"We're on the way now." She glided across the sawdust-strewn floor, her eyes sparkling. "But I couldn't leave without thanking you for the gift."

"It's not much." He shrugged, his heart rate kicking up a notch when she rested a hand on his arm.

"It is to me. It'll be the only present from home that I'll have to open on Christmas morning." Her smile slipped, and she blinked, a hint of moisture spiking her lashes.

"Hey, what's this?" Samuel dipped his head and peered into her face. "Tears just before your grand adventure?"

"Silly, isn't it?" She shook her head and sniffed. "I know you told me already, but it just hit me that this will be the first time in my life that I'll be away from my family during Christmas."

"Well, it's just for two weeks, and you'll be back." *Lord, please let her come back.* "If you don't go off and forget about us."

"I won't." She shook her head. "Thank you for the present, Samuel. No matter what it is, I'll treasure it for always." She raised on tiptoe and kissed his cheek. Her gaze searched his, and it was all he could do not to tell her that he loved her, that he didn't want her to go.

"Annabelle!" Jack called from outside. "Hurry up. Time's a wastin'."

Something akin to disappointment shuttered her features, and she turned away. Samuel could no more stop himself than he could stop the train carrying her away from him. He reached out and lightly clasped her slender wrist. At his touch, her lashes swept up and her eyes met his, a question in their depths.

He tugged, and she came willingly. She closed her eyes and tilted her face up to meet his kiss, and her lips were as sweet and tender as he'd dreamed they would be. The kiss lasted seconds, or minutes, he was never sure, but one thing he was sure of, it wasn't long enough.

"Annabelle!"

Annabelle started, her wide-eyed gaze riveted on Samuel's face. "I've got to go."

Chapter 13

Annabelle stared at the telegram from Lucy's father, telling them not to come to Illinois. A blizzard had shut down all train travel into Chicago.

"Well, if that don't just beat all," Aunt Eugenia sputtered. "Jack, you might as well turn this wagon around and take us home."

"Yes, ma'am."

Jack was uncharacteristically quiet, but what could he say? No amount of teasing or joking would change things.

Aunt Eugenia patted Annabelle's gloved hand. "What a pity, Annabelle. I know how much you had your heart set on spending time with Lucy. But you'll get another chance. Maybe this summer would be a good time to visit, much better than the dead of winter."

Annabelle nodded, not trusting herself to speak. When would she get another chance? School was due to start back in two weeks and would run all the way into May. And Aunt Eugenia didn't realize that it was a white Christmas she longed for just as much as she longed to see her cousin.

How ironic.

The very thing she longed for—snow—was the very thing that was keeping her from her dream. And Christmas only came once a year. What would next year bring? Where would she be by then? What if she never got another chance at a white Christmas?

I will be content, Lord.

She searched her heart for the bitter disappointment that she expected to feel and was surprised to discover her regret wasn't as keen as it would have been a week ago. All the way to town, she'd listened to Aunt Eugenia's prattle, answered her aunt's questions. But in the lulls, when Aunt Eugenia got wound up on one tale or another that Annabelle could recite in her sleep, her mind wandered.

Straight back to Samuel and the kiss they'd shared.

Samuel.

Like a two-by-four fresh off the saw blade, his kiss had knocked her upside the heart and made her realize what a dolt she'd been. She'd been so caught up in her own girlish dreams and plans that she'd failed to pay attention to what was right in front of her.

Well, that wasn't quite true. She *had* noticed how he'd teased her and held her close when she'd almost fallen, but she'd decided that her own romantic notions of wanting a beau had clouded her vision and that Samuel didn't feel anything more for her than a brotherly type love because he was Jack's partner.

Her cheeks flamed. His kiss had been anything but brotherly.

"Annabelle, are you listening?"

She started, realizing they'd pulled up in front of her aunt's house. "I'm sorry, Aunt Eugenia, my mind wandered."

Her aunt gave her an understanding smile. "You're forgiven. I was saying that you and Jack are welcome to spend the night with me. It'll be dark by the time you get home."

Annabelle shook her head. She just wanted to be home in her own bed to nurse her disappointment. "Thank you—"

"We'd better head on home, Aunt Eugenia." Jack jumped down from the wagon and helped their aunt down then reached into the wagon for her bags. "Samuel and I need to be in the woods by daylight."

"Of course, I wasn't thinking. You've already lost a day of work, Jack, and Annabelle and I appreciate it."

They said their good-byes, and Jack urged the horses toward home. They rode in silence for a while, before he slanted a look her way. "You're mighty quiet."

Annabelle shrugged. "Disappointed, that's all."

"Ah, Sis, I know how much this trip meant to you." Jack jostled her shoulder. "Sorry it didn't work out like you planned."

She threw him a surprised look. "Thanks, Jack."

He tossed her a teasing grin. "See, I can be just as sweet as Samuel when I want to be."

Annabelle laughed along with him, grateful for the gathering twilight that masked the blistering heat that swooshed up her neck and flooded her cheekbones. "The key is that you rarely want to be."

The miles passed quickly, the jingle of the harness and the *clop-clop* of the horses' hooves filling the silence as they topped the ridge a mile north of the sawmill. Would Samuel still be there? Would Jack stop? Her heart pounded. How could she face Samuel this soon after he'd kissed her?

She clasped her hands tightly in her lap and prayed Jack wouldn't stop.

They continued on, the wagon creaking as dusk fell quickly. Her heart pounded as the squat barnlike structure came into view, dark, no smoke rising from the smokestack. Samuel had closed up shop for the night and gone home. As they plodded on past, Annabelle closed her eyes in relief. She needed time to think before she saw him again.

Because above and beyond thoughts of the kiss they'd shared and the way his touch sent her heart rate spiraling out of control, one panicky thought rose to the surface. Why hadn't he said anything? If he cared for her, why hadn't he declared himself instead of letting her go? Her cheeks heated as the thought flitted through her brain.

Maybe he had declared himself, not with words, but with actions.

Chapter 14

Come daylight, Samuel and Jack were in the woods harvesting their first tree of the day. Jack whistled a merry tune, and Samuel poured his frustration into pushing the crosscut saw toward his partner then pulling it back with just as much gusto.

Jack had plenty to be happy about. But with Annabelle gone, Samuel didn't expect to enjoy Christmas very much. And he'd made things worse by kissing her yesterday. He clenched his jaw as he jerked the saw toward himself. Not that he regretted kissing her—not by a long shot—but now he had two full weeks to stew on how she felt about it, and what he'd do about it when she returned.

He scowled at Jack. "What are you so happy about?"

Jack grinned. "I'm going to ask Maggie to marry me on Christmas Eve. I don't have a ring yet, but she won't mind when she finds out that we're building her a house."

"We?"

"Of course." Jack pushed the saw toward Samuel. "I'll return the favor when it's your turn. Which reminds me. You haven't asked about Annabelle this morning."

Samuel thrust the blade back and sawdust flew, the rhythmic, rasping sound filling the forest. "There's really nothing to ask. I'm sure you got her and her aunt on the train without incident. They're probably in Illinois by now."

"Nope."

Samuel's gaze sharpened. "What's that supposed to mean?"

"They didn't go. Blizzard in Illinois halted all train travel." Jack gave the saw a shove toward Samuel. "So, maybe now you can see about courting my sister like you should have done already."

Annabelle hadn't gone to Illinois.

She was still here, in Mississippi, at home, less than two miles away as the crow flies. His heart pounded, and it wasn't from the push-pull exertion of working the saw. He wanted to ask Jack if she'd been disappointed, but he already knew the answer to that question. Of course she was. A white

Christmas was all she'd talked about for weeks, for months.

And he'd kissed her.

Then thought he had two weeks for the image to fade.

What was he going to do now?

Chapter 15

Annabelle unpacked her carpetbags, folded her clothes, and put them away. She fingered the thick twine tied around Samuel's present. Should she take it back and tell him to just give it to her on Christmas morning?

Taking the present back would be silly, and how would she face him, alone, at the sawmill? Or worse, in front of Jack?

No, she'd wait until Christmas Day. Since his mother had moved to the other side of Newton to live with her sister, he'd probably spend Christmas with her family anyway, just as he had for the last two years. At least on Christmas morning, her family would be around, and she wouldn't feel quite so awkward when she opened it. And maybe, just maybe, the two of them could move forward after that. If. . .if that was what he wanted.

"Annabelle?" her mother called from the kitchen.

"Yes, ma'am? Coming." She left the package on top of her hope chest and headed down the hall.

"Lilly's awake." Her mother, hands busy kneading a lump of dough, nodded at Annabelle's little sister. The toddler's grasping hands pulled at her mother's skirt. Lilly spotted Annabelle, let go of her mother, and toddled toward her sister.

Annabelle picked her up and hugged her. "Hello, sunshine."

"Run and gather the eggs, would you?" Her mother deftly flipped the dough over and continued working it with her fingers. "As soon as I set this bread to rising, I want to get some baking done. Christmas will be here before you know it."

Annabelle lowered Lilly to her pallet and handed her a pan and a wooden spoon.

Her mother cringed at the first bang. "Oh goodness, Annabelle, not that."

"Sorry, Mama, it's the only thing that keeps her busy and out of trouble." She laughed as she grabbed a coat off a peg by the door.

"And, Annabelle?"

"Yes, ma'am?"

"I know you're disappointed that your trip didn't work out, but I'm glad you'll be home for Christmas. I wasn't looking forward to having you gone, you know."

"Thanks, Mama."

They shared a smile before Annabelle hurried to the chicken coop to gather the eggs. It didn't take long, and she re-entered the kitchen, eggs in hand. Her mother peered into the basket and counted. "Hmm, I was hoping for more. We'll all have to make do with one fried egg each the next few days if I'm going to get my baking done."

"For your Christmas cookies and pound cake, I'll do without an egg all week."

Her mother laughed. "I don't think it'll come to that."

Annabelle took off her coat and put the eggs away. Lilly sat in the corner on her pallet, banging her spoon against the pan and squealing with delight. Annabelle smiled as she tied an apron around her waist. "Where is everybody?"

"They went to the gristmill." Her mother put the dough in a pan, covered it with a piece of cheesecloth, and set it to the side. "I was glad to see them go. With school out, they've been like a pack of wild coyotes. I told Hiram that when they get back, I want him to put the boys to work cleaning out the barn."

Before long, the kitchen smelled of baking bread, sugar cookies, and the pot of vegetable soup simmering on the stove for the noon meal. Annabelle went to the well and brought in a fresh pail of water, relieved that Lilly had stopped her banging.

She washed her hands, reached for a kitchen towel, and removed a sheet of cookies from the oven. The fresh-baked aroma of butter mingled with sugar made her mouth water. "Maybe we'll get all these cookies out of sight before Papa and the boys get back. Otherwise, there won't be any left for Christmas."

"Why do you think I sent them all to town this morning?" Her mother laughed as she rolled more dough, her hands covered in flour. She jerked her head toward the hall. "Check on Lilly, if you don't mind. She slipped out a few minutes ago while you were outside."

"Lilly?" Annabelle stepped into the hallway, calling for her baby sister. The family room was empty and the door to the small room where her father prayed and planned his sermons was shut. Her heart lurched as her gaze jerked to the stairs that led to the attic rooms the boys slept in. Had Lilly managed to climb the stairs?

"Lilly? Where are you, sweetie?"

The door to the room she shared with Sally was ajar, and relief filled her when she heard a rustling inside. She found her little sister seated in the middle of the room, Samuel's present clasped in her chubby little hands.

Lilly grinned at Annabelle, patting the present. "Mine."

"No, Lilly." Annabelle laughed, plucked her sister up, and examined the torn paper.

"Mine," Lilly repeated.

"No, you little scamp. It's not yours."

Lilly giggled again and lunged for the present, her grasping hands tearing the wrapping paper even more before Annabelle could get it away from her. She propped her sister on her hip and cradled the package in the other hand, the half-torn paper revealing the top of a canning jar. She frowned.

A canning jar?

Samuel had given her a canning jar for Christmas?

Unable to contain her curiosity, she pulled back the paper to peek at the contents. She gasped, letting Lilly slide to the floor. Lilly happily plopped down and played with the discarded paper. Annabelle held the jar, mesmerized by the miniature scene inside.

A tiny carved church, complete with steeple, lay submerged in water, a winding trail leading down and around as if following the curve of a hill. She turned the jar to see the next scene. Her heart lurched as she spotted what looked like the sawmill, with a lean-to tacked on the side. Miniature carved trees, painted green, pointed straight and tall toward the sky, looking lifelike behind and around the buildings. Another rotation and the schoolhouse came into view, nestled among a stand of evergreens.

She held the jar up to the light streaming in the bedroom window. Sawdust shavings covered the base of the carving like a dusting of snow. Annabelle's breath caught as she saw the tiny flakes swirling in the water as if kicked up by a gentle wind.

Mesmerized, she gently turned the jar upside down, and the sawdust floated to the top of the water. When she turned it right side up, the tiny flakes fell slowly, landing softly on the trees, the church, the sawmill, coating the entire scene just like a cascade of falling snow.

She blinked back tears as she cradled the jar in both hands. Samuel had given her a white Christmas, right here in the evergreen forest in the heart of Mississippi.

Chapter 16

The door to the sawmill creaked open and Samuel turned from putting the finishing touches on Mrs. Denson's rocking chair. "Forget something?"

But it wasn't Jack who stood in the doorway. Annabelle stood there, the sun that had just dipped below the tips of the evergreen trees casting a red and gold aura around her. She moved toward him, the canning jar in her hands, and he could only stand still and wait.

She moved closer, away from the sun that blocked her face from his view, and he saw the smile on her lips and the way her green eyes shone with joy.

A physical ache tugged at him when she looked away, held the canning jar aloft, flipped it, then righted it, letting the sawdust flutter in the small container. Her smile widened, and he swallowed, remembering how soft her lips had felt when he'd kissed her, wondering how she felt about that kiss now. Surely if she hated him for it, she wouldn't have come, would she?

Her gaze left the tiny scene in the jar and captured his. "You made this for me? Why?"

Why?

To bring you back to me.

He settled for something less risky. "To give you something to remember home by."

"It's lovely." She cradled the jar and smiled at him. "Thank you."

"You're welcome."

"And, just so you know, I didn't open it early. Lilly found it in my room." Her look was apologetic. "I hope you're not disappointed."

"I could never be disappointed in you, Annabelle."

She dipped her head and asked shyly, "Why didn't you say something?"

Samuel's heart pounded. "About what?"

"About us. About my trip." Her face flamed, and she ran a finger along the back of a chair. "Even when—when. . .you kissed me, you didn't say anything."

"Ah, Annabelle, you'd had your heart set on that trip to Illinois for so long. That's all you've ever wanted, was to have a white Christmas."

"So, you wanted me to go?"

"Well, not exactly." He choked back a laugh. "But it was what you wanted."

"What if it's not what I want anymore?"

His heart thudded against his ribcage as her eyes met and held his. He closed the distance between them, his gaze flickering to her lips and back again. He cupped her face with the palm of his hand. "What do you want, Annabelle?"

She reached out a hand and rested it against his shirtfront, and he thought his heart would pound right out of his chest.

"I don't know what I want, but maybe"—tears shimmered in her beautiful green eyes, but she held his gaze, searching, looking—"maybe between the two of us we can figure it out."

Samuel lowered his lips to hers and did a bit of figuring of his own.

Epilogue

One Year Later

The whistle blew as the train passed through another small, sleepy town on its journey north. Annabelle smiled at Samuel, slumbering beside her. The train rocked on through the night, a hint of dawn peeping through the drawn curtains. Come daylight, they'd be in Illinois, spending their first Christmas as a married couple with Lucy and her family.

Samuel stirred, and her heart fluttered. She smoothed back his dark hair, desperately in need of a trim, and then ran one finger down his cheek, rough with day-old stubble. Not much opportunity to shave on the train. But she liked the hint of whiskers on his face. His lips quirked, and she jerked her gaze upward and found him watching her through heavy-lidded eyes.

"Morning, Mrs. Frazier."

Her stomach dipped at the gravelly sound of his voice, roughened by sleep. "Mr. Frazier."

"Happy?" He wrapped his arms around her, and she laid her head on his rumpled shirt.

"Very." Annabelle smiled. She was more than happy. She was content. Very, very content.

They lay still, the rocking motion of the train lulling Annabelle back into half-wakeful, half-asleep slumber. The past year had been like a dream. Samuel had courted her in his quiet, determined way all through spring while helping Jack build a house. Jack and Maggie had married as soon as their house was finished, a stone's throw from the sawmill.

Come June, Annabelle had walked down the aisle and become Samuel's bride, and they'd moved into their own home built from lumber cut from the mill. Money was tight, but the business was flourishing, and they were blissfully happy. And then Samuel had announced they were going to Illinois for Christmas.

Annabelle smiled, listening to the steady thrum of her husband's heartbeat. Yes, she was excited about the trip, and yes, she wanted to see her cousin, but she didn't need a white Christmas anymore.

She'd always be Samuel's evergreen bride, her hopes and dreams forever planted in the pine forest way down in the heart of Mississippi.

About the Author

Pam Hillman was born and raised on a dairy farm in Mississippi and spent her teenage years perched on the seat of a tractor, raking hay. In those days, her daddy couldn't afford two cab tractors with air conditioning and a radio, so Pam drove an old Allis Chalmers 110. When her daddy asked her if she wanted to bale hay, she told him she didn't mind raking. Raking hay doesn't take much thought, so Pam spent her time working on her tan and making up stories in her head. Please visit Pam at www.pamhillman.com.

The Gift-Wrapped Bride

by Maureen Lang

Chapter 1

Chicago, Illinois
November 1848

Boom! Snap! Pop, pop, pop!

Sophie's scream echoed the sudden whinny of horses startled by shots exploding on the busy Chicago street. Despite her grip on the wagon's seat carrying her parents, the moment the vehicle bounced off the ground, she was thrown to the narrow floorboard behind her. It was the only spot of unused space between the many belongings they'd safely toted all the way from Ohio. One of her drawing pads fell from the perch where she'd left it, a stiff corner striking her on the back of her head.

Her thirteen-year-old brother, Gordy, landed on top of her, the heel of his boot smacking her shinbone. She didn't mean to shove him away, but the wagon hit another rock or rut and she plummeted toward him, her elbow smashing into his shoulder. This time they landed side by side, just beneath the seat still miraculously holding both of her parents.

Frantic, she grappled toward the bench again, adding the new pain of a splinter to her bruises. The terror on her mother's face was plain to see, just as the sinews of her father's strong forearms stood out while he fought the reins connected to the runaway horses.

"Whoa! Dink! Acer!" The horses ignored her father's desperate call. They bounded ahead, both sets of ears pressed back, Dink's mane flying, Acer's powerful neck straining against the pull of the reins.

Suddenly from beside the wagon a new shadow joined theirs, nearly flying alongside on a road littered with other horses, wagons, even pedestrians. Anything in their path parted like a terrified Red Sea to make way for their plunge farther into town.

The shadow to Sophie's right overtook the wagon itself. It was a man on horseback, his hat flying off as he jumped from his mount and onto Dink, the strong young colt Father had been so proud to drive this far. The man leaned down just as mud spattered up in all directions. He then pulled on both horses' reins, Acer not nearly as fast as Dink but twice as strong and brave. Still, reined with Dink, he hadn't any choice except to keep up with the other horse's frenzied pace that was only now coming under control.

With the shots silenced and the added weight of a rider on his back, Dink slowed at last. Or perhaps it was the drag of mud beneath them doing the job.

"Whoa there, Dink," called her father, his voice smoother than it had been a moment ago. "Good boy, Acer. That's it. Slow him down now."

"Goodness!" said Mother, righting her bonnet, which would have flown with the wind alongside their rescuer's hat had it not been for the string tied under her chin. "What in the world caused the ruckus setting them off?"

The man on Dink glanced over his shoulder once the pair of horses came to a full stop, a stop made more secure now that they were decidedly listing to one side. Sophie felt the wagon tilt. No broken wheel or axle this time; it was a slow, rather soft slide of the wagon's entire right edge.

"Ground rats, ma'am."

"Rats! Was someone shooting at them?"

"No, ma'am. Ground rats are firecrackers. They pop and sizzle and go every which way. A few landed right under your horses' hooves."

He jumped off, his own landing no doubt cushioned by the mud, but he didn't seem to mind as he patted Dink with one hand and waved a greeting to them with the other.

"Welcome to—" He stopped himself suddenly. Sophie's parents were likely the only two he'd noticed, since she was kneeling behind them and Gordy was behind her. "Mr. and Mrs. Stewart! Welcome to Chicago!"

"Look, Frank!" cried Mother. "It's Noah Jackson!"

Sophie dared another peek, her heart that still thudded from near death now pounding anew. Noah Jackson. Of all the people to greet them, why did it have to be him? That bully.

Nonetheless, she peered out, wondering if her brother Arthur might be with him. That would make the trouble that had come with their arrival worth it. But he was nowhere to be seen.

Father jumped down then moved to help Mother. Sophie watched both of them hug that wretched boy—well, she supposed he was a man now, since he certainly looked the part, with a few days of beard on his face, what she could see of it between dollops of mud. They thanked and praised him for his courage as Sophie began wondering just how convenient it was to have him play the rescuer. He'd always liked her parents, even though he treated nearly everyone else shabbily. Perhaps he'd set off a firecracker or two just to provide himself an opportunity to show off.

Knowing she must greet him, too, especially since Gordy was already scrambling over her to get out of the wagon, she sighed heavily as Noah's face lit again with another hearty reception.

"Ha! Who's this? Not Gordy!" He slapped her little brother on the back, and to her surprise, Gordy didn't seem to mind the contact. If someone had hit her that way, she'd have called it a smack. "Maybe you're a Gordon now, little man, nearly all grown up."

"Gordy's fine. Not sure I'll answer to anything else."

Then Noah's gaze left her family as if in search of the only missing member. Her. She was still peering over the seat when he spotted her.

"Sophie?"

No sense putting it off, even though he was the last person she ever wanted to greet. Here was the boy who had single-handedly humiliated her—not just once but on countless occasions. Tripping her in the middle of the schoolroom so her skirts went flying, petticoats and all, right up into her face for everyone to see. He was the boy who had tossed a spider onto her spelling test to make her scream. And who was punished for disrupting the class? Not him, even though she'd tattled on him. But she hadn't seen him do it and the teacher hadn't accepted her accusation against him, especially when he claimed innocence. So she'd gone alone to stand in the corner and had to stay after school to finish her test.

Noah Jackson had even put a frog in her lunch pail. She'd gone hungry that day, refusing to eat something that had no doubt been kissed by a frog.

She'd been sorry when her brother Arthur had left Toledo to come to Chicago for a job five years ago, but she hadn't been one little bit sorry when Noah announced he was going as well. Not a single member of his own large family protested his departure, although he'd been only sixteen at the time.

Clearing her throat, smoothing back her hair that had come loose from the braid barely tied at the nape of her neck, she ran a hand over her skirt, determined that both the skirt and petticoat would stay in place when she must jump off this wagon. She stood to her full height.

There was some measure of satisfaction to see Noah's eyes follow her from the height nearer what he likely remembered her to be all the way up to her current five-foot-three stature. His brows rose, and if she wasn't mistaken, she even saw a hint of appreciation in those eyes that had always been so filled with mischief.

Carefully, she climbed over the seat, choosing each movement ahead so that by the time she hopped gracefully from the step onto the only dry space nearby, she was sure he would see her for what she was. All grown up and not to be teased.

"You've grown some, Sophie," he whispered.

Mother laughed just as Father had to reach up to put a hand on Noah's shoulder.

"So have you, son."

The changes in Noah made her wonder how much Arthur had grown, too. Hadn't Mother sent him trousers on several occasions because the ones he left with had become too short?

Not wanting to give—or receive—any more attention to or from Noah, Sophie turned to see if the wagons that had been traveling behind them had caught up yet. She saw them ambling down the busy, mud-pocked road, a wave exchanged between Father and Mr. Hobson easing their neighbor's features from concerned to his usual placid face.

In the same sweep, Sophie also took in the sights of the street. It was just as cluttered as it had been before clearing the way for their wild ride, but Arthur was nowhere to be seen along the string of shops. Although this street offered mostly wooden storefronts and uneven boardwalks, she had to admit this town was larger than Toledo. Not that it was better—she smelled the unmistakable odor of livestock—but at least they wouldn't have to live in that wagon anymore. The past four weeks of that had been enough.

"Isn't Arthur with you?"

Sophie was glad her mother had asked what she'd wanted to, and looked again at Noah for his answer. She was surprised to see he'd still been looking at her but snapped his gaze to her mother when he caught her observation.

"He must be done at the Reaper Works for the day but likely went straight to look for you once the whistle blew."

"He got the job there, then?" asked Father.

Noah nodded. "Now that the canal is finished, a bunch of us were glad to get good jobs elsewhere, sir. I'm working with the Mechanics group myself."

Sir. Humph. Noah Jackson hadn't changed a bit. He had always sounded respectful around her father. Why didn't Noah talk to him the way he used to talk to everyone else? Clever name calling was Noah Jackson's specialty. "Squealer Sophie" had been a favorite, not to mention "String Bean Sophie" because of her skinny arms, and "Swan Sophie" because he said her neck was too long. Most of the time he'd called her "Tot," short for toddler, which sufficiently reminded her she was four years younger than Arthur. As if that would make Noah more than just two years older than her.

"Arthur wrote to us about the place to camp our wagons, Noah," Father said. "Do you know where it is?"

"Up on the Des Plaines Valley Road. I'll take you there. The site's about a half hour or so north."

"So far?" Gordy complained. "I thought we were here already. In our new home."

"And so you are," Noah said, tousling Gordy's light brown hair. "It's a spot for wagon trains going west to assemble while they purchase everything they'll need. Plenty of room for those coming to town, too, to settle in until everybody figures out where to live."

Father waved again to Mr. Hobson, who had pulled up behind them. "Noah Jackson's here," he called, "and he'll take us to a place to camp."

Mr. Hobson saluted his acknowledgment, and Sophie spotted the head of her friend Alice pop up behind him. As much as Sophie loved her best friend, she had to hide the scowl she'd just inspired. Alice was likely looking for a peek at one of the "young prospects," the main and awful reason she and Sophie and several other daughters had been dragged to Chicago in the first place. But really, did Alice want a peek at the bottom of the barrel?

Sophie meant to have a serious talk with that girl.

Noah moved back toward the horses. "We'll get you out of this mudhole first."

Sophie moved out of the way. Perhaps she would ride with Alice and start that talk right now. "I've never been so grateful for mud," she grumbled as she pulled her skirts clear of another puddle between her and the nearest wooden walkway.

Mother sent her a surprised look, Father a frown, and Noah a quizzical stare. In spite of the attention, she had no wish to call back her words. "It's what stopped us, wasn't it? The mud?"

Noah raised one of his brows but said nothing, as her mother tsked.

"That's a little like thanking the fire for a hot meal, dear. We wouldn't have anything to eat without the cook."

"What do you mean, Mother?" Gordy asked.

Sophie tilted her head, staring at her mother even though she felt Noah's gaze more strongly than any other. "She means Noah's the cook."

"Oh! Sure, that's right." Gordy's face burst into a smile. "I get it now. 'Cause it was him who saved us. Not the mud. Right, Mother?"

Sophie couldn't help but roll her eyes as she tugged her little brother along. Father went to Acer's side while Noah went around to Dink's, and between the two of them they coaxed the animals to pull the rig free of the soft, stubborn earth.

Sophie folded her arms. Noah Jackson might have grown into a strong, even handsome young man. She couldn't help but notice the way his shoulders strained the material on that gray cotton shirt he wore. He had the same bold brows, broad chin, and thick, dark hair—hair that reached past the folded collar of his shirt.

But he was no hero. She knew that as sure as she knew Chicago was the last place on earth she wanted to live.

Chapter 2

For the first time in five years, Noah Jackson was living in better conditions than the folks he and Arthur had left behind in Ohio. The boardinghouse he called home since they'd finished living in tent quarters along the canal construction wasn't much better—it was more like a dormitory above the long, wide stable below—but it had a solid roof, rope beds with straw mattresses, and real windows. All of that made it far better than sleeping under a cramped wagon or the crowded four-room home he grew up in with seven brothers and sisters.

It wouldn't be long before he and Artie introduced Artie's folks to all the possibilities that Chicago offered. Soon they'd be settled in a proper home.

Pulling on his boots, he called to Arthur, still sleeping on the cot next to his own.

"Hey, better get going, Artie. Church in a half hour."

"Huh?"

"Half hour. Let's go."

Arthur Stewart had only one thing in common with his sister: they shared the same color hair. Noah would never have bothered to describe the shade—a mix of gold and copper—until seeing it on Sophie. He wondered if he'd ever be able to look at Arthur again without thinking of her.

Which was too bad for him. She'd made a point to ignore him all the way to the campsite and forever thereafter.

Sophie had been mighty happy to see her brother, though. She'd laughed, because even though Artie was taller than she was, her brother's height had stopped at the same spot as their father. She'd teased Gordy, saying that was likely all the taller he'd get, too.

Had she noticed how tall Noah had gotten? But then, how would she, when she made such a point to ignore him?

Who would have thought that little tattler would grow into such a lovely young woman? He knew she'd matured, because Artie had shared her letters with him over the years. Letters that hadn't failed to impress, even intrigue Noah—something he'd kept to himself.

As usual, Artie was slow in the morning, even on Sunday after an extra hour of sleep. When they'd come to Chicago that was how Noah had been, too, especially on Sunday, a day both had proclaimed a day of rest, even from something like church.

But that had all changed once they'd met Ezra Pooley, the canal foreman's father. Ezra was a patriarch of Chicago who had the goodwill—some might call it bad sense—to invite young men far from their homes into his own. Tasty meals, interesting conversations, even the patience to teach whoever cared to learn the craft of leather working. He'd given Noah plenty to think about, including God.

Ezra had also helped the boys investigate land and housing available if their families did decide to come to Chicago. Noah was sure their findings had encouraged his friends' families to leave Toledo for the promise of such a growing city like Chicago.

"Better wear that tie," Noah reminded Artie, who was still sitting on the side of his cot, rubbing palms to his face against remnants of sleep.

A light of anticipation ignited on Arthur's face. "Oh yeah! We didn't take baths for nothin' last night, did we? We can reacquaint ourselves with the girls today. My parents said so themselves."

"Hush up!" called a voice a few bunks away. "Some of us are trying to sleep."

"And we're no louder than O'Hananan's snoring," Noah said back, "so hush up yourself." He pulled the duffel bag from beneath his cot, taking up his comb and facing Artie again. "I counted four, besides your sister, of course," he whispered. "That's five. Did I miss any?"

"Ha! Shows you how much you saw past Sophie. I saw you watching her. There are eight. Two in the Hobson family, three in the Cabots', one each in the Hatten and the Selway wagons."

"Two in the Hobson family? Alice is one. But you're not counting Sally, are you? She can't be any older than twelve."

"She's fifteen, and in a couple of years she'll be just as pretty as her sister."

"I'm surprised you saw anybody past Alice then, if you think I didn't see anybody but Sophie."

"It was Sophie who told me how many came along. I think the pastor brought his sister, too, but Sophie didn't count her, because she's old enough to have stayed behind." Then he cleared his throat, as if buying time to figure out what to say next. "Uh, there's something I should say about Sophie. She's not too keen on why my family decided to join us out here. Says they're putting all their daughters up on the marriage block like 'common property.'"

Noah laughed at Artie's imitation of Sophie. He'd done a good job at capturing her disdain.

"If only it were that easy," he said with an exaggerated sigh. "Just to hand over some of our savings and buy one."

Artie took a friendly swipe at Noah with the tie he would wear over one of the two new shirts his mother had brought with them—Noah was wearing the other. "Hey, that's my sister you're wanting to buy as if she's on Chicago's cattle market. A little bit of wooing will do both of you some good."

"A little bit of wooing?" Noah repeated. "You think that's all it'll take?"

Artie laughed all the way to the door.

∽

Sophie let Alice loop their arms, but it wasn't a solely affectionate gesture. Her friend surely knew that if Sophie wasn't coerced into going to this afternoon's meeting, she wasn't likely to attend at all. Why Alice and Martha and Jane and even little Sally and the rest of those who'd been brought from Ohio wanted to be here was beyond Sophie's understanding. She'd much rather stay back at the detestable wagon. At least there she could pass the time drawing the birds she'd seen on the trail here—something she hadn't been able to do during the entire bumpy ride west. She only hoped she could remember the details she'd tried committing to memory along the way.

She'd had to ignore the stares of several young men at this morning's church service behind the wagons. Not the least of which was Noah Jackson's. Word had evidently spread that five foolish families from the East had come to town ready to add themselves to the Chicago census, both now and in the future, by bringing a crop of potential new brides.

Many men of Chicago were responding, even if the first price to pay had been sitting through a church service. The pastor had welcomed his new congregation, while silly girls like Alice beamed under the attention. Sophie wished she could have crawled under Father's bench, away from the obvious scrutiny.

This afternoon's meeting was supposed to address how best to proceed with their resettlement as well as the procurement of a new church building. She'd heard her father and mother discuss such things all the way from Ohio, as if jobs and homes and the church were their only concerns.

But the real reason for coming to Chicago was the one topic they carefully avoided around Sophie. It was, in fact, the true incentive behind today's meeting. Now, boys like Noah Jackson, Alice's brother Howard, the Selway and Hatten boys—all who had come to Chicago for jobs—would be allowed to look over their sisters and neighbors and see just how mature they had become.

Wife material.

"You changed your clothes from the service this morning," Alice said as they approached the gathering spot behind their row of wagons. Tables had been added to the benches and chairs they'd used for the service, so it now looked like the setting for a party.

"I'm more comfortable now."

"And why have you pinned up your hair that way?" The disapproval in her friend's tone was clearer now. "It looks better free and down your back. Or maybe a single braid tied loosely like you did yesterday—a little softer than what you have."

Sophie was half tempted to unfasten the tight bun at the back of her head, but not for the reason Alice suggested. She'd pulled it so severely away from her face it was giving her a headache. However, that, combined with her oldest and most faded skirt and topped by a thick and unnecessary shawl on this uncommonly lovely fall day, were her only methods of protest. She wasn't here to exhibit herself.

"I can't understand why you're willing to go along with this scheme to throw us together with the boys already here," Sophie said. "It's not natural."

"Oh fiddle-faddle. What's unnatural about providing an opportunity to fall in love and start a new life? No one's forcing us to get married, you know. I think we should be grateful to be here, where brides are needed far more than they are back in Toledo. We'll have more choice here."

Back in Toledo. . . Chicago might be bigger, but Sophie had left behind the one dream that was more important to her than marriage. Mr. Allenby was like a grandfather to her. After taking her under his wing three years ago, he'd taught her more about wildlife drawing than she could ever have learned on her own. He'd assured her that her drawings were good enough to be appreciated by anyone who saw them, often telling her of his friend in New York who published such pictures in books. Real books that might have someday included her own drawings.

Each and every thought of leaving such a future behind came with a pinprick of pain. She couldn't see a bird fly or a mouse scurry across the plains without wondering what could have happened had Mr. Allenby introduced her drawings to his friend, as he'd promised to do when next he had the opportunity.

With a sigh, Sophie looked around. Others were already assembled with her parents and Alice's parents. Although Alice pulled her forward, Sophie held back, lingering near the third table. They were close enough to catch her mother's eye, however, and she gave Sophie a surprised glance at the skirt she'd worn through most of their travels. Her mother's frown sent a silent question Sophie could nonetheless hear loud and clear: *Why don't you just cover yourself in sackcloth and ashes?*

Sophie looked past her mother to a new source of resentment. The pastor's wife and three other women, all mothers, tended to the bowls and trays set off on a table to the side. On any other occasion, girls like herself and Alice would be serving the older folks. But no, not today. They didn't want the girls distracted with work when there were gazes to catch, smiles to exchange. Love to inspire.

"You're looking especially pretty this afternoon," came a familiar voice behind them.

Sophie and Alice turned around. It was Arthur, looking directly at Alice. As she giggled and thanked him for the compliment, Sophie felt like teasing him about playing Romeo. But when she saw Noah Jackson at his side, the temptation to add anything lighthearted to the afternoon abandoned her.

Arthur's eyes settled next on Sophie, where he started to smile anew but then looked outright confused. "And you, Sophie, well, you look pretty awful. That hair looks to be wound tighter than when I used to yank it. Why don't you let it go?"

"Because I like it this way." She turned around at the table, offering them her back as she took a seat and tugged on Alice to do the same. Unfortunately, rather than moving on, the boys claimed places just opposite. Arthur sat across from Alice, and Noah across from Sophie.

"It sure is nice to see some familiar faces around here," Noah said, briefly glancing at Alice but letting his gaze rest on Sophie. "I forgot how good it is to be around somebody I've known my whole life, other than just Artie."

Sophie raised her nose and looked away. "Then I suppose you know how hard it was for Alice and me to leave behind friends we've had all our lives, too."

"Aw, Sophie," said Arthur, "you brought along half the ones you know best. You weren't closer to anybody than Alice. Can't complain too much about that."

Shows you how much you know, she wanted to say. Hadn't he read any of her letters? She'd even sent him some of her favorite drawings, to show him how much Mr. Allenby had taught her. Her brother had obviously forgotten all about that. From the look on his face when he ogled Alice, she could see why.

But then he glanced back at her. "I suppose you miss Mr. Allenby. Guess I don't blame you for that."

Sophie was so surprised he'd spoken her thoughts that she wouldn't trust her voice not to reveal the depth of her loss. Alice quickly filled the growing pause.

"She certainly does miss that old man," Alice said. "Not that he wasn't kind, and a talented artist and teacher, too. But I keep telling her he was, well"—she tapped her temple—"addled. Do you know he used to call me by my mother's name? And his neighbor saw him in his bathrobe on his front stair! He said he was looking for his hat. Outside!"

"He's an artist," Sophie reminded Alice. "Artists are always flamboyant."

"I'm sorry you miss him," Noah said softly, his gaze still on her. "Arthur and I have met that kind of man here, the kind to share his time. He's taught me leather working. Guess I'd miss him if we left town."

Sophie spared him a glance but not for long. She was waiting for him to come up with a new nickname for her. If she were to think of one for herself with her hair fashioned the way she'd pulled it back today, it would be "Tufted Duck." If she drew a picture of one now, he would think of the name himself.

"And did he teach you how to make ground rats, perhaps?" She hadn't meant to say that aloud, and when all eyes turned to her, she almost wished she could recall them. Almost.

"Father told me about how Noah saved the rig," Arthur said. "You don't really think Noah set off that ruckus so he could risk his life trying to stop it?"

She didn't reply, letting her silence speak for her.

"That is what you believe, then?" Noah persisted. She was surprised to hear a touch of sadness in his voice.

It was that very sadness that angered her now, just as much as the defense her brother had launched for him a moment ago. "Why shouldn't I assume such a thing? You, who tripped me whenever you had the chance, embarrassing me in front of the entire classroom? You, who waited behind bushes until I was in range of your slingshot to shoot peas at me? You, who started that fire in the school outhouse? You, who made sure I was startled out of my wits right over a puddle and made me drop my books into it. And those are only a few of my memories of you, Noah Jackson. Why wouldn't you do something like set off a few firecrackers?"

He whistled low. "You have a better memory than I do. And here I thought you were just Tot the Tattler. Guess you had some reasons for it, though."

Such a feeble attempt to claim responsibility was hardly enough to excuse his behavior. He might have been gone five years, but she doubted that was long enough to have changed him. That would take eternity.

"Sophie," Arthur said, his tone exasperated, "Noah didn't pull such a childish—and dangerous—prank like setting off firecrackers under a horse in the middle of a busy street. That happens more than you'd imagine, with or without Noah around. Fact is, there's a group of boys in town that like creating mischief." He looked around, his gaze stopping in the direction of their parents. "In fact, I was going to warn Father to keep Gordy clear of them. Where is Gordy, anyway?"

Sophie threw a glance back toward their wagon but didn't see their brother. "He was going to stay in the wagon during the meeting—until the food is ready, of course."

"We'll talk to him directly, then," Noah said, "after we eat."

Just then the pastor called their attention to say the blessing. Before bowing her head, Sophie stole a quick look at Noah. He appeared downright pious as he prepared to join in prayer, but she didn't believe his act for a moment.

A pious bully? Huh!

Chapter 3

In the next two weeks, Sophie learned just how valuable it had been for the families coming west to have had their sons pave the way. In anticipation of their arrival, Arthur had not only helped explore housing possibilities, but also jobs and schools and the best furniture makers in town. Father was a factory millwright with experience, so his talents were in demand anywhere a factory with machinery could be found. In spite of workers already available in the city left without a job once canal work was finished, good references and the associations offered through their sons had each father a job by the end of the very first week.

Even Sophie had to admit it was only Mr. Allenby she missed, because the home Arthur had found for them in Chicago was every bit as comfortable, plus a little larger, than the one they had left behind. And she still had the company of her best friend.

At the family dinner table one evening, Noah assured her family that Chicago would far surpass Toledo.

Of course he would think so. Hadn't he helped Arthur convince their family to move here? She refused even to listen to him, leaning closer to Arthur to ask him a question she'd had nearly since their arrival.

"Is there a library here in town?"

"Several."

Sophie looked at Noah, who had usurped the answer before her brother could speak. Try though she did to avoid speaking to Noah, he seemed to have a response to everything she said, even when not directed to him.

"The libraries here in Chicago are connected to private clubs," Arthur added. "Women aren't allowed membership."

"Not at Gale and Company," Noah said. He looked at Sophie, but she averted her face even though she hung on his words. "It's a store, but they have a small circulating library, too. I can take you there tomorrow afternoon."

"I'm sure I can find it on my own," she said.

"If they don't have the kind of book you're looking for, I can introduce you to Mr. Pooley. He has quite a few books that I'm sure would interest you."

"Thank you, but I'm sure that won't be necessary." She turned her attention back to her dinner, ignoring the slight tap on her ankle from her mother.

Sophie didn't even look at Mother. She knew she would send a reminder of the gentle advice she'd offered earlier. Be pleasant, be friendly, smile at the boy. He's only trying to be nice.

Sophie had no intention of adhering to any of it. Her mother was too easily fooled by the thin veneer over Noah's bullying ways. Gullibility around someone like Noah could be downright hazardous.

⁕

"What a pleasant surprise!"

Sophie looked up from the book on the small table in front of her but offered no greeting as Noah took the empty seat on the other side. Wasn't sharing most of her family's dinners with him enough? Now he had to follow her to the library, too?

"Did you know I'm working with the Chicago Mechanics' Institute? I stop in here often because this is on my way home."

So that was the reason he'd been so eager to tell her about the library.

"It has mostly fiction, but it's a nice variety." She kept her voice polite but curt then looked again at the book before her. He did not take the hint to leave her to it. "I'm sure you'll want to be on your way, then. Good day."

He remained seated comfortably. There was only one way to end this, and that was to see about borrowing this book even though she wasn't at all sure this was the one she wanted. Exploring others would have to wait until next time.

Pulling the book closer to her side of the table, she stood. Noah jumped to his feet as well.

"In a hurry?"

"Yes," she said but was instantly convicted of her lie. "No. I simply want to speak to the clerk."

"Don't forget about the private collection I mentioned," he said. "Ezra Pooley's. Arthur knows him, too. I visited him just the other day, and I noticed he has a book you might like. A bound copy of Wilson's *American Ornithology*. Have you ever seen it, Sophie?"

Her pulse quickened. "Not a bound copy," she admitted. Mr. Allenby owned several loose plates but not the entire collection. What a treasure such a book would be! Even just to look at. . .

Her heart missed a beat at the opportunity, but she turned away. "Then

I'll ask Arthur about him. Good day."

"Sophie," he called softly after her when she took a few steps away, "are you ever going to forgive me for a few childish pranks?"

She faced him head-on. "All I've seen since we arrived is the way you used to act around my parents. Very polite, but I'm afraid not very sincere. So I'm sure you'll understand if I repeat myself. Good day."

"No, wait, Sophie." He touched her elbow lightly to prevent her from moving on again. "Even if you don't think I've changed, you must admit I've grown up. Hasn't Arthur told you that?"

"My entire family has been on a veritable campaign for you. But frankly, even if I believed a word of it, I have no intention of forgetting that you have the heart of a bully. Now really, *good day*."

Her heart pounded harder than the heels of her boots on the wooden floor. If she'd been rude, she'd given him no less than what he deserved.

Why should she believe he'd changed? She knew how busy Arthur and Noah had been these last few years, between working on the Illinois and Michigan Canal and whatever jobs they could find when canal work had been interrupted. Such labor might have made them both stronger, but work hadn't been the only thing they'd done since they left Toledo.

She'd read every letter Arthur had sent and couldn't help hearing Noah's since her mother read aloud those he'd sent to her parents. For the first four and a half years, all they'd talked about was one pub or another, often places where fights broke out. They'd lived the lives of wild young men without church or civility. Exactly how was Noah to have improved himself in a place like this?

Holding the book more gently now that she was away from him, she ventured a glance behind her, but he was already gone. Assuring herself her own rudeness couldn't possibly penetrate such a thick hide as his, she walked on. Likely he'd already forgotten their encounter.

⸭

Noah waited just outside Gale and Company. For two weeks, ever since Sophie had made it clear she remembered every foolish thing he'd ever done, he'd kept himself busier than ever. When he wasn't occupied, he tried thinking about some of the other girls who had come to Chicago with their families.

But it was no use. Even if Noah were interested, competition for polite female company was stiff in this city. If he encouraged a fledgling interest in any of them, there was already a long line of beaus waiting for her. He had

340

little desire to fight for anyone's attention except Sophie's.

The only reason he did not have to wade through a long line at Sophie's door was because she didn't seem any friendlier toward the others than she was toward him. Arthur told him when a caller came to introduce himself to Sophie, she asked her mother to send him away without seeing him.

Still, it was only a matter of time before her attitude was bound to soften about having left Toledo. Noah planned to use his close proximity to the family to his benefit around the one girl whose interest he genuinely wanted to stir.

"Fight! Fight!"

The call came from across the street, where passersby were already circling a couple of young boys locked in a scuffle. No one seemed interested in doing anything more than watch, even when one broke free long enough to land a punch against the other boy's cheek.

"Hey!" Noah jumped through the crowd, knowing all too well that a fight lasting only a few minutes could feel like it went on forever. Not to mention leave more than a little sting. He grabbed the larger of the two boys—who was still a foot shorter than Noah himself—while he staved off the other with the long length of his arm. Working on the pumps regulating the water level along the canal had made Noah stronger than ever.

"Punching each other isn't going to stop whatever gripe you have," he said. "You'd better not fight on the street, or you'll both get fined for public nuisance. Now go home and work out some other way to settle this."

He shoved off both of them. His intervention was likely nothing more than a delay to yet another fight, but at least they wouldn't be doing it with an audience of women and children. At least he hoped not.

He would have returned to the bookshop to wait for Sophie, but one of the other spectators caught his glance. This boy hadn't run off as fast as the rest of the gang of rogues.

"Gordy?"

The boy stopped, his back still to Noah. It took ten steps to reach him, and with each one Noah held out hope he was wrong. But he wasn't.

"I hope you just happened by," Noah said, but Gordy's guilty face told him otherwise. "You haven't been mixing with that group of boys, have you, Gordy? In spite of what Artie and I told you?"

Gordy plunged his hands into the pockets of his knee pants, hanging his head so all Noah could see was the top of his cap.

"They're friendly. To me."

"You don't think sooner or later you'll get in a fight with one of them, or do something you shouldn't be doing?"

Gordy squared his shoulders. "I know better than that. But a fella's got to have friends. Friends my own age."

"Gordy!"

Sophie's call came from the sidewalk on the other side of the street.

Gordy's eyes sprang to his sister then back to Noah, for the first time with a hint of fear in them.

"You aren't going to tell her, are you, Noah?"

Noah needed more than a few scant seconds to answer such a question, and Sophie joined them before he'd come close to any decision.

"Didn't you go straight home from school today, Gordy?" asked Sophie.

Gordy shook his head, even though his gaze hadn't yet left Noah's. Under any other circumstance, Noah would have had no intention of tattling, at least for now. But he was treading carefully around Sophie and wondered if withholding something she'd likely find important would sit well if she ever found out.

"I'll escort both of you home," Noah announced, and to his surprise Sophie didn't object. But she did walk in front of him, taking Gordy by the arm in just the way he hoped she would take his someday. Easily, as if it were the most natural thing in the world.

"You staying for dinner, Noah?" Gordy threw the tentative question over his shoulder.

Noah knew his answer wouldn't meet the boy's full approval, as it might have only an hour ago—before learning a good talking-to was in store.

The very same answer was likely received by Sophie with the same lack of welcome—he couldn't see her face—but he offered a broad and confident smile anyway. "Sure am!"

Chapter 4

Sophie heard only two sounds: a faint rustle from the tall, browned grass on the prairie in the distance and the scratch of the pencil against her notepad. She'd had to walk some distance to get here this morning, but the sky was clear and a southern breeze comfortably warmed the air. She'd been eager to leave behind the noise and smells along the busy streets and so had left just after dawn lit her way.

Mr. Allenby once told her real wildlife artists would use specimens from taxidermists whenever they could, or on their own might wire a small, dead animal in place to allow thorough study for recording each detail with minute precision. Other than the time Alice's cat had delivered a dead bird to her, which her friend promptly offered to Sophie, Sophie had neither the wherewithal to kill nor the desire to carry through with such measures, even in the name of art or science.

Back in Toledo she would often do what she did now. Sit quietly and study whatever God sent her way. She had to depend on her own observational skills, since most animals did not stay long to pose. But her initial drawings were always swift, and her memory was strong. She kept her drawings in her notebook, and whenever she saw a bird she'd already documented, she would check again to be sure she'd recorded it as accurately as a live bird would allow.

With her mind as quiet as her surroundings, Sophie realized she'd accepted sooner than she expected this move away from Toledo. The prairie was lovely with its tall, swaying grasses. It would provide all kinds of new animals to draw, she was sure of it. She certainly missed Mr. Allenby—he was a good teacher, after all. But perhaps what she really missed was his promise to introduce her work to an important publisher.

It still pained her to recall what Father had said when she'd protested leaving behind her opportunities and artistic aspirations. He'd claimed Mr. Allenby was nothing more than a friendly, harmless old man with no real idea how to get her drawings published. As fine as her drawings might be, there were plenty of others who would see their work published long before hers ever would be.

She knew he hadn't meant to be cruel; in his way, he might even have been trying to protect her from hoping for something he thought impossible. But as she reviewed the drawing she'd just finished, of a bird she couldn't name, with a stark red streak fringed with a contrasting white along the top of its black wings, she knew her work was true to life. It was good enough to be published. *Wasn't it?*

"Sophie! Sophie!"

Sophie stiffened at the call of her name coming from two different directions. There was no hill or canyon to make an echo. Who could be calling for her out here?

She stood.

"I'm here!"

She saw her brother first from one direction then Noah from another, both trotting closer, and each out of breath, with considerable concern on their faces.

"What's the matter?" she demanded. "Is everyone all right? Mother? Father? Not trouble with Gordy?"

Arthur exchanged a curious look with Noah before they both burst into laughter. "Everybody's worried about *you*, you great big ninnyhammer," he said, gently shoving her shoulder.

"Why in the world would anybody worry about me? I told Mother where I was going."

"Yes, and she told Father, who told me when I came by for breakfast. I started the alarm. I fetched Noah immediately and wouldn't let Gordy or even Father come along for fear of losing either one of them."

Clutching the notepad closer to her chest, Sophie cast a glance at Noah, who was still looking on with an annoyingly clear residue of concern. "I have no idea why you should have sounded such an alarm."

"The prairie's a dangerous place, Sophie," Noah said softly. "Even here, close to the city. It's easy to get lost in the tall grasses, for one, not to mention the snakes and wolves."

Lifting her chin, Sophie started back home exactly the way she'd come. "Despite what you might think, I'm not a *complete* ninnyhammer." She kept walking without looking back. "I'd know enough not to get myself lost, and as for wolves and snakes, the grasses are still a ways off, so there wasn't much risk of that either."

Although she never looked back at either one of them, she felt their presence as clearly as if they'd been breathing down her neck.

"What's that you're holding there, Sophie?" called Noah.

She pretended not to hear him.

"That's her drawing book," her brother answered. "Don't you remember? I showed you some of the pictures she sent in letters."

"Oh sure," Noah said. "You're pretty good, Sophie. So what did you draw today?"

Pretty good. He obviously shared the same tendency for meager praise her father possessed, at least when it came to her talent. What other words went with *pretty good*? *Tolerable, passable, satisfactory.* Each of those terms would hardly inspire an artist to greater effort.

Unless. . .that was all the regard her talent deserved.

She increased her pace, not speaking a word all the way back to the house, where Mother offered everyone a delayed breakfast.

Sophie went straight to her room and didn't emerge again until after Father, Arthur, and Noah left for their jobs.

⁂

"So you think they're pretty good, then?"

Noah felt little compunction about having borrowed Sophie's drawings from Arthur's letters even though he hadn't asked him. He watched Ezra Pooley's lined face for any sign that he could be wrong, that his infatuation with Sophie had fooled him into thinking her drawings were good enough to interest others besides himself and Arthur, both of whom shared definite partiality toward the artist. Ezra was as honest as he was old, and Noah knew he could depend on him for an unbiased opinion.

When Ezra raised his brows, Noah knew he was right. Sophie's talent was every bit as real as he believed it to be.

"They're very good." Ezra stroked his chin. "And you think readers will be interested in these pictures?"

Ezra's opinion had already emboldened Noah. "Don't you? There's nothing more popular than the pictures of the West in the *Democrat*. Why not give people the same visual gift about their own backyard? Newcomers and others just passing through will be interested in knowing what to look for around here, or on the prairie if they make plans to move on."

"Illustrations increase the cost," Ezra said but added a grin before Noah's hopes could be dashed. "And there won't be any colors. But I think your idea is sound, and I can suggest a name or two at the papers who can afford such a thing—starting with the *Prairie Farmer*."

Chapter 5

"And so, dear brethren, let our hearts stay warm toward the God who watches over us and sees our every action. Let us plan the remembrance of Christ's birth with love in our hearts for those outside the church, because we may be the only glimpse of God's love others will see. Amen and amen."

Sophie filed out of the pew behind her family. Everyone was jubilant over the new building Pastor Goodwin had found in the city, even though the facts behind its availability might be something they would prefer not to think about. Another church had tried establishing itself, only to fail, leaving their quarters vacant. Didn't anyone worry such a cycle might repeat itself in this muddy, stinking city?

Outside, Sophie turned up her collar against the wind. At least with colder temperatures the mud had hardened, but that was small comfort against the biting gusts.

She drew her brows together as she watched Gordy, walking ahead of them toward home, three blocks from church. Earlier in the week, he had been the cause of one of their mother's rare sour moods, but with good reason. While she and Sophie were baking bread, Gordy's teacher paid them a visit. Her brother had taken to coming home late after school, saying he was spending time with friends. But his teacher informed them he hadn't come to school at all that day.

Sophie couldn't help but wonder if Gordy wasn't taking after Noah, despite the lack of a blood tie.

"You'll help me with the costuming, won't you, dear?"

Sophie was startled when her mother put an arm around her shoulder, shaking her from her thoughts. They walked on arm-in-arm, and she was grateful to share her mother's warmth.

"What's that, Mother?"

"For the Nativity pageant. Haven't you been listening? The pastor mentioned he hopes the Christmas season will draw people to church." She sighed, her gaze on Gordy, too. "I'm hoping the fun of a pageant will keep Gordy busy with better things to do than spend time with boys who don't think school is important."

"Yes, I'll help—if I'm needed, that is. I don't think Pastor Goodwin has had much success recruiting participants." She didn't bother to veil the glare she sent her mother's way. "Those of us who came from Toledo were more concerned about bringing brides, Mother. There is only one Mary in the Nativity. Evidently we should have brought more boys than just Gordy."

Instead of being offended at Sophie's reminder of why they'd come to Chicago, Mother laughed and patted her shoulder. "All we want is to provide a happy life for our children, dear. As the saying goes, a shared life is twice as pleasant and half as hard. Jane Cabot is ready to prove that already."

Sophie grimaced. Jane was the first of the girls they'd traveled with to become engaged, and everyone was talking about their New Year's wedding. The silly way Alice and Arthur were acting, she guessed they might be next to announce upcoming nuptials.

The prospect of watching the girls go down one by one, like ducks at a hunt, seemed abjectly unjust. So obviously contrived. And yet, somehow, the thought of being the only one not to marry presented an unexpected worry.

What else was she to do but marry if she couldn't follow her dream of drawing wildlife?

∽∾

Noah grabbed the collar of the boy he recognized as having been one of the participants in the fight he'd witnessed not long ago. Holding him at arm's length, he ignored the boy's protests over having been waylaid on the boardwalk on South Water Street.

"I have a proposition for you and your friends," Noah said over the boy's shout.

"I don't want no proposition! Lemme go!"

"How do you know you don't want something you haven't even heard yet?"

Noah let go of the frayed collar, only to grab hold of the boy's shoulders. With the temperature growing so much colder, it was a wonder the boy had left whatever home he had with such thin protection—if he even had a home.

"What's your name, boy?"

"None o' your business."

"That's where you're wrong. I live in this town, and you're a troublemaker for all of us. So you made it my business."

"You're dotty! Now lemme go!"

He attempted to break free, but Noah's height and strength had the advantage. It occurred to him the boy had a right to his own freedom, and if anyone saw the exchange, he'd likely find himself—not the boy—in trouble. But he wasn't ready to give up on his idea so easily.

"Look," said Noah, "I know you must be one of the most loyal members of your pack, or else you wouldn't have had the grit to fight. You'd have let somebody else do the fighting. I want to talk to you and the rest of the boys you haunt with."

The boy's struggle eased just enough to let Noah think he wouldn't run off if given the chance. So he let go. The boy shrugged at his jacket, setting it right on his shoulders again. But he stayed put, although the suspicion on his face wasn't any friendlier than the anger had been a moment ago.

"Whata ya wanna talk about?"

"I have a job for you. It's only for a season, but worthwhile. It could lead to other opportunities." *And it might be the only way to keep an eye on Gordy.*

The boy huffed. "Sure. You got a job for a bunch o' boys when this town's filled with grown Irishmen who can't get a job since canal work got done."

"It's a job only young people can do."

"What kind o' job?"

Noah regarded the boy curiously. "Maybe you'd better let me talk to your friends. I'd rather give everybody the chance to answer without you making up their minds ahead of time."

The boy seemed to take it for what it was, a compliment on the power of a leader's influence. "Meet us back o' the tavern down the street in an hour," he said. "The Hog's Head."

Noah would have thanked him for the name, since so many streets in the city hosted more than one tavern. But the boy ran off. Noah called after him. "Hey, kid, what's your name?"

"Still none o' your business."

Then he was gone.

⁓∞⁓

"You call that a job?" Tully repeated.

The only reason Noah had learned the boy's name was because he'd heard someone else address him. He knew this was taking a chance, a "dotty" one as Tully might say, but there was bound to be a boy or two who could be convinced to join the Nativity pageant in exchange for what he had in mind.

"What's a job except an exchange of goods and services?" Noah scanned the patched clothing—near rags—some of the boys wore. "You get a meal at every practice—one you won't have to steal. You get a warm place to eat it, and at the end you get a coat to see you through till spring."

"All for dressing up like loons?"

"Shepherd boys." He looked around. "And three will get to be kings."

There was a titter here and there, a general consensus as to who should play one of the kings, but Tully stopped their rumblings with a shout. "Hey! This ain't no kingdom, so you can all make up your own minds. I think it's pure twaddle. Anybody who does it'll make a fool of hisself."

Another boy, the one Noah recognized as having been on the other end of the fight he'd broken up, stepped closer. He was taller than Tully, every bit as brash, and from something he'd said earlier, Noah already knew he was Irish. "A free meal every time we show up, ya say? And a coat to boot?"

"That's right."

The boy eyed Noah as if he were an object less than worthy of consideration. Even though his height was in his favor, bulk was not. He was as scrawny as a scarecrow.

"I'll be there."

To Noah's vague surprise, four of the nine boys told him they would be at the first rehearsal the night after next. But not Tully.

Now all he had to do was share the news with the pastor—and hope he'd meant it when he'd said he wanted to show the love of God to those outside the church.

Noah figured he couldn't get much further outside the church than the boys he was about to bring in.

Chapter 6

"I don't see why we can't just ask fully grown men from our church to fill the roles in the pageant." Was Sophie the only one wondering such a thing? It appeared so, since even Alice, next to her, looked at her with some surprise.

"The point is to invite others in," Noah said, "so you can get to know some of your new neighbors."

His gaze was settled firmly on Sophie's, once again with a light in his eyes. The man was actually proud of himself! But why wouldn't he be, if he was intent on bringing in boys just like the one he'd been himself—a rascal and a scamp?

Sophie could hardly believe both of her parents were so agreeable to a plan Noah had obviously concocted all on his own. Even though the pastor had presented the idea of a choir and pageant to the church on Sunday, he'd just now given the credit to Noah for the promise of a successful pageant. If she'd known it was Noah's idea, she wouldn't have come to this first planning meeting at all.

"The boys will always be supervised," Pastor Goodwin reminded everyone. "Noah has agreed to direct, so he'll be here for every rehearsal. My wife will conduct the music, and Mr. Stewart will take care of the Nativity scenery while his good wife will see to the costumes and our new choir robes."

"And the coats and promised meals?" Sophie asked. "Where will the provisions come from?"

"I'm sure every family will be happy to donate an item or two," Pastor Goodwin said, adding with a grin, "I've been told you make the best beef stew this side of the Mississippi, Sophie."

"That's true," chimed her mother.

Alice, next to Sophie, leaned close and whispered in Sophie's ear. "Aren't you tired of playing the grumbler every time Noah has anything to do with something? Go ahead and agree!"

Sophie knew she couldn't very well refuse, not unless she wanted it to be assumed her faith in mankind was so lacking she didn't want to help feed a few hungry boys. She *must* agree, even if it was for a bunch of rapscallions led by the Pied Piper of brutes himself.

"Actually, I was hoping for more help from Sophie—Miss Stewart." Noah corrected himself the way he used to when in the presence of polite company. For heaven's sake, he'd been calling her Sophie ever since she could remember! "I was hoping she might help with rehearsals. If she's up to the challenge, of course."

All eyes, not just Noah's, now rested on her. She was to be dared in public to participate in something that might very well be an impossible task, at Noah Jackson's side? Working with scoundrels who were likely every bit as much trouble as Noah had once been?

"I think that's a wonderful idea, dear," her mother announced. "After all, Gordy will be involved, and you've always gotten on so well with him and boys his age."

Who didn't get along with good boys? But this was altogether different. She'd already opened her mouth to agree to cook a meal or two, and somewhere along the way she'd clamped it shut. It wasn't until Alice nudged her that she realized she must open her mouth again, no matter what kind of alarm clanged inside her head.

"Yes, of course I want our church program to be wonderful. I'll help." Then she eyed Alice, who was smiling so smugly that Sophie added, "And I'm sure Alice will be happy to assist, too."

Alice's brows rose in surprise, but she smiled and agreed when Arthur took her hand from her other side. "We'll both help," he said, holding up the hand he clasped.

That was some comfort. At least she wouldn't have to spend the evenings ahead as the only nonrascal in the room.

∞

Midway through the first rehearsal, Noah was beginning to wonder if his plan would succeed. It had started so promisingly, despite only one boy beside Gordy coming from the church. All four of the street boys showed up.

That was when Sophie's face became more guarded than ever. How was he to convince her that even rascals could change?

Not helping matters was his greatest challenge so far—not from the street boys, but from Sally Hobson.

"But I only came to help with the dinner because Alice told me to come," Sally said.

"Don't you want to be part of the pageant, Sally?"

And then, to his surprise, Sophie came to his aid. "Especially in such

351

an important role? Other than the baby Jesus, who is more important than Mary?"

The girl wrung her hands. "Well. . .I never thought I could get up in front of others and. . .act."

"Oh for heaven's sake, Sally," said Alice, who evidently found it unnecessary to exhibit much patience with her little sister, "you're the right age and size. And besides, we have no one else. You'll have to do it."

Sophie reached out to caution her friend's tone, but it was Noah who lightened the mood with a laugh.

"How can anyone resist such a persuasive request?" Then he looked at Sally. "You might want to consider that at present our only alternative is to dress up one of the boys as Mary—"

"Hey!" cried Louie, one of the boys from the street. "We ain't none of us gonna put on a dress. Them shepherd robes is close 'nough."

To Noah's relief, he saw the hint of a smile hover at the corners of Sally's lips.

"Half the boys here are starting to sprout whiskers." Noah added a grin to his coaxing. "I don't think Mary would like to be portrayed by any of them. What do you think, Sally?"

The smile broke free at last, and she nodded.

"Thank you, Sally. Or should I call you Mary?"

⌒∽⌒

Was Sophie the only one immune to Noah Jackson's charm? He was like a chameleon she'd read of, a little creature able to change its colors whenever necessary.

Eyeing the boys who had come to participate, she couldn't help but remember the compassion she'd felt watching them eat, as if none of them had tasted such a meal in their lives. Although they expressed no gratitude other than finishing every last bit of the stew she'd provided, and every one of them used his shirtsleeves to wipe off his hands and mouth, she had to admit they were less threatening than she expected. None of them seemed to be carrying a slingshot, or worse.

Her greatest surprise of the evening came with how the boys treated Gordy—as if they'd known each other forever. Her mother had certainly been right to be concerned. Only when they teased him about playing the angel did she find herself less worried; at least they thought only Gordy could fit such a role.

"The shepherds are frightened at first," Noah explained. "After all, wouldn't you be if you saw someone coming down from the skies and talking to you?"

Louie laughed and jabbed the boy next to him. "Not if Lorcan swiped his daddy's whiskey jug again. We'd see all kinds of things and wouldn't be afraid neither."

Noah laughed right along with the boys, but Sophie frowned. Didn't his laugh encourage such harmful behavior?

"But they're also curious," Noah went on. "These brave shepherds. Instead of cowering or running home to hide from something they'd never seen before, they follow the angel's instructions. They go to Bethlehem, where they find the proof of what the angel told them. That's where they adore the Savior of the world." He looked around at the boys then added softly, "Our Savior, too. Mine and yours.

"So we'll begin with a narrator," he went on. "That's Pastor Goodwin. He'll speak from behind a curtain, so everyone will hear him but not see him. He'll start by telling everyone about Herod and the wise men and the reason Joseph must take Mary to Bethlehem to be counted in the census. . . ."

He continued to explain the roles, even citing their lines, having them repeat them, and asking them to remember what to say for the coming rehearsals. It would have been far easier had he distributed a script of some kind, and Sophie was determined to ask him about it just as soon as the rehearsal ended. Surely Alice would help Sophie copy such a thing.

"And when the host of angels join our angel—Gordy—we'll have the choir lead everyone in the song 'Hark! The Herald Angels Sing.' That way the audience can be part of the pageant. Afterward, with the shepherds looking on, the three wise men appear with their gifts, and they, too, worship the baby Jesus. Then the angel returns, telling the wise men to go home by a different route and not tell Herod about Jesus. He also tells Joseph to take Mary and the baby out of Bethlehem, to safety, and that ends the pageant: with Mary looking back on the scene while the choir sings 'Christians Awake! On This Happy Morn.'"

"Are we gonna have to sing, too?" asked Flynn, the boy standing next to Gordy. Earlier he'd seemed happy to be a shepherd, but he didn't look particularly interested in singing.

"We'll all sing," said Mrs. Goodwin. "We might even have a piano by then! The church's first Christmas present, from a wonderful benefactor named Ezra Pooley."

The familiar name made Sophie's gaze dart from the pastor's wife to

Noah, who wasn't even looking her way, for once. Instead, he put a hand on the concerned boy's shoulder. "We'll have plenty of time to learn our lines and the songs, too. We'll start tonight with the songs. Okay, Flynn?"

"Don't worry about your voice, Flynn," added Arthur. "I only sing loud enough for God to hear. I figure He gave me a voice that can't hold a tune, so He must somehow like it. But I'm not sure anybody else wants to hear it." He looked Alice's way, who beamed so fondly no one could have doubted she'd welcome his voice, no matter how off-key.

Sophie wondered what it must be like to have someone so blind to one's faults.

Sometime later, after the boys had departed, Noah asked Sophie if he could escort her home.

"No, it's not necessary," she said. "Arthur is coming along because Alice lives so close."

Noah nodded without trying to change her mind and turned away. So much for being a persistent suitor! She called him back.

"If you have a script," she said, "I can copy it for the boys if you like."

"No scripts. No sheet music. Nothing that requires reading."

She tilted her head. "Why ever not? It would be much easier—"

"Because half the boys who came tonight can't read. I'm hoping they are, even now, boasting about full bellies, how warm the church is, and how easy the practice was. We need another wise man and more angels. A whole host of them. We're not going to bring any more boys in if we don't spare their pride."

He crossed the three steps separating them, stopping only when his face was closer to hers than necessary. "Because most of life's problems can be traced to pride, in one form or another."

Pride? Was he accusing her of being prideful? Or confessing his own?

"And you think the rest of the angels will come from the streets?" Somehow, the question wasn't issued with the same disdainful disbelief she might have used before tonight's rehearsal.

"That's right."

His confidence made her wonder if he might just be right, after all.

Chapter 7

"I don't see why you won't let Noah take you to see Mr. Pooley, that's all."

Arthur walked beside Sophie, setting a brisk pace toward Mr. Pooley's home that he'd said was on Lake Street. For a hopefully leisurely visit with his older friend, Arthur didn't look at all relaxed.

"And while we're on the subject of Noah—"

So that was the reason for his scowl. Noah again. "That's your subject, Arthur. Not mine."

"That's just it. I guess I understood back in Toledo why you might have run the other way when you caught sight of him, but he was a kid then, and so were you. Can't you see he's changed?"

"How do you restore something that's rotten inside? He may have learned how to polish the outside, but who can say he's any different on the inside?"

"I can! You don't share the same roof with somebody for five years and not know him. Sure, he used to play pranks. But once he got a job—a real job that paid, not the kind his parents made him do without so much as a thank-you—he turned his energy to good, hard work."

Sophie harrumphed and kept walking. "Just look at the kids he's brought to the Nativity. They're all exactly like him—how he used to be. Every one of those boys reminds me of who Noah is on the inside."

"Those boys have changed in just three weeks. They laugh *with* each other now instead of *at* each other. They encourage one another." He grinned. "I even saw one of them use a napkin instead of his shirtsleeve."

"You can't make a silk purse out of a sow's ear, Arthur."

Arthur stopped and grabbed her shoulders. "You're proof that someone can change, Sophie. You used to be sweet. But now your heart is hard." His fingers squeezed her shoulders, as if in frustration. Then he let her go. "I've changed my mind about today's visit. If you want to see Mr. Pooley's copy of that bird book, you're going to have to ask Noah for the introduction."

Then he turned and walked in the opposite direction.

"Arthur!"

But her brother ignored her call.

Sophie had no choice but to make her way back home. As much as she wanted to see—to study, admire, even emulate—the drawings of such an eminent artist as Mr. Wilson, she would not suffer Noah Jackson's company to do so.

⌘

Noah eyed Tully. He'd been right about him from the first, that he was a leader, if not the top of the bunch. Several other new boys had come tonight, too, but Noah hadn't expected Tully.

"We could use another shepherd," Noah said slowly.

"Shepherd!" echoed Gordy. "He can have my spot as the third wise man, since I'm already the angel."

Noah hesitated as everyone looked at him expectantly, including Tully. Clearly they all recognized the boy's dominance and were ready to give him a prized role. Noah couldn't say exactly what he didn't trust about this boy, but a definite alarm bell sounded in his soul.

His alarm might be similar to the one ringing in Sophie's soul about him—an alarm that was groundless, based on feeling, not fact. If he believed people could change, he'd have to believe Tully could, too. So Noah patted the boy's shoulder.

"Good to have you join us, Tully. A wise man it is, then."

Eying Sophie, he couldn't help but see the disapproval on her face. Tully was just one more boy to her, one more to add to the list of delinquents working on this pageant.

He looked again at Tully, who playfully punched Gordy on the arm—a little too hard, perhaps, but in their language, a sign of gratitude for a preferred role. The rest of the boys were coming around, he was sure of it. By Christmas Eve when they presented the Nativity pageant, even Sophie would have to admit the boys showed promise—particularly if the apprenticeships and jobs Noah was working to secure came through.

But Tully? If Noah had to guess, this latecomer would need the most amount of change to reform, and Noah feared it might already be too late for time to be on his side with this one. At least to convince Sophie that all boys deserved a second chance.

By the middle of the evening, Noah was more worried than ever. In a single night, Tully managed to reignite all of the disruptive behavior Noah had successfully curbed in the past weeks. Like the leader he was, Tully's example of amusing ridicule spurred the others into matching tones—all in the name of fun.

He put an end to it when Tully teased Sally. Noah didn't hear the exact words, but given the crimson in Sally's cheeks and the horror on Gordy's face, it evidently had something to do with wanting to take the Holy Spirit's place the next time "Mary" was with child.

"That's enough, Tully," Noah said. "You haven't had the advantage the other boys have had, working together these last few weeks. We've made it clear this isn't just a performance for the church. It's portraying a holy memory. If you have no desire to act with respect for what we're doing, then I'll ask you to leave. Understood?"

The apology on Tully's face looked so sincere Noah wished he could believe him. But the boy's behavior had reminded him all too clearly of why Sophie remained wary of him, even after all these years. He'd given a few apologies like this himself back in his youth. All show and no truth.

Noah was exhausted. Working with the railroad commission all day and coming to the rehearsals in the evenings had been exhilarating until tonight. Back at his lodgings with Arthur, his feet dragged all the way up the stairs and to his cot.

In spite of that—or maybe because he knew it offered comfort—he pulled out the leatherwork tools he'd borrowed from Ezra then turned up the oil lamp beside his cot.

"Why are you doing all this, anyway?" Arthur asked, watching him work.

"What do you mean?"

"I know you started out wanting to win over Sophie, but is it worth it? All she does is turn up her nose at you. She's my sister, and I know she can be good-natured, and I'll take your word that she's pretty enough, but is she worth all this trouble? Maybe she's not meant to get married, or maybe she's meant to marry somebody else."

"You might be right, Artie," Noah said, without pause in his work. "Except the truth is, I started falling in love with her as far back as reading some of those letters she wrote to you. So it's your fault. You shouldn't have shared them with me."

Arthur lay back on his cot. "All right, then. Love's a whole different story. I just hope you can bring back the sweet sister she was in those letters."

Chapter 8

Sophie arrived early at church on Christmas Eve, hearing the excited voices of the boys who would perform tonight. Eager to join them, she stopped briefly in the coatroom to hang her coat—only to see a note tacked beneath the peg she always used.

Curious, she unfolded what looked like official stationery. Scrawled across the top, just below the address labeling it from a local newspaper, were written the bold words: *Merry Christmas, Sophie, but this isn't really a gift since your talent earned the chance.*

Breath quickened, Sophie read the body of the letter. It was an invitation to submit her wildlife drawings to the editor at Chicago's *Prairie Farmer.*

Amazed, she looked around, wondering where the note had come from. Arthur, who was just hanging his own coat, was the only one nearby.

"Look at this!"

He took the page from her, scanning it briefly as a smile grew on his face. "That's Noah's writing at the top."

She gasped. "Do. . . Do you think this is a prank?"

Her brother moaned and scrubbed his face from hair to chin. "It'd serve you right to pass up the opportunity you want most in the world because you can't believe Noah has changed."

Then he waved a hand of dismissal at her and went off in search of Alice.

❧

"Fear not! For behold, I bring you good tidings of great joy, which shall be to all people. . . ."

Sophie watched Gordy from the audience, stealing a glance from him to their parents and seeing every bit as much pride on their faces as she felt in her heart. Although the pageant had just begun, it was already a success. The entire cast had shown up, even that rascal Tully, and she felt confident Gordy wasn't the only one who knew his lines.

And the church was filled! There might be more taverns, brothels, and gambling dens in Chicago than there were churches, but on Christmas Eve it appeared even the hardest of hearts turned a little soft when it came to remembering the Christ child.

Although Sophie couldn't see Noah, she easily imagined him behind the makeshift curtains, ensuring everyone went on and off the improvised stage at the appropriate time. If her heart had swelled upon hearing her brother's sweet recitation of an angel's invitation to the shepherds, that same heart pounded anew over how hard Noah had worked on this evening's performance. All of it had been his vision, right down to the players involved.

She'd doubted him, she couldn't deny it. But every one of the boys she'd so easily mistrusted had turned out to be similar to Gordy—eager to be accepted, ready to learn his part and to help someone else when necessary. She'd seen them filled with energy and brimming with laughter—in fact, looking for something to laugh about. How could that not be contagious?

Most surprising was Tully, the latecomer she was sure would put a damper on everything. But there he was, the third wise man, offering myrrh and worshipping Mary's babe. Noah may not have accomplished such a miracle, but certainly God couldn't have done it without his cooperation. And that was a miracle, too. The heart she believed so dark inside of Noah had been washed clean. Who was she to have doubted God could do such a thing for him?

All that was left now was regret that she'd clung so long to her mistrust of him. How could she not have seen that he believed in her drawings enough to arrange for the opportunity to be published in a real city newspaper?

O come, all ye faithful
Joyful and triumphant,
O come ye, O come ye, to Bethlehem.

Sophie joined the singing with adoration, knowing that God had reminded her not only of His love, but also to trust another's love—one she'd been fighting too long.

Noah's heart hadn't been the only one in need of a washing. Her own had been too suspicious, too judgmental, too timid to realize that if she only trusted God's work in Noah, she would have admitted weeks ago she was falling in love with him.

As the pageant came to a close, applause echoed from the rafters. No one clapped louder than Sophie as she searched the edges of the stage for a glimpse of the man who had inspired the entire evening.

Noah hadn't realized the extent of his own fidgetiness until the audience burst into cheers at the end of the performance. He breathed freely for the first time that evening. There hadn't been a single blunder, if he didn't count Louie dropping the gold-painted stones at the foot of the crèche. Even Mrs. Gutierrez's baby, just five weeks old, had been quiet through the entire performance as if in reverence to his part as the baby Jesus.

As the cast returned behind the scenes, he congratulated each of them while the crowd filed out. With some disappointment, he noticed Sophie talking with her parents as they approached the door at the other end of the sanctuary. Knowing they were leaving dashed his hopes that she might have stayed, but he comforted himself, knowing he would see her tomorrow.

Some of the cast had agreed to stay late to clean up so the church would be ready for Christmas morning service. As he folded costumes, he realized Gordy was among those who had stayed, and his pulse leaped with the thought of seeing Sophie again if he took the boy safely home.

"It turned out beautifully, Noah."

The quiet, familiar voice from the dimmed sanctuary nearly made him drop the shepherd's robe.

Sophie.

Had her voice sounded nearly breathless? He took a careful step closer to her, knowing he was too eager to hope he was responsible for taking her breath away. But the way she looked at him doubled his pulse.

"It turned out well, didn't it?"

"It's a memory that will live in the heart of everyone who was here tonight." She spoke with a shyness he hadn't seen in her since they were children. "At least, I know it will always be in my heart."

Her smile went so clearly beyond her lips that he nearly approached her for a kiss. But he was too stunned to even try.

"Will it?" he asked instead, knowing he was apt to believe what he wanted with the slightest hint of hope. She was the last person he wanted to frighten away.

"Noah." Was he fooling himself to hear something new in her voice? Surely she'd never called him by name so invitingly. "You arranged for me to submit my drawings to the *Prairie Farmer*, didn't you?"

"I told you they're good. They thought so, too, when I showed them the ones you sent to Artie."

"Oh, Noah. . .I don't know how to thank you."

"You're welcome, but all I did was present the pictures. Your work did the rest."

The look in her eye multiplied the hope in his heart, and he dared another step closer, setting the robe on a nearby bench.

"I'm sorry I've been so foolish." She, too, stepped nearer, whispering the words as if they were alone, even though a few others still lingered. "About everything. Those boys were remarkable tonight. I was so wrong to think they couldn't be touched by God's love—and the love you showed them."

"Don't think too highly of me," he said. "I tried convincing myself I did it for Gordy, because I knew he was hanging around some of these boys. I know God loves them all, and they needed to be shown that. But the truth is, I was trying to impress you with how much I've changed."

To his relief, his confessions didn't erase her smile. "I think God used you in spite of me. And you let Him. I was an idiot not to see that."

Noah could no longer keep himself in check. Who would be shocked if he kissed her right here, right now? The boys would likely cheer him on. And Pastor Goodwin had surely seen the way he'd been looking at her from the moment she arrived in town.

But no sooner had his lips brushed hers than he heard the door burst open and a scuffle at the threshold.

Chapter 9

Awash with confusion, Sophie had been about to pull Noah closer when he shot away, running toward a noise at the back of the small church sanctuary. Just beyond the last pew she saw three boys tussling—Louie and Lorcan appeared to be dragging a struggling Tully back inside the church. Then Lorcan ripped open Tully's brand-new coat. Buttons tapped on the floor—along with a thud and jingle from a box landing a few feet away.

The boys behind her all raised their voices at once, whether in support of the fight or against it, she couldn't tell. Lorcan still had a grip on Tully's coat while Louie ducked clear of Tully's fist. The boy freed himself just as Noah came up from behind, grabbing Tully's arms in a stronghold. When Lorcan looked as if he might take another swing at the hog-tied enemy, Sophie cried out as Noah pulled Tully safely beyond the reach of Lorcan's punching arm.

"That's enough!" Noah shouted, Tully still imprisoned. "What's this about?"

Gordy picked up the box that had fallen during the fight. "This is the collection box!"

Pastor Goodwin stepped forward, reaching for the box. "It certainly is. I'd put it under my coat while I was helping with the cleanup."

"Here's the rat that took it!" Lorcan yelled at Tully. "I told you we weren't going in on that scheme—"

Sophie came up beside Gordy. "Scheme? Did you know about a scheme, Gordy?"

He shook his head.

"Well, I did," said Louie. "So did half the other fellas. Only we all tol' him we wasn't gonna do it—distract ever'body so he could get away with it."

"I didn't see him take it, but I guess he gone and done it anyway," Lorcan added.

Tully had the good sense to hang his head, because not one of his fellow street boys looked as if they'd offer him a smidgeon of compassion.

⚮

Noah could have moaned aloud. So much for redemption. He couldn't help but wonder if Sophie believed a bully's heart was destined to remain one, just as, it seemed, was Tully's.

He'd been so close to winning her this evening. He'd seen it in her face. He nearly didn't want to see her now, for fear her light of faith had been stamped out.

So he looked at the pastor instead. "Do you want me to turn the boy over to the constable?"

Pastor Goodwin approached Tully. "We all must take responsibility for our actions, son. Do you know that what you did was wrong?"

Tully nodded, still looking at the floor.

"Look up, son. Look at the faces of the boys who used to respect you."

The guilty boy didn't look up, and Noah adjusted his grip with a shake. "Go on."

Tully raised his head and looked at the pastor. "They're all a bunch o' mice, and I don't care what they think o' me. What's gonna happen now this is over? We all go back to empty bellies, that's what. I only took what we needed. New coats ain't gonna feed us."

"What about the jobs I'm working on for some of you?" Noah asked.

"Some of us! Not for me!"

"We weren't going to abandon you now that the Nativity is over," Pastor Goodwin said. "We want all of you to keep coming to church."

Noah increased his grip. "Didn't it occur to you that stealing isn't exactly the best way to get a good recommendation for a job?"

Tully only shrugged.

Noah exchanged a look with the pastor, and he could see the man was already willing to offer grace. But Noah wasn't eager to do so—either to prove to Sophie he saw her point about bullies or because the boy might have spoiled his own chances with her. He was still afraid to look at her for fear of seeing ready condemnation, but she stepped into his line of vision.

She eyed the boy still imprisoned by Noah's grip, staring at him until he met her gaze. At first she frowned, just the way Noah would have expected. Then, to his fascination, her frown softened into a look of pure concern.

"Is it true you took the money to help feed the others? Or did you take it for yourself?"

"Whatever I say you won't believe anyway."

"That's probably true. Which is why you'll need time to prove yourself." She looked at Noah now. "But I'm not sure the stockade is the place to do that."

"You can have a job here at the church," Pastor Goodwin said. "Sweeping the floors, dusting the benches. Cleaning up inside and out. It won't pay much, but you could sleep in the coatroom and have dinners with Mrs. Goodwin and me. But"—he looked at the rest of the boys—"I'll need help from each of you. If there is a next time, I'll want to know in advance if young Mr. Tully has any trouble up his sleeve. It's not tattling if you have his best interest in mind."

Noah couldn't tear his gaze from Sophie even to look at Tully, who he was sure was relieved over the pastor's verdict. Instead, Noah marveled at the compassion in Sophie's eyes—confirming she believed in second chances.

⁓

"But I didn't get you anything!"

Sophie stood in front of Noah, who had just arrived at her parents' house this early Christmas morning. Her mother was in the kitchen, where Sophie should be helping. But when Noah had arrived—without Arthur, who had told them he would go to Alice's for Christmas morning—Sophie's father had called her out of the kitchen so soon after the knock, she was sure Noah hadn't even announced who he'd come to see.

Abandoned by both Gordy and her father, whom had left them for the kitchen, Noah stood before her with a flat box, complete with a silk ribbon tying it closed.

"You already gave me exactly what I wanted this Christmas," Noah told her. "Hope. That's hard to wrap but just as real as what I have for you. Now open it."

They sat near the small Christmas tree that she and Gordy had decorated with popcorn and cranberries, its trunk skirted by a circle of linen she had embroidered with a Nativity scene last year. Little had she known it was bound to remind her of Noah!

She had to steady her hands to untie the ribbon before opening the box. He'd taken special care to wrap the present inside with a layer of cloth. The scent of leather greeted her immediately, and she shot him a smile.

"Did you make this?"

He nodded.

Uncovering the gift, she saw it was a book bound at the side with another ribbon. The cover made her gasp. It was intricately tooled with the images of birds. Carefully, she opened to the few pages within, surprised to find her own drawings.

"Oh, Noah," she whispered. "It's for my drawings, isn't it?"

"They're the ones you sent to Artie, the ones I showed to the *Prairie*

Farmer editor. You can add new ones as you create them. See?" He pulled the ribbon. "It comes apart. When you're finished, I can have it bound, just like a real book."

"Oh, Noah." She knew she'd repeated herself but was nearly overcome with happiness. "It's so beautiful."

Then she looked at the cover again. "These birds. . . My goodness, Noah. They're so well done."

"I can't take credit for the artwork. I'm not an artist like you are. Mr. Pooley gave me a few tissue paper leaflets from one of his bird books, and I traced the smallest pictures and placed it on top of my leather. Then I pressed my pencil into it so I could follow the image with my etching tool. See?" He pointed to each bird as he spoke. "That's a partridge, and a turtle-dove next to it. And the hen is French, of course." He laughed. "And that other one is a calling bird, but you have to use your imagination."

"Oh, Noah, it's the perfect Christmas present."

"That's the best carol for you, Sophie. 'The Twelve Days of Christmas.' What other carol has so many birds in it? The other verses are on the back, the ones without birds. I traced most of those images from children's books at the library. I went almost every day, hoping to see you there."

She turned the book over, seeing images of the remaining verses, each meticulously if roughly etched in the smooth, stained leather.

All verses but one.

"And where are the five golden rings?" she asked.

"Look inside the back cover. That was the easiest for me to etch."

She opened the book reverently, because her drawings were housed with such obvious love. A flap at the back would easily hold pencils and a knife for sharpening, but it bulged too slightly now for that. The folded top was decorated in the image of five rings.

"Open it."

Exploring inside, she caught her breath before gently pulling out a ring.

"I'll put it on your finger just as soon as you let Pastor Goodwin marry us. See? It's five strands of gold—five golden rings—all entwined together. For your wedding ring."

Noah put his hands over hers. "Will you marry me, Sophie?"

She laughed, throwing her arms around his neck. "Yes, Noah! I'm to be a bride, after all—yours!"

Stew and Dumplings

1 tablespoon butter

1 pound chuck, tip, or round steak
  cut into 1-inch cubes

3 cups chicken or beef stock

½ teaspoon salt

⅛ teaspoon pepper

2 medium carrots, cut into 1-inch
  pieces

2 large potatoes
  (approximately 2 cups),
  cut into 1-inch pieces

1 small onion, chopped

2 tablespoons flour

Melt butter in large saucepan or Dutch oven. Add beef and cook until browned, approximately 15 minutes. Add stock and salt and pepper. Heat to a boil, then reduce heat and simmer for 2 hours. Stir in cut carrots, potatoes, and onion. Add ½ cup cold water and flour. Stir to blend. Heat to a boil again, approximately 1 minute. Reduce heat and simmer 30 minutes to allow vegetables to cook.

Dumplings:

3 tablespoons shortening

1½ cups flour

2 teaspoons baking powder

¾ teaspoon salt

½ cup milk

Cut shortening into flour as you would for a piecrust. Add baking powder and salt; stir, then add milk. Dough will be wet. Drop dumplings by spoonfuls on top of stew. Cook uncovered for 10 minutes, then cover and cook for 10 minutes more. Uncover and serve.

Recipe compliments of Lora Haapapuro.

About the Author

Maureen Lang writes stories inspired by a love of history and romance. An avid reader herself, she's figured out a way to write the stories she feels like reading. Maureen's Inspirationals have earned various writing distinctions, including the Inspirational Readers Choice Contest, a Holt Medallion, and the Selah Award, as well as being a finalist for the Rita, Christy, and Carol Awards. In addition to investigating various eras in history (such as Victorian England, First World War, and America's Gilded Age), Maureen loves taking research trips to get a feel for the settings of her novels. She lives in the Chicago area with her family and has been blessed to be the primary caregiver to her adult disabled son.

The Gingerbread Bride

by Amy Lillard

Chapter 1

Ozark Mountains, Arkansas, 1870

"Madeline!"

Maddie Sinclair winced at the sharpness in her sister's tone. Grace slammed through the house they shared with their father and burst into the kitchen before Maddie could do so much as hike her skirt and run for the stairs. At least she managed to pull off her soiled apron and toss it into the sink.

"There you are." Grace's cheeks were stained pink from the Christmas Eve cold and what Maddie could only assume was the exertion of running her down in the kitchen.

"Of course this is where I am." Maddie smoothed the front of her day dress, dismayed at the smear of flour on the bodice. And was that one across her nose? She crossed her eyes to check and swiped at it just to be certain.

"You did it, didn't you?"

"Did what?" She could never keep Grace from finding out the truth. It had been that way since they were children. Her imitation innocence would only take her so far this time.

Her sister propped her hands on her hips and narrowed her gaze. "Annie Johnson at the general store said she saw you headed out toward Old Lady Farley's place yesterday."

Maddie sniffed. "I don't see how that's a problem."

"It became a problem when Pa told me that Harlan Calhoun was coming to dinner tonight."

At the mention of Harlan's name, Maddie couldn't stop the smile that spread across her face. "Of course Harlan is coming to dinner tonight. It is Christmas Eve, after all. And he doesn't have any kin near. It's only the Christian thing to do, invite him to supper."

"You're stalling," Grace said. "A sure sign that you're up to something. Now, what about Old Lady Farley?"

Maddie took a steadying breath. She could do this. "I don't know what you're talking about, Sister."

"So you're telling me that you didn't go see Old Lady Farley to get something to make Harlan Calhoun fall in love with you?"

Maddie scoffed, sort of choked, but managed to recover. She never should have mentioned her thoughts aloud. Especially not to her practical and perfect sibling. "Why, that's ridiculous."

Some of the starch melted out of Grace's spine. She smiled. "That's what I was hoping you would say." She inhaled deeply. "What's that I smell?"

Maddie gestured toward two plates of freshly baked gingerbread cookies. "You made cookies?"

"A special treat for a special day." She pushed the larger plate toward Grace. "These are for the family." She lifted the smaller plate. "And these here are for Harlan."

"Maddie." There was that warning note back in her sister's tone.

Maddie shrugged as a knock sounded on the door. "I want him to feel special."

"Maddie."

Maddie patted down her hair and pinched a bit of color into her cheeks. Then before her sister could make a move, she swept toward the parlor, a plate of cookies in her hands.

Harlan Calhoun was twirling his hat in his hands as he was prone to do. He always seemed a bit nervous when he came by their house, but Maddie didn't know why. He walked with confidence every time she saw him in their tiny town of Calico Falls in the foothills of the Ozark Mountains. Harlan had moved to their town in the spring, and Maddie had fallen immediately in love. He was tall and handsome, gentlemanly, and had a city air about him that her Arkansas suitors could never achieve. But it was more than that. He was God-fearing and Lord-loving, and she so desperately wanted to marry him.

She smiled as she cleared her throat, alerting him to her presence. "Merry Christmas, Harlan." Her cheeks grew hot with the use of his Christian name. He had told her a few weeks ago that she should call him Harlan, but this was the first time she had managed to squeeze the word through her lips when addressing him.

"And a merry Christmas Eve to you as well, Miss Maddie." He swept into a deep bow.

"I made you some gingerbread cookies to enjoy before supper." Her voice trembled as she said the words. Had he noticed? "Why don't you sit down, and I'll get you a glass of milk. Unless you'd rather have coffee."

He smiled, the action lighting the entire room. "Milk would be fine indeed." He folded his tall frame into the parlor chair. He looked ridiculously handsome in the tiny seat. Big and capable and handsome. So handsome.

Maddie set the cookies on the table next to him and sucked in a quick breath. "I'll just go. . .get the milk." She backed out of the room, never taking her eyes from Harlan as she pushed through the swinging door that led into the kitchen.

"Maddie!" her sister whispered, urgency tainting her words. "What is this?" She held up the tiny linen sack Maddie had thought she'd hidden where no one would find it.

Maddie snatched it away from Grace and tucked it behind her. "Nothing."

"You did something to those cookies. Don't even bother lying about it."

Maddie sighed, her resolve slipping. It was wrong to lie. Just as she knew that what she'd planned for Harlan wasn't the most. . .conventional method of finding a husband. "I had to, Gracie. How else am I supposed to make him fall in love with me?" The words rang between them with a hollow sound. What had she done?

"Maddie." Grace shook her head.

"I'm not like you," Maddie said, hating the envious edge in her voice. Her sister was poised and polished, as beautiful as their dearly departed mother and twice as sweet. Maddie could never win when compared with her only sibling. Once, just once, she wanted something special of her own.

Harlan Calhoun.

"You can't do that to the poor man," her sister gently said.

"But I love him."

"So it's okay to poison him so he'll propose to you?"

Maddie sniffed. "I think he likes me well enough."

Grace shook her head. "You have to get out there and get those cookies."

Maddie knew it to be true before her sister uttered the first syllable. As much as she hated to, as much as she desperately wanted Harlan's love, it wasn't right. Not like this. She nodded.

Grace nudged her toward the door. "Now, before he eats them."

Spurred into action, Maddie hustled through the door and back into the parlor.

Harlan stood as she entered, brushing the crumbs from his mouth. He swallowed hard, his lips twitching into a small smile. "I thought you were bringing milk."

"I, uh, was," she hedged, her gaze darting to the plate. Empty! "Did you, uh, eat the cookies?" She knew the answer but had to ask.

"I skipped lunch and then. . ." He gave her a sheepish smile. "Well, they were delicious."

Her heart sank in her chest, but she forced a smile. "I'm glad you enjoyed them."

"I did. Very much so." His deep blue eyes turned suddenly serious. "Listen, Maddie. I came here tonight for a very important reason."

She licked her lips, her throat suddenly dry. "You did?" she whispered.

He grabbed her hands and dropped to one knee.

Oh goodness! She hadn't expected it to work this fast.

"Harlan," she exclaimed before he could utter the one question she wanted to hear above all else. "Stand up. What's wrong with you?" Like she didn't know.

"I love you, Maddie."

She had been waiting to hear those words from him ever since he arrived in Calico Falls, and now it was nothing more than a lie. The biggest part of her heart wanted to ignore the voice of her conscience, the one that told her this was all wrong, and drop to her knees beside him.

Instead, she tugged him to his feet. "Now, Harlan, is that any way to treat your fine suit?" She resisted the urge to brush her hands across his lapels. That would be too forward. As much as her fingers itched to dance over his broad chest, it would be best to ignore that impulse until he was back to himself. Or not give in to it at all.

"Maddie, it's just that I want to—"

She shook her head. "Give me one moment. I need to get you that milk." It was the worst excuse but the only one she could think of.

"I wouldn't mind another cookie or two." He grinned at her.

"Oh, I think you've had quite enough cookies." She scooped up the empty plate and hustled from the room.

Grace was waiting on the other side of the kitchen door. "Well?"

Maddie held out the cookie plate.

"He ate all of them?"

She nodded.

"*All* of them?"

"Do you see any left?"

"Madeline Joy, don't you get all snippy with me. This wasn't my harebrained idea."

Maddie's irritation wilted. "I'm sorry, Grace. Forgive me. It's just that—"

"What?" her sister asked.

"I've waited for this for so long, and now I've gone and ruined it." Tears rose to her eyes. "What am I supposed to do?"

Grace pulled her close. "Shh. . .don't cry. We'll think of something." Grace gave her one more squeeze and let her go. "Now, how long did Old Lady Farley say this would last?"

"She didn't say." Maddie sniffed.

"So you did drug the cookies."

Maddie nodded. "It's just some harmless herbs and spices. I would never hurt him."

"Only make him fall in love with you against his will."

"Oh, Grace," she cried. "What am I going to do?"

Her sister gently pushed the door open to peek into the parlor. "You're going to go out there and keep him occupied so he can't ask Pa for your hand in marriage."

Maddie swallowed hard but nodded. Then she smoothed down her dress and pushed the escaped strands of her hair back into place.

"Here." Grace thrust a cool glass of milk into her hands. "Now go out there and keep him busy."

⁓

Harlan Jay Calhoun watched the door that Maddie disappeared behind and waited for her return. He hadn't meant to scare her, but he had been holding in his feelings for so very long. She looked particularly beautiful today. He should be used to that by now. Every time he saw her she seemed even lovelier than she had the time before. But here, today, on Christmas Eve, she nearly took his breath away.

And how had he repaid her? He'd stuffed down her cookies like they were nothing. But they were just so good. And he was hungry and nervous.

He touched the box tucked safely in the inside pocket of his jacket. He had waited two months for the treasured cameo to arrive from his parents' house in the East. How else was he supposed to ask Maddie to be his wife? He had to give her something special. Yet he had been so nervous since he'd picked it up from the post office two days ago. It had taken that long to gather up courage enough to come over here and ask for her hand.

Now all he had to do was wait for her to come out of the kitchen.

He breathed a sigh of relief when she swung into the room a few moments later. What had he expected her to do? Not come back at all?

"There you are," he said. He rushed toward her, unable to stop his feet from carrying him directly to her side. He had been denying his feelings for so long, waiting until the right time to tell her that he loved her and wanted to marry her. Waiting for the family heirloom to arrive. Waiting for a night like tonight. Now that it was here, he couldn't seem to hold his feelings in any longer.

"Here I am," she said. She shifted from one foot to the other then held out the glass of milk. "Your milk."

He looked at the glass then back to her face. She seemed as nervous as he was. Perhaps he had come on too strong. He needed to get in control of himself before he had her running for the top of the mountain.

"Thank you." He accepted the milk, though it was the last thing on his mind now. "Will your father be home soon? I have something very important to discuss with him."

A choked sort of laugh escaped her. "You don't really want to talk about important matters today."

Yes. Yes, he did.

"I mean, after all, it's Christmas Eve," she continued. "Time to celebrate our Lord's birth."

As far as Harlan was concerned, it was a perfect day to confess his love for the beautiful woman before him. Yet what if her pastor father thought differently of the matter?

He would have to see how her father felt about such things. Harlan nodded to himself. That was what he would do, sort of test the waters, see how her father responded before he dove into the proposal.

"Do you suppose he'll be home soon?" Harlan couldn't stop the shift in his stance. He had to do something to keep on his feet. He couldn't ruin this proposal now.

"I hope not," she muttered.

At least that was what he *thought* she said. "I beg your pardon?"

"I'm sure he will." She flashed him a sweet smile. He must have been mistaken.

"Good." Harlan set the milk on the side table and captured her hands in his own. He simply had to touch her. If he had to wait until her father got home to ask permission to marry her, the least he should be allowed was to rub his thumbs across her smooth skin. "I'm glad."

Something flashed in her eyes, something that looked suspiciously like. . .*panic*? She turned as if listening to something coming from the kitchen. "What was that, Grace?" she called.

He hadn't heard anything.

She turned back to him, her mouth twisted in apology. "I just need to go help Grace. . .in the kitchen. . .with dinner." She backed away from him until he had no choice but to release her. "In the kitchen." She turned on her heel and fled into the other room.

What was wrong with her?

"Good evening, Harlan."

He whirled around as Maddie's sister swept through the door that led into the hallway. "But I thought you were. . ." He trailed off as he gestured behind him toward the kitchen door.

"Thought I was what?" she asked.

He shook his head. "Forgive me," he said. "Good evening, Grace."

She smiled at him prettily.

How could sisters be two short years apart in age yet be so different in every way? Grace had hair like warm honey and pale green eyes the color of the jade statue he'd once seen on a trip to Philadelphia. Maddie's chocolate-colored hair made her meadow-green eyes shine and captured his heart like none other. God had sprinkled sweet freckles across her nose, like a fine dusting of cinnamon. Sugar and spice, they said.

"Sit, sit." Grace waved a hand toward the chair he'd recently abandoned.

He had no desire to perch his large frame on the tiny chair. It made him feel clumsy and unworthy. He needed all the confidence he could get tonight. "I think I'll just stand." He pulled on his lapels then lightly touched the box in his pocket once again.

Lord, please let her say yes. Let her father agree. Let this happen. Amen.

"Did you enjoy the cookies?" Grace asked.

"The best I ever ate."

Her eyes darkened until they were almost the color of her sister's. "I hope you didn't eat so many you spoiled your supper."

"Oh no," he assured her. "I'm really looking forward to the meal." And afterward.

"Well now, that's done." Maddie walked back into the room, smoothing her hands down her skirt.

"Wonderful." Grace rose to her feet and shot her sister a pointed look. "Perhaps now would be a good time for us to change for dinner. Before Father gets home."

Maddie smiled at Harlan apologetically. "Will you be okay here for a while, Harlan? We won't be long."

He dipped into a shallow bow. "Of course."

"Then excuse us, please." Grace moved toward her sister, linking arms as she guided Maddie toward the exit. "We'll be back as quickly as possible."

Harlan smiled. "Take your time. I have something I need to discuss with your father."

◦◦◦

Maddie raced up the stairs, Grace mere steps behind her. "I've got to hurry," Maddie wheezed. Her father would never forgive her if she wasn't dressed properly when he arrived home for supper, and she would never be able to forgive herself if he arrived home before she got back downstairs. "I can't let Harlan talk to Pa."

"Right," Grace said, her own breathing heavy. "You go get your dress. I'll redo your hair. Then you can get back downstairs before Pa gets here."

Maddie nodded. "What about your hair?"

"I'll manage." She pushed Maddie into her room and followed behind her.

In record time, Maddie was dressed and on her way back down the stairs. She took them as fast as she dared, hating the way the bustle stuck out behind her like tail feathers. She wasn't at all sure about the fashion and would be grateful when it passed. But for now, the green-and-black velvet was her best dress and perfect for a Christmas Eve meal with her family. And Harlan.

She slowed her steps as she got to the bottom of the stairs, cautiously smoothing down her dress and running trembling fingers over her hair. Had she made it?

Her gaze flickered to the large front door. Father's hat hung on the coat tree just inside. She hadn't heard him come up the steps, which could only mean. . .

She spurred her feet into motion, running as fast and as ladylike as she possibly could as she rushed toward the parlor. She swung inside to find her father and Harlan shaking hands.

"Pa!" At her shrill summons, her father and Harlan both turned to stare at her. "I mean, good evening, Father. I trust you had a good evening?" He had spent the night at the small orphanage at the edge of town, doing his best to spread Christmas cheer to the children without family this holiday season.

"Why, yes, I was just telling Harlan here about one small lad."

Maddie nodded, trying to appear interested in what he had to say. Normally she would have been, but tonight. . . Well, she couldn't keep focused on such matters when she had messed things up like she had.

"And I was just telling your father that I had something very important to discuss with him." Harlan's eyes twinkled as if he were very pleased with himself.

Lord, what have I done? Please help me make this right.

Maddie's heart gave a painful thump, but she smiled through it all. "It's Christmas Eve. We can't discuss business on such a holiday."

"She's right, my boy." Her father clapped Harlan on the shoulder.

Much to her relief, Harlan returned the smile and gave a quick nod. "Whatever you say."

Perhaps the effect of the cookies was wearing off already. She could only pray that it was.

Then a look passed between the two men, and her hopes were dashed. Had she been too late getting to the parlor? Had Harlan already talked to her father about marriage?

She closed her eyes and said a quick prayer, hoping the Lord wasn't too confused at her change of heart. She had been praying for a proposal from Harlan for so long, it was more than strange to ask for anything different.

"Y'all come t' supper." Their housekeeper, Prissy, stuck her head through the kitchen doorway, her dark eyes gleaming. Prissy had been with them so long she was less like help and more like a member of the family.

Her father nodded. "As soon as Grace gets downstairs. What is keeping that girl?" He took his pocket watch from inside his waistcoat and checked the time.

"Here I am." Grace swept into the room with a gesture worthy of her name. And once again Maddie had a hard time feeling remorse for putting the love herbs in Harlan's cookies. Without a little help, Harlan would be like the rest of the men in Calico Falls and completely besotted with her beautiful sister.

She added shame and repentance to her growing prayer.

"Ah, good," their father said, holding out his arm to escort Grace to the table. What choice did Maddie have but to slip her own through Harlan's?

He was warm and strong, solid and kindly as he patted her hand where it lay in the bend of his elbow. But as they walked toward the dining room, his steps slowed until they were well behind the others.

"I spoke to your father a little," he whispered, bending low so only she could hear. He smelled of spice and sandalwood, and it took all of her willpower not to bury her nose in the folds of his suit and inhale his tangy scent.

"You w–what?" she stammered instead.

"I spoke to him a bit. Told him how much I have come to care for you."

"You—you have?"

"Oh yes." He flashed her a dazzling smile.

Why, oh why couldn't he smile at her like that without Old Lady Farley's help? Her heart melted despite the fact she knew his gesture to be untrue.

"I told him what a surprise I received finding love here."

What a surprise indeed.

"Will you do me a favor, Harlan?" She stilled her feet, needing a moment or two more before facing the rest of her family.

"Anything, my dear."

"Please don't say anything to him at supper. Let it be our little secret for a bit."

His blue eyes twinkled at the thought. "And that will make you happy?"

"Very much so," she lied.

"Then that is what we will do."

He would never understand what lay in the chambers of a woman's heart.

He shot a quick look at her father, hoping Easton Sinclair understood his meaning. They had only talked a moment or two before Maddie had rushed back into the parlor. Long enough for Harlan to declare his love for the preacher's daughter but not long enough to state his intentions. Yet Pastor Sinclair was a smart man; he'd figure it out in no time at all. Harlan could only hope the man would keep the news to himself and allow Maddie her time for a secret.

He pulled out a chair and seated her then made his way around the table to the chair opposite hers. He wanted to see her pretty face as they dined. How wonderful it would be after they wed for him to look at her during every meal. The thought filled him with such joy, he felt heat rising in his face.

"I say," Pastor Sinclair said. "Are you all right, Harlan?"

Harlan choked back a smile then gave a discreet cough.

"It's gonna snow," Prissy said, pushing through the kitchen door, the large plate of ham nearly hiding her face.

Harlan liked the sassy housekeeper. She had spunk and spirit, and it didn't hurt any that she had saved him from having to answer the uncomfortable question.

"What makes you say that?" Grace unfolded her napkin and placed it daintily on her lap.

"My rheumatism is actin' up somethin' terrible." Prissy set the platter on the table and slid into her place opposite Grace.

"Bow your heads," Pastor Sinclair instructed, bracing his elbows on the table. "Father Lord, we come to You tonight to ask thanks for this meal we are about to receive. Make our hearts grateful and our minds open to receive the nourishment as we sup and fellowship on this fine Christmas Eve. Thank You, Father, for our beautiful and growing family."

Something touched Harlan's leg, and he opened his eyes a bit to look across the table. If it was Maddie, he couldn't tell it. Her hands were clasped together so tightly that her knuckles were white, and her eyes were squinted shut.

He closed his eyes again, sure he was mistaken.

"Father God, we ask that You bless this food, this day, and the wonderful souls sharing it."

There it was again.

He peeked a second time, his eyes centering on Grace. She caught his attention, nodding her head toward Maddie and then their father. She raised her brows in question.

Was she asking if he was going to talk to their father tonight? And here he thought he'd concealed his feelings for Maddie. He hadn't wanted to get either of their hopes up. After all, Calico Falls wasn't a large town, and he surely wouldn't be able to support her if he couldn't make his law practice survive. Fortunately his business had thrived, and he was prepared to ask for her hand.

He gave a small nod to Grace and closed his eyes again, but not before a look of panic shot across her face. What was wrong with her?

"Amen," the reverend said.

Everyone raised their heads and started passing around the platters and bowls of delicious potatoes, beans, ham, and corn bread.

It had been a long time since Harlan had had a home-cooked meal such as this, and he enjoyed every bite.

"I see the gingerbread cookies didn't spole yur appetite none."

At Prissy's observation, Maddie's father raised his head. "Cookies?"

Harlan swallowed and cleared his throat. "Yes, sir. Maddie made me a batch of gingerbread cookies this afternoon. They were delicious."

"That sounds like a fine dessert." The reverend patted his stomach.

"I apologize." Harlan coughed. "But I believe I ate them all, sir."

"I had a few of 'em myself, and they were mighty tasty." Prissy scooped up a bite of potatoes and savored it as if reliving the spicy cookie all over again.

"There might have been a few more." Maddie ducked her head over her plate.

"Just like the ones I ate?" Harlan asked.

"No, thank goodness," Grace said.

"Um, actually, yes," Maddie quietly countered, looking at Grace helplessly.

"They were delicious," Harlan repeated, and smiled to show his appreciation.

Grace stood and pushed her chair under the table, staring down her nose at each of them in turn. "I'm sure my sister can find us something else to eat for dessert." Her words seemed to challenge anyone to say differently.

"But the cookies were so delicious," Harlan said. "Life changing." He resisted the urge to wink at Maddie.

Grace shook her head. "You have no idea."

⌀

"Maddie, can I see you in the kitchen, please." Grace's words didn't quite form a request. In fact, her tone was closer to "Get in here now."

Maddie rose to her feet. "Excuse me," she said, nodding to the others in turn. Perhaps if she took off through the front door, Grace wouldn't chase her. After all, they were wearing their best dresses, and Grace had always been more of a lady than Maddie. Just like their mother, Pa always said.

Thinking better of it, she trudged behind her sister into the kitchen.

"Madeline Joy." Grace whirled on her the minute they were out of earshot of the others. "I thought you said the other cookies were. . .were. . ." She sputtered.

"Unaltered?" Maddie supplied.

Grace propped her hands on her hips. "Well?"

"I may have stretched the truth on that statement a bit."

"You lied."

Well, she wouldn't have put it like that. "I wasn't sure how much I should put in—"

"You bought a love potion from the crazy woman at the end of the lane and you didn't ask how much to use?" Grace's voice rose.

"Shh." Maddie glanced behind them, but fortunately no one burst in from the other room demanding to know the truth. "First of all, I didn't buy it, I bartered." And a right good trade she'd made, at that. Her second-best dress for the entire bag of herbs.

Grace didn't look impressed with the fine details of the transaction.

"And it's not a love potion, just some herbs to make Harlan a little more. . .amicable toward marriage." What else was she supposed to do? It wasn't like he loved another or had stated his intentions toward someone else. He worked hard and steady, barely taking off time to go to church. Someone had to save him from himself.

"Do you honestly believe that?" Grace asked, her stance wilting just a bit.

"Oh Grace, he's so handsome and wonderful and handsome."

"So you've said."

"I really didn't mean any harm."

"I believe we've had this conversation already."

"What am I supposed to do?" She only wanted his love. She hadn't meant to ruin it all.

"Find some cake." Grace frowned. "And don't leave him alone with Pa."

∽∾

Maddie pasted on a smile and backed through the swinging door from the kitchen. "Who wants cake?"

She didn't pay any attention to the answers. The gingerbread cookies were in the trash, buried under this morning's coffee grounds. She couldn't risk Harlan eating any more of them.

Grace came behind her bearing the freshly brewed coffee to end their meal.

"You girls are so sweet, bringin' in dessert like this." Prissy smiled at them, her teeth a flash of ivory in her mocha-colored skin. It might not be fashionable to allow a person of color to share a table with those who were not, but her father said they were all the Lord's children and the color of skin didn't make one bit of difference to him. Or Him.

"You take care of us all the time," Grace said smoothly. "It's only proper for us to show our gratitude when we can."

Maddie set the tray on the table, her gaze immediately drawn to Harlan. How could one man be so handsome and perfect? He loved the Lord and was successful and well learned. He was everything a poor preacher's daughter from Arkansas could ever hope for. And the Lord had sent him to her. She just knew it.

"How about we postpone this cake for a bit and go into the study for a quick smoke?" Her father pushed back from the table, his gaze trained on Harlan.

Grace shot Maddie a quick look. *Do something now,* it said.

Once the men got to the study, the women would be locked out for most of the evening. She'd have no way to intervene.

Oh, she wanted Harlan to ask for her hand in marriage, but not like this. What a moment of weakness, when she had succumbed to the urge to seek outside help in getting Harlan to love her in return.

Shame filled her. She hadn't trusted the Lord. He was all the "outside help" she needed.

"Harlan," she practically purred. Whose voice was that? She cleared her throat and tried not to sound so desperate. "Harlan, will you take me for a quick stroll? I suddenly feel the need for. . ."

"Fresh air," Grace supplied.

"Yes, that's it," Maddie agreed. "Fresh air would be wonderful."

Harlan seemed to hesitate, but thankfully the powder she had added to the cookies kicked in and took over. He wouldn't be able to deny her anything tonight. Tomorrow might be another story altogether. But she would deal with that problem then. "Of course." He stood and nodded toward her father.

"We can talk when you get back," Pa said.

Maddie took a fortifying breath. Not if she had anything to say in the matter.

Chapter 2

Only a small patch of stars shone in the night sky. Clouds covered the rest, giving hope to Prissy's promise of snow.

Maddie pulled the sides of her wool cape a little closer around her as she silently questioned the wisdom of a winter night's walk. Too bad it wasn't a fragrant June evening with birds chirping and cicadas buzzing in the heat. But she had to get Harlan out of the house before he could embarrass himself in front of her father.

"Are you warm enough?" Harlan asked. Concern colored his voice. "We can go back in, if you'd like."

"Oh no," Maddie gushed, her enthusiasm more than one person should have. She told herself to calm down and shot him a quick smile. "I want to walk all the way down to the church."

"That far?"

"Of course," she lied. Quickly asking God for forgiveness, she continued. "It's Christmas Eve, the perfect day to go to the church. Don't you agree?" At least this last part was the truth.

Harlan returned her smile and nearly took her breath away. "Perfect," he said.

She looped her arm through his, and together they started off through the small crop of trees that hid the preacher's house from the rest of Calico Falls.

"It's a beautiful night," Harlan said. His strong form moved a little closer to her. They were alone, and the action was most inappropriate, but it was cold and she relished the warmth of him drawing near. If only he was so close because he truly loved her and wanted to be by her side always. That was everything a girl could ask for. Instead. . .

"Harlan," she started as they continued their walk, "there's something I need to talk to you about." She couldn't stand the guilt any longer. So far she had tricked him into eating tainted cookies, rebuffed his sweet marriage proposal, and led him out in the cold to correct her own mistakes. These were not the actions of a woman in love but of a desperate woman who needed to get back in control of herself before she ruined Christmas for everyone involved.

She only had a short time before she would be able to send Harlan home for the evening, but she had to confess the truth before it ate up her insides.

"Yes, my love?"

Her heart tripped at the endearment, and her feet followed suit.

"Whoa, there." Harlan wrapped his arms around her. His embrace steadied her steps and kept her from falling face-first into the packed dirt street of Calico Falls. But it had done more than that. It brought them close. So close. With only mere inches separating them. Inches that could be closed in a heartbeat.

Maddie inhaled, the action only bringing them closer, their frosted breath mingling in the night air.

They had come through the trees and into town, the church steeple just visible at the end of the way.

The sight of the cross standing straight and tall against the dark, clouded sky gave her bravery she hadn't had before.

She wedged her hands between herself and Harlan, putting some distance between them and successfully ending the potential kiss that hung around them.

"I must tell you something," she breathed, hating the words before she even said them. She prayed they wouldn't change how he felt about her forever. *Lord, please let him understand that everything I did, I did out of love.*

"I went to Old Lady Farley and got some. . .ground spices and herbs to put in the cookies."

He grinned. "They were delicious."

"Not those kinds of herbs." She bit her lip, trying to come up with the best explanation and falling short. "They were ones to make you fall in love with me."

To her surprise, he threw back his head and laughed long and loud into the cold night. "You are a jewel, Maddie Sinclair."

"But—" she started, sputtering to answer. This was not how she expected him to respond. Where was the indignation, the accusations and hurt?

The poor man was so far gone he couldn't even believe the truth. Those herbs must have been more potent than she'd originally thought.

"Harlan, listen to me." She grabbed his arms, holding him still so he would face her. He had to understand how serious the matter was.

But instead of searching her face and seeing the truth, he tilted his head back and scanned the sky. "It's snowing."

Pure white crystal flakes drifted down from the clouds. They were close to the mountains, but not far enough up that they'd ever had a white Christmas that Maddie could recall. Watching the snow fall was like a miracle in itself.

"Come on." Harlan grabbed her hand, and together they raced toward the church.

Maddie couldn't stop the laugh from escaping her as they ran. The snow started to fall faster. By the time they reached the portico at the tiny white clapboard church, the ground was nearly covered.

Harlan released her hand as they stepped under the cover. He brushed the snow from his shoulders and gave her that heart-stopping smile. "I guess we should have run back toward your house."

"Most probably," Maddie said, but she wouldn't have missed the scene before her for anything. Snow fell around their sleepy little town. Candles twinkled in the windows of houses and shops alike. Pine wreaths hung on the doors, tied with red ribbon and strips of flour sacks. A hush hovered over the town, a quiet air of expectation. Tomorrow was Christmas. "It's beautiful," she whispered.

"Yes," he agreed, but he wasn't looking at the town. He was staring at her, that gleam back in his blue eyes.

"Harlan, what I said back there, I was serious."

He shook his head. "You think I asked to marry you because of something Old Lady Farley gave you?"

She solemnly nodded. At least now he was starting to understand. As much as it hurt her, she was glad.

"Maddie Sinclair, you should know better."

"I know." She had to push the words past the lump in her throat.

"You of all people should know that she's a crazy old hen. Why, she probably gave you a mess of ground-up, dried grass and charged you, to boot."

"What? No, she gave me some love herbs, and I baked them into the cookies. Then you asked me to marry you." Couldn't he understand? How many times did she have to say it before he realized she was telling the truth?

"The cookies were delicious, I might add. But not enough to make me fall in love with you." He seemed to think about it a moment. "Well, maybe. They were pretty tasty."

"Harlan Calhoun. I need you to be serious. I did something terribly wrong. You have to believe me."

"Oh, I believe you." His eyes twinkled, taking all the validity from his words. And it surely didn't help when he dropped to one knee there on the portico and clasped her hands in his. "Maddie Sinclair, would you do me the pleasure of being my wife?"

Tears immediately sprang to her eyes. Her hands were in his warm ones, and she let the tears fall. "Harlan." She nearly choked on the love and remorse clogging her throat. "I don't know what to say."

Oh, she knew what to say. She had to tell him no. As much as she loved him, as long as she had waited for this moment, she had to tell him no. And then pray like everything that he would still feel the same once the cookies lost their effect.

Not that she expected those prayers to be answered.

"You say yes," he gently explained. He released her hands to remove something from the inside pocket of his coat. A jewelry box.

Her heart pounded, and her mouth dried to ash as he lifted the lid. Nestled inside the carved box, atop a deep burgundy velvet cushion, was a cameo. It was beautiful and fragile and special. She wanted nothing more than to remove it and hold it close. Cherish it always.

"This was my grandmother's," he continued. "But I want you to have it as a symbol of my love for you."

"Oh Harlan." She clamped one hand over her mouth to keep from saying more. As badly as she wanted to declare her eternal love in return, this was wrong. "I can't accept this," she said, her choked sob escaping between her numb fingers.

His earnest smile never wavered. "Of course not. You can't say yes without my talking to your father first. Please forgive my eagerness. But I have no patience where love is concerned."

If only that were true.

She bit her lip again, this time drawing blood as she struggled to keep words she couldn't say from escaping. "I think it's time we headed back."

The ground was completely white. Perhaps it was past time to go home, weather-wise at least. But when they got back to her house, he was sure to want to talk to her father, and that was something she simply couldn't allow.

She looked out at the falling snow. They couldn't stay here much longer without scandalizing the entire town. With a sigh, she pulled him to his feet. "We have to go back now," she said. She'd worry about the rest of it later.

His smile grew positively dazzling, brighter than the snow they had to trudge through to make it back to her house on the edge of town. "I'm glad to see you're so. . .enthusiastic."

"What?" He had completely misunderstood her intentions. "That's not what I meant. It's snowing harder. If we don't get back soon, we'll never make it."

Harlan tilted his head, his expression so lost and perplexed she wanted to reach out and wipe it away with the tips of her fingers. "Are you saying you don't want to marry me?"

She opened her mouth to respond. His question had no right answer. If she said no, Harlan would forever think she didn't love him. If she said yes, then he would want to propose—for real, in front of her father and with his blessing—tonight. And what happened tomorrow when the cookies no longer had control of his emotions and his thinking was clear? How would he feel about being trapped into marriage with the preacher's plain daughter?

"Let's go," she said, turning toward the steps leading away from the church. It was best not to answer at all and say another prayer that the Lord would somehow see her through.

Yet a tiny voice inside whispered, *You got yourself into this. It's up to you to get yourself out of it.*

Maddie wasn't sure if it was the Lord or her own conscience. She suspected it might be a little of both.

Still, it wouldn't stop her from praying. And with a lot of blessing from above, she would somehow be able to stall Harlan until it was time for him to head back to his own house. Then, and only then, would she breathe a sigh of relief.

⌀

Harlan grabbed Maddie's hand, and together they dashed back through the snow. It was as if the heavens knew he needed an enchanted night to ask her to be his wife. And what was more magical than snow on Christmas Eve?

The earth glistening with the crystal flakes lent a surreal backdrop to the midnight-blue sky. It was almost Christmas, the most wondrous day of the year. Maddie Sinclair was about to agree to be his wife. And everything was perfect. He'd never felt so blessed.

Well, at least he thought she was going to agree to be his wife. But this nonsense about bewitched cookies. Ridiculous. He hoped her crazy notions about magical herbs weren't enough to keep her from saying yes.

Oh, the cookies were tasty indeed. But they weren't magical. And delicious as they were, they couldn't make him fall in love. Because he was already there. He had loved her from the first time he had seen her. She had been standing at her father's side, welcoming the congregation into their tiny church. Harlan was brand-new to town, the dust not even wiped from his shoes, but he knew he had to keep his covenant with the Lord. Despite his exhaustion and weariness from the trip west, he'd donned his best suit and walked to the church.

She had been wearing a dress as blue as the June sky, the color lending its hue to her green eyes to turn them the color of the ocean. Her deep brown hair had been pulled back with a bit of ivory lace that perfectly matched the trimmings on her dress. And in that instant, he had fallen completely in love.

He allowed his gaze to drift toward her now. She was even more beautiful, with the cold staining her cheeks a fetching pink and adding an extra sparkle to her eyes. And he loved her even more.

How silly and sweet that she had thought she could make him fall in love with her by using a crazy old woman's love potion. He couldn't love her any more than he already did. Well, that was his verdict today. Tomorrow might bring even more affection for the lovely woman at his side.

For her to go to such lengths to make him fall in love with her. . .well, that had to say something about her own feelings, didn't it?

She had yet to tell him how she felt. But she had to love him. She just had to.

They made it back to her house in record time, snowflakes clinging to their hair and clothes.

"Maddie. Harlan." Grace met them at the door, concern etched into every inch of her face. "We were so worried about you."

Maddie smiled at her sister, the action warming his heart from the inside out. "It's snowing, Grace. It's a Christmas miracle. That has to mean something, right?"

Grace shook her head. "Maddie, you didn't. . ." Her words trailed off as she helped her sister out of her wet cloak. She brushed the last of the snowflakes from Maddie's hair as Maddie whispered, "He asked me to marry him."

"What did you say?" Grace returned in the same whisper.

Harlan took off his coat but held it in his arms, waiting for the two of them to finish.

"What could I say? I told him we had to talk to Pa."

"Oh, Maddie."

"You didn't tell Pa, right? Please, Gracie, you can't tell Pa."

"What are we supposed to do?"

Maddie shook her dark head. "I don't know, but please don't tell him. He'll never understand."

"I won't tell him," Harlan said.

The sisters turned to him as if they had just remembered he was there.

"Harlan," Grace greeted, her voice overloud in the small entryway. "Let's get you into the parlor where there's a fire going." She took his coat and hung it on the rack next to Maddie's.

"Is your father in there?" he asked as Grace led him down the hall.

"He's in the study having a smoke." She wrinkled her nose as if this was the absolute worst thing. Harlan didn't partake of tobacco often. He knew it was the vogue thing in all the best houses in the East, but he'd never developed a taste for it. Still, he would much rather be in the study not having a smoke with her father than in the parlor alone. How was he supposed to ask for Maddie's hand half a house away from the blessing he needed?

He started to protest, but Grace seemed deaf as she led him toward the parlor.

"Now, you wait here, and I'll be back shortly with some hot cocoa to help warm you up."

"You don't happen to have any more of those cookies I had earlier?"

Grace's emerald eyes grew wide and her cheeks turned pale. "No," she said, her voice sounding much like a mother's to a child asking for candy. "No more cookies for you." She disappeared through the door leading back into the kitchen.

Her expression was perplexing to be sure. It was almost as if she, too, believed that Maddie had made him fall in love with her.

He had to put a stop to this nonsense. If he couldn't ask for Maddie's hand before he had to leave for the night—

He shook his head. He'd had it planned out perfectly in his mind. A Christmas Eve proposal, a kiss under the mistletoe, a spring wedding.

His fingers slipped into his coat pocket, touching the box containing his grandmother's cameo. He had imagined it pinned to the ivory lace of Maddie's wedding dress, nestled at her throat, showing the world that she was his.

"There you are, my boy." Easton Sinclair swept into the room, bringing with him the smoky tang of tobacco. "Seems Prissy was right." He nodded toward the window where the fat white flakes continued to fall.

"Yes, sir." Harlan cleared his throat, his prepared speech deserting him in his time of need.

"Get over here closer to the fire before you catch your death of cold," the reverend instructed. His voice was deep and booming even when he wasn't in the pulpit, and Harlan found himself immediately complying.

The crackling fire warmed him. He hadn't realized he was chilled. He was still floating on the warmth of Maddie's sweet smile.

"You said you had some business to discuss with me, young man." That was just like Pastor Sinclair, straight to the point.

"Not business, really. More of a personal matter." He opened his mouth to continue but was interrupted.

"Here we are." Grace pushed her way back into the parlor, a tray of treats balanced in her arms.

"Ah, something to warm us on the inside." Pastor Sinclair nodded happily.

Asking for Maddie's hand would have to wait for a few more minutes. Her father, it seemed, had something of a sweet tooth. But Harlan could wait a little longer. Despite her wild claim that she had made him fall in love with her, he knew the truth.

Ever the gracious hostess, Grace poured cups of steaming cocoa and passed out the tea biscuits shaped like Christmas trees.

"Too bad there aren't any more of those gingerbread cookies," Pastor Sinclair said.

"Too bad," Grace murmured.

Harlan was amazed that a sensible woman like Grace Sinclair would fall for such nonsense, but there it was. "Speaking of the cookies. . ."

Grace shook her head. "You promised."

"Promised what?" Pastor Sinclair asked.

"Did everyone forget I was in the house?" Maddie picked that very moment to sweep back into the room. As usual, she stole the breath from Harlan's lungs.

"Maddie, thank goodness." Grace hustled to her sister's side, whispering in her ear with an urgent hiss.

Harlan couldn't make out the words, but the intention was clear.

Maddie's eyes widened, and she gave a stiff nod.

"Girls." It seemed the reverend was accustomed to his daughters sharing secrets and thought the custom rude.

"Forgive me, Pa." Grace bowed toward him but offered no explanation.

"Since we are all here—and this seems to be turning into a family matter—I have something I need to discuss with you, Pastor Sinclair."

Maddie started coughing, choking really, though on what, Harlan could not determine. She'd had nothing to eat, nothing to drink.

Once again Grace raced to her side, patting her solicitously on the back and helping her over to the settee as she continued to cough and hiccup. "Let me get you something to drink, Sister."

Maddie nodded as another fit of whatever ailed her came upon her again. This one, though, seemed a little less genuine than the one before.

Harlan immediately regretted his assumption. Maddie was clearly in distress as she covered her mouth with an embroidered handkerchief, tears welling in her eyes.

"There, there," Grace crooned as she poured Maddie a cup of cocoa. "I hope that cold isn't already setting in. You'll catch your death being out on a night like this."

"A warm drink will spruce her right up." Pastor Sinclair nodded toward his daughters then turned to face Harlan. "You were saying?"

"Well, sir, I—"

Maddie jumped to her feet, her recovery miraculous indeed. "Harlan Calhoun, you can't stay a minute longer. You'll never be able to get home in this storm if you do."

Grace rushed from the room before he could reply, returning in mere seconds with his coat draped over one arm and his hat in her hand. "Prissy dried your coat by the fire, so you are ready to go. So glad you could join us this evening." She held his coat out to him. When he didn't immediately take it, she shook it at him.

"Would someone like to tell me what's going on in this house tonight?" Pastor Sinclair's booming words were less of a question and more of a "someone had better start explaining" command.

"Nothing, Father." Grace and Maddie murmured their reply in unison, but neither one met their father's piercing gaze.

"Mr. Calhoun will not be going anywhere in this weather." His tone brooked no argument.

It didn't deter Maddie. "But—"

She stopped as Grace elbowed her. "Perhaps we should play a Christmas game."

"Like charades."

Their father blustered. "Perhaps we should read from the Bible instead."

"Wonderful idea." Harlan rubbed his hands together. He loved reading from the book of Luke the details of the birth of their Lord and Savior. What a perfect way to spend Christmas Eve. Reading God's Word with the woman he loved and her family.

Maddie bustled off to find Prissy so she could join the festivities, while Grace continued to pin him with a warning stare.

Harlan glanced toward the preacher and tried to relax. He was anxious to state his intentions. To gain her father's blessing, to give Maddie the cameo, to start the rest of their life together on this special day. Yet it seemed all that would have to wait. But only for a while. He wanted to make Maddie his wife. And he would. As soon as he convinced her the herbs she got from Old Lady Farley were nothing more than a hoax.

⟡

"Why don't you start off, Harlan?" Pa looked to their guest and handed him the Bible.

Maddie closed her eyes as he read, his deep voice like velvet as he shared with them the story of Mary and Joseph. Of their travels to Bethlehem, of no room at the inn. Of having a child and laying the babe in a manger.

When he finished reading, Maddie was certain she had never loved him more. Why, oh why had she felt it necessary to taint the cookies? Why hadn't she left it up to the Lord? And how was she supposed to know when the effects were worn off? When he no longer wanted to marry her? It was heartbreaking. The herbs could last two hours or two weeks! How was she supposed to know?

And now he was staying the night.

"Maddie?"

She glanced up for the first time since they had gathered in the parlor. The two of them were alone. "Where did everyone go?" She had been daydreaming so much she hadn't heard the others leave.

"Your father went back to his study. Prissy said she was turning in for the night, and Grace went to find me a stocking to hang on the mantel."

"She did?"

"I told her it wasn't necessary, but. . ." He trailed off. Not that he had to say more. She knew how determined her sister could be when she set her mind to something. If Grace wanted Harlan to have a Christmas stocking, then a Christmas stocking he would have.

"At least you won't be getting coal in yours." Maddie spoke the words before thinking then clamped her hand over her mouth. "That was churlish. I'm sorry."

He smiled at her, his face lighting up with love. What she wouldn't give to have him look at her like that for now and always. Without the tricks of Old Lady Farley. "You're not going to get coal in your stocking," he said. "That I can promise you. By some chance you do, I think I know a gift that will more than make up for it." He touched his chest, close to his heart. The exact spot where she knew he had stored the beautiful cameo he'd presented her earlier.

"Speaking of," he started. He stood and stretched. With a smile, he pulled on the legs of his brown pants and the snowy-white shirt sleeves that peeked out from under his suit coat. "I have something important to discuss with your father."

"No!" Maddie tugged him back to the settee next to her. The surprise attack was most probably what pulled him off his feet, but she would take any help she could get. "Harlan, you can't."

"Of course I can." His smile was infectious, sweet and pure.

"But you promised."

A frown pulled at his forehead, and he pushed to his feet. "I did not."

"You did," she protested. "You promised me and Grace that you wouldn't say anything to Pa about the cookies."

To her surprise, he threw back his head and laughed. "I'm not telling him about the cookies. I'm going to ask for your hand in marriage."

She pulled him back down next to her. "That's the same thing."

"It is not." He was on his feet in an instant.

Maddie jerked on his arm until he agreed to sit once more. "It is."

He shook his head, but fortunately he didn't try to get away. "Is this about the herbs again?"

"That's all it's been about."

"Maddie, you're being ridiculous. There was nothing wrong with those cookies."

"Oh Harlan, I wish you were right."

"I am right." He took her hands, his blue eyes searching hers. "I want to make you my wife. And I want us to be wed this spring when the dogwoods and the daffodils are in bloom. It's not so much to ask."

"No," she whispered, caught in the warm cocoon of his voice.

He leaned toward her, and she caught the scent of his sandalwood aftershave and the spice that had seemed to follow him all night. "You will be a beautiful bride," he whispered, drawing closer still.

"You think I'm beautiful?" she asked, the words barely a whisper in the waning distance between them.

"More than you will ever know." His words washed over her, his warm breath sweet with the scent of chocolate. His gaze flickered to her lips.

He was going to kiss her!

Maddie jumped to her feet.

Harlan pulled her back down beside him. "Where are you going?"

"Uh, to help Grace find you a stocking." She was back on her feet in an instant.

"I don't need a stocking." He tugged her back down beside him. Was he even closer now?

"Of course you do." She hopped to her feet for only a heartbeat before he pulled her back down.

"Stop it, Maddie. You're making me dizzy."

She pressed a hand to her forehead. He wasn't the only one. "You can't kiss me, Harlan." Now those were words she never thought she'd say.

"You're right, of course. I shouldn't be so forward until after I've spoken to your father."

He rose to his feet, and she pulled him back down.

"Oh no," he said. "We're not going to start this again."

She laid a hand on his arm, effectively stilling him beside her. "Please, Harlan."

"Please what, Maddie? I'll do anything for you."

"Then don't ask my father for my hand." She almost choked on the words. "At least, not until the cookies—" She shook her head, unable to finish. "I'm not sure you'll want to then, but wait. . .for me."

His gaze bored into hers. "It means that much to you?"

She nodded. Couldn't he see this was for his own good?

"Then I'll wait. But only until the morning. And not because I believe in some cookie mumbo-jumbo. But because you asked me to."

That was good enough for her. "Thank you," she whispered, her heart breaking.

Lord, dear Lord, please let him still love me in the morning.

Chapter 3

Christmas morning dawned bright and sunny, the warm rays bouncing off the blinding white snow. Maddie threw back the covers and rushed to get dressed, more excited than she had ever been on the Lord's birthday.

She said a quick prayer, since her joy had less to do with God and everything to do with Harlan Calhoun. Maybe today she would know the truth.

A knock sounded on the door, and Grace quickly slipped into Maddie's room. "Are you ready?"

Maddie patted her hair in place. "Almost." She couldn't stop the smile of excitement racing across her face. She clasped her brush to her breast and turned to face her sister. "Today's the day. Oh, Grace. I prayed and prayed last night. Do you think Harlan will still love me today?"

The frown that pulled at her sister's brow was anything but reassuring. "How are you supposed to know, Maddie?"

Maddie dropped the brush on her dressing table and whirled around to face her sister. "I—I—" she sputtered. "I guess I'll just know." But her words sounded small in the space between them.

"Did you 'just know' yesterday?"

Maddie buried her face in her hands, her excitement draining away like rain off the roof. "What am I going to do?"

Grace hugged her close. "As I see it, you can get down there and tell Pa all about what happened or you can go keep the two of them apart for a while longer."

Maddie straightened, wiping the tears from her cheeks as a new determination filled her. "That's what I'll do. I'll make him take me for a walk—"

"Another one?"

"—and keep him and Pa apart until it's safe for him to go home."

"Have you seen the snow out there? He may be here for days."

"Then I'll pray for the snow to melt. Pray with me, Grace."

Her sister shook her head. "I'll pray all right, for you to return to your senses."

Maddie stuck out her tongue at Grace like she had when they were children. "I have my senses. Just pray that Harlan comes back to his."

And with that she raised the hem of her skirt and rushed out the door. Her plan would be for naught if Harlan got to her father first.

She skipped down the stairs as fast as she dared, saying a little prayer with each step that her father had somehow managed to sleep in and wasn't already—

"Merry Christmas, Madeline." Her father beamed at her from his place by the mantel. The stockings had already been filled with crunchy nuts and delicious oranges. At least she hoped that was what caused the rounded bulges in her sock and not coal.

"Merry Christmas, Maddie."

She whirled around to see Harlan casually standing by the big armchair next to the Christmas tree. He must have been sitting there the entire time, standing when she entered the room. She was too late.

"Have you been awake long?" she asked, looking from one man to the other.

"Oh, a while." Harlan's eyes twinkled as he spoke. If the look on his face was any indication, then he had been up long enough to talk to her father.

"Harlan here was just telling me about the latest fad on the East Coast."

"He was?" Did that mean he hadn't been asking for her hand? Maybe she wasn't too late after all.

"Are you ready to hear this?" her father asked with a chuckle. "Wedding cakes."

Maddie stumbled but managed to catch herself before she fell headlong onto the rug. "Wedding cakes?" she whispered, her hopes falling like last night's snow.

"It seems the bride gets this large cake all elaborately decorated with fruit and flowers. It sounds like quite a sight."

Maddie turned toward Harlan, the question she so desperately needed to ask stuck somewhere between her brain and her lips.

"It's morning, Maddie," he said, as if he could read her thoughts.

"It is," she agreed, carefully forming her words. She wanted nothing less than to jump up and down and scream in frustration. Instead, she spoke as calmly as possible. "Harlan, will you take a walk with me before breakfast?"

"Why, Daughter, it's below freezing out there."

"Please, Harlan."

He gave a quick nod. "Get your coat, my dear."

Fortunately, her father didn't protest further. Maddie donned her cloak and hustled Harlan out the door as quickly as possible.

The air wasn't quite as cold as it had been the night before, but still their breaths came out in little puffs of vapor.

"It's a beautiful day." Harlan looked up at the cloudless Christmas sky, squinting against the bright rays of the sun.

"How are you. . .feeling this morning?"

She hated Grace's logic. How was she supposed to know if Harlan was over the cookies? Maybe she should run down to Old Lady Farley's and ask.

Maddie pushed the thought away. That was no way to keep her little secret.

"I slept like a baby," Harlan replied, stepping off the porch and into the pile of snow lining the house.

"Any. . .changes this morning?"

He turned back to face her. "Is that what this is all about?"

"What?" she asked with feigned innocence. She had to know. And how would she find out without asking?

"Is this about those cookies?" He shook his head. "I was hoping you would be over it by this morning."

Me, too. "I can't believe you aren't taking this more seriously." She stamped her foot on the porch for emphasis. A small avalanche of snow fell from the roof, loosened by her motion.

"Whoa!" Harlan danced backward, but not before the snow cascaded around him. He shuffled a bit more as he tried to shake off the snow.

"Harlan!" Maddie raced off the porch. "Are you all right?" She slipped on the last step and fell headlong into his arms.

He took a step back, and another, trying to regain his balance; then the two of them fell into the snow.

The breath was knocked out of her as she fell, landing atop Harlan with a thud. It took a moment for her to regain her composure, a minute of listening to his heart beat under her ear and his own labored breathing as he caught his wind again.

"Oh!" Maddie pushed herself away and struggled to stand. Harlan managed the feat before her, reaching out a hand to help pull her upright.

"See where all this nonsense has gotten us?" He smiled as he brushed the snow from his clothes.

Tears rose in Maddie's eyes. "It's not nonsense. And what I did was wrong. Can't you see that? I'm trying to make amends, but you just won't listen." Her words ended on a strangled sob.

"Shh. . .shh. . ." Harlan pulled her to him, holding her close and rubbing a hand down her back. "Maddie Sinclair, despite your intentions and all your harebrained ideas about these cookies, I came here in love with you, and today when I leave, I will still be in love with you."

"And tomorrow?" she asked, pulling away so she could see his face.

"Still in love." He smiled.

Oh how she loved his smile. And oh how she wanted to believe what he said was true. "But—"

He shook his head. "What do I have to do to make you understand? I sent for the cameo. I came to ask for your hand. Can't you see that whatever you got from Old Lady Farley was just a ruse to take your money?"

"I bartered," Maddie started then broke off at Harlan's stern look. "I don't know," she whispered, wishing she had the answer. She wanted to believe him. She truly did, but the nagging doubts and Grace's voice of reason won out.

"I tell you what. Let's go get some of those flapjacks Prissy promised me last night, and maybe this whole thing will work itself out."

"Maybe," she murmured as he released her. She looped her arm through his and allowed him to lead her back into the house.

Harlan stepped into the warmth of the house, his mind going at full speed. How was he ever going to convince his headstrong and silly Maddie that she had been taken by the "lady" who lived at the end of the lane? Old Lady Farley was a trickster, to be sure. He had no doubt that Maddie believed that she had done something wrong. Her tears of remorse were more than enough proof of that. And even a family heirloom couldn't convince her otherwise.

"Can you two not stay out of the snow?" Grace bustled into the entryway, a towel at the ready.

Harlan looked down to see he was already standing in a puddle of melted snow. "I'm sorry," he said sheepishly. "Forgive me, I fell."

"Of course." Grace smiled at him as he lifted his feet to stand on the towel and then helped Maddie take off her cloak.

Grace took it from him, and he removed his own coat.

"I'll have Prissy hang these by the fire just as soon as breakfast is finished."

"Is that what I smell?" Maddie asked.

The entire foyer was filled with the delicious scent of vanilla and nutmeg. "Prissy's flapjacks."

"Smells delicious," Harlan said. And a bit familiar.

"Well, dry off and meet us at the table," Grace said. "Prissy is setting it now." She started toward the kitchen then stopped and turned back to face them. "And there's no time to take advantage of. . .ahem." She pointed to a spot above their heads.

Harlan looked up at the sprig of mistletoe hanging from the ceiling. Why had he never noticed that before?

Grace smiled and pushed through the door that led to the kitchen.

Harlan looked to Maddie.

She swallowed hard as she returned his stare.

He took a step toward her.

"Harlan, I—"

But he wasn't about to take no for an answer. She loved him, and despite all her crazy ideas about love herbs and cookies, he loved her, too.

He took her by the arms and pulled her close—not close enough that their bodies touched, but still near enough he could breathe in the lilac scent of her soap and the crisp smell of outdoors.

She seemed about to protest, but her eyes fluttered closed a second before he lowered his head and pressed his lips to hers.

Her lips were soft, sweet beneath his, and he couldn't wait until she agreed to be his bride.

She sighed as he lifted his head. Her eyes opened and stared into his.

"Do you believe me now?"

She pulled away, pressing the back of one hand against her lips. "Harlan, I—"

"What, Maddie?" The game was growing tiresome, but he wouldn't give up. He *couldn't* give up.

"I want to believe you," she said. "I really do."

"Do you love me, Maddie?" He had to hear her say it one more time.

"I do," she whispered.

"Then I won't give up. I won't bother you again today. But I'll be here every day after until you realize that my love for you is genuine."

Without waiting for her response, he turned and made his way to the dining room.

⌖

Maddie watched him go, the warmth of his lips pressed against hers still tingling. She had wanted to melt into his embrace, like the snow they tracked in from outside. But she held herself in check.

He would be here every day? For how long? One week? Two? Or would he walk out of her life this afternoon, never to return?

"Maddie," Grace called from the other room. "We're waiting on you."

She hustled into the dining room to find everyone already seated. Once again she sat across from Harlan. Her cheeks filled with heat as she recalled their kiss under the mistletoe. But he looked at her like she was almost a stranger. Had the cookies finally worn off? The thought made her heart ache in her chest.

"Let's pray," her father said.

Maddie bowed her head as her father thanked the Lord for the beautiful day, the wonderful company, nourishing food, and His Son who had died for them all. She silently added an entreaty for forgiveness for her transgressions and a plea that one day Harlan would forgive her as well.

"Amen," Pa concluded.

Everyone raised their heads, and the platters of food were passed around. There were stacks of sweet-smelling flapjacks with fresh butter and rich maple syrup, bowls of fried potatoes, and mounds of country ham to be shared.

Everything tasted so delicious, Maddie was soon reaching for another couple of flapjacks to complete her meal. They were just so good.

"Prissy, I say you have outdone yourself this morning."

Their housekeeper smiled at the pastor's praise. "Thank ye, suh. I put in those special spices you left fur me."

Maddie's fork slipped from her fingers and clattered onto the table.

Harlan stopped eating, his fork suspended midway between his plate and his mouth.

Grace coughed delicately into her napkin.

Only Prissy and their father seemed oblivious to the strain at the table.

"What did you say?" Maddie asked, recovering as quickly as she could. Maybe she'd misunderstood. Maybe her father really did bring their housekeeper a bag of spices from the general store. Surely Prissy hadn't found the bag Maddie had gotten from Old Lady Farley. After all, Maddie had thrown that away herself. Hadn't she?

With all the confusion yesterday over the cookies and Harlan's impulsive proposal, Maddie couldn't remember. But surely she wouldn't have been so careless with something so important.

"Why, I found a bag of spices in the kitchen yesterdee. I put 'em in the flapjacks. They came out good, huh?"

"Very tasty," Pa agreed. "But I didn't leave you any spices. Though after tasting these flapjacks, I may have to remember to do so in the future."

Maddie's heart sank. "This bag," she started, "was it small and made out of a scrap of flour sack?"

"Why yes, it was," Prissy answered.

"And was it tied with a small leather string?"

"Yes'um." Prissy continued to eat, not realizing the tragedy of what she had done.

"How could you have been so careless?" Grace hissed.

Maddie kicked her under the table.

Grace shot her a look and rose. "I apologize for interrupting our meal, but Maddie, can I see you in the kitchen." It wasn't a question.

Maddie shook her head.

"May we be excused, Pa?" Grace turned her attention to their father, and Maddie settled down in her seat a bit more.

Christmas must have put him in a good mood, or maybe it was the tainted flapjacks, but their father nodded his consent.

"But—" Maddie tried to protest, but Grace hauled her to her feet despite her sputters and dragged her toward the kitchen.

Just before they pushed through the swinging door, Maddie heard Harlan say, "If you would excuse me, too, sir?"

Grace turned on her the minute they were alone. "What have you done?"

"What have *I* done?" she protested.

They weren't alone for long. Harlan pushed his way inside. "Is she talking about what I think she's talking about?"

Maddie nodded and bit her lip.

"I told you this would come to no good," Grace scolded.

"I can't believe the two of you actually believe all this nonsense." Harlan shook his head.

"Oh, we believe it all right." Grace propped her hands on her hips and shot Maddie a look.

"What?" she asked. Then her defenses crumbled and she wilted like a pansy in August. "I'm sorry." She ducked her head and sniffed. "I never meant for any of this to happen."

"Maddie." Harlan's voice was firm and commanding. "Is this what you put in the cookies?"

She looked up to find him holding the bag she had gotten from Old Lady Farley. She nodded miserably.

He lifted it to his nose and sniffed.

"Harlan, no." Maddie rushed over to him and pulled the bag from his grasp. "Don't do that. You might ingest more of it."

He chuckled. "Maddie, when are you going to believe me?"

How could she?

He tossed the bag on the counter. "If whatever it was she gave you was supposed to make me fall in love with you, then why aren't we all in love with everyone sitting at the table? We all ate it this morning."

"Maybe it has a delayed effect." It was the best reason Maddie could come up with, and it sounded weak even to her own ears.

Grace eased open the door just a crack, only enough that she could peek at their father and Prissy still seated at the table.

"What's happening out there?" Maddie asked.

"They're drinking coffee," Grace whispered in return.

"And that's it?"

Grace jerked away from the door. It closed with a swoosh. "I think they saw me."

"He wasn't proposing or anything?"

Grace shook her head.

"See?" Harlan said. "If they both ate the herbs—and we know they did—then they should be falling in love with each other."

Hope burst through Maddie. What he was saying was logical, and yet she was afraid to let herself believe. If what he said was true, then he could really and truly love her. But she could only allow herself to believe that when she was absolutely certain. Otherwise she would end up heartbroken and alone.

"What is going on in here?"

Grace jumped back as Pa burst through the kitchen door, missing her by mere inches.

"Pa," Maddie gasped.

Grace pressed one hand to her breast, and Harlan tried not to laugh.

Maddie shot him a look. This was not funny.

"I'm waiting."

"Well," Grace started, obviously trying to stall but not sure what she should say. That was Grace, ever truthful. Maddie was surprised her sister had kept the secret this long.

"It's okay, Grace." It was time for her to step up and tell the truth. No matter the consequences. "It's my fault." The tension that had been in Maddie's shoulders suddenly loosened, and she knew this was the right thing to do. Well, she had known it all along, but there was a comfort in the telling. "I went to Old Lady Farley and bought some herbs day before yesterday."

"Her name is Eunice Farley, and you will refer to her as Miss Farley."

"Yes, Pa."

"Why did you go buy herbs at her house?" To her father's credit, he didn't so much as falter when he said the word *house* to refer to the pitiful shack that squatted at the edge of town.

"I wanted to make Harlan fall in love with me." She ducked her head as she said the words, ashamed to admit them aloud and to her pious father. What an embarrassment she had to be to him.

"And you thought Eunice Farley could help you with that?"

She nodded as shame washed over her.

To her surprise, her father laughed. "Are you saying that Eunice Farley sold you a love potion?"

"It wasn't a potion exactly. Just a bag of herbs." She was dodging the issue, but she couldn't seem to keep the words from slipping out.

"The same bag of herbs that Prissy added to our breakfast cakes this morning?"

"The very one." Harlan came to stand by her, and Maddie was immediately bolstered by his presence.

Pa shook his head. "I hope you learned your lesson."

Maddie hated when her father used that tone. That "you should know better, I thought I raised you better than this, what would your mother have to say about this?" tone he got at times like these.

"I'm sorry, Pa, I just. . ." She struggled to finish.

"You didn't trust the Lord to provide."

"No," she said, her voice small.

"Come." Her father motioned for her to follow him. "Let's go talk about this in the parlor. You, too, Harlan. It seems this concerns you as well."

⁂

The last thing Maddie wanted to do was have her father berate her reckless behavior. She deserved it, but it was still the last thing she wanted to hear.

And in front of Harlan, no less.

"I'm sorry, Father."

They had settled down in the parlor, a pot of fresh coffee between them. Grace and Prissy had disappeared into the kitchen to clean up the breakfast dishes, but Maddie had a feeling they were standing on the other side of the door with their ears pressed against it.

"I don't think I'm the only one you owe an apology."

She turned to face Harlan, her chin tucked against her chest. "I'm truly sorry, Harlan. I didn't mean any harm."

"You know I forgive you." He smiled and warmed her heart.

"Now." Her father rubbed his hands together in eagerness. "Let's get down to wedding talk."

Maddie's chin jerked up, her gaze landing on her father. "What? Wedding talk?"

"Isn't that what this has all been about?" Pa asked.

"You're not angry with me?"

"I think you've learned your lesson. You should know better than to divulge in the fanciful. You went there to get a love potion, and instead you got ground vanilla bean and nutmeg. I say that's a small price to pay to relearn what you already knew."

"Ground vanilla—"

Her father gave her an indulgent smile. "You didn't really think Miss Farley gave you a real love concoction?"

She let out a choked laugh. "Of course not." The lie was so blatant, she was surprised her father didn't make her ask for forgiveness right there on the spot.

Instead, he continued. "She has to make money when she can."

"So you're not even upset with her?"

"One can't blame the snake oil salesman, for without the buyer, how will the salesman stay in business?"

She was chagrined. She looked to Harlan, who smiled as if to say, "I told you so."

"And you still want to marry me?" she asked.

Harlan's smile widened. "More than anything."

"Now," her father started again. "It seems that we need a contract of sorts. A verbal agreement will do just fine. When shall the wedding take place?"

"In the spring," Harlan said before she could so much as take a breath to respond. "Is that all right with you?"

She smiled. "The spring will be lovely."

"I assume that you will be able to provide for my daughter, keeping her in a decent house and providing for her every need."

Harlan nodded. "That's why it has taken me so long to come and ask for her hand. I wanted to make sure my practice would flourish and I could provide. I'm looking to buy a parcel of land on the other side of the county, not too far out of town. Once the weather turns toward the warm, we can start building a house."

Maddie gasped, the reality of his feelings coming home. He did love her. Even after all her silly mistakes and crazy notions of making him fall in love with her, he still loved her.

"Are you all right, my dear?" Harlan turned toward her, concern on his brow.

"I'm just so happy," she said.

He smiled and took her hand. The warmth of his palm seeped into her skin. Love for her lit his blue eyes like the stars twinkling in the clear nighttime sky. How could one person be this happy? How could she have ever doubted that he loved her?

"Spring it is." Her father slapped his hands against his legs, his own joy evident. "God is good," he said, smiling at the two of them.

"Did we hear there's going to be a wedding this spring?" Grace and Prissy rushed into the room, raising the excitement level twofold.

"In the spring." Maddie nodded, her smile so wide her cheeks hurt. She never could have asked for more than this, would never even have dreamed she could be this happy.

Her sister and Prissy clasped hands with her, and together the three of them embraced and danced in a little circle of joy.

"Well, there is one thing I must do first." Harlan's words fell like a clump of wet clay in the middle of the room.

The girls stilled their feet and waited for him to continue. Somehow the excitement dimmed.

The room grew quiet and expectant as he stood and smoothed down the lapels of his suit. The action seemed to take forever as Maddie waited for him to reveal the one thing that would have to come before their wedding.

His eyes still sparkled but had turned darker than she had ever seen them. He walked to her and took her hands from the others' grasps and led her closer to the Christmas tree that had been set next to the window.

"Maddie," he said, his voice a little like an old bullfrog. He cleared his throat, dropped to one knee, and started again. "Maddie." He reached into his suit coat pocket and extracted the small box as he had the night before. "I have loved you since the first time I saw you standing by your father and welcoming the congregation to church. Ever since then, I have worked and toiled with one goal in mind: asking you to be my wife."

Maddie's heart pounded as she listened to his words. His confession was real this time. Well, it had been real the other two times before, but this time she knew it was real. Her hand trembled as he squeezed her suddenly cold fingers.

"Now the time has come. Maddie Sinclair, with your father's blessing, will you do me the honor of being my wife?"

"Yes," she whispered as happy tears spilled down her cheeks.

"I would like to present you with this," Harlan continued, releasing her fingers to take the lid from the ornate box. The beautiful cameo lay there, still nestled in the burgundy velvet. "It belonged to my grandmother. I want you to wear it with the knowledge that you are loved."

"I will." She tugged him to his feet. "Always," she murmured as he wrapped his arms around her. "Always and forever."

Her family surrounded them, oohing and aahing at the cameo and the love found on this Christmas Day.

"Look," Prissy said, pointing out the window. "It's snowing again."

Grace smiled at the happy couple. "Looks like we'll have the rest of the day to make wedding plans."

Maddie's heart melted a little more as Harlan smiled. "Make sure that plan includes one of those fancy new wedding cakes I've been hearing about," he said.

"Oh," Maddie gushed, certain she would be the first bride in all of Calico Falls with such a fancy offering.

"I'll get a paper and pencil and we can work out all the details," Prissy said, starting for the desk.

"Just one thing," Harlan said, stopping her in her tracks. "The wedding cake can be as big as you want, but no gingerbread."

About the Author

Amy Lillard is a 2013 Carol Award–winning author for romance. She received this honor for her novel *Saving Gideon*, set in the Amish country of Oklahoma. *Saving Gideon* is book 1 of the Clover Ridge Series. Her other Clover Ridge titles include *Katie's Choice* and *Gabriel's Bride*. Her new trilogy, the Wells Landing Series, begins with *Caroline's Secret*, releasing in August 2014. Amy is a member of American Christian Fiction Writers and Romance Writers of America. Born and bred in Mississippi, she now lives in Oklahoma with her husband of twenty-five years and their teenage son. Amy can be reached at amylillard@hotmail.com and www.amywritesromance.com.

The Fruitcake Bride

by Vickie McDonough

Chapter 1

Bakerstown, Missouri
December 1890

Sitting on the edge of her seat, Karen Briggs wiped the dust off the train window with her handkerchief and searched the crowded depot for her fiancé. With a loud hiss, the train shuddered to a stop. She'd had the whole journey to ponder her decision to marry Clay Parsons. Had she made the right choice?

No matter. It was too late to turn back now. She donned her cloak, snatched up her satchel, and hurried to the door.

The conductor grinned as he bent and picked up the step stool that rested beside the door. "You must be meetin' a feller to be so eager."

"My fiancé. He's the pastor of Bakerstown Chapel."

"Is he that Parson Parsons I've heard about?"

Karen blinked at the odd moniker. "Um. . .well, he *is* Pastor Clayton Parsons." Behind her, several other passengers lined up to exit. With so few debarking, why was such a large crowd gathered at the depot? Perhaps someone had a big family.

The conductor opened the door, allowing in a gush of chilly air. He stepped out and set the stool in place, but when he reached up to help her down, Clay rushed forward. "Please, sir, allow me."

Karen's apprehension fled, and her heart leaped like a young filly in a field of daisies as her intended smiled up at her. "Clay!"

He lifted her to the platform and into his arms for a brief hug then set her down and moved her out of the way of the other passengers. His blue-green eyes roamed her face as if looking for change. "I'm so glad you came."

She hoped she would be happy here—could make him happy. "It seems like years since you last left Arcadia instead of months."

Clay stepped back but held on to one of her elbows. A group of people crowded around them, most wearing bright smiles and all staring at her. Karen touched her hair to see if the pins had come loose. Two women to-

413

ward the back of the crowd lifted up a sign that said: WELCOME!

"These kind people are some of my parishioners. They were eager to meet you and welcome you to Bakerstown."

Karen smiled, even though disappointment coursed through her. She'd hoped for some time with Clay alone to discuss their arrangement, but being the future wife of a pastor, she knew she had to be gracious and share him. Her gaze traveled the crowd. She hoped most of these people would soon become her friends. "Thank y'all so much. It's very kind of you to come."

Clay made quick introductions then left her with the church people while he made arrangements for her two trunks to be delivered to the boardinghouse, where he'd secured a room for her.

"We just love Pastor Clay. He's such a fine young man—and handsome, too."

Was she Miss Herbert or Mrs. Wells? Karen grappled for the right name, but it flew away like a spooked bird.

"Hush, Emma Lou. She'll think you've got designs on her fiancé." A buxom woman holding one end of the sign fanned her face in spite of the chilly day.

"Why I never." Emma Lou's cheeks grew red as beet juice. "He's young enough to be my son."

"If you *had* a son," a man in back hollered in a good-natured tone.

A gentleman in a suit squeezed through the crowd, followed by a woman holding one of the sign poles.

"Emmett, slow down." She tugged on the pole as she moved forward, and a loud rip echoed across the platform as the banner split in two. Both women holding the poles stumbled.

Karen swallowed the lump in her throat, hoping the ruined sign wasn't a premonition of things to come.

"Mother, really." A pretty woman, who looked to be Karen's age, caught the toppling woman. "Must you always make a scene?"

"I declare, Helen. You've ruined the sign." The woman in back holding the other pole pursed her lips and shook her head.

"I didn't do it on purpose, Loraine." Helen straightened her bonnet.

"Never mind, ladies. We don't need a sign to welcome Miss Briggs to Bakerstown." Emmett stepped forward, hat in hand, along with Helen, still holding the stick and torn sign. "I'm Emmett Willard, mayor of Advent and a church council member, and this is my lovely wife, Helen."

He motioned to the younger woman who'd caught Helen. She stepped forward, eyeing Karen as if she were a maggot. Someone—or something—sure had put a wasp under her petticoat.

Mr. Willard cleared his voice, drawing Karen's gaze back to him. "This is our lovely daughter, Prudence."

"Prudy, Papa."

He sent her a patronizing smile with a warning in his gaze. "Prudy, then. Miss Briggs, we're happy that you've finally arrived and hope you'll enjoy living in our small town."

Prudy snorted, yanking Karen's gaze back to her. The woman covered up her action with a quick cough.

Shifting her feet, Karen wasn't sure what to make of the pretty blond woman. She reminded herself to stay in a gracious mood and turned away from Prudy. "Thank you, Mr. Willard. It's so nice of everyone to take time from your busy schedules to greet me. I look forward to getting to know each of you."

Heads nodded, smiles abounded, and Karen relaxed a smidgeon. She must have said the right thing. Learning to be a pastor's wife might be harder than she had expected. She didn't want to do or say anything that could harm Clay's ministry in Bakerstown.

Clay rushed to her side, eyes twinkling like the ocean in sunlight. "I've taken care of your luggage. Would you like to go to the boarding-house now?"

Tired from the long day's journey and stress of her situation, Karen nodded. Even though she truly appreciated meeting some of the church people, she hoped the crowd wouldn't accompany them.

Clay looked over the group, smiling wide. "I can't thank you enough for coming out to greet Karen. It was mighty kind of y'all. I know she'd like to talk with each of you, but as you can see, she's exhausted from her travels."

"It's all right, Pastor." An older man on the left, leaning heavily on a cane, stepped forward. "We know you two young'uns need time alone." He winked at Karen, and her cheeks warmed.

Prudy crossed her arms and glared at her.

"We have a dinner reception planned for Sunday after church," Mrs. Willard said. "You'll get to meet the rest of our church family and try some of our Prudy's rhubarb pie."

Karen certainly hoped Prudy's pie was sweeter than her disposition.

"Thanks again for coming out today." Clay shook Mr. Willard's hand and several other men's.

The crowd began to disperse, and the man who'd winked at her hobbled up to them and leaned on his cane. "It was a pleasure to meet you, missy. Parson Parsons sure landed himself a purty bride."

Clay beamed. "You're right about that, Jasper. Thank you for meeting the train."

"Happy to do so." He smiled a gap-toothed grin then turned and shuffled toward the stairs.

"Parson Parsons?" Karen turned to Clay and teasingly lifted one eyebrow.

A warm grin lifted his lips as he shrugged. "It's sort of an endearment some of the men use."

"It was kind of them to greet me, but is it awful of me to say I'm glad they left?"

"Of course not." He offered his elbow. "They were eager to meet you, but they respect our need to be alone."

She glanced at the train and saw two children with their noses to the window. "We aren't alone."

Clay waved at the two boys and smiled. "C'mon, let's get you settled at the boardinghouse and then eat some supper. I know you've got to be tired after your long trip across Missouri."

As he led her toward the depot steps, Karen surveyed what she could see of the small town. It looked to have only about a dozen streets with businesses lining the closest ones and then houses on the outer streets. "Where's your church?"

Clay paused at the top of the steps and pointed to the southeast. "If you look two streets over and across the tops of the buildings, you can see the steeple." He turned to face her, looking uncertain. "The church isn't very big—only about twenty-five families."

Karen patted his arm. "Size doesn't matter. Arcadia wasn't very big, either, but it was a fine town. I'm sure Bakerstown is, too."

"You don't think you'll regret moving here?"

She hoped not, but then she had no other option. "My home is with you now."

He gave her a quick hug. "I'm glad you feel that way. I have to admit being a bit worried you'd change your mind."

The tension drained from her in light of his warm welcome. Maybe things *would* work out. "I might miss climbing Pilot Knob in the summer and feeling the cool air wafting up from the mine shafts."

"There were times this past summer I wished I was back home to enjoy that with you. It was quite hot here."

She tugged her cloak closed as a gust of cool air blew across the depot. "We don't have to worry about the heat now. Not with Christmas in just a few weeks."

"Will you be able to be ready for a Christmas Eve wedding?" Clay asked as he helped her down the stairs to the street.

"I should be." If she could lose her anxiety about marrying Clay because of her situation.

"And you're not sorry we're not marrying in Arcadia?"

"I would have enjoyed having our friends there, but your parents are coming, aren't they?"

He nodded. "Ma's last letter stated they would arrive on the twenty-third. I just wish your aunt was still around to see you married. She would have been proud."

Aunt Alice would have been delighted to hear she was marrying Clay Parsons, but not so happy with their marriage of convenience—or rather, marriage of desperation. With her aunt deceased and the house for sale, she had no other options—and Clay needed a wife. She hoped their long friendship was a strong enough foundation for marriage.

"I'm glad you finally agreed to my proposal. I was starting to lose hope."

"I know a good thing when I see it." She couldn't resist teasing him, as she had so often in the past. His friendship had been one of the best things about moving to Arcadia to live with her aunt.

Clay tugged her closer as they crossed the street. "You're a wise woman."

"Wise enough to nab the preacher." She smiled up at him.

Maybe things would work out, after all.

Chapter 2

Karen closed the door to her room and leaned against it, smiling. The past hour and a half spent catching up with Clay had been wonderful. Their friendship seemed as close as ever. He'd been the big brother she never had, and that was one thing that concerned her about marrying him. She knew she loved Clay, but was it a romantic love? A love strong enough to endure a lifetime of marriage?

She'd also feared their long separation might have caused him to care less for her, but that wasn't the case, if the warm gaze in his eyes was an indication of his feelings.

Only a few more weeks and she'd be his wife. She needed to find a way to rid herself of her doubts. Clay seemed excited about their marriage, and she knew she'd never find a better man.

She crossed the room to the desk where her satchel sat, but her eyes landed on something hidden behind it. A package wrapped in brown store paper and tied with twine. She tugged the note free and read it out loud. "A present for your kitchen, to be used when mixin'. With affection, Clay."

Curious, she untied the twine and unwrapped the gift. She lifted up the smallest of the three tan mixing bowls that had a blue accent line around it. Clay must be craving some of the sweets she used to bake for him back in Arcadia. She placed the bowl with its mates, thankful for the gift but wishing it had been a bit more romantic. But the man she was marrying was highly practical, and that was one thing about him she admired. And more than likely, one of the reasons he'd proposed.

Karen wandered over to the window that looked out onto Main Street. She hoped to catch a glimpse of Clay as he walked back to the parsonage, but the street was empty. As she leaned against the cool glass, her insecurities came storming back. She knew her lack of trust stemmed from her father's abandonment, leaving her at her aunt's shortly after her mother died. She'd been a scared, confused girl of eight, but then Clay had entered her life and become her best friend—her protector. He would never desert her like her father had.

Karen yawned and turned away from the window, ready to crawl in bed. As she removed her dress, her concerns taunted her. What if she wasn't gracious enough or lost her temper with the women of the church over some petty issue? And could she make Clay happy? Did she really have it in her to be the wife he needed?

Clay pried loose one of the trim boards around the window the Langston twins had broken on Sunday after church and tossed it to the ground. Carefully, he removed the broken glass and dropped it into a bucket, where it shattered into smaller pieces. He cleaned the area around the pane, installed the new piece of glass, and then reaffixed the trim. The new addition gleamed in the morning sunlight, filling Clay with a sense of accomplishment.

"It's a blessing that you're so handy with tools."

He glanced over his shoulder, glad to see Karen. "Why is that?"

"It must save the church a lot of money."

Clay climbed down, pondering her statement. Was Karen concerned that he couldn't adequately provide for her? She had lived with her widowed aunt, who'd been left somewhat well off after her husband's passing. "If I hadn't repaired it, someone else in the church would have stepped up and done it."

"Oh." Karen's smile dimmed. "I hadn't thought of that. My aunt always hired out any work she needed done, so I assumed you'd have to also."

"I prefer to see to most of the repairs to the church and parsonage—at least, I do if I have the time."

"Well, you did an excellent job."

"Thank you." Clay warmed under his fiancée's approval. Ever since Karen moved to Arcadia to live with her aunt, he'd been her champion. She'd been so sad at first, missing her ma and constantly looking for her pa to return— but he never had. Clay eyed the basket she held over her arm. "What do you have in there?"

"I thought since it was such a nice day today, maybe we could have a picnic. Mrs. Grady was kind enough to fix an extra sandwich for you."

Clay smiled. "Having lunch with you sounds like a delight."

Karen ducked her head, her cheeks turning a comely shade of red. "It won't be long before we'll enjoy every meal together."

Clay glanced around and realized they were alone. He stepped closer and ran his index finger along Karen's soft cheek. "I can't tell you how much I look forward to that."

"Really?" She stared up at him, looking less sure than he wished. Was she having doubts?

He'd prayed about their marriage so much and felt certain it was God's will for them. "Of course. I've been dreaming of the day."

Determined to prove his affection, he made sure they were alone then swooped in for a quick kiss.

"Clay!" Karen hastily looked around. "What would people say if they saw the pastor spooning?"

He chuckled. "I doubt they'd say anything unless I was spooning with someone other than you."

She playfully smacked his arm. "You'd better not be."

He gently pulled her close again. "Karen, how can I prove to you that there's no one on God's earth that I care to marry other than you?"

She nibbled her lip and ducked her head. "I've wondered if one day you'll regret marrying me."

"I wish you could peek into my heart and see your name written there. I know you still struggle because your pa left you, but I will never leave you like that. I care too much for you."

"I believe you. I suppose I'm just nervous."

"Even if your aunt hadn't died suddenly, I would have asked you to marry me. It just wouldn't have been for a few more months."

"Truly?"

"Have I ever lied to you?"

She shook her head.

"Give your concerns to God, and everything will work out." He squeezed her hand and stepped back. Karen had always suffered with self-doubt, but she was a kindhearted person—the woman he'd grown to love. He would just have to prove to her that he meant what he said. "Let me put away my tools and wash up. Then we can eat."

Karen nodded and looked around. "What about under that tree? It's warmer today, but do you think it's too cool to sit outside?"

"Let's give it a try since there's no wind. If you get too chilly, we can go in the church."

After returning the tools and ladder to the shed behind the building, Clay found Karen on the side of the church that faced town and watched her arranging the food on a bench. He'd wanted to marry since before he went to college, and now that their wedding was close, the days until Christmas Eve seemed to be dragging by at half the speed of a normal day. If only she seemed less worried and more excited.

He plopped down on the bench next to her, and she handed him a plate with a ham sandwich, a thick slice of cheese, a pickle, and an apple. Clay smiled. "It looks wonderful. Shall we pray?"

She nodded and bowed her head while he thanked God for the food and for bringing Karen to Bakerstown. He took a bite of the pickle first, since it was making his mouth water. "Mmm. . .delicious. So, what do you think of Bakerstown?"

"It's smaller than Arcadia, but it seems nice. Things were quiet last night, so I had no trouble getting to sleep."

"I imagine you were exhausted after the long trip here, meeting some of the church folk, and spending time with me."

"I was tired, but not from being with you."

He winked at her and took a bite of his sandwich.

"Do you have services on Sunday night?"

"No, just in the morning. Some of the ranchers and farmers have a ways to travel, so they head back afterward. On the first Sunday of each month, we have a potluck dinner after the service, and most folks stay for that."

"What a wonderful idea! That gives everyone time to socialize with friends whom they don't often see."

"That's true."

Karen stared out toward the open prairie. "Are you happy here? Do the people treat you nicely?"

Clay took hold of Karen's hand. "The people here are very kind. As in all towns, there are those who think they should be treated more special, but I can handle them."

"I'm glad to hear that. I was a bit concerned about the two women who carried the welcome sign after hearing how they chided one another."

"Helen Willard and Loraine Bodine are sisters who tend to snap at each other, especially when things go wrong."

"Sisters? Well, it helps to know that."

Clay finished his food, enjoying the view Karen made. Even with a hat on, her honey-blond hair glistened in the sunlight. He loved the way her brown eyes sparkled whenever she laughed or teased him, although she hadn't done much of that since her arrival. He'd been attracted to her since the day Karen first showed up in school, looking sad and frightened. Before long they became friends. He'd never considered marrying any other woman, and he hadn't regretted that decision.

"Why are you looking at me like that?"

Clay flashed a mischievous grin. "I'm not sure you want me to answer that question."

An embarrassed smile danced on her lips; then she ducked her head.

He shouldn't tease her like that, but he couldn't resist. "How would you like to see the parsonage?"

Her head jerked up. "Do you think it's proper for us to be there together since we're not yet married?"

"I don't see why it's a problem. We'll just leave the door open and make a quick pass through so you can see the house and be thinking about what you might want to change."

"I'd love to as long as you're sure it's all right. I don't want to do anything to get you in trouble."

"You won't." He handed her the plate. "Thanks for bringing me lunch. It was a wonderful surprise."

"I couldn't stand the thought of not seeing you until this evening."

He smiled and helped her to her feet. "I can't tell you how happy that makes me."

After Karen packed the basket, Clay took it and escorted her the one block to the parsonage. He watched her face as her gaze landed on the small clapboard house painted a pale yellow with white trim.

"Oh Clay, it's lovely. I don't know what I expected, but it wasn't anything this nice."

He pulled back the screen door and propped it open with the basket then pushed on the main door. "This is the parlor, and as you can see, the kitchen is on the left side. There are two bedrooms at the rear of the house and a small washroom."

Karen turned in a circle, taking everything in. Then she spun around to face him, eyes gleaming. "Oh Clay, I love it."

Basking in her pleasure, he wasn't prepared when she threw herself into his arms. He quickly wrapped his arms around her, but he stumbled backward until he bumped into the wall. Karen kissed him soundly, and his arms tightened as he enjoyed her closeness.

A loud gasp from the porch made him realize they were no longer alone. Karen jumped away, and he straightened to look into the shocked eyes of Helen Willard and her daughter.

"Pastor, what is the meaning of this?"

Chapter 3

Karen wished she were a bird that could fly away and hide in the trees. She and Clay weren't even married yet, and she was already causing trouble for him. What had gotten into her to kiss him like she had?

He shifted his feet. "Nothing quite as terrible as you're imagining happened, Mrs. Willard."

The woman narrowed her eyes. "I know what I saw."

Prudence stood behind her mother, arms crossed, looking as if she were ready to do battle, but Karen wasn't sure whose side the young woman was on. Was she upset with her mother? Or with Clay and her?

He cleared his throat. "What you saw was Karen expressing her delight at seeing the lovely parsonage we'll be sharing. I just showed her the parlor and kitchen so she could make plans for when this is her home."

Mrs. Willard crossed her arms. "Humph! Looked more like a young couple seeking a private place to spark."

Prudy's face grew red, but she remained quiet.

"One kiss does not a spark make." Clay smiled as if trying to lessen the tension.

The woman narrowed her eyes again. "No matter. It is inappropriate behavior for a pastor and a poor example for my impressionable daughter. You can be certain the church council will hear of this."

"Perhaps it would be best for Miss Briggs to return to her hometown and come back here just before the wedding." Prudence lifted her chin.

Karen's mouth opened, but nothing came out at the woman's unexpected suggestion. She thought of all she had to do in the few weeks before the wedding and knew it wouldn't get done if she were in Arcadia worrying about Clay. And she really had no home to return to since she'd sold her aunt's furniture and belongings and had listed the house for sale with an agent.

"I don't think we need to go to such extremes, Miss Willard."

Prudence batted her long lashes at Clay. "I told you to call me Prudy."

Her mother elbowed her. "That is inappropriate, Prudence."

The young woman scowled at her mother but turned a pout Clay's way.

"I'm sure Clay is able to make up his own mind about that, Mother."

"Never mind." Mrs. Willard swatted her hand at her daughter. "The point is they shouldn't have been spooning in the parsonage."

"I can assure you, ma'am, it won't happen again." Clay shuffled his feet.

"You two should have considered that before making such a spectacle."

Karen couldn't let Clay take the blame for something she initiated. Wringing her hands, she took a step toward the woman. "Mrs. Willard, Clay is right. My joy at finding such a lovely place to call home overwhelmed me, and I expressed my delight by kissing him. Once. I'm the one who bears the blame, not him."

Mrs. Willard didn't seem to be wavering, so she tried another tactic. "Surely you were young and in love not so long ago."

Clay snorted but then rubbed his nose, looking chagrined. Prudence rolled her eyes as Karen struggled to maintain an innocent gaze.

Mrs. Willard looked from Karen to Clay and back, then sighed. "I suppose I was. But you two shouldn't be alone like this. It'll set loose lips to talkin'."

Clay nodded. Karen stepped out onto the porch, and he followed, closing the door.

"Well, now that Miss Briggs has seen the house, there's no reason for her to be in there again until after you've said your vows."

"Yes, ma'am," they said in unison.

Mrs. Willard lifted her chin. "I will overlook it this time, but don't let it happen again."

"Thank you." Clay took hold of Karen's arm and started toward the steps but paused. "Was there something that brought you two here today?" he asked Mrs. Willard.

"Prudence made some lovely curtains for your kitchen, but we can return another time to put them up." She spun, nose in the air, and hurried down the sidewalk.

Prudence remained where she was, her gaze focused on Karen. "You might want to consider going back"—she waved her hand in the air—"to wherever it is you came from. Clay could benefit from marrying a woman from these parts, not someone who knows nothing about this town."

Karen gasped.

Scowling, Clay stepped in front of her. "Miss Willard, I told you more than once that I am not an eligible man. My heart belongs to Karen and always has. It's time you face that fact."

Hurt engulfed Prudy's pretty face, and she stomped her foot. She spun around, skirts flying, and followed her mother back to the street.

Clay took hold of Karen's hand. "I'm so sorry about that. I thought that if I continued to inform Pru—Miss Willard—of my relationship with you, she'd finally take a hint, but she can be hardheaded." He escorted her off the porch. "I'd best see you back to the boardinghouse, and then I need to visit several ill parishioners."

Karen watched Prudence disappear around the far side of the church; then she turned to Clay. "I'm so sorry for getting you in trouble."

"Don't worry about it. Mrs. Willard is quick to make a mountain out of a molehill." He frowned. "Maybe I shouldn't say that, but it's the truth, and you need to be aware of it."

"Do you really think she'll keep quiet about seeing us kissing in the parsonage?"

He shrugged. "Time will tell."

"I'm sorry for my rash behavior."

Grinning, Clay looped her arm around his. "I'm not in the least."

Secretly happy with his declaration, Karen prayed the women would not gossip about what they saw. Prudence was certainly an odd duck. Did she really think she could sway Karen into leaving?

Karen determined to put the disastrous duo from her mind and enjoy her remaining minutes with Clay. "Would you like me to go with you on your visitations?"

"After we're married, I think it would be a wonderful idea, unless someone is sick with something that spreads. I'd hate for you to become ill."

She bit back a smile, but it broke loose. "Because you don't want to have to nurse me back to health?"

With a playful gleam in his gaze, Clay waggled his eyebrows. "That would be my pleasure, ma'am, but I would prefer you not get ill in the first place."

Not ready to consider such an intimate situation, Karen studied the spacious yard, a thought percolating. "Do you suppose we could get some chickens?"

Clay grinned. "That was a quick change of topic. Why chickens?"

Karen watched a trio of sparrows swoop down and snatch something on the ground and then fly up into the tree again. "I thought it might be nice if I made chicken soup for the church members who are sick or injured."

"You'd go through your flock of hens pretty fast."

"Well, perhaps I could make potato soup or stew sometimes."

"We'll see. It's a very kind gesture, but I don't want you cooking for others all the time."

"Oh? Who *would* you like me cooking for?"

"Who do you think?" He squeezed her hand then pulled a small, oblong package from his pocket. "That reminds me, here's a little something I got for you."

"I love the bowls you left in my room, by the way." She smiled. "You don't need to give me another gift."

"I want to give you nice things. I enjoy it."

Karen sighed. "I appreciate it, but I want you to know it's not necessary." He held out the package. "Humor me."

She unwrapped the small gift and stared at the odd metal object. "What is it?"

"Haven't you ever seen a nutcracker? Now you won't have to stomp on shells or hit them with a hammer."

"I remember how much you enjoy nuts, especially in my fruitcake. Thank you. This will come in handy." Another odd gift, but the gleam in her fiancé's eyes made her smile. She saw Mrs. Grady sweeping off the porch and realized they were back at the boardinghouse.

"I'm glad you like it." He bent down and placed a quick kiss on the back of her hand. "I'll see you at supper."

With a sigh, Karen watched him stride away, tall and lithe.

Mrs. Grady leaned against the porch railing. "That pastor is a fine-looking man. I imagine the two of you will have comely young'uns."

Karen spun around, stunned by her landlady's comment. "I. . .uh. . . thank you."

Mrs. Grady chuckled. "Don't look so shocked. It's merely the truth. Just watch out for that Prudence Willard. She set her cap for the parson the day he arrived." Mrs. Grady clucked her tongue and shook her head. "Poor thing didn't know the pastor's heart was already spoken for."

Heat rising to her cheeks, Karen climbed the steps to the porch. No wonder Prudy had eyed her so maliciously. The woman had hoped to marry Clay. How could Karen blame her? Clay was a wonderful man, and any woman would be happy to have him for a husband. He was quickly winning her over and making her realize that in spite of the circumstances surrounding their upcoming marriage, he was the man for her.

Her thoughts veered back to Mrs. Grady's comment about her and Clay's children. She *had* on occasion contemplated marrying him when she was younger and wondered what their children might look like, but to hear it expressed out loud was a surprise. Karen glanced to her side to discover the landlady had resumed her sweeping. "Do you need any help with dinner? I seem to have the afternoon free."

"Heavens, no! I don't allow guests to assist with the meals."

"Please, I'd like to help."

Mrs. Grady continued shaking her head. "I'm sure you must have some preparations for your wedding that need to be done."

Karen sighed. "I do have some sewing, although it's not my favorite task."

"Best you get it over and done with, then." She placed the broom in the corner of the porch and scurried toward the door, pausing just inside. "Make sure you know that pastor of yours is welcome to supper. No sense in you two eating at the café when your meals are included with your room and board."

"But Clay's aren't."

"It's a sad day when there isn't enough to feed my pastor." She turned and disappeared inside the house.

Karen leaned against the porch railing, wishing Clay had let her go with him. The long afternoon stretched out in front of her, and the thought of spending it sewing alone failed to excite her. But she had a new nightgown to finish stitching—the gown she'd wear on her wedding night. Thoughts of that evening brought warmth to her cheeks.

⋘⋙

Karen swallowed back her anxiety as she approached the Willard home. Clay had encouraged her to attend the sewing bee, and although several of the church ladies had invited her, neither Mrs. Willard nor her daughter had mentioned it or sent an invitation. Three days had passed since she'd visited the parsonage with Clay. Would Mrs. Willard use this opportunity to announce to the ladies that she'd seen Karen and the pastor kissing?

A woman who looked to be around Karen's age waved. She rushed across the dirt street and made a beeline toward her, smiling and carrying a small basket. "Good morning. You must be the pastor's intended." She stopped in front of Karen. "I'm Patricia Mullins, but most folks call me Patsy."

"I'm Karen Briggs. It's a pleasure to meet you."

Patsy's hazel eyes sparkled. "I always enjoy these gatherings. It's such fun to sit and talk with other women. My husband, Jared, is a quiet man and doesn't have much to say, and we don't have children yet." Her fair complexion turned ruby-red, making her freckles stand out. "I'm glad you came. It'll help even the odds between the older and younger women."

Karen smiled and eyed the front of the big brick house, one of the largest in town.

"Don't let the size of the place intimidate you. The ladies are always welcoming, but be warned, they'll most likely bombard you with questions." Patsy paused at the steps and smiled. "Shall we go in?"

She nodded and followed her new friend up to the porch, glad she didn't have to enter alone. Patsy knocked, and Mrs. Willard opened the door quickly, as if she'd been hovering there, waiting for them.

"Miss Briggs, it's nice of you to join us today, and it's always good to see you, Patsy." She stepped back, allowing them to enter.

As Karen's eyes adjusted to the interior lighting, she marveled at the lovely furnishings. "You have a beautiful home, Mrs. Willard."

"Thank you. Emmett does like to spoil me." She waved her hand to a room on the right. "We're gathering in the study."

Patsy took hold of Karen's arm and tugged her into the room. Three women were seated on the far side of a colorful wedding ring quilt, while two others had claimed spots on the right. Patsy led Karen around to the left side, where three chairs awaited. They took the farthest two, leaving the one beside Karen empty.

"I imagine some of you have met Pastor Parsons's bride-to-be, but in case you haven't, this is Karen Briggs," Patsy stated, as if they were lifelong friends.

Most of the women smiled and eyed Karen with curiosity. She recognized Loraine, who'd helped hold the welcome sign, although she'd forgotten her last name. Karen nodded. "It's a pleasure to meet you."

"This here's Lois Clemmons." Patsy pointed to the nearest lady and continued down the line and around the corner. "Gertrude Birch, Loraine Bodine, Sue Ellen Smith, and Paulette Davis."

Karen tried to put names and faces together. Gertrude and Loraine looked to be about the same age as Mrs. Willard, probably in their late forties or early fifties, while Sue Ellen and Paulette were at least a decade younger.

Paulette smiled. "Don't bother trying to learn our names today. We know it will take awhile to remember us all."

"I appreciate that."

Patsy sat, so Karen did, too.

"This is a lovely quilt. Have you made many together?"

"This is our seventh one," Loraine said.

"Isn't it our eighth?" Mrs. Willard stood near the study door, tapping her upper lip with her index finger. "Let's see, we've auctioned off three of them to raise money for the church and orphanage, gave one to the Henrys for their fortieth anniversary, one to the Garfields for their twenty-fifth, and one to Spencer and Julia Sloan when he retired as mayor two years ago."

"That's still just seven, Helen, counting this new one." Loraine lifted her chin.

A knock at the door sent Mrs. Willard spinning away. Karen had the feeling she was glad not to have to respond to Loraine.

A pretty young woman entered and claimed the seat next to Karen. She smiled. "I'm Carla Peterson."

"Karen Briggs. A pleasure to meet you."

"She's Pastor Parsons's intended," Gertrude stated.

Loraine rolled her eyes. "Everyone knows who she is. She's the only new woman in town."

Soft chuckles wafted around the room then suddenly quieted. All eyes turned toward the entrance. Prudence moseyed in, overdressed in her rust-colored afternoon dress with huge leg o' mutton sleeves and a bib of ruffles and lace that covered her bodice. She narrowed her eyes at Karen and took the farthest away empty seat. Confused by the woman's obvious dislike for her, Karen looked down at the quilt. Was it true that Prudence had designs on Clay? That would explain her unwarranted hostility, as well as her suggestion for Karen to return to Arcadia.

Helen sat next to her daughter. "Thelma won't be here today. Her three young'uns are ill."

"I hope it's nothing serious," Paulette said.

Helen shrugged. "I don't know what's wrong."

All around Karen, baskets clattered as the ladies removed their scissors, needles, and thread. She stared at the beautiful quilt, half afraid to apply her hand. What if her stitches were too large or not uniform?

Carla leaned over. "Don't be nervous about stitching. We all had a first day, too. Just jump right in."

"If Helen isn't happy, she'll redo the stitches anyway," Patsy whispered in her ear. Several ladies to Patsy's left nodded their agreement.

Wonderful. Now she had to worry about her sewing pleasing Mrs. Willard when they'd already gotten off to a rough start. Determined to do her best, Karen pulled out a small container and removed a quilting needle. Patsy handed her a piece of thread, and she pushed the end through the eye and found a spot to begin stitching.

"So, Miss Briggs. Where did you and Pastor meet?"

Karen glanced up, not quite sure which lady had asked the question, but by the gazes pointed at her, she suspected everyone was interested in her answer. "After my mother died, when I was eight, I went to live in Arcadia with my widowed aunt. Clay was in the school I started attending."

A smile softened Loraine's expression. "Was it love at first sight?"

Prudy looked as if she were sucking on an unsweetened lemon drop.

"No, not at all." Karen shook her head. "I felt so out of place and was missing my parents so badly that I hardly looked up from my desk for weeks. At first, Clay was one of the boys who pestered me, but I think he was just trying to pull me out of my shell."

Gasps filled the room.

"Our pastor was a hooligan?" Lois fanned her face.

"I find that hard to believe," Prudy said. "Pastor Clay is so kindhearted and courteous."

"He wasn't ever mean—just tugged on my braids and tried to get me to laugh. But at the time, I thought he was being a pest." She smiled, remembering the day she realized he wanted to be her friend. "Clay lived only a few houses from my aunt's home, so we eventually started walking to school together and became friends."

"And did he help you get over the loss of your mother?" Carla asked.

Karen thought for a moment. "I suspect he did indirectly. Becoming friends with Clay opened the door for me to be friends with the young people he knew, and that helped me to adjust to my new life in Arcadia." Still, she never forgot how her pa had deposited her at Aunt Alice's home shortly after her mother's death and never returned. She didn't even know if he was alive.

"So, you've known Pastor quite a long time. Why have you not married before now?" Loraine peeked up then glanced back down.

Karen eyed her own stitches, not liking how uneven they were. "Once Clay felt God calling him to the ministry, he left to go to college and then seminary. Afterward, he wanted to get established in his church." She hadn't realized what he meant to her until he was gone. For so long, she'd thought of him as a big brother, but as they grew older, at some point, her feelings for him shifted to something deeper. Yet until her aunt died suddenly, he had never asked her to marry him. She hadn't even known his thoughts drifted in that direction.

Patsy looked her way. "That's a long time to wait on a man. Were there no others who attempted to woo you?"

Karen shook her head. No man ever compared to Clay.

Prudy cleared her throat, drawing Karen's gaze. "But what about Clay? How do you know his feelings remained loyal after such a long separation?"

"Prudence! What an awful thing to say?" Helen turned ten shades of red.

In spite of her mother's reprimand, there was a challenge in Prudy's eyes that gave Karen pause. Had Clay merely asked her to marry him out of some sense of noble duty? There were the flashes of admiration in his gaze, and he'd even kissed her, so he must care for her. Clay wasn't the kind of man to fake his feelings. He was too honest—too good. Karen lifted her chin and aimed it at Prudy like a weapon, although she forced her tone to be civil. "Clay would never have asked me to marry him if he didn't care for me."

Prudy ducked her head, lips puckered, as if studying her stitches. Karen didn't want to hurt the young woman's feelings, but Prudy needed to know that her infatuation with Clay could lead nowhere.

Karen continued stitching and answering questions. Though the ladies were gracious, they were a curious lot. She was glad when they turned to the topic of Christmas and the annual auction supporting a Dallas orphanage.

Two hours later, Mrs. Willard pushed her chair back, signaling an end to the sewing bee. "Shall we stop and enjoy the delicious cookies Sue Ellen brought?"

Heads nodded and murmurs filled the room as the women tied off their stitches and put their supplies away. Prudy made a quick escape. Karen studied her stitches. They resembled the path a staggering drunkard might take. Patsy and Carla had done an excellent job with their handwork. Karen had little doubt Helen would be redoing hers before next session. She watched the ladies on the end and far side of the table leave the room, happily chatting. Karen missed her Arcadia friends, but in time she'd make new ones here.

Sighing, she lifted her arm to reach for her basket, but not only her arm moved, the quilt rack did, too. Suspended from the ceiling by four ropes, it swung her direction. She instantly straightened, forcing the rack in the opposite direction. Patsy reached to steady it and missed. Karen watched horrified, as the rack knocked both Gurdy and Lois sideways. The two older women struggled to stay on their feet, but both toppled sideways onto vacant chairs. After taking a moment to regain their composure, the women gaped at Karen.

"I'm so sorry." She glanced at the quilt, her cheeks blazing hot. "It seems that I somehow basted the lace on my cuff to the quilt." She peered sideways at Patsy, who was struggling to keep a smile off her face. The other women were already filing out of the room, engrossed in their conversations, oblivious to what had happened.

"Well," Gurdy said, "the first time we attempted a quilt, Helen stitched her skirt to the bottom of it. We had to help her out of the garment in order to cut it loose."

Lois nodded in agreement, a glimmer in her pale blue eyes. The humor of the situation set Karen to giggling, and soon the other ladies were chuckling, too.

"As much as I hate to ask, I need help getting my sleeve free."

Patsy and Carla quieted, although both obviously struggled to hold back their laughter.

"I guess I know where Helen will be tonight," Karen mumbled.

Patsy snorted a laugh.

Gurdy helped Lois up. "We'll see you ladies in the parlor, and our lips are sealed."

As the two left the room, Patsy mumbled, "That'll be a first."

Carla giggled so hard she could barely hold her scissors still enough to clip the threads. "There. Try it now."

Karen lifted her arm, and this time her sleeve broke free. She tugged out the loose threads and stood. "Thank you, Carla."

"Too bad the quilt rack is tied to the ceiling, otherwise we could turn it so Helen wouldn't notice." Patsy gave Karen a gentle nudge.

The three women giggled again as they made their way out of the room. In spite of her embarrassing mistake, Karen knew she'd made several new friends.

Chapter 4

On Sunday afternoon, Clay drove his buggy out of town. Karen sat next to him with a blanket covering their legs, glad to have him to herself on the cool but sunny day. "I enjoyed your sermon. You have such a lovely speaking voice."

He glanced at her, eyes twinkling. "You really think so—about the message, I mean."

"Of course I do. I wouldn't tease about something that important. You've matured since leaving Arcadia. Your sermons have more depth than when you were a youth, practicing in the field behind my aunt's home, but I'll always remember the passion you had then."

"Do you think I've lost some of that zeal?"

"No, that's not what I meant." Contemplating what to say next, Karen studied the wintry landscape as they traveled past farm after farm. Come spring, the rolling hills would blossom with wildflowers and be lovely. "You know how naive young men can be. They think they can conquer every dragon that dares to pop up its head."

"That's true. I certainly would have battled any behemoth that threatened you, my fair maiden."

He surprised Karen when he shifted the reins to his other hand and lifted his right arm, dropping it around her shoulders. "So, you're saying I've mellowed in my old age?"

"Yes, the ripe old age of twenty-three." Karen giggled and dared to lean against him, enjoying the closeness. But the memory of Prudy's snide comments and sneers threatened to ruin the lovely day. Karen had seen no special interest in Clay's eyes when he glanced at Prudy, but she obviously was smitten with him. Not that Karen could blame her.

He squeezed her shoulders. "Don't forget, ma'am, you're only a year behind me."

"We're positively ancient," she said, trying to regain her levity.

"Good thing we're getting married soon. If we waited much longer, I might have to carve you a cane for a wedding gift."

"You're funny." Karen smiled as she considered his most recent gift—a lovely quartet of teacups and saucers with a pretty violet design and a matching pot. "Speaking of gifts, I adored the tea set, but you know you don't have to keep giving me presents, don't you?"

He shrugged and tightened his grip as the buggy dipped into a rut and back out. "I enjoy it. I've never had much money—not that I have a lot now—but when I was younger and in seminary, I rarely had any. I want to make up for the times I was unable to get you a birthday gift."

Karen laid her head on Clay's shoulder. "How is it I'm so lucky to have won your affection?"

He caught her gaze and winked. "My heart has been yours since the day I first saw you."

Karen's heart somersaulted. Had he really cared for her for so long? She'd been hurting so badly back then that she hadn't noticed. "I don't know how you could have fallen for that scrawny, insecure girl I used to be." Although she had filled out to a respectable womanly form, the insecurities still plagued her. She loved Clay, too—and not in a brotherly way. Being with him again was helping her to see that, but it was her ability to be a pastor's wife that concerned her. Aunt Alice had taught her to cook and the basics of sewing, but her aunt had been a quiet woman who loved reading, so Karen had spent much of her time alone in her room. Large groups still made her anxious.

"Maybe I was attracted to you because you looked so scared and lonely. You needed a champion."

He had no idea how true that was. She was still scared, not so much of marrying him but of failing him. "You must have been desperate for friends."

"Don't say that." He paused for a long while then sighed and pulled the buggy to a halt. The horse snorted as if not ready to stop, but he obeyed. Clay shifted toward her, bumping his long legs against her skirts. "You're not having doubts about us, are you? Is my congregation pestering you too much? I know some of the ladies can be difficult."

"I won't lie to you. I had many doubts before coming here, but being with you and seeing how excited you are about our marriage has helped alleviate most of my concerns." Karen looked past him at several horses grazing in a field.

"But not all of them?"

She shook her head. "I worry that I don't have the skills to be a pastor's wife." *And about Prudence Willard.*

A red-tailed hawk swooped low, soaring over the horses before it landed on a fence post. Even with most of the foliage dried and yellow and the trees naked of their leaves, the countryside was still beautiful.

"Look at me, Karen."

She turned, giving him her full attention. His blue-green eyes focused on her, making her feel special—loved. "I have no doubt at all that you'll make a wonderful pastor's wife. You're kind and caring, patient—most of the time." He grinned when she elbowed his side. "You will have to overlook many things and try hard not to get angry when our church family intrudes on our private time, but I know you can."

Karen's heart warmed at his faith in her. Not since her mother died had anyone believed in her with the passion he did. "You're a good man, Parson Parsons."

He rolled his eyes. "Don't start with that. I might be tempted to steal a kiss just to silence you."

There had been times in the past when she'd wondered what his kiss would be like. Now that they'd shared a couple of quick, stolen kisses, she wanted to know what a real knee-bending one would be like—and she had it within her power to find out. Sheer delight wove its way through her like warm coffee on a cold morning. "Oh you would—Parson Par—"

He stopped her with his lips on hers, cold at first but quickly warming. Clay tugged her closer, illustrating his affection and pushing her doubts into the shadows of her mind. Oh how she loved this man—if only she could be enough.

Too soon, he pulled back. He caressed her cheek with his gloved hand. "I'd love nothing more than to keep kissing you, but it's not a wise idea, for now. Besides"—he smiled—"I've got a surprise. Now close your eyes."

Still rattled from his soul-stirring kisses, she blinked. "Another gift?"

"Not exactly. There's something special I want you to see, so be a good girl and comply. Eyes shut."

"Yes sir." When he faced forward again, Karen laid her head on his solid shoulder and lowered her eyelids. How could she be so fortunate to be betrothed to such a wonderful man?

They wound to the left on the country road and then back to the right. Karen listened to the rhythmic clatter of the wheels, the jingle of the harness, and tried to recognize the call of several birds she heard, all the while wondering what Clay wanted her to see. It couldn't be land for a home, because he would never want to live this far from town. As they wound around another curve, she heard flowing water.

The buggy creaked to a stop. "All right. You can look now."

Karen straightened, peered down the road, and gasped. Before her, a charming wooden bridge spanned a small river. Although there was a roof covering it, the sides rose only about four feet, allowing one to view the water. "A covered bridge?"

"It's called the Courting Bridge. Young fellows from these parts bring their gals out here to spoon or ask them to marry. I'm a little surprised we have the place all to ourselves."

She nudged him in the side, unable to resist teasing. "Which one are we here for?"

Clay chuckled. "Why, Miss Briggs, you do surprise me. Guess you'll have to wait and see."

He clucked out the side of his mouth, and the horse stepped into motion. Clay drove the buggy onto the bridge, the horse's hooves echoing on the wooden floor, and stopped. After setting the brake, he climbed out of the buggy and reached for her. She laid aside the blanket and let Clay help her down then took his arm as he led her to one side of the bridge.

Karen leaned against the wooden planks and looked down at the slowly moving water as it bumped over the vast collection of rocks. If the temperature had been warmer, she might have been tempted to climb down the bank and soak her feet. "Thank you for bringing me here, Clay. It's so peaceful."

He rested his hands on the wood railing. "Yes, it is. I sometimes come here when I'm having trouble hearing from God about a sermon topic. I don't know if it's being out among God's creation or just getting away from the busyness of people and noise of the town, but I find I can hear Him at this place."

"I can understand, but why is there a covered bridge in the middle of nowhere? Who built it?"

"The official name is the Baxter Bridge, and it's over twenty years old. I heard an easterner built it because he wanted to propose to his beloved on a covered bridge like the one near her Vermont home."

"And did he?"

"As far as I know."

"What happened to them?"

"They must have married and moved away. I don't know anyone living in this county with the Baxter surname."

Karen shifted toward him. "The bridge is a nice legacy."

Clay nodded and took her hands. "So, are you sure you want to marry me and live in Bakerstown? It's just a small town, but the people are good, at least most of them are."

"Most of those I've met have been very kind, and the size of the town doesn't bother me."

Clay studied her face for a long moment. "Why do I hear hesitation in your voice?"

Karen shrugged and glanced at the river.

"Tell me. Whatever it is, we can work through it."

How could she express all her fears and reservations? Clay had always been focused—always known he wanted to be a pastor like his grandpa. Her life had been like a rudderless boat rocked and tossed on turbulent waters. Her aunt had taken Karen into her home after her pa had left her. She missed both parents so much. That grief had shaped her and made her less trusting and less sure of things. There'd been times she'd even doubted God's goodness and had ranted at Him when she was younger.

"Karen, what is it? Please tell me what's creating the confusion I see in your pretty face." Clay's brow wrinkled.

She hated the worry that flashed in his eyes.

"Have you changed your mind. . .about marrying me?"

She laid her gloved hand on his cheek, hoping to reassure him. "No, Clay. I care deeply for you, and I'm looking forward to being your wife. But like I told you, what if I do something wrong at one of the church events? It might cause you to lose your church after you've worked so hard. How could I live with myself if that happened?"

He blew out a sigh as the tension left his expression. "My career is in God's hands, not the church board's, so please stop worrying. Just be my wife and take care of me. I don't care if you don't have anything to do with the church other than attending the services, smiling at me, and giving a resounding *amen* every now and then."

She offered a tentative smile. "Maybe you wouldn't, but the church people would. They expect certain things of their pastor's wife." She ducked her head. "And everything I do seems to flop."

Clay pulled her into his arms. "I should have married you years ago. You always were a thinker, stewing on things, contemplating how something might work out or not. I believe that God called us to be together."

"I believe that, too, but I can't shake my doubts." Karen stepped back as a picture of pretty Prudy infiltrated her mind. "Everything I do is a failure. First, Mrs. Willard caught us kissing; then I sewed my sleeve to the quilt the

Ladies Society is making. Why, even my welcome sign split in half."

Clay chuckled, and she smacked his chest. "Don't laugh. I'm serious."

"I'm sorry, sweetheart, but you have to admit that was rather humorous, watching Mrs. Bodine trying to keep up with Mrs. Willard."

"You're missing the point." She turned and walked back toward the buggy, upset at him for the first time since arriving in Bakerstown. His parents had cherished him. He was always secure in who he was and always knew what he wanted out of life. Clay had no idea what it was to struggle—to wonder if he was doing the right thing. She wouldn't be the cause of him losing his pastorate, even if it meant that she couldn't marry him. But the thought of possibly losing him made her heart crack.

"Karen, please. I'm sorry for laughing. You have to understand that those two ladies are always trying to outdo one another. Only one thing is important." He gently grabbed hold of her arms and turned her toward him, searching her features. "Do you love me?"

"You know I do. How could you doubt that?"

"You seem so troubled."

"It's my problem, not yours."

"That isn't true. You're a part of me already, sweetheart. When you hurt, I hurt." He took her hands again. "God will get us through the hard times. We just have to trust Him. *You* have to trust Him. Can you do that?"

She knew he spoke the truth. Even though she'd been mad at God for years for allowing her mother to die and her pa to leave, as she grew older, her faith in God and ability to lean on Him was what had gotten her through the difficult times she'd encountered and the long years of loneliness while Clay was gone to college and seminary. Prudy was merely another trial she must endure and survive. She smiled. "Yes, I believe I can do that."

He grinned, obviously happy with her response. "We're a good team— you, me, and the Lord. Remember the scripture, 'A threefold cord is not quickly broken'?"

She, Clay, and the Lord—a trifold braid. She latched onto the picture in her mind, and if she could only hang on to that image, maybe her life wouldn't unravel.

Chapter 5

Karen surveyed the nearly completed shirt she was making for Clay, which lay across her bed. She'd noticed his Sunday preaching shirt had dark stains on the collar and cuffs. He'd worn the same shirt both Sundays and several times during the week, so she assumed it was the only dress shirt he had and decided to attempt one for his Christmas present.

"It doesn't look half bad." Karen eyed one place that puckered where the left sleeve and shoulder met. "I can't thank you enough for your help, Patsy. I'd never have accomplished this without your guidance."

Patsy smiled as she put away her sewing supplies. "I'm glad to be of assistance. And besides, it gives me a reason to visit."

"You don't need a reason. Come anytime."

"Thank you. The same is true for you." Patsy bent over the shirt, examining it. "All you have left are the buttons and hem. Are you going to wait for Christmas or give it to him when it's done?"

Karen shrugged. "I originally thought Christmas—after we're married—but it would be nice for him to have a new shirt to wear now since there are several church events for the holidays."

"Not to mention your wedding." Patsy's eyes gleamed.

Karen touched her warm cheeks. Would she ever be able to talk about the wedding without blushing?

Patsy grinned. "I remember turning red like you do every time someone mentioned me and Jared gettin' hitched."

"How did you endure it? People sure seem to enjoy poking fun at courting couples, especially Clay and me."

Shrugging, Patsy smoothed a wrinkle in her skirt. "You have to understand that everyone in Bakerstown loves and respects Pastor Clay. The folks around here are happy for you and just wantin' to share in the fun. Folks in these parts work hard, so they need some fun and excitement and don't mind intrudin' on yours."

Some people may be happy for her and Clay, but Karen knew Prudy wasn't. Every time the woman laid eyes on Karen, she was scowling. "What can you tell me about Prudence Willard?"

Patsy stared at her with wide hazel eyes. "Why would you ask about her?"

Karen lifted her eyebrows in a "Do I have to explain it?" expression.

Patsy sighed. "I guess you deserve to know the truth. I just hope it's not gossipin' to tell you." She gazed out the window for a moment then turned back. "Prudy is a lot like her mother. Helen is used to getting what she wants. Prudy is an only child, and she's had things lavished on her all her life. It's not exactly her fault she's the way she is, but that's beside the point."

Karen twisted her hands together. "But why does she look down on me? I've never done anything to her."

"You're marrying the man she planned to wed."

Karen gasped. "But how is that possible? Has Clay given her any special attention?"

Giving her a sympathetic look, Patsy shrugged. "I don't think so, but Pastor Clay came about the time Jared and I were married. We missed his first two Sundays here because we went home to Independence for the wedding. It's possible that Prudy took one look at him and decided to woo him."

"So, you've never seen Clay encourage her?"

"No. Not at all." Patsy reached over and laid her hand on Karen's. "You don't need to worry. Anyone can tell that man cares deeply for you."

Karen resumed stitching the hem of Clay's shirt, dearly wanting to believe what her friend said. But Clay had been gone from Arcadia for years and had sent her precious few letters during that time. After Aunt Alice died, she thought she could live well in the house her aunt had left her, but then she discovered that Aunt Alice owed hundreds of dollars in back taxes and other debts. Once the house was sold and the debts paid, there wouldn't be much left.

When she explained the situation to Clay's mother, the kind woman had offered to let her live with them, but Karen didn't want to accept charity. If only she had some skill with which she could support herself. The day she received Clay's telegram, asking her to marry him, she'd thought her problems were over. She agreed to wed because of their strong friendship and because she'd cared for him for a long while. But was he merely offering her another form of charity, because as a pastor he needed a wife, or did he truly want to marry her?

But hadn't he proved that point? Even stated it out loud?

Karen hated that her father's abandonment made it hard for her to trust. But if she couldn't trust Clay, whom could she trust?

She sighed, frustrated with her confusion. Clay had always been a cherished friend and had treated her with kindness. He'd been the one to make her laugh for the first time after her father left. He'd been a confidant with whom she'd shared her deepest hurts—the brother she never had. But now she wanted him to be more. The man who loved and cherished her—her husband. So why was she doubting him? Had she allowed the needling voice of the enemy to cause her to distrust her best friend and his good intentions?

"I hate to go, but I reckon I oughta start fixin' supper." Patsy rose and gave her a quick hug. "Don't worry about that man of yours."

Karen closed the door after Patsy left and walked to the window. Before coming to Bakerstown, she'd spent several weeks deciding what to take with her and what to sell. Clay's mother had helped, but one day she showed up with some of Karen's friends, announcing that Karen needed a trousseau, so they'd switched gears and started sewing. Since her arrival, she'd been busy with Clay and finishing her sewing projects. A long time had passed since she'd spent time reading, the Bible and praying regularly. Was it possible that marrying Clay was not God's will for her life? In all her hustle and bustle, had she moved forward with her own dreams and left God behind?

On Sunday morning, Karen sat in church waiting for Clay to enter. Would he wear the shirt she'd given him last night? His surprised and pleased expression when she presented it to him had warmed her heart, as had the gift he'd given her—a pine-green apron with an embroidered bib sporting a cardinal. If he kept surprising her with gifts, she might soon become spoiled, although she secretly enjoyed them. Her aunt had always given her a birthday present and something at Christmas, but no one had ever given her random gifts before, and she cherished them even though they were practical.

A commotion to her left drew her gaze to the aisle, where Patsy halted with a tall, thin man. "Can we sit with you?"

Karen smiled. "Of course." She slid over to make room for the couple.

Patsy scooted in, followed by her husband. She yanked on his arm. "This here's Pastor Parsons's fiancée that I been tellin' you about." She turned to Karen, beaming with pride. "This here's my Jared."

"I'm happy to meet you," Karen said.

Jared nodded, the skin above his neatly trimmed beard turning red.

Patsy leaned toward her, eyes gleaming. "So, did you give Pastor the shirt?"

"I did, and he seemed quite thrilled with it."

"Did he wear it?"

Karen shrugged. "I haven't seen him. He likes to spend Sunday morning praying and studying."

The pianist took her seat and began the opening song. The chattering around the sanctuary quieted as everyone sat down and turned their attention toward the front. Clay stepped in through the side door and took his place behind the lectern, his gaze immediately seeking her out. He smiled then glanced around the room at the others. "Will you all rise and join me in song this bright Sunday morning?"

Delight soared through Karen to see the vivid white shirt she'd painstakingly stitched peeking out above Clay's waistcoat. She sat a bit straighter, glad she was finally mastering the art of sewing. Clay's mother would be proud.

He cleared his throat. "Mrs. Willard, would you please come forward and give today's announcements?" He stepped back, rolled his shoulders, and tugged on one of his sleeves.

Helen, who sat on the second aisle, stood and hurried forward. "As you all know, next Saturday evening, we'll have our annual Christmas sing-along and auction to raise money for the Buckner Orphans Home in Dallas." She cocked her head. "My daughter, Prudence, will be making several of her famous rhubarb pies, so I know you unmarried men will be eager to bid."

Karen was pretty sure Jared snorted—or maybe he had something caught in his throat. Either way, he received an elbow in his side, courtesy of his wife.

Helen continued, "I do hope all you ladies will be as generous as you have in the past to support this worthy cause. This auction helps the orphanage to provide the children with hearty meals. And don't forget the very special Christmas Eve service a week from Thursday and the wedding that follows of our own Pastor Parsons and Miss Karen Briggs."

Clay stepped forward, again tugging on his sleeve. Karen felt the blood rush from her face. Had she forgotten to remove some pins?

"Thank you, Mrs. Willard. I haven't had the pleasure of sampling the fares of the bake sale, but I look forward to it."

He glanced down at his sleeve and frowned. Karen stared at it, and her heart skipped a beat. If she wasn't mistaken, the cuff hung farther out from the end of his coat sleeve than it had before.

"If you have your Bible with you, please open it to, uh. . ." Clay rolled his right shoulder then stared at his cuff, eyebrows dipped. He gave it another tug and pulled the sleeve out a full two inches. He lifted his questioning gaze toward Karen.

She slid down on the bench, using the man's head in front of her to block her view of her fiancé. What had she done wrong?

Patsy leaned over. "Looks as if Pastor's got a problem. You did remember to stitch in the sleeve and didn't just leave it basted?"

Karen flicked a glance at her friend as she felt the blood drain from her face. Had she forgotten that step in her haste to finish before she and Clay had dinner last night?

Clay chuckled. "Pardon the distraction, folks. It seems I'm having garment troubles today."

Face burning, Karen hunkered down on the bench, praying no one had overheard Patsy's loud whisper about her making the shirt. Why, oh why had she thought she could tackle such a project? Even on her best day she'd never been a good seamstress. But Clay needed a shirt so badly—and he'd given her so much.

Patsy rose, and Karen realized she hadn't heard a single word of Clay's sermon. She stood on shaky legs, hoping to make a quick getaway and not talk to anyone.

She dared to peek at Clay, and the horrid sleeve now covered his fingertips. As he talked to a man who'd sat on the front row, he surreptitiously folded the cuff in half so that it didn't look so bad.

As soon as Patsy stepped into the aisle and moved aside, Karen squeezed into the crowd, making her way to the back door. She was supposed to have dinner with Clay, but at the moment, she couldn't bear to see him. No matter what she did, she was a failure.

Chapter 6

Karen wished she could ignore the knocking on her door, but she couldn't abide being rude. She swiped her eyes and pinched her cheeks then opened the door. Fragrant aromas from downstairs drifted in the door, making her stomach gurgle in spite of her lack of appetite.

Mrs. Grady lifted one brow. "Must have been one troubling message the pastor preached."

A tiny smile tugged at one corner of Karen's mouth. "It's not that. I'm surprised you haven't heard what happened yet."

"Tell me later. Gotta get our Sunday dinner dished up, and the pastor is waiting in the parlor for you."

"I don't suppose you could tell him I'm not feeling well?"

The landlady's expression sobered. "You're sick?"

Karen shrugged. "Truthfully, no. Just sick at heart."

"Did that charming rascal do something untoward?"

"No! No. Nothing like that." She glanced away, feeling her cheeks warming again. She sighed. She had to face up to what she did and explain what happened.

Mrs. Grady's eyes widened as Karen told her about the sleeve slipping down Clay's arm. Then she burst out in a belly laugh.

"It's not funny." Karen frowned and crossed her arms. "I'm humiliated."

Tears glistened in the older woman's eyes. "I'm sorry, but that's the most amusing tale I've heard in a long while." She patted Karen's shoulder and wiped a tear from the corner of her eye. "Remind me to tell you about the first shirt I made for Mr. Grady." She turned and bustled toward the stairs, still chuckling.

Karen hurried over and peered into the mirror, not liking what she saw. Her face was splotchy, her eyes puffy, and her nose red. She didn't want Clay to see her like this, but there was nothing to be done about it. She could hardly keep him waiting until her complexion returned to normal.

Downstairs she paused at the entrance to the parlor. Clay stood at the window, looking out. He'd changed from her shirt to a plaid one. She couldn't blame him for wanting to remove that dreadful thing. He must have heard her, because he turned and smiled. "I looked for you after church."

Karen ducked her head, afraid any sympathy on his part would set her crying again. Why couldn't he be angry? It would make her feel better.

He crossed the room and stopped in front of her. "Are you all right?"

She shrugged but didn't look up.

"Tell me what's wrong."

"Surely you know. I sat through the whole service, watching your sleeve slide farther and farther down your arm."

He chuckled. "That was unexpected. I wasn't quite sure what was happening. I thought maybe I'd torn it off with all of my tugging."

A ray of hope pushed away her misery. Could his tugging have caused the sleeve to come loose? "Why *were* you pulling on it?"

His eyes widened, and his ears turned red. "Uh. . .it's a very nice shirt."

"You don't have to spare my feelings. I know something was wrong."

"Uh. . .well. . .it pinched my underarm a bit."

"Oh. I should have made it bigger."

His taut expression eased. "When we're married, you'll be able to try things on me before you finish them so you can adjust them if needed."

Karen snorted and looked away. "You're such an optimist, Clay. I don't know as I'll ever attempt to make you another item of clothing."

He took her hands. "I hope you do. It's a fine shirt. It just needs a few adjustments. Even when I buy ready-made shirts, they sometimes need tweaking."

It was impossible to stay angry in light of his encouragement. "Tweaking—as in needing a new sleeve?"

He grinned. "Well, maybe not a whole sleeve, but sometimes they need to be shortened or the buttons moved."

"I'm mortified. Everyone must think I'm a buffoon."

He took hold of her shoulders. "Karen, no one even knows you made the shirt, so how could they think that?"

She shrugged. Perhaps he was right. Once again she was making a mountain out of a molehill.

"Dinner's ready," Mrs. Grady called from the dining room.

Footsteps sounded upstairs as the other boarders made their way across the hall and down the stairs.

"Better put on a smile, or those other boarders will be booting me out the door, thinking I did something to upset you."

In spite of her misery, a smile lifted her lips.

"That's my girl." He glanced past her then dipped down, stealing a kiss and setting her heart dancing. "Stop worrying so much. I love the shirt and hope you'll make the needed adjustments once we're married."

"Just don't blame me if it falls apart again."

He chuckled. "All right. I'll lay the blame on Mrs. Willard."

A giggle bubbled up and spilled out. "Shame on you, Pastor."

He winked then looped her arm through his and escorted her into the dining room. This was the Clay she remembered—the one who could always make her feel better, no matter the situation. The only man other than her father whom she had ever loved.

Karen deposited the last of the half-dozen fruitcakes she'd made for the auction on the crowded table, feeling a bit proud of how nicely they'd turned out. At least her cooking skills couldn't be questioned.

"Those turned out lovely. After smelling them baking all afternoon, I just might have to purchase one." Mrs. Grady leaned over and sniffed. "Mmm. . ."

Karen lifted her hand to her mouth. "Oh my, I should have thought to make you one. It was so kind of you to allow me to use your kitchen and some of your supplies."

Mrs. Grady swatted her hand in the air. "You saved me some extra work. I always attend the auction and donate something. It's for a worthy cause. And my donating supplies while you did the baking worked out well."

Clay walked up to them. "I sure hope you made one of those for me. How long has it been since I tasted your scrumptious fruitcake?"

Karen smiled, inwardly delighted. "Probably the Christmas before last. But if you want one now, you'll have to buy it. This is all I baked."

Clay stroked his chin, a mischievous expression on his handsome face. "I just might have to do that." He glanced around the crowded room. "Although, with all the people here, the competition should be quite stiff."

Karen patted his arm. "Have no fear. If you don't get one today, I'll make a special one for you after we're married."

"I'll look forward to that."

Mrs. Willard and two other women halted on the opposite side of the table, followed by Prudy, who looked as if she'd been chewing on fresh rhubarb. Karen couldn't help admiring her lovely, dark green velvet dress.

"Looks like we'll be making another fine donation to the Buckner Orphans Home this year." Helen Willard's gaze swung along the four tables filled with sweet-smelling baked goods. "It was kind of you to donate six fruitcakes, Mrs. Grady."

"Oh, they're mostly from Miss Briggs. I just provided some of the supplies and my kitchen. Karen did the baking."

Helen lifted her chin but managed a somewhat grateful look. "How kind of you, Miss Briggs, with you so new to town and all." Her gaze swiveled away. "Pastor, did you happen to see that Prudence baked *eight* rhubarb pies?"

Rue-barb was more like it. Karen crossed her arms, feeling the poke of the woman's barb and her pride that her daughter had donated more than Karen had.

"They look mighty tasty, Mrs. Willard, but I have to say, I prefer cake to pies." Karen straightened. Bless Clay's heart.

Mrs. Willard harrumphed then moved down the table, most likely searching for other victims to lord her daughter's efforts over.

Prudy stared down at the fruitcakes. "They look absolutely delicious. What all do you put in them?"

Karen relaxed. Had Prudy finally decided to be civil? "Um. . .well, besides the basics like flour and sugar, I add raisins, currants, mace, nutmeg, and candied lemons and cherries."

Prudy's brow dipped, and she tapped one finger against her mouth. "You don't use brandy in it? I was certain I spied you buying a bottle at the mercantile. Surely you don't drink the stuff."

"Of course she doesn't." Clay straightened, obviously upset by Prudy's accusation. "How could you ask such a thing?"

Mrs. Willard and her cronies moved back toward Karen and Clay.

Karen's face flamed. Some women took offense to brandy being used in fruitcakes, so she'd refrained from mentioning it. "I do use it, because the brandy keeps the cakes from molding and prolongs their life. But I merely soak the raisins in it. The potency cooks out, so you can't even tell it's there."

Gasps surrounded her. Prudy glowed proud, but her mother's face paled. "You put liquor in your fruitcakes?" Lois Clemmons fanned her face with her hand.

Karen stared at the floor, wishing she was an insect and could crawl under the table. She'd tried to do something nice—something to support the church's event—but once again she failed.

"Now, Lois, don't make such a stink. Using brandy for baking is quite common." Mrs. Grady sent Karen a smile.

Karen backed away from the table, fearing she may well have cost Clay his job. All around her, the crowd pressed in and people grumbled. She spun. "Excuse me, please. I need some air."

"Karen. Wait!" Clay called out, but she continued squeezing through the throng.

She pushed her way outside then ran all the way back to the boardinghouse. It was no use. She was the wrong bride for Clay, and it was time he faced the facts.

Chapter 7

Clay longed to go after Karen—to soothe the wounds the church ladies had carelessly inflicted—but he had responsibilities here. Everyone seemed to be talking at once. He lifted two fingers to his mouth and whistled. The noise quieted instantly, and everyone looked at him. "Let's not forget this is a church event, even if we are not in the church. Please quiet down, and we'll begin the auction. Where's Elmer?"

"Back here, Parson Parsons. Let me through, folks. I'm the auctioneer."

"Everyone knows that, Elmer." Fred Smith chuckled, as did half the crowd.

Clay relaxed as the tension of the crowd eased, but there was still one person he had to confront. He searched for Prudy and was not surprised to see her making her way toward him, smiling like a child who'd stolen a pie from a windowsill.

She batted her long lashes at him. "I'm so sorry, Clay. I had no idea that the mention of brandy would upset everyone."

He crossed his arms, fighting hard not to lose control. "Lying doesn't become you, Miss Willard. I know exactly what you were doing. And it won't work."

She pouted and swirled her skirts, obviously struggling to maintain an innocent gaze. "What won't work?"

"Trying to chase Karen away. She's the woman I intend to marry, and if it means leaving my church to do so, I will."

She paled. "Why would you want that mouse when you could have me? I've practically thrown myself at you. Any other man would have married me months ago."

Clay shook his head, feeling sorry for the woman. "You don't understand. Karen has owned my heart for more than a decade. There is no other woman for me."

She ducked her head. He hated hurting her, but she had to stop chasing after him and pestering Karen.

A ruckus behind him drew his attention. Bart Tremble waved a dollar in the air. "Start with them fruitcakes. I want one."

"Me, too." Silas Hightower stepped in front of Bart. "I'll bid two dollars."

"Three!"

Clay looked up front at Mrs. Willard's stunned face and smiled. It looked as if Karen's fruitcakes were a winner—at least with the men. He turned back, and Prudy was gone. Good. He needed to find Karen and tell her the good news.

⟡

What a mess she'd made of things. Karen slapped a blouse into her satchel but then jumped at a knock on her bedroom door. As far as she knew, she was alone in the house.

"Open the door, Karen."

Clay. She didn't want to see him—to break his heart. "Go away."

"I'm not leaving, so you might as well open the door."

Sighing, she did as ordered. "You shouldn't be here. If anyone found out—"

"I don't care what anyone thinks." He stepped into her room, eyes beseeching her to believe him. "I love you. I should have told you years ago, but I wanted to get settled—to have a home for us first."

Karen shook her head. "It's too late. I can't be the wife you need. I'm leaving, Clay."

"Leaving! You don't mean that. Where will you go?"

She shrugged and turned back to the open satchel on her bed. "I'm sorry, but I won't be the cause of you losing your church."

"I can get another church, but you're the only woman for me. Can't you see that? I've loved you for as long as I can remember."

She shook her head. She loved him too much to bring about his demise. "I'm sorry. But it won't work."

He stepped closer. "Karen—"

Steeling herself, she spun around. Better to hurt him now than later. She held up her hand. "I'm not changing my mind."

His deep sigh and sad eyes were almost her undoing.

"Fine. I won't force you to marry me." He spun around and was gone.

⟡

Clay walked down Main Street, confusion warring within him. He thought marrying Karen was God's will, but had his love for her overruled his ability to hear God on the subject?

Silas Hightower moseyed toward him, holding one of Karen's fruitcakes and chewing. He slowed as he neared Clay. "This is the best stuff I've ever eaten. You'd be a fool, Pastor, not to marry a woman who can cook like her."

The man's comment didn't help his crumpled emotions. As much as he wanted to head home, hide out, and nurse his wounded heart, he needed to check on things—and the Christmas sing-along was to start soon. He was expected to get it going, but then maybe he could sneak out after that.

Clay returned to the building where the auction was being held and scanned the table. Most of the items had already been claimed. Mrs. Willard spied him and moved in his direction. She was the next-to-last person he wanted to talk with now. He backed out the door, ready to tuck tail and run.

"Pastor, wait. Please."

Her contrite tone slowed his steps, and he turned. Helen approached, along with her sister and Lois Clemmons. Helen cleared her throat. "We'd like to apologize."

"It's my fault." Lois ducked her head. "My father was a drunkard, and I can't abide alcohol. But I do feel we overreacted and owe Miss Briggs an apology."

"I agree. You'll find her at the boardinghouse."

Lois nodded, and she and Loraine turned that way.

Helen moved closer. "Pastor, I do hope you won't hold any hard feelings against Prudence. She's a woman scorned and was desperate to gain your attention."

Clay crossed his arms. "Your daughter's games hurt a good woman and may have jeopardized our marriage. I forgive her, but I also made it clear that I am not now, nor have I ever been, interested in her as a potential wife. Karen is the only woman for me."

Helen ducked her head and nodded. "I understand. She won't bother you again."

Clay watched her hurry to catch up with the other two women, feeling only marginally better. It was good the women were on their way to apologize. He probably ought to be there—just in case. First, he had to get something from his home—one last gift.

Persistent knocking at the front door drew Karen from her room. She didn't want to answer, but it might be a prospective boarder, and she wouldn't be the cause of Mrs. Grady losing business.

She opened the door, stunned to see the trio responsible for her latest woes.

Lois quickly explained and apologized.

"And we want you to know we're sincerely happy to have you here in Bakerstown," Mrs. Willard said.

Loraine nodded. "You make Pastor Clay happy."

Karen's chilled heart began to thaw. "Thank you so much for coming. You can't know how much it means."

The women left as quickly as they came, but a foot slid into the opening before she could close the door. She stepped back, and Clay pushed into the room.

She crossed her arms. "Why are you back?"

"Because I can't let you leave. We belong together—we always have. This is for you." He held out a package—too small to be something for her kitchen.

"Clay. . ."

"Please. Just open it."

Even though she knew she shouldn't, Karen unwrapped the paper and opened the tiny box. She gasped. A beautiful ring with a blue sapphire gleamed in the light shining through the door. "Oh, Clay. It's lovely."

He stepped forward. "I love you, Karen. Please don't go. Stay and be my wife."

Leaving him was wrong. She knew it. All it would create was misery for them both. She loved this man and didn't want to live without him. Tears coursing down her face, she nodded.

Clay smiled and took her into his arms. "Oh sweetheart, you don't know how happy that makes me. I love you so much."

"I love you, too, and I promise never to make another fruitcake."

Clay threw back his head and laughed. When he finally stopped, he captured her gaze. "I certainly hope that's one promise you don't keep."

⤙⤚

Late Christmas Eve, Clay lifted Karen off the porch and carried her through the door of the parsonage—their home. He kicked the door shut then claimed her lips, kissing her as he'd longed to do for years.

After a while, Karen pulled back, gleaming in the love of a newly married woman. "I have a gift for you."

"Oh you do?" He grinned.

"It's not what you're thinking. Please put me down."

Reluctantly, he set her on her feet. She opened the satchel he'd placed on the table earlier and pulled out a box and handed it to him.

Curious, he lifted the lid, delighted at the fruity aroma that greeted him. "A fruitcake!"

Karen smiled.

He set the cake on the table then waggled his brows. "I'd love some later, but right now, I prefer to enjoy my wife—and she's much sweeter than fruitcake."

Fruitcake by Measure

2 scant teacupfuls butter

3 cupfuls dark brown sugar

Half a grated nutmeg

1 tablespoon ground
cinnamon

1 teaspoon ground cloves

1 teaspoon mace

½ cupful molasses

½ cupful sour milk

6 eggs, whites and yolks
beaten separately

1 cupful lemon and/or orange
juice

4 cupfuls sifted flour

1 level teaspoon baking soda

1 pound raisins, seeded

Currants, washed and dried

½ pound citron, cut in
thin strips

Cream butter and sugar; add nutmeg, cinnamon, cloves, and mace; add molasses and sour milk. Stir well; then add egg yolks and juice; stir again thoroughly. Add flour alternately with egg whites. Dissolve baking soda and stir in thoroughly. Mix fruit together, and stir into it 2 heaping tablespoons flour; then stir it in cake batter. Butter two baking pans carefully, line them with parchment, well buttered, and bake at 350 degrees for 2 hours. After it is baked, let cake cool in pans. Afterward, put in an airtight container, or cover tightly in pans.

Mrs. S. A. Camp, Grand Rapids, Michigan

About the Author

Bestselling author Vickie McDonough grew up wanting to marry a rancher, but instead she married a computer geek who is scared of horses. She now lives out her dreams in her fictional stories about ranchers, cowboys, lawmen, and others living in the West during the 1800s. Vickie is the award-winning author of more than thirty published books and novellas. Her books include the fun and feisty Texas Boardinghouse Brides series and *End of the Trail*, which was the Oklahoma Writers' Federation, Inc., 2013 Best Fiction Novel winner. Her *Whispers on the Prairie* was a *Romantic Times* Recommended Inspirational Book for July 2013. Vickie has been married for thirty-nine years. She has four grown sons and one daughter-in-law and is grandma to a feisty eight-year-old girl. When she's not writing, Vickie enjoys reading, antiquing, watching movies, and traveling. To learn more about Vickie's books or to sign up for her newsletter, visit her website: www.vickiemcdonough.com.

The Snowbound Bride

by Davalynn Spencer

I have set the LORD always before me:
because he is at my right hand, I shall not be moved.

PSALM 16:8

Chapter 1

Spruce City, Colorado
1885

Arabella Taube clutched her small carpetbag as tightly as her breath and turned her back to the coach car. The man in the brown bowler had watched her all the way from Denver. He was watching her now through the window. She was certain of it.

Blowing snow swirled around her skirts, and the cold nipped at her ears. Oh, to have her trunk and be off to the hotel with the other passengers. She rubbed her jacketed arms as couples claimed their baggage and trudged through the snow toward waiting hacks and buggies. With this delay, there might be no rooms left when she got there.

Stomping her freezing feet against the platform boards, she looked again for a porter. She had assumed the train would press on to Leadville without stopping for the night. *"Assumption is the devil's joke on the unwitting."* Her grandmother's brittle warning chafed, and the woman's disapproving *tsks* rang in Ara's ears. Or was that the pop and snap of the engine as it cooled?

Horses whinnied and tossed their heads as they pulled from the station. She stiffened against the bluster of wind and panic. She *would* make her own way without her uncle's ordering of her every step and Grandmother's resentful regard—as if Ara could go back and change her parentage. The train heaved a dying breath, and the engineer stepped from his cab. The conductor followed. Where were the porters with her trunk?

The brown-bowlered man exited the car, looked both ways, and skimmed over her as if she didn't exist. She was not fooled and turned quickly for the depot. An inside bench would serve if need be, but she'd not be ogled by that man any longer.

The fine hairs on her neck sprang like porcupine quills. He was following her. *"Ladies do not run."* She lifted her skirt and quickened her pace. As she neared the depot door, the clerk reached for the shade. Casting off

Grandmother's drill, she ran and grabbed the brass doorknob. "Please," she mouthed.

He shook his head, jerked a thumb over his shoulder, and dropped the shade. The light dimmed within, and she turned to see the bowlered man a few paces away, lighting a pipe. The flare of his match lit pale eyes that watched her askance. Her stomach knotted. She didn't know his name, but she knew he was one of her uncle's lackeys, one willing to do for a price what her uncle would not.

Well, she'd not be bullied back to Chicago to be sold as a bride to the highest bidder. Uncle Victor could solidify his latest business alliance some other way. With tight resolve, she raised her chin and walked calmly toward the end of the building. At the corner, she turned and ran, skirts a-flying, to the nearest wagon. Tossing in her bag, she grasped the side but stopped short at the bared and snarling teeth in her face.

A scream lodged in her throat, but she scuttled to the harnessed horse where she dared draw in a desperate breath. A dinner biscuit from her skirt pocket abated the nag's nervous whinny. "There now, old girl," she whispered, her voice betraying her racing heart. A velvety nose rippled over her shaking hand, lipping up the broken bread. "You wouldn't give me away, would you?"

Pulling in great gulps of cold air, she spied the dog watching her from the wagon bed, head cocked and sharp ears pointing.

She dug in her pockets for another bribe but found only a hanky and a paper with the name of the Leadville banker she was to contact upon her arrival. She had to get her belongings, guard dog or no.

Easing closer to the board, she sent up a silent prayer and cooed at the beast. It seemed to warm to her voice and laid its ears down. The tail wagged. "Good boy you are, guarding your master's wagon. Might I retrieve my bag, please?"

Suddenly the dog crouched and turned from her with a chilling growl as the brown bowler came round the depot. Ara dropped to her knees and crawled under the wagon. Pipe smoke pinched her nostrils, and her chest seized.

The mongrel lunged against the side boards, drawing uncivilized expletives from the man's throat and distance from his feet. In his fright he dropped his pipe and stooped quickly to retrieve it. Ara feared she'd been found out, but he showed no sign of spotting her and fled the area, leaving a trail of curses behind.

Returning to its previous position, the dog waited quietly for a moment then rumbled a low beckoning. Ara crawled out, peered into the shadows hugging the depot, and slowly straightened. Brushing off her skirts, she spoke again in soft tones.

"You old love. If I had another biscuit, I'd let you have it for sure." Afraid to pet the animal, she eyed her bag so foolishly thrown into the wagon before she knew what else was there. "Will you let me get my things?"

The ears flattened again and the cur smiled, if that was possible. But in Ara's unsettled condition, she believed—and hoped—anything was possible and made for the back of the wagon.

Black-and-white paws matched her steps and stopped by the carpetbag.

"There's a good boy. I'll just be taking my—"

The dog clamped upon the handle, dragged the bag to the center of the wagon bed, and sat protectively beside it.

"Well, I never!" Narrowing her eyes, she drew herself up. "I'll not be had by a dog."

A slight woof puffed from the pointed snout.

"We'll just see about that." She marched around to the wheel, yanked her skirts above her knees, and climbed the spokes. The dog looked away as if scandalized.

Ara stepped into the bed and froze as mangled strains of a Christmas carol rose from the alley, coming her way. She glared at the dog, who again seized the handle in its jaws. With no other recourse but to leave her belongings and risk running into her uncle's shady minion, she dove to the rough boards, flattened against the outer edge, and jerked a loose tarp over her feet and head.

"God rest ye merry, gentlemen, let nothing you dismay—"

She clapped her hands over her ears. *Dismay, indeed. Have mercy!*

The dog howled then shook the wagon as it bounded to the edge.

"That bad, ol' boy? I don't sing any worse than you."

A muffled woof and exuberant wiggling indicated its master had returned. A decided tilt as the man climbed to the seat threatened to roll Ara like a Yule log from her hiding place. Whoever he was, he was either rotund or robust. At least he wasn't the brown bowler.

With a light slap and a hearty "giddyap, ol' girl," the mare took to the road. Ara sucked in a dusty breath. Should she rise and call out? Demand the driver take her to the hotel—where there may be no rooms? What if her uncle's hireling was watching? With a drawn-out groan, the dog settled its warm body against her. O Lord, what had she gotten herself into?

Chapter 2

Nate Horne bunched his shoulders and pulled his hat down. A ground blizzard would drift what snow they already had at the ranch and close the road he traveled. He called Beetle, but the dog didn't respond. A quick glance found it curled against a tarp, tail wrapped round its nose like a squirrel in a knothole. Nate reached back and rubbed the speckled ears and re-counted the crates and barrels he'd taken on at the mercantile before going to supper. He roughed the dog's side with hearty approval. It'd sooner take a man's hand off than let a thief steal their stores.

He didn't recall, but whatever lay in the tarp would be frozen before he got home. Just like him. Thanks to all the train passengers, he wouldn't be staying at the hotel as planned. Rooms had disappeared like cabbage in the chicken yard.

"Get on, girl. No sense dragging it out." The wind cut cold against his face, freezing his lashes. He pulled his neckerchief over his nose and ducked his head.

Atop the first of many hills into the backcountry, a hearty gust cleared the air for a spell and a black vault opened above him, sparkling like a diamond-littered canopy. The spectacle took his breath away—that and the muffled sneeze from the wagon bed.

Beetle didn't sneeze like that.

Nate eased off the road and set the brake. He tucked his coat flap behind his holster, settled a hand on his gun, and stepped over the seat. Beetle flattened his ears and looked away as if caught chewing the tablecloth from the clothesline again. Nate waved him off, and he slunk to a corner, guilt painted all over his mottled face.

The gun slid smooth, and the cold hammer click spurred movement beneath the tarp. "Out." He raked his eyes the length of the roll, searching for the business end of a gun. Something squirmed then stilled. At the top, the canvas tucked down, and a woman's green hat peeked out, followed by two enormous dark eyes. "Stand up."

Gloved fingers tugged the tarp under a pointed chin. "But it's s–s–so cold."

"Now." Relieved to see the rest of her clothes matched her hat and not some saloon gal's get-up, he eased the trigger back but kept the gun trained. He'd heard about women with derringers in their skirts or handbag or wherever. His neck warmed as a few wherevers piled up at the back of his mind. "Drop the tarp and show me your hands."

She complied and shivered against a hard-hitting gust. He waved the gun toward the seat. Looking away while she maneuvered over the bench, he met the dog's reproachful glare. "I'll deal with you later," he said under his breath. It dropped its head and grunted down on its front paws.

Nate holstered his gun. "Scoot over."

She scooted. He sat on her right, keeping his gun from her reach. As tall as she was, if she'd a mind to wrestle him for it, she might put up a good fight. He had never hit a woman—or knocked one out of a wagon—and he didn't want to start tonight. He pulled the tarp over the seat and handed it to her. "It'll be a couple hours before we get to the ranch, and you'll freeze to death in those fancy riggin's."

Her eyes grew even bigger. "Two hours? Ranch? But I must stay in Spruce City!" Her teeth chattered as she stood and wrapped the tarp around her like a squaw then hunched on the seat next to him.

"Closer to three, and we're not turning back."

She blinked, and tears bunched up in her eyes.

"Quit that, or your eyes'll freeze shut."

She stared at him, rubbed her face with gloved fingers, and jabbed out her chin. "They will not."

"Suit yourself." He gathered the reins, released the brake, and clucked Rose on. They'd be even later now.

⁂

Ara had read about ranchers out West. They all wore spurs and chewed tobacco and slurred their speech. Of course, she'd kept her dime novels well hidden from Grandmother and Uncle Victor—beneath her unmentionables. And when she left, she'd tucked them into her trunk.

Her trunk. Would she ever see it again? Would she ever make it back to Spruce City and on to Leadville? She'd given her word to arrive mid-November. She turned to the stranger whose face was swathed in a knotted neckerchief and nearly hidden beneath a wide-brimmed hat. "We have to go back."

He grunted and kept driving. It was like talking to the dog.

"Please, I have to be on the train tomorrow morning. I'm meeting someone in Leadville."

He slanted her an eyes-only look she'd expect from a bandit. What kind of person had she attached herself to? She snugged the tarp tighter and squeezed her eyes shut against the wind. How foolish she'd been to toss her bag willy-nilly into an unknown wagon, and then herself. She'd been so desperate to elude the bowlered man that she'd let go of her wits and now bounced along next to a horrific singer who draped himself like a bedouin. A sudden jolt shot her eyes open. Snow danced in swirling eddies against the wagon and across their path.

"Badger hole."

Another jolt knocked her against the man's shoulder, and she jerked back. His eyes slid her way. "I won't bite."

Looking over her shoulder, she envied the dog snug and content in its thick coat.

"But he might."

The stranger did not laugh outright, but she heard it in his tone. How dare he.

"What were you doin' in my buckboard?"

She gritted her teeth. Could she trust him? She peeked his way, allowing that he hadn't put her out along the road to die from the cold or Indian attack or some other unthinkable fate. "I was trying to get my bag."

He turned in the seat, searching the wagon's contents. "What's it doing back there?"

"Your dog dragged it to the center where I couldn't reach it."

Another shaded look. "And how did Beetle get it?"

Beetle? What an odd name for a dog. "He dragged it there."

The man pulled his neckerchief over his nose and mumbled something behind his hand. She was certain he'd sworn.

"You put it in the wagon?"

She pressed her lips together and tugged the tarp higher. "Yes."

He leaned closer. "What?"

She leaned away. "Yes. I put it there."

"Look, ma'am, you'd best tell me what's going on 'fore we get to the ranch. It'll make a difference in what happens once we get there."

In spite of the *ma'am*, fear shot straight from her frozen backside to the roots of her elegantly pinned hair.

Chapter 3

Nate looked at the woman hunched beside him. "What's your name?"

She turned her big doe eyes on him. "Ara."

It sounded like *air-uh*, like a breath. "Ara what?"

She hesitated. If she said Smith, he'd know she was lying.

"Taube. Arabella Taube." The panic had dimmed.

He slid her another look. She started battin' her eyes again. No wailing, just a small jerk with every silent sob. Finally, she pulled the tarp over her green hat and buried her face in her hands. Hang fire, he could sober a bawlin' calf but not a crying woman, not even his own ma. What was he supposed to do with this one?

Something deep inside him wanted to wrap her in his arms and hold her close. He gripped the reins tighter. Not happening. He'd as soon rope a rattler than tangle with a female who misunderstood his intentions.

A fat flake dropped on his knee and quivered into a wet spot. He raised his head and another fell on his face. The clouds had dipped low and thrown open their shutters, about to empty their load.

❧

Numb all over except where she slept against him the last hour, Nate pulled up in front of the ranch-house steps. He'd tucked the gal under his arm to keep her from sliding off the seat, and she'd murmured but didn't rouse. She fit against him as if she were made special order for his long, lanky frame. Leadville, she'd said. Maybe she was some rich man's bride-to-be, but tonight he'd make sure she was warm and safe.

A shadow crossed one of the two front windows, and the wide door swung open. His ma hurried out, wrapped in a quilt and holding a lamp. "You're home." The wind snatched at her words.

He ducked his hat against the snow and tied off the reins. "Out," he told Beetle, and the dog flew over the wagon boards and into the house. His ma leaned from the top step and held up the lamp. As gently as lifting a newborn foal, Nate scooped Ara into his arms, stepped down with a slight jostle, and carried her inside, tarp and all. His ma followed and

THE *12 Brides of* Christmas COLLECTION

shouldered the door closed.

A glowing fire warmed the parlor, and he laid his bundle on the settee. "Is she hurt?"

The cold knots in his back and legs kinked tighter as he straightened. Moving to the fire, he rubbed his hands together and turned to warm his back. "Not far as I can tell."

"Where'd she come from, and why did you bring her out here in a blizzard?"

"I didn't know she was in the back of the wagon till she sneezed."

His ma raised an eyebrow.

"She rolled herself in the tarp. By the time I heard her, we were too far out to turn around." He backed closer to the fire and flexed his shoulders in the warmth. "The hotel filled up with train passengers, or I'd be in town, too."

His ma held the back of her hand to the woman's forehead. "Do you know anything about her?"

"Said she was on her way to Leadville to meet someone. But I'll be danged if I know why she threw her satchel in the wagon. Said Beetle wouldn't let her get it." He rubbed his hands over his head and down his face. "Maybe you can get more out of her."

"Did you get her name?"

"Ara Taube."

His ma's hand drew back, and her voice dropped to a whisper. "Taube? She must be German."

He added a log to the fire and poked around it until it flamed. "You're up late. Is everything all right?"

She set the lamp on a small table and pulled a footstool close to the settee. "We're all fine here. Buck went to bed hours ago. But I knew you'd be home." She patted her chest.

Nate couldn't count the times his ma had "known."

"I'll take the wagon and Rose to the barn. The stores'll keep for tonight." He glanced at the mantel clock about to call the hour. "Be back 'fore long." He hitched his collar up, called the dog, and ducked into the wintry blast as the New Haven clock began to chime.

⁓∾⁓

Ara bolted upright at the striking tones. Her heart jammed her throat, and she clutched at the tarp. The culprit perched on a broad mantel above a roaring fire. Where was she?

"Hello."

Startled, she jerked around to a kind-eyed woman with a smile as warm as the hearth. Relief weakened her shoulders, and she slumped, waiting for her heart to find its way back to her chest.

"I'm Nate's mother, Lilly Horne. You're at our ranch, and this is my home."

Nate? The wagon driver? "P–Pleased to make your acquaintance." Ara cringed. This was no social call. "I mean. . ." She fingered her hat, askew on the side of her head, and held out her hand. "I am Miss Arabella Taube. From Chicago."

Lilly's eyes brightened, and she took Ara's hand. "Oh, it's been so long since we've had guests. I do hope you'll stay awhile and visit. There's so much I'd love to hear about. The latest fashions. The theater—" She swept Ara with a worried look. "Please forgive me. Here I am thinking only of myself." Standing, she helped Ara rise. "Let's get you out of this dirty thing. Land sake, look what it's done to your beautiful velvet suit." Crumpling the dusty tarp in her arms, she continued. "Oh my, but that deep green is absolutely lovely against your dark hair."

Ara sat again. The tarp soon found its way to the door, and Lilly pulled the small quilt from her shoulders and draped it over Ara's lap.

"I have a kettle on the stove, and I'll be right back with a cup of tea." She paused at the door to the kitchen. "You do drink tea, don't you?"

Ara tugged the fingers of one glove. "Yes, ma'am. Thank you."

The woman's smile broadened, and then she hurried through the door in her trousers.

Chapter 4

Ara blinked. Lilly Horne was wearing britches.

The second of her gloves joined its mate on the cushion, and Ara laid aside the quilt. Gingerly standing, she tested her legs for balance before moving closer to the fire. With her back to the luscious warmth, her stiff joints relaxed, and she took in the cozy room. Log walls bore lovely paintings of forested landscapes, and above the mantel hung a portrait of a dark-haired man astride an exquisite horse. A large desk sprawled beneath one wide window, and as she watched, snow built up on the sill, reminding her of the long cold ride. But she didn't remember arriving.

"Here we are, dear." Lilly brought a tray to the small table.

Ara returned to the settee, and Lilly took the footstool rather than one of two large leather chairs. With a warm smile, she handed Ara a delicate cup and saucer. Such contrast. A woman in trousers crouching on a stool serving tea in fine china. Beautiful artwork covering rough log walls, and a blazing fire dispelling the cold of a stormy night. Somehow it all seemed so natural.

"The paintings are lovely."

Lilly appeared pleased. "Thank you." She lifted her gaze to the portrait above the fireplace. "I haven't done much since Nathan passed."

Heavy footsteps on the porch jerked Ara's attention to the door, and her cup rattled on its saucer. Had the brown-bowlered man found her?

"Don't worry." Lilly touched her hand. "It's only Nate dusting the snow from his boots."

With a whoosh, the door flew back. Flurries raced over the threshold to die in the entryway. Beetle darted in, and the stranger followed with Ara's carpetbag in hand, looking for all the world like a fairy-tale giant. She'd not realized earlier how big he was. Freezing to death had been more on her mind than appraising his stature. He set her bag against the wall, hung his coat and hat on the hall tree, then pulled his boots off in a metal jack that looked like a large beetle. That couldn't be where the dog got its name.

A cold nose touched her hand, and she sloshed her tea. Beetle eyed her, that odd grin tugging his jowls, then he trotted to the hearth and curled into a ball.

The driver passed behind her, smelling of leather and snow. A dark wool shirt hugged his broad shoulders, and the scarf still circled his neck. Without his hat, blond hair fell across his brow, and bright pink tipped his ears and nose. He stood with his back to the flame, and blue eyes swept her with bridled appreciation. He nodded once.

Rattled by his obvious assessment, she returned his nod as curtly as possible. She could be just as tight-lipped as he.

Lilly chuckled. "Nate, Miss Taube is from Chicago. I'm hoping she'll stay awhile as our guest and bring me up to date on the latest happenings in the city."

Not wanting to offend her hostess, Ara quickly arranged her refusal. But not quickly enough.

"She'll be staying." He looked toward the window. "Storm's comin' hard. We'll all be staying."

Ara's heart leaped back to her throat. She sprang from the settee, spilling tea on her skirt, and rushed to the window. Ice lashed the pane like tiny claws across a hardwood floor, and the drift on the sill swept twice as high as before. Cupping a hand to her face she leaned against the glass but saw only swirling white assailing the house. Tears stung her eyes, and she gritted her teeth, determined not to appear childish and ungrateful.

A log gave way, and the fire crackled. Beetle sighed heavily, but the Hornes remained silent. Straightening, she faced them. At last she'd fled her uncle's dominance, only to be held hostage by the weather, a captive houseguest of a family she knew nothing about in a wild and mysterious land.

Oh Lord, if only I had wings like a dove, for then I would fly away.

Nate rolled his shoulders and stretched his neck. The gal's hair lay knotted on her shoulders, and the fine dress was smudged from being wrapped in that old tarp. He still wanted to wrap his arms around her.

His ma rose from the stool. "Come stand by the fire, dear. You'll catch your death over there by the window."

Nate stole into the kitchen for coffee he knew would be waiting. Cradling a tin mug in both hands, he returned to the parlor door. Ara slumped on the footstool near the fire, staring at the copper flames. The hat shared the table with the teapot, and his ma was working through the tangled hair the same way he'd pulled cockleburs from a mare's mane one spring.

He pressed his fingers to his thumb, felt again the prickly burs that itched for days. His uncle had laughed at him for not wearing gloves. Next time he did.

She looked at him then, those doe eyes filling up her face. He moved closer to the fire and gentled his voice. "You hungry?"

"I set a plate in the oven for you, Nate. There's enough to share between the two of you." His ma spoke quietly, intent on untangling that mess of brown mane. He returned to the stove, grabbed a towel, and pulled out a tin platter heaped with beef and potatoes and carrots. He scraped some onto a plate and added a fork and napkin. She was probably a dainty eater.

When he returned, her hair hung smooth and shiny over her shoulder and pooled like dark water in her lap. "Thank you, Lilly." Weariness edged her eyes and voice.

His ma patted Ara's arm and handed her the pins. "My pleasure. Always missed having a daughter to fuss over." She stood, took one of the plates, and handed it to Ara. "Though Nate here kept me plenty busy, growing out of his clothes faster than I could make them." She pulled the leather chairs closer to the fire so each one angled toward the warmth and gestured for Ara to take a seat in one. "Do you have more than the satchel Nate brought in, dear?"

"My trunk is still on the train." Easing into the nearest chair, Ara sent Nate a worried look. "What do you think will happen to it?"

He took the other chair, ducking her pleading eyes. "They'll offload it in Spruce City or take it on to Leadville."

"And then?"

She made him feel responsible. "They'll hold it." He forked in a mouthful.

Ara relaxed against the high leather back, fitting to it like she'd fit beneath his arm.

"Morning will be here before we know it." His ma smoothed her hands down the front of her britches and picked up the lamp. "Your room is on the right as you go down the hall, Ara. Mine is across from yours. Just knock on my door if you need anything. I'm a light sleeper."

Ara laid down her fork and gave his ma a weak smile. "You've been very kind."

As his ma left the room, darkness leaped into the corners where the fire's light didn't reach. Ara stiffened and gripped her plate with both hands.

He leaned toward her, close enough to hear her quick, shallow breaths. Softly he spoke, like he would to a jittery colt. "It's all right. You're safe here." He had a need to touch her, but he held back.

She turned her head, and the fire glinted off her dark eyes like a flame against obsidian. He'd seen that look before.

"I'm not afraid."

He returned to his meal, determined not to argue the point. Arabella Taube might not know it, but she was scared to death.

Chapter 5

Sparrows twittered, water dripped, and a dove called, insistent in its beckoning. Ara rolled to her side and burrowed into the warm feather tick. Her elegant bed in Uncle Victor's mansion could not compare. Hoping to see the same log walls that had housed her for a week, she opened one eye then offered a silent thank-you. Somehow, the Hornes made her feel wanted.

"It's all right. You're safe here." Nate's deep, soft words spun a tight coil in her stomach each morning when she rehearsed them. He'd tried to ease her worries—quite unlike his frightening demeanor on that dreadfully cold ride. He was different here in this house. No longer the cloaked bedouin or masked bandit, his very presence commanded safety. And next to him and his mother, Ara felt less the gangly giant that towered over others. She fit in.

But she was far from where she needed to be, and Lilly had seemed to understand when Ara explained she'd taken a position as a private tutor for a Leadville banker's children. Even Nate and Buck had nodded mutely at that dinner conversation. Everyone knew that when the snow melted enough for the wagon's passage, she'd be on her way to Spruce City and the train.

A part of her dreaded that day.

She tossed back the quilt and tiptoed across the cold floor toward the incessant dripping. Beyond the heavy lace curtain, icy rapiers clung to the eaves, pouring themselves one drop at a time into tiny pools beneath the window. A sapphire sky spread over the mountain-rimmed valley, and the brilliant landscape shone like a blue willow dream. Eyes aching, she turned from the window with Nate's warning in her ears. *"Don't stare at the snow. It'll blind you."* She squeezed her eyes tight and drew in a crisp breath. Winter was so different here. In Chicago, all was gray for weeks on end.

And the tall horseman was different from any man her uncle had pushed upon her. Had she met Nate Horne in the city, she might never have left. A wrenching shiver sent her to the foot of the bed where a blue calico dress and two flannel petticoats lay over the footboard. More of Lilly's kindness. That first morning the woman had brought black coffee on a tray. Her blue eyes smiled over her cup brim, and she pulled Ara in with a motherly gaze.

"From the size of that satchel, I imagine you don't have another change of clothes, and your traveling suit is ruined. Would you accept something from me to wear for the time being?"

Embarrassed, Ara considered refusing. But what choice did she have? Lilly took the dress and petticoats from a chest against the wall. "I wore this dress the day I met Nate's father, and I saved it back for my daughter." The last word faded with a shadowed pause. "It's been packed away so long it has creases where it shouldn't." The simple style and fabric spoke of a young woman not well-to-do by any means.

"It's lovely." Ara took the dress and held it against her breast. "You wore it when you met Nate's father?"

Lilly picked up the tray. "I was a mail-order bride and wore that dress on the train, all the way from New York." A sad smile drew the corners of her mouth. "Nathaniel Horne met me at the Spruce City depot with my picture in his hand and a promise in his eyes."

Ara's heart pinched at the thought of such risk, but from the look on Lilly's face and the sprawling log house, their marriage must have worked out for the best.

"Those were wonderful years, and the good Lord blessed us with Nate."

Who, with his uncle, ate nearly as much as the foaling mares kept close in the barn, Ara had since learned. The rest of the horses and a few cows wintered beneath the mountain.

Shedding her gown with a shiver, she stepped into the petticoats and dress again, flouncing the skirt over the warm flannel layers. Lilly had worn nothing but britches since Ara arrived. What might that be like?

Nate drove the team into the barn, and Buck unhitched the sled. Haying the horses took near all morning after they bogged the runners. At least the band was close, on the south side of the mountain. He pulled the heavy harness from the Clydes and led them to their stalls. A good brushing, a can of corn, and a pile of hay paid them for their labor. A pitchfork-full to Coffee one stall over, and Nate paused to run a keen eye over the bay's distended belly, ready to drop any day. She whiffled her thanks as she nosed into the sweet grass, her long, dark neck as smooth as Ara Taube's eyes. Coffee black and lit from the inside out, they were. Longing sneaked in and curled around Nate's heart like Beetle near the fire.

It'd only been a week, but if he could, he'd take Ara in his arms and beg her to stay. Then he'd ride out, whistle up a bear, and make a winter coat from its hide. He huffed at the likelihood of either prospect.

The close warm air splintered with a sudden crack. Buck lifted the ax and moved to the next bucket in line down the alleyway. "It's thinner this mornin'. Too bad we can't keep this ice for summer when your ma makes lemonade and we're sweatin' like the Clydes."

Nate grunted in agreement.

His uncle paused and tugged on the galluses holding up his pants. "That little gal seems to like it here."

Nate tossed a fork of hay and shot him a look.

"Your ma was hummin' in the kitchen this morning." Buck's ax rang through the barn like a rifle shot. "I ain't heard her hum in years. Not since your pa died."

Nate kept his thoughts to himself.

"You think a city gal would take to the high country?"

He ignored the question, moved on to Rose, and rubbed between her ears. She tossed her head and blew warm air in his face. No foals for her, but she'd earned her hay.

"Lilly's bakin' cookies today." Buck set the buckets in the stalls, hefted the ax to his shoulder, and grinned beneath his wide brim. "Think I'll go in and help her out with 'em." His whiskered face bubbled on the sides. Made Nate laugh every time.

He hung the fork on the wall. "Be right behind you. Need to check a couple things first." Like what he was going to do around Ara Taube until the road was passable. In a short week he'd grown partial to her gentle ways and lively eyes. He'd like her to stay, forget about Leadville. A frozen knot in his belly thawed at the notion. He dug through a box of rawhide and horsehair bundles, hoping he could untwist his thoughts by twisting mecate reins or building a headstall. He felt near loco thinking about her.

Beetle woofed at him.

"It's all your fault."

The dog looked away.

"If you'd scared her off like you were supposed to, she wouldn't be here, and I wouldn't be feeling like I had hot coals in my chest."

The dog grinned. Nate snorted and headed outside.

Chapter 6

At the porch, Nate stomped his boots and side-stepped Beetle as the dog skedaddled through the front door. He shed his coat and hat, scrubbed his hands through his hair, and smoothed his mustache. Anticipation had him all bowed-up. Laughter snagged him like a dried thistle bush and pulled him to the kitchen, where his ma was taking cookies from the oven. Buck and Ara sat at the table drinking coffee, and Beetle lay at Ara's feet, the turncoat. As Nate stepped through the doorway, his ma laid a pan of gingersnaps atop a towel on the table. Then she knifed under each one to loosen it from the tray. His mouth watered like it had when he was a boy.

Caught in conversation, Ara looked up with a laughing smile that melted like a pale sunset the moment their eyes met. His chest tightened. She dropped her gaze and pushed at the braided twist of hair at her neck. Buck caught the sudden shift and cocked a ragged brow at Nate.

But his ma chattered on. "Take a seat, Nate. My brother is going to get most of them if you don't scoot to the table."

He grabbed a cup from the counter and straddled a high-back chair. Buck poured the coffee, and his ma flipped a cookie in the air with her knife. Nate snatched it and watched Ara's eyes and mouth go round with surprise. His ma flipped one to Buck, paused with a look at Ara, then flicked one her way. To her credit, Ara caught it and laughed aloud. The sound shimmied up Nate's back and down his arms like cool rainwater. Dunking his cookie in the coffee, he leaned over to take a bite.

Ara's brow pulled down. "Do you always dunk your cookies in your coffee?"

"Don't you?"

Buck choked trying to hold back a laugh.

"Ara, I must apologize for the men of this house. They've always dunked my gingersnaps. My dear Nathan taught them his atrocious manners, and living way out here in the high parks, I couldn't see any point in spoiling their fun."

Ara dunked her cookie, but it broke in half and sank.

"Like this." Nate repeated the move. "In and out." Then he popped the softened part in his mouth.

She mimicked him, grinned with her success, and puckered her lips around the bite.

His pulse bucked and ran. Wanting to run himself, he went to the parlor to check on the fire. By the time he returned, his uncle was gone and Ara was pouring hot water in the sink while his ma scraped the cookie sheet. He stopped at the doorway.

"Your family seems to enjoy one another." Ara set the coffee cups in soapy water then unbuttoned the cuffs of her blue dress and rolled up the sleeves.

His ma chuckled and shook her head. "A merry heart is medicine indeed. It's so much easier to laugh and joke and carry on. I can't imagine living any other way."

Ara pushed a rag inside the cups and nearly washed the color clean off.

His ma looked over her shoulder. "Is it different in your family?" The question came out quiet and gentle, in that way she had of getting at the truth.

Ara sighed. The blue fabric stretched across her back as she drew in a deep breath. "Yes, very. That's why I'm on my way to Leadville. Trying to start a happier life on my own."

Nate turned on his heel and made for the front door with Beetle close behind. He had to get outside, away from that tall, slender woman who wouldn't leave him be, whether he was drowning in her dark eyes or trying to drive her from his thoughts.

But it was hopeless. He was already roped and snubbed to the post.

⌒∞⌐

Ara had fallen easily into the rhythm of ranch life. She rose early to help Lilly with breakfast, listened without blushing as the men talked about the latest foaling, and decided once and for all that Nate hated her.

He kept darting off to complete some chore rather than remain in her company for any time at all. And he had every right to hate her. She had stowed away in his wagon, won over his dog, barged into his family, and was traipsing around in his mother's dress. Not that Ara had any choice over what she wore, but resentment was a bitter and familiar enemy. She didn't want to be the cause of anyone else's gall, but there wasn't one thing she could do about her situation other than set out on foot for Spruce City.

But that was no longer what she wanted.

She placed four dripping cups on the counter, and a heavy sigh escaped before she could stop it.

Lilly touched her arm. "Leave those, and come sit. I need more coffee."

The woman clearly ran this ranch just as Grandmother ran Uncle Victor's household, but with a far gentler touch. Ara dried her hands on her borrowed apron and took a seat at the table, cradling the cup Lilly had refilled.

"Tell me what troubles you." Lilly swirled her coffee, looking into its depths, leaving Ara free to speak without scrutiny.

Avoiding her suspicions about Nate, Ara chose the safer of two troublesome thoughts. "I gave my word to Mr. Lancaster that I would arrive before the holidays and take over his children's education. Yet here I am, snowbound far from the train and unable to even send a telegram. He must think I've gone back on our agreement."

Lilly's eyes shadowed with worry. "Is it so bad here?"

Remorse flooded Ara's heart and burned her cheeks, due retribution for a partial truth. "Oh, please, that is not what I meant. You have been nothing but kind to me."

Lilly reached across the table and patted her hand. "Don't fret, dear. The Lord tells us to let Him take care of the things we can't. And we can't do a thing about the weather."

Mutinous tears crowded Ara's throat. "This is all my own foolish fault for hiding in Nate's wagon. For not showing myself and begging him to take me to the hotel as soon as I knew he was a good man."

With motherly pride, Lilly leaned in. "And when did you know my Nate was a good man?"

Now it was Ara's turn to stare at her swirling coffee. She'd not even admitted the truth to herself. "As soon as I heard him sing."

Lilly sputtered and covered her mouth. Ara squirmed with embarrassment.

"It's a wonder his singing didn't send you running in the opposite direction." Lilly shook her head and her eyes crinkled shut with laughter. "You should hear Buck. He's worse. I don't know how Beetle stands it when they ride out after the mares. All that caterwauling."

"I did cover my ears, but his tune was less of a threat than the man following me."

The news stilled Lilly, and a sharp line formed between her brows. "Do you know who he was?"

"He's one of my uncle's henchmen, sent to drag me back to Chicago. Uncle Victor had his own ideas of whom I should marry, but I chose not to accommodate his business dealings."

Flushing with anger, Ara gripped her cup tighter. "That's why I hid in Nate's wagon." The surface of her coffee rippled. "I'll not be traded like chattel."

Chapter 7

Wind licked the mountain's summit, and snow danced up like white dust devils. After a month of alternating cold and snot-slick thaws, the weather's siege appeared to be over. Ara Taube might be on her way back to town. Out of Nate's sight and out of his life. And he'd go plum out of his mind longing for her. He leaped onto the porch and reached for the door, but it opened on its own, and he nearly stepped on his ma's boots. His eye ran the length of sheepskin coat and found Ara peeking over the collar. It still caught him off guard.

"Beg pardon." Habit shot his hand to his hat brim.

"No—it's altogether my fault." She clutched the scrap can with a smaller tin inside it and peered at him with her big brown eyes.

His insides turned to marmalade. "You huntin' the chickens?"

She nodded. "Lilly said they're in the back of the barn."

The gal had set her hand to every other household chore. Might as well see the coop. "Come on."

She followed him off the porch and along the sloppy path to the barn, where she plowed into him when he stopped at the doors. "Oh!" Her breath puffed out like a new heifer's.

He tipped his head back and squinted at her.

"I know," she said with a deep sigh. "I'm not to stare at the snow. But it's so beautiful, I can't help it."

Neither could he. He dragged his eyes from her perfect lips. "No smokestacks."

Curiosity lifted her brow. "You've been to Chicago?"

"Shipped some horses there. Rode along on the train." He unlatched the barn door and held it open for her. "I saw enough."

Curiosity gave way to judgment, and her brows dipped. "You make it sound like a horribly disgusting sight."

"Truth is—" The words caught in his teeth. It wasn't her fault he didn't take kindly to crowded streets and close-packed buildings.

She held out the small can. "Truth is you like it better here." Her voice dropped. "So do I."

Shocked by what he thought she'd whispered, he thumbed his hat up a notch and took the can. "You do?"

She walked inside and switched leads without a stumble. "Lilly said you can make a star-shaped cookie cutter out of that tin."

"I can."

She moved deeper into the barn. "The chickens back here?"

He led her to the back of the barn and held the wire gate open while she tossed in the scraps, then pulled it shut. "We open that wide door to the outside yard when it's not so cold."

Curling her fingers through the mesh, she watched the chickens scrabble. The top of her head came to his nose. He leaned toward her to catch a whiff of her hair. She noticed.

He jerked back.

"I won't bite." She tipped her chin toward the chickens. "But they might." With a wry smile, she left him standing by the coop holding an empty peach can and a bucketful of foolish.

⁘

The next storm frosted Ara's window with fernlike patterns and bound her to the house. She and Lilly did nothing but cook for the men, who did nothing but shovel snow and feed horses. Dreams of Leadville faded as if they belonged to someone else, and tallies in the back of her Bible marked off four-and-a-half weeks. She'd never been happier.

In the kitchen, Lilly punched down a creamy mound of bread dough, puffing yeasty goodness into the air. She folded two smooth loaves into baking pans, smeared butter on each top, and set them on the back of the stove. Then she wiped her hands on her apron and went to the small pantry off the kitchen while Ara peeled potatoes for dinner.

"I imagine it will be hard without your family this year at Christmastime."

Ara's mouth went dry with distasteful memories of Christmas in her uncle's mansion. Cold. Formal. Forced. Slicing back the tight skin, she peeled away her family's facade. "Not really."

Lilly returned with canned green beans, strawberry preserves, and a face full of curiosity. Ara accommodated her.

"I was as much a decoration in Uncle Victor's home as the towering tree he insisted upon each year. Something to flaunt when his associates came to parties. I abhorred them."

"His associates or the parties?"

"Both."

Lilly gathered her apron in hand and took hold of a jar, twisting against the tight seal.

"Grandmother saw to it that I was properly schooled and churched, but I learned at an early age that she resented me."

A choking noise fell from Lilly's lips, and she sloshed bean juice down her apron and onto the floor as the lid gave way. Ara reached for a towel.

"Lately these jars are a fight." Lilly turned aside and swiped her face with the back of her hand. "I do believe they're sealing tighter, or else my hands are getting older." She pulled a thin smile across her lips.

Ara stooped to mop up the water. "Let me help you."

For a moment, Nate's eyes looked out from beneath his mother's graying brow. A longing washed over the woman's face that shot an unnamed ache deep into Ara's chest.

Lilly gathered herself, set out a large skillet, and filled it with strips of salt pork. "We'll add onions and the beans. It's Buck's favorite." She checked the fire and situated the skillet. "What of your parents?"

Heat licked Ara's face like fire beneath the cast iron. Would she never be free of her past? Halving the peeled potatoes, she took a deep breath. "My mother died unwed in childbirth. She was Grandmother's only daughter, and I was hers."

Ara filled a kettle with water, added the potatoes, and waited for judgment to stab with a pointed remark or a disgusted *tsk*. Instead, a breathy "Oh my" followed her explanation. Pity was as distasteful to Ara as resentment. She moved the kettle to the stove and prepared for the onslaught.

Lilly sliced an onion into her skillet. The pork sizzled. "That explains how you ended up on the train to Leadville alone." Not a speck of disapproval seasoned the woman's words, as if Ara's background made no difference at all. Ara's brow relaxed and cooled, and condemnation drained from her heart like the water she poured off the green beans.

Chapter 8

By the time dawn blushed the sky, Nate was dressed and holed up in the barn, looking for peace in the familiar scent of horseflesh and hay. Lantern light haloed the stalls as he fed, and Coffee greeted him with a deep rumble.

"I see she's done tangled your spurs."

Buck's sleepy voice rolled down the alleyway, and Nate turned to see him leaning against the doors, daylight licking his boot heels. Nate grumbled a greeting.

"That kinda talk ain't gonna win her."

Nate flexed his grip on the pitchfork. "I don't know any other."

Buck ambled to the corn bin, scooped out a can, and gave it to the Clydes. "Sure you do. Just tell her how you feel."

Nate jammed the pitchfork into the ground. "What if she doesn't feel the same?"

An honest stare drove his uncle's point marrow-deep. "Would you be any worse off than you are now?"

Nate made for the door and tromped across the frozen mud to the chopping stump. The smooth ax handle in his hands and the snap of the splitting log helped ease the burn in his gut. And if that burn didn't let up soon, they'd have enough firewood for three winters with some to spare.

An hour and half a row later, a hearty mix of steak, potatoes, and coffee lured him to his seat at the table. Ara set out the serving dishes, and her arm brushed his shoulder when she drew back. He cut his ma a look to see if she'd noticed fire sparking on his sleeve, but she took her seat smug and satisfied as a milk-fed cat, holding her hands out for prayer. Ara's soft fingers slipped into his, and he bowed his head as Buck said grace. No calluses on Ara's hand. No cuts or rough edges. Could she survive on a horse ranch in the Rocky Mountains, or would she resent him for filling her life with hard work and worries?

A canyon stretched between holding her hand and asking for it.

"Nate, have you got a cookie cutter for me yet?" His ma's question startled him, and he dropped Ara's hand. Buck coughed and helped himself to the fried potatoes.

"Almost." Regretting the lie, Nate knifed a slab of beef and tried not to look guilty. He hadn't even started on it.

"Good. Christmas is only ten days away, and Ara and I have plenty of baking to do. Buck, have you seen any promising trees yet?"

"Saw a little bunch at the mountain's base when we hayed the mares."

"Good. I'd like to get our tree up early this year since I have help decorating." Her eyes sparkled like tinsel when she looked across the table at Ara. "You men won't be bothered."

Buck drooped his face like a hound pup. "Now Lilly, you know I was countin' on helpin' you put those doodads on the tree again."

"I'll remember that, little brother."

Nate concentrated on his beef, washing it down with hot coffee.

"Did you see the trees, Nate?"

He glanced at his ma and nodded, grateful for a full mouth.

"Good."

That was her third *good* in less than two minutes. Something was up.

She snagged Buck again. "And you're still working on the new crèche I asked for, aren't you?"

"Yes, ma'am. Got a fine piece o' willow and started Joseph last night."

"Will you have all the pieces finished before Christmas with all the other chores you have?"

Nate filled his mouth. There were hardly any chores at all other than shoveling snow and mucking out stalls. He shot Buck a look in time to see something pass between him and his ma.

"We can't have missing pieces in the crèche. It wouldn't be right." Without so much as a sidestep, she collared Nate. "Why don't you cut the tree today? Take Ara with you. It would do her good to get some fresh air, and we may have only one clear day before the next storm hits."

Ara's fork stopped in midair the same time as Nate's, and they both stared at the innocent-looking woman at the head of the table.

"I've got some old trousers I think will fit you just fine, Ara. We'll get you bundled up good, and I'll trust you to pick the best tree for the parlor. Can't be taller than Nate, though, to fit in the corner by the window." She gave Ara a winning smile and completely ignored her son.

Buck took great interest in buttering his bread and kept his head tucked. Nate couldn't see his mouth, but his whiskers twitched. That was a dead giveaway.

479

Chapter 9

The denims scuffed when Ara walked across the bedroom, and she giggled behind her hand. Grandmother would be scandalized. But the trousers didn't chafe as she'd expected, and already she was warmer in the wool shirt and belt that held everything together. The thick socks Lilly had given her weeks ago were now comfortable old friends, as was the sheepskin coat she wore almost daily.

After her initial embarrassment dissipated at breakfast, Ara found herself giddy with anticipation. She could not have planned a better outing. This time, Nate couldn't run off without her. And she would know for sure if he hated her or felt the same tug in his heart as she.

Or maybe he felt nothing at all.

The cold thought ushered in a more worrisome concern: she'd never ridden astride. If she fell off and broke her arm or leg, it would be even longer before she was fit to take the train to her promised employment. Guilt wagged a pointed finger at her as Ara wrapped Lilly's red scarf around her throat. Instead of riding out to find a tree for the parlor, she should be riding into Spruce City to send a telegram.

Boots stomped onto the porch, and she took one last look in the halltree glass. Beneath the wide-brimmed felt with her hair tucked up, she could pass for a boy. The door swung open, and Nate's presence consumed the close entryway and most of her breath. "You're ready."

She raised her chin to his typically abrupt statement. "Of course."

His eyes snapped with amusement, but he didn't laugh outright. Lucky for him, for this morning, dressed as she was and near as tall as he, she felt certain she could set him down.

"Come on, then."

Would he ever speak to her in more than three words? Warmth spread through her chest at the thought of one three-word phrase she wouldn't mind hearing.

Rose and another horse stood tethered to the front porch railing. Nate stopped next to the mare. "Grab the saddle horn with your left hand and the cantle with your right."

Stunned by the lengthy explanation, her eyes followed as he touched each part of the saddle.

"Then put your left foot in the stirrup and pull yourself up."

Gripping the horn that looked nothing like a horn, she did as he said. For once, her height proved a definite advantage. Rose danced sideways.

"Relax." Nate pulled her foot back until only the front rested on the stirrup. "Keep your heel down." He stepped around and repeated the process on the other side.

"Why?"

Blue eyes squinted up at her. "You want to get dragged?"

She gasped and gripped the horn with both hands.

"Relax," he said again but gentler. "Rose can feel your tension. The boot heel will keep your foot from slipping through the stirrup." He pulled the reins from the railing and looped them over Rose's head. "Hold these in your left hand. Don't pull back unless you want to stop."

Evidently, Nate Horne didn't mind talking about horses. Gathering his own reins, he mounted, leaned forward, and patted his horse's neck. "Badger will lead." A near smile tipped his mouth. "Do what I do." With that he turned toward a snowy peak across the valley.

Rose didn't follow well. Ara tried to relax, but the mare trotted to catch up, pounding Ara's teeth and body with each jolting step. At last she settled alongside Badger in a more relaxed gait. If Ara were a gambling woman, she would bet Nate was silently laughing.

⚬⚬⚬

Ara was no horsewoman, but she had promise. Nate imagined her riding the high parks with him, becoming confident enough to help drive the mares down. This was what he'd been missing—someone to be his partner other than Buck. And someone who was easy to talk to as long as he wasn't looking at her. As they cut across the open valley side by side, her dark eyes and perfect mouth didn't distract him. He huffed and shook his head. Half the morning she'd had him dishing up more words than he'd used in a month.

"Have you always lived here on the ranch?"

He slid her a look. She was taking in their surroundings and sat a little easier.

"Don't know anything else. Pa started with that sorrel stallion in the portrait over the fireplace. High Park King." He patted Badger's neck. "Direct descendant here."

She eyed his mount. "Shouldn't his name be Prince or Duke with King for a sire?"

Nate laughed. "Too sissified."

She looked straight at him and cocked one brow. "And King isn't?"

"Nope." He held back a grin trying to figure her next comment.

"What happened to your pa?"

Danged if she didn't get right at it. He swallowed a sharp pain in his throat and reined Badger around a gnarled cedar stump. "A horse fell over backward with him. Broke his neck."

She gasped and jerked on the reins, but Rose ignored the impulsive tug. "I'm so sorry."

Her comment was to be expected, though *sorry* didn't cover what he'd learned to live without the last twelve years. "I've been as long without him as I was with him." He reset his hat, squinted at the mountain. "Buck moved in after the accident. Helped Ma and me with the ranch and just stayed on. He's got a good head for horses."

As they neared the mountain, evergreens flaunted their heavy robes among the naked aspens. Any of a dozen young trees would suit the parlor. Nate pulled up.

Ara stretched her back and neck. "I'll probably hate you and Rose tomorrow."

Her comment jabbed a fearful dart, but he held his tongue, stepped off Badger, and dropped his reins to the ground. Ara threw her leg over then buckled beneath her own weight.

He reached for her arm. "Give yourself a minute to get your land legs. You'll be sore, but it'll wear off."

She grimaced and rubbed one thigh. "It's not that I don't believe you. It's just that I highly doubt it."

He laughed outright and impulsively reached for her hand. "Come on. You need to pick a tree."

Chapter 10

Ara's heart sang. Nate didn't hate her. His spontaneous grasp was as good a proof as anything, and nearly as perfect as the tree she chose.

After he felled the spruce, he tied off the bigger end and looped the rope round his saddle horn. Then he returned the hatchet to his saddlebag, loosed a tarp from behind his saddle, and spread it on a snowless patch away from the horses. "It's too cold to stay long, but we might as well eat sittin' as ridin'."

Ara knelt on her heels, her stomach threatening to consume itself. Nate dropped cross-legged in the opposite corner and unrolled the bundle between them. Sliced bread and roast and cookies made up the fare. She'd never tasted better.

Nate drank deeply from a canteen and passed it to her. The water was cold and sweet. "Thank you," she said, handing it back.

He smiled as if relieved she'd accepted his offer, twisted on the lid, and laid the canteen beside him. Then he pushed his hat up and rested his arms on his knees. "What do you think of this country?"

Disappointed that he wouldn't speak of something besides the scenery, she held in a sigh and scanned the horizon, admitting that it had no rival. "It's magnificent. I had no idea the Rocky Mountains were so breathtaking."

He rumbled a wordless response, apparently pleased that she appreciated the raw and rugged terrain as much as he did. Leaning back on her hands, she boldly stretched out her legs and squelched a vision of Grandmother coming down with the vapors. A blue swath spread above them, jays sassed from the near trees, and the horses nibbled at bare spots in the snow. Chancing a look at her companion, she found him as majestic as the land on which he lived—strong and tall and silent. Like the stand of dark pine on the mountain that braved harsh storms, he survived on his own, and she admired him for it. A sorrowful heat filled her chest. His loss was greater than hers, for he had known and loved the parent he lost. She had not.

"I didn't know my parents, but I can imagine the pain of losing a father you so admired."

He flinched ever so slightly, as if she'd touched a bruise, and fingered a

483

hole in the tarp. "Your uncle raised you?"

At last—a personal question. "With his mother, my grandmother."

He glanced up from beneath his hat brim, and his eyes flashed like the darting wing of a blue jay. "Why'd you leave?"

Ara chose her words carefully, not wanting to spoil the moment by speaking too intimately. "Uncle Victor arranged a business deal contingent upon my marriage to the other party. I refused."

He grunted and worked his jaw with obvious disapproval.

"I was running from his hireling when I dared to hide in your wagon." The confession brought his eyes to hers, and he held her gaze for a long silent moment. A question dangled in the air. He cleared his throat and fiddled with the tear, working it bigger with his finger. His nervousness sparked her own, and as he worried the tarp, an unseen thread tightened between them. She tucked her fingers beneath her legs to keep from slapping his hand from the growing tear.

He cleared his throat again and shot her a look. "Could you live here?" He frowned, and his hand jerked back, ripping the hole farther. "I mean, do you still have your heart set on going to Leadville and teaching that banker's young'uns?"

Breath froze in her lungs. Of course she could live here, but what did he mean? Stay on the ranch and help his mother or stay in Spruce City as a teacher? Or something else? Her heart began to pound, and she tucked her feet beside her and folded her hands in her lap. "I made a commitment to tutor Mr. Lancaster's children."

Nate smoothed his mustache and mumbled under his breath. She leaned toward him expectantly. "Excuse me?"

He slid her a quick look. "If you liked it well enough here on the ranch, I thought you might want to. . ." Again he mumbled and looked away.

She leaned closer, forcing him to face her, and tried to hear what he wasn't saying. "Might what?" If he had intentions toward her—and she hoped he did—he'd have to put them into words. She needed to know if he was looking for a ranch hand or a wife.

He huffed out a breath and looked her straight in the eye. She held his gaze, and her heart thrummed with anticipation. Yes, he was a man of few—hardly any—words, but three would do if strung together in the right order. Suddenly he jumped to his feet and towered over her, his hands working like billows. She stood as well, a spiny tingle ringing her neck and running down her arms on fiery feet. The heat in his eyes left no doubt. But instead of coming for her, he stooped and made quick work of the tarp, rolling it into a tight bundle, remains of their lunch and all.

"Sorry 'bout that." He pulled his hat down and strode to his horse where he retied the tarp behind his saddle and mounted. Badger danced in a circle, proving a horse does indeed sense its rider's distress.

Deeply embarrassed, Ara looped the reins over Rose's head and attempted her earlier success at mounting without assistance. But now she fumbled and could not pull herself and her heavy heart into the saddle.

Nate leaned from his saddle, grabbed her around the waist from behind, and hefted her up. She looked to catch his eye, but he turned away. The rope tightened on his saddle horn, and the beautiful blue spruce dragged behind them with a scolding swoosh as they rode wordlessly back to the ranch.

◈

Ara would never accept him after the dust-busting he'd just put her through. Hope had risen like mist in the morning, but Nate said something wrong or didn't say something right, and now that hope had burned off, leaving him dirt-dry and empty. From the corner of his eye he caught her stiff back and shoulders, that pert chin squared out over her hands. She was right. She'd hate him and Rose tomorrow. Him more than Rose.

Daylight was running the ridge by the time they reached the barn. Without a word, Ara jumped down, tied the reins to the rail, and politely thanked him for the ride and lunch. Then she walked away and left him standing with his heart in his hands and a tree tied to his horse.

485

Chapter 11

Ara made it to her room and managed to shut the door with a quiet tick without alerting Lilly. Throwing herself across the bed, she buried her face in the feather pillow and pounded her fists on the ticking. She wanted nothing more than to stay on the ranch with Nate. But he hadn't even professed affection, let alone love. She could have had that kind of marriage in Chicago.

And what of Mr. Lancaster's children awaiting their teacher? *Oh Lord, what am I to do?*

"Don't fret," Lilly had said. Ara growled into the pillow. How not to? Pushing herself up, she rubbed her face then went to the washstand. Tepid water stood in the pitcher, and she filled the basin and bathed her face and neck and hands. Then she changed out of the denims and put on Lilly's calico. She didn't even have her own clothes. The least she could do was wear her own worth.

Freshened, she drew her Bible from the nightstand and sat on the bed. The thin pages fell open to her favorite psalm, and she read the words aloud, as much from memory as sight. "'I have set the Lord always before me: because he is at my right hand, I shall not be moved.'" That's what she needed—to not be moved from her goal. But was tutoring in Leadville the Lord's goal for her? Had she answered Mr. Lancaster's ad simply to escape her uncle's dominance?

"Oh, Lord, have I made a mess of things?" She rubbed her temples and thought back over her path to the Hornes' ranch that seemed only a series of missteps. Had God been directing her? She looked again at the familiar scripture, and it soothed the ache, just as it had countless times when Grandmother blamed her for her mother's death. Ara truly believed she was never alone, but she longed for something more, something she feared she might never have. Closing her eyes, she whispered a prayer for guidance. If the storms cleared and the ground dried enough, perhaps Buck would drive her to the train.

Revived and encouraged, she returned her Bible to the nightstand and marched down the hall and into the parlor. Lilly held the tree, and Nate lay half hidden beneath its branches, tightening the screws of an iron tree stand.

"Ara, you outdid yourself. It's beautiful." Lilly's face shone, like the angel atop Uncle Victor's enormous tree in the great hall. "Tonight we will pop corn over the fire. I have cranberries saved in the root cellar, and when Nate finishes the star cutter, we can add sugar-dusted cookies."

Ara's brave plans melted like butter on warm bread. She could no more leave now than fly to the rafters, for she refused to dampen this generous woman's Christmas. Mr. Lancaster surely had other resources, a man in his position. And how much studying would two eager children accomplish anyway, so close to Christmas? The Leadville banker would simply have to wait.

That evening Ara strung fluffy corn and red cranberries and lost more blood from pricked fingers than she'd thought possible. Even Nate set aside his muted manners and joined the festivities. But Buck kept his distance in the corner, where he sat whittling a figurine, gathering the shavings to toss on the fire and twitching his whiskers every time she caught him watching her.

In spite of the tension with Nate, Ara had never known a Christmastime as warm with Grandmother and Uncle Victor. With a twang of sadness, she doubted they knew such a family hearth was possible.

∽⧉∾

The next morning, Nate's neck and shoulders cramped like a froze-up well pump. His belly felt full of prickly pear, and even his fingers itched. He sat on a stump at the barn, soaking up borrowed sunlight and making a set of short ties for Ara's hair. They'd be her Christmas gift if she didn't refuse 'em like she'd refused him.

"Didn't go so well?"

Nate's hands stilled, breaking his rhythm, and his heart dropped to his belly. His uncle read sign like he was tracking a six-toed lion. The man came up from behind, leaned against the wide door, and pulled a figurine and his knife from a pocket. Nate frowned and went back to twisting the red and gray hairs into a pattern. These heart-to-hearts were rubbin' a sore on his temperament.

After a few fumbles, his hands fell against his thighs, and he blew out a heavy breath. "I figured she knew. That look she gets when she takes in the land—I thought she'd like living here with me."

An extra-long piece slid from the willow. Nate tied off the hair, set it aside, and rubbed the back of his tight neck. Then he stood and kicked the stump he'd been sitting on.

"Don't spit the bit now, son. She's not gone yet."

Nate stashed his work and beat it outside, scratching at the stinging itch in his fingers. He couldn't reach the one in his heart.

Chapter 12

Anticipation hung in Ara's heart like diamond icicles, sparkling and pure. Cradled as they were on the breast of the mountain, glitter and glamour didn't fill the house. Instead, the special care given to selected recipes and homemade gifts graced this home. The scent of cider and cinnamon and cloves curtained the kitchen, and star-shaped cookies winked from red yarn on the popcorn-and cranberry-laced spruce.

She shrugged into the sheepskin coat and tucked the denims into her boot tops before making her way to the barn with the scrap can. Another snowfall had chased her out of the calico and into the borrowed britches.

Just inside the barn's wide door, she paused by a new wooden manger filled with fresh hay as if awaiting a heavenly guest. Bending to breathe in the grassy perfume, she closed her eyes and marveled at the simple pleasure. A scuffling step said Buck was near.

"It's an offering." He stopped beside her and fluffed the hay with his large, rough hands. "He came to stockmen, you know. Like us. And His ma made His bed in a barn."

Ara's heart warmed at Buck's uncharacteristic tenderness. "It's a wonderful gift. Exactly what the Christ child would need."

His thick brows rose with hope. "You really think so?"

"Of course. Warmth and shelter and love. The same things we all need. I'm sure He would have been most comfortable in this crib you've made."

A smile puffed out his whiskers, and Ara swallowed a laugh. Such pleasure in a modest gift made from what one had at hand.

Her gifts would be far less than modest, for she had little else but her efforts to give this generous family come Christmas Eve. If there were enough dried fruits in the larder, perhaps a stollen each? Her stomach fluttered at the idea of giving Nate a part of herself, even if only her labor. She longed to give him more.

At the barn, she tossed the kitchen scraps to the hens and watched them vie for the choicest bits. Once she'd stopped scraping and scratching over Leadville, peace had settled in her heart. Worry did not help clear the road or ward off the storms. Nor did it get her to the Spruce City depot. What a waste to miss all the joy of the season worrying about something over which she had no control.

Returning along the alleyway, she stopped to visit each mare and foal. Three had delivered beautiful, long-legged youngsters since she'd been at the ranch, and Ara delighted in the mother-and-child atmosphere that filled the barn.

A shadow suddenly darkened the doorway, and a man stood backlit against the sun. The breadth of his shoulders and the line of his hat brim gave him away. Her breath quickened. "Good morning." She smiled, hoping he would join her at the stable's half door to watch Coffee with her baby.

Nate came to stand beside her, smelling of wood smoke and leather. His gloved hands folded over the edge of the door as he regarded the dark brown mare and her foal. "Named him Bean."

Laughter burst out before she could stop it, and she covered her mouth. The tilt of his mustache said he'd intended the joke, and she admired his wry wit. "With those gangly legs, it's a wonder he can stand at all."

Nate huffed a brief laugh. She'd grown accustomed to his silent conversation. No wasted words, no foolish prattle. Just a deep and quiet presence. She would miss it.

He looked at her, and she listened with her eyes for what he was thinking and feeling. Her pulse thrummed with what she thought she saw in the way he held his mouth and the intensity of his blue gaze, but his words stilled the song.

"Ma wants greenery for the parlor."

She let out a deep breath. "Well then, we'd best be at it."

Following him into the deep snow toward a clump of trees, she spared herself some effort by stepping inside his large footprints.

"Take the small branches from the bottom." With a quick twist and snap, he jerked off the tender shoots and cradled them in his arm. Ara had no gloves to protect her from the prickly needles and sticky sap, but she bent beneath the spreading boughs and broke off what she could.

Watching Nate ahead of her, surrounded as they were by pillowy snow, she gave into a childish urge. Laying her few short branches in a neat pile, she formed a large snowball from stiffer, melting snow, stood up, and took aim. The missile hit him in the neck, and he stopped. Delighted yet terrified, she muffled a shout with icy fingers. He slowly faced her with heat in his eyes and a curl in his lip that she took for a playful threat. Or was it real? She turned and ran.

His first round hit her squarely in the back of the head, knocking a gasp from her lips. She ducked, but not before a second snowball pummeled her and then a third. Feeling as mature as Coffee's colt, she took cover behind a wide spruce and began amassing ammunition. During a brief lull in Nate's barrage, she counted eight snowballs in her cache. Snow crunched behind her, and she turned with a cry.

Like a hat-wearing grizzly, Nate lunged, knocking her into her carefully piled snowballs. The sound of his laughter set her heart free, and they tossed fistfuls of snow at each other until they fell together, exhausted by their battle. He elbowed himself up and leaned over her, his eyes simmering, his quick breath close and warm. And then he pressed his lips against hers.

Everything she'd ever wanted pulsed with the heartbeat of this mountain horseman. He drew slowly back and searched her face, his cheeks as red as a robin's breast. Then he offered his hands to help her stand. Unable to contain herself, she threw her arms around his jacketed waist and laid her head against his shoulder.

"You're shivering."

With delight. "I don't have my gloves."

He removed his. "Take mine."

She slid her fingers into one unmanageable leather casing. "They'll never work. You keep them."

"I'll get yours." He cupped her cheek with a hand, and she leaned into his warmth. "Wait here."

She nodded and shivered anew when he left her side and trudged off through the snow. Did he know where to look? Stepping forward, she raised her head to call after him, but a different gloved hand clamped across her mouth and nose, cutting off her voice and breath. She fought to free herself, but an arm circled her waist and threw her onto the snow where again her mouth was covered with a smooth doe-skin glove. Her muffled scream and clutching fingers drew a snarling leer across the man's face.

How had he found her? And where was his brown bowler?

Squirming beneath his weight, Ara sank her teeth into the fine leather. He jerked away with a curse. Ara filled her lungs with the burning cold of mountain air and split the sky with her scream.

Chapter 13

Nate's heart and footsteps froze. That was not a playful taunt. Terror cut through the forest beyond the ranch house, and Nate turned and charged down the path he'd just made. Coyotes? A cougar? What had drawn that blood-chilling cry from Ara's throat?

He shouldn't have left her, should have carried her to the house. His hands balled into stony fists as he crashed through the trees, jerking to a rough stop at the sight of a man holding Ara by the waist with a gun at her temple.

"Stop or she's done for," the man yelled.

Hurt her and you're bear bait.

Nate's breath cut sharp into his chest, and his arms flexed defiantly as he forced himself still. He ached to feel the rough's neck in his hands.

Yellow teeth winked beneath a mustached sneer as the man began walking backward, dragging Ara with him. She clawed at his hand.

"You'll not be takin' another step," her captor shouted.

He must be the man Ara had told them about, but how had he found her? A movement in the trees snatched Nate's eyes to the left.

"Don't be tryin' to fool me with that old trick." The scoundrel laughed and squeezed Ara up against himself with a cocky grin. "I know there ain't no one out here but the two o' ya."

He snickered again. "The lass thought she could fool me, too, but I saw her hidin' under the wagon. Took me awhile and a bit o' silver, but I found her, and her uncle will be repayin' me kindly when I bring her home."

Helplessness clutched Nate like an iron spring trap. He spread his open hands waist high to show they were empty. "Don't shoot."

"I won't if I don't have to, but if I do, the second bullet is for you." On the last word, he pointed the muzzle at Nate. Beetle leaped.

Sharp teeth pierced the thug's gun hand, and a cracking flash sent a bullet thudding into a tree. Ara broke away and fell to the snow, scrambling on her hands and knees.

Screaming and cursing, the man dropped the gun and pounded his other fist into Beetle's head. The dog didn't weaken but shook the man's hand as if to tear it from his body.

"Call him off! Call him off!"

Nate grabbed the gun and leveled it on the frantic fellow. "Down!" Both Beetle and the man dropped to the snow. Nate slapped his leg, and Beetle ran to him, human blood reddening his lip. Nate held his eye and aim on the weeping man and stooped to pet his dog. "Good boy, Beetle. You've earned your keep today."

The clearing snow that allowed the bully to reach the ranch also allowed Nate and Buck to haul him back to town trussed up on his horse. Ara insisted she ride along so she could wire Mr. Lancaster and check on her trunk.

At the depot she eyed the telegraph operator, recognizing him as the man who wouldn't let her inside on that blustery night so long ago. She wanted to kiss him for his stubbornness, but he was startled enough by her trousers. Instead, she described her trunk and asked if it had been left at the depot. He checked a list of unclaimed items then took her to a small storeroom. Relieved to find it stacked with other forgotten baggage, she drew an earnest promise from him that he would hold it a few days more. Then she dictated a brief apology to Mr. Lancaster regarding her formerly stranded state. She wished him well in finding another tutor, but pressing matters prevented her from taking employment with him.

Matters like her heart that pressed against her ribs every time a certain lanky horseman looked her way.

She paid for the telegram and walked the short distance to the jail where Nate and Buck were turning over their prisoner with a less than glowing report of his conduct.

That evening after supper, Ara pulled on the familiar coat and slipped out to the porch. Countless stars blazed from one horizon to the other—fuller, brighter than any she'd seen in the city. A deep longing surged through her to make those stars her own from this vantage point, and a sigh slipped out in a puff of white as she tugged the wool collar around her neck. Her future was less certain than it had been upon her arrival at the ranch six weeks ago: no employment in Leadville, and no idea of what she would do instead. But peace had settled within her. She was free, her own woman, and the Lord was with her.

Like an ill-timed intruder, the memory of Nate's fervent kiss sent shivers up her spine. He loved her. She was certain of it.

The familiar creak of the wide front door turned her head. Warm light silhouetted a man as he stepped outside. Ara hugged herself to keep her heart inside her chest, but her confidence dissipated in a frosty puff. Perhaps Nate had simply been caught up in the moment and yesterday's kiss meant nothing after all. The fine hairs on her arms prickled as he approached, and his warm breath at her ear loosed a deep yearning.

"Cold?"

Before she could answer, his strong arms enveloped her from behind, and he whispered her name against her hair. "When I came so close to losing you, I knew I couldn't let you go."

She closed her eyes and tipped her head back, wrapping his arms in her own.

"Marry me, Ara."

As her heart rose to accept, it quivered on a disappointing note. Would he never say he loved her? She turned in the circle of his arms, clinging desperately to her fragile belief that he did. Reaching up she smoothed his mustache then laid her hand on his chest, drawing strength from his steady heartbeat and resigning herself to his ways.

He looked out at the night, scanning the wide, sparkling band that stretched over the mountains. "Beetle knew it before I did, but he was right." His eyes returned to her, dark and solemn. "I love you, Arabella Taube."

Surprise, relief, and delight flooded her soul, and she threw her head back and laughed at those wonderful words. Pulling her closer, he caught her lips with his own. Her lips, her heart, and her life.

Epilogue

Ara tucked Lilly's note in her coat pocket and met Nate at the wagon for their run to Spruce City. Instead of handing her up, her scooped her into his arms and kissed her soundly before setting her on the bench and joining her there. She took a deep breath and gripped the seat. He may be a man of few words, but he knew perfectly well how to get his point across.

Beetle sat proudly in the wagon bed, and Rose pranced out of the yard as though confident of her errand—Ara's trunk, fabric for a wedding dress, and a preacher to do the honors. Nate wrapped his arm around her and tugged her closer, and Beetle bounded over the seat to plant himself beside her. Ara laughed aloud at Nate's scowl.

"I hear a war of words between you two."

Nate snorted. "He's too smart for his own good."

Ara gave the dog a quick hug. "Well, I'm certainly grateful for him. He saved my life and yours."

Another snort. "I had the gent where I wanted him."

Rolling her lips to squelch her laughter, she regarded her black-and-white bench mate. "You've never told me how Beetle got his name."

Nate's mustache rose on a crooked grin. "He was a sneaky thing as a pup. Waddle up behind you like a beetle without you knowin' he was there." Blue eyes studied her with a twinkle in their corners. "Quite the watchdog."

Beetle woofed and tilted his snout higher, and Rose flicked her ears at the laughter that rang in the chill morning air.

By midafternoon they were home, Ara's arms full of bundled fabric and ribbon as she stepped through the front door of the sprawling log house.

"Back here." Lilly called from her room—a room Ara had never entered. She stopped at the threshold, awed by the paintings. In one, a woman and child stood in a meadow, and in another a small dark-haired girl sat in a swing beneath a large tree. Ara's heart broke with sudden memories of hushed words and shadowed smiles. Swallowing an ache, she stepped into the room.

Lilly looked up from her treadle sewing machine and caught Ara's expression. "Her name was Emily. Such a delicate thing." She set aside her sewing. "These paintings are how I imagine she would have looked had she survived that first hard winter."

"I'm so sorry," Ara whispered.

Lilly pressed her palm to her heart. "We loved Emily for the time she was with us, and I love her still." She rose and went to her bedside table and picked up a small, fabric-covered box. "Like so many parents who have buried their children in this vast land, I've entrusted her to the Lord's care."

Ara set her purchases aside and shrugged out of the heavy coat. Lilly reached for her hand and wrapped Ara's fingers around the box. "This is for you. I can't wait for Christmas Eve."

Ara warmed beneath Lilly's smile and thought of the burgundy silk cord and brocade she'd bought to make a small reticule for this gracious woman.

"Please, open it."

Ara drew off the white satin ribbon and removed the lid. Two porcelain doves perched on a polished wooden base, so lifelike that their unheard cooing hung in the air. She lifted them from their velvet-lined nest and glanced up to see joy brimming in Lilly's eyes.

Ara's throat tightened. "They are exquisite."

"Nathaniel gave them to me on our wedding day." Again her fingers rubbed a spot above her heart, and a youthful memory warmed her eyes. "He said I was his fair dove."

"Oh, Lilly, this is too much—"

She shook her head, cutting off Ara's protest. "I have long asked the Lord to bring Nate a dove of his own. I just did not expect her to come in the back of the wagon."

Laughter eased Ara's discomfort and brought a light to Lilly's eyes. "You are that dove, Ara. I knew it the night he carried you in, wrapped in that old dirty tarp." Lilly swiped her cheeks with a quick hand. "I knew as soon as he told me your name."

Ara's breath caught. So accustomed to her German surname, she rarely if ever thought of its meaning. "Taube," she whispered. *"Dove."*

Lilly smiled and pulled Ara into her arms with a laughing sob. "The Lord brought you to us, Ara. He answered my prayers and brought my Nate a dove."

∞

On Christmas Eve's eve, Buck replaced the New Haven clock on the mantel with his hand-carved figures and arranged the pieces just so. Ara scattered cedar twigs and pinecones among them. When she finished, he pulled a handful of sweet grass hay from his pocket, gently lifted the sleeping figure, and filled the manger before returning the Babe to His bed. Ara linked her arm through Buck's and gave it a squeeze. "It's perfect. What a wonderful talent you have."

His whiskers puffed out, and his eyes twinkled. "That's not all I've got." From his shirt pocket he pulled a mistletoe sprig with red yarn tied round the end. Then he tacked it to the low beam between the parlor and the entryway and gave Ara a wink.

She laughed behind her hands and hurried to the kitchen. They would celebrate that night with wild turkey and stuffing, squash and beans, pies and cookies, and enough cider and stout coffee to serve all of Spruce City. And well they might, for on Christmas Eve after the service, Ara would wed Nathaniel Horne II.

⌒∾⌒

The next evening, the small church was alight with candles on the altar, the windowsills, and small tables against the walls. Pine boughs and red ribbons adorned the pews and perfumed the air with promise. Ara and Lilly stood at the back as Nate and Buck took their places in front, dwarfing the dear pastor. Ara smoothed her creamy satin dress marveling at the delicate doves Lilly had embroidered on each sleeve and the white fur muff the woman had pressed upon her.

With a catch in her heart, Ara gazed at the strapping cowboy who stood so straight and tall, like a mighty pine. Lilly touched her arm and placed a delicate kiss on her cheek. "Welcome to the family, Ara. The Lord continues to bless us."

Ara blinked away her tears. "Merry Christmas, Lilly."

At her cue, Ara stepped into the aisle and halted in surprise as the congregation rose and began singing "God Rest Ye Merry Gentlemen." Nate's face lit with delight, and he tilted his head back to join in on "tidings of comfort and joy." His may not have been the most perfect pitch, but his deep voice flooded Ara with exactly what the song declared—comfort and joy. As she gained the front of the sanctuary and stretched her hand toward the man who held her heart, Ara thrilled to know exactly what it felt like to fly on wings like a dove.

About the Author

Davalynn Spencer is the wife and mother of professional rodeo bullfighters. She writes Western romance and inspirational nonfiction and teaches writing at Pueblo Community College. She and her handsome cowboy have three children, four grandchildren, and live on Colorado's Front Range with a Queensland heeler named Blue. Find her at www.davalynnspencer.com.

The Yuletide Bride

by Michelle Ule

For Rachel Durham,
And the fine musicians of St. Mark Lutheran Church
Including
Lynn, David, Marianne, Lou, Helen,
and the Jubilate choir

Chapter 1

Fairhope, Nebraska, 1873

Ewan Murray's fingers shook so much, he had trouble tightening the tuning nut on his fiddle. After four long months, the moment he'd dreamed of beckoned. Surely she wouldn't be late to church.

He plucked the strings, winced at one out of tune, adjusted the instrument, and picked up the horsehair bow. When the front door opened, a breeze blew in the scent of ripening corn, and Ewan's heart began to hammer.

"As soon as the MacDougalls are seated, you can start," Reverend Cummings said. "We're pleased to have you and your violin back."

Ewan nodded, but he scarcely took in the words, so transfixed was he by the refined young woman coming down the aisle behind her burly father. With her auburn hair swept into a knot, his childhood playmate, Kate MacDougall, had grown into a woman.

Her eyes widened. He laughed to watch her bite back a delighted squeal. She'd seen him, too.

With bow poised over the strings, he waited as Kate, her older brother, Malcolm, and their parents filed into a second-row pew. Kate smoothed her blue silk skirt and lifted her face—and heart, he was sure of it—to him as he slid through the opening notes of "Amazing Grace."

Had he ever played with such emotion? Ewan's heart soared with joy and hope, God's grace bestowed upon the hundred church members, and for Kate.

He played only for her.

And God, of course!

Reverend Cummings raised an eyebrow at Ewan's breathless finish. Ewan took a seat in the first pew, acutely aware of Kate directly behind him. He struggled to concentrate, but eventually God's Word focused his thoughts and he spoke the Lord's Prayer with enthusiasm. The sermon, as always, engaged his mind and left him excited at what God had ordained for him.

And for Kate, too. He tossed a sly look over his shoulder.

She dimpled. He caught a whiff of lilac.

Duncan MacDougall cleared his throat. Ewan faced forward.

During the passing of the plate, Ewan played "Blest Be the Tie That Binds," lingering perhaps too long on the vibrato, but happiness swelled and he could scarce contain himself.

Until he looked across the aisle at Josiah Finch and his fingers faltered. Why was the son of the wealthiest man in the county casting eyes at his Kate?

He swayed to look in her direction. She batted her thick eyelashes and blushed.

So there, Josiah.

Reverend Cummings spoke the benediction, and Ewan launched into "Jesus, Lover of My Soul" to end the service. Perhaps he sped through it, but he needed to speak to Kate.

And also to Duncan MacDougall. Ewan gulped and thought of his mother's prayer: "I put this situation in your hands, Lord, come what may."

As the congregation filed out, Ewan rubbed down his instrument with his mother's old embroidered handkerchief and nestled both into the battered case.

"Will you play next week? Perhaps you and young Kate could perform a duet. We've missed your fine music this summer."

Ewan tugged on his coat, the last garment his mother had sewn, now a little tight with his nineteenth birthday. "I'll speak to Kate. It's sheer joy to play with her."

"You wear your heart on your sleeve, Ewan. Be careful."

He tucked the case under his arm and thanked the minister who had been so kind through the last difficult years. Reverend Cummings had buried his parents and given him a bed in his barn. He knew Ewan's circumstances, and Ewan trusted him.

Ewan put on his old summer hat and stepped onto the wide church porch to survey the area. Golden fields surrounded the churchyard, while on the wide lawn facing town, ladies spread a potluck luncheon across makeshift tables. Ewan ignored his grumbling stomach to search for his prize.

She'd put up a parasol while politely listening to Josiah Finch, but her attention flitted his way. Her proud mercantile-owner father stood behind, his satisfied hands tucked into his linen vest and a straw hat pushed back from his forehead.

"Ewan, it's good to see you again." Mrs. MacDougall carried a basket of heavenly scented biscuits. "Have you returned for good?"

"I hope so, ma'am." He took the basket and set it on the closest table. "Kate looks beautiful."

"She does." Mrs. MacDougall's voice lowered. "Josiah Finch who works for the bank in Clarkesville, has come calling. Duncan is pleased."

His stomach roiled. Ewan cleared his throat. "How does Kate feel about him?"

"It would be a good match."

Ewan's heart sank. She'd always been kind.

"But who can know a young woman's heart?" Mrs. MacDougall's dimple matched her daughter's as she glided away.

"Ewan!" Kate danced across the grass to grasp his free hand. "You've been gone so long. I've missed you. I've had no one to make music with."

An auburn curl had escaped her hairpins and dangled above her rounded shoulder. He tucked it behind her ear, nearly catching the lock on her sparkling earbob. "We'll have to remedy that." His voice sounded hoarse.

She leaned forward. "Are you back for good?"

"I hope so. Are you glad to see me?"

Kate glanced toward her father. "Absolutely. I've made three sweet new flutes. Call after the social and bring your fiddle; so much has changed this summer."

"I can see." His heart hammered and tongue twisted. It was safer to stay with simple answers.

She bit her full, pink lips. "Will you sit with me at supper? Josiah will probably join us, but you won't mind, will you?"

He could see Finch glowering at him. "I must speak with your father, first."

"Hurry. He's always hungry after the service."

Ewan took a deep breath and approached the Fairhope founder.

"You played well," MacDougall said. "Your parents would have been pleased."

"Thank you, sir. May I have a word with you in private?"

"Now?"

"If possible."

MacDougall indicated the plain wooden church topped with a bell. "We can speak on the other side of the building."

As far as the eye could see, a healthy crop of corn stretched golden and ripe under the clear blue sky. As the son of a farmer, Ewan knew the harvest would begin soon. "A good crop."

"A fine one. I assume you've come to work."

"Yes, sir."

"I'm sure we can find you a spot."

"Thank you, sir, and I'll take you up on that, but. . ." Ewan took a deep breath and tried to calm the nervous butterflies Mr. MacDougall always provoked. "I'd like to talk about Kate."

The older man beamed. "My girl is growing up. She's doing a fine job at the mercantile. Our little schoolhouse taught you well." MacDougall frowned. "Other than Malcolm, of course. But he'll come into his own when he runs the mercantile."

Ewan raised his eyebrows. "Malcolm will run the store?"

MacDougall scratched the back of his neck. "He just needs time to grow up. He'll drive a wagonload of goods to Sterling tomorrow. You remember how he loves horses."

"Yes."

"He could use a teamster. Perhaps you'd like to help him? It'll be overnight, but I'll pay you five dollars."

"I'd like the work."

"Good. Let's eat."

"I have another question."

MacDougall tapped his toes.

"I'd like to ask for Kate's hand."

The large man stared. "My Kate?"

Ewan removed his old hat and brushed the unruly dark curls off his brow. "I've loved her since I was a boy. I'm a man now and would like to wed her."

"Ewan, you've had a rough go of it, but you're just a grasshopper of a boy. You've no land, no prospects, no money. All you've got is your fiddle and a willing heart. It's not enough to court my daughter."

"We love each other, sir. You know we do. We've always planned to wed."

"Childhood fantasies, Ewan. Surely you can see how ridiculous this suggestion is? Josiah Finch is a much better prospect. How would you support my daughter?"

"I'll do anything. I'm a hard worker."

MacDougall frowned and stared at the ground. "I can't do it, Ewan. You can't live on love. Unless you can support my girl, I'd be a poor father to agree."

Ewan clenched and unclenched his hands but kept his voice steady. "What would it take, sir? How can I prove myself?"

Behind them, the scratchy sound of insects in the corn caught Ewan's ear. A soaring red hawk called from above and came to rest on the top of the church. Enormous piles of white clouds built across the horizon. Ewan waited, praying for God to give him the desire of his heart.

MacDougall sighed in a great gust. "I mark your words, Ewan. I knew your family, good people. I've always been sorry for your loss. But unless you can earn seventy dollars by Kate's Christmas birthday, I cannot agree to a match."

"Seventy dollars?" Ewan had never earned so much in all his fiddling days. He barely had fifteen dollars to his name, and it needed to last the winter. To suggest a lesser amount, however, would insult Kate and worsen his chances. He swallowed across an enormous lump in his throat. "It's a deal. Seventy dollars and Kate will be my yuletide bride."

The older man winced. "I'm sorry it has to be this way."

Ewan put out his hand. MacDougall shook it.

"Know this, Ewan," MacDougall said as they walked to the tables. "Josiah Finch has already asked."

Chapter 2

Kate tried to be patient, she really did, but she hadn't spent any time with Ewan since he'd finished the June planting and left to find work. She could hardly wait to play her flute and accompany him on his fiddle. It had been hard to sit still in church, she so itched to join him. Perhaps Reverend Cummings would let her sing next week with Ewan. Without Ewan's music, the long summer had been empty and quiet.

She paced along the edge of the grass, watching Ewan and her father. What could they be discussing to take so long? Josiah could swoop in and spirit her away if Ewan didn't hurry.

"Malcolm," she whispered. Her brawny older brother always smelled of his prized horses. "Go distract Josiah."

He grimaced. "What can I talk to him about?"

"Tell him about your team."

"He doesn't want to talk to your brother, but I'll try."

Kate closed her parasol and thrust it at him. "Take this with you and tell him it needs to be tweaked. He loves to pretend he can fix things."

With a grunt, Malcolm strolled to the well-dressed young man loitering at the lemonade table. Josiah eagerly snatched the parasol to examine it while her brother stood motionless and awkward, hands in his pockets. Kate glanced back to the church where Ewan and her father shook hands.

Kate took a deep breath and felt the pinch of the new stays. Her blue silk dress belled out in the breeze, and the scent of ripening corn filled the air. The busiest time of year was coming. Would Ewan have time to play?

Ewan carried his battered fiddle case and rubbed his chin with his right index finger as he walked across the grass. Ewan's hands were always in motion, practically a blur when he played a fast tune.

He set down the case, propped his hat on top, and took her hands. She rubbed his finger calluses even as she felt an unexpected jolt at his touch. "Why so sober? Can my father not help you?"

"In this one, no." His sky-blue eyes looked troubled, his black brows tense. Ewan's shoulders had broadened during the summer though he still stood only several inches taller than Kate. His confident merriment usually buoyed her, but today he seemed tentative.

"What is it? Do you need a place to stay?"

He shook his head. "Reverend Cummings has given me the extra room in his barn. It's a good place for now. But not for the future." Ewan wrinkled his tanned forehead.

"Mama's made fried chicken and her featherlight biscuits. I churned the sweet butter myself. Let's fill our plates and you can tell me about your summer. Where have you been?"

"I must speak with you alone."

She dimpled. "Here I am. Speak away."

Ewan swallowed and lowered his rich tenor voice. "Haven't we always made beautiful music together?"

"Yes." Mirth bubbled.

"Would you like to do it forever? With me?"

"Of course."

His mouth dropped open. "Then you'll do it? Just like that?"

"Play music with you? Of course. I've missed you so much. I made three new reed flutes this summer, but it wasn't the same without you here."

Ewan squeezed her hands. "No. I mean, yes. But that's not what I'm asking."

She scrutinized him. His thick black hair was rough with curls, but he gazed with such intensity and, could it be, longing? Josiah stared at her the same way, as if he would swallow her whole. She always slipped away from him, uncomfortable. But this was Ewan with whom she'd laughed, sang, and fluted so many happy days.

She caught her breath at a new thought.

Ewan took a matching breath.

Kate gripped his hands as the idea surged through to her soul. "Are you asking me to wed you?"

His hands shook, and he nodded.

She leaned toward him. "Were you discussing marriage with Papa?"

He nodded again. She'd never known Ewan to lose his tongue.

Excitement poured through Kate. If she married Ewan, dear, darling Ewan, they could have a home of their own filled with music. Ewan could fiddle every night and she would accompany him. Music would surround her all day long. The children they could produce, musicians all!

"Oh, Ewan," she sighed. "Most definitely, yes."

"It's time for the potluck, Kate." Josiah's deep voice, a bass, broke into their conversation. "I'll escort you."

Dazed, she faced him. "What?"

507

"Sunday dinner." Josiah pressed his lips together in disapproval. "You played well today, Ewan."

"Thank you. Kate is dining with me."

"With me."

Kate cut them off. "With both of you. Shall we get our plates?"

Her heart beat so fast, Kate thought she would faint. She led the two men—suitors, she realized—to the potluck line. Her father waited with arms crossed.

"Papa, do you know?"

"We'll discuss this later. Reverend Cummings is about to pray."

As it did no good to antagonize Josiah or his family, Kate followed him to a seat with Ewan right behind. "We need three seats together, Josiah."

Josiah waved his free hand. "Ewan can sit anywhere."

"I'll bring a chair from another table." Ewan set down his plate and retrieved it. Josiah scowled until he realized how close Kate needed to sit to him.

As she nestled between the two handsome men, her toes danced in her slippers. She yearned to hear Ewan's stories, listen to his fiddle, and dream about the future. Stories about the summer would do for now. She'd spent so much time listening to Josiah talk about his activities, he could listen to Ewan's adventures with her. "Tell me where you've been," Kate asked at the same moment Josiah demanded, "Why did you come back?"

Ewan's eyes twinkled at Kate. "I've played for summer dances and church festivals in four counties. One of the camp meetings featured a choir of plump women who loved the fiddle. They sounded splendid and full voiced on 'My Faith Looks Up to Thee.' I kept looking to the sky myself, thinking Jesus must have been smiling down."

Josiah tried again. "What will you do in Fairhope?"

"I'm looking for work. Do you have a job I could do?"

"What can a fiddler do other than play his toy?"

Ewan stuck out his chin. "I have a teaching certificate. I'm good at ciphering. I can work in a store, help with the harvest. Tomorrow I'm teaming with Malcolm to haul a wagonload of goods to Sterling."

"You are?" Kate squeaked. "Malcolm will be so pleased."

Josiah relaxed. "Is that what you were discussing with Mr. MacDougall?"

"Yes."

The stilted conversation continued. Josiah expounded on issues at the small bank where he worked in Clarkesville, the county seat, and his travels around the county "drumming up" business.

"So you don't live in Fairhope?" Ewan asked.

"I ride the train home on weekends to worship in this fine church." He paused. "And to see Kate, of course."

She blushed. He'd begun paying attention to her only since her schooling ended in June, and had shown a marked interest when she put up her hair.

"I think you'd enjoy living in Clarkesville, Kate."

Kate frowned. She hated it when Josiah acted pompous. "I've never given Clarkesville any thought. I love Fairhope. I know my neighbors here."

"But you're so friendly and welcoming. I'm sure you'd be popular wherever you lived."

Kate didn't know how to answer. She touched Ewan's arm and stood. "Could we sing? Get your fiddle and we'll start a sing-along."

Ewan retrieved his instrument. He rosined the bow and quietly began a favorite: "In the Sweet By and By."

"There's a land that is fairer than day," Kate sang.

The folks still sitting under the trees sang in four-part harmony. Ewan's fiddle led the melody, and they sang for half an hour.

Kate swayed with the tunes. When she met Ewan's gaze, happiness coursed through her. Surely helping Ewan lead worship is what God had created her to do.

They packed up the baskets and their possessions as the afternoon grew late. First Josiah and then Ewan pressed her hand, promising to call later. Kate sighed as her family carried baskets full of leftovers, plates, cups, and cutlery down the wide dirt road to their home behind the mercantile.

"Ewan said he spoke with you, Papa. I'm so happy."

"What did he say?" Mama asked.

Papa shifted the basket from one hand to the other. "He'll ride teamster with Malcolm tomorrow. I'm paying him five dollars for the trip."

"Great," Malcolm said.

Kate set her jaw. "He asked for my hand, Papa. I told him yes."

Mama gasped.

Kate turned toward her. "You know I've always cared for Ewan."

She nodded.

Papa's brows drew together. "There's a catch, Kate. He cannot marry you unless he's earned seventy dollars by your eighteenth birthday."

Kate went still. So much money! No wonder he'd seemed worried. She drew herself up tall. "I have confidence in my Ewan. He'll earn the money, and I'll be a Christmas bride. I know it."

Papa raised his eyebrows. "We'll find out, won't we?"

Chapter 3

Ewan met Malcolm behind the MacDougall Mercantile early the next morning. They filled his wagon with a pickle barrel, crates of dry goods, bags of flour, and other staples. Malcolm retrieved his well-brushed horses, harnessed them to the wagon, and they set off on the long dusty road to Sterling.

Already, farmers worked their fields, preparing for the harvest. A torrent of jackrabbits scattered as they passed. Calling birds sailed on the wing as the sun rose slowly in the eastern sky. Ewan savored the cool, fresh scent of a September morning.

"You still got your mare?" Malcolm asked.

"Yep. Tess is cropping grass in the Reverend's back forty today. We traveled a far distance this summer."

"I remember when your pa got that horse. I never saw one so beautiful in my life. You let me know if you ever want to sell her."

His throat thickened when he thought of his parents now two years gone. "She's a beauty all right."

Malcolm nodded. "I'd rather spend all day with a horse than sit in the mercantile. If my pa has his way, I'll go crazy."

Ewan watched his old friend chew on a piece of fresh straw. "What's the problem?"

"I never did learn how to cipher. The numbers swim in front of me and I get lost. Horses are better. They don't care if you can add or subtract."

"Adding and subtracting is the problem?"

He shrugged. "I can do it if I think long enough. But I don't well remember how to multiply and divide. You remember how Mr. Bellows used to hit me with a cane?"

"Yes." Ewan often felt the slash of the same cane for not sitting still in class. "What if I helped you?"

Malcolm sighed. "No one can help me. I'm stupid."

"Once you understand the concept and memorize the multiplication tables, it starts to make sense. The trick is to get into the rhythm. Try it.

One times one is. . ."

He waited.

Malcolm shrugged.

"One," Ewan said. "One times two is?"

"Two?"

"Exactly." Ewan sang through the times tables in time to the harness jingle. "Two times two is four; two times three is six; two times four is eight."

They worked on memorizing the multiplication tables through twelve. Ewan beat on the wagon, sang to the rhythm, called out the numbers, and encouraged his friend. The *clip-clop* of the horses' hooves provided a steady beat.

"It can't be that simple," Malcolm said.

"I'll work with you. You're intelligent. We can do this together."

Halfway to Sterling they stopped to water the horses. Ewan collected pebbles. While they ate their dinner, he demonstrated multiplication with piles of small stones. "Two times three is taking two piles of three stones and putting them together. How many do you have?"

Malcolm ran his tongue around the inside of his mouth, pondering. "Six?"

"Perfect."

While Ewan bit into his slab of spiced beef and thick, chewy bread, Malcolm arranged the stones into three piles of four each. "Twelve?"

Ewan nodded. "Try five times six."

The young man's brow furrowed as he moved the stones around. Ewan shook his head. Twenty years old and no one had ever explained how arithmetic worked. When Malcolm shouted and grinned, Ewan knew he had grasped the concept—probably for the first time.

"Five times five is twenty-five; five times six is thirty. I just have to memorize the answers and I know?" The wonder in Malcolm's voice troubled Ewan.

"Exactly. We'll practice all the way to Sterling. I bet you'll have it down by the time we get there."

He did.

"How come no one ever explained it like this before?" Malcolm asked as they put up the sweaty horses that night at a livery stable.

Ewan shrugged. "You keep singing the song and memorizing the numbers. The next time we team together, we'll work on division."

"Wouldn't that be something?" Malcom said. "But I still don't want to leave the horses. I love them."

Ewan felt the same way about his fiddle.

⌒⌒

"I know Ewan can earn the money," Kate said. "He's always been clever and resourceful."

"Seventy dollars is a large sum," Mama said. "How much does he earn fiddling?"

Kate didn't know, and she'd hardly had time to talk to Ewan alone since his stuttered proposal on Sunday. "He can work the harvest and find other odd jobs. People always need help."

They sat together quietly while Kate chewed on her lip and tried to think what Ewan could do.

Fairhope was a small town. The mercantile was the biggest enterprise, and most folks lived on farms. Ewan couldn't be the minister. He had received a primary teaching certificate last fall, but dedicated spinster Doris Hall schoolmarmed the grammar school east of town near the bend in the stream. Mr. Storner taught the secondary school in town.

"Maybe he could work at the train station?"

Her mother frowned. "Those jobs are taken."

"I'll give him my job," Kate declared.

"Your father wouldn't agree," Mama said. "You know he wants Ewan to demonstrate he can provide for you without our help."

Kate threw herself onto the soft velvet settee. "What am I going to do? How can I help him? Don't you think he's the perfect man for me?"

Mama sat beside her. "I loved his mother as my dearest friend. I know he's a fine young man. If you're adult enough to wed, Kate, you need to think about what it means to be a helpmeet."

She pondered the word *helpmeet*. Obviously the Bible passage meant a wife should assist her husband. How could she help him? What could she do to encourage Ewan to work hard for them both?

Kate savored the thrilling thought he was working for her. It was like Jacob in the Bible. Except, he wound up with two brides. Kate chuckled. That wouldn't happen. Ewan only looked at Kate; he never even saw other girls.

"Could I make my wedding dress? It would cheer him if he knew I expected to wear the dress at Christmastime."

"What a lovely gesture," Mama said. "There's fabric in your grandmother's old trunk. Let's see if it's suitable."

Kate pulled the trunk from the dark corner of the attic and set it on the floor of her bedroom.

"After your grandmother died, your father couldn't bear to remember his heritage. It made him feel too sad."

"Will Papa mind?"

"No. He's always meant you to have *Guiddame's* prize possessions."

Kate lifted the lid. Her father's mother loved the dried lavender tucked inside.

"Such fine cloth." Mama unfolded the red-and-green plaid with lines of royal blue. "Perfect for Christmas."

Kate lifted the soft wool to her shoulders. "There's plenty for a dress."

"Your Guiddame would be pleased you like it."

"What have we here?" Papa stood in the doorway.

"Kate needs a new dress for winter, and I remembered this fabric."

"The MacDougall tartan," he said. "I once had a cap made of the plaid."

"Do you mind, Papa?"

He shook his head. "Let's see what else is in the trunk." He pulled out an old leather volume. "The family Bible." Turning the musty pages, he paused at the names written in dark ink. "Her death was the last item on the list. Your birth the one before." He turned the book for Kate to see.

"Why is it in the attic instead of in the parlor where we can read it?"

He shrugged. "It should come out. Enough time has gone by I don't miss her with such a sharp ache. She'd be on me for hiding away this Bible."

Kate knelt beside her mother and reached into the chest for a large deer-skin bag. "What's this?"

She struggled to contain the bundle of old leather and wooden sticks as she lifted it out. She turned to her father, who barked a bitter laugh. "I'd think you, of all people, would recognize a musical instrument. Bagpipes."

She peered closer and saw round holes in one of the sticks. Turning the bundle over, four wooden tubes jutted out the back of what appeared to be a flattened sack covered in the MacDougall plaid. One stick had small holes on the capped end, and the other three tubes had knobby endings.

"You must blow in these holes, but what is this sack the sticks are attached to?"

He pursed his lips in distaste. "Bellows. You blow into the mouthpiece, place the bag under your arm, and manage the sound by squeezing out the air." He pointed to the finger-holed stick. "You play the notes there on the chanter. The longer tubes on top are drones. They make low bass and tenor notes under your melody."

Papa helped her hold all the awkward pieces in place.

The short mouthpiece smelled musty and reedy, but when she blew into it, the bag expanded under her arm. She blew and blew to fill the bag until her lungs ached and she felt dizzy. A squawk sounded, and Mama's hands flew to her cheeks.

Papa laughed. "After all this time, you'll need to make new reeds if you want to get any sort of melody. I give them to you, Kate. The pipes are your heritage, but I will not listen to such caterwauling in my house. Take them away!"

Kate clasped the jumbled instrument to her chest. "Thank you."

He laughed again. "We'll see if the neighbors feel the same."

Chapter 4

Ewan winced as Kate blew into the bagpipes. The scolding, harsh sound grated on him as she wavered the tone, trying to find a clear note.

She spit out the mouthpiece in a gasp. "Don't you love it?"

"If you must make music with multiple tubes, I like the panpipes. How about a fiddle and flute duet?"

Kate set down the awkward bundle. "I'll get one."

Ewan picked up the "instrument" to examine. He observed dings and dents in the wooden tubes, and was that blood on the cloth? With a little care and perhaps a new cover, it would look presentable in public, but the noise! He shuddered. His musician's ear could be both a godsend and a curse when it came to musical notes.

He tugged at the chanter and it came apart, exposing an old reed. Ewan blew, amazed it still produced a sound. He popped out the old one to study better. Surely a new reed would help the tone. In the meantime, without a reed, Kate couldn't make any noise. He grinned.

Sitting across from him, Malcolm laughed. "Thanks."

Kate sashayed into the parlor with the cane flutes she and Malcolm had constructed during the summer. Ewan knew this instrument and blew a tentative breath into the largest one. Ah, a much more satisfying sound.

The reed flutes always reminded him of his mother. She'd escort them to the creek near the school when they were children, carrying a thick knife. She'd cut the cane, whittle out holes, and they'd make music on the riverbank. Kate took to it the best, though Malcolm wasn't bad. Ewan's favorite childhood memories were of sunny days along the chattering creek piping the flutes.

"Let's play your mother's song." Kate blew the opening notes of "The Bonnie Blue Bells of Scotland." Ewan joined in, modulating his tone to ensure the notes were in tune.

Mrs. MacDougall clapped. "It reminds me of Bonnie to hear her song. You have her gift, Ewan, and it's a pleasure to hear."

"And me?" Kate asked.

"You've been well taught." Her lips lifted in an indulgent smile.

Kate made a face and laughed with her merry mother.

Malcolm closed his eyes. "Play the number song."

Ewan tried a few notes to find the right pitch and then piped quietly while Malcolm ran through the multiplication tables.

MacDougall entered the parlor and frowned. "What's this children's song?"

"Ewan taught me to multiply."

His father challenged him on several. Malcolm got them right.

"Do you understand what it means?" MacDougall asked.

Malcolm reached for a collection of his mother's silk embroidery threads. "I'll show you. Two times two is four." He deftly moved the floss hanks into groups as he sang the multiplication tables to ten.

"So, if I have a box three feet by two feet by one foot deep, what's the volume?" His father asked.

"Take it by steps," Ewan said. "First, three times two; then the answer times one. You can figure it, Malcolm."

Mrs. MacDougall blinked rapidly.

"Three times two is six. Six times one is six. The answer is six?"

Ewan played a piper's congratulations tune.

MacDougall stared at his son. "I don't believe it. Come to the store tomorrow and I'll put you to work."

Malcolm shook his head. "Got to get the horses shod. Sorry."

MacDougall stomped out of the room, but his wife approached Ewan. "How?"

"He needed encouragement. I don't think he'd ever grasped the concept before. He's on his way."

"But I still don't want to work in the mercantile." Malcolm rose and went upstairs.

Kate tucked her hand into Ewan's elbow as she walked him to the porch. "I'm so proud of you. Thank you for helping Malcolm."

"He'll do fine." Ewan leaned closer to her, sighing at her lilac scent, so like his mother's.

"What will you do tomorrow?"

"I'll be harvesting the Reverend's crop this week. That'll pay for my room and board," he paused, "until we're married, of course. Once I'm finished there, I'll seek work at the other farms."

"I ask everyone who comes into the store if they need a worker. I'll help you."

Ewan jerked. "What type of work?"

"Anything. Right?"

He nodded. "I suppose so."

Kate inspected her slippers peeping from beneath her dark skirt. "I've found fabric to make a dress."

"You're a good seamstress."

"I know about my father's arrangement with you, and I know you can do it. I'll support you any way I can. I'm sewing a wedding dress."

Her confidence caught him by surprise. "You have such faith in me?"

She glanced toward the lighted window and dared a kiss to his cheek. "God brought us together. He'll see us to the wedding."

Ewan pressed her hand to his chest.

"Good night, Ewan," Mr. MacDougall called.

He kissed Kate's hand and jumped off the porch into a night studded with approving stars. He danced all the way to Reverend Cummings's hay-filled barn.

Kate spent her afternoons working at her father's mercantile. She loved cutting fabric for the farm wives and watching the shy grins on children's faces when she slipped them a piece of penny candy.

When the teamster from Clarkesville stopped by with the weekly order, Kate compared the bill of lading to their ledger list. She checked off each item as she unpacked it from the crate and signed her name at the bottom. Kate swallowed when she saw the freight charges marked "C.O.D." Her father was out of the store. "How do I pay this?"

The gruff bearded man pointed to the letters. "Cash on Delivery. You pay me cash from the till, and I'll write you a receipt."

She opened the lock box, counted out the bills, and waited for the teamster to sign. He tipped his hat and left the store.

Kate tapped her fingers on the receipt. Something wasn't right.

The bell above the door rang, and a sweaty Ewan entered. "Hello, pretty girl. Have you got a drink for a thirsty man?"

He smelled of summer crops and hard work; his sunburned face shone. She reached for a tin cup under the counter. "The pump is outside."

When he returned, she showed him the bill. "Does this look correct to you?"

Ewan examined the numbers. His eyebrows rose, and he pointed to the freight charges. "Does it really cost this much?"

"That's what he said."

"You're paying a high percentage versus the cost of the items. It would be more economical to hire Malcolm to haul your freight."

"He'd like that," Kate said.

Ewan rubbed his chin. "This is the usual cost?"

Kate shrugged. "My father always pays this bill." She collected the papers and stuck them into the ledger. "He'll check them. I have another problem."

She pulled out the bagpipes from a basket under the counter. "I've been trying, but they won't make a sound."

He nodded.

"I asked Josiah to look at them last night. He doesn't know anything about musical instruments and didn't want to help me. Do you know why they would have stopped playing?"

Ewan's hands went into his pockets. "What have you done different?"

"Nothing. Watch."

She gathered the three drones and leaned them against her left shoulder, slipping the air bag under her arm. She pointed the finger-holed stick, the chanter, toward the ground and adjusted the mouthpiece. She blew and the bag expanded but produced only an empty whoosh.

Kate moved her fingers over the holes. No sound, only air rushing between her fingers. If she pushed her elbow hard against the bag, the air came out faster, but the drones only emitted a low groan, hardly music and unaffected by her fingering.

"At least it doesn't hurt anyone's ears now."

The way he said it, a sort of flippant remark, made Kate suspicious. She pushed out the air from the bag and stared at him. "What did you do to my bagpipes?"

"Do you have a piece of twine? Let me help you."

She set the poor bagpipes on the counter and retrieved a spool of hemp twine from the shelf. Ewan arranged the instrument like a skeleton on the counter, each part pointing in the correct direction. He tied the three drone sticks together, "so they'll stop flopping around," and then tugged apart the chanter.

Kate gasped. "Did you break it?"

He pulled a birch bark box from his pocket. "Here's your problem. You need a new reed."

She examined the roughly shaped bagpipe reed. No longer than her little finger, the reed part looked like two tiny fans glued together on the side with a narrow slit at the top. A piece of thread tied them together at the base of the fan and around an inch-long narrow tube.

Ewan plucked it from her hand and blew into it, producing an airy duck quack. "It works. I copied the old reed I found inside the chanter the other night. I could see you needed a new one."

He put the pieces back together. "Try it now."

He set the instrument into her arms. Tied together, the three drones no longer flopped out of control. Kate blew into the mouthpiece to fill the bag, and a wailing squeal sounded.

Delighted, Kate ran her fingers up and down the holes. The noise screeched like a wild cat, and Ewan clapped his hands on his ears. "Enough!"

She let the mouthpiece drop from her mouth. "You don't like the sound?"

"No. Doesn't it hurt your ears?"

Her thick braids wound around her ears muffled the sound. Kate recognized it wasn't a pleasing tone, but she'd only blown the instrument a couple of times. What did Ewan expect?

"Wouldn't you rather play your flutes?"

Kate considered him. Ewan's fine ear enabled him to tune her reed flutes with tiny knife cuts. She loved the light happy sound of the small flutes, but these bagpipes gave her a feeling of power. The loud, uncontrolled noise, the heaving bellows, the floppy sticks, made for a physical experience. She loved the bagpipes, even if she couldn't play them yet.

"I adore my flutes," Kate said. "But I want to master the bagpipes. These are part of my heritage."

Ewan grimaced. "You have until Christmas, then, if you want to marry me. I can't live with a noisemaker that roars so loud and makes my ears hurt."

Kate laughed. "You must be joking."

Ewan shuddered. "I'm not sure."

Chapter 5

After he finished harvesting Reverend Cummings's fields, Ewan moved across the countryside: cutting, threshing, stacking, and stowing other farmers' crops into barns. Some days he teamed with Malcolm to tote loads to Clarkesville or Sterling for sale, other days he manned a pitchfork and spread straw. His strong arms grew more muscular and brown in the golden late summer. He slept well at night, exhausted from the labor.

Each morning, he woke before the sun to read the family Bible and play hymns on his fiddle. The Word of God fired his brain; the music of God lubricated his spirit. By the time he reached the worksites, Ewan felt cheerful and strong, ready to take on the day with gusto.

Sundays were spent as a Sabbath rest, playing his fiddle in church, visiting with Kate and usually the officious Josiah, eating a hardy meal with the MacDougalls. His money stash was growing, but not fast enough.

On Saturday nights, even though he hated to leave Josiah visiting Kate, Ewan took to riding far into the county and playing at local harvest dances. He didn't get paid much, but every bit counted. Ewan even contemplated putting his savings into Josiah's bank. Compounding interest would help, too.

Most of Fairhope had finished the harvest by the end of October, and on the final Saturday night, Ewan stayed in town. He'd be fiddling for the local dance, and while he was part of the entertainment and getting paid to play, he'd still get to see Kate in her finery. Maybe he could even find an old-timer to take the fiddle and he could steal a dance himself.

A big harvest moon shone down, and lanterns hung from the trees. A crackling fire sent friendly smoke into the air and provided coals to roast ears of corn. Ewan stepped up to the church porch. The dancing would take place in the open area in front of the church. He tuned his instrument and struck up the first dance, "Turkey in the Straw."

Folks had traveled from the outlying areas and brought picnic suppers. The dozen school children ran among the trees playing hide-and-seek, but when the music began, they circled back to watch the first reel.

Kate wore a red dress with a matching bow in her hair. Josiah Finch bowed, a stiff bend because he'd buttoned his tight vest all the way up. Ewan fingered the strings and pushed his bow fast in irritation. Finch might get every dance.

A bevy of young women he hadn't seen in months stood beside the porch, swaying with the music, tapping their toes, and laughing up at him. They smelled of sweet soap and flowers, a bouquet of happiness at his feet. Ewan smiled in return at their enthusiasm and hoped the young men lurking by the livery stable would get up the nerve to dance with them.

Malcolm stumbled up and reached for one woman's hand. She tittered and followed him into the reel. Ewan picked up the pace. For such a large man, Malcolm danced with nimble feet. Ewan laughed. He knew Malcolm would soon drop his jacket and turn as red as his hair from the exertion. Malcolm swung the petite girls so fast, their feet left the ground.

Ewan played favorite tunes from "Skip to My Lou" to "Barbary Allen." The dancers spun and sang as they moved across the grass. Children lined up, adults came and went, but always Kate danced before him. When he needed a break, he signaled to Mr. MacDougall, who called for refreshments.

Kate brought him a cup of lemonade. "That was so much fun. We haven't had a dance since you left. If you're here this winter, perhaps we can do this more often."

Perspiration beaded her brow and her auburn hair tumbled around her shoulders. She looked adorable.

"What do you mean if I'm here?"

In the lamplight, he saw Kate blush. "Of course you'll be here. When the cold weather sets in, we can dance at the schoolhouse."

Ewan shook his head. "The grammar schoolhouse would be large enough if you pushed back the desks, but it's a ways out of town. Would people go so far when they can meet here at the church?"

"We'll ask Reverend Cummings if dancing is allowed. Are you tired?"

He grinned. "I'd fiddle for hours to watch you dance."

Josiah loomed up, tall and lanky with a sniff above his waxed mustache. "Aren't we paying you to play?"

Ewan nodded. "Back to work."

Kate caught his arm. "Can I join you? I've brought a flute."

He grinned. "You're on. 'Irish Washerwoman'?"

Dimples. "Fun!"

He began the complicated piece slowly, deliberately, as Kate found her key. She played a cane flute made from a thick reed cut that summer. The shrill sound always modulated under her breath, and he savored the string and reedy duet. After one round, he picked up the tempo. Kate kept pace, hitting all the notes cleanly and on time.

Faster.

The crowd stopped dancing to listen. Several clapped when they got to the end of the round and Kate kept up.

Faster. Faster. On the final round, she tossed back her head and laughed. "Ewan wins."

The crowd cheered.

They played several other duets together, his fiddle calling to her flute. It felt so right to make music with her, and Ewan knew the audience appreciated them. When the moon shone full on his face, he turned to Kate and winked. Flustered, she lost her place and put her fist on her hip in mock anger.

Laughter from their audience and then a shout: "We want to dance, Ewan. Stop teasing the girl. Play another reel."

Kate pretended to pout, but when Josiah stepped up and took her hand, she departed the steps for the dance area. She made a face at Ewan and then attended to her steps.

His heart swelled. It was enough.

⟡

"You're making too much of the fiddler." Josiah held her too tight and too close on the promenade.

"If you were musical, you'd understand."

"You should not make a spectacle of yourself. Just because everyone knows you, doesn't mean they approve of your behavior. He winked at you."

"I would have winked back if I knew how." Kate broke away.

"He flirts with all the girls. Look at him now."

Sally Martin and Priscilla Trenton hovered by the porch. Ewan leaned his fiddle at them as he played and grinned.

"He's friendly with everyone," Kate said.

Mary Standish approached with a cup. When he finished the song, Ewan drank it in one gulp. He tapped her chin and grinned. The young woman scurried away, giggling.

Kate burned. Should he welcome and tease those girls if he loved her?

Josiah drew her into the shadow of a stand of trees. "He's a country hick. All he knows how to do is fiddle. He can't support you with catgut and wood.

Why don't you marry me and I'll take you on the train to Lincoln to hear real music."

"I don't want to marry you."

"Your father thinks different. You're young. You don't know your own mind yet."

"What does my father have to do with this? I do know my mind. I want," she caught back Ewan's name and modified her words, "to make music. You don't even sing."

He put his elbow on the tree trunk and leaned into her. "I sing at church, where it belongs. Music is for children. Adults don't need panpipes and fiddles to make them happy."

"You are misinformed," she said coldly. "Music draws me closer to God. It makes me happy. I sing all the time and play my flute and bagpipes daily. Maybe if you made more music, you'd be happier, too."

Josiah grabbed her wrist as she tried to spin away. "He has nothing. His dead parents were Indian lovers who lost their property. I can give you a future. He has nothing to give."

Kate twisted out of his grip. "Ewan has what I desire: music in his soul and love for God."

A shout went up, the dancing stopped, and excited jabbering filled the churchyard. Ewan tucked the fiddle under his arm and waited. Kate hurried to her mother. "What's happened?"

Mama's fingers went to her lips. "The schoolmarm ran off with a farmer from Dixon. She's abandoned the school."

"What will we do?"

Malcolm joined them. "Pa's talking to Reverend Cummings and Mr. Finch right now. The school board will have to find a replacement. They should hire Ewan. He could teach the little students."

"What a wonderful idea," Kate said. "Let's go tell them. You can demonstrate how much he's taught you."

"You think they'd hire Ewan because I can multiply?"

Papa thought Malcolm's improving arithmetic skills were the miracle he'd been praying for. She knew Ewan helped the little Cummings girls with their arithmetic. It couldn't hurt to ask.

She smiled at him across the churchyard and tried to wink. Surely that's what being a helpmeet meant?

Chapter 6

Ewan cleared his throat. The eleven students regarded him with serious expressions. He already knew most of them, particularly the two Cummings girls who had walked him to school. Five boys and six girls ranging in ages from six to twelve were his class.

"I'm your new teacher. We're going to have fun learning to read, write, and do arithmetic."

Charity Cummings, six, raised her hand. "What do we call you?"

His lips twitched, but he swallowed the grin. "During the school day, I'm Mr. Murray."

Miss Hall had worked for three weeks and obviously planned her elopement. She'd left notes about the students and thus Ewan knew their abilities. The job paid twenty dollars a month and, with his savings, would put him within range of the seventy he needed to claim Kate for his bride.

He must not think of Kate. He had a class to teach.

Still, his thoughts drifted to the cinnamon-scented bag she'd pressed into his hands this morning. Charity and Grace, the older Cummings sister, had giggled when Kate darted out of the MacDougall house carrying the sack, her glorious hair drifting in clouds and her delicate feet bare.

Ewan cleared his throat again to discipline his mind. He led the students in prayer, played a hymn on his fiddle to get their souls stirring, and then asked Grace to read the Bible story. She stumbled on the name Zaccheus. Ewan noted she read without expression and with rigid shoulders. He'd have to help her; reading should be fluid and engaging.

"Please open your *McGuffey Reader* to your lesson and I'll take you in turn at the blackboard." Ewan beckoned to the two youngest children.

Ninety minutes into the morning, he had to clench his fists to keep from fidgeting. He gazed out the east window toward the prattling creek, remembering how school days lasted an eternity during his childhood. He'd loved the lessons but had yearned to escape to recess.

As he took the older boys through the arithmetic lesson on the dusty blackboard, he noted the same hesitancy Malcolm had shown. Tommy and

Jimmy were smart boys, but Ewan wondered if they had memorized the answer, rather than understood the concept. After three tries to solve the problem, he declared the lesson finished.

"Let's run around outside for five minutes."

Tommy's mouth flew open. "Short recess?"

"Five minutes. When I call, each of you should go down to the creek and find ten small pebbles. Wash them and bring them back. I'll help you, Charity." He grasped her soft, tiny hand.

The settler who gave the land ten years before had ten children and lived on the eastern side of town. He'd been a cantankerous man and deliberately lived a fifteen-minute walk over a hill from MacDougall's mercantile, the first building in Fairhope. By the time townspeople built a new schoolhouse closer to town, too many students had reached the upper grades and filled the new building. The younger children's school remained out in the country.

Ewan nervously glanced to the rutted road leading past the schoolhouse into town. He knew the school board might not approve the surprise recess, but Ewan itched to get outside, and the pebbles would be part of the next lesson. Singing "Blest Be the Tie That Binds" under his breath told him when five minutes were up, and he called the students down to the creek. They clomped back to the wooden building ten minutes later to find Josiah Finch waiting for them.

"Good morning, students. My father asked me to stop by to see you on your first day with a new teacher."

"Why are you still in Fairhope?" Ewan asked.

"I'm on my way to the train. I stopped in to see how you're doing in your new job."

He gestured to the students. "We're about to work an arithmetic lesson. Gather around my desk." He directed the giggling children to set their pebbles in straight rows.

Josiah snorted.

Charity and Silas, the six-year-olds, slowly counted their rows to make sure they had ten. Ewan directed them to take their pebbles and count them into two even piles. While they counted, he showed the remaining nine children how multiplication worked.

Two girls hesitated. They didn't want to get their hands dirty, but the boys seized the idea. Tommy reminded Ewan of Malcolm, grabbing pebbles and putting them into the appropriate piles. Ewan finally stood back and let Tommy show the other students how it worked.

He glanced at Josiah, who returned a sneer. "You teach school by letting the children play with rocks?"

"Only to get the concepts down."

He showed the youngest children how to add simple groups of pebbles.

When the wall clock showed noon, Ewan sent the students outside to eat dinner. He grabbed his sack and followed them with Josiah trailing behind.

Josiah clasped a hat onto his head and untied his horse. "I don't give you much hope for success. My father said if they're not ciphering by the end of the month, he'll have you fired." Josiah patted his pocket. "I've got his letter here, ready to be sent back east looking for another schoolmarm. Women do better with small children anyway."

The proverb the class had read that morning and copied onto their slates flashed through Ewan's mind: "A soft answer turneth away wrath."

He took a deep breath and quickly counted to ten. "Why don't you like me, Josiah?"

Josiah swung onto his horse and bent down to Ewan's eye level. "Because you have ideas above your station, fiddler boy." He kicked the horse onto the road to town. A cloud of dust remained behind.

Ewan shook his head and joined his students. He could hardly wait to devour Kate's treat.

⌒◦◦⌒

Malcolm had advanced to long division—he and Ewan worked together two nights a week on arithmetic. Papa watched with a mixture of pride and astonishment as they scratched on slates around the kitchen table. Kate embroidered a collar for her dress and talked with Ewan in between problems.

She basked in his happiness about teaching school, delighted to be a helpmeet to a young man so enthusiastic about his job. He loved all her suggestions, particularly having the students memorize poetry. "Musical words," he called poetry, "perfect for making reading fluid."

Once Malcolm finished his problems, Kate and Ewan retrieved their instruments and played music together. The evenings always ended on a merry note, even though Ewan refused to let her play the bagpipes in his presence. It was the only discord between them.

Other than Josiah, of course.

She could never explain about Josiah to Ewan, who grew stormy faced whenever Josiah appeared or was mentioned. Wasn't it obvious she preferred Ewan? Didn't he know she loved him alone?

Malcolm often slipped outside to give them private time, but Papa usually stormed in before they could exchange many intimacies.

"It's for your own good," Papa said one night after Ewan left. "Until the boy shows me his hard-earned cash, you're not betrothed. I gave Josiah my word."

Kate clenched her jaw. "I told Josiah no. I'm the one getting married, and I know who I love."

"You can't live on love, girl. He needs to be able to support you."

"He works hard."

Lines crossed Papa's forehead. "I know. He's using newfangled ways, though, to teach arithmetic, and Sam Finch doesn't like it."

"If it works, why does it matter?" Kate asked.

"He's one-third of the school board. We'll have to see how much the students learn."

⁓∞⁓

While chilly mornings were the norm and rain blew in frequently, surprising days of warm sunshine appeared in early November. Kate untied her apron one afternoon and excused herself from the mercantile. She and Malcolm were joining the grammar school students on an outing. Ewan needed their help.

Malcolm carried two sharp knives from the kitchen and a basket of Mama's warm biscuits. As they walked down the hard-packed road lined with fields gone to straw now the harvest was done, he muttered division problems under his breath. "Do you know how easy it is to divide by ten?"

"You take away the zero or you move the decimal point." Even as she said the words aloud, a memory tugged at her mind. Kate frowned. Had she seen a similar mistake somewhere? At the mercantile?

They heard the fiddle before they reached the school, and Malcolm chanted the times tables to the tune. They rapped on the door, and Grace Cummings let them in. Once the students and Malcolm reached "twelve times twelve is one hundred forty-four," Ewan finished the song with a nimble run up and down the fiddle strings. "Time to visit the creek."

Ewan led them around the schoolhouse and down to the water.

Tall willows sagged above the stream along with hickory, walnut, and fading wild plum trees. The hawthorn trees had lost their yellowed leaves and reached like spindles to the sky. The creek took a wide swing below the schoolhouse, and reeds grew thick. Ewan directed the children to remove their shoes.

"We've come to make reed flutes," Kate explained. "My brother and I will do the cutting and whittling and then teach you how to blow. Find a reed about this long." She held her hands eighteen inches apart.

Tommy Miler stepped into the water and pointed at a reed. With a sawing motion, Kate cut it clean.

Malcolm did the same while Ewan showed the children how to rub the ends of their reeds in the rough sand, "to smooth."

When they had their reeds, she told the children to measure two inches down from the node closing the end of the reed. "This is the mouth hole. We'll put five finger holes into your flute the width of your thumb apart."

Using the tips of their knives, the adults carved holes and rolled the flutes in the sand to smooth the cuts. They cut two pinholes in the node ending, and Kate demonstrated how to blow through them to produce a tone.

The children blew into their flutes. They positioned their fingers over the holes, and Kate helped them hear the different tones. Their eyes grew round with surprise. Several boys blew too hard, little Charity blew too softly, but after ten minutes, they all could get a clear tone.

After eating Mrs. MacDougall's biscuits, they trooped back into the schoolhouse.

Once inside, Ewan drew a picture of their reed flutes on the blackboard. "First we're going to teach you to play the multiplication song. Tomorrow we'll start on other music. It's a secret, but I'm going to teach you to play 'Joy to the World' in time for Christmas."

Three children took to the flutes as Kate had so many years before. Others mangled the fingering like Malcolm, but their eyes sparkled. Ewan winced at some of the notes, but Kate encouraged the children to hear the changes in tone patterns. Ewan clapped, they blew, and after another half an hour, everyone needed a drink.

Ewan marked each flute and collected them into a basket. "Remember, these are a Christmas secret. Today we'll demonstrate how you can spell for Mr. and Miss MacDougall. The spelling bee commences now."

Malcolm started to protest, but Kate took the proffered teacher's chair as the children lined up on either side of the room.

"Since the boys are one short, I'll join them. The MacDougalls will run the bee." Ewan took his place at the end of the line.

The girls protested, but Kate laughed. Ewan was an atrocious speller. She knew which side would win.

Unless she thought of another way to help him.

"I'll use the word in a sentence," she explained. "You'll repeat it after me then spell. *Bagpipes* will be the first word. 'I love the sound of bagpipes.' Mr. Murray?"

He shook his head but spelled *bagpipes* successfully.

Kate laughed. "Next?"

The girls won.

Chapter 7

Ewan liked to stop at the mercantile after school to say hello to Kate. One late November day, he had a gift. Before the weather turned cold, he'd returned to the stream and fashioned three new reeds for the bagpipes.

He hoped they'd improve the sound.

Nothing could make it worse, and it was a sore spot between them. How could a girl whose flutes sang with high, silvery magic endure the raucous, out-of-control dead swan blather from the bagpipes? They'd never be a match for his fiddle's call and response.

He appreciated Mr. MacDougall's insistence she play far from civilization.

Though, of course, Ewan couldn't stay away from his pretty girl and certainly didn't want her off by herself in a field.

Ewan stuffed his ears with cotton and watched from a smug distance.

At least the bagpipes had frightened Josiah away.

The store was nearly empty on the wet day, the friendly smell of hickory wood burning in the stove making it feel cozy inside. Malcolm stacked goods on the shelves while Mr. MacDougall and Kate stared at a swirl of papers on the counter. Mr. MacDougall's lip curled up. "What made you think of this?"

"Ewan suggested if they'd made an error once, they might have done it in the past."

MacDougall scribbled down figures. He glared at Ewan. "You've seen the numbers?"

"Only those on the one bill."

The mercantile owner pushed the paper toward him. "Tote these up."

Ewan provided an answer.

"Kate says you're good at the percentage. What are they charging me per load?"

Ewan reviewed the numbers and told him.

MacDougall dropped onto the stool behind the counter and scowled at the pouring rain. "I haven't been paying close enough attention. I knew my profit was down; I didn't know why. They've been cheating me."

"For how long?" Kate asked.

"Nearly a year. Malcolm, do you want a job?"

Malcolm set the final sack of beans onto the shelf. "I'm working now."

"I need you to be my teamster. You'll drive horses to Clarkesville next week to get our provisions. I'll let this company know their services are no longer needed." He nodded at Ewan. "Will you accompany him and figure the numbers?"

Ewan thought of his not-full-enough money pouch and sighed. He couldn't miss school to make the trip. "Malcolm can figure the bill. I'll help him unload here. I could use the work."

"Mrs. Trenton needs you to butcher her pig," Kate said. "She can't pay, but she'll give you meat."

Ewan swallowed. He hated butchering animals. "Thanks. I'll talk to her."

"She wants to make sausage, so you'll need to stay into the night to tend her smokehouse. I told her you'd do it."

Ewan stared at her. "I have a job, Kate, and the school board is coming to test the students the end of next week. I need to prepare them. I may be too tired if I stay up all night tending the smokehouse."

She sniffed back tears. "But I thought you needed money. I did this for us."

"I need every cent, but I have a responsibility to the students. If they don't cipher as well as Mr. Finch expects, I'll be out a job."

Mr. MacDougall watched him with a bland expression. Ewan hated having this conversation in front of the school board head. "We'll need my job after Christmas to live on."

"Where do you plan to live?" MacDougall asked. "You can't expect Kate to create a home in Cummings's barn."

"Yes, where?" Kate asked eagerly. "I could be putting a home together. I could measure the windows for curtains and start sewing them now."

Ewan examined his boots.

"Are you thinking of the old soddy near the school?" MacDougall asked.

Kate's eyes widened. "Oh."

He watched Kate's enthusiasm evaporate.

Ewan put back his shoulders and faced them. "I'm fixing it up as best I can. It will be simple, but it won't be the last place we'll live. I promise."

Kate nodded, but he saw the tears building.

Ewan set the box with the reeds onto the counter. "These will help, I hope. I'll leave you to it, then."

He walked out the door into the rain and felt his spirits slip down his cheeks into a puddle of mud. He still wasn't sure where he'd earn all the money. If it meant staying up all night to earn Kate's hand, he'd do it. A squealing pig couldn't be any worse than Kate's bagpipes.

⌒∞⌒

"Josiah offers a warm wood house in Clarkesville. You'd have a fancy carriage, fine clothing, and a place in society."

"I don't care." Kate stamped her foot.

"We like the boy, we know he's a hard worker, but he's got nothing anchoring him. Do you really want to live in the old soddy?" Papa smacked his big hand onto the counter.

"No," Kate sobbed. "But it won't be forever. Ewan's clever and smart, and I love him. It's not his fault his parents died."

"Caring for the least of them is what Bonnie did." Mama had entered the store. "We should all be ashamed. The Murrays gave their lives nursing those Indians and asked for nothing in return. We could have died of diphtheria, too. We owe the young man a little help."

Kate dabbed at her eyes. "Mama agrees. Can't we help him?"

"This is not easy for me," Papa said. "One day you'll have children of your own and you'll understand. We have to look at facts. I'd be a poor father to let you live in a dirt hut when you could have a comfortable home."

"What did you have when you came to Nebraska? You didn't always own a fine store. Guiddame told me stories about the hardships your family suffered. Why can't you give Ewan the benefit of the doubt? I'll be his helpmeet. We'll work together."

"Making music? You'd be like the grasshopper who plays away the summer to scramble in the winter and beg for help. I won't see my only daughter reduced to poverty when she has a perfectly eligible suitor asking for her hand."

"A boring, opinionated man who looks down his nose at everyone. You would shackle me with a Josiah Finch who thinks music belongs only in the occasional hymn at church? I'd rather die than marry a man like him."

Papa stood up. "You don't know what you're saying. You're being childish."

"Josiah always calls me childish. I'm not a child. I'm a woman who loves a hardworking man, and I resent your attempts to marry me off to a..." she stuttered, "a pompous banker like Josiah Finch."

Mama put out her arms, and Kate went into her comforting embrace. "You've seen his skill with numbers, Duncan. You know how well he's done with Malcolm. Reverend Cummings cannot speak more highly of him. It will do Kate good to make a simple home at first. She needs to learn how to manage on what her husband can bring."

"In a soddy in the winter? Have you gone mad?"

"Ewan has different prospects than Josiah. He has a winning personality, excellent taste in music, and a heart for the Lord." Mama rocked her.

"That ought to count for something," Malcolm said.

"Exactly. Maybe another place will come up before Christmas, but in the meantime, he's looking ahead and preparing what he can afford. You can't fault him, even if it isn't where you would want to live. The question is, will Kate be happy there?"

Kate closed her eyes and breathed in her mother's fresh-from-the-baking yeasty scent. She tried to imagine life in a dark soddy far from town. The snug sod house wouldn't have room for anything save a stove, bed, and table. It couldn't be much larger than her bedroom.

They wouldn't have much, but every night and day Ewan would be there. He would play his fiddle and she would sing,, and they'd bring beauty and happiness even into the most humble home. God would be with them, and that was more important than anything. Confidence stirred in her heart.

Kate raised her head. "I can do it. I can be happy as long as Ewan is there."

Mama touched her cheek and kissed her on the forehead.

Papa scratched the top of his head and pulled his hair into tufts. He rose and paced. He smacked his right fist into his left hand and muttered.

Kate, Malcolm, and Mama looked between themselves in confusion.

"What is it, Duncan?" Mama asked.

"I cannot give my permission or blessing or help. A deal's a deal," Papa finally said. "We'll see what Ewan's made of first."

Chapter 8

The three school board members filed into the schoolhouse: Mr. MacDougall, Mr. Finch, and Reverend Cummings. Josiah Finch slunk in behind them and Ewan frowned. He'd been praying about his attitude toward Josiah when he'd realized with a sinking spirit that, for Kate's sake, he needed to make peace with the man.

Ewan's money purse wasn't as fat as it needed to be for him to earn Kate's hand in twenty-two days.

He'd taken to going door to door at farmhouses outside of town looking for odd jobs after school. Reverend Cummings had paid him a small amount for whitewashing the inside of the church and for chopping firewood, but the minister didn't have much money himself.

Malcolm had volunteered to give him funds, but Ewan shook his head. A deal was a deal. He needed to earn the money.

Ewan wasn't sure what he could do. He'd have to trust God to provide for him and Kate. It felt a little too thin for comfort, however. Worry wouldn't help; he'd let the day's cares take care of themselves.

Today he needed to support his students. He nodded to the four men and introduced them to the class.

"This will be akin to a spelling bee," Sam Finch explained. "We will provide the arithmetic problems, and you will answer them. We will begin with the youngest students."

Charity and Silas stepped to the board. Mr. Finch directed Josiah to write the problems. Reverend Cummings's warm smile helped calm the children and Ewan.

The first two children worked their way through simple addition problems without any difficulty. Charity stopped and counted on her fingers twice, but the men smiled indulgently. Silas surprised them when he asked for a double digit problem, probably to show off. Josiah wrote the numbers, and before Silas could answer, Charity called it out.

The school board members chuckled. "Thank you," Mr. MacDougall said. "The next class, please."

"Why are those boys fidgeting?" Mr. Finch asked while Tommy and Jimmy worked on multiplication.

"I suspect they're singing under their breath," Reverend Cummings said.

"Singing?" Mr. Finch's voice rose.

"Speak up, boys," Mr. MacDougall said. They sang the times tables to him as they worked the problems. Their long division skills were not as strong as their multiplication, but they found the correct sums. The girls were just as good.

Two hours in, Ewan insisted on a recess. He followed the children outside into the chill air and watched them run around. He thought they'd done well, but there was no telling what the Finches would say. He muttered a quick prayer about his attitude. If he couldn't earn enough money, Kate would become Mrs. Finch. Ewan needed to be happy for her prospects.

Even if the idea broke his heart.

As he expected, when they returned to the schoolhouse, the board had made their decision. Two to two, Finches versus MacDougall and Cummings.

"Congratulations, Mr. Murray." Mr. MacDougall shook his hand. "Your students have learned a lot of ciphering. Your methods may have been unorthodox, but you have taught them well. We look forward to your return to the school after the Christmas holidays. The parents expect to hear a poetry recitation soon, I understand. You've done well."

The men put on their hats and coats and shook his hand. Reverend Cummings was the final one.

"But the vote was two to two," Ewan whispered.

"Josiah isn't on the school board," Reverend Cummings said. "You're a good teacher. Keep up the good work."

❧

In the December cold, Kate brought her bagpipes to work. As long as no one, particularly her father or Ewan, was in the mercantile, she could practice.

She'd experimented with the different reeds Ewan carved for her and found one produced a better sound than others. She'd learned how to modulate her breathing and pressure on the bag to release air into the pipes. Sometimes the clashing sounds sounded like music.

"You're getting better," Malcolm said. "I could almost hear the melody."

Malcolm still worked in the mercantile on the days he wasn't hauling goods. He'd grown a bushy beard, and the rest of his face turned red whenever Sally Martin stopped by. On slow days he pulled out a slate and worked math problems. Ewan had found a book of Euclidean geometry, which Malcolm said made better sense than long division.

As the days grew shorter, Ewan's visits became abbreviated. Kate didn't know how much money he still needed to earn and she didn't ask. When he came by, she put away the bagpipes and pulled out one of the reed flutes. The man she loved was discouraged, so she played to cheer him up.

That afternoon he shuffled in as she filled a jar with striped Christmas candy. She set it on the counter and pasted a bright smile on her face. She'd finished sewing her dress. Should she tell him?

His sad smile resembled a grimace as he tapped his long fingers on the jar. "When I was a boy, this candy meant Christmas. Ma called them Yule logs painted in Christmas colors to celebrate the holiday. I've since learned Yule logs burn in the fireplace, but seeing this candy is a happy memory."

Kate plucked a piece out of the jar and handed it to him. "Merry Christmas."

He clutched the candy and recoiled. "What's the date?"

"December 15th. You have plenty of time."

Ewan opened his fist and stared at the candy, now crushed. He scooped it into his mouth, his hand shaking.

"Are you okay?" Kate reached for him.

He rubbed her hand clutching his arm. When he'd finished the candy, he cleared his throat. "'In the world ye shall have tribulation,' Jesus said, 'but be of good cheer; I have overcome the world.' I remember that verse when I'm discouraged. Ten days. God will have to do a miracle. I've been praying for Josiah."

"Why?"

Ewan lifted his head and gazed at her with those clear blue eyes. "Because I love you and I want only the best for you. If you married Josiah instead of me, you'd be safe and could have a good life. So, I've been praying he'll become the man you need him to be."

"You needn't bother. I love you, no one else. If I can't have you, I won't marry. I'll stay here and work in the mercantile. This isn't the end. If you don't have the seventy dollars by Christmas, you'll earn it next month at the school. Please don't be discouraged."

Ewan shook his head. "He said your eighteenth birthday, December 25th. We gave each other our word. How could I look your father in the eye after I pledged to meet his requirement?"

"If you truly loved me, you wouldn't care. There are other ways to come up with the money. Can you sell one of your possessions? I'll buy something from you. What do you have?"

"Here. I owe you money." Malcolm rose from his chair at the back of the store. He handed Ewan two silver dollars.

"What's this for?" Ewan stared at the heavy coins.

He held up *Euclid's Geometry.* "My book. How much will you charge to curry my horses? How much do you need? I don't want Josiah Finch in my family." Malcolm walked out the door and slammed it after him.

They were alone. Kate came around the counter and took Ewan's face in her hands. "Ten more days. Mama, Malcolm, and I are rooting for you. God will provide."

"Thank you," he whispered. Ewan's arms came around her, and the kiss was worth all the anguish.

Maybe even better than making music together.

Chapter 9

Ewan tossed the last log into the schoolhouse stove. He planned to borrow Malcolm's wagon after school and haul firewood. A teacher's job involved more than classwork in Fairhope's school.

He didn't remember being so chilled while attending classes. Of course, he'd shared a desk and students huddled together when they felt cold.

"Okay, let's try it again. Top left index finger on the front hole, blow through your flutes, and let's play 'Joy to the World.'"

It was a tricky song with only five holes to play, but Kate had carved holes in the back of the flutes and shown the children how to place their thumb over half the hole, which gave them an octave-higher sound. It also turned the flute into a sharp whistle the boys enjoyed too much, but Ewan had convinced them to play softly for the Christmas carol. He knew their parents would be surprised and pleased.

The children had written poems in honor of Jesus' birth, and they had memorized the second chapter of the Gospel of Luke. Ewan planned to purchase a stick of Christmas candy for each of them with his limited resources. He was going to miss the mark to satisfy Mr. MacDougall, and eleven pennies wouldn't make much of a difference.

"'In every thing give thanks,'" he whispered. Ewan had taken to quoting scripture when he felt discouraged.

"I'm cold, Mr. Murray." Grace Cummings shook. "Can I put on my coat?"

"What happened to the window?" Tommy asked.

So caught up in the lesson, Ewan hadn't checked the window lately. Like the rest of the class, he stared. It was perfectly white, as if someone had whitewashed the panes.

He peeked out the door. Whiteout conditions. He couldn't see any farther than the end of the porch. He slammed it shut. Eleven pairs of frightened eyes stared at Ewan.

You could hear rain pounding on the roof and bouncing off the stove pipe, but not snow. Snow came on quietly, tumbling from the sky in soft, fat flakes that landed as gently as a feather. They hadn't heard a sound.

Ewan's mind raced. The last wood already in the fire, the room cooling rapidly, town a ten-minute run in good weather but not in bad. He had eleven children to care for. Would anyone come to help?

"We need to pray." He called the children together, and they knelt in a circle. "Dear God, the snow makes it hard to see. Please give us wisdom and help us make it safely back to town. Amen."

"Amen."

Surely someone would come for them. Should they stay? But it would be dark soon. If they could find their way to the road not twenty feet away from the north end of the schoolhouse, they could follow the ruts into town.

"Put on all your warm clothing and huddle together," Ewan said. He had an ax, a coil of rope, and eleven children.

And eleven flutes.

Staying made more sense. He stuck his head out the door again. He could make out the bush beside the road. He jerked up his head. What was that sound?

Ewan grinned in relief. "Grab your flutes and get into a line. I'm going to tie you together."

He put little Charity and Silas in the front and Tommy at the end. "We're going outside, and you need to blow your flutes as loudly as you can. Turn them into whistles. We'll walk together to the road and head to town. You make as much noise as you can then stop to listen with me."

They stepped out slowly onto the porch, Ewan leading Charity and tugging the rest behind. He could not risk losing anyone in the swirling white. "Blow," he shouted.

They blew, high and loud.

He waited.

A honking, screaming, squabbling noise responded. Bagpipes! Ewan turned his face in the direction of the sound. "Let's go. Pipe."

They shuffled through the snow, already three inches deep, and the cold seeped into their feet. Charity clutched his hand and blew her whistle. He did the same.

Honk. Squawk.

Ewan walked in the direction of the sound. When he tripped on a furrow, he knew he'd found the road.

"Pipe!"

Eleven whistles. Ewan added a twelfth. "Silence."

The shrill trembling noise sliced through the falling snow, calling like a beacon. Ewan pulled the roped children in the sound's direction.

So they went for an endless time in freezing solid white. The snow fell upon them like shawls, blowing into their faces and clinging to their clothing. The pattern remained. Whistle, pause.

Bawl, shriek, screech.

Shuffle, shuffle, whistle.

Peep, shrill, squeak.

Tug, trudge, stumble. Whistle.

The piping slit through the snow like a knife, and the answering yammering squeal beckoned them.

By the time the first building appeared, a shroud of darkness in the impossible white, Charity and Silas were crying. Tommy and Jimmy, however, hooted when they weren't piping, and soon the answering honking, oinking squeal was loud. Never had he been so happy to hear an off-key note sounding more like a bleat than music.

Malcolm reached them before they stumbled to the steps of the mercantile. He scooped up Charity and blundered into the rope, falling with a yell.

Up on the covered porch, Kate dropped her bagpipes and shouted for her father. Mr. MacDougall, Reverend Cummings, and two farmers ran out of the store. They seized the children and carried them into the warm room, where Mrs. MacDougall waited.

"God be praised," she cried.

Ewan sighed as he sank to the wet, snowy floor. "Amen."

∞

Kate shivered violently when she entered the mercantile. She felt frozen, and her lips ached. The warm air entered her sore lungs, and she gasped in great gusts. The bagpipes clattered beside her into a blubbering whoosh. She felt dazed from the exertion. Where was Ewan?

"Share my cup?" Covered in snow and with blue lips, Ewan croaked his invitation. He held a tin cup to her lips filled with hot tea, but she barely registered the warmth.

"Ewan, get by the fire." Mama bustled up with another cup and a blanket. "You'll both have frostbite before this day is done."

Ewan's voice cracked. "Only if my favorite bagpipes player will join me."

Malcolm picked up Kate and carried her to a bench beside the fire where she joined the children and Ewan. They'd removed their sodden garments and huddled together, trying to get warm. The adults pressed hot tea to the children's mouths and held them close while everyone told their story.

Ewan put his arms around Kate and kissed her forehead. "How did you think to play those pipes? We wouldn't have found our way without them."

"I was practicing and noticed the snow coming down," her teeth chattered. "I didn't think much of it until Reverend Cummings came in looking for Malcolm. He wanted him to take his wagon to get the children. When we saw how fast it was coming down and how little we could see, I remembered how sound carried. I thought if I played, you might hear me."

"I wouldn't have left if I hadn't heard you squawking. You saved us. We might have frozen in the schoolhouse."

"Or you could have lost all those children on the road," Mr. MacDougall said. "You took a mighty big risk."

"I took a calculated risk," Ewan said. "The bagpipes could bring us home as long as Kate played them. You must have heard our piping?"

"Not at first. I was about to give up when I heard the whistle. I recognized it and kept playing."

"You're my heroine." Right in front of her father, Ewan kissed her.

"I'm your helpmeet." Kate laughed with relief. "After all that bagpiping, I was afraid my lips wouldn't work!"

Ewan rubbed his cheek against hers. "Your lips work just fine."

Chapter 10

The snow fell for two straight days, and the school board declared school finished until the New Year. Ewan traipsed from house to house in Fairhope looking for anyone to hire him to do anything. On December 23, he cleaned his fiddle for the last time, wrapped it in the newly washed and pressed white cloth, and closed the case.

He tucked the worn purse with $66.78 into his pocket and stepped out into the shining afternoon. Ewan had only one hope, and a faint one.

The entire MacDougall family was in the mercantile when the tiny bell rang his entrance. He nodded at Mrs. MacDougall and Malcolm, gazed a moment at Kate, and then extended his hand to Mr. MacDougall. "I've come about our deal, sir."

"Very good. Do you have the money to show me?"

"No, sir. I'm a little short, but a deal is a deal. I wonder if you would buy my fiddle for five dollars. I'd have enough then."

MacDougall crossed his arms. "I don't have any use for a fiddle."

"Papa," Kate cried. He put up his hand to silence her.

Ewan swallowed. "Malcolm, would you like to buy my horse?"

Malcolm bolted upright. "Yes! But I don't have any money, I just bought new harnesses."

"Do you have $3.22?" Ewan kept his eyes on Mr. MacDougall.

"No."

"How would you earn your keep," MacDougall asked, "if you sell the two assets you need to work?"

"Do you have any job I could do to earn $3.22 by the day after tomorrow?"

Duncan MacDougall looked him up and down. "Josiah Finch was in yesterday telling me about his house in Clarkesville and all the plans he's made to wed Kate. Do you know what I said?"

Despite his curdling stomach, Ewan answered as calmly as he could. "No, sir."

"I told him Kate had a better offer. My answer to him was no."

Kate gasped.

"Josiah Finch could give Kate a houseful of possessions, but he can't feed her soul. He can't give her the music she craves. He's a taker, not a giver."

Ewan willed himself to remain steady. "What about our deal?"

"The way I see it, there's two ways to make money. There's the money you earn and then there's the money you don't spend. Do you understand what I'm saying?"

"No."

"The Good Book says a worker is worthy of his hire. A man deserves decent pay for hard work. You saved eleven children from freezing in the schoolhouse. You led our church in worshipping God with your fiddle."

"Kate saved the schoolchildren," Ewan said. "She made their flutes and called us with her bagpipes."

MacDougall pulled a handkerchief from his pocket and wiped his face. A log shifted in the stove with a crunch, and the hot cider pot on top bubbled.

"A joint effort. You taught my son how to cipher, and by helping us find the errors with the haulers, you gave him a profession," the mercantile owner said. "But more importantly, you make my daughter happy and she loves you. I'd be a fool not to count your bill paid in full."

Ewan stood tall and smiled at Kate, who gazed back with proud adoration.

"Except," MacDougall said, "we had a deal."

Ewan's heart sank.

"Oh, Duncan," Mrs. MacDougall cried. Kate cleared a sob from her throat.

MacDougall reached under the counter. "I have an envelope for you from the school board. Sam Finch wanted you to have it after your students' impressive display last week."

Ewan slit open the heavy envelope. Five silver dollars fell out. His lips parted and he stared, first at MacDougall and then at Kate.

"After Josiah left, the school board voted again. Sam Finch, like me and Reverend Cummings, is no fool. Your newfangled methods may not make sense to us, but those students have a stronger grasp of ciphering than they ever had before. You've earned a Christmas bonus from all of us, Ewan." MacDougall began to laugh.

Kate squealed and shuffled into a little dance.

"Your hard work earned Kate's helping hand. She's all yours, a bagpiping, helpmeet of a bride. Tell him about your dowry, Kate."

"While my dress is made in MacDougall tartan and I'm ready to wed, I've been practicing how to be a good helpmeet."

Ewan thought of the teaching job and the smokehouse meat he'd helped prepare and nodded.

"While you've worked so hard to prove yourself, I've put up food from the harvest and bought winter supplies from the mercantile. We won't starve."

"I only have $71.78 to my name," Ewan laughed. "But I have a heart full of love and music for you. Will you marry me?"

"You realize if we wed, you have to take the bagpipes, too?"

Ewan took her in his arms for a confirming kiss.

He didn't really care.

Kate was worth any sort of music: fiddling, fluting, singing, or squawking—as long as she was his.

"Is that a yes?" Kate dimpled and batted her beautiful eyes.

"I love you and your bagpipes." He laughed again and kissed his yuletide bride. "Yes."

About the Author

Michelle Ule took her first piano lesson at the age of six and has been playing musical instruments ever since, usually woodwinds. She even marched in the UCLA Band! These days, she sings in the choir and plays her clarinet at church. Despite all her musical experience, Michelle has the worst arithmetic skills in her family—for whom she bakes a Ule log cake each Christmas in northern California. You can learn more about her at www.michelleule.com.

For further informtion about *The Yuletide Bride*, including a video of Michelle playing the bagpipes, see her page: http://michelleule.com/books/yuletide-bride/